PENGUIN BOOKS

ROSIE

By the same author

Rosie

LESLEY PEARSE

PENGUIN BOOKS

PENGUIN BOOKS

Published by the Penguin Group
Penguin Books Ltd, 80 Strand, London WC2R 0RL, England
Penguin Group (USA) Inc., 375 Hudson Street, New York, New York 10014, USA
Penguin Group (Canada), 90 Eglinton Avenue East, Suite 700, Toronto, Ontario, Canada M4P 2Y3
(a division of Pearson Penguin Canada Inc.)
Penguin Ireland, 25 St Stephen's Green, Dublin 2, Ireland (a division of Penguin Books Ltd)
Penguin Group (Australia), 250 Camberwell Road, Camberwell, Victoria 3124, Australia
(a division of Pearson Australia Group Pty Ltd)
Penguin Books India Pvt Ltd, 11 Community Centre,
Panchsheel Park, New Delhi – 110 017, India
Penguin Group (NZ), 67 Apollo Drive, Rosedale, North Shore 0632, New Zealand
(a division of Pearson New Zealand Ltd)
Penguin Books (South Africa) (Pty) Ltd, 24 Sturdee Avenue,
Rosebank, Johannesburg 2196, South Africa

Penguin Books Ltd, Registered Offices: 80 Strand, London WC2R 0RL, England

www.penguin.com

First published by Michael Joseph 1998
Published simultaneously in Penguin Books 1998
Reissued in this edition 2010
2

Typeset by Rowland Typesetting Ltd, Bury St Edmunds, Suffolk
Printed in England by Clays Ltd, St Ives plc

ISBN: 978–0–141–04601–3

www.greenpenguin.co.uk

To Peter, Lucy, Sammy and Jo, with love

Acknowledgements

Thanks to Gerald Lockyer, retired Superintendent of the Somerset and Bath Constabulary, whose help, advice and knowledge of the police and their procedures during the fifties proved invaluable. Thanks also to *News Beat*, the Avon and Somerset Constabulary magazine, who so kindly helped put me in touch with Gerald Lockyer.

Chapter One

Somerset, 1945

The privy stunk worse than usual because of the heat, so Rosie pulled her knickers down out in the orchard, before opening the rickety door. Then, holding her nose with one hand and her dress up with the other, she backed in, that way avoiding seeing the fetid, bottomless hole.

A large brown spider weaving a web from one of the beams to a crack in the door swung past her right cheek. Rosie laughed. She considered all living creatures as friends, even the less attractive ones.

'Hullo, Syd,' she said in nasal tones, because she had to hold on to her nose. 'Why d'you stay in this smelly place? You could catch just as many flies if you made your web on one of the apple trees, and you'd have a nice view of the moors too!'

Rosie's home, May Cottage, was at the heart of the Somerset Levels, a low-lying area of fertile moorland criss-crossed with rivers and man-made rhynes. For some, such an isolated place, however lovely, would be daunting, especially if they were forced to be entirely alone here as often as Rosie was. But she didn't mind, not even when darkness fell. To her, each snuffling, barking, squeaking or grunting sound was the voice of a friend, whether it be rabbit, bird, bullfrog or hedgehog. They didn't gossip or turn up their noses about the Parkers, unlike the people in Catcott village further up the road.

The male Parkers intrigued, horrified, frightened and

1

yet somehow excited their neighbours. Cole Parker, Rosie's father, often remarked that if it wasn't for him there would be no conversation in the Crown. He claimed too that they were jealous of him. There was an element of truth in this: Cole was a handsome man and had a way with the ladies. He also had the luck of the Devil. Somehow he'd managed to convince the conscription board he was unfit for active service, then spent the war years making good money out of it. But behind the envy was fear too; mysterious accidents seemed to befall people who spoke too volubly about the Parkers, especially those who dared say that Cole's lads weren't just wild, but twisted, and twice as dangerous as their father.

As the war slowly creaked towards its end, however, even the people of Catcott had found something more to talk about than the Parkers. The men were expected home, rationing and the blackout would soon be just a distant memory. There were frantic preparations for the victory celebrations: chickens and pigs to be fattened, hoarded sugar, flour and currants dug out for cakes. Spring cleaning took on a new fervour, and in the village school there was a rash of compositions handed in based on childish sweet-toothed fantasies of a world where chocolate bars hung on trees, rivers flowed with lemonade and streets were paved with fruit gums.

In the drunken revelry of the village Victory Party there had been a conviction that a wonderful new era was just dawning. But now in June, just one month later, that vision was already tarnished. Many servicemen were still overseas, and of those who had come home a great number were finding it hard to adjust to family life. Rationing was worse than ever and shortages of paint, bricks and building materials prevented city dwellers from repairing the war damage to their houses.

Rosie was more aware of how it was for families in the big cities than any of her school friends, because her father often went to Bristol and London, fixing up deals to clear bomb sites. When she felt a little lonely, afraid or hungry she tried to remember stories her dad had told her about poor, skinny kids he'd seen scavenging wood and coal. In big cities they didn't get the odd rabbit or duck to supplement their meat rationing like they did down here. They went hungry.

Cole was in London now. At least he was on his way back after a three-day stay. He'd left Rosie in the care of her brothers. But Seth was seventeen, Norman sixteen and they had a great many better things to do while their father was away than to play nursemaid to an eight-year-old. So their little sister's curly, coppery hair hadn't seen a comb in days. Her bare feet and knees were ingrained with dirt, her dress so tattered it was only fit for the rag-bag, yet despite these clear signs of neglect, Rosie looked robustly healthy, if a little small for her age. She also had a remarkable air of happy self-assurance, even here in such undignified surroundings.

A familiar distant rattling, rumbling sound made Rosie forget the spider and run out to the orchard, pulling her knickers up as she went. Jumping up on the log pile beside the chicken house, she peered across the moorland in the direction of Burtle. The shimmering heat and tall grasses growing along the rhynes and ditches prevented her from seeing if the approaching vehicle was definitely her father's pickup truck. But it was unlikely to be anyone else's; few trucks, indeed motor vehicles of any kind, came to this part of the Somerset Levels.

Despite the beauty of the surrounding flower-speckled moors, May Cottage, the Parker home, was not the picturesque chocolate box cottage its name suggested. It was a dilapidated, turn-of-the-century farm labourer's house, almost concealed by mountains of scrap metal flanking it on both sides. Old tractors, broken-down rusting cars and motorbikes, timber, filing cabinets, bedsteads, worn tyres and ancient farm machinery. Cole Parker saw nothing incongruous in piling such objects in a place where herons and kingfishers fished in the tranquillity of the ditches and rivers. He didn't see his forest of junk as ugly or grim. It was his living.

As the familiar rust-red cab of the pickup truck came into view, Rosie darted back up the orchard, scattering the hens, and through the side gate from the back yard, skirting round the piles of junk to arrive at the front of the cottage just as her father pulled up with a squeal of brakes.

'Daddy!' she yelled in welcome, waving both hands excitedly. She was just about to jump on to the running board, when she realized her father was not alone.

A woman was sitting in the passenger seat beside him. Rosie backed away in fright to the shelter of the overgrown may trees in the front garden.

Cole leapt from the cab, but instead of sweeping her up in his arms for a hug as he usually did when he'd been away for a few days, he stopped short and frowned at her.

'Come now, Rosie. That's no way to behave,' he bellowed at her, his usually slow speech quickened with irritation. 'Come over here an' say hullo to Heather; she's come all the way from London to be a ma to you.'

Rosie stared at her father in stupefaction. Her father had never before encouraged visitors to May Cottage, indeed he'd brought her up to view strangers with suspicion. Now, with no advance warning he had brought home a new mother!

'Ma, to me?' she blurted out.

'That's right, so give her a welcome.'

Rosie may have been stunned, but she knew better than to show her father up in public. So she took a few reluctant steps forward and forced a smile as the woman climbed down from the cab.

On closer inspection she wasn't that old, Rosie decided. She wore a crumpled floral dress and her bare legs were mottled as if she'd spent the winter sitting too close to a

4

fire. She was nothing like the women Cole usually went for; there had been several of those over-made-up, brassy ones in the last two years. This one was hefty, with wide hips and a big plain face. The only remarkable thing about her was her hair; it was beautiful, thick, long and butter coloured.

''Allo,' she said, her big face breaking into a disarmingly warm smile. 'I'm 'Eather Farley, and I've 'eard all about you from yer dad. Don't be scared of me, luv, we'll soon be mates.'

Rosie was amazed at the girl's peculiar accent. 'Why do you talk so funny?' she asked, her timidity retreating in the face of curiosity.

''Cos I'm a cockney, ain't I?' the girl laughed. 'Born in the sound of Bow Bells. We all talk like that. You and yer dad sound real funny to me an' all!'

Rosie looked into the girl's warm brown eyes, then back to her father. He was smiling too, one of his rare, real, from-the-heart smiles. She instinctively knew he really liked this girl Heather, and that pleased Rosie because he didn't take to many people. Although plenty of women took to him.

Even at forty-one his hair was still as thick, black and glossy as it had been when he was eighteen. His body rippled with muscle, even though he had a slight paunch from the quantity of cider he drank daily. Dressed as he was now in his Sunday trousers and boiled white shirt, he was a handsome man. He often spoke laughingly of his mother's claim that the gypsies must have taken her baby and replaced it with one of theirs, for his strong features and dark skin tone were more Romany than English.

'Come on now, lass,' he said to his daughter in a softer voice, catching her up in his arms and hugging her. 'You've been too long without a ma, and Heather's got no kin. Let's be givin' it a go, eh?'

Looking across at Heather from the safety of her father's

5

arms, Rosie decided the girl would make a change from talking to chickens, spiders and birds. She looked and sounded jolly, and she was young enough to be a big sister. So after only a moment's hesitation she slid down from her father's arms and walked over to her. ''Lo, Heather,' she said, blushing a little. 'D'you wanna see the house and have a cup of tea?'

'Not 'alf,' replied Heather as she took Rosie's hand and squeezed it with real warmth. 'I feel like me throat's been cut I'm that thirsty.'

Leaving her father to follow with Heather's bag, Rosie led her through the maze of junk round to the back yard and into the kitchen.

Heather gasped as she stepped over the threshold and stopped dead. Rosie couldn't imagine why the kitchen evoked such a response, the dishes were all washed. Maybe she didn't like chickens?

Grabbing the brown hen which was pecking at a loaf left on the kitchen table, Rosie flung it out of the door and turned back to Heather. 'They're not supposed to come indoors. But that one's a bit saucy. Did he scare you?'

Today was the first time Heather Farley had ever been out of London, and she'd been enchanted at the sight of fields, rivers and wild flowers. She hadn't been the least bit put off by the dilapidated outside of May Cottage, nor the piles of junk around it, because on the long drive down here Cole had explained he made his living from scrap metal. Besides, compared with bomb-damaged, dirty London houses it looked pretty enough to her.

But her first glimpse of the kitchen stunned her. She had never ever before witnessed such filth, and she'd been brought up in the slums of Poplar, and seen sights that would make most people turn green. On top of the dirt it was blazing hot from a kitchen range, and it stunk worse than an abattoir.

It was a large room with a low-beamed ceiling, and its

furniture – a dresser, a large chest of drawers, central table and chairs – had probably been brought here at the time the house was built. Everything was covered in a thick film of grease, there were chicken droppings on every surface, and greasy cobwebs hung from the beams. The stone floor could not have been swept in weeks, let alone scrubbed, and the windows were so dirt-encrusted it was difficult to see through them.

'No, I ain't scared of the chicken,' Heather said slowly. She guessed this child didn't get invited into other people's homes very often and she probably had no idea what a clean house looked like. 'It's just so 'ot in 'ere it gave me a turn for the moment.' She wiped her forehead with the back of her hand to illustrate this point.

'I lit the stove 'cos Dad was coming home,' Rosie explained. 'I thought he'd want sommat hot to eat, and a bath, after London.'

Cole stepped into the kitchen, his towering frame blocking out the light from the doorway. 'You did right to light it, Rosie,' he said. 'We'll be needing lots of hot water tonight.'

Rosie sensed that Heather was shocked and disappointed, whatever she said. But her father's expression and behaviour puzzled her still more. He looked almost cowed and he was shuffling from one foot to the other as if he were embarrassed. She had never seen him like that before.

'Rosie does her best, but she's only a babby,' Cole continued. 'Me boys are lazy buggers an' all, can't get'm to do a hand's turn without a stick to their backs. Where're they too, Rosie?'

'Gone to Bridgwater on the motorbike,' Rosie replied, hoping he wouldn't grill her about what they'd done every day since he'd been gone. If he discovered the truth he'd lay into the boys with his belt the second they walked through the door. And Seth would round on her later in retaliation. 'I'll just fill up the kettle,' she added and grabbing it quickly, scuttled past her father out into the yard to fill it from the pump.

Over the splashing of the water from the pump Rosie couldn't hear what Heather and Cole were saying in her absence, but she had a creeping feeling it wasn't happy chat. So it was a surprise when she walked back into the kitchen with the kettle to find Heather bending over by the range, twiddling the tap on one side experimentally. Furthermore she had tied her hair back with a ribbon and put on an apron.

'So there's 'ot water, that's sommat,' she stood up, putting her hands on her hips. 'This place needs a good bottoming, and something stinks an' all, so you two 'ad better clear off and get some grub and cleaning stuff in, while I do it. Never mind the tea. I'll make do with water.'

Rosie looked to her father expecting him to say something sharp. He didn't like bossy women. But to her surprise he took the kettle from Rosie's hands and placed it on the hotplate.

'I didn't mean you to start working today, Heather.'

'Well, I can't sit about in this midden,' Heather laughed and the sound rang out around the gloomy kitchen. 'And you'll be wanting a meal soon too. So let me get cracking.'

Rosie wondered what a 'midden' was, but she had a feeling it was better not to ask, so she followed her father out to the truck without another word.

Once Cole and Rosie had gone, Heather stood in the middle of the kitchen and sniffed. The foul smell was strongest away from the range, but it was a minute or two before she realized that the open back door, in fact, concealed another door, and it was from behind this that the stink was coming.

Holding her nose, she pulled it open, jumping back in horror as a dozen fat bluebottles came shooting out like fighter planes. There, on a shelf, was the source of the smell: a piece of meat left so long on a tin plate that it was

8

alive with wriggling maggots. She gagged, slammed the door shut again and ran out the back door for fresh air.

Heather Farley was a little slow, in so much as she had never quite mastered reading and writing. But what she lacked in education she made up for in common sense. As she filled her lungs again with sweet-smelling air, she took stock of her situation.

The rest of the house was probably even worse than the kitchen. The little girl Rosie looked like a tinker's kid; she might even have lice. It had to be at least two miles to the nearest house; it didn't bear thinking about how far it was to the closest town. She was a city girl and she didn't know the first thing about country life. It was only today that she'd seen her first cow. How could she even think of staying here?

On the other hand she was a hundred miles from London and she had nothing but a few shillings in her purse. Besides, it wasn't as if she had anyone or anywhere to run to! In any case Cole Parker hadn't lied to her. He'd said again and again that his cottage had no modern conveniences, and that he and his boys couldn't cope with looking after it alone.

But, above all, there was the little girl. Heather smiled to herself as she remembered how rough Rosie's hand had felt in hers. She seemed a nice little thing, even if she was filthy, and she needed someone to look after her. Wasn't that good enough reason to stay?

Heather lifted her face to the sun and the warmth on her skin felt good. She had never been anywhere so tranquil before – all she could hear was the buzzing of bees and the hens clucking in the orchard. The utter peace boosted her determination. She'd spent the whole war dreaming of living in the country. Well, she was here now, even if this cottage was a tip. 'So you'd better get cracking,' she said aloud, and went back to the kitchen.

She scooped the rotten meat on to a newspaper while

holding her nose. Once that was dealt with, she stacked every piece of china, each pot and ornament on the table, and took all the chairs outside. Then filling a bucket with hot water from the stove, she picked up a bar of yellow soap and began to scrub the walls and shelves.

Heather Farley was only two, her brother Thomas seven, in 1929 when their father died from tuberculosis. Home was two rooms in a tenement building in Poplar. They shared a tap and lavatory with four other families. Rats and mice played on the stairs – to leave food uncovered for just a second or two was to lose it. But Maud Farley, their mother, had been a proud woman. She didn't sit and cry about her misfortune but went out and found cleaning jobs to keep her family from starving. Heather supposed it had been a tough childhood, but yet she had nothing but happy memories, with Thomas at the centre of all of them. He had looked after her when their mother was working, taken her to school, played with her and protected her. Other children sometimes jeered at her because she was a dunce, but Thomas never did. All she could remember was him praising her for her sewing, cooking and cleaning.

When war broke out in 1939, Thomas had been working in Smithfield Market for three years. He was very much the man of the house. Heather could remember crying because Thomas said he was going to join up as soon as he was eighteen and she didn't think she could live without him.

But she did learn to live without him, and her mother too. Thomas joined up in 1940 and was sent overseas almost immediately. In October of the same year before Heather was even thirteen, her mother was killed in an air raid on her way home from work, while Heather was waiting for her down in the shelter.

Neighbours often said that Heather was from the same mould as Maud. As devastated as she was, she stayed in their home, took over her mother's two cleaning jobs and just carried on, ignoring the bombs, dismissing the idea that she too might be killed, just waiting for the day when her brother would come home on leave and tell her what to do next. But Thomas never came home, he was in the Far East somewhere. Heather got a neighbour to read his infrequent letters out to her and dictated cheerful letters back. Then just as she thought nothing worse could happen, in January of 1942 their tenement building took a direct hit, reducing it to a heap of rubble.

She had been fourteen then. She took a job as laundry assistant in Whitechapel Hospital and found a tiny room in Bethnal Green. In February of that year she heard the news that Singapore had fallen, but she didn't know definitely if that was where Thomas was and anyway all the post from the Far East took a long time to get through.

The year had worn on, but still with no word from Thomas, Heather had become increasingly worried. The last letter she had received from him arrived just days before the flats were bombed. She made inquiries at the post office to see what they did with mail arriving for an address which no longer existed and they assured her they kept it till it was claimed. Other people urged her to keep sending letters to Thomas; they said the army and Red Cross worked together to make sure men got their mail, wherever they were, but still she heard nothing. Not even one of those brief notes to inform her that her brother had been taken prisoner. She felt deep inside that Thomas must be dead; he had always been so conscientious and resourceful, she was sure he would have found some way to let her know he was safe.

Finally a kindly priest investigated for her. The information she eventually received in 1944, over two years after Thomas's last letter, was the worst and most bitter blow she'd ever been dealt. Thomas Farley had gone missing when Singapore fell and as they had no record of him in any prison camp, he was presumed dead.

Heather had always been a buoyant and optimistic girl but this news wiped her out. There seemed to be no point in anything then; she had nothing to look forward to, no one to care for, or to care about her. It was only in January of 1945 that she managed to pull herself together enough to leave the laundry and find a new job in a cafeteria in Piccadilly. This was where she had met Cole Parker.

It was in late April, just a couple of weeks after her eighteenth birthday. Everyone in London was in a state of excitement anticipating that victory would be declared at any time. The pubs and clubs were getting in stocks of beer and spirits for the celebrations, the tube stations were finally closed as bomb shelters and men loaded up trucks with mountains of obsolete sandbags. Heather had found the excitement to be infectious. She trimmed her hair, put on some lipstick and even began to feel a stirring of her old optimism.

The cafeteria had been very busy that day, not just at lunch time, but all day. As fast as she cleared the tables, more people came in and filled them again.

At about four in the afternoon she saw the big dark-haired man standing with a tray of food, unable to find a seat, and she hurried over to him, directing him to a corner table that she'd just cleared.

He seemed to want to talk, asking her for directions to Victoria, where he said he had to pick up some goods. Heather always talked willingly to everyone, but it was the man's rolling, country accent which struck her more than his conversation. She'd never heard anything like it before. He told her he came from Somerset and he teased her about her cockney accent too.

He was still there when it was time for her to have a break, and on an impulse she joined him at his table. That was when he told her how his wife had been killed two years earlier when she'd come up to London for a visit. He said his boys, Seth and Norman, were old enough to fend for themselves, but that his little girl Rosie was only eight and he worried about her growing up without a woman's influence.

He said he'd tried to find a housekeeper, but joked that no one would stay once they saw the state of his cottage. Heather's heart went out to him and his little girl.

The wild celebrations on Victory Day and the turmoil in the days that followed put the man out of her mind. She certainly never expected to see him again. But one afternoon almost three weeks after they'd first met, he came back to the cafeteria, and this time it was clear he'd come especially to find her. He asked if they could meet up when she'd finished work, and although all the other waitresses said he looked a bit dangerous, she agreed to go.

He took her to the White Bear on Piccadilly, packed full of servicemen, and he told her so much more about his home and family.

'Seth's a bugger,' he said with a grin. 'Just like me at the same age. It'll do him good when he's called up for his National Service later this year, put some discipline into him. Norman's not much better, but as thick as a plank. Rosie's a bright little thing though. Always reading and asking questions. She deserves better.'

Heather couldn't help but view the whole family in a romantic light. Two boys as dark and handsome as their father, a little girl growing wild because she had no mother to guide her. She didn't even think to ask Cole why he hadn't been called up during the war, she was sure there must be some very good reason. When he asked if she would consider coming to look after them, she said she'd think about it, and give him her answer in two weeks' time when he returned to London.

The two weeks seemed endless. Each day it became clearer to her that there was nothing for her in London. Her room was tiny and dark, she had no real friends, no family or boyfriend, and she felt she was too plain to ever find one. London was full of sad, painful memories too. Maybe in time she would forget the terror of the Blitz, the exact sound of a doodlebug or that pungent gas and plaster smell that hung in the air after a bombing, but she knew that whatever else might ease with time, her lost brother's face would be as clear in her mind in another twenty years as it was now.

She had her bag packed with her few belongings two days before Cole arrived for her answer.

Heather was sitting outside in the sunshine drinking a cup of tea when Cole and Rosie came back. She had worked like a slave for two hours, and she was just resting while the floor dried. She still hadn't gone beyond the kitchen. An unpleasant smell from behind the henhouse in the orchard directed her to the lavatory. It was quite the worse she'd ever seen, a stinking, dark, spider-ridden privy, but she hadn't the strength to tackle that today.

Rosie came rushing through the gate, excitement in her periwinkle-blue eyes.

'Dad got lots of special things because you've come,' she blurted out breathlessly, sitting down beside Heather and sliding her hand into the older girl's. 'It took us a long time because Dad had to get some of the things from people he knows.'

'The black market?' Heather asked, looking up. Cole held a bulging canvas bag and a sack stuffed with something.

'Kind of,' he grinned. 'Rationing don't bother us too much round here, we got our own ways.'

Rosie disappeared into the kitchen but burst out again almost immediately, her eyes huge as millstones. 'Dad! Dad! Come and see what Heather's done. It looks real grand.'

Cole put his load down by Heather and went in to inspect. Like his daughter he came back grinning from ear to ear. 'It looks like I got your number right,' he said, patting her shoulder. 'I ain't seen it looking like that for many a year.'

Heather glowed. She felt certain that Cole was as unaccustomed to doling out praise as she was to receiving it. 'I've put the curtains in to soak and those easy chairs need new covers,' she said, but the questions she'd intended to ask him were immediately forgotten as she opened the sack beside her and saw two dead rabbits staring up at her.

She'd seen rabbits hanging in butchers' shops of course, but she'd never imagined buying the whole animal and having to deal with skinning it.

Cole laughed at her horrified expression and fished them out by the back legs, dangling them teasingly in front of her face. 'They'll need to hang for a coupla days, but I'll skin them for you, don't you worry. Take a look in the other bag.'

Heather had never seen so much food outside a shop in her life. Flour, sugar, dried fruit, jam, margarine and bread, a parcel of fresh meat, butter in waxed paper, cheese and bacon, and a whole heap of vegetables. He had got cleaning materials too: more soap, soda, wire wool, Jeyes fluid and a tin of beeswax polish. She could hardly believe what she was seeing – the shortages in London were so chronic it would take a fortnight going from queue to queue to get just half of these items. She looked at Rosie helplessly and the child smiled.

With that one smile Heather knew she would grow to love this child.

'We get the eggs from the hens,' Rosie said. 'I collect them up. I know all their hiding places, and I'll show you an' all.'

It was after eight that night when the whole family sat down around the kitchen table to eat the liver and bacon and mashed potatoes Heather had cooked. She was a bit tiddly as Cole had given her a couple of glasses of cider,

15

but perhaps that was just as well because it took the edge off his two sons' rudeness.

Their arrival at seven had shattered the peace. First the roaring of a motorbike, then the stamping of heavy boots across the yard. Both boys were filthy dirty with mud up to their knees and Seth, the older one, had slung two huge, still-wriggling eels into the sink before he so much as glanced Heather's way.

As Cole had already said, the boys were so alike they could have been twins. An inch taller than their father, but with the rangy slenderness of youth, they shared the same black hair and eyes, olive skin and razor-sharp cheek bones. But although they were undeniably handsome with their tanned faces and perfect teeth, somehow the special something which Cole had, that sparkle which drew the eyes and warmed Heather's heart, was missing in his sons.

'So you're the bint from London?' was Seth's first remark to Heather, his cold black eyes travelling up and down her body making her squirm inwardly like one of his eels. 'Shouldn't think you'll take to it here.'

Norman wasn't quite so unpleasant. He remarked on how nice the kitchen looked and told her not to worry about the eels because he'd skin them later. But even he gave her the impression that he was fearful of how a woman in the house would interfere with their freedom.

Heather asked them both nicely if they would mind taking their boots off out in the porch, but they ignored her and flopped down in the two easy chairs regardless of their muddy trousers.

'Rosie, take Heather upstairs,' Cole snapped and Rosie, who had been helping peel the potatoes, jumped to it, grabbing Heather's hand and leading her to the narrow winding staircase in the corner of the kitchen.

'Dad's going to blast them,' Rosie said as she led Heather into the small bedroom they were to share. It contained nothing more than a double wooden bedstead and a small chest of drawers. There weren't even curtains at the window and the bed was unmade, grubby sheets exposed. Yet the room pleased Heather for she had been just a little anxious that a country man like Cole would think a housekeeper should share everything with him, including his bed.

'Blast them?' Heather repeated; for a moment she thought the child meant Cole was going to take the shotgun she'd seen in the porch to his sons.

'You know, bawl them out, clout them,' Rosie said nonchalantly. 'He just don't want to do it in front of you.'

The walls and floorboards might have been thick enough to blot out the row that ensued, but the windows and doors were wide open and Heather heard every word.

'We don't want some cockney tart bossing us around.' Seth's voice was sullen.

'This is my house and I'm master in it,' Cole roared. 'Heather ain't no tart, and if you don't like her being here, then you's can just piss off out of here for good.'

'But Dad,' Seth was whining now. 'We was gettin' on just fine on our own.'

'We lived like pigs, and you two were wallowing in your own filth. But I didn't bring Heather here for your benefit, I brought her here for our Rosie. I don't want my daughter growing up like you two ignorant beasts. Now get those boots off, and put them in the porch, wash up and go and change your clothes before supper, or you'll get nothing. And take those blasted eels outside, they're enough to terrify anyone.'

The sudden silence in the kitchen then the splash from the pump in the back yard proved that the boys were obeying, however reluctantly.

'Are your brothers always like this, or is it just because of me?' Heather asked. Even before the boys came home she had been apprehensive about them. Rosie had shown her their bedroom and it stunk worse than a stable, of a mixture of stale urine and sweat. Rosie had airily explained it away by saying Seth often wet the bed when he'd been drinking. Heather hoped she wouldn't be expected to wash his sheets; she drew the line at grown men's messes.

'Norman's not so bad, when you get him on his own,' Rosie said, anxiously touching Heather's arm as if afraid she was about to run off. 'But Seth's horrible. I'll be glad when he gets his call-up.'

Heather's cooking pleased all three men. They wolfed it down and mopped up the gravy with thick slices of bread. Heather didn't like the way the boys ate with their mouths wide open or their many belches, but at least they seemed more kindly disposed towards her. Whether this was due to 'the blasting' or just satisfied hunger, she didn't know, but Seth said she was a good cook as she cleared the table, and Norman invited her outside to see him skin the eels.

They were still alive, wriggling and squirming even though Seth had cut their heads off.

'It's just like peeling off a girl's stockings,' Norman said with a lascivious grin and proceeded to run his knife down one of the eels' underbelly and show her what he meant. 'Ever eaten eels?'

'Jellied ones,' she said, thinking she'd never eat another one as long as she lived. 'Is that what you're going to do with them?'

'No, these are for a mate of mine, he smokes 'em. Me and Seth don't like 'em much. We only catch 'em to sell 'em. You wait till the nights we go for them proper. We catches hundreds on the right night of the year when they're trying to get back towards the sea. We can make fifty quid from a good night's work and Dad takes them up for the Yids in London.'

Heather looked down at the two skinned eels still wriggling in the basin and shuddered. She had a feeling that before long she'd be witnessing many more country skills that would make her want to run back to the civilization of London.

*

'What about having a bath and letting me wash yer 'air?'
Heather suggested to Rosie after the men had disappeared
off to the pub. She had gathered that this pub was some
two miles away, and she had a feeling the men wouldn't
return until after closing time.

She still hadn't given Rosie the fairy story book she'd
brought with her from London. Cole had said Rosie was
a good reader and she'd already demonstrated this by
reading out something from the *Picture Post*. Heather
almost wished she hadn't brought the book now, as it
would mean she'd have to admit she couldn't read any
more than the simplest words herself.

'But Sunday is bath night,' Rosie said, her blue eyes
wide with astonishment. 'It's only Saturday.'

'Where I come from we 'ave a bath when we're dirty,'
Heather said. 'And I don't believe that 'air's bin washed
since Christmas.'

'It has,' Rosie said indignantly. She didn't feel intimidated by Heather; she was nice, and it was good to have
company – the evenings always seemed very long on her
own.

'Well I fancy a bath 'an all.' Heather decided she must
make certain she didn't embarrass the girl. 'So let's lug it
in, shall we? I'll let you go first!'

As Heather sat beside the tin bath washing Rosie, she
was reminded poignantly of her mother, and all she had
taught her. She could remember being bathed like this
herself, her hair washed, then rolled up in rags, and being
made to clean her teeth with a little salt. Heather's clothes
had been just as shabby as Rosie's and she'd often gone
without shoes too, but her mother had instilled in her the
need for hygiene, and that was one thing which was badly
lacking in this household.

Heather lit the oil lamp before taking her turn in the
tub. Rosie was sitting on a chair wearing a too short
tattered nightdress. Her damp hair looked so beautiful
in the lamp light, spring-like coils of burnished copper

19

bouncing on her thin shoulders and framing her pink and white face. As Heather washed herself she became aware that the little girl was looking curiously at her.

'Will I get those big things?' Rosie said at length.

Heather giggled. 'Of course you will, luv, all girls do when they get to thirteen or fourteen.'

'Why?'

Such a question saddened Heather: it showed just how much Rosie had been deprived of by losing her mother.

'They're for feeding your baby when you get married.'

'What, like cow's udders?'

As Heather had never seen a cow before today, and that only from the truck, her knowledge of their anatomy was limited. But as milk came from them she assumed they did serve the same purpose. 'Yeah, I suppose so. They fill up with milk after you 'ave a baby. Up till then they are just like mine. Ain't you ever seen a mother feeding her baby?'

Rosie shook her head. 'What's the hair for on your tummy, then?'

Heather didn't know the answer to that and said so. 'It just comes around the time you get breasts, it's all part of turning into a woman.'

Rosie was thoughtful for a moment. 'Why do Dad and the boys have those dangly things then? We haven't got those.'

Heather blushed. At Rosie's age all she'd known was that Thomas's thingy was called his 'Johnny' and hers had been called her 'Millie'. She certainly hadn't had any idea why they were different, or what they were for. She had eventually found out from girls at the laundry during the war, and most of that seemed very rude. It didn't seem right to try and explain any of it to someone so young, certainly not on her first night.

'They're connected with 'aving babies,' she said. 'But you are too young for me to explain any of that just now.

20

I've got a book in my bag for you. Let me get me nightie on and this water chucked out, then we'll look at it.'

Rosie was still awake long after Heather had blown out the candle and fallen asleep beside her in the double bed. The window was wide open and a full moon was shining right into the room. She wished it was bright enough to read some more of the lovely book.

She was really glad her dad had brought Heather back with him. She was lovely. Funny, chatty and kind, even if she couldn't read. She hoped very much that Seth and Norman wouldn't upset her, and that Dad wouldn't get into one of his tempers and frighten her.

Three months later on a warm September evening, Rosie was up in the hayloft in the barn at Shank's farm in Burtle with all the other young children from the surrounding villages. She felt like a princess in the new apple green dress with puffed sleeves and smocking across the bodice that Heather had made her. She had no intention of getting into any rough games which might spoil it.

It was the Burtle Harvest Home, an annual night for celebrating the crops that had been safely gathered in. Everyone was here, even the very old people. It was a time to talk and laugh with old friends, to eat, drink and be merry, and for the younger, single ones it was an opportunity to look for romance. But this year it was a double celebration, as the war was finally over, most of the men were home again and everyone was looking forward to lasting peace.

The decorations this year were the best that anyone remembered: boughs of greenery, garlands of Michaelmas daisies, goldenrod and chrysanthemums nailed to the wooden walls, paper streamers and bunting swathed across the rafters. The long trestle tables of fast disappearing food were festooned along the front with swags of more greenery and orange ribbons.

Most of the men had already drunk a good deal of cider from the barrels set up outside, and now they were ready to join the women for dancing. The music was supplied by the Burtle silver band, and Jack Dunkie played his accordion whenever the bandsmen went for refreshments. The light from dozens of hurricane lamps fixed up high out of harm's way spilled a warm golden glow over the whole scene, and Rosie felt so happy she thought she might burst.

Ever since Heather had arrived back in June, Rosie's life had taken a sharp upturn. It began with the pleasure of coming home from school to find Heather there in the kitchen with everything bright and clean, and good smells coming from the oven. She would get up in the morning to find a cooked breakfast rather than just a slice of bread and marge, her school dress had the buttons sewn on, and clean white darned socks were waiting to be put on. But gradually it had become far more than just a feeling of comfort and being relieved of the heavier chores. Heather had become mother, big sister and friend all rolled into one.

She had changed everything. The kitchen was white-washed, bright new curtains hung at the windows. The back yard was pretty now because Heather refused to allow the men to bring any junk in there. She swept it daily and encouraged Rosie to plant some flowers in an old sink by the back door. Norman had rallied round and painted the old wooden settle. You couldn't even smell the privy any longer because Heather had found some special stuff to put down it. The may trees at the front of the cottage had been cut back to let more light into the parlour, and there was always a jam jar of wild flowers on the kitchen table. Once Rosie had slept in the same sheets for months before they were washed; now they were changed every Saturday morning without fail.

Cole didn't go down to the Crown so often, but sat outside on warm nights with his pipe and a pint of cider, while Heather sewed or knitted. Once school had broken up for the summer holidays, he often took time off from working when it was hot and took them all down to Weston-super-Mare or Brean for the day in the truck. Heather would pack a picnic, and even Seth and Norman stopped sneering and swanking long enough to paddle, swim or play football on the beach.

But it was the long days alone with Heather, when Cole and the boys were out dealing in scrap, that Rosie enjoyed most. Heather made all the chores fun. She loved to wash, lighting the fire under the boiler out in the shed early in the morning long before Rosie got up, tossing in sheets and pillowcases, shirts and underwear with absolute delight. Her arms were so strong, she could hook out the steaming washing as though it weighed nothing, then feed it through the mangle, singing as she worked. When she rinsed it in the tin bath under the pump, she would splash water at Rosie with childlike glee.

They made pastry and cakes together, listened to 'Children's Hour' on the wireless, played cat's cradle or card games, and Heather made a rag doll for Rosie, looping thick yellow wool for hair and painting eyes on to big white cotton-covered buttons.

Rosie found it mystifying that Heather couldn't read or write properly when she had so many other skills. She had tried to teach her a bit, but Heather formed letters back-to-front and she still couldn't recognize any words that were longer than three letters. But it didn't seem to matter much. Rosie read out recipes from magazines, she could add up a row of figures for Heather, and her learning took a great leap forward through the encouragement of an appreciative audience.

Sometimes Cole brought home sacks of old clothes picked up in his capacity as rag-and-bone man in Bristol. Before Heather came these sacks had just piled up in the outhouse until he had enough to sell on to a rags dealer, but Heather went through them meticulously, sorting out those items which could be used. Buttons were removed and stored in jam jars, buckles in another. Skirts of good cotton dresses were unpicked, washed and ironed ready to be made into something new for Rosie. Men's shirts had the collars turned as work shirts for Cole and the boys.

They made jam together from raspberries and blackcurrants, and bottled gooseberries. Heather got Cole to teach her how to rub saltpetre on rabbit skins so they could sell them and she even overcame her fear of eels and helped the men with the skinning when they got a big load one night.

But perhaps the best thing of all to happen was Seth getting his call-up papers, and finally leaving back in August to become a gunner with the Royal Artillery at Larkhill. Almost the moment he'd left, a new lightness and gaiety seemed to sweep through the house. Heather was released from the burden of Seth's sullen antagonism, and his endless wet sheets. Rosie no longer had to hide her few toys and books to ensure he didn't maliciously destroy them as he had so often done in the past, or flinch when he walked in the room.

Norman had always been overshadowed by his older brother, so much so that until now he had no identity of his own. Now he began to talk and laugh more, willingly helping with chores that once he would have sneered at.

But Rosie noticed even more remarkable changes in her father. He rarely flew into a temper these days. He seemed content to just be with his family and was far more interested in both Norman and her. He was happy, Rosie decided, and she felt Heather was entirely responsible for that.

Looking down into the barn from her vantage point at the edge of the hayloft, Rosie saw that Cole was dancing with Heather again. He had always been a much sought-after partner at these parties because he enjoyed dancing and he was light on his feet, but it was the first time Rosie remembered him choosing the same partner over and over again. Heather's face was flushed and she looked almost pretty with her yellow hair flowing loose over her shoulders. She had made herself a new dress for tonight – blue and white check with a low neck – and she looked like a milkmaid.

'Is your dad going to marry Heather?'

Rosie looked round in surprise to find that the unexpected question came from Florrie Langford, a girl two years older than herself who thought she was a cut above the other children who lived out on the moors. Florrie lived in Catcott village and her father ran the post office. With her ringlets and big satin hair ribbons, she always looked a real madam. Tonight she wore a blue velvet party dress, not a handmade cotton one like Rosie's.

'I dunno.' Such a thought had never entered Rosie's head before. Marriage wasn't a subject that ever came up in May Cottage.

'Well, he can't marry her, can he?' Florrie looked down at Cole swirling Heather round and her lips curled in scorn. 'He's still married. His wife ran off with another man, didn't she?'

'What do you mean?' Rosie felt an unpleasant prickle in her spine. 'My mum was killed in London two years ago.'

Florrie gave her a scathing look. '*Your* mum might have been. But she wasn't Mrs Parker, was she? She was just one of his women. Seth and Norman are only your half-brothers.'

This was news to Rosie. She didn't understand what Florrie was getting at, but she sensed it was intended to rattle her. 'So what if they are?' she said defiantly. 'And if you's know so much already, why bother to ask if my dad's going to marry Heather?'

'Because my mum thinks it's a disgrace the way he carries on with women.'

It had often been said that Rosie was as hot-headed as her brothers and father. She didn't stop to think about her new dress, or that Heather had said she was to try and be ladylike tonight. She just sprang up and threw herself at Florrie, knocking her down on to the hayloft floor, then she leapt on top of her and pummelled the girl with her fists.

Florrie screamed as if she was being murdered and all the other children gathered round.

'Your mum is a fat, lazy old cow,' Rosie said, pinning Florrie down beneath her, suddenly aware that she had only seconds to make her point before a grown-up intervened. 'And your dad is so scared of mine that he shits himself every time he has to deliver letters at our house. Don't you ever say anything about me or my family again or I'll make you sorry.'

Fortunately for Rosie it was Norman who came rushing up the ladder to see what was going on. 'Let her up, Rosie,' he said, barely able to hide his amusement. He turned to Florrie, who was struggling to get up. 'And you'd better keep your mouth shut in future, fancy-pants, if you know what's good for you.'

Norman's remark suggested he had a good idea what had sparked off the fight. He took Rosie's hand, dusting the straw off her dress and hair. 'You'd better come down where I can keep an eye on you,' he said. There was a touch of approval in his dark eyes.

Once in the barn, with a glass of lemonade in one hand and a jam tart in the other, Rosie told Norman what Florrie had said. 'Is it true?' she asked.

'Yeah,' Norman muttered. 'Thass right, me and Seth ain't got the same mum as you. I thought you knew that!'

'Did your mum really run off with another man?' Rosie found that hard to swallow. All women liked Cole, even if they were a bit scared of him too.

'Yeah, so they say.' Norman looked embarrassed now.

26

'But Dad was glad to see the back of her, and don't go talking about that stuff to anyone else or I'll give you a belting.'

As the night wore on Rosie watched Cole and Heather with new eyes. They were dancing slowly now, looking into each other's eyes and smiling at one another. She hoped they were falling in love. That way Heather would stay for ever.

Norman was so drunk when it was time to go home that Cole dumped him in the back of the open truck and said he could sleep there. The glasses of cider Rosie had sneakily drunk when no one was looking must have caught up with her too, for she didn't remember getting home, and had only a vague memory of her father carrying her upstairs in his arms.

The rooster's crowing woke Rosie, and she got up sleepily to pee in the chamber pot. It was only then that she saw she had slept in the bed alone. She crawled back in, wondering where Heather might be, and she was nearly asleep again when she heard a rocking sound.

It was gentle and rhythmic, almost like someone rocking a cradle. It appeared to be coming from across the landing and her father's room. She strained her ears to listen, and identified the noise as her father's headboard banging on the wall.

Above this sound was something else too, a grunting, heavy breathing which made her feel very uncomfortable. She knew instinctively what was going on. Heather was in bed with her father, and they were doing that thing that made babies.

Yet her overriding feeling was of puzzlement rather than horror. Heather had often spoken in shocked tones about girls having babies before they were married, so why was she doing it herself now? On top of that Heather had said on more than one occasion that her ideal man would be like her lost brother Thomas. She said he was gentle, sensitive towards women and children and he liked to paint and draw. Cole Parker was not remotely like that!

But as Rosie slipped back into sleep she allowed herself to imagine a baby in the house. It would be lovely, she decided, and that way Heather would never go back to London.

Chapter Two

Seven years later, 1952

Thomas Farley sat down on the stile, dropped his stick, jacket and haversack down beside him, and pushed his hat on to the back of his head. He hoped it wasn't much further to Catcott; it was so hot and his leg was giving him gyp.

Flapping the front of his shirt to cool himself, he looked around. He had never been to Somerset before and it was very different from what he had expected. The man who gave him directions from Bridgwater station had pointed out that this part of the country was the Levels, a vast area of moors prone to flooding, but that just a few miles away the flatness gave way to rolling hills and woodlands. Thomas thought that the seemingly endless miles of flower-studded moorland looked very beautiful now in the June sunshine, but he guessed that in winter it would be a bleak, windswept place.

He was puzzled as to why Heather had chosen to come and work here. Girls born and bred in the East End of London, used to shops, cinemas, markets and throngs of people, didn't adjust well to the country. Bridgwater, some five miles back down the road, was one of the dreariest towns Thomas had ever seen, and he doubted Catcott was more than a handful of cottages.

A middle-aged woman came waddling down the road towards him, the only person he'd seen over the last two miles. Thomas pulled himself up on his stick and limped towards her.

'Is it much further to Catcott?' he asked, forcing himself to smile. She had a sullen, sallow face, with a few dark hairs bristling on her chin. Her print dress was stained red down the front: he thought perhaps she'd been picking strawberries, although she wasn't carrying any.

'A coupla miles yet,' she said, staring at his stick. 'You looking for some place in particular?'

Her rolling accent was far more pleasant than her appearance. It reminded Thomas of Sam Gurney from back in the camp in Burma. Sam had come from the West Country and often at night he told the other men tales about the farming community he'd grown up in. Sam had never got to see his home again.

'May Cottage,' Thomas said. 'Would you know that?'

She smiled, showing two blackened stumps of teeth.

'Thass Cole Parker's place I reckons you means. You'll knows when thee's there by the heap of junk round it.'

As Thomas walked on, he sensed that the woman was watching him speculatively. People always did.

Thomas Farley was only thirty, but three years in a Japanese POW camp had aged him prematurely, and he had shrunk a couple of inches from his original six foot. He'd put on some weight to his emaciated body since the end of the war, but his face remained haggard. When he looked in a mirror now, he could see no resemblance whatsoever to the burly eighteen-year-old who couldn't wait for his basic training to be over so he could be sent out to fight. He'd become an entirely different man.

After the camp was liberated, more than one army nurse had remarked on his similarity in looks to the actor Leslie Howard. Sometimes he could even see it himself. His face had become long and thin, years in the hot sun had etched deep lines which tended to give him a doleful expression, and on rare occasions when his fair hair had grown out of its customary short back and sides, it had the same droopy quality as the actor's.

But Thomas didn't linger in front of mirrors. It was bad enough when he undressed to see the scars of beatings and tropical ulcers, to be forced to strap on his artificial leg and know he was unlikely to ever find a girl foolish enough to marry him – a cripple – even if women did keep telling him there was something mysteriously attractive about him. He struggled instead to keep in his mind the few advantages the war and imprisonment had given him: resourcefulness, patience, a deep understanding of other men, and the loss of his once strong cockney accent, He hadn't actually noticed that his accent had gone until after he returned to England, and he put it down to a close relationship with an officer who had often teased him about his dropped 'aitches, and had got him to read poetry and literature to him because his glasses were broken and he couldn't see to read himself. Thomas told himself almost daily that losing his leg and youth for his country was nothing. He might have lost his life out there, like poor Sam and so many of his other friends. He told himself this so often that sometimes he almost believed it.

Thomas was not used to walking so far and he knew he had rubbed his stump raw even before he finally saw the piles of junk ahead.

If it hadn't been for the woman's description, he wouldn't even be considering that this might be the place; when Mrs Lovell, an old friend of his mother's back in London, had given him the address, he'd imagined a pretty thatched cottage with roses around the door.

There were no roses, not unless you counted a wild one scrambling up over a rusting tractor.

Pausing some ten yards from the house, he leaned heavily on his stick, hoping the woman had been mistaken. The plain red-brick building was almost hidden behind overgrown sprawling trees, but there on the broken gate was the sign, May Cottage, confirmation that he had indeed found the right place.

Mrs Lovell had told him Heather had left London to come here, soon after VE day in 1945. Thomas felt a prickling of unease as he gazed at the farm labourer's cottage.

Pushing his way through the overgrown trees he knocked on the front door. There was no reply. He knocked again, and again, but he could hear no sound from within. Peering into the lone downstairs window he was somewhat taken aback to see incongruous grand furniture: large armchairs, a huge oil painting above the fireplace, and a highly polished oval dining table very similar to one he remembered seeing in an officer's home in Singapore. Thomas took a step back and looked at the house reflectively. It was all very odd.

He was just about to make his way round the back of the cottage to see if there was anyone out there, when he heard a rustle. It came from a bush at the side of the house. He sensed that someone was behind it, watching him.

'Hullo there,' he called out. 'I'm looking for Heather Farley. I believe she came to work here after the war.'

No reply. Bees buzzed amongst the weeds and wild flowers; there was a faraway bleat of a sheep and the plaintive cry of a bird.

He called again, louder this time. After all, it could be someone old and hard of hearing. But still there was no reply.

'Just call out if you're scared of me,' he yelled again. 'I can't run after you, I've only got one leg.' To prove this point he waggled his stick in the air.

'Heather left, three years since.'

Thomas almost lost his balance with surprise. He stared at the bush from where the voice came. 'Come out and talk to me,' he called back.

'No, I won't. And go away now. Me dad don't like strangers calling at the house.'

The girl's voice was bold and Thomas had a feeling she was probably more afraid of her father than a stranger. He turned and limped exaggeratedly out of the gate.

'I'm not calling at the house,' he said over his shoulder. 'All I want is to find out where Heather is. I've come all the way from London.'

The bush quivered, some tall weeds parted and out came a girl. She looked about thirteen or fourteen, small but robust, wearing a woman's shabby faded cotton dress several sizes too large for her. She was barefoot with a mane of copper-coloured tangled curls and freckles across a small snub nose. Thomas smiled, she reminded him very much of the kind of children he'd grown up with in the East End of London – not just her shabby clothes and bare feet, but the sharply suspicious expression in her blue eyes.

'That's better,' Thomas said, keeping his distance in case she ran away. 'I never was much good at holding a conversation with a bush.'

The girl giggled. Thomas thought there was something rather enchanting about her, as he leaned back against an old oil drum.

Rosie had been watching this man's approach for some time. She'd seen him coming up the lane while she was hanging out washing in the orchard and she was curious about him even before he knocked at the front door. Holidaymakers didn't usually bother with this part of Somerset and men with bad limps and a stick didn't go in for hiking. Besides, he had an intriguing face. Not exactly handsome, but interesting.

He looked too smart to be looking for work; his trousers were neatly pressed, the white open-necked shirt spotlessly clean and his boots were well polished too. Something about the tilted-back angle of his trilby, the nonchalant way he'd slung his jacket over his shoulder along with a canvas knapsack, suggested he was an ex-serviceman, a wounded one at that. She wondered how he knew Heather.

'You've got two legs,' she said reproachfully.

'One and a bit to be precise,' he said and bent down and pulled his trouser leg up a couple of inches to show her the dull beige artificial one. 'I lost my real one when a wound became infected during the war.'

'They chopped it off?' she said in horror, but moved closer as if she wanted to inspect it.

'Sawed it off.' Thomas had been very lucky that the infection only got a grip on him after the camp had been liberated. He'd witnessed several amputations at the hands of the Japanese, and every one of the men concerned had died slowly and horribly, as the foul-smelling gangrene crept through their bodies. His own amputation had been without anaesthetic, but at least it had been carried out in reasonably sterile conditions in a field hospital, with proper dressings and clean water to wash the wound. 'I was a prisoner of war in Burma, then in hospital for a long time afterwards. But never mind me, where did Heather go, and why?'

The girl put her hands on her hips. 'What's she to you?'

Thomas didn't think she was afraid of much, even though she'd said that about her father.

'I'm her brother, Thomas Farley.'

The insolent look vanished. She clamped one hand over her mouth.

'You can't be! She said you was dead, and anyway you don't sound or look like her.'

'I thought she was dead too, until a few weeks ago,' Thomas shrugged. 'I heard our old home was bombed and when I didn't get any letters from her in the camp I thought she must have been killed there. The war certainly messed up a lot of people's lives. As for us not looking and sounding the same, well, brothers and sisters aren't always alike. Now where did she go? I must find her.'

'She went back to London,' the girl said. 'Like I said, three years since.'

Thomas felt a dull thud of disappointment. He slumped back against the oil drum, wondering what he should do next.

He wished he'd thought of some contingency plan in case he lost touch with Heather. But then no one had expected there to be so much destruction in the East End, or that so many civilians would be killed, and he certainly hadn't imagined he'd be captured by the Japs either. Of late the phrase 'If only' seemed to pepper his speech and thoughts. If only he'd been able to get compassionate leave when their mother was killed in the Blitz, if only he hadn't been in Singapore when it fell. If only there'd been medicine at the camp he might not have lost his leg. If only he'd gone straight to London after the war.

He'd been shipped home to a hospital in Bournemouth in the spring of 1946 where he remained for almost a year. Believing there was nothing and no one left for him in London, he stayed on in the town after he was discharged from the hospital, living in a hostel for ex-servicemen, hobbling around on crutches, waiting for the time when he could have an artificial leg fitted. During that time he had heard the government were offering re-training courses for men like himself, and he managed to get on one to learn clock and watch mending. He might never have left Bournemouth but for hearing about a job in a clock and watch repairers in London's Hampstead, with a small flat above the shop thrown in.

It had been in an attempt to rid himself of the memories that haunted him that he eventually went back to Poplar just a couple of months ago. Perhaps if he walked through the streets he grew up in, once more, he would come to terms not only with losing his mother and sister but also with his disability.

He hadn't wanted to linger when he saw the devastation: whole rows of houses gone, weed-filled areas where tenement buildings, including the one he'd been born in, had once stood. He tried to tell himself that the wholesale destruction was a good thing, that at last slum dwellings and all the deprivation that went with them would be wiped out for ever. Yet as he looked at the pictures on hoardings of the blocks of flats the government was intending to replace them with, he felt even more saddened. They might have electricity and bathrooms, but old folk couldn't sit on doorsteps eight or nine floors above the road, neighbours wouldn't drop in as they used to. He looked sceptically at the pictures of children's playgrounds and wondered how far away the parents would be. In the old East End children had been almost shared, watched over as they played by often exasperated but always caring neighbours. The new health service might wipe out diseases, and fear of the workhouse and the means test become a thing of the past, but would the welfare state support and nurture in quite the same way as the old community spirit had?

He heard from a man in a paper shop that most of his old neighbours had been rehoused out in Dagenham, and he might have just turned away and put aside his past for good, but for stopping for a pint in the Nag's Head and bumping into old Jack Crowhurst.

Jack Crowhurst owned a fish and chip shop down by the West India docks, and Thomas used to peel potatoes for him after school. Jack had looked about seventy then, a small, stooped, bad-tempered man with a permanent frown. But he'd been kind to Thomas, often giving him parcels of fish and chips to take home to his mother and sister.

Jack hadn't changed a bit. He still looked about seventy, even though twenty years had passed, and was just as grumpy. When Thomas told the old man who he was, Jack looked as if he was seeing a ghost.

'We all thought you'd copped it out in the Far East,' he said. They chatted for a while about how Jack had kept his fish and chip shop going right through the war, only to lose it to a fire in 1946. He said how sorry he was that Mrs Farley had been killed, and asked if Heather had got married.

When Thomas said he thought she was dead too, Jack shook his head. 'Never! She came in for some fish and chips one night just before the end of the war,' he said. 'She was on her way round to see Ada Lovell. She told me she was working up West somewhere in a cafeteria.'

That news was more thrilling to Thomas than hearing he had won the Pools. Jack Crowhurst told him Ada Lovell was now living with her daughter in a prefab on the Isle of Dogs, and Thomas was off there immediately, knocking on doors until he eventually found her.

It was Mrs Lovell who filled him in about all that Heather had gone through back in the Blitz. Of his mother's death and how Heather had taken on her jobs and kept the flat going. Of the day their tenement was bombed, and how his sister had found a room in Bethnal Green and work in a laundry. She spoke too of the agony Heather had been through when she heard nothing from Thomas, and finally her devastation when she heard he was 'Missing, presumed dead'. It made Thomas very angry to think she'd suffered such unnecessary grief, just through some slip-up in administration.

But with these thoughts there was also terrible guilt for Thomas. He'd been back in England for six years. He could excuse himself for the first of those because he'd been too sick and weak to do anything but lie staring at the ceiling. But the truth was that he'd continued to wallow in self-pity and apathy instead of getting help and advice on how to find out what exactly had happened to Heather. He'd been afraid of finding confirmation that she was actually dead, so he'd chosen instead to slip into a deep depression of denial.

*

Thomas was suddenly aware of the young girl again; she was standing silently, watching him. 'What made Heather decide to chuck it in here?' he asked.

'I dunno exactly,' the girl said with a shrug. 'Dad said she missed London.'

This seemed a fair enough explanation to Thomas. After the mayhem of London during the war it must have been bliss to come here and live in the peace and fresh air. But given time any young girl would begin to yearn for company of her own age, for dancing, freedom and fun.

'I'd better come back when your dad's here, then. To see if he's got her new address in London.'

Thomas was astonished to see the girl's face blanch.

'You'd best leave now if you know what's good for you.' She put her head on one side and looked sharply at him like a little bird. 'Our dad ain't exactly a gentleman. He can't tell you nothing about Heather because he don't know where she's gone. All you'll do is rile him up, speaking of things that upset him. So he'll just get mad and kick you out.'

'Well then, you'd better tell me about her yourself,' he said. He hoisted himself up on to the oil drum, guessing that settling down in full view of anyone coming up the lane would make her nervous. 'She is my only living relative, and until a few weeks ago I thought she was dead. I've come too far to leave without learning something about her, and I don't give up easily. So I can either sit here and wait till your dad gets back and take my chance with him, or you come somewhere else where we can talk in private. You see, Heather was just about your age when I last saw her, thirteen, a schoolgirl with pigtails. I want to know what she grew up like.'

'I'm fifteen,' she snapped. 'And I've left school.'

'I'm sorry.' Thomas smiled at such indignation. She had the maturity of an older girl but her body was as undeveloped as a child's. 'So what's your name then?'

'Rosie.'

Thomas thought her name suited her perfectly. Her skin was the colour of pale pink rosebuds, her blue eyes were as brilliant as the summer sky; even the freckles across the bridge of her nose reminded him of golden pollen. She was prickly too and every bit as wild as the briar rose scrambling over the ancient abandoned tractor. Somehow he doubted she'd ever learn to tame that mop of unruly curls, or develop a little sophistication, but there was no doubt in his mind that she'd turn into a very pretty, desirable woman. Years ago he would have wanted to paint her, there was such strength and determination in her little face. But once he'd lost his leg he found he'd lost the will to paint too.

'Your mum named you well. You're as pretty as those wild roses,' he said, pointing to a bush scrambling over the tractor.

Rosie blushed, and her eyes dropped to her dirty bare feet. Thomas guessed she wasn't used to compliments.

'I'll let you come round the back for a cup of tea because you look tired,' she said. She bit her lip nervously as if already sure she would regret her kindness. 'But promise me you'll go afterwards and that you won't tell anyone you've been talking to me?'

'I promise,' he said.

The back yard was a total contrast to the scrap yard, neat and tidy, concreted over and well swept, with a colourful mass of flowers planted along the inside of the rough fence of wooden palings. Opposite the gate into the yard was an outhouse which seemed to be used as a workshop. Another fence and gate separated the yard from an orchard in which chickens were roaming free.

Beside a stone porch which presumably led into the kitchen, there was an old sink planted with more flowers, a wooden settle bleached white in the sun, and an old pump. Thomas glanced into the porch and saw a collection of waterproof coats and boots, but more ominous, three shotguns fixed into a rack.

'Stay there,' Rosie said warily, pointing to the settle. 'I'll just go and put the kettle on.'

Thomas sat down gratefully, easing his artificial leg out in front of him. He was concerned about the soreness; he didn't think he could make the long walk back to Bridgwater station this afternoon, and wondered if there was a pub near by that would let him have a room for the night.

He could hear Rosie in the kitchen, the clinking of cups and a hissing noise as if she was putting a wet kettle on a solid fuel stove. The only other sounds were those of insects and a clucking of hens.

Looking at the flowers Thomas wondered who was responsible for them. There was nothing willy-nilly about the planting, the colours, heights and shapes had all been taken into consideration by someone with an artist's eye. He couldn't imagine a man who piled junk outside his house doing such a thing. Could there be another woman here?

He looked around him for any evidence of this. Down in the orchard was a line of washing: six men's shirts, three pairs of vests and underpants, two sheets and a striped dress. There were a couple of smaller items too, but no other female things.

'Who's the gardener?' he asked as Rosie reappeared. 'It's very pretty.'

'Me,' she said, and her face warmed as if she rarely got any appreciation for it. 'I just love flowers. I'm going to have a go at the front garden soon. But the ground's as hard as the Devil and I don't have much time with the boys and Dad to look after.'

'I expect you wish you had a sister?' Thomas said.

Rosie sighed as if in agreement.

'What are your brothers' names, and how old are they?'

'Seth's twenty-five, Norman's twenty-three and Alan's five.'

Thomas raised one eyebrow. 'So Alan was born while

Heather was here?' He thought Mrs Lovell must have got hold of the wrong end of the stick, saying Cole Parker was a widower.

'Well, of course he was, she had him.'

Thomas stared at Rosie. 'You what?'

'Clean your ears out,' she said cheekily. 'I said of course she was here. She had him! Alan is Heather's little 'un.'

Thomas's stomach seemed to plummet to the floor like a runaway lift in a movie. He wanted to ask her to repeat what she'd said again, but yet he knew he'd heard it right. He could no more imagine his little sister having a child of her own than he could imagine her flying a plane or going to a royal garden party. If she'd left the child here and skipped off it was no wonder Cole Parker wouldn't want to talk about her.

'So Heather married your father?'

Rosie looked at him with an expression somewhere between amusement and bafflement. 'Marry Dad? Not likely.'

'Then she married one of your brothers?' It occurred to him that the eldest son must be around the same age as Heather.

'She didn't marry no one, not while she was here.'

His stomach plummeted further. Heather getting herself into trouble wasn't something Thomas had ever considered. The girl he'd carried in his mind all these years had been just a schoolgirl, not unlike the girl in front of him now. It wasn't right to fire questions of an intimate nature at her, he knew, but he had no choice.

'So who was Alan's father? Do you know?'

'Dad, of course,' Rosie said.

There was absolutely no trace of embarrassment on her young face. It was as if she was unaware of the normal social pressure to have babies in wedlock. Before Thomas could ask her anything more, the whistle of the kettle blasted out and Rosie was off into the kitchen leaving him shell-shocked. He was an uncle!

'Rosie, why didn't Heather take Alan with her when she left?' Thomas asked when she came back with two thick china mugs of tea. 'Didn't she care about him?'

'Of course she cared.' Rosie's voice was indignant. 'I don't suppose she had anywhere to take him to, and she knew I'd look after him right enough.'

'Where is Alan now?'

'At school,' she replied, looking at him as if she considered that a daft question. 'And you'd better drink your tea and go. I've got the ironing to do and a pie to make.'

Thomas drank his tea. He felt Rosie was telling the truth, at least as far as not knowing where Heather had gone. He decided he would ask questions elsewhere, sleep on the problem and decide what to do about it in the morning.

'Did Heather ever tell you about me?' he asked her as he got up to leave.

Rosie nodded. She was shifting from one foot to the other impatiently, but the look she gave him was curiously gentle.

'She said you were clever and that you looked after her when she was little.'

Thomas sighed. 'One more question before I go. Did you like Heather?'

He didn't really know why he asked this, yet it seemed all-important to him.

To his surprise and consternation Rosie's eyes welled with tears.

'I'm sorry,' he said quickly, afraid he may have asked one question too many. 'You don't have to tell me if you don't want to.'

'I don't mind telling you,' she replied in a small, shaky voice. 'I loved her and I had all the best times I remember with her.'

A lump came up in Thomas's throat and he reached out and squeezed the girl's small hand. Whatever had happened here, if the child had loved Heather, it was almost certain Heather had loved her back. That made him and Rosie allies, and as such he knew he would have to honour his promise that he would keep their meeting secret.

But it made Heather's disappearance all the more odd. He wasn't going to leave Somerset until he knew more.

At eight that evening, Rosie sat by her bedroom window and allowed herself to think about Heather for the first time in months.

It was still very warm, the pink sky promising another hot day again tomorrow. She never tired of the view of the moors from her window; she saw it as her extended garden. A heron was standing as still as a statue on the edge of the ditch just beyond the orchard, and a few moments ago she had glimpsed a flash of turquoise which she knew was a kingfisher. Later as dusk fell, an owl would come to perch on the washing-line post as usual, waiting for his supper when mice came out to nibble at the chicken feed.

Living here on the Levels had taught her how precarious the balance of nature was, and how dependent every single living thing was on the chain of life. If the men didn't clear the rhynes and ditches of weeds, the fields became flooded in the winter, drowning the livestock, destroying crops of vegetables and the fruit trees. She supposed that was why so many of the people here were tough and brutish like her father and brothers. They had to be, to survive.

She thought that Thomas Farley must be equally tough and single-minded to have survived that prison camp. She'd read about them and she knew how many men had died in them. Such a strong-willed man wouldn't go back to London until he had discovered every last thing about his sister's time here. That made Rosie feel very uneasy. There was an awful lot she hadn't told him, and maybe she should have curbed her nosy streak for once and stayed hidden.

Yet deep down she wasn't sorry she'd spoken to him, not even if it stirred up some trouble. Heather had told her so many stories about her brother, so it was lovely to discover he hadn't died in the war. Maybe if Thomas could find Heather he'd also help her to take Alan away from here. That would be so good for Alan, and it might also mean Rosie could get a proper job.

Miss Tillingham, her teacher, had been very disappointed when Cole made her leave school as soon as she was fifteen. She said it was a wicked waste of a fine brain for her to stay at home just to be a housekeeper for her father and brothers. But even Miss Tillingham wasn't brave enough to express her views directly to Cole Parker. Everyone knew he considered it unnecessary for girls to have anything more than a rudimentary education.

But Rosie hadn't quite given up on learning. She always had the wireless on while she worked in the kitchen and she read every newspaper and magazine she could get her hands on. While most girls of her age could only cite King George's death back in February as the major news of the year, Rosie knew about the ins and outs of the Korean war, the spy scandal with Burgess and Maclean, and even the Mau Mau out in Kenya. One day she intended to be something more than a housekeeper.

'Rosie!' A high-pitched shriek from Alan startled her.

'What is it?' she called back, already halfway across her room towards his room next door to hers.

'I can't get to sleep,' he bleated.

Rosie squeezed past her two older brothers' single beds towards Alan. There was little space in this room. Alan's camp bed was squashed up against the window, and its position showed what little regard the men of this household had for its youngest member.

Seth and Norman had grown into carbon copies of their

father in the course of the last few years. Their respective two-year stints in the army and the hard manual work of hauling heavy loads of scrap metal had built up their muscles, and they drank and fought like Cole did too. Until such time as Alan showed signs of becoming a thug like them, and took an interest in handling guns, hunting and snaring, Rosie didn't think they'd ever find a kind word for their little brother. While Cole was merely indifferent to his youngest child and mostly ignored him, the boys actively despised him.

'You should go to sleep,' she said, sitting on Seth's bed and leaning over to stroke her little brother's forehead. 'You've got school in the morning.'

Earlier as she was putting Alan to bed, she'd been tempted to tell him about his Uncle Thomas calling here, just so he'd know there was someone in this world aside from her who was interested in him. But Rosie knew better than to risk telling him something he might blurt out accidentally.

She looked at her brother now, searching for a resemblance to Thomas, but she couldn't see one. Alan was a pallid, sickly looking boy with large, sad brown eyes and pale ginger hair. Thomas had sad brown eyes too but that was the only real similarity. In fact Thomas had put her in mind of Ashley Wilkes in *Gone with the Wind*. A sort of lean, aristocratic, intelligent face, so very different from the ruddy, coarse-featured men around these parts. She thought she remembered Heather saying he was five years older than her, so that would make him about thirty.

'I could sleep if I was in your bed,' Alan said, his big mournful eyes pleading with her.

'Now you know what Dad would say to that,' Rosie said gently. Cole had stopped Alan sharing her bed and room a few months back, part of a new regime intended to toughen the little boy up. Rosie always obeyed her father – to do otherwise would be foolhardy – but in this case she had been tempted again and again to disobey him because she knew her older brothers used every possible opportunity to frighten, ridicule and hurt Alan. Trying to get him off to sleep long before they got home from the pub wasn't a certain way of protecting him from his brothers' viciousness, but it went a long way towards avoiding it. 'I'll read you a story, that'll make you sleepy.'

The book was the same one Heather had given Rosie on her first day here. It was falling apart now, the pages loose and odd ones missing. They both knew almost all the stories by heart. Each time Rosie read it to Alan she was reminded sharply of Heather.

Three years ago when she left, the bright spark which had always burned in her father went too. To everyone else he seemed the same, but Rosie knew he was sad, blaming himself for everything. She didn't know then how to tell him she understood how he felt. She still didn't know, for Cole was an intimidating man, hard, unpredictable and usually totally uncommunicative. Yet despite that Rosie knew there was a tender place inside him for she'd seen glimpses of it many times. He loved her too, in his own way, and he was proud of her. The only way she knew how to help him then, and now, was to look after him and the boys as best she could. At least that way he wouldn't bring yet another woman to the house. He didn't have much luck with women.

From that night of the Harvest Home in 1945 when Florrie Langford had informed her Seth and Norman were only her half-brothers, and later on when she'd found Heather had joined her father in his bed, Rosie had gone out of her way to find out about her family history.

It hadn't been easy. People were too scared of Cole to gossip to her. But along with being nosy, Rosie was also persistent, and bit by bit she pieced it all together.

Ethel Parker, Seth and Norman's mother, was reputed to have been the beauty of the county with long dark hair and sultry eyes. Her father who was a farmer somewhere out beyond Glastonbury had thrown her out when she became pregnant by Cole, and she came to live at May Cottage with him and his parents. They got married just before Seth was born in 1927. In 1934 Ethel vanished, leaving her boys, then seven and six, with their father. Legend had it that she ran off with a Welsh travelling salesman.

By the time Ruby Blackwell arrived in answer to an advertisement for a housekeeper in the autumn of 1936, the boys were running wild and out of control. By all accounts she did her best to be a mother to them, and bring order into a chaotic house, but within a year Rosie was born.

Rosie wished she could remember more about her mother; it seemed awful not to have strong visual pictures in her head of someone so important. But all the images she had from her early childhood were just cloudy fragments, a striped blouse, auburn fluffy hair, a small nervous woman who, when she wasn't cooking and cleaning, sat in a chair by the stove knitting.

Yet she could recall in great detail the day her mother vanished, even though she was only six. She had gone to play with Janice Mirrel after school, and it was tipping down with rain. Mrs Mirrel got very cross in the evening when Ruby didn't turn up to collect Rosie, she kept muttering something about 'taking advantage'. Seth turned up eventually to collect her, which in itself was a very unusual event; he was sixteen then, he'd come on his bike and was soaked to the skin. Rosie overheard him explaining to Mrs Mirrel that he'd only just got back from working in Bridgwater to find the house empty and Ruby still out.

Rosie rode home on the crossbar of Seth's bike and it was very scary because it was so dark and wet. At home the stove was out, and Seth told her to go to bed straight away before her father got back.

Cole and Norman must have come home late that same night because they were downstairs when she woke the next morning. Cole said her mother must have gone up to London to see a relative and she'd be back in a few days.

But of course Ruby had never come back, and eventually Cole said he thought she must have been killed in an air raid.

Until then the war hadn't really affected Rosie personally. For as long as she could remember, the sounds of planes roaring overhead, grown-ups talking about rationing, evacuees, clothing coupons and being called up had just been a part of life, the same as it was for every other child of her age. Sometimes she was jarred into realizing that elsewhere there were some very bad things happening because adults' eyes filled with tears when they spoke of deaths in air raids or soldiers being killed. But her father wasn't away fighting like many of her schoolfriends' fathers, and even when a stick of bombs was dropped on the moors near Burtle, no one was hurt.

When her father said her mother had been killed in an air raid, war became suddenly very real, not some distant threat. She couldn't understand why her mother should be singled out to die, when every other mother she knew was still safe at home.

The two years between her mother's death and Heather's arrival were blurred. Rosie remembered being on her own a great deal, but nothing more. It seemed to her that her bank of memories only really started with Heather. Certainly in September of 1945 they were all happy ones.

Heather had moved permanently into Cole's room the day after the Harvest Home and everything was wonderful for a whole year. Cole stayed home a great deal of the time and the cottage rang with laughter as he repapered the bedrooms and Heather made new pretty curtains. Even when Seth came home on leave from the army he couldn't manage to spoil things, or even influence Norman against Heather.

But as Heather's belly swelled with her expected baby,

that autumn things began to go wrong. Maybe it was because for the first time ever Cole was finding it hard to make money. Perhaps it was partly because he dreaded Norman going off on his National Service too, leaving him without any male assistance. But it certainly seemed that Cole was suddenly resentful of the burden of another expected child.

He had begun to find fault with everything. He started to disappear off to the pub the moment he'd eaten his evening meal and sometimes he didn't come home at all. Before long Rosie was often woken late at night by her father shouting and furniture being overturned. She would hear Heather crying and she knew Cole had slapped her.

It was those noises which brought back vague memories of similar fights between her own mother and her father, and Rosie became very frightened. Heather had seemed to change overnight; she became pale and listless and although her belly was huge, her face, arms and legs were very thin. She always seemed to be tired, sometimes sinking into a chair at midday and unable to get up again, and her situation wasn't helped by heavy snow falls in January of 1947 which made all her chores, like the washing, so much more difficult. Rosie did her best to help her, but she found it hard to pump the water. Turning the handle of the mangle outside, in temperatures that were below freezing, was beyond her.

The snow continued. That winter was the coldest on record and animals were freezing to death in the fields. Rosie remembered seeing Heather trying to dig a path in the heavy drifts to get to the coal shed and falling down with exhaustion before she'd even managed to fill a bucket. There were many times when there was no fire and little to eat because the local shops could get no provisions, and Rosie scooped up snow to melt over the oil lamp because the pump was frozen up.

Heather went into labour in February and it lasted for

two long days. The road to the village was blocked with deep drifts of snow, and even if Cole had attempted to get a doctor for her, it was doubtful he could have got through in his car. All Rosie knew of childbirth was watching lambs being born, but even though she partly believed her father when he said Heather was making a fuss about nothing, it didn't seem right to her that he let her go on and on with that terrible screaming and just stayed downstairs, drinking cider and ignoring her. It was she who finally got help; she trudged through the snow to the vicarage which had a telephone and the midwife arrived a couple of hours later on a tractor.

'Let's hope the little bastard is born dead,' Cole mumbled before he finally passed out in his chair. 'What do I want with any more kids?'

There had been times in the last couple of years when Rosie had thought of her father's horrifyingly callous words that night and almost wished Alan hadn't survived either, because it seemed his birth was the moment everything went finally and irreparably wrong. But Rosie had only been ten then; a baby was like a dolly and she loved Alan from the first moment she held him in her arms.

Cole never took to Alan. It didn't help that he was small and sickly, crying almost continuously, and that the bitter winter went on and on. But Cole studiously ignored him, and ignored Heather too for that matter, unless he was picking a fight with her. She couldn't do anything to please him. When the hens refused to lay, it was Heather's fault. If the stove went out it was because she hadn't laid it properly. Then in the autumn of 1947, Seth returned from his National Service and added to Heather's problems with his wet beds, drunkenness and surly behaviour.

Perhaps it was a premonition that Heather would run away too that turned Rosie into a little mother. Once she asked Heather if she would take her and Alan if she left, but the girl just looked blankly at her.

''Ow can I go?' she said, her eyes filling with tears. 'I

ain't got nowhere to go to, Rosie, and I sure as 'ell ain't got no money.'

Alan was one, Rosie eleven when her feelings of dislike for her older brothers turned to hatred. She was sent home from school early one afternoon in February because snow was expected. Walking in the back door she found baby Alan screaming his head off in his pram, yet even above that noise she heard something else from upstairs. A banging, thumping sound that chilled her, and before she lifted Alan from the pram she crept up the stairs to investigate.

What she saw was so shocking she almost wet herself, as she shrunk back against the wall on the landing out of sight. The mirror on the wardrobe in her dad's bedroom reflected back what was going on in there. Twenty-year-old Seth was fully dressed in his dirty work clothes, Heather was on all fours on the bed, her skirt tossed over her back, held there by Seth, his fingers digging into her flesh. He was mounting her from the rear, just like the bull did out in the fields. Seth was grimacing and grunting, Heather was crying, a pitiful heartbroken cry that cut through Rosie like a knife.

Worse still, Norman was standing there beside the bed watching. He was on his National Service then, and had come home on a forty-eight-hour pass the day before, still in uniform. His flies were unbuttoned, he was rubbing himself and urging his older brother to hurry so he could take over.

Rosie had tried hard to blank that memory from her mind, along with the guilt that she didn't try to do something to stop it. But she'd been so shocked, so appalled that she could do nothing but creep back down the stairs to comfort her screaming baby brother.

She wanted to tell her father, but she was too afraid of what Seth might do to her or Alan in retaliation. She didn't even dare tell Heather that she had been a witness.

It was only when Heather had run away a year later that Rosie began to suspect her own mother hadn't been killed in an air raid after all, but had fled for the same reasons as Heather, because she could no longer bear the cruelty of Cole and his boys.

She fully understood why both women had left. She didn't blame either of them for deserting her, but one thing troubled her deeply. Why did Heather leave Alan behind? Rosie had got home from school to find him still strapped in his pram down in the orchard, screaming fit to bust because he was wet and hungry.

There were good enough reasons to explain why Rosie's own mother had left her behind. She was six after all and her father's pet. But Heather knew Cole didn't love Alan. How could she have left him to the mercy of three men whom she knew to be dangerous and without the slightest interest in his well-being?

Seth had once viciously remarked that Heather was a tart, that she had men in the cottage all the time during the day, and left Alan behind because she'd gone off with a man who didn't want the kid around. But Rosie never believed it. Heather might have been a little simple, but she had loved her baby.

For a long time after she went Rosie fully expected her to reappear one day to collect Alan when the men were out, but she never did.

So Alan had become, to all intents and purposes, Rosie's child. Cole paid a couple of shillings a week to someone in the village to mind him while she was at school, he paid for clothes and shoes, albeit begrudgingly. But he took no interest in the small boy and left everything else, including protecting him from the older boys, to Rosie.

Later, downstairs, Rosie laid a blanket on the kitchen table, spread a sheet over it and plugged the iron into the overhanging light. The electricity had only been put in last year and she still thought it was a miracle. It was good to have running water in the kitchen too, but that had been here for two years now, and she'd got used to that.

She dampened down her brothers' shirts and rolled them up tightly while she waited for the iron to get hot, but her mind wandered on to what was going on in the Crown and if Thomas was in there too.

Thomas was in the Crown, tucked into a corner with his second pint of cloudy rough cider. Sam used to talk about this cider all the time in the camp, and although Thomas wasn't wild about the taste, he felt he owed it to Sam to sup at least three before the night was out.

He'd knocked on the door of the pub earlier in the afternoon after he'd left Rosie and asked if they had a room. Mrs Hilda Colbeck the landlady had been very wary at first. She said she didn't usually bother with paying guests, unless they would be staying a full week, but she relented when Thomas admitted he couldn't walk much further. It seemed she had a soft spot for wounded ex-servicemen.

Over a robust dinner of steak and kidney pudding with both Colbecks, Hilda had quizzed him as to why he was in Somerset. Thomas thought it judicious to keep quiet for now about Heather and told them about his friend Sam Gurney and how he'd planned to look around the area before moving on to search for his family in nearby Henton.

With his leg feeling a little easier, and a large dinner inside him, Thomas was now watching and listening to Cole Parker and his sons who'd arrived at about seven-thirty.

He didn't need to wait for someone to greet them by name to know who the three men were; the moment they swaggered through the door he guessed. All shared the same shiny black hair, dark hooded eyes and swarthy skin. A handsome trio, taller, with wider shoulders than any other man in the bar and a certain dominance that told him they saw themselves as the lords of this particular manor.

Yet however they saw themselves Thomas knew immediately they weren't popular. The temperature seemed to drop a few degrees as they came in; the smiles of greeting looked strained. No one actually met their eyes.

The bar was full, but then it was quite small, with a low beamed ceiling and an inglenook fireplace which took up enough room for half a dozen more drinkers. Aside from Hilda, behind the bar, there were no women. Most of the men were farm workers, still in their rough working clothes with muck on their boots, and they all had the same rolling Somerset accent. But everyone paled into insignificance next to the Parkers.

The two boys were so similar they could easily pass as twins, an inch or so taller than their father and far leaner, their complexions smooth and tanned a golden brown. But though the boys had youth on their side, still perfect teeth and firm bodies, their features were bland compared with Cole's. The boys had thin lips and narrow noses; Cole's mouth was wide, fleshy and sensual, and his nose was broad. He smiled easily, his laugh was deep and throaty, belying the bad temper Rosie had hinted at. In fact if she hadn't warned Thomas her father wouldn't be receptive to questions about Heather, he would have had no compunction at approaching the man right now.

But the boys were different. They didn't seem to hold conversations as such, but greeted other men with the kind of sarcastic banter that suggested they were incapable of real friendship, and they looked around them constantly to check the effect they were having on everyone. Thomas smiled to himself at this. He'd met so many men like these during his time in the army. Strutting, dim-witted bully boys who, if you could separate them from their sidekicks and give them a dose of their own medicine, would turn into snivelling runts.

'Come on, Stan, get the pints in. It's your shout,' one of the boys called out suddenly. Thomas guessed this must be Seth and the object of his attention was a very small man in a Norfolk jacket who looked distinctly nervous.

There was a sudden hush. The little man had only come in to the bar in the last fifteen minutes and he certainly hadn't been stood a drink by any of the Parkers.

'I can't tonight,' the man replied, licking his lips nervously and clutching his pint mug in front of him. 'I've no money on me. I only came in for a quick one.'

Seth grinned. 'Well, let's make it quicker for you then,' he said and with that grabbed the man's hair with one hand, tilting his head back, and seizing the pint from Stan's hand began to pour it into the little man's open mouth.

There was a titter of uncomfortable laughter, several men turned their heads away, but no one lifted a finger to stop it. Stan's arms flayed wildly, he was choking and spluttering, beer running all down his jacket.

Thomas started to get up out of instinct, but Hilda shot him a warning glance from across the bar.

'Now then, Seth,' she said reprovingly. 'Stop that this minute. Thass no way to behave.'

Thomas noted from the faces of all the other customers that they were in total agreement with Hilda, but no one attempted to back her up.

Seth ignored Hilda and continued to pour the beer in the man's mouth.

It was Cole who stopped it. He laid one hand on his son's forearm. 'Enough, son,' he said quietly.

Stan backed away, still spluttering, reached for the door latch and was off without a word. Thomas sunk back into his seat and pretended to look at an old photograph on the wall beside him. He guessed Seth would be looking around, hoping to challenge anyone unwise enough to pass comment.

By closing time, Thomas had the Parkers' full measure. All three men had consumed at least eight pints of cider each and their voices became louder with each one. They bragged constantly, about horses they'd backed, women who fancied them, deals they'd done. He heard they were off to London next week collecting up Anderson shelters. Apparently they could get as much as ten pounds for each one they dug up, along with often getting the owner to pay them on top for disposing of it for them. Seth made a crack about knocking off lonely housewives too, while Norman said something about giving old ladies a couple of bob for old furniture and silver.

As the bar closed on the last customer and Thomas got up to go to his room he felt sickened that his young sister had lived in a house for four years with such creatures. They seemed worse than animals to him. Women were there to be used and abused, as they conned, lied and cheated their way through life. He wondered too how Rosie had managed to turn out so nicely, and also how safe she was in the company of those two brothers.

'Weren't you lonely stuck in that corner alone?' Hilda asked him as she followed him up the stairs. 'You should have sat at the bar. We're a friendly bunch really.'

'I was happy enough watching and listening,' he replied. 'Those three dark men particularly. They were characters!'

She stopped at the top of the narrow staircase and turned to look at Thomas, her narrow, bony face full of contempt. 'Just between you and me,' she said, 'if I had my way they'd never step over the threshold here again. Blaggards the three of them, they'd sell their own grandmother for tuppence. But Harold's scared of 'em.'

'Don't cut that bread so thin,' Cole snapped at Rosie the next morning. He was washing at the kitchen sink, but he must have been watching her in the mirror. 'Those sandwiches are for men, not a bloody garden party. Seth! Norman! Get down here, you lazy buggers!' he roared up the stairs.

It was half past six. Rosie had been up for an hour

already. She'd lit the stove, collected up eight new-laid eggs from the hens, and three huge fried breakfasts were waiting in the oven, the kettle nearly boiling for tea.

Cole was so big he blocked out all light from the kitchen window. He wore the same dirty grey trousers he wore every working day, his braces hanging down at the sides as he washed his armpits. People said he was a fine-looking man, and at times when he was dressed in his Sunday suit Rosie agreed with them; but not in the early mornings, with thick black stubble covering his entire lower face and his hairy paunch hanging over his trousers.

Rosie silently put the three plates of breakfast on the table as Seth and Norman came into the kitchen, wearing just their trousers.

'D'you want a flask too?' she asked her father. He had put on his clean shirt, combed his hair and his braces were back on his shoulders. She was nervous now her brothers were in the room. She was never comfortable in their presence any more. The girls in the village might find them handsome, but she didn't.

Seth stunk of urine, and that meant he had wet the bed again. There was a strong smell of stale sweat too, and it sickened her to think they would probably put the clean shirts she'd just ironed over their unwashed bodies. Neither of them ever cleaned their nails, or brushed their teeth. Cole might have a vicious temper but at least he was fastidious.

'Don't you go getting no lads in here today while we're gone,' Seth said. 'Or we'll cut off their balls when we get back.'

'Leave her alone,' Cole scowled at his eldest son. 'Our Rosie's got more sense than that. And you, lad, can wash yerself proper before we leave. You stink worse than pig shit.'

Rosie slipped silently out the door and off up the stairs at that comment, not even waiting for Cole's answer about a flask. When Seth was reprimanded by his father, he usually took it out on someone. She had no intention of being the target.

She gagged as she went in to see Alan. As she expected Seth had wet his bed and the smell of ammonia was disgusting. He never apologized, much less stripped the sheets. But then he was an animal in every way. He often vomited on the floor and left it for her to find, just as he would sometimes do more than just pee in the chamber pot and leave that too. She suspected if she wasn't there to change the sheets and clean up after him, he'd just go on wallowing in it like a pig.

As she pulled off the sheets, Alan woke.

'Shush,' she whispered, putting a finger up to her lips. 'Stay there till they've gone out, then we'll have our breakfast together.'

Ten minutes later Rosie heard her father bellow out her name. She ran down the stairs. 'I was just making the beds. Are you going now?'

Cole smiled at her and held out a half-crown.

'We'll be at the auction all day, and we won't be back until late, so we'll get sommat to eat there,' he said. 'It's a hot 'un again, so after you've done the chores, take a walk down to the village and get yourself an ice-cream.'

The unexpected treat and consideration pleased Rosie. On impulse she ran down the last few stairs to hug him. Fortunately Seth and Norman had gone outside to the pickup truck. Cole was never as warm when they were in earshot.

'You're a good 'un,' he said, hugging her back. 'Now don't you go forgetting to shut the hens up this evening, there's foxes about. And get that lazy little bugger up, he should be helping you at his age, not lying abed.'

She followed her father outside to wave him off. It was a beautiful morning, a light haze hanging over the moors. She suddenly felt very happy. With the men out till late and no evening meal to prepare, it would be like a holiday.

*

Rosie held Alan's hand as they walked along the lane to the village school. It was the best part of the day for her, a chance to see a few people, even if no one stopped to speak. But today as Cole had given her half a crown, she could buy a newspaper and Mrs Willis the shopkeeper might have a few old magazines for her.

She saw Thomas long before she reached the Crown. He was sitting outside on the bench as if he was waiting for the bus into Bridgwater. The bus didn't arrive until half past nine, so the only reason he could be there now was to wait for her to pass by on the way to school.

Suddenly she was glad that she'd put on her better dress – the blue and white striped one she'd ironed last night.

Keeping a tight hold on Alan's hand she walked on, willing Thomas not to draw attention to them by calling out to her. When he opened a newspaper in front of him she knew he had spotted her, but he merely nodded and then appeared to be reading.

Her heart thumped so loudly as she walked right past him, she was sure he'd be able to hear it, and she covered her confusion by pointing out a couple of white doves sitting on the roof of the Crown to Alan, pausing just long enough so Thomas could take a good look at the small boy. She glanced towards the man, putting one finger to her lips and, understanding, Thomas winked back at her.

Thomas felt a surge of unexpected emotion when he looked at Alan. It was like looking back at himself as a small boy. The same dark brown eyes, which his mother had always said were too big for his face, the knobbly, much scarred knees and the pale, thin face. Alan's hair was more red than blond though, and he looked nervy which Thomas had never been.

Late last night Hilda had given him the full nine yards on Cole Parker, his sons and his disappearing women. It was alarming stuff, even taking exaggeration and spiteful gossip into account. Thomas had woken this morning after a disturbed night knowing this was one situation he couldn't walk away from.

It had dawned on him during the night that the word 'avoidance' summed up what was different about him now, compared to how he'd been before capture by the Japs. Once he took everything head-on. Trouble was faced with courage and belief in himself. If a mate got in a fight he'd join in too, right or wrong. He would stand against injustice, even at risk of losing his own liberty; running or avoidance to him was rank cowardice. When he first arrived in the camp in Burma, even after a gruelling march with little food or water, he still believed it was his duty to his country to fight the Japs every step of the way.

He was flogged twice in the first two months for refusing to obey the guards' orders, left in the hot sun with his back in ribbons until he thought he heard the clank of the Pearly Gates. But gradually the futility of rebellion sunk in. He saw so many good men die because of stubborn pride or sheer cussedness. Captain Gregson allowed himself to be strapped to a bamboo frame and left to die slowly and horribly in the boiling sun rather than apologize for insulting a Japanese officer. Another man was whipped to death when admitting he had a wireless hidden in his hut would have saved him. The Japs found the wireless anyway, and punished every man in the hut. Still more men died for far less noble reasons, just disease and slow starvation.

It was the many camp funerals which finally made Thomas truly value his own life. Nothing was worse than to take the corner of a makeshift bamboo coffin on his shoulder and, with each step towards the freshly dug grave, endure the horror of his face, shoulders and chest becoming splattered with the dead man's putrid bodily fluids, which were considerable if he'd died from beriberi. There was no dignity or glory in such an end, and Thomas vowed then that survival was all, that avoiding trouble was not cowardice but sanity.

But in the early hours of this morning Thomas realized it was time he found his old spirit and stood up again to be counted, whatever the personal cost.

As Rosie drew her brother on to the school gates, Alan looked back over his shoulder at Thomas. For just a moment their eyes met and Thomas smiled.

He knew then that, come what may, he would get Alan out of Cole Parker's clutches. He just wished he could do something for Rosie too. From what Hilda had told him she had a hell of a life.

Chapter Three

'Vic's early today,' Rosie said to Alan as she heard a vehicle draw up outside. It was Saturday morning, just after nine, and she was polishing the parlour table. 'I'd better go and get some money off Dad.'

Vic was a travelling greengrocer. He called in his van every Saturday, but he didn't normally get to May Cottage until eleven or twelve.

Alan climbed up on a chair to look out the window. 'It's not Vic,' he said. 'It's policemen.'

Rosie was startled, and quickly checked to see if her brother was right. 'So it is,' she exclaimed, seeing PC Nutting, the local policeman, putting on his helmet. To her consternation he was accompanied by another man she did not know. He was wearing a peaked cap and he had stripes on the sleeve of his uniform. She thought he must be senior to Ernie Nutting.

Her father and brothers had only arrived home late last night after two weeks working away in London. They were tired and filthy but in high spirits, with a full lorry-load of Anderson shelters. For once they didn't even go down to the pub, but climbed into the tin bath out in the yard, one after the other, then went straight to bed.

Seth and Norman were still in bed, Cole was in the kitchen eating his breakfast. For the police to call so soon after their return seemed very ominous, especially in a car. It was a common enough occurrence for Ernie Nutting to call in on his bicycle while on his beat; he'd dropped by just last Monday because he'd heard Rosie was alone with Alan in the cottage. But he wouldn't call with another officer unless it was official business.

Pausing just long enough to tell Alan to stay where he was, Rosie ran out to warn her father.

Cole was just wiping the egg off his plate with a lump of bread as she blurted out the news. His braces were dangling down by his sides, but he was wearing a clean white vest and he'd shaved.

'Don't look so worried,' he said, grinning broadly. 'Your dad ain't done nothing.' He merely picked up his tea and swigged it down noisily.

He stood up at the loud rapping on the door, hoisted his braces on to his shoulders and wiped the egg off his face with the back of his hand.

'Let's go and find out what they want,' he said, and slinging one big arm round her shoulder he led her out of the back door with him and round to the front of the house.

Rosie was no fool. So maybe Cole didn't have anything 'hot' in the house this time, but she knew that whenever he used her as a prop, he did have something to hide. When Ernie Nutting called to make inquiries after someone fitting Cole's description had been seen bagging a brace of pheasant on the big estate over by Wells, or when car tyres had mysteriously disappeared from a neighbouring village, it helped Cole's cause greatly having her around as a distraction, or to back him up with an alibi for the night in question. Rosie had always enjoyed these little bits of play-acting, it made her feel important.

'Can't open the front door, I'm afraid. Long since seized up with age, just like me,' Cole joked to the two policemen. 'Hullo, Ern! What brings you round here so early, and where's the iron horse?'

Nutting grinned sheepishly and tweaked at his helmet. He was a big man with a round weather-beaten face that made him look much older than he was. Cole always claimed he was a pillock, but Rosie liked him because he was kind, jolly and a keen gardener. He often gave her seedlings he'd grown in his greenhouse. She wondered why he didn't answer her father's question about his bike.

The man in the peaked cap with Ernie was looking hard at her.

'Is this your daughter, Mr Parker?' he asked.

'Yes, this is our Rosie,' Cole smiled down at her affectionately, clamping his hand firmly on her shoulder. 'Why, have you come to arrest her? What's she been up to?'

Rosie suddenly remembered Thomas Farley. It was nearly three weeks since he was here, and in the two weeks her father had been away she'd hardly given him a passing thought. All at once she guessed this police visit was precipitated by him; it had nothing at all to do with Cole's business activities. Her stomach churned.

'Nothing, at least as far as we know. I'm Sergeant Headly from Bridgwater. I've called today with PC Nutting to make some inquiries about a missing person, Heather Farley.' The policeman looked right at Rosie and smiled. He had bright blue eyes and a narrow dark moustache. Rosie thought he looked nice. She had a gut feeling that the smile was intended to reassure her he wasn't going to tell Cole that Thomas had spoken to her already. 'We believe she was your housekeeper, Mr Parker, for some four years? We'd also like to talk to her son Alan. As we understand it, Miss Farley left him in your care.'

Rosie held her breath for a moment, expecting her father to fly off the handle. But to her surprise he looked unconcerned.

'Dunno that I can be much help,' he said with a shrug. 'As Ernie will tell you, she shot off three years since without a word to me or anyone else. You'd better come indoors to see the boy.'

As they walked around the house Rosie grew more anxious. She wished she'd had some warning so she could have dressed Alan in his school clothes. The patched grey shorts and too small flannel shirt he was wearing today made him look neglected.

It was the first time Rosie ever remembered her father taking anyone into the parlour. He always said he didn't want people seeing the nice things he had in there because they might think he'd pinched them. It certainly was odd in that case to take a policeman in there. But even odder was that instead of looking irritated that Alan was cowering behind one of the armchairs, he picked him up in his arms.

'This is my boy Alan. Say hullo to the policemen,' he said and wiped a smudge off the boy's face with a display of parental tenderness.

Alan was rendered rigid and speechless by his father's unusual behaviour. Rosie was too; she'd never seen Cole pick Alan up before. He was far more likely to kick him out of the way.

'He's a bit shy,' Cole said. 'We don't get many visitors out here.'

Rosie stood in the doorway of the parlour, not knowing whether to go right in, offer to make tea, or run for it. Ernie Nutting looked uneasy, he had taken off his helmet and he stood, turning it awkwardly in his hands. He avoided looking at Cole or Rosie.

'How old are you, Alan?' Sergeant Headly asked, taking a step nearer to Cole and the boy.

'Five,' Alan replied, looking towards Rosie for an explanation.

'Well, let's see how big a five-year-old is.' The policeman indicated that Cole was to put him down.

Rosie was on tenterhooks. It was quite possible that Thomas had found people in the village a great deal more eager to talk about her family than she had been. Suppose someone had told him Cole and the boys were cruel to Alan? What if the policeman pulled up Alan's shirt and saw the stripes on his back from the last caning he'd got just before they went to London?

But to her relief the senior policeman sat down on the sofa and chatted to Alan for a moment or two, asking him about school, how he was getting on with his reading and sums, then he patted the small boy's bottom and told him to run along because he wanted to speak to his dad.

Rosie took Alan out into the kitchen and began to clear away the breakfast things. Once the parlour door was shut she could hear nothing but the low rumble of voices, too indistinct to allow her to eavesdrop.

'Why did he talk to me, Rosie?' Alan asked, taking the butter dish to the pantry to put it away. He looked puzzled rather than alarmed. He wasn't used to being singled out for attention.

Rosie didn't know what to say. She couldn't explain that their visit was connected with his mother, as that might upset him. Besides, Seth or Norman might come down at any minute.

'He was just being friendly,' she said. 'I expect he likes little boys.'

It was some ten minutes later just as Rosie was about to go down into the orchard with a bowl to pick some raspberries that she heard the bellow of Cole's voice raised in anger.

'Who said that? Give me the bastard's name and I'll drag him round here to make him admit he lied. I could've dumped the kid at an orphanage, but I've looked after him, fed and clothed him, even though his mother didn't want him.'

Rosie wanted to stay and hear more, but she took one look at Alan's stricken face, and knew she must get him out of earshot before he heard more.

Once down amongst the raspberry bushes Rosie considered the cause and likely outcome of this police visit. It was obvious from her father's indignation that someone had been talking. It would almost certainly mean a good hiding for both Alan and herself.

Rosie was very scared of her father when he was angry

66

and his good hidings were terrible, but her main concern now was for Alan. Cole was like the Devil himself when he laid into him, and it wasn't right for such a little boy to be punished for something he knew nothing about.

Looking around her she tried to think of somewhere to hide Alan, but in her heart she knew that would be a pointless exercise as it would only make Cole even more angry when he finally found him.

Then an idea came to her.

For a moment she dismissed it as too extreme, but a glance sideways at Alan made her mind up for her. He was just standing there, white-faced, looking back at the house, his dark eyes wide with fright. There was nothing she could do to distract him. He knew just as she did that there was trouble brewing, and knew too he would get the worst of it.

Heather had spoken about Thomas so often that Rosie felt she knew him well. Just that one brief chat with him had confirmed that Heather hadn't exaggerated his good qualities. This visit from the police was proof that he not only intended to find his sister, at all costs, but that he felt responsible for Alan's welfare too.

Rosie had always tried to shield Alan from her father's rages, but she hadn't been able to prevent the last beating he'd received. All he'd done was drop a couple of eggs in the yard and Cole had taken the cane to his back. Now she suddenly understood that by hiding her father's and brothers' cruelty to the boy she was actually condoning it. That made her as bad as them.

Her idea was drastic and she'd be in deep trouble with her father once he found out. But for Alan's sake, she had to do it, whatever the consequences. Thomas cared enough to send the police here, so he would look out for Alan whether or not he found Heather. Yet all the same Rosie felt heartsick. She loved her little brother so much, she couldn't bear the thought of being separated from him.

One further glance at him was enough though. He was trembling, unable even to pick a few raspberries. She knew then that his safety today and in the future was far more important than her own feelings. Maybe his Uncle Thomas wouldn't be able to look after Alan himself, but even putting him in a children's home was better for him than staying here.

Blinking back her tears she dropped down to her knees and caught hold of her brother, looking right into his eyes. They were soft and trusting. Maybe if he went away now he would grow up to be different from Norman and Seth. She owed Heather a great deal; the least she could do now was make sure she acted in her little boy's best interests.

'Alan,' she said, holding him to her tightly. 'I want you to do something very quietly, very cleverly, so no one sees you.'

She gave him his instructions, making them as simple as possible.

He listened carefully, his head cocked to one side, the sunshine on his hair making it glow like burning embers in a fire.

'You mean now?' he asked, looking anxious, but not opposed to the idea.

'Yes, now, while Dad's still indoors talking. When he comes out with the police I'll pretend you are still down here picking raspberries.'

'But why can't you come too?'

Rosie wished she could. 'I have to stay here so they don't suspect anything.'

'But when will I see you again?' Alan's eyes were suddenly wary. His fingers reached out to cling on to her.

'I don't know,' she said honestly. 'Just do what I said, tell them what I said. Now go and keep right down under the fence.'

Helping him through the barbed wire on the fence at the side of the orchard she kissed him one more time and patted his bottom in the direction of the road when he hesitated. She just wished she could tell him that there was someone else out there who loved him, but there was no time for that now.

'Clever boy,' she said, biting back tears. 'Go on, now.'

Rosie waited behind the raspberry bushes until she saw the policemen coming out of the kitchen door. As she had half expected Cole followed them, smiling genially.

She sighed. Cole had a knack of bending people to his will. She had no doubt he'd managed to convince the sergeant that he was a wonderful father to Alan, and Ernie Nutting would go along with it because he was just as scared of Cole as everyone else around here. She forced herself to run back towards the yard as if the two policemen were visiting neighbours she wanted to say goodbye to.

'I'm just sorry you were dragged out on a fool's errand,' she heard Cole say as he shook the men's hands. 'There's people around here who would accuse the Pope of wrong-doing. Between us, I was a fool over Heather; I should have known better than to think I could make a city girl settle out here. She hurt me very bad when she ran off, but that don't mean I'd take it out on our little boy. But I suppose I've earned my reputation as a hard man, and I have to live with all the suspicion that comes with it. If the boy's uncle wants to see him, that's all right with me.'

Sergeant Headly turned towards Rosie as she came running up with a bowl of raspberries in her hands. 'Hullo! What've you done with Alan?'

'He's down there picking raspberries,' she said, waving her arm vaguely in the direction of the orchard.

Headly stepped closer to her and took a raspberry from her bowl. 'Umm,' he said appreciatively as he ate it. 'My favourite. Keep up the good work.' He smiled warmly at her. 'Your father has been telling us what a good little mother you make. And that you're something of an expert on flowers.'

Rosie blushed and looked down at her feet. As usual she was barefoot and they were very dirty. She felt ashamed, not only of her feet but also her stained and torn dress.

'We'll be off then.' Sergeant Headly spoke directly to Cole, and put his cap back on. 'Sorry to have taken up so much of your morning.'

Rosie held her breath until she heard the car drive away. But just as she took the first big gasp of air, Cole rounded on her.

'Get that little bastard and bring him here,' he snarled at her, his face taking on a purplish hue. 'I'll teach him to complain he's been ill-treated!'

'What do you think then, sir?' Ernie Nutting asked as the senior officer drove back towards Ashcott where Ernie was stationed. Ernie had been very surprised yesterday when he'd been given orders to accompany the County Sectional Sergeant from Bridgwater on this inquiry. As the local beat officer he knew all the Parkers well, and all the old stories about them, but he felt that most of those about Cole were exaggerated. In his book the two sons were black-hearted rogues, but Cole was a character. Maybe he didn't keep his house in order, he drank too much, he was hot-tempered and possibly a bit unscrupulous in his business dealings, but he added a bit of colour to the community. As for Rosie, she was one of the nicest kids Ernie had ever met. How could she be like that if her father really was such a blaggard?

Ernie hadn't met Sergeant Headly more than three or four times before, but he knew he had a reputation for being highly intelligent and intuitive. Ernie was a bit puzzled now he'd seen him in action. On the way over here he'd given him the impression that this was a very serious inquiry, yet the minute they got in the door of the Parker place, he'd seemed entirely on Cole's side, chatting as if it was just a social call. When he finally got around to raising the point about suspected cruelty to Alan, and asked why Cole hadn't reported the two women missing, he'd even sounded embarrassed. Ernie had expected that a senior officer would be much tougher.

'I think the man's a –' Headly paused mid-sentence at a rustle from the back of the car. Both men jerked their heads round.

'Well I never,' Headly exclaimed, as he glimpsed Alan crouching down behind the front seats. He pulled over to the side of the road immediately, and leaned over the seat. 'What on earth are you doing in here, sonny?'

'Rosie told me to do it,' Alan squeaked. 'She said I was to hide in here and tell you things.'

'A police car is no place for pranks,' Ernie said in the pompous voice he always kept for small bad boys. He might have cuffed him round the ear too, but before he could move, Headly got out of the car, pulled his seat forward and held out his arms to the boy.

Sergeant Ronald Headly was a family man with five children ranging from fifteen down to three. In over twenty years in the force he'd seen countless frightened children, but he didn't remember ever having been quite so moved as he was by this small boy's fear.

Alan cringed back into the car, arms held up to protect his head from the expected blows. His white face was taut with terror and he was quivering.

'Its okay, sonny,' Headly reassured him. 'I'm not cross with you and I don't smack little children. Come on out a minute.'

Alan moved only slightly, but enough for Headly to see he had a big, dark stain on his grey flannel shorts, and urine was dripping down his skinny legs.

'Don't worry about your trousers,' Headly said. 'We'll find something for you down at the station. You are a good boy to do what your sister told you. So come on out here and tell me all about it.'

When Thomas Farley had called in at the police station in Bridgwater almost three weeks earlier and told Headly the story about his sister and her child, the Sergeant's first

71

reaction was that it wasn't a police matter, but something social workers could deal with.

During the war a great many young women had come from the big cities to the area for one reason or another. Some of these women had got themselves into trouble and in a few cases they had vanished leaving the baby behind them. As far as Headly could see the only thing separating Heather from these other women was that she hadn't abandoned the child in a church, field, or shop, but left him with his father.

But there was something very upright and straightforward about Farley. He had an exemplary war record. Headly felt he owed the man a full report.

'Let's slip these off,' Headly said, unbuttoning the boy's trousers for him there by the side of the road. 'I expect your shirt will keep you decent.'

As Headly removed the wet shorts and underpants, he saw tell-tale marks of an old beating across the boy's bony buttocks. He lifted Alan's shirt and saw that his back was criss-crossed with thick brown scars, probably at least a couple of weeks old now and therefore healing over. But whoever gave him the beating had broken the skin at the time.

'Who beat you, Alan?' Headly tried to keep his voice light, even though he was consumed with a fierce anger.

'My dad.' Alan's eyes filled with tears and spilled over. 'Rosie said I was to tell you so he couldn't do it again.'

Headly picked him up and held him tightly to his chest. He looked hard at Nutting who was still sitting in the passenger seat, staring straight ahead. He thought the constable needed a kick up the pants, but this wasn't the moment. 'You drive, Constable,' he said. 'The boy can sit on my lap.'

At five that afternoon, Headly once again drove out to Catcott. This time he wasn't accompanied by PC Nutting, but by Detective Inspector Dunn from CID. Their intention was to inform Cole Parker that Alan was in the care of the local authority and warn him that charges of cruelty to a child were likely to be laid against him. Although Headly was far from happy that a child had to be hurt before he could prevail upon a senior officer to take a more active interest in his investigation into Cole Parker's activities, he was certainly glad of a good reason to be returning to May Cottage. Detective Inspector Dunn was a hard-headed man, unlikely to be taken in by Parker's charm. He'd chalked up thirty years with the force and like Headly he followed hunches.

Alan was now safely and quite happily in the care of Miss Pemberton, the local social worker, and on his way to a temporary foster home in Taunton. He had been very upset at first to find himself the focus of so much attention, and he kept asking when he'd see Rosie again. But by the time he'd been washed and found some dry clothes and given some dinner, and realized that he wasn't about to be punished in any way, he had become quite talkative.

To police officers with children of their own who had never done more than give their offspring the odd clout or smack on the leg, it was horrifying to find such a young child totally unaware that all children were not beaten with sticks for merely wetting the bed or dropping an egg. Again and again Alan's reports on both his brothers' and father's behaviour were slanted as if he thought himself entirely bad and therefore deserving of such treatment. When asked if Rosie was beaten too, he admitted that she was sometimes, but not so often as him because she was a girl and anyway she looked after them all.

'Have you ever known a man left alone with a child who didn't report the mother missing, sir?' Headly asked some minutes into their journey.

Dunn shook his head. He was fifty-seven, but looked younger, with cold grey eyes, thin lips and a full head of dark brown hair. His wife had once commented that the reason he stayed looking so young was because he didn't have any emotion. She was probably right; he didn't get worked up like other men. He looked at things calmly and logically.

Since Headly came back this morning with the boy, he'd studied Parker's record scrupulously. Aside from several fines for poaching and a six-month spell in Shepton Mallet prison for assault, way before the war, Parker had somehow managed to wriggle out of all the many other charges brought against him over the years. He'd been accused of black-marketeering and looting during the war, burglary and innumerable assaults, in many of which the victims were so badly hurt they had needed hospitalization. But all charges had been dropped. All too often the witnesses seemed unable to attend the court, or to make a positive identification, and in two cases the arresting officers backed down from their original statements.

'Parker certainly isn't the rough diamond PC Nutting took him for,' Dunn said scathingly. 'Damn fool! If he knew three women had disappeared from that house, why the hell didn't he bring our attention to it?'

Headly thought carefully before speaking. Privately he thought Nutting to be a little dense and extremely unobservant, but at the same time he had a little sympathy for him. It was hard getting anything out of people who lived on the Levels; they were an insular and closed community who did not readily speak out against one of their own.

'I think you might understand why Nutting overlooked it once you've met Parker,' Headly said. 'He can be a likeable bloke and on the face of it he is devoted to all his kids.'

'I'll bear that in mind,' Dunn said. 'But I've got no intention of pussy-footing around with this family. I want the whole lot of them brought in for questioning. The girl included.'

*

74

The ancient pickup truck piled high with Anderson shelters was gone from the grass verge where it had been that morning.

'Looks like we're out of luck,' Headly said as he pulled up in front of the cottage. 'His truck's gone.'

'Or in luck.' Dunn raised one eyebrow and grinned sardonically. 'It gives us a chance to poke around.'

Headly led Dunn straight round to the back yard. There was absolute silence, aside from the clucking of hens, but the back door was open.

Headly knocked but when no one came he stepped straight in, stopping in surprise at the mess on the table. A piece of ham lay on a plate, a few flies buzzing round it, and bread, butter, cheese and pots of pickles with the tops off were left there amongst the crumbs. It gave the impression that someone had snatched a meal in haste, before running out. Could they be out looking for Alan?

'Is there anyone home?' Dunn bellowed out.

Headly went out again into the back yard and looked thoughtfully at the enamel bowl lying upturned by the gate and the spilt raspberries. He went back inside and pointed it out through the window to Dunn.

'Rosie had that in her hands when we said goodbye this morning,' he said. 'I don't understand why she would just leave them there if she'd spilt them? Unless of course her father whacked it out of her hands, then gave her a beating.'

He suddenly felt afraid. Not for himself, but for Rosie. She'd organized getting Alan away; it was very likely she'd been punished for it.

Dunn was infected by the Sergeant's anxiety and opened the narrow door to the stairs. 'Anyone up there?' he yelled.

Headly pushed past him. The hunch he'd had even before seeing Alan's scars was growing stronger. He could feel something very wrong here.

He took the stairs two at a time, Dunn followed closely behind him, their heavy boots falling noisily on the bare wood. He glanced in the first bedroom, but it was empty, a double bed neatly made. In the front main bedroom the bed was unmade, but it too was empty. He rushed to the third one at the back and pushed open the closed door.

His exclamation of horror and that of Dunn, behind him, were simultaneous. Rosie was lying spread-eagled, face down across one of the two unmade beds. Her dress was pulled up over her waist, knickers wrenched down and her small naked buttocks were covered in glistening red weals. The back of her dress was soaked in blood.

There had been a violent struggle in the room. A camp bed lay in pieces on the floor, a dressing table was over-turned. There was also a strong smell of urine, worse than a public urinal on a Saturday night.

Headly leapt over to Rosie and took her pulse. 'She's alive! Rosie! Can you hear me?' he asked as he gingerly opened the buttons on the back of her dress. The blood was already congealing so that the material was sticking to her wounds. He felt he was to blame for this terrible beating. He hadn't given a thought as to what might happen to Rosie when her father found out Alan was gone. But he should have! Why hadn't he taken Alan to safety, then come right back here immediately?

A low groan proved she was conscious, and her head moved slightly so both men could just glimpse her slit-like eye in a mound of red raw tissue.

She seemed to recognize Headly. 'Will you take me away too?' she croaked.

Contrary to everything he'd ever learned about first aid, Headly hauled her up enough to get his shoulder beneath her chest in a fireman's lift, straightened up and made for the stairs.

'We should call an ambulance,' Dunn said, putting a restraining hand on his shoulder.

'Maybe,' Headly grunted. 'But do you want to leave her here another minute?'

*

Dr Willis stared down at the lacerated back and buttocks of the young girl in cubicle two of the casualty department in Bridgwater Infirmary and winced. Sister had already cleaned the wounds and he'd seen far worse injuries during the war when he was an intern at Bristol Royal Infirmary, yet the knowledge that a father could inflict such a beating on his daughter made his blood run cold.

'How are you feeling, Rosie?' he said, patting her bare arm. Sister had already said that the girl hadn't even whimpered as her dress was eased from her back. She had just lain there face down, hiding her face with her hand.

'A bit better now,' she whispered.

'It's going to be sore for a few days,' he said, wondering how anyone so small and young could be so stoic. 'But I'm going to put a dressing on your back and give you something for the pain, then we'll take you up to a ward.'

'It wasn't my dad that did it,' she said, lifting her head a little and squinting at him. Both her eyes were buried in puffy flesh; she'd have two shiners by the morning. 'He hit me so I'd tell him where Alan had gone. But it was Seth who beat me after Dad had gone out.'

Rosie had been aware that the man who carried her downstairs and out to a car was the policeman with the moustache who'd been with Ernie Nutting that morning, but she hurt so much she couldn't say anything. It was as if she had a red-hot iron on her back and all she could concentrate on was the hope that soon someone would remove it.

She didn't know or care where they were taking her to, it was all a jumble of shooting pain and being jolted around as she lay across the policeman's lap. But once she was brought in here and the nurse bathed her back, the pain had retreated enough for her to remember clearly what had happened.

Cole had struck her across the face when she said she

didn't know where Alan had gone. They were still out in the yard and she'd fallen back against the fence with the force of his blow.

'Tell me where he is!' Cole shouted at her, pulling her up by the shoulders. 'Don't play stupid games with me!'

Something snapped inside Rosie. She didn't even care if he hit her again. 'I told him to get in the police car. I told him to tell the police all the things you and the boys do to him so they'll take him away for good and let him live with his uncle.'

She had wanted to see him frightened, but his reaction to what she'd said floored her. He just backed away from her and slumped down on to the settle, holding his head in his hands.

Rosie couldn't stop then, everything she'd bottled up for years came out in a torrent. 'Heather was lovely and you made her run away. You made my mother go too and you lied to me when you said she died in London. All I do is work here, cooking and cleaning. I don't have any nice clothes, books to read and I haven't any friends, and I'm scared of Seth and Norman in case they do what they did to Heather, to me.'

He still had his head in his hands but at that last sentence he jerked up quickly. 'Whass that? What did the boys do to Heather?'

Something told her then that she'd gone too far, but there was no turning back now. 'Sexing her,' she said, not knowing what the right word for it was. 'I saw them both forcing her. Heather was crying. And Seth scares me most because he's always touching me here.' She put her hands on her breast. 'He says he's just checking to see if I'm ripe for it yet.'

Cole got up. Rosie thought he was going to hit her again and she was off out the gate and down the road running as fast as she could.

But her bare feet stopped her; the stones hurt and when she paused to look back, fully expecting Cole to be just a few feet behind her, there was no sign of him. The lane was deserted. Reason got the better of her: she couldn't go to the village without shoes, and Cole couldn't be that angry with her if he hadn't chased her, so she went back.

As she crept round the junk she could hear her father shouting, so for safety's sake she crouched down behind the old tractor and listened.

'Rosie's lying, Dad. We never did that to Heather.' Seth's voice was high and whining. 'She's trying to shift blame on to us because she told on you to the police.'

'She ain't lying,' Cole roared at him. 'No one would even think of something like that unless they'd seen it. You fuckin' animals. And what's this about you touching Rosie up? She's your sister, for Christ's sake!'

There was a whistling noise and a crack followed by a yelp. Rosie realized the sound was her father's leather belt and he was laying into both boys with it.

There was pandemonium up in that room, yells, swearing, thuds and scuffling. She heard something crash, then a part of Alan's camp bed came hurtling through the window. Rosie had heard enough. She wriggled out of her hiding place and ran for it, down through the junk yard and out on to the moor.

She dangled her feet in a ditch, and wiped away the tears trickling down her cheeks. She felt so small, so alone and scared. She wasn't sorry she'd sent Alan away; at least he was safe, but without him to cuddle and care for what had she left? Long, lonely days of washing, cleaning and cooking, no trips to the school to break it up, no one to tell stories to, no one to help her feed the chickens or get them back into the henhouse. No purpose in her life other than trying to appease three men who took everything she did for granted.

The grass around her was so long now that her eyes were on a level with the feathery fronds on the top. Looking around her it was almost like being in the middle of an ocean, with the wind creating waves and ripples. In the

79

past this sight had pleased her, but today it made her feel as though she was drowning. And there was no one anywhere to hold out a helping hand.

She guessed by the position of the sun that it was around two when she made for home. There was no point in staying out any longer. She had all the men's dirty work clothes to wash, she hadn't even made their beds yet today and they'd only get angrier if she was late starting the evening meal.

The mess she found in the kitchen cheered her a little. It meant they had all gone out in a hurry, probably to Bristol to dispose of the Anderson shelters. She sighed with relief; at least she'd have some peace until tea time and if they got a good price for the shelters they might just forgive her about Alan and all she'd said.

She ran upstairs to collect all the dirty clothes.

There was nothing to warn her she wasn't alone in the house. Not a sound from anywhere. But as she walked into the boys' bedroom the door slammed shut behind her.

Seth was there. She smelled him even before he spoke. 'So you came back then? You little bitch,' he snarled.

He was standing behind the now shut door, wearing only a pair of trousers. His right eye was red and swollen, he had congealed blood on his lip and there were bright red weals on his shoulders and chest from Cole's belt. In his hands he held the thin stick he always used to terrorize Alan.

'I th-thought you'd g-g-gone out with Dad,' she stammered. As usual the smell of stale urine was overpowering in the small room.

'How can I go anywhere looking like this?' he said. 'And it's all your fault, so I'm gonna teach you not to tell tales.'

There was nowhere to run to. She backed away from him over a pile of dirty clothes towards the window where the broken remains of Alan's camp bed lay and, finding herself trapped, she covered her head with her hands protectively.

'Please don't hit me, Seth,' she begged, but such a plea was pointless for Seth was already raising the cane.

He swiped and swiped at her bare arms, first one, then the other, making her hop with the pain.

'Hurts, don't it?' he taunted her, prodding her cheek with the tip, then flicking it back to her side to hit that too. 'It's going to get a lot worse before I've finished.'

Seth had always been a bully, but now she saw that inflicting pain actually excited him; he was flushed with it, grinning menacingly.

Rosie tried to make a run for it as he raised his arm to bring the cane down harder, but as she tried to dodge him she tripped on the pile of clothes on the floor and fell sideways on to Norman's unmade bed.

'I'll tell Dad!' she yelled.

'You won't be alive to tell him anything,' Seth yelled back, and as the cane swished through the air Rosie just glimpsed his mouth wet with spittle and his black eyes alight with hate.

There was no counting the strokes, or trying to avoid them. They rained down on her so fast it was just one endless, agonizing explosion of pain.

'Pleeease,' she called out.

She felt him roughly pull her dress up and his hands grabbed the back of her knickers and pulled them down. She bucked furiously as her buttocks were exposed, fearing he was now going to repeat what she'd seen him do to Heather.

'Please what?' he said sarcastically. 'Will I "sex" you? That's what you called it, wasn't it?'

The cane came down again, harder still on her bare bottom, cutting into her like a knife. She tried to get her hands round to protect herself, screaming now with the pain, but he merely swiped her hands away and slashed at her again.

'You'll go to prison for this,' she screamed.

When the next expected blow didn't come, she moved her head slightly to see what he was doing. To her absolute horror he had his penis in his hand, and he was rubbing himself, just the way Norman had been doing that day while Seth attacked Heather. Aside from then, she'd never seen an erect male penis, and she'd been too shocked to notice anything about it. But Seth's looked huge, nothing like the soft, floppy thing she'd observed sometimes when he was bathing. She covered her eyes and screamed again.

'Scream again,' he said hoarsely. 'Go on, scream. I like that.'

Even through the agony of the wounds he'd inflicted upon her, Rosie's mind assimilated a message. He was mad, dangerously mad, he had no fear of what his father might do to him for this. He was beyond any kind of reason. She knew she must say nothing further to provoke him. Do nothing to encourage him.

She let out one more scream, forcing herself to control it instead of thinking about what he was doing, and closing her eyes tightly so she couldn't see his jerking wrist or his demented face. Slowly she let the scream die, hoping she was faking losing consciousness effectively.

Rosie heard him make a guttural groan, but she didn't dare open her eyes to look. She heard the twang of bed-springs as he slumped down beside her, and for a moment there was silence, punctuated only by a long-drawn-out sigh.

When his hand touched her cheek, it was all she could do not to scream again. It was sticky with something and it smelled sour. She braced herself, expecting him to pull her up, or to start beating her again, but instead she heard something which sounded very much like a sob.

Then he went. He just stood up and walked out of the room and down the stairs. Without another word.

*

82

It was Monday afternoon, two days since Sergeant Headly had found Rosie, and he was back in the same bedroom at May Cottage, leaning out of the window. It was partly to get a breath of fresh air, as the room still stunk as much as it had on Saturday, but mostly it was to watch the men below attaching chains to an old tractor to move it. They had already cleared much of the area, there were yellow and white bald patches amongst the weeds showing where the heaps of tyres and old machinery had been.

Headly felt as if he hadn't slept for a month, but then he hadn't had more than a couple of catnaps since Saturday afternoon when he'd found Rosie up here.

Cole and Norman Parker had been arrested when they arrived back at the cottage late on Saturday night. They were both very drunk and it was just as well that six officers had come along to apprehend them, as both men resisted violently. One officer sustained a black eye and a bloodied nose, Headly a cracked rib.

Cole Parker's attitude to his arrest was puzzling. He admitted almost immediately that he'd been harsh with Alan, his excuse being that boys needed discipline to toughen them up. But he showed no remorse, or even fear, that he was to be charged with cruelty. Yet when told what Seth had done to Rosie he became almost incoherent with rage, and after ranting and raving about what he'd do to Seth when he got his hands on him, he finally burst into tears, sobbing and claiming that he'd always loved Rosie, and that she was his favourite.

Norman, on the other hand, once in a cell on his own, was docile and even penitent that he'd lashed out at the police. He came across as a simple-minded boy who followed his father's and older brother's lead blindly. As he spoke about what they'd been doing in London, he used words like 'conning' and 'leaning on people' so openly that it was clear he had no real idea that this was wrong or shameful.

Neither did he seem to understand the concept of cruelty

to a small child. He just looked vacant and said Alan 'only got the stick and belt the same as me and Seth did'. Likewise when asked if his father had hit Ruby and Heather, he said, 'Well, they just got slapped when they needed it.'

Seth still hadn't been found, and this was creating something of a mystery. He hadn't been spotted by anyone and he had no transport. Like all the Parkers he knew every nook and cranny out on the moors, so it stood to reason he was holed up somewhere in a makeshift camp. But it had been raining heavily from early Sunday morning until an hour or two ago when it turned to drizzle, and though he may well have taken some provisions with him and a waterproof coat, it was doubtful he could hide out for long. More worrying still, a shotgun was missing from the porch.

Headly walked slowly down the stairs once the tractor had been moved. His rib hurt and he wished he could go home. There was no real reason for him to stay; he'd done his bit and searched the entire cottage for anything which might offer them a lead. But aside from finding a cashbox behind a loose brick in the parlour chimney containing nearly a hundred pounds, an old ration book of Heather Farley's stuffed down the back of one of the parlour chairs, a pale blue silk scarf caught up on a rough piece of wood at the back of a chest of drawers in Cole's bedroom, and a thin gold wedding ring among some cheap beads in a trinket box, he'd found little evidence there had even been grown women in the house, let alone anything which might point to murder.

Yet without any evidence Detective Inspector Dunn had organized the search and dig party on Parker's land, calling in all available men in the area to help. He said Cole couldn't account for where he was on the days his women disappeared. Neither could he give a plausible answer as to why he didn't report them missing. Headly was as convinced as Dunn that all the women were dead, but he thought Dunn very brave to play his hunch right up to the hilt and start digging. His career wouldn't shine so brightly in future if he was wrong about this.

The back yard was muddy now, tramped through by the men after yesterday's heavy rain. In the mud were various implements the Parkers had used as weapons to resist arrest – fence poles, an axe and a couple of broken bottles. And amongst the debris was Rosie's ruined garden. Every flower crushed by heavy boots. Even the ones in the old sink were squashed flat as if someone had fallen on them. It was almost symbolic of what had happened to her.

Headly didn't see how Rosie could recover, any more than those flowers could. The doctors and nurses could treat her external wounds, but he doubted whether any medicine would wipe out the memory of that beating. And there was worse to come, he knew that with utter certainty.

Detective Inspector Dunn stood back from his men and watched them dig.

'How's it going, sir?' Headly asked him. 'Any sign it's been dug before?'

Dunn shook his head. 'That junk has compressed the ground and with three years of snow, frost, rain and sun it all looks the same. But one of the lads has just found the remains of a woman's shoe down the bottom of the heap of tyres.'

Elsewhere in the Levels the ground was soft and spongy with peat, but May Cottage was built on slightly higher ground which was rock hard. Yesterday's heavy rain hadn't softened the soil that much, and it looked as if it would be a long, back-breaking job.

At half past ten that night the drizzle turned once again to heavy rain, forcing the men to retreat into a makeshift tent they'd erected just off the lane. Until now they'd carried on regardless of the wet, slipping and sliding in the mud, but now it was impossible to continue.

The top layer of compressed grass and soil had been removed from the whole area now and as the rain collected on the harder, less porous sub-soil it resembled a large paddling pool in the light of a few hurricane lamps. The senior officer ordered the men who had been on duty since that morning to go home, keeping the six men who'd joined the job in the early evening to stay on as guards.

By first light the rain had stopped, but as the men emerged with their spades to start again, they noticed an interesting phenomenon. In two places, some ten feet apart from one another, the rainwater that had collected was draining away faster than elsewhere, leaving a curiously similar rectangular shape in each case.

'Well, I'll be buggered.' PC Sam Kenting, who came from Bristol, had been amusing the men during the night with tales of a job he'd once had in a sewage works. 'If that ain't the spot where she'm laying, then I'll go back to shovelling shite tomorrow.'

When reinforcements arrived soon after six o'clock, amongst them Headly, who'd found it impossible to stay in bed, they found the six men digging furiously, three at each spot. They were already down some four feet, caked with mud from head to foot.

It was just on seven when Sam Kenting struck on a bone. He was alone in the hole, as it had become too cramped for more than one man to dig. He had been told to go off duty, but he'd ignored the order and as his yell rang out, all spades were dropped, cigarettes hastily stubbed out and everyone rushed to see what he had found.

'Don't say it ain't human,' he said, bending over and scraping away the heavy clay with his hands. 'If that ain't a bleedin' femur, then my name's Dr Crippen.'

The men circled the hole, watching as Kenting carefully

86

edged the soil away further with a trowel. Slowly they could all see a human thigh bone taking shape.

'Come on out, now,' said Headly, the first to come to his senses, holding out a hand to Sam Kenting to help him. Judging by the small size it was a woman's thigh bone, and that was enough for him now. 'I'll have to get hold of the DI and he'll want to get hold of the top brass at Taunton and the forensic boys. But well done, Sam, and all of you. I'll stand you all a pint later.'

Sister Dowd guessed the girl was crying as she made her way round the ward just after eleven-thirty in the evening of the same day. There was no sound, but her sixth sense told her what the slight quivering of the bedcovers meant. Everyone except the old lady in the bed at the far end of the ward was asleep, and her first thought was that she should allow the girl the dignity of crying alone.

But Sister Dowd was Irish, with six brothers and sisters – a warm, poor family where they shared each other's sorrows and joys. Since the news had broken at six this evening that two women's bodies had been found buried out at Catcott, a whisper had gone round the entire hospital that the young girl who'd been brought in here so badly beaten was also the daughter of the murderer. Sister Dowd was horrified that people should make such quick assumptions without any real proof to back it up. She was even more disgusted when one uncharitable soul suggested the girl should be taken somewhere else. In Sister Dowd's opinion, young Rosie was entitled to sympathy and understanding. She'd have enough to face when her father was tried.

'There now, Rosie,' she murmured, lifting back the bedclothes from the girl's face. 'Would you like to tell me about it, rather than crying all on your own?'

'I'm not crying,' Rosie insisted, her hands coming up to cover her swollen eyes. The ward was dimly lit by just a green shaded lamp over Sister's desk in the middle of the ward. 'I just can't sleep.'

'You don't fool me,' Sister said. 'I've got eyes in the back of my head and hidden antennae under my apron that tell me when someone's in pain, whether it's their injuries or their heart breaking.'

Rosie didn't answer immediately. Being in hospital was a strange and entirely new experience for her. For the first time in her life she was the centre of attention, waited on and fussed over. She had been in terrible pain for the first twenty-four hours, but even so all that caring eased it.

On Monday, she had begun to feel a little better, even hopeful for the future. A policewoman who had come in to see her said that when she was well enough to leave hospital, a social worker would help her to find somewhere else to live and, in time, a job. She said too that Alan was settling down well in his new home and that his foster parents might be able to bring him up to see her.

Sergeant Headly had been in to see her too. He brought her a pretty nightdress and a big bar of chocolate, and they talked about his children and Alan. He said that her father and Norman had been arrested on Saturday night, but Seth had disappeared. He asked Rosie to suggest places or people she thought he might have gone to. Yet he didn't once hint that he suspected Cole or her brothers of anything worse than cruelty.

Then earlier today he had returned to say that they had found two women's bodies under the junk at the side of the house which they believed to be Ruby's and Heather's, and they were charging her father with murder.

She couldn't believe it was true. She said it must be a mistake. Then she began to cry and she was so cold the policeman had to get her another blanket.

All the afternoon after he'd gone she just lay there on her tummy wishing she was dead too. It was like one of those nightmares that comes back again even after you've woken up, turned over and told yourself it isn't real. She could see the junk yard so clearly in her mind's eye, playing hide and seek with Alan there, climbing on the piles of tyres, sitting on the tractor, making camps with bits of timber and old blankets.

And all the while she had believed her mother and Heather to be living in London, they'd been there. Worms crawling over them, maggots eating their flesh. She and Alan had been playing on their mothers' graves.

Sister Dowd sat on the edge of Rosie's bed, even though she was always admonishing the nurses for doing so. 'What your father has done is his sin, not yours,' she said. 'You must keep that firmly in your mind at all times.'

'But I sat on his lap, I hugged and kissed him,' Rosie whispered. 'I loved him. How could I love a murderer?'

Sister Dowd didn't know how to answer that one and she guessed that it would be a question that would trouble the child for the rest of her life. Hate was a far easier emotion to deal with sometimes. It burned fiercely and eventually died. Love stayed.

Chapter Four

As Miss Violet Pemberton drove towards Bristol she glanced sideways at Rosie sitting in the passenger seat, concerned by her silence. The girl hadn't said a word since they left Bridgwater Infirmary almost an hour ago.

Violet was the social worker who had found a home for Alan, and now two weeks after placing him in Taunton she was taking Rosie to one too. The physical wounds she'd suffered from the beating were healed now, but Violet was afraid that the invisible, mental scars might be too deep to ever heal.

'Have you been to Bristol before, Rosie?' she asked.

Rosie wanted to reply; she knew she must appear very rude, perhaps even stupid too, just sitting here staring out the window. She didn't know why she couldn't speak; she had enough questions milling around in her head to keep her talking for days, yet she couldn't seem to articulate them. She took a deep breath. 'Once, Miss, but it was a long time ago,' she managed to get out. 'Heather took me there once on the bus, to see Father Christmas.'

Violet almost wished she hadn't asked. But then in the three previous meetings with this poor child almost every question she'd posed seemed to involve one of those people Rosie had loved and now lost.

'I don't suppose you'll recognize it then,' she said. 'Central Bristol took such a hammering during the Blitz, and now they're beginning to rebuild it. But it's a very beautiful city with some fine, big shops. I always find it an exciting place.'

Violet didn't suppose a fifteen-year-old girl who had spent her entire life tucked away in the country would share her excitement at seeing a war-damaged city resurrected, or understand that the Fifties might very well prove to be the era when momentous changes took place. Violet could feel it starting already, despite continuing rationing and austerity. The new National Health Service, the concept of a society which cared for one from the cradle to the grave, and the influences from across the Atlantic – big cars and modern labour-saving homes – were going to change traditional British working-class ethics. Before long, she felt, any man would be able to rise above that which he'd been born to. There was work for all, vast new housing estates cropping up overnight like mushrooms, and the government was delivering messages that family life was all-important, encouraging those same women who'd worked so hard in factories during the war to stay at home now and focus their undivided attention on their children and husbands. It was becoming the idealists' era.

Violet was something of an idealist herself. A short, stout woman of forty-five, she didn't do herself any favours by having her straight brown hair cut in a severe Eton crop, or choosing to wear tweed suits which advertised her stoutness, as they both created an image of an unapproachable, rather masculine woman. Yet in point of fact Violet was kind-hearted, sensitive, with a lively mind and a handsome face. Her skin was as clear and unlined as a girl's, with pretty hazel eyes and clearly defined cheekbones. But Violet Pemberton had little interest in her own appearance. She put all her energies into helping others.

Finding a home for Rosie had been extremely difficult. Setting aside most people's objections to taking in the daughter of a possible murderer, she was too old at fifteen for a regular foster home, and yet too young to fend for herself.

When a social worker colleague in Bristol suggested the

Bentleys, who she knew through her church, Violet was relieved. She would have preferred to place Rosie with someone known to her personally, but time had run out, the hospital wanted her bed, and it was important to get her right away from the Somerset Levels as feelings were running high there about the Parkers. Until something more suitable turned up, Rosie was to help Mr and Mrs Bentley around their house in Kingsdown, Bristol, in return for her board and lodging.

'Do these people know about my dad, Miss?' Rosie finally managed to blurt out.

'Yes, dear.' Violet always endeavoured to be truthful to children in her care. 'But don't let that worry you. They are good, kind Christian people and they offered to help you.' She really hoped that the Bentleys would live up to the recommendation her colleague had given them, but her one and only meeting with them hadn't been long enough to gauge if their motives for offering Rosie a home were pure altruism, or just image-enhancement.

Until five years ago, Violet had rarely needed to consider people's motives. Nursing had been her life, and that profession wasn't attractive to the vainglorious.

She'd begun in St Mary's in Paddington where she'd risen to the position of theatre sister, and then on to the Queen Alexandra's Royal Nursing Corps at the outbreak of the war. She had loved the Q A s and all the opportunities for travel that came with it. She'd been to India and Egypt and seen sights few of her present colleagues could even dream of.

In 1947, aware that time was running out for her, she'd left the Q A s. She wanted a husband and children, and although nursing in the Army brought her into close contact with men every working day, all the suitable ones were already married.

Going home to Somerset and becoming a social worker hadn't turned out quite as she'd hoped. She bought a little cottage, learned to drive and adjusted to a civilian life, but an appropriate husband somehow eluded her. She was looking for a strong, dependable man, who had been in the Forces, preferably officer class, though she was prepared to consider an NCO. He had to have travelled as extensively as herself, and share her passion for classical music. She didn't mind if he already had children from a previous marriage.

She had met several widowers in the course of her work, and had she dropped her standards a little, two or three of them might have almost fitted her requirements. But Violet wasn't the kind to drop her standards under any circumstances. Now, five years later, she was a little disillusioned. Not at the lack of husband or child, that was just her fate, but because her work brought her face to face with some of the most unpleasant aspects of human nature.

She had been brought up in Somerset, yet she had no idea that incest was so prevalent in the country. In one appalling family she'd visited, the father had made all three daughters pregnant. Neither had she had any notion that there were so many slovenly and unfit mothers. At times she wanted to run back to the orderly world of hospitals, slip into a theatre gown and once again mix with intelligent, dedicated people who shared her high standards.

Yet when she was called into Bridgwater police station to see Alan Parker, she hadn't an inkling that the few remaining strands of belief she held that truly barbarous acts only happened in cities were about to be pulled out by the roots.

Within twenty-four hours of taking Alan to a foster home in Taunton, she got the message that his sister was in hospital following a terrible beating and that the police were digging up the land surrounding May Cottage.

Even now, two weeks later, everyone was still agog about the discovery of two women's bodies buried there. Rumours were flying around that there were still more out on the moors. The police had made an appeal for Ethel

Parker to come forward, so they could rule out her being another possible victim, but as yet she hadn't responded.

Cole was being held at Bristol prison, loudly protesting his innocence. Seth had finally been caught a week after the bodies were discovered. He had holed up out on the moors and the police eventually captured him because he made the mistake of building a fire at night. He was only charged with grievous bodily harm against Rosie, but Violet understood that the police were convinced he too was involved in the murders.

Norman, however, had been released. The police were satisfied that he neither knew about nor was party to the murders. Violet had heard he had gone to Cardiff to work. May Cottage had been emptied of its contents and boarded up as it had become something of a Mecca for morbid sightseers.

But the adult Parkers, their guilt or innocence, were not Violet Pemberton's concern. Her role was to ensure the safety and well-being of the two children. Alan had been easy to deal with. Although he had asked for Rosie countless times in the first few days with his foster parents, he had quickly adjusted to his new life, and indeed responded well to Mrs Hughes, his new foster-mother.

Rosie, however, was an entirely different kettle of fish. Violet wished she'd met her before all this happened. She seemed so calm and controlled. Was that an act, a way of preventing anyone getting too close to her, or was she naturally so? While she was very relieved that Rosie was taking it all so well – she found disturbed adolescent girls difficult to deal with – she thought the girl's quiet acceptance, her lack of tears or emotional outbursts, a little odd under the circumstances.

'Are we nearly there, Miss?' Rosie asked suddenly, interrupting Violet's reverie.

'Nearly. About five more miles now. Did I tell you that Kingsdown where the Bentleys live is only a short walk down a steep hill to the shops and the docks? Near by there are some very old quaint places, and an area called Clifton which is rather splendid.'

Rosie stared out of the window dejectedly. Everywhere seemed grey and miserable because it was raining; it looked and felt more like autumn than July and the middle of the summer. She didn't believe she'd find anything or anywhere splendid, ever again. She didn't think that she'd like living in a city either, and she was frightened of going to live with strangers.

'When can I see Alan?' she asked a few minutes later. She was deeply suspicious about Miss Pemberton taking him to Taunton, then placing her in Bristol. She had a feeling that the big distance between the two places was intended to separate them permanently.

'We'll talk about that in a few weeks when you've both settled down,' the social worker said crisply. It was touching that Rosie clearly cared more about her little brother than herself, but also a little irritating. 'Mrs Hughes feels that he needs time alone with them to adjust properly. But I've already told you, dear, that he's very happy with them. He's stopped wetting the bed, he's eating well and looking forward to going to a new school in September.'

That all sounded very good to Rosie. She was quite satisfied he was being looked after properly. She just wished she could put into words how she needed to see Alan, just so she felt she still had somebody.

Then there were the nasty, dirty thoughts which tormented her all the time. Like remembering what Seth and Norman did to Heather, and Seth rubbing his 'thing' while she was screaming. She knew in her heart that Seth was really bad, perhaps even more dangerous than her father. Every time Sergeant Headly came to see her in hospital a little voice in her head kept telling her she should tell him this and explain why she thought it. But she just couldn't. He was her brother after all, even if she did hate him. Yet all the same she kept hoping Seth would do something,

95

anything, while he was in prison to make the police realize just how nasty he was.

As they drove into Bristol and Rosie saw big buildings, fancy shops and masses of people, she tried to put her problems aside and look enthusiastic. No one would know who she was here, they couldn't point her out or whisper about her. Maybe Bristol would be a good place to live.

'Here we are then,' Miss Pemberton said brightly, finally stopping in a terrace of tall, grey Georgian houses. 'Now, before we go in and I introduce you to the Bentleys, I just want to remind you of one or two things. I'm here to help you, Rosie. If you have any problems, anything you want to talk over with me, just drop me a line and I'll come to see you.

'You'll be safe here. No one knows who you are. Mrs Bentley will just tell her friends you're helping around the house. Just try to be a good girl, do as you are told, and you'll be fine.'

Twenty minutes later Rosie was having a cup of tea in Mrs Bentley's sitting-room. She'd seen over the entire four-storey house, from the kitchen in the basement to the room she was to have on the top floor, but now she was looking out of the window, aware that Miss Pemberton and Mrs Bentley were discussing her, but too engrossed in the view to listen to their conversation.

Kingsdown Parade ran along the top of a hill, but that wasn't apparent until you stepped into the house and looked out of the back windows. Even in the summer rain it was a spectacular panoramic view of the city rooftops, with green hills in the distance and the river Avon winding its way through the city like a silver snake. Rosie hadn't known Bristol was so huge; it looked as if there were enough houses for a million people and dozens of church spires. But better still than the view was the Bentleys' garden down below; it was a bit overgrown with lots of trees and bushes, but it invited exploration.

'Are you listening, Rosie?' Miss Pemberton said, forcing her to turn back to the two women and appear interested. 'Mrs Bentley was just asking me about your clothes. I explained that I've found you a couple of dresses and new shoes and I'll get you a coat as soon as possible.'

Rosie blushed. She didn't like being a charity case. Because the dress she'd been wearing when Seth beat her was ruined, Miss Pemberton had brought in the green dress, shoes and underwear she was wearing now, and another everyday dress and change of underwear. They were all lovely, the sort of clothes she'd always wanted, but she hadn't expected Mrs Bentley would need to know they weren't really her own.

She didn't like the look of Mrs Bentley either. She was a big stern-faced woman dressed all in grey and held in firmly by strong corsets. Her hair was grey too, and that was kept in place by a hair net. She had said earlier that she had three grown-up daughters and boasted that she kept all their bedrooms ready for them just in case they came home unexpectedly, yet Rosie thought she sounded far too snooty to be motherly.

'I expect Rosie's frightfully overwhelmed,' the woman said, looking at Rosie with one of those phoney, kindly expressions. 'This house must be *so* very different from what she's been accustomed to.'

Rosie smarted. She had been terribly aware of her Somerset accent from the moment she walked through the door because Mrs Bentley's was so posh. Yet the suggestion that she came from a hovel riled her. The Bentleys' house was big, but the carpets and furniture were all very shabby. The parlour at May Cottage was a great deal grander.

'Rosie will soon find her feet here,' Miss Pemberton replied, and Rosie had a feeling she didn't like Mrs Bentley much either. 'She's been used to looking after her entire family, cooking, washing, and cleaning, and as I under-stand it, a very good job she made of it too. I'm sure she'll be a great help to you, Mrs Bentley. Now suppose you tell her the house rules. Bedtime and so forth.'

Edith Bentley was an ideas person. She had a different one every three or four months. Her past ideas had ranged from collecting old Bibles to send to the missions in Africa, to knitting rugs for refugees and helping 'unfortunates'. Her position in the local church usually meant she could get others to actually do the work, she merely co-ordinated it. Just after the war there had been a glut of unmarried mothers, and she'd found homes for most of them, only to find that most of the young mothers complained they were expected to do so much housework they had no time to look after their babies. Then there was a brief flirtation recently with ex-prisoners. She persuaded people to give them homes in return for odd jobs and gardening until they got on their feet again. Unfortunately some of them got on their feet in a more literal way than finding a permanent job: one wealthy woman in the parish came home one day to find her family silver gone, along with her maid.

When Mrs Bentley heard from a social worker acquaintance that Violet Pemberton was looking for a home for the murderer's child, she immediately saw a golden opportunity to refresh her flagging reputation at the church, and get a little help around the house. Of course no reasonable person would assume the child to be dangerous just because of what her father had done, but most of Edith Bentley's friends at St Matthew's were twittery spinsters and they would be impressed by her bravery and compassion.

Edith was a little disappointed to find that Rosie Parker was an attractive, seemingly intelligent girl, despite her appalling rustic accent: she'd expected someone plain and a little simple.

'I'll expect you up at seven.' Mrs Bentley lowered her glasses to peer at Rosie over them. 'I shall make a list of tasks to be done in the mornings. We have lunch at one o'clock sharp as Mr Bentley comes home for it. After washing up the lunch things you can have some free time until five. I would expect you to be in bed by ten. I'm sure I don't need to say that you must remain indoors during the evening. I don't approve of young girls *raking* the streets. I shall give you two and sixpence pocket money on Saturday morning. You will have all your meals with us, but I think you'll probably be happier down in the kitchen during the evening; there's a wireless there you can listen to.'

Rosie sensed she was expected to say something. She looked quickly round the sitting-room, hoping for inspiration. She saw the many books and for the first time that day managed a real smile. 'Can I read some of those?' she asked.

During the first three weeks at the Bentleys' house, Rosie contemplated running away many times. Mrs Bentley didn't hit, starve or overwork her, but she never stopped carping from morning till night.

The woman found fault with everything, from the way she spoke to her lack of table manners and even the way she approached the simplest job. Rosie had long since given up trying to hold a conversation with her. Every sentence she uttered was corrected.

'It's "I didn't", not "I never". We say "That is" not "thass". Stop rolling those r's! You sound like a farm worker.' It was easier to stay silent than be reminded constantly of her ignorance.

She stood over Rosie as she ironed a shirt, insisting the collar had to be tackled first, then the cuffs. Embroidery on hankies or tablecloths had to be done over a thick wad of blanket. She screamed in horror when Rosie plunged dirty plates into hot water, they had to be rinsed off first in cold. When Rosie was making a bed, dusting a room or sweeping down the stairs, the woman watched her, keeping up a barrage of instructions. Not one word of praise ever came her way, and by the evening Rosie would go to her room and sob herself to sleep.

On the evening of the day she arrived Rosie had been buttering the bread for tea when Mrs Bentley went up to answer the front door. As she left the kitchen she told Rosie to lay the table.

Although the kitchen was in the basement it was a pleasant, bright room, painted light green with cream cupboard doors. They had all the modern equipment – a gas cooker and boiler – and not one piece of china was cracked. Rosie laid the central table for the three of them and made sure the knives and forks were the right way round. To her astonishment Mrs Bentley shrieked when she came back in and saw her handiwork.

'What are you thinking of?' she exclaimed, pursing her lips in utter disgust, as if Rosie had disembowelled the cat in her absence. 'I meant the dining-room table. Only servants eat in the kitchen!'

Rosie was sent staggering upstairs to the dining-room on the ground floor with a tray piled high with things that looked absolutely unnecessary, but Mrs Bentley soon put her straight about the 'niceties' of table-laying and introduced her to previously unknown items such as jam spoons, butter knives, tea strainers, sugar tongs and napkins.

Since then every single meal had been an endurance test, as Mrs Bentley kept up a constant flow of instructions. 'Don't hold your knife like a pencil. Don't you dare turn your fork to scoop up food. Use your right hand for drinking, bread and butter in the left. Sit up straight. Keep your elbows in.'

Mr Bentley never joined in these instructions, he just sat and ate his meals in silence. He was a dapper little man with a complexion like pale parchment, a thin moustache like a pencil stroke and dark hair shiny with brilliantine. He had a printing business in Bristol and even when it was hot, and after climbing the steep steps from town, he never looked flushed. He never sat in his shirt sleeves, belched, swore or shouted.

Rosie wondered now after observing him during so many meals whether he had grown silent for the same reason she had, because his wife had worn him down. If she asked him a question he rarely said more than 'Yes dear' or 'No dear'. When Mrs Bentley passed on a snippet of gossip, or mentioned something she'd heard on the wireless, he raised one eyebrow and replied 'Really?' But however odd Rosie found his silence, he always smiled and thanked her when she did something for him. She had a feeling he was sympathetic towards her.

Until her first Sunday with the Bentleys, Rosie had never been inside a church. She knew about God and Jesus because she learned about them at school and said prayers in assembly. But Cole hadn't believed in churches. Rosie was pleased when Mrs Bentley said she had to go with them; it made her feel as if she was accepted as a member of their family, and she was curious about what a 'service' meant. But the moment she walked in, between the Bentleys, she saw heads turn to look at her and heard the whispers. 'That's her,' 'Here she comes!' and 'She looks quite ordinary, considering.'

Throughout that first interminable service she had smarted with shame and anger because Mrs Bentley had obviously told everyone who she was. She kept her eyes tightly closed during the prayers so she couldn't see all of those nosy people watching her, and offered up one of her own that she should find the strength to rise above the stares, Mrs Bentley's constant criticism and her terrible sense of guilt.

Perhaps there was someone up there listening to her after all, because it was a couple of days later that she thought of writing a list of all the good points in her new life as opposed to the ones that made her want to run.

There were quite a few once she thought about it. She had her own small room up on the top floor with a wonderful view of Bristol. She had enough to eat, and there was a real bathroom and indoor flushing lavatory. Until she was taken to hospital, she'd never known what it was like to have a real bath, and there were plenty of books to read, and newspapers. The work wasn't hard. There were no filthy grease-covered clothes to wash, no one tramped mud into the basement kitchen, and the Bentleys ate like birds compared with the Parker men so there were no mountains of potatoes to peel. Then there was the garden. When Mrs Bentley wasn't watching her like a hawk she would wander around it, pulling up a few weeds or stopping to sniff the roses, and it almost made up for not having the moors on her doorstep.

In the afternoons she could go for walks and she soon found that there were compensations for town living. She'd never seen such big, fancy houses before, glimpses into windows gave her a whole new insight into how rich people lived, and many of them had wonderful gardens too. Clifton was every bit as splendid as Miss Pemberton had said, with majestic Georgian terraces with superb views of the city. There were the Downs too – acres of grass so it felt like being back in the country.

She came across Clifton suspension bridge quite by accident, after wandering through an intriguing area with dozens of smart little shops, and her heart nearly stopped at the magnificence of it. She stood for ages on the bridge, looking down into the formidable gorge with the river so far below. It scared, awed and inspired her all at once. Somehow after seeing that place her own problems and anxieties seemed almost trivial.

Sometimes she would walk down the steep steps from Kingsdown that led right into the heart of Bristol's shopping centre and could hardly believe the huge variety of goods available for those with the money to buy them. Catcott had only the general store and the post office and they had barely changed since the war, stocking up with only the most basic essentials.

Here the shops had rail after rail of pretty dresses. Rows of shoes in every colour of the rainbow. Jewellery, cosmetics, and food shops laden with items she'd never even seen before. She observed elegantly dressed women going into smart little cafés for afternoon tea, and marvelled at their attractive hats, high-heeled shoes and stockings with nice straight seams. There were so many cars too, cinemas and dance halls. It was, as Miss Pemberton had said, an exciting place.

Yet as much as she liked to see the shops and watch the people, it was here her feelings of loneliness were most intensified. She saw mothers and daughters shopping together, groups of girls her own age giggling and chatting as they looked at make-up and jewellery in Woolworth's. Everyone seemed to have someone, except her. She would look at toy shops and wish Alan was looking with her. She missed him so much.

A letter arriving during her third week in Kingsdown Parade finally stopped Rosie from thinking about running away. Mrs Bentley came down into the kitchen where she was washing up and handed it to her.

'For me?' Rosie asked in astonishment, hastily wiping her hands on her apron. It was the first letter she'd ever received.

'Well, it's addressed to you,' Mrs Bentley said with a sniff. 'It's a London postmark. I didn't know you had any relatives there?'

'I ain't,' Rosie said. 'I mean, I haven't,' she said quickly, then opened the letter with fumbling fingers. When she saw Thomas Farley's signature she was frightened, certain it would be a nasty letter about her father. But as she began to read she found to her delight it was nothing of the kind.

He said he was going down to see Alan in Taunton on the following weekend, and as he would be changing trains at Bristol on Sunday afternoon, with a two-hour wait between them, perhaps she'd like to meet him there. He said he understood she hadn't been able to visit Alan herself and he thought she might like to hear how he was first-hand.

'Well?' Mrs Bentley said. 'Who's it from?'

'Mr Farley,' she said, and because she was so overwhelmed by his kindness she handed the letter to Mrs Bentley for her to read.

'Isn't that nice of him?' Rosie said, grinning from ear to ear and expecting the older woman to agree with her. But to her dismay and embarrassment Mrs Bentley winced.

'How very strange,' she said in her snooty voice, handing her back the letter. 'If I were in Mr Farley's shoes, the last person I'd fraternize with would be the daughter of the man who gave my sister an illegitimate child, then murdered her. I shall have to discuss this with Miss Pemberton.'

Later, alone in her room, Rosie wondered how a woman who talked continually about Christian kindness could be so cruel. She was already crushed by the enormity of what they said her father had done, she didn't need to have her nose rubbed in it too. In fact she was so terribly ashamed that she didn't know whether she had the nerve to see Mr Farley anyway.

By the next morning though, she felt defiant. She would meet him, even if Miss Pemberton forbade it. If he was big enough to suggest it, she would be cowardly to refuse. Besides it would be a relief to talk to a real human being again after being trapped in this house for three weeks with a woman who belittled her every effort to please. And of course she was dying to know how Alan was.

On the morning of the Sunday when Thomas Farley was to come to Bristol, Rosie awoke feeling jittery. Mrs Bentley had been as cold as ice ever since Miss Pemberton agreed to the meeting. There was church to get through, then lunch. Both would be ordeals. The morning service seemed even longer than usual. She kept fidgeting during the sermon, and Mrs Bentley rapped her on the knee several times. It was very hot too, and someone close to their pew smelled of sweat. She kept imagining the moors, thinking how nice it would be to go paddling in a ditch with Alan and catch a few tiddlers. She wondered how she was going to get through lunch and then the washing-up without screaming.

As usual when they came out of the church, everyone gathered in the churchyard to chat. Mrs Bentley stopped to speak to a woman in a large blue hat. Mr Bentley stood at her side offering nothing but his usual polite nods.

Rosie looked around her with interest. She saw the same faces each week and liked to check what they were wearing. As she had only one dress fit for wearing to church and Mrs Bentley always wore the same navy blue and white dress, and a white hat with a blue band, she thought the women who wore a different outfit each week must be very rich. Some of the ladies were very fashionable, wearing slim straight skirts and waisted jackets, others wore the new ballerina-length full skirts with wide belts nipping their waists. All wore hats and such pretty ones too. One had what looked like a wide feathered Alice band in a brilliant salmon pink to match her dress. Rosie looked hard at it, wondering what bird had feathers of that colour.

The prod in her side took her by surprise.

'Don't stare at people,' Mrs Bentley hissed. 'It's very rude.'

'They stare at me,' Rosie replied without thinking. 'You'd think I'd got two heads!'

Then she saw Mr Bentley smiling. He was standing just a little way back from his wife in his usual subservient manner, but he was looking right at Rosie and his smile was pure amusement. Rosie had never noticed until then

105

what nice eyes he had; they were grey-blue and kindly. She smiled back, and in that brief exchange, she knew he was on her side.

Rosie had to stand on tiptoe to see through the windows of the refreshment rooms on Temple Meads station. She could see herself reflected in the mirrors behind the long wooden counter, the glass domes covering cakes, a Kia Ora orange squash machine with artificial oranges bobbing around and the backs of a few heads. They were mostly ladies' heads though, all wearing hats. Rosie thought perhaps men preferred to wait for their trains out in the fresh air; she didn't much like the pungent smell of stewed tea and cigarettes either which escaped each time the door opened.

She hesitated before pushing open the glazed door, partly because she was again reminded of Mrs Bentley's nasty insinuation about Thomas Farley, being odd because he wanted to see Rosie, but mostly from surprise to find he was already there waiting. The table he'd taken was just to the right of where she'd looked in the window and he was looking down at a train timetable.

He looked different from how she'd remembered him. Maybe it was because he wasn't wearing the trilby, or that his tweed jacket, shirt and striped tie were so much more formal than the open-necked shirt he'd been wearing on their first meeting. Yet it struck her what a good face he had. Bushy fair eyebrows and a straight refined nose. His face was too thin and lined to be conventionally handsome, yet at the same time those lines suggested strength of character, and there was something compelling about him which set him apart from other men.

He must have sensed her presence because he suddenly lifted his head and his eyes caught hers. He smiled, and for a moment he looked like Heather, the same soft brown eyes and that special sparkle she had.

All at once Rosie knew she mustn't allow Mrs Bentley

to influence her about people, she was too mean-spirited to see good in anyone. There was nothing odd about this man, unless it was that he was unusually kind.

He pulled out a chair for her as she reached the table. 'I was afraid you wouldn't come,' he said. 'I'd resigned myself to a long dull wait between trains.'

'I was a bit scared of seeing you again.' Her voice trembled with nervousness. 'But I so much wanted to hear about Alan.'

'And you shall hear about him,' Thomas said as she sat down. 'Just as soon as I've got us some tea and cake.'

In fact Thomas was finding it difficult not to stare openly at her. He could hardly believe that this pretty girl in a well-fitting green print dress, polished shoes, dazzling white ankle socks and with her coppery hair brushed and gleaming, was in fact the same dirty ragamuffin who'd given him a cup of tea at May Cottage. She looked like the child of solid middle-class citizens, who'd never seen a day's unhappiness in her entire life. Even her Somerset accent seemed to have faded a little.

Yet when she blushed and hung her head, Thomas was saddened. She had been so bold at their first meeting.

When he came back from the counter with a tray, she still seemed uneasy, sitting bolt upright as if poised for flight. He launched right into his news of Alan, hoping that would put her at her ease.

'He's really happy with Mr and Mrs Hughes, so don't you go worrying yourself about him,' he began, then went on to describe the bright sunny modern house with bay windows and a big back garden complete with sand pit and swing. 'Alan shares a room with Raymond, he's eight; then there's Jennifer who's four in a smaller room. You should see the toys they've got, Rosie, as many as in a toy shop, and dozens and dozens of books. Alan likes the tricycle best, he rides it up and down the garden. He calls the Hughes Uncle and Auntie.'

Thomas told her about a dog called Rex, a playhouse

made out of old clothes-horses and blankets, even that Alan had started to learn how to tell the time.

Rosie found her nervousness fading as she listened to this man she hardly knew talk with such warmth and interest about her brother, reassuring her how happy the little boy was.

'I think I've just about exhausted Alan as a subject,' he said eventually. 'So now it's your turn to tell me all about yourself and what's been happening to you.'

Rosie couldn't remember when anyone last wanted to know anything about her. She sometimes felt the police had put her through a mangle, to squeeze out every last piece of information about her father and brothers, but they hadn't any real interest in her personally. Mrs Bentley was the same, asking questions about the men, but caring nothing about Rosie's feelings. In fact there had been nights when she'd lain awake wondering if her lot in life was to be someone who people whispered about behind their hands, something of an embarrassment whom they felt they had to help but would prefer kept out of sight.

It felt good to talk, to share all the new things she'd discovered since leaving the Levels, with someone else. She told him about the Avon Gorge, the suspension bridge, and climbing up Cabot Tower to see the panoramic view of Bristol. She spoke of wonderful shops she'd seen, of beautiful gardens and all the books she'd read. She wanted him to think she was happy.

But Rosie soon discovered Thomas Farley was as perceptive as he was kind. He had a way of picking up a hidden thread of a story woven into her conversation, then pulling it. One time was when she was describing a meal, another was the incident that morning at church. In both cases she'd told the story for laughs, imitating Mrs Bentley's posh voice and starchy manner. But though he laughed with her, it seemed he sensed her underlying shame.

'Do you feel all the church people know who you are?' he asked.

'I know they do.' She shrugged her shoulders. 'Mrs Bentley's told 'em. I bet it makes her feel really daring having a murderer's kid staying in her house.'

'So how do *you* feel about yourself?' he asked. A doctor had asked him this same question once and he'd had a surge of relief from openly admitting that after his time in the POW camp he felt he was only half a man.

Rosie hesitated. It was the first time anyone had asked her such a thing.

'It's important to get it out in the open,' he said gently. 'Then you can tackle it.'

'If you really want to know, I feel like I've got tainted blood, Mr Farley,' Rosie said in a low voice, glancing around her to make sure no one was eavesdropping. There were around twenty or so people near by, and like in church she felt they all knew who she was, even though common sense told her they couldn't possibly. 'I could change my name, move away somewhere, and maybe for a while people wouldn't know who I was. But I can't change who I really am, or my dad. I'm marked for life, aren't I?'

'That's rubbish,' Thomas said firmly. 'People will forget about your father, and so will you in time.' Privately he knew she was right of course, it was almost insulting her intelligence to argue with her. But it was a very heavy burden for such a young girl to carry. 'Let's forget this Mr Farley stuff,' he suggested, changing the subject. 'It's plain old Thomas to you. Now tell me more about the Bentleys.'

Rosie thought the name Thomas suited him very well. All the Toms she'd known at school had been daring and fun and she had a feeling he'd been that way too. When he smiled his whole face lit up just as Heather's had. She found it oddly comforting.

'Mr Bentley's okay, he just doesn't talk much,' she said.

'But *she* is so very proper. The table has to be laid just so. I mustn't run downstairs, or go without my shoes. She's always correcting things I say, and she doesn't think much of my table manners.'

'I found it hard when I first joined the army,' Thomas said in understanding. 'I was tough and strong and I couldn't stand being treated as if I was second rate just because of the way I spoke and where I came from. There were weedy young officers as thick as two short planks, only there because they'd been to a posh public school, and they got to order me about.

'But my sergeant gave me some advice on how to deal with them. He said, "Keep your gob shut, Farley, and salute them smartly. If they give you an order, jump to it, but make sure you do it better and quicker than they ever could. Watch those upper-class prats and learn from them. Remember, no experience is ever wasted."'

Rosie opened her mouth to say that she didn't see recognizing the difference between a teaspoon and a jam spoon as being vital to her education, or that living with the Bentleys was a valuable experience. But a look in Thomas's eyes made her bite it back. All at once she realized he truly understood what she was going through, and that could only be because he'd been on a similar road to her once or twice in his life. She thought it was amazing he wasn't bitter about his missing leg; even more astounding he had a big enough heart to meet the daughter of the man suspected of killing his sister.

'Got any ideas about what job I could do then?' she asked instead with a flash of her old cheeky grin. 'All I can do is cook and clean.'

'I was in much the same boat as you after the war,' Thomas said. 'I didn't have any real skills, all I knew was meat portering in Smithfield market, before I became a soldier, and I couldn't go back to humping sides of meat, not with only one leg. I was beginning to despair, but then someone told me about government training schemes especially for ex-servicemen. You could do all sorts – bricklaying, plumbing, carpentry – but I chose clock and watch mending because it meant I could sit down.'

'Do you like it?' Rosie asked. Somehow she couldn't see him crouched over a work bench doing something fiddly; despite his disability he still looked the outdoor sort.

'Yes, I do,' he said after a moment's thought. 'It's quite engrossing. And I get to live in Hampstead which is one of the best areas in London. Mostly I think myself pretty lucky. But getting back to you, is there any kind of job you especially fancy?'

'I'd like to be a nurse,' she admitted. This idea had come to her in hospital after her chats with Sister Dowd. 'But you have to be eighteen for that and I'm not sure I can bear the Bentleys for another two years.'

'Stay with them until your dad's trial is over and you're sixteen,' Thomas suggested. 'Make sure you work hard enough and smile sweetly so they give you a good reference, then find another job, maybe in a boarding school or nursing home, until you are old enough.'

Rosie dropped her eyes to the table. She really liked this man. She wished she knew how to show her gratitude towards him. But she didn't know where to begin.

'You are a very nice man,' she said eventually, a blush staining her cheeks.

Thomas reached across the table to put his hand over one of hers. 'And you are very brave, Rosie.'

Her eyes prickled. 'Thank you, Thomas,' she said in a shaky voice. 'But I ought to go now.' She saw by the clock above the door that it was already ten to five. 'It's a long walk back to Kingsdown and Mrs Bentley told me to be back by half-past.'

She got up, kissed him shyly on the cheek and was gone in a flash. Thomas limped to the refreshment room door, reaching it just in time to see her handing her platform ticket to the guard at the barrier. From a distance she

111

looked what he was, a skinny child, yet all the time he'd been with her he'd had the sense he'd been in the company of an adult.

Sitting down again Thomas felt suddenly very tired. Travelling down from Paddington yesterday, a night in a cheap boarding house, and just a few hours with Alan – if it hadn't been for Rosie, he might have thought the trip was a waste of time, money and energy.

The glowing picture he'd painted for Rosie of Alan's happiness with Mr and Mrs Hughes was an accurate one. But he hadn't been able to tell her that he viewed it as an awkward stranger, there under sufferance. Alan had barely looked at him, he'd been too busy with his tricycle and a wooden train.

Thomas was very aware that people didn't know what to make of him. He had been described in the past few years as dour, sober, lugubrious, humourless, a loner, mysterious and standoffish. In fact he was really none of these things, except perhaps a loner, and he wasn't that by choice, only circumstance. If he didn't talk, laugh and go out of his way to make friends it was because he was constantly aware of all those he had lost.

He was just like any other eighteen-year-old recruit when he joined the Royal Fusiliers in 1940, a fun-loving lad looking for adventure, who until then had spent his spare time hanging around street corners with his mates, watching the girls or playing football. He was thrown in at the deep end in war the moment his basic training was over. His regiment was sent to Dunkirk to fight in a rear-guard action. He saw two good friends killed, just a few yards from him, but there was no chance to run to them, not even time to shed a tear on their behalf. He grew up fast in France.

To be sent to Singapore early in 1941, when so many other regiments were being sent to North Africa, appeared to be a cushy number. The Japanese weren't there then and it was thought that if and when they did come, it would be from the south and the great naval guns were trained that way in readiness. For Thomas's regiment it was a time of comparative ease; there was plenty of food, fun to be had with pretty girls in the many bars, swimming in the warm sea, and a whole new country and culture to be explored.

But the designers of the great guns were wrong and the Japanese surprised everyone by approaching from the north through Malaya. The guns were useless in Singapore's defence and she fell in February of 1942. Thomas was one of thousands of men rounded up and herded into Changi gaol. Later he was moved on to Burma to build roads. The journey, part train, mostly forced route march with little food or water, claimed many lives. But the deaths on that endless march were nothing compared to the later daily death toll in the camp.

Thomas was asked on liberation why he thought he'd survived having fallen prey to dysentery, tropical ulcers and malaria. He had laughingly claimed it was cussedness, that he felt he was too young to die in some sweaty jungle when he knew so little. He'd admitted he'd spent most of his imprisonment planning his exploration of the rest of the world, imagining all the women he would love, all the delicious meals he would eat, all the sights he would see.

After they amputated his ulcerated leg, however, he found his mind could no longer construct those cheering images which had sustained him so well in the camp. It stayed stubbornly on those friends who had died. Dozens and dozens of them, their gaunt faces like some grim frieze along the walls of the ward. He even felt sorry he'd managed to survive and he began to avoid contact with people.

Solitude became a habit once he left the hospital and took up a place in an ex-servicemen's hostel. Girls often made eyes at him, other men tried to get him to join them at the pub. But he didn't want to make friends for fear they insisted on questioning him about his experiences during the war. He certainly could not even think of making love to a woman now he was crippled. So without really being aware of it, he built an invisible wall around himself that no one could breach.

But when he discovered Heather had gone to Somerset, part of the wall collapsed. Eight weeks ago he had set off joyfully to find her. For the first time in years he was aware of others, even interested enough to speak to them. Good pictures came back into his mind as the train chugged westwards, pictures of his childhood in Poplar, of school friends and indeed of his old ambitions to become a famous artist.

Yet just a few days later on his return to London, his mind could barely stand the conflicting emotions he felt. Rage at his own suspicion that Cole Parker might have killed his sister. Tenderness for the small motherless boy he had only glimpsed briefly. Anxiety that Alan was being ill treated, and impotence too that he could do nothing about anything himself. But yet as demented and angry as he felt, it was good to feel *something* again. He'd lived in a vacuum for so many years, he had feared he was incapable of feeling much ever again. Then he got word from the Bridgwater police that they had taken Alan into care, and all at once he felt a strong sense of real purpose.

A man needed something more in his life than just his work. Alan needed a home. Thomas found himself thinking about where he could put a bed for the boy in his tiny flat, considering how he would plan his day with a child to look after.

When the police found the two women's bodies, it hadn't come as a real surprise, as he'd been convinced almost from the start that Parker had killed them. But the news of Rosie being in hospital following a severe beating from her older brother had floored him. It was almost as bad as the grief he felt for Heather. He felt deeply responsible because it was all connected to his visit to the police. He couldn't forget either that it was Rosie who had

had the courage and initiative to get Alan to safety, without any thought for her own, while he was still thinking about what to do next.

A voice of reason had begun to speak in the last couple of weeks, since he'd learned that Alan was safe and well cared for. He'd realized that a mere blood tie didn't mean he was qualified to become father and mother overnight.

He had been puzzled that the boy had shown no interest in the fact that Thomas was meeting Rosie on his way home. He didn't ask one question about her, or even send a message. In private Mrs Hughes admitted that he had stopped talking about her just a few days after his arrival, and that perhaps he had chosen to block out all memories of May Cottage, good and bad.

Small children were remarkably resilient, Thomas couldn't help thinking.

It seemed ironic that while he and Rosie needed someone in their lives, the child who was the tenuous bond between them didn't appear to need either of them. But then life was full of irony, and few people got what they deserved, or needed.

'Rosie, we don't put our knife in the jam pot,' Mrs Bentley said sharply. 'You must use the spoon! Put a little on the side of your plate, then spread it on your bread.'

'I'm sorry,' Rosie replied. She privately thought her way of doing it was a lot less messy and saved washing up another spoon.

She wished she'd described Mrs Bentley to Thomas. She thought he might have found it funny how everything about her was kept firmly in place. Smiles were strictly controlled, for church and visitors, and her conversation was stilted. Even her elbows seemed to be attached to her sides. The only time Rosie had seen them move from that position was when she gave her a lesson in hanging out washing *her way*.

Rosie knew she must be about fifty because she had

once mentioned watching a parade of men going off to the First World War when she was Rosie's age. Her face was still unlined, but she wheezed and held her sides walking up the stairs. She couldn't imagine Mrs Bentley as a young girl. But she liked to imagine how she might be after she'd drunk a couple of pints of cider. That might loosen her up!

Mr Bentley was as silent today as he always was. In fact when she thought about it, the most he'd ever said to her was on her first day here. He had cleared his throat and mumbled something about 'her unfortunate circumstances', then said if she needed anything she was to ask, and to remember to say her prayers each night. Another time he had nervously asked, out of his wife's hearing, if she wished to visit her father and brother in prison, because if so he would arrange it. He looked very relieved when she said she didn't.

Rosie remembered his smile today though; it had given her the idea that outside his home Mr Bentley might be quite different.

'Rosie! Sit up straight at the table.' Mrs Bentley gave her a poke in the spine through the back of the chair. 'And cut that slice of bread in half before you attempt to eat it!'

Rosie sighed inwardly. She was so hungry she could eat the entire plate of thinly cut bread and butter. By the time she'd played around dolloping the jam on the plate, then spreading it on the bread and cutting it, it was hardly worth the effort, one mouthful and it was gone.

The dining-room was as depressing as Mrs Bentley. Even on the warmest days it was cold and inhospitable. The chairs seemed designed to make sure no one lingered on them. Horsehair prickled her legs, and the knobbly bits on the carved backs dug into her spine. The room overlooked the street, and the wallpaper was a sombre brown, made even more dismal by many pictures with dreary scenes from the Bible. 'Salome', with John the Baptist's severed head on a silver salver, seemed a very odd choice of picture for a dining-room. It made her shudder.

Mrs Bentley cut the fruit cake and looked at Rosie as if she'd finally decided it was time for conversation. 'Now, my dear,' she said starchily. 'How did your meeting go with Mr Farley?'

Mr Bentley looked at Rosie too with the politely interested expression he always put on when a conversation was being held in his presence. Rosie wondered if he listened, or was his mind a million miles away?

'It was nice to see him again,' Rosie said. 'He looked tired, it had been a long journey for him. Did I tell you he's got an artificial leg? They sawed off his own one when he was a prisoner of war.'

'*Limb* is a much politer way of referring to a leg, my dear,' Mrs Bentley corrected her. 'And we don't mention such things as amputation at mealtimes.'

Rosie couldn't see what was offensive about the word 'leg'. Or indeed why she shouldn't mention it being sawn off, when there was John the Baptist's severed head right above them. But now she had Mrs Bentley's attention she was happy to launch into an enthusiastic account of how happy and settled Alan was, including the details of the tricycle and train set.

'Well, that is good news. Isn't it, Herbert?' Mrs Bentley said to her husband as Rosie came to a halt.

'Very good, my dear,' he replied, helping himself to a slice of fruit cake.

'Well, now we know your little brother is happy and safe, we must think about your future,' Mrs Bentley said, fixing Rosie with her cold watery-blue eyes. 'We're very happy to have you here of course, for the time being, but it isn't exactly ideal for any of us.'

The truth of the matter was that Edith Bentley found Rosie disconcerting. She worked hard enough, faster and better than a woman twice her age. But it was her bold manner which upset Edith. She had fully expected a child in her position to be so ashamed of what her father had done that she couldn't look anyone in the eye. Instead she asked questions, stared at people openly and quite often looked as if she expected to be liked.

On top of that she wasn't even grateful. And Edith suspected the girl was laughing at her silently.

'I thought I'd drop Miss Pemberton a line tomorrow and suggest she finds another place for you.'

Rosie looked at Mrs Bentley, wondering what she'd done wrong. Her eyes began to well up. It wasn't that she wanted to stay here, just the injustice of it. She tried to bite back the tears, but they came anyway, first one slipped out, then another and suddenly she was sobbing.

Edith Bentley had prepared herself for some cheek, so she was astounded to see tears instead. 'Come now, my dear,' she said, unsure of what to do or say. 'You knew this home was only a temporary measure.'

'But I thought I was to stay here until after the trial,' Rosie sobbed. 'I thought you were satisfied with me too.'

'Now, Edith, let's not be hasty,' Mr Bentley said.

Rosie was so surprised to hear Mr Bentley speak, her mouth fell open and she swung round to look at him. He looked more animated than usual, a pink tinge to his parchment-like complexion and his eyes glittered.

'Rosie is a great help to us,' he said with a shrug. 'I see absolutely no reason to send her away now just as she's beginning to settle in.'

After Mr Bentley spoke, Rosie was sent out of the dining-room, so she didn't hear what passed between the couple. But some time later Mrs Bentley came down to the kitchen with the tray of tea things, and for once she didn't have much to say for herself.

'We've decided you shall stay here, for the time being at least,' she said quickly, as if anxious to say her piece and be gone. She had a pinched mouth as if she didn't actually approve of this decision. 'So you'd better pull your socks up if you don't want me to regret it.'

Rosie didn't know why she hugged Mrs Bentley. She wasn't in the habit of hugging people, and the woman hadn't really said anything nice enough to warrant it. But it seemed to be the right thing to do. Mrs Bentley didn't exactly respond; Rosie might just as well have hugged a post box, they were both equally rigid. But she did get her head patted, and that was an improvement on yet another lecture.

Although the first three weeks in Kingsdown Parade had seemed endless, the rest of the summer flew by. There were even times on sunny days when Rosie was content to be there. Mrs Bentley was heavily involved in organizing a fête to be held at St Matthew's at the end of August, so she was out a good deal of the time. Without anyone breathing down her neck, Rosie flew through the daily chores and most days she found enough time before lunch to do an hour or so of weeding out in the garden, and still more in the afternoon.

She knew she would never grow to like Mrs Bentley, but she adored her garden. As the house was built on a hill and the garden sloped steeply towards the town, it could easily have ended up a wasteland like others further along the road. But someone at some time had planned and laid out the series of terraces with great care. Rockery plants tumbled over the retaining walls, the strips of lawn between terraces were lush and soft. High stone walls around the entire garden gave it shelter and privacy, and there were many lovely trees. To Rosie though, one of its main attractions was that you couldn't see it all from the house: there were rose-covered arches, dozens of different flowering shrubs, and perennial flowers which could only be seen when wandering right down to the bottom. But the Bentleys didn't appear to care much for it. Mr Bentley mowed the lawns religiously, but weeds had hidden many of the smaller plants.

Rosie had always had an instinctive knowledge about

plants and her first attempts to tidy this garden up were tentative. A clump of weeds pulled up here, a little thinning out of plants which needed more room. But as she saw the improvement, and the Bentleys didn't appear to notice, so she became bolder. In the evenings she often buried herself in one of the many gardening books she found in the house, learning about flowers she hadn't come across until now. She began to think of the garden as hers, and took it upon herself to do more.

Working in the garden, she could forget her father and Seth were only a few miles away in Bristol prison. She found that the small voice which kept suggesting she must admit all she knew about Seth to someone didn't speak to her out here. Even thoughts of Alan were just tender memories rather than anxious ones. She liked to feel the soil in her fingers, to see things flourish under her care. The warm sun on her back, the smell of roses, pinks and freshly cut grass, and the beauty of the trees and flowers, erased some of the more ugly images in her mind.

Her feeling of contentment was helped by Thomas writing to her every week. She felt less isolated, more optimistic knowing he cared enough to sit down every Sunday afternoon to write to her. He described Hampstead, the part of London where he lived, so well, she could almost see the quaint little shops, the steep High Street which went up to the heath and the cottages with pretty gardens. He sometimes described the people who came into the clock repairers, picking on the snootiest ones as if he knew she'd laugh about them.

She thought he must be lonely, and wondered if it was because of his missing leg that he hadn't got married. He had been to see Alan again, and although he said Alan had been away for a week's holiday in Cornwall with his foster parents and their children, and that he'd seen the boy's new school uniform, Rosie had a feeling Thomas hadn't made much headway with him.

Rosie wrote back each week too. She told him about

the garden, and books she'd read, and new things she'd learned to cook. Often she felt like complaining about Mrs Bentley's harshness, sometimes she wanted to ridicule the woman, but she stopped herself. Thomas wouldn't want to hear such things. Besides, Mrs Bentley wasn't all bad, she was growing quite kindly at times, allowing her to make cakes all on her own and helping her make a dress for herself in the evenings on her treadle machine. As for Mr Bentley, Rosie had no complaints there; in his quiet way he seemed to like her. He often brought her home the *Reader's Digest* or *National Geographic* because he saw that her reading tastes stretched beyond women's magazines. He even fixed her up a bedside lamp in her room so she could read in bed. The days just drifted by pleasantly; even the newspapers had run out of anything further to say about her father.

If it wasn't for Miss Pemberton's fortnightly visits, Rosie might almost have been able to believe she was in Kingsdown to stay. But the social worker brought reality with her on her visits, reminding Rosie that she was no longer a child and soon she would have to fend for herself in the outside world.

On one visit she said she felt Rosie should think about her future and produced career leaflets which ranged from jobs in offices to joining the women's army, and asked her to read them all and see if any of them appealed to her.

On another visit she explained the facts of life, in detail, unperturbed by Rosie's embarrassment, and seemed concerned to discover she hadn't yet had a period. In these visits they had never yet talked about Cole or her brothers. Rosie didn't bring up the subject because she was too ashamed to, and Miss Pemberton didn't mention what she knew because she felt the child was happier in ignorance.

It wasn't until a visit in the middle of August, nine weeks after Rosie's arrival, that Miss Pemberton felt the necessity to speak of them. She knew the date for the trial would be set any day now.

They were in the kitchen, Rosie cleaning the silver. Outside it was pouring with rain as it had been for several days. Over a cup of tea they discussed the awful flooding in Devon. Just that morning Rosie had read in the newspaper that thirty-one people had been killed in Lynmouth. She asked the social worker how things were on the Somerset Levels.

'Very bad. Lots of fields are flooded,' Miss Pemberton replied. 'People living by the River Parrett have a foot or two of water in their cottages.'

Rosie was just about to launch into an account of one family she knew who got flooded out most winters and merely moved upstairs after Christmas in anticipation, when she sensed the older woman had something on her mind.

'Is there something wrong?' she asked.

Miss Pemberton folded her arms on the kitchen table and cleared her throat. 'Not wrong exactly. I just have something I must discuss with you. You see, I went to see your father in prison a few days ago.' She paused, looking a little flustered. 'I thought it was essential that someone acted as a go-between. I'm sure there are things you both wish to say to one another.'

A cold chill went down Rosie's spine. She sensed that what Miss Pemberton wanted to add was 'before he's hanged'.

'I haven't got anything to say to him.' Rosie couldn't even bear to call him 'Dad'. 'I try to forget him.'

'I think you do have things to say to him,' Miss Pemberton said gently but firmly. 'He is your father!'

Rosie said nothing.

'I think that if you don't, you might regret it in years to come. We both know that he is almost certain to be found guilty at his trial. And we both know all too well what that means.'

Rosie gulped. She knew exactly what that meant. A rope around his neck and a long drop. 'What did he say about me?'

'He said he loved you. That he wished he'd done better for you. He said to say how sorry he was about hitting you that day.'

'He's just a murderer to me,' Rosie said stubbornly. 'I wouldn't care if he was ill, mad or turning green. I just hate him.'

Violet Pemberton looked at Rosie and felt desperately sorry for the girl. There was something upright, strong and bright about her. She'd come to this house under the worst of circumstances, yet she'd actually made the best of things. Her diction had improved, she always looked clean and tidy with well-brushed hair, she enjoyed learning new skills. Violet didn't subscribe to the idea that character traits were all inborn, but believed much was learned by example and upbringing. As Rosie's mother disappeared when the child was only six, she could hardly have been much of an influence. So it stood to reason that Cole Parker had to be responsible, at least in part.

In her time as a social worker she'd visited several men in prison to discuss their families with them. In the main they had been some of life's weasels, unpleasant, shady characters who were so inadequate she felt little compassion for them. But Cole Parker wasn't a weasel, he was a big powerful man who even in a prison uniform had managed to look dignified and proud. He looked her right in the eye as he was speaking, he hadn't once lapsed into self-pity. He confessed that his relationship with Heather had fallen apart before Alan was born because he had reason to believe the child wasn't his. Yet he said he was ashamed that he hadn't found it in his heart to love the boy as his own. And somehow this man, for all his many faults had managed to pass on to his daughter his finer qualities. Courage, determination and pride. She found herself moved by that.

'Well, you just think over what I've said.' She gave Rosie a pat on the hand. 'I'm not suggesting you go to visit him, prisons are no place for young girls, but maybe you might like to write to him.'

Herbert Bentley came home early from work on the 1st of September. Miss Pemberton had telephoned him at his office with the latest news about Cole Parker just as he got back from lunch. Knowing his wife would be out for the afternoon with one of her church committees, he thought it best to go home and take the opportunity to talk to Rosie himself. He didn't quite trust his wife to be diplomatic.

Herbert wasn't quite the little mouse that his wife's friends and acquaintances took him for. He just bowed to her dominance because it was easier than confrontation. If his marriage was cold, empty and unsatisfying, his printing business more than made up for it. He was in charge there, looked up to by his staff whom he considered more friends than employees. He made a decent living, he kept others in work, he enjoyed it and he'd long since realized that he was luckier than most men.

He let himself into the house with his key and stood in the hall listening for a moment. The house was silent and he thought perhaps he'd come on a fool's errand and Rosie had gone out to look in the shops.

Walking into the sitting-room, he dumped his briefcase on a chair and took off his jacket. It was hot again; it looked as if an Indian summer was on its way. He went over to the windows to open them, but stopped short as he saw Rosie below in the garden. She was on her hands and knees, planting out something in one of the beds.

Standing back a little by the curtain so Rosie wouldn't spot him if she looked up, he watched her for a while. She was kneeling down, tenderly placing the plants in a way he could remember doing himself once, before Edith's griping had driven him to spending more time in the print room. Rosie had proved to be worth helping; she was a brave little thing and as bright as a button. Anyone who could tolerate Edith's constant criticism and learn so quickly deserved a medal.

Her hair looked like burnished copper coils today in the sunshine. Such pretty hair – it was a good job he'd stopped Edith from cutting it short as she'd once suggested. He wished now that he hadn't rushed home. She looked so happy and what he had to tell her was going to ruin that.

Rosie jumped guiltily to her feet as he came out through the kitchen to the garden. 'Hullo, Mr Bentley, er, um, would you like some tea?' she said falteringly. He never came home at this time of day and she was embarrassed to be caught unawares.

'I'll make some for both of us,' he said with a shy smile. 'You get back to the plants. I was wondering who the good fairy was that had been looking after them for me.'

Rosie was now stunned because Mr Bentley had said a whole sentence and offered to make *her* tea. She knew too she really should have asked before touching things in the garden.

Curiously he didn't seem cross at all. In fact he seemed pleased. 'I'm sorry I didn't ask you first,' she said, hopping nervously from one foot to the other. 'I should, I know, but I couldn't bear to see so many weeds.'

Ten minutes later Mr Bentley came back down the garden with two mugs of tea. Rosie looked askance at them. She'd been told by Mrs Bentley you should only ever give a mug to a tradesman.

'Better than those prissy teacups,' he said with a smile, sitting down on the steps which led to the next terrace. 'Now tell me what are those things you're planting?'

'Lupins,' Rosie said. 'The ones at the bottom of the garden had seeded themselves, so I dug them up and thought I'd replant them here. They're all blue ones. I thought they'd look pretty here next year amongst the marguerites; perhaps we could plant something red with them too. That would be nice for the Coronation. I read in one of the magazines you brought me home that all the gardeners in the big parks are planning red, white and blue displays for next summer.'

Herbert felt as if he'd been stung. He hadn't imagined that she ever thought more than a couple of weeks ahead. Now she was talking of next June.

'Come and sit down,' he said, patting the step beside him. 'I've got something I need to talk to you about.' He wished now he'd taken Miss Pemberton up on her offer to break the news to Rosie. Yet just an hour ago he had thought it was kinder to tell her himself.

Her face clouded over. 'Is it the trial?'

Herbert nodded. 'Miss Pemberton telephoned me today, and I came straight home. The trial has been set to start on the 24th of September. And it will be here in Bristol. Not at the assizes in Wells or Taunton as we expected.'

'Oh,' she said, and cupped her hands round her mug as if suddenly chilled.

Herbert didn't know quite how to proceed, even though he'd had it clear in his head on the way home.

'The trouble with it being here in Bristol is that it's going to attract a great deal of local attention. I can't remember when we last had a murder trial here. People are ghoulish about such things and it will dominate the newspapers.'

Rosie turned on the step towards him, her eyes looking right into his. 'You won't want me here then,' she said without a trace of bitterness, only quiet acceptance. 'Is that what you wanted to say, Mr Bentley?'

'No. That isn't what I meant,' he said, blushing furiously.

Rosie said nothing, just looked down at her feet; they were bare and very suntanned and she flexed her toes so the grass sprang up between them.

'What about Seth and Norman?' she asked eventually.

'Will they be in court too?' She had refused to ask about either of her brothers in all this time, and Miss Pemberton hadn't volunteered any information about them either.

'Norman will be called as a witness of course. But didn't Miss Pemberton tell you that Seth has been charged jointly with your father?' he asked.

'She said he would be tried at the same time,' Rosie said, then, as if a thought had just come to her, she looked at Herbert sharply. 'Does that mean the police think he helped Dad do the murders?'

Herbert squirmed. He thought Miss Pemberton should have made this plain to Rosie some time ago. He couldn't think why she hadn't. 'Well, yes, Rosie, I thought you knew that.'

'No. I didn't,' she said. She was thrown entirely. 'I thought he had only been charged with hurting me.' She paused for a moment, a strange sense of relief flooding through her that her prayers had been answered and Seth's wickedness had been seen and would be punished. 'Will I have to go to court too?'

Herbert noticed she had grown very pale; the freckles across her nose stood out more clearly. He didn't think it was advisable to try and explain now why the police had dropped some lesser charges against her brother. In point of fact the decision was partly to protect Rosie: to save her a harrowing court appearance and to keep her anonymity. But the police believed that by concentrating their entire efforts on the most serious offence, that of joint murder with his father, Seth would hang anyway and it wasn't necessary or advisable to spin out the trial and possibly confuse the jury with lesser offences.

'No. You won't have to be there, not now. They have enough witnesses without you. Apparently the police have finally tracked down Ethel Parker, so she'll be one of them.'

'Will she?' Rosie exclaimed. Her feelings about this piece of news were mixed. It was a relief to find that Cole hadn't killed her too, but at the same time Ethel was unlikely to say anything in court which might help her father. 'It's going to be very strange for her coming face to face with the two boys she left behind,' she said. 'Maybe if she hadn't run out on them, they wouldn't be the nasty pieces of work they are now?'

Herbert looked sharply at Rosie. That was a remarkably adult observation. He wondered what her real feelings were about her father and brother. Did she believe them innocent? Or did she know they were guilty? He felt ashamed of himself that he'd had her under his roof all this time, yet he hadn't tried to communicate with her. But it was too late now to try and discover what was going on in her head.

'Well, Mrs Bentley won't want me here if there's going to be a terrible fuss, will she?' Rosie said after a moment's deep thought.

Herbert sighed. Rosie had hit the nail right on the head. His wife might bask in reflected glory at taking in 'an unfortunate', but her kind of charity was the fair weather variety.

'I haven't spoken to her about it yet,' he said, but his forlorn tone told Rosie what the outcome would be.

'It's okay, Mr Bentley.' Rosie touched his arm tentatively. She was grateful that he cared and she was reminded then that but for his previous intervention on her behalf she would have been shipped out weeks ago. 'I understand.'

'Do you?' He looked at Rosie raising one eyebrow. She had been brought up with a man who killed women who got in his way. Did she secretly despise him for being so weak with his wife? What sort of woman would she grow into? A tyrant like Edith, or a long-suffering victim like her mother? He fervently hoped she could steer a middle course.

'Yes I do.' She suddenly smiled at him. 'It hasn't been wasted being here with you. I've learned such a lot, about laying tables, gardening and all sorts of other things. I'll be all right wherever I go. Don't you worry about me.'

Herbert drank his tea, then walked around the garden with Rosie. He let her show him all the plants she'd uncovered amongst the weeds, then went back indoors, pretending he had some letters to write.

He felt afraid for Rosie. Cole and Seth Parker might be the ones facing the death penalty, but poor Rosie was going to hear things in the next few weeks that would destroy any remaining good memories she had of her family and strip away the last shreds of her innocence. Worse still was the fear that the evidence the police had compiled against her brother Seth would be insufficient for the jury to find him guilty of murder, and that he'd be out on the streets in a few weeks looking for the person whom he felt to be responsible for his father's plight.

Herbert sighed. Miss Pemberton had the right idea in getting Rosie right away from the West Country with a brand new identity. She'd also been acting in Rosie's best interests by convincing the police how damaging it would be for her to be forced to stand up in court and give evidence against her father and brother. But her plan of shielding Rosie from any further harm and humiliation sounded almost as bad as incarcerating her in a prison.

He could think of no worse fate than being sent to work in a lunatic asylum.

Chapter Five

Rosie peered through the tall iron gates of Carrington Hall and shuddered. She had imagined that a private mental home with such a grand-sounding name would be a kind of stately home set in beautiful grounds. Instead it was a rambling, ugly building which looked like an old work-house. The garden was overgrown and very neglected.

Peeling paintwork, dark red brick showing through damaged stucco, the tall fir trees surrounding it and the barred windows added a menacing note to the already melancholy character of a place used to lock away the feeble-minded.

It was pure instinct that made her turn and walk away, back towards the pretty road she'd come along from Woodside Park tube station. The semi-detached houses there were all newly built since the war, with keyhole-shaped porches, neatly cut lawns and tidy flower borders. When she saw them she'd even begun to think things were going to improve for her. Hadn't life thrown enough horror at her already, without Miss Pemberton betraying her trust and sending her to a crumbling madhouse?

She had gone some twenty yards when common sense prevailed. She stopped, put her suitcase down for a moment, and considered her options.

Where else could she go at seven in the evening? Thomas's home in Hampstead couldn't be that far away, but would he welcome her turning up uninvited on his doorstep?

She had no idea about how to get another job or a place

to live. London was so huge too, and she had only a couple of pounds in her purse, and was too tired to think clearly. Maybe she was overreacting? Besides, it was a bit spineless to run before she'd even set one foot over the threshold.

Taking a deep breath, she turned back, this time trying to be more positive. The house appeared to have been extended over the years in a haphazard fashion. Even the roof was at two different heights. On the lower side there were two main floors with a row of tiny attic windows below a conventional roof. On the other side there were three floors all with smaller windows and pointed gables up above.

On the ground level other single-storey buildings had been added to the main house; they sprawled round a concrete area which was enclosed by an eight-foot chain-link fence.

Rosie pushed open the gates and began to walk cautiously up the weed-filled concrete drive. It had been raining all day until just an hour ago, and water dripped on her from the overhanging trees. The drive was about forty yards long and as the ground-floor windows had net curtaining on their lower half, Rosie couldn't see anyone, but she had the distinct impression she was being watched.

She rang the front-door bell, but it was a long time before the door was opened. A fat middle-aged woman in a navy blue nurse's dress and starched frilly cap perched on iron grey hair scowled at her.

'Yes?' she said, as if she suspected Rosie of hawking brushes door to door.

'I'm Rosemary Smith,' Rosie said, so nervous now that she could barely raise her voice above a whisper. 'I've come here to work.'

The woman's sour expression did not change. No sudden welcoming smile or an apology, just a cold stare. 'I expected you hours ago,' she said curtly. 'We've all had our tea and the kitchen's shut up. I'm Miss Barnes, the matron, and I'm much too busy now to deal with you. I'll call someone to show you round. Come in and wait.'

After her long journey and then her hesitation outside, this cold reception instantly stripped Rosie of her last shreds of self-confidence, and it was all she could do not to burst into tears. She stepped warily into a small area with a black and white tiled floor. It was enclosed by a wooden and wired glass partition. Matron shut the front door and locked it with one of the many keys she had on a chain attached to her belt. Then without saying another word, she went on through a door in the partition and locked it behind her, leaving Rosie trapped in what was virtually a cage.

The day after Mr Bentley had told Rosie about the date of her father's trial, Miss Pemberton had called to tell her she'd fixed her up with this job. Rosie hadn't liked the sound of it one bit, in fact she'd pleaded with Miss Pemberton to find her something else, but the social worker talked her round. She pointed out that Mr Lionel Brace-Coombes, the owner of the home, was an old friend of hers and he was prepared to accept Rosie purely on her recommendation, without checking her background. It was also a step in the right direction towards getting into nursing.

Once Rosie realized that no alternative would be offered her, she tried to be optimistic by looking at all the attractions the job offered. It was in north London, and Thomas Farley was only a bus ride away. She was to be paid one pound ten shillings a week, with everything, including her uniform, found for her. But perhaps the best thing of all was that absolutely no one there would know who she really was, not even Mr Lionel Brace-Coombes. Miss Pemberton had somehow managed to get her a national insurance card in the name of Rosemary Smith, and together they'd composed a whole new background for her. Rosemary's mother was to have died from an infection following a miscarriage when she was six and her father had died last year from a heart attack. Rosie was amazed at how simple it was to change identity. Like a snake shedding its skin.

Miss Pemberton could not have been more encouraging or kind; she was determined that Rosie should make her new start with all the right clothes. She took her up to Bright's department store in Clifton and bought her, amongst other things, the dark green raincoat she was wearing now. It had a warm tartan lining and a hood, and she could hardly believe she owned something so smart. Her suitcase might be a battered old one of Miss Pemberton's but almost everything inside it was new. She even had a photograph of her 'parents' in a frame to give her new family history credençe. Granted the small curly-haired woman and the tall man with a droopy moustache were just friends of Miss Pemberton's, but the woman had a similar country-girl look to Rosie.

'You can refer to me as your Auntie Molly, your father's unmarried sister who helped care for you after your mother died,' Miss Pemberton suggested, laughing as if she almost wished she was. 'And give my address in Chilton Trinity as your home address. I'll write to you just as an aunt would, so if anyone feels like snooping, as people do, they won't be any the wiser. I can pass on information about Alan. You can always tell people he's your small cousin.'

Mr Bentley had asked if she would keep in touch with him too. He suggested that she send the letters to his office, and he would reply as Uncle Herbert. Rosie knew by this that he didn't want his wife to discover where she had gone, or his interest in her. Sharing her secret destination with him made her feel warm inside, as did looking at the leather writing case he'd given her as a leaving present.

But the happy, excited feeling she'd had when she left Bristol this morning was now replaced with terror as she waited, locked in. Through the wired glass which was at eye level, she could see a wide uncarpeted staircase. To the right and left of it were other closed doors, all with a small wired glass panel. The walls were painted a dull pea-green colour, the doors cream. It looked inhospitable enough, but it was a distant noise which really intimidated her. A wailing sound, not crying or screaming exactly, but a bleak sound of someone deeply distressed.

'Is this what it's like for you, Dad?' she thought.

She had done what Miss Pemberton suggested and written to him. Thinking deeply on what she felt about him and putting it into words had soothed the torment inside her a little. She told him bluntly that she felt no sympathy, only deep shame, and that the only thing which might change the way she felt was if he was man enough to admit to his crimes and show some real sorrow for what he had done. Yet for all that she still softened her harsh words towards the end of the letter by saying she would keep the good memories of him in her heart and try to forgive him.

His reply had made her cry. He wrote like a child in big printing with no punctuation and almost every word spelled wrong. But his message to her was strong and clear: he had always loved her, he was proud of her and was very sorry he hadn't been a better example. He neither protested his innocence, nor admitted any guilt, but said he was glad she was leaving Somerset because he wanted more for her than he'd got living on the Levels. He hoped she would marry a man who would cherish her and keep her happy.

Rosie had read and re-read the letter before she eventually destroyed it. Somehow those few, inarticulate words said so much about the man. He did have a gentler, decent side, he dreamed dreams, he ached for more than life had offered him. Rosie looked back and remembered the pride he took in his parlour. The furniture he'd bought at country house auctions during the difficult Thirties had been too grand really for a working man's cottage. He used to run his big hands lovingly over the polished table and point out the skill of the craftsman who'd made it. She remembered too that it was him who'd awoken her interest in nature, telling her all he knew about birds and animals while they were out tramping the moors together.

She thought perhaps he was as much a victim as Ruby and Heather were, forced from when he was just a young boy to rely on his physical strength, all sensitivity knocked out of him by the harshness of the life into which he was born. She didn't know why that should make him turn killer, but maybe too much frustration could do that to a man.

Just as Rosie was on the point of screaming and hammering for the door to be unlocked, at last she saw a girl coming down the stairs. She looked about nineteen or twenty, an exceptionally plain girl, painfully thin, with badly cut, short mousy brown hair and wire-rimmed glasses. She was dressed in a maroon uniform dress. Like Matron she had a bunch of keys on her belt.

With her unprepossessing appearance Rosie was surprised when she waved and smiled before opening the door. 'Don't look so scared,' she said with a giggle as she let Rosie out. 'It is a madhouse, but it isn't quite as bad as it looks.'

The girl's cheerfulness was a slender ray of hope, but once through the partition, the door was locked again behind her, the wailing noise was much louder and there was an unpleasant smell like stale vomit.

Rosie quaked visibly and the other girl laughed. 'Don't you go worrying about that noise,' she said. 'It's only old Mabel, but they'll shut her up soon. I'm Jackson. We get called by our surnames when we're on duty, but I'm Maureen out of Matron's hearing. I didn't realize you were going to be so young. Rosemary Smith, isn't it?'

Rosie nodded and tried to smile but tears filled her eyes.

'Come on, love.' The older girl patted her on the shoulder and took her case. 'Let me take you up to our room –

you're sharing with me. You look as if you're all in.'

Maureen led her up the stairs; the sound of their feet on the bare varnished wood almost drowned the wailing sound from above. She stopped on the first landing by a door. 'This is the way through to the ward where you'll be working,' she said letting Rosie look through the viewing panel. Another similar heavy door was directly inside, beyond that a long passage. 'It'll seem like a prison to you for a while as all doors, the ones inside as well as these ones, have to be locked when you go in and out. But in a couple of days you'll be so used to locking and unlocking you won't even think about it.'

'Are the patients dangerous then?' Rosie asked nervously.

'Some can be,' Maureen said with a shrug. 'But mostly the locking up is so we know exactly where they all are and what they are doing.'

The wide staircase ended abruptly on the second-floor landing, just past the door that Maureen said led to the ward for the more disturbed patients. From there on the staircase leading to a final door was narrow, carpeted and clearly a more recent addition to the house. Rosie realized as Maureen unlocked the door that they were entering the taller part of the building she'd noticed from outside.

'This is the staff wing,' Maureen said. 'We all live up here, except for Matron, who's got a flat on the ground floor. Because it's separate from the rest of the building it's very quiet. All hell can break loose downstairs and we can't hear it.' The door led into a dark narrow corridor and she opened the first door she came to. 'And this is our room.'

After the bare wood staircase and the institutional bleakness of the rest of the place, the room Rosie was led into looked pleasingly comfortable, with twin beds with heavy cream bedspreads, two easy chairs, a dressing table and a big chest of drawers. There was even carpet on the floor and cheerful yellow checked curtains at the window.

'The bathroom is right next door,' Maureen said, sitting down on the bed nearest the window. 'This is my bed. You get the two right-hand drawers on the dressing table and the two bottom drawers in the big chest. There's bags of space in the cupboard. I haven't got many clothes.'

Rosie just stood in the middle of the room looking about her and suddenly the events of the long day all hit her at once and she began to cry.

She had believed she was old enough and tough enough to cope with being sent to London alone, but she wasn't. No one had warned her how crowded and frantic it would be, or how confusing the underground trains were. She went all the way to a place called Gloucester Road before she realized she was going the wrong way and by the time she found her way back to Leicester Square and the right train, she was on the point of tears. Everything was different from back home. People pushed and shoved, they had paler faces, smarter clothes and they sounded strange. She looked at the women's high heels and sophisticated costumes and felt like a little country mouse in her heavy black lace-up shoes and white ankle socks.

Now she was in a place where dangerous people were locked away. In a couple of weeks her father and brother would be tried and hanged and she'd have absolutely no one she could confide in. She was so very scared. How was she going to cope?

Maureen looked aghast at the younger girl's tears. She got up off the bed but hesitated, as if wanting to offer a comforting hug, but afraid of rejection. 'Don't cry. It's okay here,' she said, putting a tentative hand on Rosie's shoulder. 'I know no one really wants to work in a loony-bin. But it's not as bad as it looks and we have lots of laughs. I'll go and make a cup of tea while you unpack your case. Later I'll show you round.'

'I'm sorry,' Rosie sobbed, dabbing at her eyes ineffectually. 'It's just that,' she stopped short, unable to pinpoint exactly what had upset her.

'That you've never been away from home before? That Matron made you feel about as welcome as a dog flea? The locked doors and Mabel wailing? I know. It's all too much when you're tired,' Maureen said sympathetically.

Rosie managed a weak smile. She thought Maureen was kind, perhaps it was just the unexpectedness of that which made her cry. 'I suppose now you'll think I'm such a baby?'

Maureen looked at Rosie appraisingly. She had gentle grey eyes behind her glasses and her warm smile made her pale spotty face seem less plain. 'No, I don't. Everyone's the same when they first come here. I'm really pleased to see you; it's been lonely in here on my own. Now put your things away and settle in; that will make you feel better.'

Maureen was gone for some ten minutes. As Rosie couldn't hear anything, she assumed she must have gone back downstairs. Rosie hung up her clothes, put her case on the top shelf of the cupboard, then sat down on her bed.

Maureen had even fewer belongings than she did. No photographs, books or other clutter. She wondered if everyone who came to work here was an oddball, with nowhere else to go.

It was dusk now, and looking out of the window she saw their room overlooked the back garden. It was better cared for than the front, with a well-cut lawn, flower-beds and several wooden bench seats. It was some hundred foot long, surrounded by a high stone wall, with jagged glass along the top. There were many trees and a small summer house. Beyond the trees were fields. She began to feel a little less frightened.

Maureen came back in with two mugs of tea in one hand and a plate of buttered toast. 'I thought you might be hungry, but this was all I could rustle up,' she said with a wide grin. 'I put extra sugar in your tea. It's good for shock.'

Over tea Maureen rattled out the pecking order of the staff. 'Starting at the top, there's Matron, Miss Barnes that is, the witch who let you in. Then there's Dr Freed, who comes in a couple of times a week. Sister Welbred and Staff Nurse Aylwood come next, but you won't have much to do with them. Mrs Trow handles all the administration stuff, she comes in daily. Then there's two trained nurses, you can tell them by their striped dresses. Below them are the chargehands, that's us. We wear maroon, and you'll get your uniform tomorrow morning. Then below us are the domestics. They do cooking, laundry and cleaning; some wear white overalls, some green, depending on what they do. Two of them, Clack and Simmonds, have a room downstairs, but the rest live out and work part time.'

Rosie thought this sounded like an army of people. She asked why she hadn't seen anyone else around on her way in.

Maureen smirked. 'They aren't all here at any one time. They work different shifts and in the evenings there's no need for so many. Whatever Matron or the nurses might tell you, us chargehands do most of the real work. Dishing out the patients' food, feeding those who can't manage it themselves, dressing them, washing them and cleaning up those who poop themselves.'

Rosie shuddered. Miss Pemberton had told her all that, and it hadn't seemed that bad then, just like nursing, but now she was here it seemed horrible.

'You'll soon get used to it,' Maureen said with a shrug. 'They can't help it, after all. I try and think of the patients as big children, I find it helps. One or two of the staff are a bit mean to them. I hate that, and I'm sure you will too, but don't speak out, not if you want to keep your job, and try to keep in with Matron, otherwise she'll make your life a misery. But most of the staff are okay. Linda Bell and Mary Connor are young like us. They've gone out to the pictures tonight, but they'll be back later.'

Maureen went on to explain a little more about Carrington Hall.

'It isn't a bit like the state loony-bins,' she said, 'as people pay to keep their loopy relations here there aren't hundreds of patients, only about thirty at the most. There's plenty of staff, the food's better, and it's not so scary. I know what the other places are like. I worked in one.'

By the time Maureen said it was time for her tour of the building, Rosie was beginning to think working at Carrington Hall might not be as bad as she'd feared initially. But as they got down to the second-floor landing she heard some muffled banging and shouting noises coming from behind the locked door and shuddered.

'We're not going in there,' Maureen said reassuringly, taking her firmly by the arm and leading her on down the stairs. 'In fact you may never go in there. Matron doesn't like the younger staff working there. I've been here three years and I only get sent in there occasionally when they are short-staffed. And don't worry about the noises either – the people in there are nuts, remember, and it's just their way of letting off steam.'

Through the two sets of locked doors on the first floor was a long wide corridor with highly polished brown lino and many doors leading off it. Although it smelled nasty, stronger still than it had downstairs, it was light and spacious with a long narrow window overlooking the front drive.

'The dormitories are down there,' Maureen said, waving her hand vaguely. 'Women in one, men in the other. The other rooms are isolation, treatment and bathrooms, but I'll show you all those later. First I'll show you the patients, they're all in the day room.'

As it was peaceful on this landing with only a background hum of voices to show there were people close by, Rosie felt no sense of alarm. She stepped into the day room behind Maureen quite confidently, but before she'd even had a second to glance around, or catch her breath, a man lunged at her. He enveloped her in a bear hug, lifting her right off her feet, holding her so tightly she thought her ribs would be crushed. She screamed in terror.

'It's okay,' Maureen called out over Rosie's screams. 'He's perfectly harmless, just over-friendly. Now put her down, Donald.' She slapped at the man's shoulder. 'Smith's come here to help look after you, and she won't stay if you scare her.'

To Rosie's intense relief the man dropped her instantly, and backed away looking crestfallen. She saw he was quite young, perhaps in his twenties, and tall with fair hair. 'I only w-w-wanted to s-s-say hullo,' he stammered and slunk away with his head down.

Still reeling from the shock of this attack, her heart thumping like a steam hammer, Rosie got her first sight of the rest of the inmates, and as she did, her legs buckled beneath here. Nothing she'd ever encountered before had made her feel quite so revolted, or so afraid. She cowered and retreated back against the locked door, fighting the desire to scream again.

Fourteen or so ugly, misshapen faces and all of them staring at her. Dull eyes, sloppy mouths, some with runny noses too. Some were sitting, others stood frozen to the spot as if halted mid-shuffle by her unexpected appearance. The room was unbearably hot and stuffy, stinking of a pungent mixture of stale food, sweat and farts.

There was absolutely nothing to distract her gaze from these pathetic human rejects either. Not a picture on the grubby cream walls, no curtains at the barred windows, not even a rug on the brown lino floor. Aside from a dozen or so easy chairs there was nothing more than a stack of tubular chairs in one corner, and a table by the window.

'Are you all right?' Maureen asked, breaking the silence. 'You've gone as white as a sheet! Let me introduce you to Brownlow. She's another chargehand.'

Rosie forced herself to smile at the middle-aged woman

coming towards her, even though she wanted to run. The woman looked weary. The many lines on her face all had a downturn as if she had never smiled in her entire life. She wore a maroon uniform like Maureen's, but also a cap and apron. Her hair was grey, her eyes dull.

Maureen rattled out a hasty explanation as to how Smith had just arrived from Somerset. Brownlow held out a limp hand and made a very brief and stilted welcoming speech, but it was obvious she was disinclined to chat and soon went back to her chair.

Trying very hard to control her fear and disgust, Rosie looked around her. To her surprise, Donald, the man who had crushed her, was not only the youngest of the patients, but the only one of them who looked anything approaching normal. In fact if it hadn't been for his sloppy mouth and a somewhat vacant look in his mournful blue eyes, he could almost have been called handsome. He was at least six foot tall, of a slim, very straight-backed build with floppy blond hair which badly needed a cut. Compared with the other men he didn't look scary.

There were fewer men than women, but aside from Donald the rest of them looked over forty, wearing the same grey trousers and loose battledress-type flannel jacket over a shirt. One was rocking backwards and forwards in his chair, muttering something under his breath and rubbing his hands on his groin. The others remained staring at Rosie; one was dribbling.

The women began to move again first, clustering in groups of two and three, and whispering to one another as they watched her. Unlike the men there was no uniformity about their clothes or their ages. The youngest appeared to be in her mid-twenties, the oldest perhaps over sixty. Some wore print dresses and cardigans, others wore skirts, blouses and cardigans. But all of them looked neglected with food stains down their fronts and unkempt hair, and they moved slowly, awkwardly, almost as if their limbs ached.

'I'd better tell you who they all are,' Maureen said, catching hold of Rosie's elbow and drawing her away from the door. 'Don't be scared, they are all quite harmless, and some of them are kind of sweet when you get to know them.'

Rosie couldn't believe this. A wild-eyed woman of maybe thirty sat in a chair knitting furiously. She had coarse red hair which stood up like a brush. In one corner two very much older women stood huddled together, their arms linked. One had a terrible scar from her temple to her jaw line which pulled at her flesh so her eyes were on different levels. Her companion was so thin she was almost skeletal. But most frightening of all was a very fat woman sitting on the floor. Her partially bald head was terribly misshapen, with a huge bulging domed forehead. Her eyes were just narrow slits and she had virtually no nose, just two holes. Her dress was rucked up, showing long pink drawers, and she was picking at a nasty scab on her thin, mottled leg and grunting to herself.

Maureen behaved as if she was just walking about amongst a class of children. Still holding on to Rosie with one hand, she bent to speak to some of them, telling them who Rosie was; others she just touched on the shoulder as if to acknowledge their presence. 'This is Aggie,' she said, stopping by the fat lady with the strange-shaped head. 'And these are Alice and Patty,' she said of the two older women with linked arms. Jacob sat rocking in his chair and totally ignored Maureen's attempts to get him to speak. The wild-looking woman knitting was Tabby. 'Like a cat,' she chortled, knitting even more furiously. 'I claw people too, so watch out.'

'She does too, sometimes,' Maureen agreed with a smile and patted Tabby's shoulder in an affectionate gesture. 'But that's not why she's called Tabby. It's just short for Tabitha. But you aren't going to hurt Smith, are you, Tabby? Because she's nice.'

The woman looked up at Rosie as if considering whether

or not to strike out. 'She's got pretty hair,' she said in a dull monotone. 'Matron won't like that.'

That remark appeared to be based on an understanding of Matron, and as Tabby was the only one to speak aside from Donald, Rosie plucked up some courage and bent down towards the woman. 'What are you knitting, Tabby?' she ventured.

'A dress,' Tabby replied, and stopped knitting to hold up her work. 'It's nice, isn't it?'

Rosie agreed out of politeness. It was in fact just a long multicoloured strip no more than ten inches wide, with many holes where she'd dropped stitches.

Donald seemed to have recovered from being told off. He came back to Rosie and this time put his hand in hers like a child. It was hot and sweaty, but the broad smile which accompanied it was friendly and unthreatening. 'Wh-wh-what's your n-n-name?' he asked.

'Smith,' Rosie said in a faint voice. It sounded so peculiar saying a name she'd hardly got used to yet, and even stranger talking to a giant of a man who behaved like a small child. 'And you're Donald, aren't you?'

He nodded and grinned. 'Are you g-g-going to be my f-f-friend?' he asked.

'Er, yes,' she replied hesitantly, hoping that she might find it in her heart to care for at least some of these people eventually. At least Donald wasn't ugly, and maybe his fierce hug was his way of getting attention. 'Yes, of course I'm going to be your friend,' she added with more conviction than she felt.

'Smith will see you all tomorrow,' Maureen called out in a loud voice. 'And I want you all on your best behaviour, or else.'

The relief at leaving the room was so great that Rosie slumped against the corridor wall outside as Maureen locked the door.

'Tough, eh?' she said with some sympathy.

'They scared me,' Rosie whispered. 'I know I ought to

feel sorry for them, but all I wanted to do was run out. I'm not going to be a bit of good here. I won't even be able to touch them. I don't know how you stand it.'

Maureen smiled in absolute understanding. 'Everyone feels the way you do the first time they visit a mental asylum,' she said. 'But we've never yet had anyone come here to work who didn't get used to it within a couple of days. In a week I bet you'll tell me you can't remember any more what it was that gave you the creeps. But we'd better go and see Sister Welbred now, before I show you the rest of the place. By rights she should be in there now with Brownlow as they do the nights together. But I expect she's having a fag in the office.'

It was after nine-thirty when the girls got back to their room. Maureen lit up a cigarette and it seemed as if she intended to talk all night.

Rosie was too stunned and sickened by all she had seen and heard to ask any further questions. They had run into Matron again who had curtly told Rosie she was to tie back her hair otherwise she'd insist on having it cut short. That at least made sense of Tabby's remark. It seemed Matron didn't approve of any femininity. Sister Welbred was odd too, a big, red-headed woman in her fifties with a slight cast in one eye. She'd been reading a magazine when they came across her in the office; a cigarette was hanging out of the corner of her mouth and she smelled of alcohol. She'd squeezed Rosie's arms and said she'd soon get a few muscles in them, then laughed almost manically.

Rosie had seen everywhere Maureen thought she needed to, the bathrooms and dormitories on the first floor, the staff dining-room and rest room on the ground floor, a treatment room and an isolation room. Rosie's flesh crawled when Maureen waved one hand at some locked doors and airily said they were padded cells, and then the other at a place for electric shock treatment. She wondered too why no one opened any windows, for there were nasty smells lingering everywhere which weren't entirely banished by the strong aroma of disinfectant.

Finally they came to a sitting-room on the ground floor overlooking the front garden, which was for visiting relatives. It was homely and comfortable with chintz-covered armchairs. Rosie asked if the relatives ever saw the patients' upstairs day room and compared it.

'There's very few of them ever get visitors,' Maureen said with a shrug. 'They stick them in here, pay the bills and then forget them. Donald's parents used to come every three or four weeks, but even they only come about once every three months now. The saddest thing is that I don't think he needs to be in here at all, he's only a bit simple. But no one is interested in my opinion.'

But now the tour was over and they were back upstairs with Maureen rattling out stories about patients and gossip about staff. When Rosie yawned, Maureen blushed furiously. 'Oh gawd, I'm sorry, you must be so tired and here I am gabbling on. Get into bed, love. We can talk some more tomorrow.'

Rosie was almost asleep when Maureen spoke again.

'Do you think you can bear it?' she asked softly.

'I don't know,' Rosie replied, wondering how she was ever going to conquer her squeamishness. 'But you learned to like it, so maybe I will in time.'

She thought Maureen was as odd as everything else here. She didn't seem like a young girl. She gave the impression she was almost in charge here, yet terse remarks she'd made about other staff suggested she might be unpopular with them. It was strange too that she hadn't once mentioned anything outside Carrington Hall, almost as if she never went out.

'I don't know what it's like outside of asylums,' Maureen said. 'I was put in an orphanage when my mother died, and sent straight to Luckmore Grange when I was only fourteen. This place is paradise next to that.'

Rosie wanted to hear all about Maureen but she couldn't stay awake any longer. The last thing she thought before she sank into unconsciousness was that as soon as she was sixteen in October she'd get out of here. She wasn't even sure that she wanted to be a nurse any longer.

Maureen was awake for a long time after Rosie fell asleep. There was a great deal more she could have told this new girl, but she hadn't dared. She would find out soon enough, and in the meantime at least it meant Maureen had some company. But she had been truthful when she said it was paradise compared with Luckmore Grange. She still had nightmares about that place.

Maureen Jackson was nineteen and she was happy enough working here in Carrington Hall. But then her idea of happiness was not being verbally or physically abused, and having three good meals a day and a decent room of her own. Until she came here, she'd never had any of those things.

She was six when war broke out, living in two rooms in Peckham with her two older brothers and her mother. Maureen had never known her father, but very early in life she'd realized that her mother didn't like her, because of him. 'You're just like your father,' she would rage as she took a belt to her.

When Maureen's whole school was evacuated to Bognor Regis, all the other mothers were tearful, but not hers. Peggy Jackson was off up the road and into the pub before the crocodile of children were even ushered out of the school gates.

Between September of 1939 and 1943 Maureen was sent to eight different homes, finally ending up on a farm near Bodmin with a crazy old couple who didn't even bother to send her to school, much less feed her with any regularity. She was still there, a skinny, plain girl of ten, when she got the message that her mother had been killed. Not by a bomb, which might have gained Maureen a little sympathy, but knocked over by a car on her way home from the pub.

She was moved then to an orphanage in Yeovil where she stayed until the war ended, then for some reason which was never explained to her, she was packed off back to London, to Northwood, another orphanage in Dulwich. When Uncle Ted, a man that did the gardening, began cuddling and fondling her, she had a vague feeling there was something bad about it, yet it was nice that at last someone cared about her. Ted was simple, but he used to give her sweets, and called her his little girlfriend. She trusted him and considered him her best friend.

Then one day just before she was fourteen he pushed her down on some old sacks in his potting shed, and forced himself into her. It hurt terribly, but worse still than the pain and shock was the awful feeling that she'd been betrayed. She ran away from him crying when he'd finished hurting her, and kept well away from him after that.

It was at a routine medical that they found she was five months pregnant. Maureen had innocently wondered why her tummy seemed to be getting fatter, but she'd never made the association between that and the horrible thing Ted did to her. When the doctor questioned her she was too scared to admit anything, and she just kept saying she didn't know how it had happened.

That was how she came to end up in Luckmore Grange out in Essex. They said she was mentally defective and it was the only place for her.

She went into labour prematurely, and the baby girl died a few hours later. She was only fourteen and a half, and not one person showed her the slightest sympathy.

Maureen was in that dreadful place for almost two years. Spending days in a gloomy locked ward surrounded by old shuffling women who peed on the floor and shat in their beds. She saw women so deranged that they pulled out their hair and tore at their flesh with their nails, and she heard them screaming from brutal electric shock treatments. For a while after losing the baby, she sat motionless, refusing to speak to anyone.

But then one night as she lay in that dormitory, her skin crawling at the horrible sounds of madness all around her, the cackling laughter, sinister rustlings and strange moans, she knew if she didn't do something, she'd soon be as mad as they were.

All at once she saw she'd have to fight to prove she was sane. Any violence would mean electric shock treatment and a strait-jacket – they wouldn't listen to any protests. The only other way was being sneaky.

Offering to help the staff was the first step. They were a hard cruel bunch, doing a job that no one else wanted to do. At first they only belittled her, making her do the vilest jobs like cleaning up after the incontinent patients. But slowly she saw they were coming to rely on her and soon she was feeding the more helpless patients, making beds and running errands. A new young doctor was her real salvation; without him she might have been trapped in a twilight world for ever, expected to work, yet still locked away.

The very first day he came into her ward, she saw that light in his eye that said he hadn't yet been worn down by the hopelessness of mental institutions. She listened to him telling a belligerent nurse that the mentally incompetent were still people and that they must be treated with compassion, and she knew he was the one to help her.

She dogged his footsteps every time he did his rounds. Offering him assistance with difficult patients, volunteering information about them. Then finally the day came when he asked her to tell him about herself.

That was how she got the job here at Carrington Hall. She could barely read or write, which ruled out almost every other job, and she'd grown used to looking after the mentally ill. So she was sent here on a month's trial, and now she'd been here for almost three years.

She looked across the narrow divide between her bed and the new girl's and felt so very envious of her. She had everything: she was pretty, she had nice clothes and even the photograph on her bedside table showed that she had loving parents. She wouldn't stick it here for long.

Watching the girl sleep with one arm curled around her head, Maureen felt a little guilty that she'd agreed to tell Matron every last thing about her. Rosemary seemed nice and it didn't seem fair to spy on her and pass back information. But then Matron had insisted there was no other way, not unless she wanted to end up in another place like Luckmore Grange.

Rosie awoke with a start as a bell rang.

'Time to get up,' Maureen said, leaping out of bed. 'Put something plain on for now. You'll get your uniform after breakfast.'

Rosie rubbed her eyes and got out of bed. She picked up her washbag and towel and went next door to the bathroom. By the time she got back, Maureen was already fully dressed.

'Hurry up,' she said. 'We've got to be downstairs in five minutes.'

Rosie wondered where the girl had washed and brushed her teeth. There didn't appear to be another bathroom anywhere. She hastily pulled on her navy skirt and a white blouse, then brushed her hair and secured it at the back of her neck with a rubber band.

Everywhere was silent as they walked down the three flights of stairs, presumably all the patients were still asleep. But Rosie could smell that distinctive odour of ammonia wafting out from under the locked doors and it was an unpleasant reminder not only of what this job would entail, but also of her brother Seth.

At the foot of the stairs they turned left into the single-storey part of the building where Maureen had taken her last night to show her the staff rooms and laundry.

Breakfast was laid in a small dark room just off the kitchen. The clock on the wall said it was only six-thirty and the small strip of sky she could see beyond a thick bush outside the barred window was dark grey. Rosie and Maureen were the first to arrive, and took seats at a table laid with eight places, but they were joined a few minutes later by two girls in their twenties, both in the chargehands' maroon uniform.

Maureen introduced them as Mary Connor and Linda Bell, the girls who she'd mentioned last night. She explained to them that Rosie had arrived while they were out and she'd shown her round.

They appeared to be entirely disinterested, merely nodding at her. Rosie wasn't sure if this was hostility or just because they were barely awake.

Linda Bell looked the eldest, a buxom girl with short dark hair and bad skin. She sat down opposite Rosie and began pouring herself a giant portion of cornflakes.

Mary Connor hesitated before grabbing the cornflakes box, and, perhaps aware that they were being rude, she looked at Rosie and passed it to her first. 'You'd better tuck in too. You want to eat everything on offer at breakfast, it always seems for ever till dinner time,' she said.

Her accent was a soft and melodious Irish one. She looked a couple of years younger than Linda – small and dumpy, but pretty, with fluffy blonde hair and grey-blue eyes. Rosie liked the look of her.

She was too nervous to be hungry, and poured only a tiny amount of cereal. But when a much older woman wearing a white overall brought in plates of bacon, eggs and fried bread and silently plonked one down in front of her, just as she finished the cornflakes, it smelled and looked so appetizing that she began to eat it.

'That's Pat Clack,' Mary Connor said as soon as the older woman had disappeared back into the kitchen. 'She was a patient here at one time, but now she does the cooking. She's a funny old bird. She hardly speaks, sometimes she doesn't seem to hear either, but she's a good cook.'

'All the domestic staff are a bit –' Bell put her finger to her head implying they were simple. 'Matron finds them. She likes to have people she can control.'

As Rosie ate in silence, wishing someone would speak again, she became aware of the noisy way in which Maureen was eating. A glance sideways at the girl made her feel nauseous – she was chewing with her mouth wide open, smacking her lips and barely swallowing one mouthful before stuffing in the next one. It was a disgusting sight and a sixth sense told her that Linda and Mary hated it too. Maybe that was why they weren't too friendly?

Over a second cup of tea and a third piece of toast, Rosie felt brave enough to speak and ask where Mary and Linda came from, and if they liked working here.

Mary smiled, her eyes holding enough warmth to banish any idea that Rosie might not be welcome here. 'Linda's from London. I'm Irish as I'm sure you guessed, from Cork. Do we like it here? Do we hell! You'd have to be mad to *like* it. What about you? Your accent sounds like West Country. What makes you want to work in a nut-house?'

Rosie grinned at this string of explanations and questions. 'I want to be a nurse, so I thought this would fill in till I'm eighteen.'

'Gravedigging would fill in just as well,' Linda said darkly, her cockney accent reminding Rosie sharply of Heather. 'You won't last 'ere till you're eighteen.'

The arrival of Matron in the doorway halted any further conversation.

'Jackson, Bell, upstairs!' she said curtly, her expression saying *now, not when it suits you*. 'Connor, help with the breakfast trolley. Smith, come with me.'

Rosie looked back before meekly following Matron. Linda Bell was pulling a face at the woman's back, and

152

she winked at Rosie as if to say they were all united in their dislike of their superior.

Matron led Rosie along the narrow passage, past the staff sitting-room and the laundry. Two older women in dark green overalls were in there, one stirring a giant steaming copper, the other feeding dripping wads of clothing through a big wringer. They looked round as Rosie passed. The one stirring waved.

Matron did not speak until she'd unlocked a door some ten feet from the laundry. Then she turned to Rosie, looking her up and down. Last night Rosie had been more concerned with this woman's formidable presence than her physical appearance, but now she noticed too that her looks were as unattractive as her sour manner. Dark beady eyes were set too close together and a lifetime of scowling had furrowed her forehead and puckered her mouth. Her skin had an unhealthy grey tinge, and a dark moustache seemed to emphasize her large yellow protruding teeth.

She wasn't evenly fat all over, but lumpy; indeed she had a roll of fat around her hips which jutted out like a shelf. More fat squished over her lace-up shoes, and from beneath the white starched cuffs of her uniform on her upper arms, another roll squelched out. Yet more worrying than the woman's appearance was a sense of antagonism which wafted out of her like the unpleasant smells everywhere in this place, and worse still it appeared to be directed right at Rosie.

'All the uniforms will be too big for you,' Matron said in a tone which implied this was Rosie's fault. 'Are you any good with a needle?'

Rosie could darn socks, sew on buttons and she'd made a blouse in needlework at school, but she wasn't sure she could take in a uniform. 'I don't know,' she said.

'Well, either you are or you aren't,' Matron snapped. 'I can't stand indecisive people.'

'I can sew. I meant I wasn't sure I could take in a

uniform,' Rosie retorted. Then, remembering what Maureen had said about 'keeping in with her', she added, 'I could try.'

Matron opened the door she'd unlocked, snapped on a light and went in, leaving Rosie in the passageway. It was a vast cupboard, the walls lined with wide shelves. On one side were neat piles of staff uniforms in all the different colours Maureen had described. On the other side were more assorted clothes – skirts, grey trousers, jumpers, underwear, nightdresses and pyjamas. Rosie thought that these must be for the patients.

Matron rummaged through the maroon pile and pulled out two dresses, holding one up to Rosie. 'That's near enough,' she said, even though it was several sizes too large and almost to Rosie's feet. Three of everything came next – white starched aprons and caps, thick knickers, black lisle stockings – then one maroon cardigan and a black elastic belt. 'Has Jackson explained about the laundry?' she barked.

Rosie nodded. She was staggering under the pile of clothes. 'It has to be in on Mondays. And aprons each day.'

'You must sew a name tag in each item tonight.' Matron handed her some tape and a marker pen. 'Give me that back tomorrow morning.'

She was ordered then to go upstairs and to change into her uniform. She was to take no longer than fifteen minutes and then report back to Matron in Mrs Trow's office in the hall, with her insurance card.

As they went back along past the dining-room Matron stopped by a small cupboard and unlocked it. It was full of keys and she took down one bunch and jingled them at Rosie. 'These are yours now,' she said. 'If you lose them the cost will be deducted from your wages. The colour tag on each signifies which floor they are for. Red for down here, green for the first floor, blue for the staff wing. The number corresponds to the numbers on each door.

You are only entrusted with keys to the rooms you need to go into.'

There was no time for Rosie to do anything more than dump the stuff on her bed and quickly change. The knickers were the large fleece-lined type she'd worn at school, and she looked at them in horror wondering who had worn them before her. As a compromise she pulled them on over the nice white cotton ones Miss Pemberton had bought her.

She had no suspender belt to hold up the stockings, so she couldn't put those on. As for the dress, as she had expected, it reached almost to her ankles and it was several inches too wide.

She managed to hitch up the dress a little once she'd got the apron on and the belt round her middle, but when she looked in the mirror she didn't know whether to laugh or cry. She looked ridiculous, like a small child dressed in adult clothes. And the maroon colour clashed with her hair. As she anchored the white cap to her hair she wondered if Maureen knew anything about altering clothes.

Matron was waiting for her in Mrs Trow's office.

'Where are your stockings?' she asked, looking down at Rosie's ankle socks with distaste.

'I'm sorry but I haven't got a suspender belt,' Rosie stammered.

'Garters are good enough. Make some tonight.'

Matron sat at the desk but didn't offer Rosie a seat, or even look at her directly as she barked out all the 'never's: never to leave the day room unattended (two staff must be there at all times); never to bring in anything for a patient from outside, however innocent the request might seem; never to smoke in the day room and never to give the patients cigarettes or matches; never to discuss Carrington Hall with anyone and she must behave in a dignified manner at all times.

Rosie had fully expected the matron to be like Miss

Pemberton, a bit brusque maybe, but interested enough in her staff to ask some personal questions, and how she was settling in. But to her dismay Matron seemed incapable of even the most lukewarm welcome.

'You will have Tuesdays as your day off for the time being,' she said eventually, giving her a look that suggested she hoped Rosie wouldn't still be here in a week's time. 'You may go out on evenings when you aren't working, but you must be back here by ten-thirty. Don't think for one moment that your connection with Mr Brace-Coombes will give you any privileges. If you are late coming in or you break any of the rules, you will be sacked immediately. Now it's time you got to work.'

The remark about Mr Brace-Coombes made Rosie wonder whether this could be the reason why Matron appeared to resent her. She opened her mouth to protest that she had no real connection with the owner of the home, but shut it again, aware that such a statement might make her position even more precarious. Instead she thanked the woman, although she hadn't the slightest idea what she was thanking her for.

By the time she got up to the first floor to start work, many of the beds in the two dormitories had been stripped, but the pungent smell of ammonia still lingered despite wide open windows. Rosie was very glad she'd missed the first part of the day. She wasn't sure she could cope with reminders of Seth's wet beds on top of everything else.

All the patients she'd seen the night before, except for Aggie, were already dressed and sitting at the table in the day room waiting silently for their breakfast. Like last night they all stared vacantly at her. Aggie was dressed, but sitting on the floor in exactly the same place she'd been last night, rocking to and fro, cackling to herself.

Maureen was pouring out mugs of tea from an urn on a trolley, while an older woman called Simmonds, wearing a green overall, dished out bowls of porridge. Rosie couldn't see Linda anywhere.

'Pass the porridge round,' Maureen ordered her, then looking sharply at Aggie she yelled, 'Get up now, Aggie, otherwise you won't get any.'

Aggie made some unintelligible reply, turned over till she was on all fours and crawled towards the table. Rosie thought this must be her normal way of getting about as no one appeared to see anything odd in it. As Rosie put a bowl and spoon in front of each of the patients they just fell on it as if they hadn't eaten for a week.

Aggie eventually hauled herself up on to a chair, but there was obviously something badly wrong with her legs; she didn't appear to be able to stand on them and there were several nasty-looking weeping lesions on them. She put her mouth right down to the bowl and virtually sucked in the porridge. It turned Rosie's stomach.

Next came scrambled egg with tiny cubes of fried bread. Rosie had to assume it was cut like that to eat with spoons. But many of them ignored the spoons and ate it with their fingers, cramming it into their mouths so fast she thought they couldn't possibly be chewing.

As Rosie spread slices of bread and marge with a thin layer of marmalade, she found herself thinking back to Mrs Bentley and her continual carping about 'table manners' and wondering what she'd make of this lot. Donald was the only one who ate with some dignity, and Rosie wondered why that was. Had he only recently been admitted, or was it because he was a bit brighter than the others and so retained things he'd been taught as a child?

Mary came down from the second floor at nine to join them, complaining bitterly that one of the patients had eaten her breakfast, then vomited it up all over her, forcing her to change her entire uniform and even her stockings too. She flopped down in a chair and said she was already exhausted. It seemed that Linda was staying on the second floor today.

Matron had informed Rosie that as part of her duties as a chargehand she was to mop over the day room, dormitories and corridor floors with disinfectant, make the beds and scrub out the bathrooms. She'd said that Rosie was to look at the rota and see what jobs she'd been allocated. Maureen, however, didn't seem to care what was on the rota; she said that Simmonds was already making a start on one of the dormitories and that she and Mary would tackle the day room. Rosie could join Simmonds and do the rest.

Rosie agreed willingly. She suspected from Mary's raised eyebrows that this wasn't exactly a fair allocation of work, but to her it was preferable to being locked in the day room with the patients. The feeling of revulsion hadn't diminished. It made her flesh crawl to watch them shuffling about aimlessly, scratching at themselves, picking their noses. She wondered if she'd ever be able to talk to them. They didn't even appear to communicate with one another.

'You could take Donald to help you,' Mary suggested. 'He's good at cleaning and it gives him something to do. He always helps me.'

Rosie shuddered. She had visions of Donald grabbing her again as he had last night, and no one being around to stop him.

'He's quite safe,' Mary said quietly. 'Just look at him!'

Rosie turned to see Donald standing by the door. His face was anxious; he was smoothing down his blond hair as if trying to make himself look more attractive to her. Something clicked inside Rosie. She'd seen that very same expression on Alan's face so many times in his older brothers' presence. Wanting to be liked, ready to do anything.

'Okay, Donald, you'll be my helper,' Rosie said with some reluctance, but she was rewarded with a wide, merry smile.

*

Within half an hour of being alone with Donald in the first dormitory, Rosie found that she was not only very glad of his help, but she saw that Maureen was probably correct in saying he didn't really need to be here at all.

He knew exactly what to do. He had the clean sheets and pillowcases out of a cupboard and on to a trolley before she could even think where to start. Then he led her down to the end of the row of beds, quickly threw the blankets and pillow on to the next one, then spread out the clean bottom sheet.

'L-l-like this,' he stammered, showing her a special way of doing neat corners. 'Hospital c-c-corners. S-s-sister showed me.'

He said very little as they worked, but Rosie found herself smiling at the pride he took in his work. The top sheet had to be turned down just so, and the pillow plumped up and positioned carefully. He was quicker and more efficient than many of the nurses she'd observed during her stay in hospital. When they'd finished the women's dormitory they joined Simmonds in the men's to help her, and Donald showed Rosie which was his bed, the only dry one, down by the window.

'I l-l-like to look at the g-g-garden in the morning,' he stuttered. 'I w-w-wish I could g-g-go out there, wh-wh-when I like.'

This wistful remark put Donald's and the other patients' predicament into perspective. Already just a few hours into the day, Rosie was hankering to go outside and breathe in the fresh air. Her entire life there had been wide open spaces just beyond the back door. But she could go out this evening, sniff flowers in gardens, walk in streets and fields if she chose, yet poor Donald, through no fault of his own, was destined to spend all day, every day trapped in here, viewing the outside world through a window.

Later Donald showed her where the buckets, mops and cleaning materials were kept, and sped off into the sluice room to fill the buckets with hot water. Simmonds took one bucket from him and began to mop down the corridor, and Rosie and Donald worked side by side along each of the dormitories. Again he was thorough, taking care to wring out the mop properly. Rosie felt his silence was probably because he was very aware of his stutter, yet he was agreeable company, and she found his way of taking the bucket from her to empty and refill it rather touching.

Simmonds had left the ward to help down in the kitchen when they moved on to clean the lavatories and bathrooms. To Rosie's horror someone had defecated on the floor just inside one of them.

Rosie retched, and Donald grabbed her arm pulling her back. 'I'll d-d-do it,' he said.

She almost let him, but a glance at his face proved he was as squeamish as she was about such things. 'No, Donald,' she said, and smiled reassuringly at him. 'It's my job. You just get some more hot water.'

By the time he came back to the lavatory, Rosie had managed to scoop up the offending mess with some toilet paper and flushed it away. Donald looked relieved. 'It's S-s-sister's fault,' he stammered. 'She d-d-doesn't always unlock us in t-time, not even wh-wh-when we shout that w-w-we want to go.'

Rosie couldn't imagine that was the reason for this mess; if a patient had got as far as the lavatory, to her mind he or she could manage to sit over the bowl. But all the same Donald's remark stuck in her mind and when they got back into the day room just after eleven having finished all the cleaning, she thought she'd ask the other girls if what he'd said about Sister Welbred was true.

Maureen and Mary were busy repositioning the armchairs after the floor had been washed. But when Rosie put her question to them, to her amazement Mary, who was bending over, jerked upright, her face tightened, then said, as if she hadn't heard the question, that it was time she made the 'elevenses'.

As Rosie watched Mary's unduly rapid departure from the day room, Maureen moved nearer to her. 'You'll make a lot of enemies if you start asking too many questions,' she said crisply.

Rosie frowned, she didn't understand what Maureen meant. 'But surely if we have to keep cleaning up messes that aren't necessary, we should do something about it?'

Maureen just looked at her for a moment, sighed and then sat down in an easy chair, beckoning for Rosie to join her. 'Look,' she said wearily. 'It's true that some of the patients are a bit scared of Sister so they don't call out at night or first thing in the morning when they want to go. If you want my opinion, I'd say we'd get no more than two wet beds a night and hardly ever a messed one if there was a lav the patients could get into on their own.

'But on the other hand, we find messes like the one you found quite often, at all times of the day. I reckon it's Archie, he's got some disgusting habits as you'll soon find out. So don't go giving your opinions about anything until you know how it really is here, not unless you want to find yourself very unpopular.'

Rosie didn't say any more, but images of helpless patients too afraid to call out to use the bathroom for fear of upsetting a trained nurse stayed in her mind. It smacked of that same kind of intimidation Seth and Norman had inflicted on Alan.

After elevenses, disturbing noises were coming from the second floor. Mostly it was just banging and bellowing, but every now and then there was a real scream. It was strange that neither the patients nor Mary and Maureen appeared to notice it, but Rosie found it very distressing.

'It sounds like they are being tortured,' she blurted out at one point to Maureen.

She just laughed. 'They aren't, it's just the way they try to get attention. Some days it's worse than others, they set each other off, you see, but you'll get used to it. In a week or so you won't even hear them.'

Simmonds brought the dinner up on a trolley at twelve-thirty. It was a stew followed by jam roly-poly and custard. Once it was on the table Maureen said that she and Mary were going down to the staff room to have their own dinner, leaving Rosie to oversee the meal with Simmonds's assistance.

Rosie was aghast. She didn't feel capable of coping with the patients without experienced help and Simmonds made her even more nervous than some of the patients. The woman was very tall and broad, with a face like undercooked beef, wide shoulders like a man's and an antagonistic look in her eyes. Over the bed-making Rosie had felt cowed by her cold silence punctuated only by loud sniffs, and as Mary had informed her the woman was another ex-patient, Rosie had a feeling she was someone that you didn't turn your back on.

Maureen must have guessed what was on her mind, because before leaving she patted Rosie's arm and grinned. 'Simmonds is quite safe,' she said. 'Just silent, but very capable. Let her do things her way and just follow. After they've finished their dinner, she'll take them in twos out to the lavs and to wash their hands. You just stack up the plates on the trolley and when I get back you can take it down with you and go for your dinner. There's a lift just by the staircase. Now don't panic, especially if you find yourself on your own for a few moments. Just be firm with them all.'

Dinner was an even more nauseating sight than breakfast had been, and several times Rosie actually gagged. The patients crammed the food in, chewed it with mouths wide open and often took it out again for examination. Patty, the old lady with the scarred face, half chewed several pieces of meat then spat them back on to her plate. To Rosie's horror Jacob snatched them up and ate them. Only Donald was bearable to watch. As at breakfast, he ate with as much dignity as any man could manage when being forced to use only a spoon. Rosie wondered how

162

much longer his good manners could last surrounded by such animalistic behaviour.

Yet as appalled as she was by these people, however much she wished she was a hundred miles from here, she could feel a prickling of sympathy for them too. She had thought she knew how it felt to be an outcast from society, yet these poor wretches were so much worse off than she had ever been. She might be as unwanted and as unloved as them, but she had a keen mind, she was young and healthy. She could find a happier way of life one day soon. They never could.

Pat Clack was just giving Rosie her dinner down in the staff dining-room when Linda Bell, the London girl she'd met that morning, joined her.

''Ow's it going?' she asked as she sat down at the table beside her. They were the only staff in the dining room. 'I 'ad 'oped I could keep you under me wing today and show you the ropes. But bloody Matron sent me up to the second floor.'

'It wasn't quite as bad as I expected,' Rosie lied. She didn't want the other girl to think she was a misery, or feeble, especially if she was kind enough to want to look after her. 'But I think the time will drag this afternoon with no more cleaning to be done.'

'Get yourself a book,' Linda suggested. 'That's what I do. Mary knits. As long as you're there, it don't really matter what you do. I read a couple a week, more when I'm upstairs.'

'But Maureen doesn't read,' Rosie said. She didn't think anyone should bury their nose in a book when they were supposed to be watching people, however boring that was.

'Well she can't, can she? She's a bit simple 'erself.'

Rosie was stunned by this. She hadn't thought of Maureen as simple.

Linda laughed at her shocked expression. 'She's weird an' all. She don't wash, she eats like a pig and sucks up to Matron. I'm just glad I ain't got to share a room with 'er. You wait for a day or two. She 'ad a bath yesterday, but that was only because we made 'er. She stinks.'

Rosie blanched. She recalled wondering where Maureen had washed that morning; obviously she hadn't bothered. Heather had instilled a need for cleanliness into her. She'd made Rosie wash every morning and night, right up until the time she disappeared, and Rosie had never lost the habit.

'Perhaps no one ever told her about those things,' Rosie said gently. 'Her mother died when she was little.'

'I was dragged up in a tenement with four of us sharing a bed,' Linda retorted. 'We were so used to dirt we didn't notice it. But I managed to work out for myself when I got to about thirteen that soap and water made you a little more attractive.'

'If she gets smelly I'll say something,' Rosie said evenly. She didn't feel right dishing the dirt about Maureen behind her back. 'I thinks she's kind anyway. She was nice to me when I arrived and she's sweet to the patients.'

'Just watch your step with her,' Linda said darkly. 'Don't tell her anything, and hide your money away somewhere safe.'

Rosie bristled. She knew from school how bitchy some girls could be, she'd been on the receiving end of it many times. In fact Linda looked none too clean either; her hair needed a wash and it looked as if she picked her spots all the time. Suggesting Maureen was a thief and a tell-tale sounded like pure spite. 'That's not a very nice thing to say,' she said tartly.

'You'll find out soon enough that she ain't very nice,' Linda smirked. 'Just don't say I didn't warn you. Now to get on to something more bleedin' cheerful, what's up with that uniform of yours? It's big enough for an elephant!'

Rosie had to smile. She had already been teased by Mary. She told Linda what Matron had said about altering it and her fear that she might not be able to do it.

164

'I'll take it in for you if you want,' Linda offered unexpectedly. 'I did a spell as a machinist before I came 'ere. There's a sewing machine in the staff sitting-room. I'll do it tonight. And don't think I'm an evil cow saying that about Maureen. You might thank me one day for warning you.'

Rosie discovered in the next day or two that boredom was one of the worst things about Carrington Hall. Cleaning and making beds was quite pleasant, and she surprised herself by very quickly becoming used to the disgusting way the patients ate, their nasty personal habits and the occasional puddle on the floor. The horrible noises from upstairs still worried her and Matron's malevolence made her very uneasy. But sitting in a stuffy room for hours on end watching patients shuffling about or rocking in their chairs made her feel she might just go mad herself.

Yet if it was boring for her and the other staff, at least they had one another as a diversion, with meal breaks and little jobs to do. The patients had absolutely nothing with which to amuse themselves. Not a book or a puzzle or even pencil and paper. It was no wonder most of them moved so slowly. Rosie felt they all badly needed some exercise. She felt like a caged tiger herself, but after work she could go outside and walk if she wanted to. The patients never got that opportunity.

On her third afternoon, however, the sun was shining and Matron sent a message up to the ward that Rosie and Mary Connor could take those able to manage the stairs down to the back garden.

The ripple of excitement which went round the day room proved that this was a rare treat, but Rosie was surprised to find that Maureen was not in the least put out at having to stay upstairs with Aggie and a few others. She said that Rosie would soon find out what a chore it was.

It took almost an hour to organize outdoor shoes and

coats for eight of the patients and get them down the stairs, and Rosie could only suppose that this was what Maureen meant. But once outside, they all seemed suddenly more animated, grabbing each other's arms and excitedly pointing things out as if they'd been taken on a holiday. Patty and Alice sat primly on a bench. Tabby put down the knitting she'd insisted on bringing down with her and prowled around peering into the bushes. One of the older men got down on his hands and knees examining the grass minutely. But it was Donald who really seemed to get the most out of it; he ran around like a small boy pretending to be an aeroplane.

At first Rosie didn't dare relax for a second, her head swivelling from one side to the other watching out for everyone. She had visions of them eating snails or tripping up and hurting themselves, but in no time at all they seemed to be calmed by the fresh air, happy to just wander, or sit and look around them. Mary was sitting with Patty and Alice, looking at a magazine.

It was force of habit that made Rosie start deadheading some of the pansies and dahlias, and pulling up a few weeds, an almost unconscious action she couldn't help.

Donald startled her by suddenly appearing at her elbow. 'Can I h-h-help?' he said, reaching out for a lupin.

'Not that one,' Rosie said. 'That's a flower. I'm only pulling out the weeds. They don't belong here, you see. They are horrid things which choke the pretty plants.'

'B-but it's got no f-f-flowers,' he said, looking at the spiky leaves in some surprise.

'That's because it's flowered already this year,' she said evenly. 'If we leave it here, next June it will have big blue or pink flowers again.'

She showed him which ones were weeds and he surprised her by catching on quickly and pulling out dandelions and chickweed with enthusiasm.

'I like g-g-gardens,' he said. 'I had a lovely one once, b-b-before I came here.'

'Can you tell me about it?' she asked. He was kneeling down beside her now and he had colour in his cheeks from running around. Although she hadn't forgotten the incident on her arrival in the ward, he had wiped out her initial fear of him by proving himself to be very gentlemanly and capable. He intrigued her, she wanted to know more about him.

'It had a pond, with fishes, and lots of trees,' he said. He looked very thoughtful and he'd quite lost his vacant expression. She also noticed he'd said a whole sentence without stuttering. 'I wish I still lived there.'

'I had a nice garden too,' Rosie said, thinking of the Bentleys. 'I felt so happy when I was out in it digging and planting. We could pretend this is our garden, couldn't we? Watch things growing together, learning the names of the flowers.'

Donald smiled suddenly, showing perfect white teeth. 'You're nice, Smith. I like you. Sh-sh-show me some f-f-flowers now.'

'Tell me about Donald,' Rosie said to Maureen later, once they were back in the day room. It was nearly five and Mary had gone down to the kitchen to get the tea trolley. Although Mary was the friendliest of the staff, happy enough to talk about her family back in Ireland, nights out at the local dance hall and boys she'd been out with, she didn't want to speak about the patients at all.

Rosie had come to the conclusion that she was a bit of a dolly daydream. She was too lazy to look around for a more appealing job, so she blanked out the aspects she didn't like about this one, just marking time until the off-duty hours. Maureen was quite different, she lived, breathed and slept Carrington Hall; in fact she had no other interest.

'His parents are stinking rich,' she said and pursed her lips as though she resented that bitterly. 'They live in

Sussex somewhere. They've got another older son and daughter who are quite normal. Dr Freed thinks Donald was brain-damaged by forceps at birth. He lived at home until he was about fifteen, but he started wandering around the village, talking to people and stuff, and I suppose he made people nervous. You remember how he hugged you on your first night here? Well, he does that when he gets excited, and he's very strong. What I heard was that some girl went home crying to her mother and they thought he'd hurt her, you know.' Maureen stopped, blushing furiously.

Rosie knew Maureen was hinting about rape and a picture of Seth flashed into her mind instantly. But she squashed it; she might be ignorant about mental patients' behaviour and their sexuality, but Donald didn't seem a bit dangerous to her.

'I can't really believe he did that,' Maureen went on. 'He's never showed any sign of anything like that since I've been here, all he does is hug people. Some of the men here are horrible, they get their things out and play with them and stuff,' she grimaced. 'But Donald never does. Anyway I suppose someone talked his parents into sending him here, just in case.'

Rosie thought that was very unfair and said so.

'I know,' Maureen agreed. 'And if he stays in here much longer he'll get as bad as old Jacob and the others. Still, I suppose he's luckier than most; if his parents couldn't afford to send him here, he'd be in a State asylum.'

Maureen was very fond of talking about the State asylums. According to her the patients there were treated like cattle; if they couldn't feed themselves they went hungry, left in their own filth for days on end and at the mercy of any sadist who happened to take a job there. She spoke with authority, but Rosie wasn't sure she could entirely believe everything she said. In truth she couldn't really believe people would allow such terrible places to exist.

'What about all the others?' she asked. 'Why is Patty's face so badly scarred?'

'She got that in another loony-bin,' Maureen's voice dropped to a whisper. 'Her family are rich too. She was quite normal until she got some illness, when she was in her twenties. I don't know what it was, but anyway it made her go peculiar. Apparently she got very sexy with men, started running around without any clothes on and eventually they got her committed.'

Rosie wanted to smile at this. Carrington Hall might be Maureen's absolute favourite subject, but sex and sexual deviants were her second. 'So was it a man patient who scarred her?' Rosie asked, almost expecting to hear he was some sort of pervert too.

'No, of course not,' Maureen scoffed. 'In State asylums the two sexes are segregated. It was a woman. She attacked Patty with a knife, opened her face right up and judging by that scar the doctor who stitched her up must have known as little about sewing as I do.'

Rosie's knees went a bit wobbly at this. 'Is that why she came here?' she asked.

Maureen nodded. 'She was one of the first patients when this place opened. I've heard that she used to help with the meals and everything back then. But her brother was alive then and by all accounts he came to see her almost every week. When he died, no one else came instead and she just withdrew into herself. She looks about sixty, doesn't she? But she isn't, she's only forty-three and according to Matron her family are always late paying her bills now. So I expect soon she'll be shipped off somewhere else.'

Rosie felt very sad as Maureen told her about other patients too, and ashamed at herself for being so revolted by them. She had always imagined that mental asylums were full of totally insane people, maniacs who would attack on sight, like those in horror films. Now she was finding that although there were some like this – Maureen said there were dangerous patients on the second floor – the vast majority were merely of limited abilities. Many of them were brain-damaged at birth or as a result of childhood illnesses, so that while their bodies had become adult, they had retained the mental age of a small child. Perhaps even more pitiful were those like Tabby who had once lived a normal life, gone to school and then on to a job, but something had pushed them into depression which had rapidly worsened into mental illness. From what Rosie could gather there was no real treatment or medicine, and it seemed to her the patients would only get worse from being understimulated and virtually ignored.

But saddest of all to Rosie was the discovery that every single patient in Carrington Hall came from a well-off family. She could remember families on the Somerset Levels who had a simple son or daughter, but poor and uneducated as they were, they did not have their feeble-minded offspring put away, they just accepted them, with all their limitations.

Chapter Six

The six-thirty alarm bell rang in the corridor. Like a robot Rosie sat up, rubbed her eyes and sleepily swung her legs over the edge of the bed. Then she remembered. It was Tuesday and her first day off. Maureen was dressing, but without even bothering to speak to her, Rosie slumped back on to her pillow, and closed her eyes.

Later, when she woke again, she thought it must be mid-morning. But a check on Maureen's clock revealed it was only eight. She stretched out luxuriantly, smiling to herself in happy anticipation of the day ahead.

Today was only her eighth day at Carrington Hall. But it seemed to her as if she'd been here weeks. Each day had brought new shocks and sometimes she felt like she was edging her way round an active volcano which could erupt at any minute.

Nothing, aside from meal times and Matron's hostility, was predictable. The day could start calmly with all the patients sitting quietly, then suddenly with no warning, and for no discernible reason, one of them would hurl a shoe or a plate at the window, or grab another patient, and all at once mayhem would break out.

The first time it happened was on Rosie's fourth day. The other girls said that the patients had all been on their best behaviour until then, because she was new and something of a distraction. Tabby started it. She found that someone had pulled her knitting off her needles and she leapt on Maud, the youngest woman, presumably because she happened to be closest. Mary and Rosie jumped up to separate them, but as they moved so did everyone else in the room and George, one of the older men, fell over Aggie as she sat on the floor. Aggie screamed at the top of her lungs and started everyone else off. Archie seized the opportunity to try and throttle George.

It was Donald who rang the bell for help; neither Mary nor Rosie could get to it, surrounded as they were by clawing, yelling people. Rosie was absolutely terrified in the few moments before the day room door burst open and Simmonds, Maureen and Gladys Thorpe, one of the nurses, rushed in. She had no idea what to do for the best and was paralysed with fear by the screaming all around her. Although she felt a surge of relief as the reinforcements arrived, she was appalled to see Simmonds punch Tabby in the mouth, and Maureen grab Archie's arms, twisting them up behind his back.

That day both Tabby and Archie were dragged out of the day room, Archie to be put in one of the isolation cells along the corridor, Tabby to be plunged fully dressed into an ice-cold bath and held there by force until she was quiet again.

Back in the day room it was left to Rosie and Mary to calm the other patients down, which involved separating the men from the women and forcing them to sit at opposite ends of the room. As Rosie had received no prior warning that this sort of fracas was common, or any instructions about how to deal with an emergency, she felt helpless, shaking with fright for some hours after it had all quietened down.

She learned later that she should have rushed to the bell first, before even attempting to intervene and then she should have gone up behind the perpetrators and caught them securely by the arms, and pushed them hard against the wall, if necessary banging their heads against it. Such brutality was unthinkable to Rosie, and she didn't believe she'd ever be able to do it.

One thing she soon learned, though, was that patients

involved in such incidents were always punished. Tabby not only got the cold bath, but spent the rest of the day in isolation without any food and her knitting was taken away. Archie got similar treatment, but without the bath as he wasn't considered hysterical, only an opportunist who used any upset to attack someone. Rosie heard too that in extreme cases they got electric shock treatment, but apparently the threat of this was usually enough to silence anyone, without the necessity of going through with it.

After that first fight, Rosie found she handled herself better in similar incidents, grabbing the person who started it before anyone else became involved and shouting for silence like a sergeant major, the way Maureen did. She began to see why Sister Welbred had made that remark about developing muscle on her first night here. She also learned to read advance signals from the patients that they were likely to lash out, and often by leading them away from the rest of the group to talk gently to them, it was possible to defuse them.

Rosie remained very anxious about the second-floor patients. However hard she tried to stop lurid pictures from forming in her mind when she heard patients up there screaming, they came anyway. When the laundry bin was being wheeled downstairs each morning, the stink of faeces wafted everywhere. She had seen for herself a line full of rough linen shifts hanging up and was told that was all the patients up there wore. A hamper marked 'strait-jackets', the odd-shaped feeding cups used for patients unable to hold ordinary ones, all these things served to create unwelcome images in her head. A veil of secrecy seemed to surround that floor. Again and again she had asked questions, only small unimportant things like, could the patients feed and bath themselves? What sort of treatments did they receive? But her questions were always evaded, or fobbed off with a joke.

Although Rosie had learned to pick up the early warning

signs of trouble and brace herself for it when it came, it was far harder to cope with the nausea which came with the vile jobs. Rosie didn't mind wet beds, she was used to that. But to deal with a grown man who had messed himself was quite another matter. It didn't help reminding herself that she'd cleaned Alan's bottom hundreds of times in the past. To be cloistered in a bathroom with an unattractive stinking adult and to be forced to scrape the mess off him, then wash him was absolutely disgusting, and she didn't think she would ever get used to it.

But perhaps the most disconcerting thing of all in Carrington Hall was confirmation that there was no treatment or medicine that could cure the patients or even make them a little happier. There was a doctor, Dr Freed, who came a couple of times a week and treated any injuries or infections, but the reality was that these poor people were only fed and cleaned, imprisoned in a ward with no mental stimulation or physical exercise, until death released them.

It was an awful job. Rosie thought it must rate as one of the worst in the entire world, but as Maureen had said on her first night there were lighter moments too, and it was those which made the job bearable.

Like when Maud emptied a bowl of rice pudding over Albert's head because he kept begging her for it. A heart-stopping moment when Aggie went missing, only to be found later sitting in the broom cupboard, singing to herself. As Aggie could barely walk, how she'd managed to shuffle through the day-room door when it had been left unlocked for only a few moments and hide herself quite so quickly was still a mystery. Then there was Alice and her new shoes. She liked them so much she insisted on carrying them instead of putting them on her feet.

And Donald. He was always at her side wanting to help. His merry smile was real, not the dopey, vacant grin the others had. There was nothing physically repulsive about him; in fact, when he slipped his hand into hers it felt very much like having Alan back beside her. She really liked him.

But at the end of the day it was Linda and Mary who cheered Rosie most. She hadn't had another girl to chat to since she left school and she'd forgotten how good it was to have female company.

Linda Bell was one of the funniest people Rosie had ever met. Her humour was the dry kind – startlingly wicked observations, sharp one-liners – rather than clowning. Upstairs in the evenings she would mimic people so accurately she actually seemed to become that person, with the facial expressions, the movements and the voice. On one particular occasion she'd stood outside the bathroom door while Rosie was in there, and launched into a tirade of complaints in Matron's voice. Rosie had slunk out, apologizing profusely, only to find it was Linda, and Mary Connor was further along the landing doubled up with laughter.

Mary was a tonic too. She could take the most trivial of incidents and turn it into farce or tragedy with a little of her very Irish embroidery. During afternoons in the day room she giggled a great deal too and Rosie found it infectious.

If it wasn't for them, Rosie might not have been able to rise above the shock of finding Jacob lying in bed one morning rolling excrement into balls in his hands. Or Albert frantically masturbating in a corner of the day room, or Maud dripping with blood from wounds she'd inflicted on herself after finding a sharp piece of glass out in the garden. Linda and Mary made her see the humour in even the blackest moments, and assured her that one day she'd be as casual about such things as they were.

Rosie hadn't formed a real friendship with Maureen though. She was fine to work with, but her dirty habits made it impossible to really like her. Linda had been right in saying she didn't wash; the smell of stale sweat hit Rosie each time the girl undressed. She often sat on her bed picking her nose then eating her findings, then moved on to squeeze her spots, or pick at her feet. On top of these habits which made Rosie cringe, Maureen was very dull company. She lived, breathed, ate and slept Carrington Hall. She didn't care what was happening in the world, at the pictures or even further down the road. All she could talk about was work.

Rosie found she couldn't stay in bed any longer. The sun was shining outside, a beautiful misty September morning, with the promise of another warm day. She got up, had a bath and washed her hair, put on the new green checked skirt and toning sweater Miss Pemberton had bought her, made her bed and Maureen's, then went down to get some breakfast.

She had her day off all planned. This morning she would explore Woodside Park and find the nearest library. She intended to buy a suspender belt so she could throw out those uncomfortable garters, and get her first pair of nylons. In the afternoon she was going to take the bus to Hampstead and find the shop where Thomas worked. She hoped he might be free later in the day so they could catch up on each other's news.

Breakfast was officially over at seven, but there was an understanding that on a day off, as long as the staff turned up before nine they would still get something to eat. The food for the staff at Carrington Hall was something Rosie couldn't fault. It was well cooked and plentiful, as if there was no such thing as rationing. Yet the moment Rosie walked into the dining-room and saw Matron sitting there reading a newspaper and drinking tea, she wished she'd gone straight out.

A week of working at Carrington Hall had changed her views on some of the things which had intimidated her on her arrival, but Matron wasn't one of them.

Mary Connor summed Matron up perfectly in one word – 'odious'. Linda had gone a stage further to describe her as a putrid smell which tainted the very air the staff breathed. Everything Rosie had observed about the woman so far had led her to believe that she thrived on spite. She was always watching, lingering outside the staff room door, peeping through glass panels on doors, waiting to catch people out. Worse still for Rosie, she sensed the older woman was singling her out for extra nasty treatment because she resented that Mr Brace-Coombes had employed her without consulting her. As Mary had laughingly pointed out, Rosie was *in for it*. She didn't look meek enough, she was too attractive and, even worse in Matron's eyes, some of the patients had taken a great liking to her.

Nothing Rosie had done so far had met with Matron's approval. Not the taking in of her uniform with Linda's help, or the way she'd mastered putting her hair up in a tight bun. She hadn't liked it when she came in the day room and found Rosie teaching Patty and Alice to do cat's cradle with a piece of string, and she claimed that Rosie got the patients over-excited when she heard she'd been playing 'Oranges and Lemons' with the whole group. Yet even Sister Welbred, who disapproved of anything which might make her charges anything less than docile, had remarked on how contented and amenable they had all been that evening when she came on duty. Rosie had been blamed for Aggie's disappearance too, even though it was Maureen who'd forgotten to lock the day room door.

According to the other girls Matron had a perfectly good kitchen of her own, or she could ask Pat Clack to bring her meals to her private flat, but they assumed her only reason for using the staff dining-room was so she could keep a closer watch on them.

'Couldn't you sleep?' Matron said sarcastically over her newspaper, her thin lips curving into a sneer.

'I wanted to,' Rosie said. She knew most of the staff spent a good deal of their day off in bed and she felt Matron was implying she was abnormal. 'But I've always had to get up early. I suppose it's a hard habit to break. Anyway I wanted to go to the library.'

She sat down nervously at the other end of the table from Matron and helped herself to corn flakes. Pat Clack came in with a fresh pot of tea and didn't help the strained atmosphere by giving Rosie a beaming smile. The cook had decided Rosie was her friend ever since she had commiserated with her over a nasty burn on her hand a couple of days earlier. Rosie guessed Matron didn't like that either.

'Scrambled eggs, lovey?' Pat suggested, but her tone implied she would get her anything she desired.

'Whatever you are doing,' Rosie replied nervously.

Matron picked up her newspaper again. Rosie ate her cornflakes and hoped the older woman would ignore her. But a gasp and a rustle of the paper suggested she was about to say something more.

'Those murdering monsters from your part of the world are coming up for trial next week then!'

Rosie knew instantly who the woman was referring to and her blood seemed to turn to ice.

'Who's that?' she asked, trying to sound innocent. She hoped she wasn't blushing.

'The Parkers. The father and son who murdered two women and buried them on their land. Surely you know about it?'

'Oh, them.' Rosie nodded and put another spoonful of cornflakes in her mouth, hoping that would be a good enough excuse for not speaking.

'All the strangest people seem to come from the West Country. They're all interbred of course. I worked in Stoke Park in Bristol. Half the staff there were as mad as the inmates.'

Rosie felt this was a deliberate attempt to goad her, so she merely shrugged and didn't reply.

'I'm surprised you didn't go there to work instead of trailing all this way to London. Why was that?'

Rosie almost choked on her cornflakes. 'A friend of my family's suggested I came here, because I wanted to work in London.'

'But this is so far out of London, and hardly a well-known institution. I find it a bit strange your mother should agree to allow you to go so far from home.'

Rosie's heart began to flutter. It sounded as if Matron was digging for information. 'My mother died when I was little,' she said with a touch of defiance. 'My aunt wasn't very keen for me to go so far away, but I wanted to come to London.'

Matron sat back in her chair and her smirk was almost triumphant. 'So you were rebellious even at home?'

Pat Clack's return with the scrambled eggs was the perfect excuse for not answering the question. Rosie began to eat quickly, intending to make her escape as fast as possible. She kept her eyes on her plate, aware Matron was studying her.

'Girls often try to fool me,' she said after a few minutes' silence. 'They apply for jobs here to cover up something they've done. You see, people believe no one looks too closely in mental homes. We've had them all here. The thieves, the runaways, the ones who've just had babies adopted and those just out of prison. I always find out though. I've got a nose for such things.'

Back in her room ten minutes later, with Matron's words ringing in her ears, Rosie was hastily making certain there was absolutely nothing amongst her belongings to give Matron grounds for further suspicion. A sixth sense told her that her room would be searched today. She took out the letter from Miss Pemberton that had arrived on Saturday. As she had promised she had signed it 'love and kisses, Auntie Molly', and there was nothing in it to make anyone doubt that it was genuine. Just a caring note saying she hoped Rosemary was settling in and not finding London too big and strange, and that she hoped to hear all the news soon.

Rosie refolded it very carefully, noting how she had done it, putting a pencil spot on the top fold, then slid it back in the envelope. She put it in the drawer with her underwear, carefully placing a hair grip on top of it, so she could tell if it had been moved. Then taking a couple of sheets of writing paper and an envelope from her writing case, she put those in her handbag.

She would write to Miss Pemberton in the privacy of the library and post it while she was out. Suddenly she didn't trust the system of leaving letters to be posted downstairs. She would make a bet that Matron steamed them open and read them, before they reached the post-box.

By mid-morning Rosie was sitting on top of a bus on her way to Hampstead. She'd been to the library and she had *Gone with the Wind* and the first of the series of *Jalna* books, which she'd always wanted to read, in her bag. She had also bought a pretty white suspender belt and a pair of nylons and put them on in a public lavatory before catching the bus.

The excitement of wearing her first pair of nylons and seeing London at last from the top of one of the red buses she'd so often seen in picture books had driven Matron and Carrington Hall right out of her mind. From talking to Linda who knew London well, she had discovered that this whole part of north London from Woodside Park, through Finchley and on to Hampstead was one of the best areas and not exactly a representative view of the city. But she wasn't anxious to see the drearier, poorer parts today, or even famous places like the Tower, Buckingham Palace or Trafalgar Square. She would find them all on other days off. Today she was happy to see fine big houses and flower-filled gardens and revel gleefully at how surprised Thomas would be to see her.

The last time she had written to him was just after Mr Bentley had told her about the trial being in Bristol. She had said she would be moving on, but at that time she didn't know where. She said she would write again once she was settled. But she hadn't written – a surprise visit was much more exciting.

The conductor called out 'Henlys Corner', and the bus went across a wide, very busy road, with a big showroom full of gleaming new cars to her right. All at once Rosie found she was in the *real* London, as seen so often in films and the *Picture Post*: long rows of shops, with three or four floors above, interspersed with rather grand blocks of flats with names like Albemarle Mansions and white marble steps leading up to them.

Flats were intriguing to Rosie. Until she went to Bristol to live, the idea of several homes on top of each other was totally alien to her. She thought she'd like to live in one of these places; through the glass doors she could see tantalizing glimpses of thick red carpets, glossy varnished doors and a lift beyond, and she supposed the flats themselves must be even more posh.

The shops too were quite different from those in Bristol: elegant dress shops, restaurants and milliners. She saw one selling nothing but flowers, and so many jewellers. She imagined the people who lived around here were all very, very rich.

Even the old bomb sites here and there, seemed less ugly than ones she'd seen in Bristol. Ivy and rosebay willowherb had scrambled up over the piles of rubble and seemed to transform them from eyesores into ancient ruins. Rosie suddenly got the feeling that in London anything was possible. She could get to be a nurse, a secretary, or even run that lovely flower shop, if she wanted it enough. Maybe she might end up living in one of these smart flats too.

The bus conductor directed her where to get off. He said the place was called Swiss Cottage and pointed out she could catch another bus or walk up a hill into Hampstead from there. Rosie was happy to walk; the tree-lined avenue was steep but the sun was warm on her shoulders and it was interesting looking at all the big houses. Some of them were very dilapidated, with overgrown gardens, and they seemed to be shared by many families. Others still maintained a kind of faded grandeur with peeling paint on the front doors but white-stoned steps, stone bird-baths and huge urns full of flowers. There were several bomb sites here too, which, judging by makeshift playhouses built out of old timbers and packing cases, were now used as playgrounds by the children. Although this avenue didn't have the neatness or even the affluence of the well-kept suburban houses of Woodside Park, Rosie liked it. It was more like the London of her imagination, a street of character and just a little mysterious.

Her excitement grew as she came to Hampstead village. It was far lovelier than the image she had stamped into her mind from Thomas's descriptions. Such quaint old shops, enchanting tiny courtyards, cobbled alleyways with dear little cottages, but yet so busy compared with any village she'd ever seen. The women here were so very sophisticated compared with their counterparts in Somerset. Not a head scarf covering curlers, or an apron in sight, but elegant hats, costumes and high-heeled shoes. She lingered in shop doorways listening to their posh voices, noting the way they had pencilled their eyebrows, their glossy lips and manicured nails. Even the mothers pushing prams with a couple of smaller children in tow were attractive and smartly dressed, and she wondered how they found time to make themselves look so nice.

It took her some time to find Flask Walk, as she kept being distracted by the many fascinating shops. Books, clothes, art materials and jewellery – she felt she could wander here for days and not see everything.

But finally she found Bryant's. It was tucked away between a grocery shop and yet another book shop, its tiny bow window full of old clocks and watches. Peering into the gloomy interior she could see only an old man with snow-white hair. He was perched on a stool behind the counter, peering into a watch with a magnifying glass stuck right into his eye. She thought this must be Mr Bryant who Thomas worked for.

The old man took the glass from his eyes as she stepped into the shop. 'Good afternoon,' he said, in a deep resonant voice which didn't seem to match his frail appearance. 'What can I do for you?'

For a moment Rosie hesitated, suddenly struck by the thought that Thomas just might not appreciate a surprise visit after all. But it was too late now to back away. The shop was musty smelling and very dusty. Scores of old clocks stood on shelves, some with a label attached showing the owner's name, others marked 'For Sale'. Under the glass of the counter were dozens of watches and a large velvet pad displaying pieces of jewellery.

'I just popped in hoping I could see Mr Farley for a moment,' she said. 'Is he here?'

'He certainly is. I'll call him for you.' The old man beamed at her and got up from his stool. 'What name shall I give?'

'Rosemary Smith,' she said nervously, wondering if he'd guess who that was.

The old man disappeared out the back. It sounded as if he was going upstairs. He called out, but his voice was muffled so Rosie didn't hear what he'd actually said.

The old man returned to his stool, and Rosie could hear Thomas coming down. His slow pace suggested the staircase was a narrow, tricky one. As he came through the doorway behind the counter and saw her, he looked stunned.

'I was just passing,' she said quickly, feeling very foolish. Thomas was wearing a long brown apron over his clothes and he needed a shave. He didn't look like the smart gentleman she'd kept a picture of in her head. 'I'm sorry if I've interrupted your work, I only wanted to say hullo.'

The old man was standing there watching them both

183

with keen interest. 'I'm working near by,' she added lamely.

'It's good to see you, Rosemary,' Thomas said, but his tone was very stilted. 'What a surprise. I had no idea you were in London.' He looked across at his employer. 'Would you mind if I popped out for half an hour with Miss Smith?'

The old man smiled warmly at Rosie, but she sensed he was very curious. 'Of course I don't mind. I wish I had pretty young ladies calling on me.'

Thomas went back into the passage and came back a few seconds later with a jacket replacing his apron and carrying his walking stick. Then opening the door he ushered her out. Once in Flask Walk he took her arm with his spare hand and led her away from the shop as if he was in a hurry. 'You shouldn't have come like this,' he said in a low voice. 'You've caught me on the hop.'

It wasn't the warm welcome Rosie had expected. 'I'm sorry,' she said in a small voice. 'I just wanted to surprise you.'

'You did that all right,' he said and without saying another word led her right to the back of a nearby café.

It was only once they were seated, well away from the other customers, that he leaned nearer to her and spoke in a low voice. 'I am pleased to see you, Rosie. But you should have written and given me some warning. Mr Bryant must be wondering who you are now, and it's hard to think up a plausible tale on the spur of the moment.'

His eyes hadn't met hers as he spoke, and for the second time that day Rosie was reminded sharply of just who she was. 'I didn't think,' she said, and to her dismay her eyes began to prickle with tears.

'For goodness' sake don't cry,' he said quickly and patted her hand. 'It's just that word's got around I'm a key witness in the trial next week. It's made everyone interested in me.'

Along with feeling awkward, Rosie now felt surprised

and very stupid. In all the time they had been corresponding, Thomas had never mentioned the trial, or being a witness. She didn't know why it hadn't occurred to her that he would be, it seemed perfectly obvious now. But maybe she wasn't as smart as she'd always supposed.

'They couldn't guess I'm Cole Parker's daughter, could they?' she whispered.

As the waitress picked that moment to come to their table, Thomas couldn't answer. Rosie watched him closely as he ordered tea and two ham sandwiches. He had a natural, easy way with him, smiling at the woman as he spoke as if she was very important to him. She realized it was this gentlemanly quality along with his thin face and blond hair which had made him so much like Ashley Wilkes in *Gone with the Wind*. She thought women must find him very attractive.

'I doubt they'd guess who you were just by looking at you,' Thomas said once the waitress had left with his order. 'But I've had several reporters sniffing around me already. I've been astounded by how much they know about me, Heather and your family. Maybe I'm getting paranoid, but I do feel as if I'm under a microscope. Now just imagine if one of them should amble by today and see me with a pretty young thing like you – aren't they bound to wonder who you are?'

Rosie looked at him bleakly. Thomas blushed and dropped his eyes. 'I'm sorry, love. I must sound ridiculous to you. But just imagine if someone did make the connection? It could make me unbelievable as a witness, not to mention blowing the cover Miss Pemberton has arranged for you.'

Rosie hadn't considered that. 'I'm so sorry. I'd better go,' she said, getting up from her chair. She was afraid she just might cry and that way she would certainly draw more attention to herself.

'No,' he said, catching hold of her arm. 'No, you can't go now.'

Thomas was so overwrought he couldn't think straight. In the last couple of weeks as he'd prepared himself for the trial he hadn't eaten or slept. Childhood memories of Heather plagued him. The camp in Burma and all the atrocities he'd witnessed kept coming back, however much he tried to banish them from his mind. He had believed he'd worked all the rage out of his system about that a long time ago, but now he found he'd just suppressed it.

In calmer moments he realized he was using Cole and Seth Parker as whipping boys for every single thing that haunted him and to a certain extent some of that hatred had begun to wash over on to Rosie too.

But now that she was sitting here in front of him, her blue eyes brimming with unshed tears, he was brought up sharply. She was just a child, one who'd been stripped of everything – her home, family and her innocence. It was him who'd held out the hand of friendship to her in the first place, and maybe with hindsight that was fool-hardy, but it wouldn't be right to turn his back on her now.

'It will look even odder if you go rushing off now,' he said hastily. 'Besides, I want to know about what you're doing here in London. Stay and tell me.'

Rosie told him about her job.

Thomas immediately pictured a ward he'd been in for a time. It was full of men who'd lost their minds during the war, and it was another ugly picture he had no wish to recall.

'It's not so bad,' she said when she saw the horror in his eyes. 'It's just another kind of nursing.'

Thomas had been in regular contact with Miss Pemberton regarding Alan and from her letters he'd formed an opinion that the woman was very wise and caring. But now, on hearing where she'd sent Rosie, he wondered if he was mistaken about this social worker. Hadn't Rosie been through enough already without subjecting her to more horror?

He thought for a moment before making any comment. 'Yes, I suppose it *is* just nursing,' he said guardedly. 'I'm probably prejudiced about mental asylums like most people. But are you happy there?'

'Yes, really happy,' she said, unconvincingly. 'I like being in London. The other girls are nice. I've got a lovely room. Some of the patients are kind of sweet.'

Thomas looked into her eyes and saw the truth clouding them. She loathed it, but she believed she had no right to anything better. Any antagonism he'd built up in the last couple of weeks for her being part of that appalling family vanished in sympathy for her. 'Oh Rosie,' he said, shaking his head sadly. 'You don't have to pretend to me. It's awful, isn't it?'

Rosie gulped hard.

Until today she had thought of Thomas Farley as almost god-like. Courageous, intuitive, compassionate, all-seeing and so very strong, and she'd wanted to cling to him for security. But all at once she realized the strain of the forthcoming trial had sapped his strength. His skin was grey, his eyes had dark circles beneath them and she guessed he was living on his nerves. He chose to befriend her because he was a generous-hearted man, but yet she could only serve as a constant, bitter reminder of the men who killed his sister. She had to back away from him, it wasn't right to allow him to worry and concern himself with her at such a difficult time in his life.

'It isn't awful at all,' she said, forcing herself to laugh gaily. 'Strange, a bit disgusting sometimes, but it's a great deal better than putting up with Mrs Bentley's constant criticism. I like working with other girls, we have lots of laughs and I'll soon get used to the weirdness of it all. In fact the main reason I called around today, besides telling you I'd come to London, was to suggest we give up writing to each other.'

Thomas raised one eyebrow inquiringly. 'Why?'

'Well, I don't get much spare time for a start,' Rosie

said. 'But apart from that the other girls reckon Matron steams open their letters, and we wouldn't want that, would we? We could always pass any messages on to each other through Miss Pemberton if we need to.' She paused breathlessly, hoping she'd managed to create the right light tone. 'Now, have you had any news from Alan?'

If it hadn't been for the waitress coming back with a tray, Thomas might have pursued the subject further to make sure Rosie meant what she said. But a moment or two's respite gave him enough time to see it was the ideal solution to his dilemma. It was also possible Rosie needed a clean break with the past.

'Mrs Hughes wrote on Saturday,' Thomas said once the tea and sandwiches were on the table. 'Alan's settled in well at his new school. He didn't even cry on the first day and when she picked him up at three-thirty he was full of it. It sounds like he's very happy.'

Over their sandwiches Rosie steered the conversation well away from personal matters. She told him about the girls she worked with and Thomas spoke of painting the living-room of his flat above the shop.

'It can't have been touched since the turn of the century,' he said with a smile. 'I've painted it white now and it looks so different. I'm going to tackle the kitchen next.'

Rosie looked at his thin, unshaven face reflectively. She had always disliked seeing her father or brothers that way. It seemed brutish somehow. Yet for some odd reason Thomas looked quite the reverse; in fact she wanted to reach out and caress his bristly chin, and tell him not to worry about anything. She thought his life above the shop mending watches must be very lonely and she wondered if he cooked proper meals for himself. 'You should find a lady friend,' she said reprovingly.

'And you ought to find yourself a boyfriend,' he retorted, waggling a finger at her. 'Get out dancing with some of those other girls.'

'I don't know how,' she admitted a little shamefacedly.

'Then why don't you learn?' he suggested. 'There're often classes advertised. It doesn't cost much.'

When they parted outside the café Thomas waited before walking back up Flask Walk, and watched Rosie dart nimbly through the traffic on Haverstock Hill. An unexpected lump came up in his throat, catching him by surprise. In her checked skirt and sweater she looked no different from any other pretty adolescent girl. She appeared so carefree, it was hard to believe that she was nursing such a huge, dark secret. He wondered who she would turn to when her father and brother were hanged, for it certainly couldn't be him.

'That's not your problem,' he told himself firmly as he turned away. But somehow he knew Rosie had dug herself a little place in his heart and he wasn't going to be able to forget her that easily.

The shine seemed to have gone off the day after Rosie left Thomas, but she still looked in all the shops in Hampstead High Street, and made her way up to the heath as she'd planned. But sitting there in the sunshine by Whitestone pond, she suddenly felt utterly desolate.

There were women and children all around her, girls only a few years older than herself with babies in prams, other women playing with toddlers and a whole family with five or six children sailing boats on the pond. She could sense all these women's happiness, and felt that not one of them had anything more serious to hide than maybe spending a little too much housekeeping money.

Until now she hadn't thought beyond her father's and brother's trial. It was like a high fence blocking out the view. But all at once it was as if she could see over the fence, and she didn't like what lay ahead one bit. Thomas was wary of being seen with her now, and she doubted he'd ever want to clap eyes on her after the trial. Just about every person in England would follow the court case, the names Cole and Seth Parker would go down in history and every detail of Rosie's family and home life would become common knowledge.

It was all very well for Thomas to urge her to go out dancing and find herself a boyfriend, but had he for one moment considered what a potential minefield that might be? So maybe there wasn't any harm in going out dancing with Linda and Mary. But just suppose she did meet a boy she really liked? What then? Should she carry on with the same story she'd told the girls?

Rosie felt desolate. Telling lies to keep a job was one thing, but she didn't like the thought of deceiving someone if she grew to care about them. But who would want her if she told the truth? Looking even further ahead, no decent boy would want to marry into the Parker family.

She remembered how she had thought her father's crime was like an indelible mark on her forehead. Now she knew Seth was involved too, it was far worse than that. It was like being a carrier of a hereditary disease; she might have no symptoms herself, but no sensible man would risk having children with her.

It was after six when Rosie got back to Carrington Hall. She used her key to go in the side staff door, and hearing Mary Connor's laughter coming from the dining-room, she went straight along there instead of up to her room.

Mary, Linda, Brownlow and Thorpe were just having their tea. They all looked up at her as she came in the room.

'Where've you been today?' Mary asked.

'To the library, then I caught a bus to Hampstead,' Rosie replied.

'Sounds fun-packed,' Mary said with heavy sarcasm.

'It was nice,' Rosie said indignantly. 'Hampstead is really lovely.'

'Well, sorry if this is gonna spoil it for you,' Linda chimed in, 'but Matron wants to see you in her office. I think she's bleedin' well on the warpath.'

Rosie immediately thought of this morning's events and her blood went cold.

'What have you done?' Mary asked, her blue-grey eyes widening.

'Nothing that I know of,' Rosie shrugged. 'I suppose I'd better go and find out.'

'Come in,' Matron replied to Rosie's tentative knock on the office door. By day this room was the domain of Mrs Trow who did all the administration work, but Matron had a habit of going in there around this time of day, the girls said to snoop on Mrs Trow's work.

Rosie walked in and found Matron sitting at the desk. The office was very small, a partitioned-off part of a much bigger room which had no real windows, only a pane of glass looking out on to the staircase. A large desk with a typewriter took up most of the space, metal filing cabinets the wall behind, and crammed into the remaining space was a series of pigeon-holes, one for each patient, with medical reference books and stationery piled on top.

'Bell said you wanted to see me,' Rosie said from the doorway.

'So I did, you disgusting wretch,' Matron spat at her. She leapt out of her chair and caught hold of Rosie by the shoulder, dragging her in and kicking the door shut behind her before Rosie could even blink. 'I've met some filthy girls in my time. But never one to equal you.'

'What have I done?' Rosie asked indignantly, wriggling away from the woman. She couldn't think of anything which would warrant such a vicious attack on her.

'This.' Matron caught her by the neck of her jumper and dragged her towards a cardboard box on the floor. Flicking it open with one finger in a gesture of utter distaste, she pushed Rosie's head down towards it.

Rosie gagged at the strong smell. It appeared to be two pairs of maroon uniform knickers, and a pair of blood-stained white ones. Surrounding them were four or five unwrapped soiled sanitary towels.

'That's nothing to do with me.' Rosie jerked herself away from Matron. 'Why should you think it was?'

'Because I discovered them under your bed and you own several pairs of white knickers identical to those.'

Rosie was so shocked by the accusation she stared stupidly at Matron for a second.

'Don't gawp at me like that, girl,' Matron roared. 'Explain yourself.'

'They aren't mine,' she said. In fact after a moment's thought she had a feeling the white knickers were indeed hers and she also realized who was responsible for leaving such a disgusting collection for someone else to find.

'Don't lie to me,' Matron hissed. 'I know they are yours.'

'I am not lying, and I do share the room in case you've forgotten,' Rosie snapped back angrily. She could hardly believe that another girl would even think of helping herself to someone else's knickers, but as angry as she was, she couldn't actually bring herself to name names.

'Just as I expected.' Matron was red in the face now and her already close-set eyes looked like one dark slit across her nose. 'You would try and put the blame on someone else. They are yours. Don't deny it.' She lifted her hand and slapped Rosie's cheek hard.

Rosie's temper flared up at such injustice. 'I will deny it because it's the truth,' she shouted out. 'I haven't even started my periods yet, and how dare you slap me for something I couldn't possibly have done.'

'You liar,' the older woman yelled back, picking up the box and shoving it into Rosie's hands. 'I'll be reporting you first thing tomorrow morning to Mr Brace-Coombes.'

Rosie didn't stop to think, but flung the box back at Matron, its disgusting contents spilling on to the floor. 'Report me to who you like. But those things are not mine and if you want someone to remove them, find the filthy person they really belong to.' She ran to the door and rushed out before Matron could catch her.

When Rosie burst into the bedroom a couple of minutes later, Maureen was sitting on her bed. Her head jerked up guiltily and Rosie reached her in two strides, slapping her hard across the cheek before the girl had a chance to move.

'You can get downstairs and tell Matron who those towels and knickers belong to,' she roared, so angry she was unable to control herself. 'Go on, now!'

When Maureen didn't move Rosie grabbed her by the shoulders and shook her until her teeth almost rattled and her glasses fell off.

'Do you hear me?' she shouted. 'You are an animal, Maureen. You already disgust me because you don't wash, and now you've left those stinking things there for Matron to find and get me blamed. And how dare you take my knickers and wear them? Haven't you got any pride or decency? If you don't go down now and tell Matron the truth, I'll make such a commotion that every single person in this place will know how filthy you are.'

'I'm s-s-s-sorry,' Maureen stuttered through the shaking, her grey eyes wide with terror. 'I didn't say they were yours; Matron just assumed that and I was too scared to tell her the truth.'

'I haven't even started my periods yet,' Rosie snarled. 'But even if I had, I would never leave such things lying around, neither would any decent person. Now get down and tell Matron, or so help me I'll swing for you.'

Maureen slunk out, giving Rosie a wide berth, her terrified expression saying that she preferred taking her chances with Matron to staying here for more punishment.

Once Maureen was gone, Rosie sunk down on her bed and began to cry. She was furious with Maureen and Matron, but even more horrified with herself for losing control. She'd never known she was capable of such rage, and it was just another reminder of the Parker blood running through her veins.

The door opened and Linda looked round it. 'I 'eard all that,' she said. 'Good for you.'

'Go away,' Rosie said, struggling to compose herself. 'This is a private matter.'

'Suit yourself,' Linda pouted. 'I only wanted to say I admire your spunk. Me and Mary thought you had the makings of another bleedin' doormat.'

It was over an hour before Maureen slunk back into the room bearing an angry red hand-print on her cheek where Matron must have slapped her. She was quivering with fright and clearly thought Rosie was going to lay into her again.

But Rosie had calmed down and her anger was now directed more at Matron than a girl who'd never been taught basic cleanliness. She had found her letter from Miss Pemberton had been read. The hair grip was gone, the letter put back in the envelope the other way round.

'I'm sorry,' Maureen whined and burst into tears. 'We're supposed to take them down to the incinerator, but I always forget. And I'm really sorry too that I wore your knickers, but I didn't have any clean ones of my own.'

Rosie softened then. She could guess what Matron had put the girl through. Maureen might be much older than herself, but she wasn't very smart. She took the girl's hand and led her over to her bed.

'It's okay. I'll forgive you. But you've got to learn about washing and stuff,' she said softly. 'It's important. No one likes smelly people, it's horrible. So you've got to do what I tell you.'

Later that night when the light was turned off, Rosie thought how ironic her situation was. Maureen really believed she came from a nice home, with a proper bathroom, and that a loving mother had given her all the knowledge on feminine matters that Rosie had passed on to her.

Rosie wondered what the older girl would think if she was to get a glimpse of May Cottage in the middle of winter when her father and brothers' boots turned the kitchen floor into a sea of mud. If she saw them coming in late at night, drunk as lords, vomiting into the sink or even on the floor, or if she found herself on the receiving end of their foul language. She wished she could admit that most of her knowledge came from women's magazines, that bath night for Rosie had been a tin bath on the kitchen floor, and that until a few months ago her knickers had been only suitable for rags and no one in their right mind would want to borrow them. Maureen had said too how much she admired her fancy table manners and Rosie almost laughed aloud. Mrs Bentley could take the credit for those!

After Rosie had made some tea and Maureen had had a bath, she'd opened up more about herself, telling Rosie about the man who had raped her and how she had ended up in a lunatic asylum. It was a harrowing story and one she guessed the girl had never told anyone else. It was so very tempting then to admit to her own background if only to point out that people could actually learn to live differently.

But she hadn't, and she never would. One thing she had learned in recent months was that you shouldn't put complete trust in anyone. Miss Pemberton, Thomas and Mr Bentley all invited trust. But Miss Pemberton had sent her here. For all she knew Mr Bentley might betray her later on if the price was right. Thomas seemed to have changed his mind about being her friend. She couldn't trust anyone but herself.

Almost two weeks later and a whole week into her father's trial Rosie discovered just how fragile her invented past was, and the dangers of letting people get too close to her.

It was Sunday evening and all the girls who were not on duty had gathered in the staff sitting-room after tea. Linda, Mary and Maureen were there, along with Gladys Thorpe, one of the nurses. The room was intended for all the staff but in practice it was only the younger ones who used it.

Present and past staff had done their best to make this room a cosy retreat by adding pictures, cushions and books, but their widely differing tastes and furniture which had been passed on by well-intentioned people when they grew tired of its ugliness or shabbiness, gave it a forlorn air. Bars on the window, a noticeboard with staff rotas and Matron's many curt memos were a constant reminder that they were all almost as institutionalized as the patients upstairs.

Sundays seemed twice as long as any other day because for some reason for which no one could offer an explanation, the patients always played up.

There were theories: that there were fewer domestic staff on duty and therefore the chargehands were distracted by having to fill in for them. Because a vicar came and gave a service in the day room, or that this was the day visitors usually called and brought back to the patients vague memories of life before Carrington Hall.

Whatever the reason, there were always more puddles on the floor, messed pants, tantrums and fights. So when six o'clock came, all the staff coming off duty were too weary to do anything but flop into chairs and commiserate with one another. Fortunately Matron always went to Evensong, and rarely came home before ten because she had supper afterwards with a friend, so they tended to gather in the staff room drinking endless cups of tea and smoking cigarettes until minutes before she returned.

Rosie's run-in with Matron had moved her up a couple of notches in the other members of staff's estimation. As they saw it, she'd not only been courageous enough to stand up to Matron, but she hadn't said a word against

Maureen afterwards to anyone and had even managed to persuade the girl to wash at last.

All of them were aware that Matron was out to get Rosie – she didn't take kindly to one of her staff showing her up – and this bothered them. The only way they had of showing their allegiance to Rosie was by befriending her, sharing tea and cake after work and by encouraging her to tell them about herself.

After being lonely and isolated for so long, Rosie found it wonderful to not only find herself accepted but liked, so when the other girls asked her questions about her home and family, she had to give them something more than just a skeleton story. Without really being aware of it she slipped into describing an almost fairytale childhood in a pretty cottage with a doting father and maiden aunt looking after her. In one or two moments of nostalgia she told true stories about her father, allowing them to glimpse his joviality, strength and charismatic personality. It pleased her to see that they liked the man she portrayed, and it soothed her sense of loss.

But as the trial began, and Seth and Cole Parker became almost as infamous as Jack the Ripper, Rosie was brought down to earth with a bump and forced to see the worst aspects of her family. Everyone at Carrington Hall, from Matron right down to the lowest domestic, was avidly following the trial. They listened to the news on the wireless and read all the newspapers. Each day as some new revelation came to light, it was chewed over at length, and because Rosie came from Somerset and they supposed she might have some inside information, she was often asked for her opinions. Rosie shrugged off their questions with pretended disinterest, but the burden of knowing so much became heavier and more distressing each day.

On Thursday when Ethel Parker was called to the witness stand to give evidence of her husband's cruelty, Rosie found it almost impossible to keep her views and knowledge to herself.

Ethel was forty-eight now, and the court artist's sketches captured not only her gaunt face and grey hair, but also the livid scar on her cheek which she claimed was caused by Cole holding a hot flat iron to it. Rosie had looked at this picture in stunned disbelief. The woman bore no resemblance to the raven-haired beauty she'd heard gossiped about in Catcott, and her vitriolic account of her violent and unhappy marriage didn't match up to the accounts Rosie had heard of the artistic and fun-loving woman from neighbours. Ethel made much of being forced to run away and leave her sons, yet under cross-examination it transpired she had indeed run off with another man, and in eighteen years had made no attempt to discover how her boys were. Even as she stood in the witness box with Seth just feet away from her in the dock, it was reported that she showed no emotion at being confronted by the son she'd abandoned so long ago.

Today the Sunday papers had gone to town on the story, with headlines like 'The Marsh Murders' and 'Satan in Somerset', and there were background profiles on Ethel, Ruby and Heather, so that inevitably the evening's conversation turned to them.

Linda took centre stage as she lay on the settee, cigarette in hand, a newspaper on her lap. 'I reckon both Blackwell and Farley were gold-diggers,' she said airily, blowing smoke rings towards the ceiling. 'I don't mean I think that gave the Parkers a right to kill 'em for it. But if I was a man and I 'ad a few bob, I'd be savage when I found out that's all they were after.'

'What on earth makes you think that?' Mary asked incredulously.

'Well, look at their backgrounds,' Linda said, pointing to the newspaper. 'They both came from the East End of London, they 'ad nothing before they ended up as his 'ousekeeper. I come from there. I know 'ow it is. You can't tell me they thought, "Ah, the poor man needs 'elp with 'is motherless children." They saw it as a way of getting a good, easy life.'

'If that's what they wanted,' Gladys said gently, 'why didn't they clear off the moment they discovered it wasn't going to be like that?'

In the three weeks Rosie had been here she had learned a great deal about the other girls' characters in discussions like this. Linda had lived through the war in the East End of London, and though her family had been rehoused out in Romford in 1945, she had retained a tough, cynical view on life. Rosie often wondered why she came here to work. She wasn't a carer by nature, her personality was better-suited to working in a factory than kowtowing to the likes of Matron Barnes. But whenever Rosie had tried to broach the subject Linda had just laughed and claimed it was easy work.

Mary, on the other hand, had been well educated at a convent in Ireland, but she was a romantic dreamer, soft-hearted, lazy and gullible too. She had come here with the intention of filling in time before nursing training, but for one reason or another – it seemed to Rosie to be mainly because of falling in love frequently – she hadn't moved on.

Nurse Gladys Thorpe was a kindly but dim girl of twenty-six, the oldest in the room. The other girls, perhaps unkindly, said she'd gone into training as a psychiatric nurse because she hadn't got the brains for general nursing. She was the plodding type who didn't look ahead any further than her next pay-day. Placid, unimaginative and plain as a pikestaff with a moon-like face and lumpy body, Rosie felt she'd still be here in another twenty years.

'They stayed because they knew Parker 'ad money tucked away somewhere,' Linda argued. 'They were working out 'ow to get their 'ands on it.'

'You're daft, Linda,' Mary piped up indignantly. 'Women don't think like that. They must have fallen in

199

love with him. Why else would they both have had a child by him?'

'Because they were both tarts and I reckon Farley knew 'e'd killed Blackwell.'

Rosie had distanced herself from this conversation, steeling herself to make no comment whatever the other girls said. But at the insult to Heather her anger rose. 'Neither of them were tarts, and of course Heather didn't know what Parker had done to Ruby. She was a simple girl.' Rosie stopped short, suddenly aware that by using the women's Christian names and speaking out with such passion, she'd revealed not only her interest but perhaps some secret knowledge of the women.

There was absolute silence for a moment, the other girls looking at one another in surprise.

'You seem to know a lot,' Maureen said, looking at her curiously.

'I don't,' Rosie said hastily. She was particularly wary of Maureen, she might be virtually illiterate but she was quick to pick up on intrigue. 'I just don't like people speaking ill of the dead.'

''Ow the 'ell do you know that Farley was simple?' Linda asked pointedly, her dark eyes narrowed. 'I've never read that anywhere.'

'I come from down that way, remember.' Rosie wished the floor would open up and swallow her. 'You hear things on the grapevine; everyone was talking about the women when the bodies were found.'

The conversation resumed but Rosie was painfully aware that all the girls were watching for any further reaction from her. She tried to black out what they were saying, but each time she heard something she knew to be untrue, her stomach contracted agonizingly.

She had read every single account of the trial, trying hard to keep an open mind. She doubted the truth of a great deal of the vindictive things that Ethel Parker had said about Cole, and in fact the defence lawyer had argued that the scar on her face was a fairly recent one, certainly not one of eighteen years' standing. Yet Rosie knew the police evidence to be sound, and who would have killed the two women and buried them on Parker land, other than the Parkers? So she hovered in uncertainty, waiting for something which would finally prove their guilt or innocence.

Meanwhile, however, the press were creating a background to the story which prevented anyone else from being fair-minded. May Cottage had been recreated as a kind of hell-hole, a dark and sinister place where its sub-human residents wallowed in filth and perversion, and imprisoned young women against their will.

Rosie remembered how clean the kitchen had been, the well-scrubbed floor and table, Heather's bright curtains at the window, Ruby's crocheted rugs – even Ethel had left behind hand-painted storage jars up on a shelf. Were those the work of unwilling slaves?

She could see in her mind's eye Cole smiling into Heather's eyes at the Harvest Home. She could hear their laughter as they repapered the bedrooms that first summer. She could visualize the orchard in springtime when pink and white blossom fluttered down on to the grass like confetti, and Heather running barefoot through it shouting to Rosie how much she loved it. She wished there was some way she could create a few of those prettier images for the jury.

'I wonder what they've done with Parker's other two children?' Gladys said thoughtfully some time later. 'I bet they could tell a few tales!'

'Stuck them away behind bars somewhere I 'ope,' Linda said. 'They 'aven't got an 'ope in 'ell of being normal.'

Again Rosie felt anger rising, but she squashed it down firmly.

'The little boy's probably too young to be affected that much,' Mary said with a deep sigh. 'But the girl must know the whole truth. I wouldn't be in her shoes, not for all the tea in China. I'd want to top myself with a father and brother like that.'

During the second week of the trial Rosie felt nauseous almost all the time. She went through the days automatically, doing what she was asked to, cleaning, feeding, making beds, wiping up urine and chivvying the patients along. But her heart and mind were in that courtroom a hundred miles away.

Thomas gave his evidence and in the course of it he spoke of his meeting with her at May Cottage. She couldn't help thinking that, but for her disobeying her father that day by speaking to a stranger, Cole and Seth wouldn't be in the dock now, and she'd still be in ignorance of the fate that both Ruby and Heather had met. Yet even as she thought it, she felt ashamed of trying to bury her head in the sand. Maybe they weren't proved to be murderers yet, but they had been cruel to Alan and she ought to be glad that through her one act of disobedience he'd been rescued.

The newspapers maximized on Thomas, with a photograph of him when he first joined the army and then another taken soon after his camp in Burma was liberated. She was struck by his similarity to Heather in the first picture, the thick fair hair, the wide smiling mouth and plump cheeks. In the second picture taken just five years later, he was unrecognizable, almost skeletal, a lined and weary face, leaning on crutches with his amputated leg bound in bandages, old before his time.

Rosie guessed that Thomas must be cruelly embarrassed by this tug on people's emotions, and it brought it home to her that long, long after this trial was over, people would still remember his part in it. She was certain their friendship was now over. She wondered if he could even bear to still see Alan.

It was the court artist's sketches of Cole and Seth, however, which demonstrated to her just how confused she was. Seth's true character showed in the insolent way he lolled in the dock. The events of that last day at May Cottage came back with such force she trembled from head to foot. She could believe every last thing he was suspected of. She wanted him found guilty.

But the sketches of her father made her melt inside. There was dignity in the upright way he sat, not insolence. His dark eyes seemed to say to her that whatever other bad things he'd done in his life, he hadn't bludgeoned her mother and Heather to death as the police said he had.

It was hard to resist cutting out just one of these pictures, a keepsake to hold on to for old times' sake, but even that was denied her because of Matron's prying. She wished too that she could see him one last time, to put aside what was happening now and just be father and daughter again.

On the Friday evening of that same week Rosie went into Linda's and Mary's room. Mary was lying on her bed reading the *Evening News*, dressed and made up to go out dancing in a pale blue satin sheath dress, but with her hair still in curlers. Linda was standing in front of the mirror wearing an off-the-shoulder 'Goosegirl' blouse and a red circular skirt, straining to reach behind her to dab some angry-looking spots on her upper back with Pan Stik make-up.

'Do this for me?' she pleaded, pushing the stick into Rosie's hands. 'I can't reach. But mind you don't get any on me blouse.'

Rosie complied, but as she glanced over to Mary she noticed she was reading something about the trial. 'What's the latest?' she asked, hoping she sounded casual enough.

'It looks like the son couldn't have been in on it,' Mary said without looking up. 'Some farmer gave evidence that he was working for him 'til gone seven on the day Ruby Blackwell went missing. I'm beginning to feel sorry for him. It sounds like he had a terrible childhood.'

Rosie's hands shook.

'Watch what you're doing!' Linda screeched as she saw Rosie behind her in the mirror waving the Pan Stik dangerously near her blouse.

Rosie pulled herself together and apologized. She wished she could grab the paper from Mary's hands and read it herself, but she knew she'd have to wait until they'd gone out.

'She'd say Jack the Ripper was a good sort really, if she 'eard his mother drank and went with men,' Linda said, checking over her shoulder in the mirror to see Rosie had done her job properly. 'But for once I'm going along with her. The son was too young, for a start; you can't tell me a sixteen-year-old boy could 'elp his dad with something like that and never let it slip to anyone.'

Rosie felt a cold chill running down her spine. She knew Seth was perfectly capable of doing just that. He might be many things, but he'd never been a blabbermouth; none of the Parkers was, herself included. 'Can I read it when you've finished?' she asked Mary.

Mary made a disapproving face. 'You should be coming out with us, not staying in and reading papers,' she said. 'What's the point in working in London if you never go out the door?'

'I do go out the door,' Rosie protested. 'I just can't dance and I'd only show you up.'

'Then we'll teach you on Sunday night,' Linda said, fixing a wide black belt round her middle and pulling it in tight. 'You only need to know the waltz and the cha-cha, none of the blokes can do anything else. Now, 'ow do I look?'

Rosie smiled. Linda looked plain by day, but after setting her dark hair in pin curls and putting on some make-up she was suddenly transformed into a voluptuous glamour girl.

'Like a beauty queen,' she said. 'Now can I have the paper?'

Mary threw it at her. 'So you're just as hooked on it as us!' she said triumphantly.

'I'm not,' Rosie insisted. 'I want to look at Situations Vacant so I can leave this madhouse.'

'Then pick out a job for all three of us,' Mary laughed. 'Somewhere with good pay, little work and lots of men!'

It was absolutely silent on the staff landing once Linda and Mary had gone out. Maureen and Gladys were down in the staff room listening to the wireless, and if Staff Nurse Aylwood was in her room further along the landing she was as quiet as always. Rosie stretched out on her bed and read the report on Seth's defence, relieved that she was unlikely to be interrupted.

Earlier in the trial the prosecution had made much of Seth's reputation as a fighter, troublemaker and bully, driving home the point that he idolized his father and emulated his behaviour. The barrister defending Rosie's half-brother didn't seek to deny these charges, but set out to show that Seth had another gentler side which he chose to hide because he was afraid of his father.

He questioned Seth at length about the two years after Ethel Parker had left May Cottage, when he and his younger brother had been left to fend for themselves, often hungry, always neglected. By the time he got to the point where Ruby arrived, Seth's answers implied that the nine-year-old boy saw her as a longed-for replacement mother. He spoke of her cooking meals, knitting him warm jumpers and making the house a real home again, including the addition to their family of a new baby sister.

A tear ran down Rosie's cheek as she heard Seth's fond words about her mother. She believed it all because it struck a chord about the joy she'd experienced when Heather came into her life. As the barrister probed ever more deeply into the years when she was a small child, she was chastened to hear Seth's affectionate references to both her mother and herself and she felt she may have misjudged him. She certainly didn't think he could have killed the woman he obviously had such a high regard for.

As Mary had already said, there was a testimony from the farmer in Bridgwater that Seth had worked on his barn all that week in which Ruby disappeared, and his farm accounts in which Seth's wages had been paid to Cole were submitted as evidence. The barrister played on this for some time, showing that between fourteen and eighteen, Seth worked long hours out in all weathers, but yet was paid no wages by his father for his efforts, only a scant amount of pocket money. He then went on to draw attention to Seth's excellent National Service record, suggesting that but for the boy's fear of displeasing his father, he would have become a mechanic in civilian life and moved away to the city to become self-sufficient.

Moving on to the time of Heather's death, he laboured heavily on the point that Seth was in Bristol working all that week, and that he stood to gain nothing by killing the woman, only becoming more firmly entrenched in helping his father run his business and taking more responsibility for the younger children.

As the prosecution had previously brought up Seth's alleged cruelty to Alan and Rosie, the defence had no choice but to come back to it. To her surprise Seth didn't attempt to deny it, but somehow the carefully worded questions on the subject created the image that her brother was merely acting on his father's behalf, endeavouring to instil some order in a household where all sense of discipline and orderliness had flown. He sounded severe, but caring.

Rosie lay on her bed for a long time after reading the newspaper, her head and heart reeling with conflicting emotions. She didn't think Seth could have killed her mother or even known about her death. He was the same age then as she was now, too young for such things. But she wasn't so sure of his innocence in Heather's death.

Looking back she recalled Heather often saying he bitterly resented her, and Rosie remembered so well how much happier all of them had been once he went into the army.

In that moment she suddenly saw how wrong she was not to tell Sergeant Headly or even Miss Pemberton everything about Seth. Maybe that scene she'd witnessed in her father's bedroom did not prove he helped her father to murder Heather, but it showed quite clearly what kind of a man he had grown into. The police still believed that the beating Rosie received from her brother was merely for making Alan run away. If they'd known the whole story the prosecution might have taken on a whole new turn, and Seth's barrister wouldn't be able to sway the jury into believing he was just a simple-minded country boy who lived in fear of his father's displeasure.

But what could she do now? Miss Pemberton had gone to great lengths to keep her out of the trial. And Thomas too! What would it do to him to hear that both Seth and Norman had raped his sister?

Rosie awoke in the night from a terrible nightmare. She was walking down a dark street towards some brightly lit shops at the end, when suddenly Seth came up behind her. She ran and ran, but instead of reaching the safety of the shops, they seemed to move further and further away, and Seth was closing in on her. He grabbed her round the waist and flung her down to the ground; she saw his grinning face looming above her and his mouth coming down on her throat as if to tear it out like a mad dog. Just as his teeth sunk into her flesh, she woke up.

As she lay awake, too frightened to close her eyes again for fear the dream would continue, she remembered that her father knew about Seth and Norman. It was up to him to reveal it, and if he then asked that she be called to the witness stand she would go.

But however much she wanted to believe in her father's innocence, and however distressed she was that he hadn't yet given his lawyer anything substantial to fight his cause with, she had to face the unpalatable truth that he must have murdered both women and that Seth was almost certainly involved too. There was no escaping that.

It made her realize it was time that she thought of herself. As Sister Dowd and Thomas had pointed out, she wasn't responsible for anyone's deeds but her own. She would be sixteen very soon, old enough to decide on her own future. Perhaps then she should make a clean break with the past, forget her disreputable family and move on somewhere else, leaving everyone, even those who had sought to help her, behind.

The next morning as she got up, Rosie discovered her periods had started. But as she looked at her blood-smeared nightdress, she felt no dismay, just a kind of confirmation that her thoughts during the night had been rational, adult ones. For the first time ever she felt as if she was in control of her life. And she had no intention of letting anyone take that control from her.

Chapter Seven

Freda Barnes was not a very intelligent woman, but what she lacked in brain power, she made up for in guile and determination. Her father had been a doctor with a country practice in Herefordshire. Until she was fourteen and the First World War broke out, her childhood had been a very pleasant one. Although her father wasn't rich and their home was a little shabby, they had a maid, and a governess who came in daily to teach herself and her three sisters. Because of her father's position all five girls were often invited to many of the wealthier neighbours' homes for parties, picnics, dances and tennis. Freda had always assumed that in the fullness of time she would turn into a beauty like her two older sisters and that one of the sons from these rather grand houses would ask to marry her.

But the war changed everything. Her father felt compelled to offer his services for the good of his country, and one by one she saw all the young men in the neighbourhood join up too as patriotic fever swept through the small villages. Her mother upbraided her many times for being far more distressed by the lack of parties or tennis partners than by the casualty lists posted weekly in the village. She said it was high time Freda thought about someone other than herself and ordered her to roll up her sleeves and give a hand at the surgery, helping out old Dr Mayhew who'd come out of retirement to take her father's place.

Freda grudgingly complied with her mother's wishes, and waited for the war to end so everything would get back to normal. But her father didn't come back from

France, he contracted cholera and died in 1917 while helping the wounded in the trenches.

She was eighteen when the war finally ended, but to her dismay she saw that life was never going to return to how it had been before, and she felt bitter and resentful. She hadn't even turned into a beauty. Her hair was lank, straight and mousy; she had a plain face with thin lips and close-set eyes. While her sisters had hourglass figures and shapely legs, she was as hefty as a carthorse. Fewer than a quarter of the young men returned and many of them were mere shadows of the gallant gentlemen who'd joined up in 1914.

The maid and the governess left soon after her father went to France, but on his death her mother could no longer afford to live in such a big house, and made plans to move into a small cottage. Rachel and Hester, her two older sisters, both went off to London and found jobs. Grace, the sister a year younger than Freda, married the son of a local farmer and her mother made it plain that Freda must pay her own way too.

Dr Mayhew pulled some strings to get her trained as a nurse in Whittington Hospital in London. Freda had no desire to be a nurse, but it was better than being a shop girl or governess, and it was the only thing she had any experience of. She fully believed too it would be only a matter of time before she found a doctor to marry her so she could be the envy of her more attractive sisters.

She barely scraped through her exams, but she had the kind of authority, breeding and poise that were admired by her matron. The years passed and slowly she worked her way up to becoming a staff nurse and finally sister. Freda loathed the children's wards, and midwifery, though she spent a year specializing in each, still hoping for that elusive doctor to sweep her off her feet. She wasn't keen on surgery either, and a spell in the theatre made her want to run away from nursing for good. She felt that life had cheated her; she didn't see why her life was only work, with no hope of anything better. She wanted money and position, and she believed she deserved them.

She had been on the point of moving into district nursing in 1931, when she attended a lecture on mental illness and saw the opportunities there.

All the mental asylums were grossly overcrowded and badly run. The war had swelled the numbers of patients and there were few nurses of Freda Barnes's background anxious to enter into such a gloomy and unglamorous field. Freda had no desire to improve the lives of the mentally incompetent – as far as she was concerned they deserved to be locked away out of sight. But she thought there would be real possibilities to shoot up the ladder, even to the post of matron in a few short years.

Freda was then thirty-one. She had come to realize that there was little chance now of making a good marriage; she was too plain and she had no fortune either. On top of that the country was in the grips of a depression. If she stayed in general nursing, it might be another twenty years before she saw herself rise higher than ward sister. So she applied for posts in several large mental hospitals, and settled for Stoke Park in Bristol because it seemed more civilized than any of the others.

Hope turned to bitterness when she discovered that Stoke Park was a pioneering mental hospital, intent on breaking away from the barbaric image asylums had acquired. They were looking for dedicated and compassionate people in the senior positions, and hard, domineering women like Barnes were purposely overlooked in promotion. She hated everything about Stoke Park. The deranged patients, the common untrained women she had to work alongside, but most of all the young doctors hardly out of medical school who looked down their noses when she tried to instil some discipline into the place.

Freda had been at Stoke Park for seven long, miserable years, when a chance meeting there with Lionel Brace-Coombes changed her life. He owned a small private

211

mental home in London with the kind of genteel patients Freda could identify with. He appreciated her experience and background, and she charmed him into offering her a post of sister, a spacious flat of her own and excellent wages.

Lionel Brace-Coombes was the kind of man she would have liked as a husband. Ten years older than herself, with inherited wealth, unfortunately he already had a wife, Ayleen, who had been diagnosed as being schizophrenic some five years into their marriage. He had tried so hard to keep her at home at Foxhill, but the many nurses he'd employed just wouldn't stay, not once they found how difficult Ayleen was. He couldn't bear the thought of committing his beautiful wife to any of the terrible asylums he visited and as time went on opening a private home seemed to be the only alternative.

The old house at Woodside Park had been lying empty since the early Thirties. It was near enough to his home for him to visit regularly and its owner was glad to have it taken off his hands. Lionel converted it with great care, landscaping the gardens and installing the best equipment available. Originally he had intended to have no more than five or six women patients only, imagining them all to be distressed gentlewomen like his wife. But the cost of providing a doctor and nurses to look after so few patients proved prohibitive and by the time Freda joined him, the numbers had swelled to twelve.

Sadly Ayleen died of pneumonia in 1940, two years after Freda arrived. What with the war and other more pressing business interests, Lionel distanced himself from the place then. When his matron left he gave the vacant post to Freda, with the full control she'd worked so hard for.

'You look very nice today, Freda,' Lionel Brace-Coombes said as he poured tea for them both from a silver teapot. His compliment wasn't truly sincere. He thought Freda looked impressive in her navy Matron's dress and starched cap – they suited her stern, humourless character and gave her dignity. But in a pale blue costume and lace-trimmed blouse she looked what she was: a fat, plain, middle-aged spinster who was trying to disguise her underlying toughness with a layer of false femininity. He felt however that as she'd gone to such lengths to please him – she'd had her hair washed and set for this visit, and she was even wearing a little lipstick and rouge – the least he could do was show some appreciation.

'Well thank you, Lionel,' Freda Barnes simpered. Her new navy blue high-heeled shoes were pinching her corns and her corsets were laced so tightly she couldn't sit right back in the seat, but the discomfort was worth it if he thought she looked nice.

Lionel Brace-Coombes, her employer and owner of Carrington Hall, was the only person whose opinion she valued, and a visit to his home Foxhill House in Borehamwood in Hertfordshire was a rare treat. She thought he was still a fine-looking man with his thick white hair and bright blue eyes, even if he was sixty-two. He had put on some weight in the last ten years, yet this had only made him more distinguished-looking. But then Freda Barnes admired everything about her employer: His appearance, impeccable manners and his intelligence. She also envied his gracious home and his adventurous ancestors who had made a fortune in shipping and left it all to him.

The garden beyond the large windows of the drawing-room was glorious, a lawn as smooth and green as a bowling green, the many old trees turning to gold and brown in autumnal splendour.

Lionel's great-great-grandfather had built Foxhill House two hundred years before when Borehamwood was just a tiny hamlet, surrounded by woodland. It wasn't a grand place by rich people's standards in those days, just eight rooms in all, but he was a man with an eye for symmetry and beauty, and the graceful Georgian style was timeless. He had also commissioned craftsmen to make much of the beautiful furniture that still graced each room. Subsequent intrepid Brace-Coombeses had brought back many intriguing artefacts from every corner of the world, the thick-fringed rugs from Persia and India, and a fabulous collection of jade figurines from the Far East.

All the downstairs rooms had been redecorated since Freda's last visit. The walls had been covered in pale gold watered silk, with new cream and gold soft furnishings.

'Do you like the new décor?' Lionel asked, noting the way her close-set eyes scanned the room, missing nothing. He passed her a dainty bone china teacup and saucer.

'Very much so. It's so very elegant and tasteful,' she gushed. Foxhill House had been requisitioned by the Home Office during the war and although Lionel had removed much of his furniture to places of safety, it had become very shabby. She felt it was a good sign that Lionel was asserting his character on his home at last. He was a quiet, genteel man, with a passion for art, music and nature, and she had always considered the previous décor of the drawing-room with its dark Regency stripes too overpowering for a man of his sensitivity.

'I felt it was high time I took myself in hand,' he said with a shrug. 'To be honest, Freda, I've let things slide in recent years.'

Freda gulped nervously. He might of course be merely referring to his home at this moment, but she knew his interest in Carrington Hall had waned some years ago. She was afraid he might want to close it down.

Freda had asked for this meeting today on the pretext of discussing some of the more long-term patients whose families were behind with their fees. But her real motive for seeing her employer wasn't to involve him in things she could handle perfectly well herself, but simply to find out a little more about her newest member of staff, Rosemary Smith.

Rosemary Smith had been at Carrington Hall for a whole

month now, and although the Matron could not really fault the girl's work or behaviour, she found her puzzling to the extent that she intruded on her thoughts almost constantly.

Freda had been at Carrington Hall for fourteen years, twelve of those in the post of Matron, and in that time she had never known a young girl who did not break down in tears on occasion, or one who did not disobey some of the rules. Rosemary Smith had never done either of these things, and it wasn't normal for a girl of not quite sixteen to be so controlled and conscientious. Even that regrettable incident with the soiled sanitary towels which had made Freda look extremely foolish had passed by without any further repercussions. What girl of that age wouldn't make a complaint to her family and demand an apology?

Furthermore, Freda did not like the way the girl had gained a certain status amongst the rest of the staff, or how she was always asking questions about aspects of the home which didn't concern her. At times it felt almost as if she was compiling a dossier on the running of Carrington Hall. Looking at all these things objectively, she was deeply suspicious of Smith. The only explanation seemed to be that the girl had been placed there as a spy.

'Nothing is sliding at Carrington Hall, I can assure you,' Freda Barnes said soothingly to her boss. 'It's going from strength to strength and is a credit to you. If we do have a weakness it's merely that we may be just a little too charitable. I know you don't like to be ruthless, Lionel,' Freda continued, in the gentle and persuasive voice she kept for him and the relatives of new patients, 'but these people have entrusted us with their relatives and we can't do that job properly unless they pay the fees. Patty is a case in point. Since her brother died no one else in the family has visited her, and they are almost a year behind with her fees. They must be made to face up to their responsibilities, Lionel. Either they pay up, or Patty must go into a State institution and leave a bed free for someone who values the kind of care we give at Carrington Hall.'

'But Patty has been with us right from the start, she was Ayleen's friend,' Lionel said quickly.

Freda looked at her employer's horrified expression and smiled inwardly. In most people she despised sentimentality and weakness, but she found it attractive in Lionel. She knew he could well afford to keep a dozen Pattys without feeling the pinch, but that wasn't the point.

'You are such a kind man,' she said. 'But Lionel, Patty doesn't really know where she is, or who is looking after her. If we start keeping one patient for nothing, soon everyone will stop paying, and then where will we be?'

Lionel shrugged. He was ashamed to admit he had toyed with the idea of selling the home. It held too many sad memories of Ayleen and in truth he found mentally defective people terribly distressing. He was so very glad he had someone like Freda Barnes to look after it for him. It meant he didn't need to keep going there. 'What do you suggest we do?'

'Nothing too unpleasant, just a firm letter stating our position. I'm sure that will do the trick. It isn't as if her family are short of money, is it?'

Lionel agreed. They moved on to discuss other patients, then slowly Freda brought the subject round to staff.

'The new girl, Rosemary Smith, is shaping up well,' she said with a beaming smile. 'Quite a find on your part, Lionel!'

'Oh really?' He raised one eyebrow in surprise. 'I was a bit concerned about her age. Fifteen is very young.'

'Is she the daughter of one of your friends?' Freda said, daintily sipping a second cup of tea.

'No.' He shook his head. 'She was recommended by Violet Pemberton, a nurse who once looked after Ayleen for a short while here, long before I opened Carrington Hall. A good woman, and one I would very much have liked to employ when I started the home.'

'She didn't want to work for you then?'

'Unfortunately she was firmly entrenched at that time in St Mary's in Paddington, and anyway psychiatric nursing wasn't really her forte. She was a great help to me though, advising me on staff, equipment and other such things. We kept in touch and she was very kind when Ayleen died.'

Freda bristled. It sounded very much as if Lionel had been a little sweet on this woman. 'Is she still at St Mary's?'

'No, she joined the QAs when war broke out; now she's a social worker down in Somerset. When she contacted me about this young girl, I was only too happy to give her a trial. I trust Violet's judgement entirely.'

'So Smith is one of her cases then?'

For the first time in their long and agreeable association Freda saw Lionel look furtive.

'Oh no. Of course not.'

Freda changed the subject then. She knew Lionel well enough to know when he had nothing further to say on a subject.

She was just leaving to catch the bus back to Carrington Hall when she had an idea. 'Could you give me your friend's address?' she asked. 'I'd very much like to drop her a line and tell her how well Smith is getting on. I always think people appreciate hearing that their recommendations have been sound, don't you?'

Lionel was heartened by Freda's appreciation of Rosemary Smith. He felt she must be mellowing with age as she hadn't always been generous with her praise in the past. And Violet Pemberton would be delighted to know her protégée hadn't let her down.

'Now that would be a nice gesture,' he said with a broad smile, and promptly turned to his desk to find Violet's address. 'Give her my regards too when you write.'

As Freda waddled down the lane towards the bus stop she looked at the address Lionel had given her again: 1, Chapel Cottages, Chilton Trinity, Near Bridgwater,

Somerset. She suspected there was something odd going on as this was the same one that Smith had given as her aunt's address.

'Unless the girl's aunt and this Miss Pemberton share a home,' she muttered to herself, 'there's something very fishy here.'

Rosie heard the news that her father had been found guilty on the wireless in the staff dining-room.

It was Thursday, the 23rd of October, and she and Maureen had just walked in to have their tea when the rich tones of the BBC newsreader rang out with the headlines.

'Cole Reginald Parker was today found guilty of the murders of Ruby Blackwell and Heather Farley at Bristol Assizes. Judge Draycott said as he passed the death sentence, "You wilfully and cruelly murdered these two defenceless women, and cold-bloodedly buried them on your own land to hide the evil deed you had committed."'

Rosie gasped involuntarily. The room swum around her, and she blindly reached out for Maureen to cling on to.

'What's up?' she dimly heard Maureen say.

'Seth Parker, Cole Parker's son, was found not-guilty by the jury and acquitted,' the newsreader went on and a humming sound in Rosie's ears prevented her from hearing anything more. Yet she was aware of Pat Clack staring at her open-mouthed. She knew it was Gladys Thorpe's hand on her elbow supporting her. And she sensed Maureen's curious gaze.

'I just went all dizzy,' she managed to get out and groped for a chair to sit down.

Gladys pushed Rosie's head down between her knees. 'Get her a cup of tea,' she ordered.

Rosie could only see their legs as she struggled to pull herself together, but the fact that Pat Clack didn't move towards the kitchen suggested that the three women were all looking at one another.

'It was that news,' Pat said. 'Fair chilled me too.'

Rosie sat up again. 'I'm okay.' She tried to smile but her face was too stiff and frozen to move. The news had moved on to the Mau Mau emergency in Kenya. She thought the newsreader might come back to her father's trial and sentence and she had to divert attention from it. 'I felt a bit odd earlier this afternoon. Perhaps I'm just hungry.'

Rosie forced herself to eat a ham sandwich even though each mouthful stuck in her throat. Maureen was looking at her very suspiciously and things weren't helped by Mary and Linda coming in and being regaled with the story, of both her near faint and the death sentence on Cole Parker. She was so close to breaking down. They were all so ghoulish discussing how long it took to die by hanging, and what it must feel like to wait for the moment when the hangman put the hood over your head and the noose around your neck.

'Do you remember when Timothy Evans was hanged?' Linda asked. 'Me mum kept saying 'e was innocent, and that 'e was too feeble-minded to kill anyone.'

'One of the chargehands here, a woman called Lily Stoops, hanged herself just a few weeks after I first came here to work,' Gladys said. 'She did it in the treatment room. You know that pulley thing that's up on the ceiling, for lifting patients into the bath – well, she climbed up on a stool and put the rope through that. Matron found her.'

'When was this?' Linda gave Gladys her undivided attention. 'I've never 'eard that one before.'

'Five years ago,' Gladys said. 'I hadn't been here long enough to know much about Lily, who was a bit odd by all accounts. The other girls reckoned she'd been jilted and they found she was pregnant at the post-mortem. Don't let on to Matron I told you though. That's one of the grisly secrets of Carrington Hall she likes kept quiet. Same as she doesn't like people talking about that patient who jumped out the window and broke both her legs.'

Rosie forced herself to sip her tea. The girls' conversation washed around and over her, but she cut it out, concentrating her mind on looking and reacting normally, until the moment she could get up and leave the room without drawing any further attention to herself.

Although she hadn't read another newspaper since the night she dreamt about Seth chasing her, she'd still heard enough from the other staff to know what was going on.

While Seth had built up a strong defence with his apparent lack of motive and sound alibis and managed to gather some sympathy because of his mother's neglect and bullying father, Cole's defence was very weak. His alibis at both murders could not be corroborated by anyone but his sons. In the case of Heather's death, he had first said he was away in Bristol all week, then later admitted he'd come home for a couple of nights leaving Seth alone in the digs.

Pathologists had found that both women had been struck by a similar weapon, they thought the blunt end of an axe. Ruby appeared to have been hit several times either before or after the fatal blow to the base of the neck. Heather on the other hand appeared to have been hit only twice, again at the base of the neck. Although there was no witness to either murder, or indeed proof that Parker had dug the graves, testimonies from Ethel Parker and other neighbours about his violence towards his women weighed heavily against him. But it was the fact that he had reported neither woman missing which sealed his fate. Clearly the jury didn't believe that an innocent man would just accept that his women had run off leaving their children behind, without making some attempt to find them.

'What's the matter?' Maureen said as she got into bed that evening. Rosie had gone to bed early, explaining that she was overtired. Maureen had stayed downstairs in the staff room for a while, but she came up unexpectedly around nine and found Rosie not only wide awake but with eyes swollen from crying. 'You can tell me. I won't tell anyone else.'

Rosie would have given anything to have someone to confide in, but she knew there wasn't anyone she could trust, and least of all Maureen.

'I'm just homesick,' she said, trying to smile.

In a way that was true. For the last couple of hours she'd thought of nothing else but home, and precious memories of her father.

Sitting on his shoulders, high above the crowds of people at the Christmas Eve fair at Midsomer Norton, the dozens of stalls lit by hurricane lamps. Hands sticky from toffee apples, tightly clutching a bag full of tangerines, nuts and pomegranates. She could remember loading the goose he always bought at the auction, the new barrel of cider, and a box of vegetables into the truck, and then having a blanket tucked round her while Cole went for one last drink of whisky before he drove her and the Christmas treats home.

Days at Weston-super-Mare in the summer, paddling in the sea, building sandcastles, riding donkeys and eating candyfloss. And the nights by the fire in the winter when the wind howled round the cottage and Cole would tell her of his childhood when the River Parrett burst its banks every winter and turned the moors into one big lake.

'You aren't thinking of leaving here?' Maureen asked, and the anxious look in her eyes made Rosie feel even guiltier because she didn't trust her. 'I don't think I could bear it if you were to go.'

'No, I'm not thinking of leaving,' Rosie sighed. She wished she could truthfully say she'd grown as attached to Maureen as Maureen obviously had to her, but she couldn't. She tolerated Maureen, stuck up for her to the others, but she couldn't really like her. As Linda had said, Maureen was odd; she might be cleaner now, and too loyal to Rosie to steal anything or get her into trouble, but there was something underhand and sneaky about her.

'You know that Parker family, don't you?' Maureen said in an accusatory tone.

Rosie felt another cold chill go down her spine.

'What on earth makes you think that?' she said quickly, hoping she wasn't blushing.

'Because you haven't once talked about them, like we all do. And I know it was that news which made you go all faint.'

'You've got too much imagination for your own good,' Rosie said with a sniff. That phrase had been a favourite one of her teacher's, and it seemed appropriate now. 'If you must know, I think there's something weird about people who are obsessed with murder. Now for heaven's sake stop keeping on at me.'

Rosie was very glad she'd had her day off changed to Friday, as it meant that the next day she'd be able to get out of Carrington Hall and escape any further discussion. But even though she wanted to just walk in the countryside, she awoke to find it pouring with rain and the library seemed the only sensible place to go.

There were no more than four or five people in the whole place, and only one old man reading the newspapers. Rosie hung her soaking raincoat up on a peg, and taking a seat as far away from the old man as possible, read one paper after another until she felt she had the complete picture of what had taken place in the courtroom over the past weeks.

She wondered how her father could stick to his plea of innocence, when he freely admitted that he was hot-tempered and sometimes hit women. He hadn't denied any of the things Ethel said he did, except branding her with a hot iron, which had been virtually discounted by medical evidence anyway. His coarse words were that 'she asked for trouble'. His barrister managed to cast doubt on her testimony because she ran off with another man and showed no concern for her children. But where Ruby and Heather were concerned, he could offer nothing substantial to sway the jury into believing in his client's innocence, other than that Cole had no reason to kill them.

The barrister had played long and hard on Cole's fierce masculinity and asked him questions to try and bring out his deep shame and hurt that two more women he loved had left him, to try and show that this was the only reason he hadn't reported their disappearance. But Cole had remained unemotional and inarticulate. His plea that he was afraid his daughter might have been taken away from him didn't ring entirely true, particularly as he had freely admitted he had no time for Alan.

When the prosecution summed up the evidence there was really no debate or deliberation necessary to find him guilty. As the barrister pointed out, 'Maybe someone with a grudge against Cole Parker could have come to the cottage and killed his women. But were they then likely to bury the women tidily and efficiently on his land, all before he got back from his work?'

Rosie could just about accept that her father may have killed both women in a fit of temper because they said or did something he didn't like. But when she read the lies that both her brothers had told about Heather she almost screamed out her anger right there in the library. They claimed that Heather was a loose, slovenly girl who had preyed on their father's vulnerability, citing how quickly she had ended up in his bed and produced another child for him to keep. According to them she drank cider all day, and they'd heard it rumoured that men were seen calling at the cottage during the day when they were out. Seth even said he believed Alan wasn't Cole's son.

Rosie's heart went out to Thomas. She could imagine what it had done to him to hear such filth. She had never been more ashamed and disgusted by her brothers.

When Norman spoke of the night he and Cole had come home from Birmingham to find Ruby gone, he was speaking the truth, because it was just as Rosie re-membered it. She had been left with a neighbour called

Mrs Mirrel that day, while Ruby went to visit a sick friend. Norman said Cole had only said Ruby was killed in an air raid because he thought Rosie could deal with death better than abandonment.

Norman could not comment about Heather's disappearance as he was away doing his National Service, but he'd been told that his sister had come home from school to find Heather and her belongings gone and baby Alan still strapped in his pram down in the orchard.

The prosecution drew Norman's attention to the testimonies given by several neighbours and the village school mistress who all said that both women were conscientious mothers who would never walk away from their children. He asked Norman to consider this. Norman pointed out that these same neighbours had also claimed his own mother was conscientious, yet she most definitely had cleared off and left two small boys on their own.

When Rosie saw a photograph of Seth grinning triumphantly outside Bristol court after his acquittal, she felt sick. He looked the way he always had when he'd got away with something. He didn't even care that his father was on his way to a condemned cell. She knew then without any doubt that he was guilty. Maybe he hadn't actually killed the women, but he had created the trouble which had led to Cole losing his temper. She was certain that he'd helped dig the graves too. Rosie just knew her father wouldn't have gone through that alone.

She spent the afternoon walking in the rain, unaware of where she was going, taking paths across fields as she came to them, almost blinded by tears. In a few weeks' time her father would be hanged in Bristol prison, his body sprinkled with quick lime and buried there without a marker or prayers.

But it was her own guilt which stabbed her like a knife through the heart. She should have gone to the police and told them about Seth, just as she should have told her father what she'd seen Seth and Norman do to Heather when it happened. She should have been brave enough to insist on being a witness; perhaps if she'd been able to tell the judge and jury her view of her family, the outcome might have been different.

But it was too late now. Seth couldn't be tried for the same crime again. It wouldn't save her father and all it would do would be to hurt Thomas more.

She wondered how Thomas felt today? Another less sensitive man might celebrate, but she knew he would be too keenly hurt by the things her brothers had said about Heather to even feel satisfaction at the verdict. She doubted she would ever hear from him again.

There was no doubt in her mind either that Seth and Norman would soon be in some sort of trouble again, now they no longer had their father to hide behind. She never wanted to see either of them again as long as she lived.

As Rosie was walking through rain-sodden fields, crying to herself, Matron was in her sitting-room, her stockinged feet up on a stool in front of an electric fire, smiling triumphantly to herself.

The newspaper was on her lap, but she'd read everything she wanted to. She knew now who Rosemary Smith was.

There was no hard or fast proof of course, just guesswork, and a couple of pointed remarks from Maureen Jackson. But nurses and doctors often made an accurate diagnosis based on nothing more than a few symptoms, some pertinent questions, and guesswork.

The girl was the right age, from the right area, shielded by a social worker, and of course mental homes were ideal places to hide away misfits. They hadn't even had the intelligence to change her name dramatically. Rosemary Smith was Rosie Parker, the only daughter of the man dubbed the 'Moorland Monster'.

But what was she going to do with the knowledge?

Her first thought had been to call a staff meeting and

denounce her in public now while the news was hot. But after a moment or two's thought she guessed Lionel would be very angry with her if she did that. If it got around it might place the future of Carrington Hall in jeopardy. Besides, just throwing the girl out would be a hollow victory. On top of that the girl was also a good worker and she'd be hard to replace.

Weighing it all up, Freda thought she'd do just what she always did when a juicy bit of information came her way and keep it to herself for the time being. It might be a trump card to have up her sleeve at a later date. She folded the pages of the paper containing the story and pictures of the Parker men and tucked them away in her desk.

On Saturday morning of the following week Matron swept into the day room just as Rosie and Simmonds were stacking the breakfast things on to the trolley. Maureen was moving the chairs back against the wall assisted by Donald. The rest of the patients were scattered around the room, some merely standing and staring at nothing, others in chairs rocking themselves. Tabby was knitting frantically. It was tipping down with rain outside again and both Rosie and Maureen had already discussed that it would be a long day today as they wouldn't be able to take any of the patients out into the garden.

'Smith, come here,' Matron said curtly.

Rosie moved over to the older woman, expecting some sort of complaint. She hadn't been herself all week, even though she'd tried to hide it. The least little thing had set her off crying – a difficult patient, a sharp word from one of the other girls – and her mind had been continually on her father, imagining him in that cell awaiting death.

Her sixteenth birthday had come and gone and she hadn't had the heart to mention it to anyone, much less plan some kind of celebration. There had been a white fluffy angora jumper from Miss Pemberton and a nice card signed by Auntie Molly, but that was all and so it had gone unnoticed by everyone.

Even the weather depressed her; it had rained almost constantly, the trees were losing their leaves and when she looked out of the windows the views were as bleak and cheerless as her future. She thought Matron must have heard she was off-colour and was going to take her to task for it.

To her surprise, Matron smiled at her. It completely changed her face, everything grew wider, her eyes and her mean mouth, and for a brief second she actually looked quite attractive.

'Mr and Mrs Cook, Donald's parents, are coming to see him this afternoon,' she said in a low, almost conspiratorial tone. 'I want you to make sure he has a bath, and give him his best clothes. I'd also like you to accompany him for the visit. Mrs Trow will let you know when they arrive.'

'Yes, Matron,' Rosie replied. When a patient had guests, a chargehand or nurse had to be present throughout the entire visit. Rosie had heard about patients who got agitated, sometimes violent when relatives called, but in Donald's case this was very unlikely. She wondered why Matron was singling her out for a job which normally went to the senior staff.

'Make sure your apron is clean and your hair neat and tidy,' Matron said, looking her up and down. 'I want to create a good impression for the Cooks. I told them on the telephone that you seem to have formed a close relationship with Donald, and it was they who requested to meet you.'

Coming from anyone else, Rosie would have considered this praise. But Matron was a very odd woman and Rosie had a feeling that today was to be some kind of test.

'Can I tell Donald?' Rosie asked. 'Or will you?'

'You can inform him, but for goodness' sake don't get him too excited,' she said as she turned to walk away.

It would have been too much to expect Matron to just

leave without finding fault with anything. Ignoring Alice who shuffled over to speak to her, she crossed to the windows and ran one finger along the sill, moved a couple of chairs and sniffed.

'The chairs are supposed to be moved when the floor is washed over,' she said tartly. 'Jackson! The hem of your uniform is coming down. Fix it before I catch sight of it again.'

'Witch,' Maureen muttered once the woman had left, Simmonds close behind her with the breakfast trolley. 'Have you noticed she never even speaks to the patients, you'd think they were just bits of furniture. What did she want you for?'

Linda often joked that Maureen would be a natural successor to Matron if she learned to read. She certainly made it her business, like Matron, to know everything that went on in Carrington Hall. Yet Rosie thought Linda was too harsh; in her view Maureen was to be pitied because she was in fact more like one of the inmates than a member of staff. Because of this Rosie never told her to mind her own business when she asked questions, as the others did. So she related the entire conversation between her and Matron.

'Why did she pick on me do you think?' she asked.

Maureen shrugged. 'Search me! But don't complain, Mr and Mrs Cook are nice and you'll have a far better afternoon than I will up here. Some people get all the luck.'

Donald got very excited when Rosie told him the news. He jumped around the day room like a kangaroo and finally flopped down on his back, drumming his heels noisily on the floor.

Rosie suddenly felt a little better as she watched Donald with affectionate amusement. She felt he had the personality and behaviour of a large puppy. Many of the patients like Aggie and Archie still repelled her, some were exasperating, but Donald was just lovable. If he wasn't nearly six feet tall, and didn't have to shave every day, anyone could just think of him as a child. He had been assessed as having a mental age of eight, but Rosie had discovered he could read a little and she was privately convinced that if books, jigsaw puzzles and board games were provided in the day room, then he could learn a great deal more than he already knew.

'Get up, Donald,' she said, resisting the temptation to tickle him and make him laugh more. 'You can come and help me with the cleaning and making the beds. If you carry on like that all morning, everyone will get cross with you. Me included.'

One of the saddest things of all in Carrington Hall, as far as Rosie was concerned, was that all the patients were lumped together and treated as being on the same level as the most severely retarded ones. Even though she'd only been here for such a short time, with no previous experience of people with mental handicaps, she felt there should be times in the day when the more able ones should be separated and given things to do. She had suggested this to Mary once, but she just laughed at her, and said Matron wouldn't like it because they'd need more staff.

Rosie wasn't brave enough to do anything Matron didn't like; she sensed that would be asking for trouble. Besides, no one else on the staff shared her views; they all liked to just sit, chat, read, or knit while the patients shuffled about aimlessly. Even Maureen, who did talk to them, was as bone idle as the rest. That was why Rosie ended up doing almost all of the daily cleaning.

But Rosie had worked on Donald quite a bit, particularly during the last week when she'd wanted something to take her mind off her father. She had brought in a gardening book to read and showed Donald the pictures of the flowers, getting him to learn many of the names. Another time she had let him do a dot-to-dot puzzle in a magazine and had been surprised to find that he recognized most numbers. In the main, however, her progress with Donald had been in talking to him as they made the beds and cleaned. Sometimes he dropped the stuttering for long periods and he loved playing a game with her where she made up a few lines of a story, then made him finish it. Sadly his imagination didn't stretch beyond Carrington Hall. She might start a story with two little girls going on a train to London, eating their sandwiches and having a drink of lemonade, but invariably when he continued it would always be with something like, 'Then Matron told them to put on their shoes and coats because it was time to go down to the garden.'

Perhaps it was purely because she knew her father would never see the outside world again that her thoughts had turned to wanting freedom for Donald. He had done nothing wrong, yet he was imprisoned too and it wasn't fair. She wished that she could take him out to the shops, or just for a walk in the countryside, to buy him a comic, take him on a bus, or let him see a field of cows. She wondered if she might get a chance to broach this subject with the Cooks.

As they washed over the dormitory floor that morning, Rosie sang to Donald. She began with 'Molly Malone', then as that pleased him she sang 'The Teddy Bears' Picnic'.

'I kn-kn-know that one,' he said, interrupting her. To her surprise he began to sing along with her, no stutter, no hesitation, and he knew most of the words.

'Who taught you that song?' she asked, after they'd been through it several times.

'Mother,' he said and his face glowed with pleasure. 'Sh-sh-she used to s-s-sing it when I went to b-b-bed.'

Rosie prompted him to tell her more. He remembered feeding ducks, going on a swing and rolling out pastry.

Some of the other patients occasionally recalled things from their childhood. Tabby remembered the seaside, Archie talked about trains, but their reminiscing was very disjointed and it was impossible to guess how old they were at the time, or even who they'd been with. With Donald the memories were very lucid. She felt the song had been the key which unlocked them and Rosie wondered briefly just how much more she could achieve with him if she had a free hand.

At two-thirty Mrs Trow came to say that Mr and Mrs Cook were waiting downstairs. Donald had been bathed, his hair washed and his fingernails cleaned before dinner. Now in his own pale blue sweater, grey flannel slacks and a white open-necked shirt he looked very smart, quite different from how he looked every other day. He held Rosie's hand very tightly as they went downstairs, and she was almost as nervous as he was.

The visitors' sitting-room overlooked the front garden. Because of so many trees growing close to the window, it was a rather dark room, but as it was raining hard outside and someone had lit a cheerful fire, it looked very cosy and, compared to the austerity of the rest of the building, extremely comfortable.

Mr and Mrs Cook were both older than Rosie had expected; she thought they were in their early sixties. Mr Cook was a big man, with a ruddy complexion and a large stomach. Although his hair was thin and grey he had very dark bushy eyebrows which gave an impression of sternness. His wife was a small, dainty woman dressed in a dark blue fitted coat and a matching cloche hat. Her hair was more white than grey, indicating she had been a blonde like her son, and her skin was very soft-looking, not lined exactly but more like a peach once it is past its best.

Donald ran straight to his mother, enveloping her in one of his bear hugs and sniffing rapturously at her perfume. Rosie stood back, feeling self-conscious and superfluous. She knew why a member of staff had to stay in the room, but she couldn't see Donald escaping or throwing some sort of tantrum, not when he was so thrilled to see his parents.

Mrs Cook had tears in her eyes when Donald finally let her go. Rosie glanced at Mr Cook as Donald went to embrace him; his eyes were swimming too, although he tried to hide this from both Rosie and his wife.

'This is Smith,' Donald said suddenly, taking Rosie by surprise as he bounded back across the room towards her and caught hold of her hand. 'She's my f-f-friend.'

'Then Miss Smith had better come over and sit with us.' Mr Cook smiled at her, and it warmed Rosie.

For the first part of his parents' visit, Donald chattered non-stop, about what he'd had for meals, the other patients, even about the rain and how it stopped them all going into the garden. His parents seemed quite happy just to listen, though Rosie felt it was sad he wasn't asking them questions about home. Then quite suddenly Donald jumped up from the settee where he'd been sitting with his mother and, holding her hand, dragged her over to the window.

'Those are M-M-Michaelmas daisies,' he said, pointing out a clump of the purple flowers just outside the window. 'Smith s-s-said they are p-p-perennials, that means they come up every year.'

This display of a remembered lesson astonished Rosie, but Donald went on, pointing out other flowers. There weren't many, as the front garden wasn't kept well like the back, but he got all the names right.

Mrs Cook looked at Rosie quizzically.

'I like gardening,' Rosie said by way of an explanation. 'I've been telling Donald a bit about it when we're out in the back garden.'

'And you show me the book,' Donald reminded her excitedly. 'Smith is nice, Mummy, she gets me to show her the words I can read in magazines and she tells me stories and sings songs.'

The most extraordinary thing was that Donald didn't

stutter once in that last statement. His father sat up straight in his chair, seemingly more aware of that than the content of what Donald had said.

As the visit went on, Donald talked more and more about 'Smith', to the extent that Rosie began to squirm. Pat Clack brought in tea. Mr and Mrs Cook told Donald about his older brother, Michael, who had a new baby called Robin, and they got out some photographs to show him. Rosie felt easier then as Donald was at last weaned off her as a subject.

Rosie hadn't lost her curiosity since coming to Carrington Hall, and as Donald chattered to his parents she was glad of the opportunity to study them. She had never met anyone rich before and she had expected wealth to show on people like a badge. But it didn't show on the Cooks, at least not in the flamboyant way she had imagined. They had good clothes – Mrs Cook's blue coat looked as if it had been made to measure and the cluster of blue stones on her brooch weren't just glass. Her shoes were dainty crocodile ones which matched her handbag, and there was the big, gleaming black car outside in the drive. But they didn't put on any airs and graces.

Donald had the same sad blue eyes, wide mouth and fair hair as his mother, but he'd inherited his father's height and his slightly jutting jaw. But what pleased Rosie most about these people was their real pleasure in being with their son. She didn't once see them sneaking a look at a watch, or hear a yawn; they laughed with him, encouraged him to talk. This was no duty visit from rich people who'd abandoned their child because he was an embarrassment to them. They really did love him and they were reluctant to leave him.

She wondered if they knew Donald hadn't worn the clothes he had on today since their last visit, or that the rest of the time he wore whatever happened to fit him from the store room. She wondered too if they had any idea how bleak the day room was, or how many scratches and bruises he'd had from other less placid patients. Would Mrs Cook be shocked if she saw he had to eat his food with a spoon, or spend the night smelling other patients' urine or worse until the morning? She was pretty certain they knew none of this.

At four Rosie tactfully reminded the couple that Donald had to go back to the ward. Donald got up, hugged both his parents and made for the door quite cheerfully, without any protest. But as Rosie went to follow him Mrs Cook caught hold of the sleeve of her cardigan.

'Miss Smith,' she said in a low voice. 'Could you come back down after you've taken Donald upstairs? We'd like to speak to you in private.'

Rosie felt very uneasy as she returned five minutes later. Matron didn't approve of staff becoming involved with patients, her excuse being that the patients suffered when the member of staff left. Rosie thought this might be why Matron had asked her to meet the Cooks today, guessing that Donald would make too much of her and upset them. Matron always took Saturday afternoons off, so she was probably sitting somewhere gloating over the thought of her most junior chargehand getting a dressing down.

But as Rosie came back into the sitting-room, both Mr and Mrs Cook beamed at her.

'We've never seen our son in such good spirits,' Donald's mother said, patting the settee for Rosie to sit beside her. 'I just felt compelled to say thank you for taking care of him.'

'You taught him flower names and he remembered them,' Mr Cook said. 'In fact today he seemed almost, well, normal.'

'He is normal,' Rosie said with some indignation. 'He's just a bit simple, that's all.'

Almost the second the words left her mouth she regretted them. She had no business to be airing her views on a patient. That was the doctor's or Matron's job. She waited to be slapped down, not daring to look at either parent.

'I'm sorry,' she said, still hanging her head. 'I shouldn't have said that. It's just that I like Donald.'

'You should say what you think,' Mrs Cook said, and her voice seemed to have a smile in it rather than anger.

Rosie glanced up and saw the woman was indeed smiling, and those eyes which had looked sad before were now sparkling with amusement. 'You've just said words that every mother in my position wants to hear,' she said. 'But I'm very curious as to why you think you shouldn't have said it.'

'Because I've only been here a few weeks. Because I'm too young and inexperienced to have an opinion about Donald.'

'It couldn't be that you are afraid of displeasing Matron?' Mr Cook asked pointedly, raising one thick eyebrow. 'Anything you might like to say to us, Miss Smith, we will treat as confidential. We asked you to come back down because we sensed you really were our son's friend. So we want your opinion, regardless of whether you feel too young or too inexperienced for it to be of any value.'

Rosie looked at Mrs Cook, then back to her husband. They both had identical open expressions on their faces, and she knew they really did want the truth.

'I don't think he needs to be here,' she blurted out. 'In fact, if you don't mind me saying so, I think it's going to make him worse if he stays here much longer.'

Suddenly she didn't care if she got the sack, there was a fiery ball of anger inside her which she had to let go. The world was full of injustice and prejudice and maybe giving her opinion on Donald wouldn't change that, but if she did speak out, his life might improve.

She told them everything – the lack of stimulation, of Donald being subjected to seeing and hearing disturbing things. She couldn't quite bring herself to tell the tale Linda had reported, that Archie had been caught once or twice trying to make Donald masturbate him, or that all the girls were a little anxious about what went on in the

235

dormitories after the patients had been locked in for the night. But she said how she wished she could take him out to the shops or on a bus ride, of her certainty that with a little help he could learn a great deal more. Finally she told them how he'd sung 'The Teddy Bears' Picnic' and said that he remembered his mother singing it to him.

'I'm so sorry,' she said, as Mrs Cook dabbed her eyes. 'I didn't mean to upset you by telling you that. It's just that he has got a good memory and he's capable of doing so much more than he gets a chance to do here.'

'Miss Smith, you are very young,' Mr Cook said, putting one big hand on her shoulder. 'You are also disturbingly frank. But we are touched by your concern for our son and very grateful to you for sharing your views with us.'

'We never wanted to send Donald away,' Mrs Cook said in a quavering voice. 'We were coerced into it. People talked about him, blamed him for all sorts of things and we were afraid for him. A year ago Matron said she thought it would be kinder to him if we were not to come so often. She said he was always distressed afterwards. But it hurts us so much to stay away.'

Rosie was tempted to say she was certain this was rubbish, but she knew she'd said too much already. 'I can't say anything about that as I wasn't here last time you visited,' she said. 'But if it will make you feel better I could drop you a line in the next day or so and tell you how he was after this visit?'

'You'd do that?' Mrs Cook looked very surprised.

'Only if you promise not to let on to Matron,' Rosie said. 'But don't write back to me, will you, because someone might see the letter.'

The couple looked at one another for a moment. Rosie thought she'd gone too far.

Mr Cook cleared his throat. 'I'll tell you what,' he said, reaching into the inside pocket of his suit jacket and drawing out a card. 'This is our address and telephone number. Could we impose on you to telephone us sometimes in

236

the evenings, that way we could talk about Donald more easily. You can reverse the charges.'

Rosie had never had any cause to use a telephone. She didn't have the first idea about how to go about it. But she wasn't going to admit that. She would find out how to do it.

'Okay,' she said, slipping the card into her pocket. 'But I ought to go now, if that's all right with you.'

'Thank you so much.' Mrs Cook got up and took Rosie's hand. She didn't shake it but pressed it between her two hands. 'We'll sleep a great deal easier knowing Donald has you as a friend.'

Rosie left them, hurrying out before someone noted how long she'd been speaking with the couple. She glanced at the card, saw an address in Sussex, and put it away in her pocket, reminding herself she would need to tuck that away from both Matron's and Maureen's prying eyes.

On Monday evening Rosie made her first telephone call to the Cooks from the telephone box outside the library. She was surprised to find it very easy, and even more astounded to hear Mrs Cook's voice as if she was just a little further down the street. It was a happy call. Donald had suffered no ill effects from their visit; if anything he was brighter and more contented than he'd been before. Rosie promised she would telephone again next month, unless his parents managed to get up again before that.

As she walked back later to Carrington Hall she saw some girls of her age waiting at a bus stop. They were giggling and pushing one another, excited as if they were going somewhere special. She paused in a shop doorway to watch them, and felt a pang of envy. None of them was any better dressed than she, they were all wearing quite shabby old gabardine school raincoats left open to show off their quite ordinary dresses, but the way they'd made up their faces and curled their hair reminded her that every other sixteen-year-old in London probably knew more about make-up and hairstyles than she did.

As the bus came along Rosie walked on thinking that perhaps it was time she dropped her country-girl look and took up Linda's and Mary's offer to take her dancing with them. If nothing else it might take her mind off her father. It might even make the ache inside her a little less, and the future a bit brighter.

She hesitantly broached the subject with Linda and Mary and they gave her no opportunity to back out at the last moment and bought a ticket for her for the dance on the following Saturday at the local parish hall.

'It won't be anything to be scared of,' Linda insisted. 'There's always more girls than fellas there and all you can drink is lemonade. But it's a good place to give you confidence.'

The following evening Linda taught her the rudiments of the waltz, and Mary went through her few clothes to sort out what she would wear.

Rosie couldn't say she truly enjoyed the dance. The hall looked pretty enough decorated with balloons and streamers, but she felt silly shuffling around the floor with Mary, trying hard to pretend she could really waltz. The girls outnumbered the boys two to one and she felt very old-fashioned in her print summer dress next to the local girls who were all decked out in copies of American fashions with tight sweaters and full skirts. The mascara Linda had insisted she wore made her eyes feel sore and her feet ached in a borrowed pair of Mary's high heels. But she liked the band. They all wore dark blue jackets and dickey bows and they played after the fashion of Victor Sylvester, which seemed terribly sophisticated. She made up her mind she would learn to dance properly and spend all her wages on some fashionable clothes before she ventured out with them again.

*

November passed very slowly. Eisenhower won the American presidential elections on the 4th. On the 18th, Jomo Kenyatta was charged as head of the Mau Mau, but though Rosie tried to interest herself in world news, she could see no further ahead than her father's impending execution. The other girls spoke expectantly of Christmas. Each night in the staff room the sewing machine whirred as Linda made dolls' clothes for her nieces, and Mary's knitting needles clicked away as she struggled to finish a cardigan for her mother before her visit to Ireland.

But Rosie had no one she wanted to make a present for. Her father was on her mind from first thing in the morning, until she fell asleep at night, but somehow she had to keep up the pretence of being interested in anything and everyone. There was an appeal, but it was lost, and she was aware that Cole would now be in the condemned cell, watched every minute of the day and night.

Rosie wrote him one last letter, enclosing it with one to Miss Pemberton, asking that she got it to him. She had so much to say, but yet so very little. Finally all she managed was to say he was in her thoughts and that she loved him.

On the eve of Friday, the 4th of December, she didn't sleep a wink. Cole was to be hanged at eight in the morning. She kept the night-long vigil with him, turning over and over in her mind all the good memories, and praying silently that he would stay calm and his death would be quick.

As Friday was her day off, Rosie feigned deep sleep when the alarm went off at six-thirty. Once Maureen had gone downstairs she sat up in bed with the clock in front of her and watched the hands moving slowly towards the time of her father's execution.

By five to eight she was sobbing uncontrollably with fear and grief. Cole's face was so clear in her mind, it was almost as if he was standing before her. Dark, dark eyes full of sorrow, all bravado and swagger gone. She mentally kissed and hugged him, recalling the soapy smell of him in the mornings and offered up a prayer that he would sense her presence too at his moment of death.

She seemed to see him being brought out of his cell, hands tied behind his back and flanked by two prison officers. In her heart she knew he would keep his courage and pride even when they put the sack over his head and the rope around his neck.

'God bless you, Daddy,' she whispered as the hands finally reached eight. 'I love you. And I forgive you.'

Chapter Eight

'Get this down you, Smith.' Linda pushed a tumbler of gin and orange into Rosie's hands and passed another to Mary who was putting on her make-up at the dressing table.

It was New Year's Eve and the three girls were going up to the West End to join in the celebrations. Linda insisted they all got 'tanked up' as she called it, before they even left Carrington Hall as the pubs would be very crowded.

Rosie sipped the drink and shuddered. 'That's vile,' she exclaimed.

'So's sex the first time,' Linda said with a snigger. 'But that don't stop people getting the taste for it. Look at Mary! She's put the frilly knickers she had for Christmas on, just in case.'

Mary turned on the stool at the dressing table, her face pink with a combination of a liberal layer of Pan Stik make-up and indignation. 'Are you saying I'm easy?'

'Bejesus no,' Linda replied in a mocking exaggerated Irish accent. ''Aven't I been told you convent girls never let a man's 'and creep beyond your knees? So I reckon you must be gonna strip off and jump in Trafalgar Square fountain.'

'Eejit,' Mary scoffed. 'It's freezing tonight, so it is. If you must know, I was tempted to put on the warm ones Mam gave me. But I'd die of shame to be sure if I got run over and they had to peel those off me.'

Rosie sat back on the bed and sipped the sweet sticky drink. She felt happy tonight. A fun night out, a brand

241

new year ahead of her. She had already made her new year's resolution and that was to become a Londoner, in appearance, mentality and behaviour.

Londoners, as she saw it, were first in line for everything. New films and plays, fashions, crazes, all began here. Elsewhere in England people were still living in much the same way as they had before the war, seemingly unaware that a whole decade had passed by. Yet here in London, despite the wholesale destruction caused by bombs, they were moving on, clearing the bomb sites, tearing down damaged houses and rebuilding. Rosie felt that Londoners were faster and more forward-thinking than their country counterparts. They embraced the new ideas from America with enthusiasm – modern housing, refrigerators, vacuum cleaners and motor cars alike.

Their exuberance for life and progress was clearly illustrated in the newspapers, where even the most momentous news story was swiftly eclipsed and forgotten by something more dramatic. This point was driven home to Rosie at the time of her father's hanging. It commanded space on every front page on the day, but the next it dropped like a stone in favour of the names Christopher Craig and Derek Bentley. They had shot a policeman while robbing a sweet warehouse in south London and they were portrayed as young hoodlums who had grown up on a diet of American gangster films. Both boys were found guilty of murder on the 11th of December, but although sixteen-year-old Craig actually fired the gun, his companion, nineteen-year-old, simple-minded Bentley, was deemed to be equally guilty because the pair of them had set out on a felonious enterprise together. Because of Craig's age he was sentenced to be detained at Her Majesty's Pleasure, while Bentley, despite a recommendation for mercy from the jury, was given the death sentence.

Rosie had been very relieved that the public's attention was being diverted away from her father. It was difficult enough hiding her grief and coping with the feeling that she would never, ever get over it, without constant jolts. As Christmas had crept closer and all the staff spoke of their families, her main preoccupation was getting through each day without breaking down over hers.

Yet much as she had dreaded Christmas, it had in fact been a turning point.

Two days before, the girls had decorated the day room with paper chains, garlands and balloons. On Christmas Eve the entire staff including Matron sang carols to the patients on the first floor and each of them was given a small bar of chocolate and a tangerine.

On Christmas morning after breakfast the verger from the local church had arrived dressed as Santa Claus with a sack of presents. The patients were thrilled, they clapped their hands, stamped their feet and for once there were no fights or squabbling. Everyone had two presents – whether these came from their families or were arranged by Matron, she had no idea – but they all had a remarkably similar value and content, mainly cardigans and slippers.

Even the Christmas dinner was a jolly occasion with the day-room table laid with red paper, crackers and paper hats. All the domestic staff on duty came upstairs to help wait at the table. As Rosie cut up food and passed it round, she suddenly realized that she no longer felt repelled by any of the patients. Seeing them sitting around the table in their party hats, faces lit up with excitement, she felt affection and indeed amusement, for it was a little like watching a chimps' tea party.

She was still wary of Tabby. Archie could be absolutely disgusting what with his dribbling, masturbating and the often soiled pants, but she had overcome her revulsion enough to talk to him, brush his hair and jolly him along. Aggie with her bad legs, no nose and dome-shaped head was strange, but no longer scary. Maud was just like a little girl, old Patty and Alice were harmless, gentle souls, and as for Donald, well, she'd grown so fond of him she couldn't quite imagine a day without him.

Perhaps Carrington Hall was a place where human rejects were dumped so as not to offend the sensibilities of so-called normal people. Maybe some of the staff were almost as batty, but at that moment Rosie was glad she was there.

It crossed her mind later that for the severely disturbed patients upstairs it was probably just like any other day, as there was the usual muffled screaming and wailing. No one sang them carols and there was no mention of Santa Claus going on up there. But she asked no questions. She felt she'd had her share of sadness in the past few months, without looking for more things to upset her.

The day staff had their Christmas dinner in the evening. Fortunately Matron had been invited out and Staff Nurse Aylwood, who was equally forbidding, had chosen not to join them, so Linda said that was worthy of a celebration and scooted off to her room to collect a hidden bottle of sweet sherry.

It was a good evening. Everyone was in high spirits, and Pat Clack had surpassed herself in cooking a truly memorable meal. They gave each other little presents, pulled crackers and wore the paper hats. Mary made everyone laugh with her exploits in Ireland; she'd been over there for four days and only arrived back on Christmas Eve. Linda gave a hilarious speech, pretending to be Matron giving her last talk before retiring, in which she revealed where she got her training for Carrington Hall: lion-tamer in a circus, governor of Holloway prison, chief torturer in the Gestapo and a missionary in Africa bringing 'the word' to a tribe of cannibals.

Rosie was a little tiddly when she went to bed that night. After the sherry, Pat Clack had brought in some home-made gooseberry wine. It tasted so nice she gulped down two large glasses without realizing how potent it was. Mary told her the next day she'd been singing Ruby Murray's 'Softly, Softly' very loudly as they went up the stairs, and they'd had to gag her. But it was just as well she was a bit drunk, it stopped her thinking about Alan in the midst of his new family. Or how Christmas used to be at May Cottage with the table in the parlour all laid nicely and Dad carving the goose, wearing the tiny toy policeman's helmet he dug out every year.

When the shops opened after Christmas, Rosie had bought the new outfit she was wearing tonight, New Year's Eve – a black and white houndstooth-checked dress with a fashionable gored shirt and white collar and cuffs. She felt sophisticated wearing lipstick, mascara and her hair tied back at the nape of her neck with a black velvet bow. Linda had said she looked like a London girl now, and Rosie believed if she could achieve the right look so easily, she could just as easily stop herself looking back over her shoulder, and become whatever she wanted to be.

'Drink that!' Linda ordered as she saw Rosie staring into space, the glass in her hand still nearly full. 'Wherever do you pop off to? I never saw anyone drift off into a dream world as often as you do.'

'She's away with Donald, to be sure,' Mary said with a giggle.

Rosie pulled herself together, all at once aware that she had been doing exactly what she'd planned not to – drifting back into the past. 'I was not dreaming of Donald,' she said, and laughed because all the staff pulled her leg about the two of them. It was true she had become very fond of him, and Donald missed her terribly on her day off. She just wished they wouldn't make smutty jokes about him and call him her boyfriend.

'I was just thinking how gorgeous you both look,' she went on, hastily gulping down some of the drink. Mary was wearing a pale blue shirtwaister dress her mother had made for her; it matched her eyes perfectly and with her blonde hair set in sleek waves she looked like a plump beauty queen.

Linda, although not naturally pretty, looked very

attractive tonight in a slinky red wool dress and her face made up. Mary had set her hair for her. It was a froth of dark curls, swept over to one side and secured with a glittery hair slide.

Linda beamed at Rosemary's compliment. To her mind one of the best things about this new girl was her knack of making others feel better about themselves. She was even touched by the patience and affection she had for Donald. Heaven knows none of the others could be bothered with him. Normally she wouldn't want to be bothered with carting someone as young as Rosemary out for the night, but the girl was intriguing. She came across as an innocent country girl, yet there was something very strong and adult about her too. Every now and then Linda got the feeling she had some big secret. There was nothing unusual about that in Carrington Hall – most of the staff had something they wanted to hide, that was exactly why they were there. But she had resisted the urge to try and find out what Rosemary's was. She had enough secrets of her own to give her the screaming hab-dabs, without discovering anyone else's.

'Are you nearly ready now?' Linda turned her attention to Mary who was now curling her eyelashes with a pair of tongs. Mary couldn't even go out for a walk without lipstick. A night out in the West End needed a full beauty treatment.

'Five minutes,' Mary mumbled, grimacing at herself in the mirror. 'Have another drink and calm down. There's no point in going out too early and hanging about in the cold till midnight.'

Maybe it was the reference to hanging around in the cold, or just because she'd been wondering about Rosemary, but Linda was suddenly taken back to those nights in Cable Street.

She was fourteen when the war ended and just starting an apprenticeship with Cohen's Gowns in the Mile End Road, when her mum and dad got offered a council house out in Romford. While her entire family was jubilant about this step up, Linda had her misgivings. All her friends still lived in Bethnal Green, and it would be a long train journey to work. When her Auntie Babs offered her a room of her own in her flat, just five minutes from Cohen's, she saw it as a chance to gain independence.

Her ambition was to become a court dressmaker and one day make gowns for the nobs in Knightsbridge. Mr Cohen said she was the best apprentice he'd ever had, so her dream didn't seem too unrealistic and she made pin money on the side by making frocks for neighbours in her spare time.

Everything was fine until she met Sydney Greenslade. She only went out once a week dancing, visited her family each Sunday, and she was always at work on time. But Syd changed all that. He was twenty-three with black hair and merry blue eyes, and his way of life turned hers upside down. Syd was a 'Spiv'. He made his money in 'deals' in pubs and clubs at night and he wanted a girl on his arm while he made them. At first she insisted on being home by eleven, but Syd was very persuasive and he laced her up with gin so she forgot about the time and her job. Auntie Babs would have protested had she known, but she liked a drink too, and mostly she was out cold by eleven, and never guessed that Linda didn't come home until the early hours.

Soon she was in trouble with Mr Cohen, late most days and falling asleep over her sewing machine. Mr Cohen said if she didn't pull her socks up he'd sack her.

Linda tried, but she just couldn't say no to Syd. Almost every day she promised herself an early night, but as soon as she heard him blasting the horn of his car out in the road, off she would go without a second thought. Of course she couldn't hold back from going the whole way with him either, not once she'd fallen in love with him.

When she told Syd she was pregnant, she really thought he'd marry her; after all, he said he loved her every time they had it away in his car. But he just laughed at the suggestion and gave her some money, telling her to go and get herself fixed up by Ma Purdy who saw to all the girls down Cable Street.

No one warned her how much it would hurt when the baby came away. Or how weak and weepy she'd be afterwards. Mr Cohen sacked her, and on top of that Syd disappeared.

She was just sixteen when she went with a man for money. It seemed the only solution to get a few bob and tide her over until she found another job. She told herself just once wouldn't hurt, that no one would ever know. Yet it didn't work out like that.

Once she got over the disgust of the first time and realized she could earn more in five minutes than she could in a week at dressmaking, she just couldn't stop. Before long Auntie Babs found out, and slung her out. Her parents heard too, and when she turned up at Romford hoping to move back in with them, they called her a trollop, and told her in no uncertain terms to sling her hook.

So she stuck her nose in the air, said she didn't care and carried on. It was good that first summer; she was young and very much in demand, and for the first time in her life she had money. Not just a bob or two, but pounds and pounds with no one holding out their hand for some of it. She bought nice clothes, got herself a little room in Cable Street where no one cared what she did, and when she had a guilt attack, she went out drinking with the other girls.

Of course she didn't intend to stay in Cable Street; it was the worse place in the whole of the East End, dirty, smelly and rough. There were illegal gambling dives, opium dens and brothels, all patronized by sailors, dockers and villains. Almost every night she said she was going up West to find some toff who knew how to treat a girl like a lady. She boasted to the other girls she'd end up with a fancy place in Park Lane, and she believed it too. But something seemed to prevent her from getting away. Perhaps deep down she knew that a cockney tart with a plain face was never going to set the world alight.

Her second abortion nearly killed her. She was taken into the London Hospital in Whitechapel with a haemorrhage. When she was discharged nearly three weeks later, her room had been taken by someone else and all her belongings had been stolen. Another girl let her doss down on her floor for a few nights, but then she slung her out too.

Looking back, Linda couldn't imagine how she survived that winter of 1947. She was trapped in a vicious circle from which there was no way out. To get money for a room for the night she had to take the punters down for a knee trembler under the arches in Cable Street, but her rough appearance got her nothing more than the most squalid of accommodation, shared with other terrifying down-and-outs. As she became more and more unkempt and dirty it was finally only the foreign sailors who'd pay her, and sometimes they used her, then robbed her, often beating her for good measure.

Drinking gin was a temporary release from the nightmare she was living, but at four in the morning when she awoke with the cold to find herself huddled up in some derelict building or an alley, death seemed preferable to struggling through another day of humiliation and utter misery.

It was a church army woman who saved her. A funny skinny little woman in a grey coat and hat who found her early one morning lying vomiting in the gutter. She took her arm and hauled her up and said she was taking her somewhere warm to get her cleaned up.

It took six months to get her healthy again. She had lice, the clap, and a chronic chest infection. She had to hand it to those church army women – they might have looked like little grey ghosts, but they were tough. They put her in their hostel, nursed her, fed her, prayed for her and talked to her until finally she broke down and admitted she really wanted their help to change her life.

It was through them she finally came to work at Carrington Hall.

Matron knew what she was. And Linda knew what Matron was too. They reached a compromise. Matron didn't ask her to grass anyone up, and kept off her back. Linda, in return, didn't tell tales out of school about the second floor, and kept any other potential troublemakers amongst the staff in line.

Working in a loony-bin wasn't satisfying or creative like dressmaking, but it had its compensations. She was away from the East End and sordid reminders of how low she'd sunk. The pay was good, she had a decent place to live and her family managed to forgive her once they'd seen she'd turned over a new leaf.

Mostly she felt secure now, five years on. Yet every now and then, particularly when she was confronted with a little lamb like Rosemary, she was reminded of how she'd been at sixteen. Rosemary would be easy prey for anyone unscrupulous, be that Matron or some fast-talking man in a sharp suit. She had every intention of warning Rosemary about men, but she didn't quite know what she should do about Matron.

'Isn't it wonderful?' Rosie gasped as they stood in Piccadilly a couple of hours later. She could barely see Eros because of the people climbing on to it. The pavements were packed with a vast noisy, jostling, but good-natured crowd, and above and all around her were the famous neon lights she'd heard so much about but never seen before. Her neck was already aching from looking up at the ever-changing messages and advertisements flashing green, red, yellow and blue. She could stand here all night and never grow tired of it.

'It won't look so bleedin' wonderful to you if you get

lost,' Linda shouted back. 'Keep a tight 'old on my belt, and if we do get separated, come back 'ere to Swan and Edgar's so we can find you.'

They managed to squeeze into a pub later. Mary was complaining she was cold and her feet hurt. Linda was thinking to herself that she'd rather be down in the East End having a jaw with people who spoke her language, than being pushed and shoved by upper-class berks with braying voices and college scarves.

Rosie thought it was the best night of her life.

There was something in the air here in the West End that thrilled her right to the end of her frozen toes. The wisps of fog floating across the brightly lit buildings, the lights, smells and the wafts of music coming from every direction. So many people, all with cheerful faces despite having to move along at a snail's pace. The red buses, the big black taxis. It was all so marvellous.

A smell of chestnuts roasting on a brazier took her right back to market days at Midsomer Norton, but there was so much more here than she'd ever seen in Somerset. A barrel organ on one street corner, with a pet monkey in a little red coat jumping up and down on it, an old gypsy lady selling sprigs of white heather and a one-man-band marching along as proud as a louse with a drum on his back, thumping out a steady beat.

As they tried to elbow their way towards the bar, a big dark-haired man with a long white evening scarf tied rakishly round his neck turned to watch them. Rosie thought he looked a bit like Errol Flynn, the same kind of wicked grin and sparkly eyes. He saw their predicament at once. Linda was jumping up and down trying to catch the barman's eye, but she was too small to be seen behind the burly shoulders of the men who were drinking there.

'Let me buy you a drink, girls,' he called out. 'What'll it be? I'm just getting one in.'

Mary lit up like a Christmas tree to see such a good-looking man. She giggled and batted her curled eyelashes at him. 'To be sure that's very kind of you, sir. We'll have three gin and oranges, please,' she said.

Because of the density of the crowd, Rosie was edged away from Mary and Linda. She heard the man tell Mary his name was Mitch, and the way he was looking down at her and smiling attentively as she spoke back suggested he was instantly taken with her.

Rosie's drink was passed over heads to her, and as more people pushed their way towards the bar so the distance between her and her friends grew larger. She wasn't alarmed as she could still see both girls: Mary was gazing up at the big man and fluttering her eyelashes, and Linda was right next to her, waving her hand from time to time to let Rosie know they hadn't forgotten her. But Rosie was happy just to sip her drink and watch the other people in the bar. After the cold outside it was good to feel her toes getting warmer. Everyone was very jovial, considering the crush; she really didn't mind if they stayed right here until twelve instead of going down to Trafalgar Square as they'd planned.

It was some ten minutes later that Rosie noticed Mitch was leaning very close to Mary, saying something in her ear. She stood on tiptoe for a moment and saw Mary clearly; she was laughing and appeared to be agreeing with the man. A few people left the bar, creating a space and in that brief instant Rosie caught sight of Linda. Unlike Mary she wasn't laughing, in fact she looked frosty-faced. Rosie was just about to edge her way closer to find out what was going on when Linda suddenly caught hold of Mary's arm and began to drag her through the crowd, away from the man.

Rosie looked back to Mitch. As he stood a head taller than any other man around him she could see his face clearly; he looked astonished and he was saying something, but she couldn't hear what it was over all the other noise around her.

'Drink up, we're going,' Linda said curtly as she reached Rosie, still holding on tightly to Mary who looked none too pleased. Rosie obediently downed the rest of her drink in one and followed them outside.

It was less crowded on the pavement outside the pub compared with how it had been when they went in. It felt very cold after the heat inside and everyone was surging in one direction, she assumed down to Trafalgar Square.

Mary struggled to get free of Linda's grip. 'I don't want to go down there,' she said in a sullen voice. 'It's too cold and it will be more fun at his party. You two go to Trafalgar Square if that's what you want. I'm staying with Mitch.'

Rosie was very surprised. It had been Mary's idea to come to the West End tonight, she who had persuaded Matron to extend the ten-thirty curfew by a couple of hours. She was just about to ask what was going on, when Linda rounded on Mary.

'You bloody ain't goin' nowhere with that bloke,' she snapped, catching hold of her friend and shaking her. 'Sometimes I think you've got bleedin' sawdust between your ears. If you get in a bloke like that's car, 'eaven knows where you'll end up. There ain't no party. 'E's just looking for someone to shag. Surely you can see that?'

'You're just cross because he didn't fancy you,' Mary retorted.

'Blimey, girl, I know you're a sodding Mick, but try and use your noddle,' Linda said, grabbing Mary's arm and forcing her to walk with her. 'That bloke is a ponce. 'E 'eard your Irish accent, saw your pretty blonde 'air and big blue eyes and thought 'e won first prize in the raffle. Now come on, we're going to Trafalgar Square, we'll sing "Auld Lang Syne", 'ave a bit of a knees-up, then we're off 'ome on the last tube.'

Mary fell asleep on the tube home, her head falling on to Rosie's shoulder. Linda was sitting opposite them. The carriage had been crammed to capacity at the Strand, but

253

now they were past Camden Town there were only around ten people left.

'Enjoy yourself?' Linda asked, lighting up a cigarette and stretching her feet up to tuck them between the two other girls.

'It was marvellous,' Rosie sighed happily. She had never experienced such an enormous, yet happy crowd. Everyone kissing each other, dancing and shouting. It made her feel that 1953 would be a wonderful year. 'I never thought there were so many people in the world, let alone London.'

'You ain't seen 'alf of it yet,' Linda said with a smile. 'It's about time I showed you round a bit more and taught you a thing or two.'

Rosie liked the sound of that and said so. They chatted a little more, Linda talking about dance halls, big shops in Oxford Street and Battersea Pleasure Gardens on the other side of the river.

'Linda,' Rosie asked tentatively, 'what's a ponce?' The word she'd heard earlier had stuck in her mind. She vaguely remembered Heather using it too, in connection with Seth. But then Linda and Heather had a very similar vocabulary.

'It's a bloke what makes girls go on the game, then takes the money they earn,' Linda said.

'The game! What game?' Rosie asked.

'Prostitution,' Linda said with a deep frown, then went on to graphically explain what that meant.

Rosie's eyes widened in astonishment. 'Women do that for money? How could they?'

'Because they are 'ungry, because they've got kids to feed. Sometimes they do it because they don't know any better,' Linda said. 'But what I 'ate is the geezers who get 'em into it in the first place. And there nearly always is a geezer too. See, sometimes when you're lonely, a bit scared or just plain daft, you forget stuff you've been told by your ma. Most men are animals. Don't you forget that, Rosemary. Your Dad might've been a good 'un, same as mine is, but there's more nasty ones than good and they'll do anything, say anything, to get your knickers off.'

Linda lapsed into silence after that little outburst and Rosie didn't press her further. She wondered how Linda had come to be so cynical. Had she met a few Seths and Normans in her life too?

Although 1953 started well for Rosie, on the 28th of January she was jolted back to her father's execution when Derek Bentley was hanged for the murder of policeman Sidney Miles at Wandsworth prison. She shared his parents' and sister's grief, and felt utter rage that the legal system was so warped it could send a simple-minded boy to his death, even when he hadn't killed anyone.

Just days after Bentley's hanging there were more tragedies to make her weep: an Irish ferry sank and one hundred and twenty-eight people drowned; in early February widespread flooding in Holland caused over a thousand deaths; and at the same time a hurricane hit the east coast of England and three hundred people died. Mary and Gladys, both Roman Catholics, rushed off to church to pray for the souls of these people. Rosie wondered how they could even think of praying to a God that had allowed such things to happen, and gave her entire week's wages to a fund to help the survivors.

It was her sense of impotence at these disasters which made Rosie remember the resolution she'd made at New Year. While she could do nothing to prevent injustice, or acts of God, she had got the ability to take her own life in hand and strike out for what she wanted. While thinking about what that might be, she looked long and hard at herself in the mirror. She saw a pale freckled face, an untidy mop of uncontrollable hair and a boyish shape. It certainly wasn't the kind of look to open doors to a job with better prospects.

Throughout the cold bitter weather in February, Rosie spent her spare time studying fashion magazines and discovered there were two distinct looks at present. One was the voluptuous, busty blonde kind, created by Diana Dors, and then there was the cool sophisticated look of the model Barbara Goalen with her swept-back hair, elegant hats and long gloves.

Rosie knew both of these styles were out of reach. She had only the tiniest of breasts, she couldn't think of taking a bottle of peroxide to her hair, even though two thirds of the women in Britain seemed to be doing so. As for the sophisticated look, that was way beyond her too. Her hair didn't stay swept back, stray curls always crept out, and besides she'd never seen anyone who was only five-foot-three with freckles across their nose look sophisticated.

Then she saw a picture of a French model and read that the *gamine* look with very short hair was much favoured in Paris. Linda, Mary and Maureen didn't believe such a drastic style would suit her, and said that her hair was too pretty to cut off. But night after night Rosie wet her hair and pinned it back, teasing only tiny tendrils around her cheeks to see how it looked. She believed it was right for her.

On the 1st of March she opened the curtains to find a touch of spring in the air on her day off. The sun was shining again at last and she could see the first tiny green buds coming on the trees and bulbs pushing their way through the soil. That decided her, and less than an hour later she was walking out the gates towards the bus stop and the smart hairdresser's she'd seen in Finchley Road.

The only hairdresser's Rosie had been to before was the men's barber in Bridgwater. It was a gloomy, scary place – the men lying back in chairs with their faces covered in shaving soap, while the razors, clippers and sharp snipping scissors all had a kind of menace. It was no wonder Alan always cried when she took him there for a haircut.

The hairdresser's in the Finchley Road called Sally's Salon was quite different. Rosie had seen into it from the bus as she passed by and admired the pink and white décor, the glass-topped gilt reception desk and the Hollywood-style photographs of elegant models on one wall. She had to assume that the haircutting and setting business went on behind the pink curtain, as the photographs and a display of setting lotions were the only real evidence it was in fact in the business of doing hair at all.

A sophisticated Barbara Goalen lookalike was sitting behind the desk as Rosie went in. She had chiselled cheekbones and eyebrows that were just a stroke of pencil and wore her dark hair in a sleek chignon. She agreed they could fit Madam in now as they'd had a cancellation and she looked at the magazine picture Rosie had brought with her and nodded.

'Oh yes, Madam, that style is absolutely perfect for you,' she agreed.

A strong smell of something was wafting out from behind the pink curtain. Rosie thought it must be perming lotion. She was whisked through the curtain, her coat removed and replaced by a pink overall and towel, then led down past a row of cubicles with several ladies sitting under huge domed hair-dryers to meet Miss Sally.

Miss Sally was about thirty. She was a peroxide blonde, with conical breasts and a wide belt pulling her waist in to a handspan. Her skin was like white marble, and her eyebrows were thin, surprised-looking arches. Rosie immediately felt awkward, plain and embarrassed, as the woman looked at the picture she'd brought with her, sighed as she looked back at Rosie, then beckoned for her to sit down.

She spent a moment or two combing Rosie's hair through and examining it closely. 'Are you sure you want it cut that short?' she asked eventually.

Rosie assumed the woman didn't believe it would suit her, but she had no intention of backing down now. 'Yes,' she said, more bravely than she felt. 'I'm tired of it the way it is.'

As the coppery curls fell to the floor making a thick rug around the chair, Rosie tried not to consider that it might be a disaster. Miss Sally asked her a great many questions as she snipped away. Where did she work? Had she a boyfriend? Where did she come from? Rosie could hear other women shouting over the noise of the hair-dryers, so she thought question-and-answer time must be the order of the day in a hairdresser's.

However, once she told Miss Sally she worked in a mental asylum the questions stopped abruptly. Rosie was quite glad. She wanted Miss Sally to concentrate on her hair.

It was the lightness of her head which struck Rosie most as she left the salon over an hour later. Miss Sally had enthused about how the short 'urchin' style showed off her delicate features and drew attention to her pretty blue eyes. But Rosie felt an affinity with a shorn sheep.

She stopped in front of a jeweller's window to look at herself more objectively and to her delight she saw that Miss Sally's opinion and her own intuition had been right. Her long, curly hair had always been her most remarkable feature. It dominated everything else – she couldn't count how many people had described her only as 'the girl with the hair'. Without that fiery mane she had a whole new identity. Less pasty-faced, more adult. Her hair was shinier, and with just a hint of curl rather than a halo of frizz. She decided she loved it and as she walked around that day in the spring sunshine she felt a surge of new confidence and optimism.

Two weeks later Rosie received a letter from 'Auntie Molly' asking if she could come down for a holiday with her at Easter at the end of March. As usual she'd worded her letter carefully with only the most casual reference to Alan. But reading between the lines Rosie felt Miss Pemberton's reason for inviting her down was that she wanted to take her to see Alan and perhaps discuss both his and Rosie's futures.

Straight after her dinner break, Rosie went to Matron's office. She usually shrank from any contact with the woman and today she was even more nervous of speaking to her than usual. She fully expected Matron to fly off the handle at her request for time off and dismiss her out of hand.

Matron was sitting behind her desk, her arms crossed just below her big bosom, creating the effect that she was pushing them up. The close-set eyes swept over Rosie as if she were a small rodent and her thin lips were pursed in readiness to deny any request, however humble.

Rosie had learned to accept many of the things she didn't like in Carrington Hall, but she was no closer to finding common ground with this woman than she had been on the day of her arrival. She stammered out her request, half expecting a slap round the face for her cheek.

'A week's holiday!' Matron exclaimed, before she'd even finished, unfolding her arms and placing her hands on her hips in indignation. 'But you've only been here seven months.'

Rosie squirmed. She wanted to go so badly she didn't know what she'd do if Matron refused. 'I won't ask for another holiday,' she pleaded.

'You won't get it if you do,' Matron said curtly.

In fact she had seen the letter for Smith amongst the post that morning and ironically she hadn't steamed this one open, mainly because previous letters had been so disappointing. She wanted to refuse this request point-blank just to assert her authority, but she had a strong feeling the girl would get her 'aunt' to intervene on her behalf, and that could only result in loss of face, just like the regrettable incident with the sanitary towels.

'If I let you go, I shall expect you to work your next two days off on your return. That's the only way I can adjust the rota,' she said in a cool crisp voice, already picking up some papers dismissively.

Rosie knew there would be some price to pay, but that one seemed remarkably low. She nodded her agreement. 'So I can go then?' She wanted it confirmed now so she could write to Miss Pemberton.

'Yes, you may.' Matron gave her a disparaging look. 'But in future you will have time off only when I allocate it.'

Rosie didn't care about that, she didn't intend to be working here much longer. 'Thank you so much, Matron,' she said breathlessly, and left before the woman had a chance to change her mind or offer some spiteful criticism.

Once back on the first floor Rosie let out a whoop of delight before she let herself back into the day room. Since having her hair cut her life seemed to be charmed. Two boys had asked her for a date at a dance she went to with Linda and Mary, she'd had a pay rise of two shillings a week and her bust seemed to have grown another inch. She didn't like either boy enough to see them again, but it was nice to be asked. The bust and the rise in pay had satisfied her more.

'You look pleased with yourself!' Maureen said spitefully as Rosie came rushing into the room with a wide grin on her face.

Rosie paused at Maureen's tone, all at once aware of a tense atmosphere. Maureen was mopping the floor; obviously someone had had an accident. The patients were all down at the far end of the room huddled together looking cowed. Rosie wondered if Maureen had been shouting at them as she sometimes did, frightening the life out of them. There was no sign of Mary.

'I've got a week's holiday at Easter to see my aunt,' Rosie said reluctantly. As Maureen didn't go anywhere on her days off, and never mentioned holidays, she didn't want to rub in her own good fortune. 'Who had the accident?' She assumed Mary must be with whoever it was.

'Patty. That's the fifth time she's done it this week.

She doesn't seem to even know she's doing it.' Maureen frowned in irritation. 'She ought to be upstairs.'

Rosie was just about to say she didn't think being incontinent was reason enough to incarcerate someone with severely disturbed people, when an ear-piercing scream ripped out from the floor above. She stopped short, looking up, and unusually so did all the patients.

Normally such loud screams were short-lived, but not this one. It went on and on, too fierce and strong for it to be someone just disapproving of having their hair brushed. George and Alice put their hands over their ears and started rocking in their chairs. Donald looked very alarmed.

'Hell's bells,' Rosie exclaimed. As everyone predicted, she had grown used to disturbing noises from upstairs, mostly she didn't even notice them. But this one was exceptional; it made her blood run cold. To her mind it could only be someone in terrible pain. 'What on earth's going on up there?'

'As if I'd know,' Maureen snapped.

Rosie looked at Maureen in surprise. For all this girl's faults, she did normally seem to care about the patients. 'Well, do you think I ought to go up there and see? It might be an emergency!'

'It's none of your business,' Maureen replied sharply and she moved towards the door, almost as if she intended to stop Rosie from rushing out. 'Aylwood won't thank you for sticking your nose in.'

Such an odd reaction disturbed Rosie even more. Maureen looked frightened; her grey eyes were blinking furiously behind her glasses and her usually pale face was flushed. The screaming grew louder still. Aggie began to wail in fright, and when Rosie looked round at her she saw all the patients were huddling closer still to one another like a flock of frightened sheep.

'I'm going up there,' Rosie said, so alarmed now that she felt she had to do something.

Maureen blocked her way. 'Oh no you don't. You'll get us all into trouble,' she said, gripping Rosie's arm to restrain her. 'You're the nosiest person I ever met.'

The screaming stopped abruptly, just like a gramophone record being snatched off. Aggie stopped wailing. Maureen let go of Rosie's arm.

For a second or two the day room was totally silent, not a sniff, grunt or even the sound of breathing. Rosie glanced behind her and seeing the patients like statues, too terrified to move, she saw their need to be reassured was of far greater importance than tackling Maureen, or concerning herself with something happening elsewhere.

She wheeled round, walking down the room towards them. 'All better now,' she said soothingly.

Donald moved first, getting out of his chair and lumbering towards her. His eyes were wide with fright and as he reached Rosie he slid his hand into hers. The door opened and Mary came back with Patty in tow. Archie shuffled his chair along the floor making the feet squeak on the lino.

The almost palpable tension in the room vanished as the usual noises began again. Alice got up to go over to Patty. George began to creep across the room, Maud started to talk to herself again. But Donald, who was usually quicker than anyone else to adjust to sudden changes, was still clinging to Rosie's hand. Rosie guessed whatever was troubling him had happened before the screaming started.

'What's up, Donald?' Rosie asked quietly. He was hanging his head as if afraid to speak out. Normally he confided in her about everything that happened in her absence. 'Did something happen while I was out of the room?'

'Jackson s-s-smacked Patty,' he whispered. 'She sh-sh-shouted at us all too and told us to sit d-d-d-down or we'd be s-s-sorry.'

Rosie was still smarting at Maureen's remark about her nosiness. Hearing she'd hit an old lady just for wetting herself added to it, but as she soothed Donald she noticed Tabby.

All the other patients were moving again, yet she was still sitting in a chair just staring blankly into space, her knitting lying on her lap.

Tabby was never motionless. She either knitted frantically or paced about, and Rosie felt a pang of disquiet. Leaving Donald for a moment, she went over to sit beside the woman. When she asked what was wrong, Tabby didn't reply but caught hold of Rosie's hand and held it tightly.

This was entirely out of character. Most of the patients liked to be touched. They responded eagerly to having their heads stroked, their hands held or a hug, but Tabby always shied away from any physical contact.

'What's wrong, Tabby?' Rosie asked again.

Tabby pointed to the ceiling.

'It's okay, it's all quiet again now,' Rosie said. 'There's nothing to be frightened of.'

'I don't want to go up there,' Tabby spat out, her tawny eyes flashing the way they often did just before she lashed out at someone.

Tabby was one of the patients with whom Rosie had made almost no headway. Although she was articulate and capable of holding a proper conversation when she chose, most of the time she merely grunted at people, Rosie included. Her nature was as fiery as her hair, one minute quiet and docile, the next flaring up for no apparent reason and clawing whoever happened to be closest. All the staff treated her with caution.

'No one's going to send you there,' Rosie said evenly, wondering if Maureen might have threatened this.

Tabby turned conspiratorially towards Rosie, still holding her hand. 'There's a bad man there,' she said in a low voice. 'He hurt me.'

Rosie thought she was just confused and after a few soothing words encouraged her to pick up her knitting again. Maureen had left the day room now, perhaps to have a cigarette, so seeing Mary was sitting alone reading a magazine, Rosie went over to her.

'Was Tabby ever upstairs?' she asked.

Mary nodded. 'Yes, just before I came here. Why?'

'Just wondered,' Rosie replied and walked over to the window to save the necessity of explaining herself, or being accused again of being nosy.

There were daffodils out in the front garden and a forsythia bush was a mass of bright yellow flowers, but for once Rosie wasn't heartened by these clear signs of spring. She was all too aware of something ugly lurking unseen in this building.

She thought that the combination of Maureen shouting at the patients, Patty being smacked, and then hearing that screaming from upstairs, must have triggered off an old memory for Tabby. Could the male chargehand called Saunders who worked up there be the bad man she spoke of? Or had there been a different man working there before?

In the entire seven months Rosie had been here she hadn't had any contact with the male chargehand at all. He lived out and came in minutes before seven, going straight to the ward. His dinner break never coincided with hers, the most she'd seen of him was the odd crossing on the stairs. Even at Christmas he hadn't put in an appearance in the staff room.

Considering that men were the main topic of conversation amongst the chargehands, it was odd that they didn't speak about the only male one. Rosie had always assumed that the lack of information about him – whether he was married, where he lived and suchlike – was just because he was so unattractive. He was a big, heavily built man with short cropped sandy hair and pockmarked skin. She certainly hadn't been interested enough herself to ask anyone about him.

But then, now she came to think about it, Staff Nurse

Aylwood who worked alongside him was equally mysterious. A tall, gaunt-looking woman in her forties with slate grey hair, she had her breakfast before anyone else, had dinner sent up to the wards, and often took her tea up to her room. In the evenings she always shut her door firmly with a bang, then switched on her wireless as if to drown out the noise of the younger members of staff's chatter. Rosie hadn't even discovered her Christian name.

In the light of what Maureen had said just now about Aylwood not being likely to thank her for sticking her nose in, it now seemed more probable that these two members of staff kept their distance because any familiarity with other staff might expose the way they ran that ward.

Rosie frowned; that didn't really make sense. After all, Gladys Thorpe, Linda and Mary all spent several hours up there each week too. Yet as she mulled it over in her mind she realized that floor must be seriously understaffed for most of the day, because the other girls only went up there at meal times.

A horrifying image of people locked in cages like animals, shot into her mind. She tried to shake it out, sure her imagination was getting the better of her, and she vowed then silently to herself that after Easter she would find a new job.

It was a bright, sunny but chilly afternoon when Rosie got off the train at Bridgwater two weeks later. Miss Pemberton was waiting on the platform wearing a tweed coat and a brown felt hat. Like many people she had a black band sewn on her coat as a sign of mourning for Queen Mary, who had died just a few days before.

Rosie's emotions had swung like a pendulum between joy and apprehension on the long train journey. She was excited at having a holiday, and at seeing Miss Pemberton and possibly Alan, but coming back to an area which held such a wealth of memories was frightening. After Bristol she had her nose pressed up against the window, anxiously awaiting the first glimpse of the Levels. As the train chugged across the familiar flat landscape, her mouth had become dry with nerves, yet her eyes prickled with tears as she saw again the place she loved.

The sun glinted on the rhynes and patches of floodwater that were still lying in the fields. She saw new lambs gambolling around their mothers, herons standing like statues on the banks of the rivers. There was blossom on fruit trees and clumps of primroses were growing on banks, all so beautiful and serene. Yet everything she saw was a reminder of her father and brothers. She knew too that down here people had long memories: they wouldn't have forgotten the brutal murders as had the people in London.

'You look marvellous,' Miss Pemberton exclaimed, taking Rosie's small case from her hand and putting it down on the platform for a moment. Then taking both Rosie's hands in hers, she smiled warmly. 'Let me get a really good look at you!'

Violet hadn't actually recognized the chic young girl with an urchin haircut and an apple-green costume getting out of the train. Not until Rosie waved and she saw the familiar cheeky grin. This new Rosie looked like a fashion plate.

Rosie giggled with embarrassment as Miss Pemberton studied her. 'You look like a real city girl,' she said. 'I'm proud of you, Rosie.'

A lump came up in Rosie's throat, not so much at the praise but at the warmth in the older woman's eyes and voice. It made her feel as if this really was her auntie, welcoming her home after a long absence.

Rosie didn't speak as they drove out through the town because she was so engrossed in looking at everything. Bridgwater had seemed a magical place to her as a child, bustling with people, cars and buses and dozens of exciting shops. There was the barber's shop she took Alan to, the gunsmith's where Dad bought his shot, the greengrocer's who sold home-made toffee apples and the little flower stall where she used to stop to sniff the flowers and ask the names of ones she didn't recognize.

She remembered standing on the bridge watching the river and the boats, wishing she could live here. It was less than a year ago that she'd last seen it, on leaving the hospital, but it wasn't as she remembered.

'I expect you think everything's shrunk. As I've found, some places improve by leaving them and then going back. Others are best left in memory,' Miss Pemberton said drily. 'I felt just as you must now when I came back here in 1947. I had a wonderful memory of a sweetshop with rows of gleaming glass jars filled with every kind of sweet you could imagine. The old lady who owned it wore a big white apron, and when I was a young girl she used to tell me to close my eyes and open my mouth, and she'd pop something delicious into it.

'I couldn't wait to find it again. During the war I'd dreamed of her toffees and coconut ice. I planned to go in and buy pounds and pounds of different sweets –' She broke off to laugh.

'Did you find it?'

'I did, but what a disappointment! It was dark and dingy, hardly any stock what with sweet-rationing. There was another old lady in there, in a rather dirty overall. All I bought was two ounces of bull's eyes.'

'I wonder what I'd think if I went by May Cottage,' Rosie said thoughtfully.

'There's nothing there now. They pulled it down back in January,' the older woman said hurriedly. 'I drove past the other day and I couldn't pinpoint where it was exactly: weeds and grass had covered any bare soil.'

Rosie knew she would be able to pinpoint it. She knew that even when she was as old as Miss Pemberton she'd be able to pace out exactly where the front door of May Cottage had stood. But she made no comment.

*

'So what do you think of my little home?' Miss Pemberton asked once she'd taken Rosie on a quick tour of the little two-bedroom cottage in Chilton Trinity. They were in the tiny kitchen and she was lying a tray with tea things.

'It's lovely,' Rosie said with enthusiasm. 'Can I go out in the garden?'

The cottage wasn't quite as old and quaint as Rosie had expected. Miss Pemberton said it had been built in 1880 and it had the plain no-nonsense look of the artisans' cottages of that period. Grey stone, a trellised porch around the front door. One window up, one down. Inside there was one big room with the staircase going out of it and a small lean-to kitchen. Originally there had been no bathroom, but Miss Pemberton had had the back bedroom divided in two to put one in. What Rosie liked best about it was the simplicity: walls painted white, polished wood boards downstairs and a thick colourful fringed rug to make it cosier. Each piece of furniture looked as if it had a story attached to it. There were a couple of low carved tables Miss Pemberton said she'd brought back from India, a highly polished desk with a leather top which had been her grandfather's. The settee was an old brown leather one, and two armchairs which didn't match had buttoned backs and looked very old.

Miss Pemberton unlocked the back door. 'I'd forgotten how much you love gardening. I wish I had more time to spend in it. But spring is always a good time to see it, with all the bulbs coming through and before the weeds shoot up.'

The moment she stepped outside and saw the secluded garden surrounded on all sides by six-foot-high thick hedges, Rosie knew that she and Miss Pemberton had far more in common than she'd originally supposed. Only real flower-lovers planted their daffodils in clumps in the grass that way; pretend gardeners put them tidily in beds. It made her heart ache to see that mass of yellow against the lush lawn. As she walked down the path with Miss

Pemberton just in front of her she noted with approval the bird table with a hunk of coconut for the blue tits, the way purple aubretia was pushing its way out of the crazy paving, and the dozens of rose bushes with shiny new leaves.

She stopped to take a deep breath, savouring the clean, sweet-smelling air, with just a faint whiff of farmyard manure coming from the fields beyond the hedge. It took her straight back to May Cottage; if she closed her eyes she could imagine she was down in the orchard. Then she saw the tree beside the shed.

'What is it?' she asked in awe. Pinkish-white candle-like flowers were just beginning to open on almost bare branches.

Miss Pemberton turned and smiled. 'It's a magnolia. Do you like it?'

'It's the most beautiful tree I've ever seen,' Rosie whispered, and to her embarrassment she felt tears well up in her eyes.

Miss Pemberton slid her arm around Rosie's shoulder. 'There's not a lot wrong with your heart and soul,' she said in a soft voice. 'That tree has moved me to tears many a time. To me it's God made visible. And you'll see it in all its full glory too before you have to leave.'

Later that evening as they sat companionably in front of the fire, Miss Pemberton told Rosie she was taking her to Taunton the next day to see Alan.

Rosie yelped with excitement and hugged the older woman impulsively.

'You'll find him very different,' Miss Pemberton warned her. 'He's grown in every direction, bigger, more confident, sometimes even a little cheeky. You may find he ignores you, as he does Thomas.'

'Does Thomas still come down here to see Alan then?' Rosie asked. As the social worker hadn't mentioned him, Rosie assumed he'd cut himself off entirely since the trial, just as he had with her.

'Of course, my dear.' Miss Pemberton seemed surprised by the question. 'In fact he's coming down tomorrow too. We'll be meeting him at the Hugheses' and I offered him the couch here for the night so you'd have the opportunity to see him again.'

Rosie was astounded. When she hadn't received so much as a Christmas card from Thomas she'd presumed that her brothers' lies in court had killed any interest he'd once had in her. Just the thought of meeting him again made her feel jittery.

She explained this to Miss Pemberton and asked why he should want to see her now.

'I think you are forgetting what an honourable and courageous man Thomas is,' Miss Pemberton said soothingly. 'I think once he'd hit rock-bottom emotionally he realized just how bad it must have been for you too. He said he needed to face you again if only to square things up.'

Rosie took a deep breath to try and stop the butterflies in her stomach. 'He's probably right, we ought to meet again, but I'm still scared of seeing him.'

'You don't need to be, my dear. Although I haven't yet met Thomas in person, I've come to know a great deal about his character from our correspondence. He's a gentle, lonely man; the many tragedies in his life have given him great reserves of compassion and endurance. You won't find him hostile towards you. Besides, the greater part of this meeting will be to discuss Alan's future, and I'm sure that is one area where you will be in complete harmony.'

'Alan's future?' Rosie sat up straight. 'Does Thomas want to take him back to London?'

'No, my dear, Alan is far too happy to even consider that as an option. Mr and Mrs Hughes would like to adopt him legally.'

Rosie gasped.

'I'm sorry. I didn't mean to upset you, Rosie, by throwing something like that at you,' she said quickly, patting the girl's hand reassuringly. 'Wait till you see Alan with his new family, and discuss it with Thomas before you pass judgement. Alan is very, very happy and settled with them, my dear, and the Hugheses adore him. Adoption would give him absolute and permanent security.'

Rosie's first thought when she saw Alan was that this sturdy little boy was an impostor, not her baby brother. Nothing was the same. His hair was a shade darker, more brown now than red, he had rosy plump cheeks and the dark brown eyes which met hers were bold and fearless. Even his clothes were different – smart grey shorts which fitted properly, a neat little checked shirt and navy blue handknitted jumper.

'Hullo, Alan,' she said, almost overcome by emotion. She wanted to scoop him up in her arms. 'Do you remember me?'

The Hugheses' sitting-room was like one from an Ovaltine advertisement. Very post-war, chintzy and comfortable. The garden beyond the french windows had a swing and a sandpit. A tricycle stood on the path, washing on the line.

'You're Rosie,' he said, without smiling. 'But your hair's different.'

'I had it cut because it got so messy,' she said. 'Yours has got darker. And you must be two inches taller.'

He came and sat next to her on the settee later. He told her about his school and demonstrated that he could read with his Janet and John book. Thomas sat in an armchair watching. Miss Pemberton had gone out into the kitchen with Mrs Hughes.

It felt very strange too to see Thomas again in such unfamiliar surroundings. She wished they could have met up before being confronted with one another here. He made her feel jumpy and uncomfortable as they'd had no opportunity yet to clear the air. He looked strained and

271

pale and she couldn't tell if that was because he was tired or nervous.

It wasn't helping that Alan was totally ignoring him. He hadn't spoken to Thomas directly at all. He said things politely for both their benefit. But when Thomas asked him questions, he looked at Rosie as he replied. Mr Hughes had apparently taken his son and daughter out soon after Thomas arrived, because he thought it would be easier for Alan with less of a crowd. But Alan only seemed to want to talk about Jennifer and Raymond and the dog Rex.

It hurt Rosie to see that Alan had transferred all the love he once had for her to his new family. She was sure he hadn't forgotten that she had once been important to him, because on several occasions she noticed him looking at her thoughtfully. But if he recalled any incidents he didn't speak of them, and Rosie didn't dare prompt memories in case it upset him.

Mr Hughes came back later with the other two children and it was almost a relief to have the pressure of talking to Alan alone lifted from them. Seen together, the Hugheses looked like the kind of ideal family portrayed on holiday posters: Mrs Hughes in twinset and tweed skirt with tightly permed hair; her pipe-smoking husband a head taller, wearing a handmade Fair Isle pullover; Jennifer a dimpled five-year-old blonde in a blue wool pinafore skirt; and Raymond, typical of all nine-year-old boys with thin much-scarred knees and drastically cut hair.

Alan made it quite clear where his affections laid. He climbed on to Mr Hughes's lap and leaned back comfortably against his chest, smiling rather smugly at Thomas. Jennifer was more interested in Rosie, admiring her hair and her costume and asking if she had any lipstick in her handbag that she could try.

As they all had tea and a slice of fruit cake, it seemed to Rosie that she had at last stumbled on the kind of happy, warm, uncomplicated middle-class family hitherto only glimpsed in Enid Blyton books. Alan fitted in as if he'd always been one of them, he even spoke like them now. He had a slight West Country accent but not the broad one he once had. She felt a stab of envy, yet the sorrow at losing him was greater. In her heart she knew this was the last time she'd see her little brother.

When they got back to the cottage Thomas saw to lighting the fire while Rosie helped Miss Pemberton prepare ham, eggs and mashed potato for supper, and although all three of them chatted comfortably, about the cottage, living in the country as opposed to the town, and the forthcoming Coronation, Alan wasn't mentioned.

'Well, I think it's time we discussed Alan,' Miss Pemberton said as she handed round cheese and biscuits. 'One of the main reasons Mr and Mrs Hughes are anxious to adopt Alan now, rather than waiting a few years, is because they fear as he grows older he might begin to ask difficult questions about his family.'

'Adopting him won't stop that,' Rosie shrugged.

Thomas and Miss Pemberton looked at one another and Rosie suddenly realized what she meant.

'You mean, if he doesn't see Thomas or me there's no reason for him to ask questions?'

Miss Pemberton nodded.

Thomas put his hand over Rosie's on the table. 'So you see the Hugheses' point?' he asked.

'Yes,' Rosie said in a small voice. 'I don't want him ever to know either.'

Helping Miss Pemberton clear away the supper things later, Rosie mulled things over again in her head. She found Thomas confusing. Each time she'd seen him he'd been slightly different. In some ways he was very assertive, in others he seemed weak. Sometimes he was boyish, sometimes like an old man. She had thought at first that she knew so much about him and his character, but now after all these months away from him she felt she didn't really know him at all. It bothered her.

The next morning, after Miss Pemberton left the cottage, Rosie made another pot of tea for herself and Thomas. It wasn't nine yet, a cold but sunny morning. Miss Pemberton had just gone into her office for a couple of hours, but would be back in time to take Thomas to the station at eleven.

Thomas was prodding a little more life into the fire and Rosie brought the tray of tea over to him.

'When will Alan's adoption be?' she asked. Yesterday she hadn't been totally convinced it was the right thing to do, but she'd woken this morning knowing for certain it was.

'I think it ought to be as soon as possible, don't you?' Thomas said with a sigh. 'But let's leave that subject for another day. I want to know about your job. You haven't said a word about that.'

Thomas had sensed Violet had gone out specifically to give them time to talk alone. He had no idea what she thought he ought to discuss with Rosie, but he knew it wasn't just Alan's adoption.

'There's nothing much to say,' Rosie shrugged. 'I'm going to look around for a new job when I get back.'

'That bad, eh?' Thomas pulled a face.

'It's not all bad,' she smiled. 'One patient called Donald I really love, some of the others I've got quite attached to. I like the other girls and there are times when it's quite good fun. I've learned a lot there. Last year when I saw you I thought I'd never get used to some of the awful things. But I have.'

'All of them?' Thomas raised one eyebrow.

'No.' She dropped her eyes from his. 'There's Matron, and the secrecy about what goes on upstairs.' She told him just a little, but brushed it off with a tight little laugh. 'The trouble with me is that I am a nosy parker. If I could be like everyone else and just do my job without wanting to know the ins and outs of everything, I'd be a whole lot happier.'

Thomas thought Miss Pemberton would probably winkle all this out of her and she was better-placed to advise Rosie what to do about it. 'Well, I'd be a whole lot happier if you'd meet me in London,' he said. 'How about we arrange a regular evening, say once every three weeks or so, and I'll take you out to supper somewhere?'

'Why would you want to do that?' she asked.

'Because I think we need one another.'

Rosie looked at him and frowned. She knew she wanted to see him, but she couldn't imagine why he should want to. 'To talk about Alan, do you mean?'

'Well yes, but not just that. There's a great deal of unfinished business between us. I haven't told you why I didn't contact you before.'

'But I know why that was,' she said.

All at once Thomas knew what Violet wanted them to talk about. 'Maybe you think you do, but we haven't discussed it,' he said. 'Perhaps too I just want you as a chum. Or don't you fancy a one-legged old crock as a friend?'

'Of course I do,' she said indignantly. 'I just don't see how we can be, not after all that stuff in the trial.'

'That's exactly why,' he said, his voice dropping. 'Have you told *anyone* how you felt the morning Cole was hanged?'

'No,' she whispered. 'And I couldn't tell you either, because we're on opposite sides of the fence.'

Thomas shook his head. 'No, we aren't. We both loved Heather, so how can we be?'

Rosie felt a sudden surge of anger. She was prepared to spare him hurtful details of things she'd witnessed between Heather and her father, but she wasn't going to pretend she was glad Cole had been hanged just to make him feel better.

'Well, you tell me how *you* felt the morning Cole was hanged then,' she retorted. 'Can you talk about that?'

'Yes, I can.' He frowned at her sudden hostility. 'If you really want to know, I wanted to feel elation. I believed I would gladly have been there to see him drop. But at the end it wasn't like that at all. I felt absolutely nothing. I lay on my bed watching the hands of the clock tick round and I felt numb. I thought a big weight would rise from my shoulders, but it didn't. I felt more when your bloody brother got off. That made me so angry I could have killed him if he'd come anywhere near me.'

Rosie stared at Thomas. She knew that remark came straight from the heart.

'If it makes you feel any better, that made me angry too,' she blurted out. 'I don't know whether he really was guilty, but I hated him so much I wanted him to hang.'

'And your father?'

He immediately regretted asking such a question. She hung her head and twisted her fingers together.

'I cried for him,' she finally burst out defiantly. 'I loved him, whatever he was.'

Her words seemed to hang in the room. They couldn't look at one another and only the crackling of the fire muted their heavy breathing.

Thomas spoke first, his voice hoarse and rasping. 'Rosie, I want to be able to forgive him. I know I must if I'm ever to get over it. Could you help me?'

For months now Rosie had kept her feelings about her father squashed down so low, that at times she believed she had actually eradicated them. But Thomas's plea had the effect of a knife being pushed under the lid of a jam pot to let the air in, and suddenly they sprang up, as sharp as they had been on the morning of Cole's death. 'How can I help you?' she shouted at him through tears. 'I can't even help myself.'

'We can help each other,' she heard him say, then his arms went round her and he was holding her to his chest, smoothing her hair, just the way Heather used to. She realized he was crying too. 'We can recover,' he whispered. 'I know we can if we learn to trust one another and become real friends. We do need each other.'

Chapter Nine

Rosie shivered with excitement as she watched the huge crowds of people packed shoulder to shoulder down below in Piccadilly. It was Coronation Day, the 2nd of June 1953, and later today the royal procession would pass right by this very window on its way back to Buckingham Palace. She could hardly believe that she had been singled out by Donald's parents to see something so momentous and thrilling.

Even the heavy rain couldn't put a pall on the day. Here she was in the comfort of a very grand apartment, a guest at the Cooks' family party, with an enviable front-row seat. Looking down into the crowd it was impossible to see as much as a spare inch of pavement behind the barricades. Across the street, even the railings of Green Park were almost hidden by people who had found ingenious methods with lengths of rope and boxes to get to a higher vantage point. Beyond them, still more people were coming across the park. The noise was incredible, a roaring sound of hundreds and thousands of voices, shouting, laughing and singing. Many of them had camped out overnight on the pavements to make certain of getting a good viewing position. They had primus stoves to make tea, deckchairs or boxes to sit on, blankets to wrap round them and umbrellas to protect them from the rain.

It was a sea of red, white and blue. Hats, ribbons, streamers and crêpe-paper wavers. And as if that wasn't enough to show patriotic fervour, a great many people had gone beyond a few accessories and dressed themselves in the three colours too.

Rosie dragged her eyes away from the view out of the window and back to the people she was spending the day with. Mr and Mrs Cook sat together on one settee, Mrs Cook cradling her youngest grandchild, a fourteen-month-old baby called Robin. Michael, Donald's older brother, and his wife Alicia sat opposite them, with the other two children, Clara and Nicholas aged eight and six respectively, squeezed in beside them. Donald was sitting quietly in an armchair, and Susan, his sister, perched on the arm showing him a picture book. Susan's husband, Roger, had slipped out for a walk.

Rosie had never known a family quite like the Cooks. She thought the Hugheses, Alan's new parents, were nice, but they were a little prim and restrained. The Cooks were very open, warm and jovial, so interested in one another and her. They'd even suggested she called them all by their Christian names as so many Cooks were confusing. Several times this morning she had found herself wishing that she could miraculously become a permanent member of their clan instead of just a guest for the day.

Michael was thirty-eight, Susan two years younger, and they were both very like Donald. All three were tall and shared the same floppy blond hair, blue eyes and wide mouths. If Donald was able to control his loose, wet mouth, and his jerky movements, no one would guess he was any different from his older brother and sister.

The three grandchildren had the same blue eyes too, but they had their mother Alicia's dark brown hair and smaller features. Clara and Nicholas were chatty and sunny. Rosie was touched they didn't seem to find anything odd about their Uncle Donald whom they'd only seen once or twice before.

Mr Cook had borrowed this second-floor apartment from a friend who was in America on business. He must have been a very good friend as Rosie had overheard Mr

Cook telling Michael that rooms with such excellent views of the procession route were being let out for as much as three thousand pounds for the day. She also thought that the Cooks' own home must be every bit as splendid because they were all so casual about it. But she, on the other hand, was astounded. To her mind it was fit for royalty or at least a film star.

The drawing-room they were in was big enough to hold at least twenty-five people. Decorated in pale blue and cream, the armchairs and settees had the softest cushions Rosie had ever sat on. There were beautiful landscape paintings framed in gilt and a luxurious cream carpet. She was particularly impressed by the curtains; she thought there had to be a hundred yards of blue velvet as they were at least ten-foot long and there were three wide windows. She had never before seen such pelmets either. The velvet was draped in soft swirls, each one held up by a slightly darker blue rosette. She wondered what the owners of the flat did when the curtains got dirty. She couldn't imagine how anyone could wash and iron them.

On top of all this magnificence there was also television. Although Rosie had heard and read a great deal about this amazing invention in the last two or three years, it was the first time she'd actually seen one, other than in shop windows. When Mr Cook opened the cabinet doors and turned it on this morning, she had gasped aloud at the miracle of seeing a close-up of Queen Elizabeth in the state coach on her way to Westminster Abbey.

But after two hours, the novelty of watching the small screen was beginning to pall for everyone. They had all marvelled at the pageantry and imagined the colours of the ermine-trimmed coronation robe, the golden coach, the plumed horses and the heralds in their scarlet and gold ceremonial uniforms. They had spotted each member of the royal family, but everyone was becoming a little fidgety and they had begun to chatter amongst themselves, and even made irreverent jokes.

'I wonder what would happen if the Queen wanted to spend a penny?' Alicia said, looking thoughtfully at the screen. The choir were singing an anthem and the cameras kept homing in on the young queen who still managed to look as serene as if she had only been there for ten minutes.

'Only you would wonder about that!' Michael laughed and playfully slapped her knee. 'You have an extremely lavatorial mind.'

Rosie laughed too, she thought Alicia was fun. Although she was over thirty with three children, she was still very slender and girlish. She wore her long, dark hair loose, and her pink dress with a sweetheart neckline and puffed sleeves gave her a look of an American high-school girl.

'Well, it would be very difficult,' Alicia retorted indignantly. 'Imagine trying to cope with that long dress and the cloak?'

'I expect she's been trained to wait,' the elder Mrs Cook said. In fact her daughter-in-law had voiced her own thoughts. She had come to the conclusion that Elizabeth had probably been denied anything to drink until the ceremony was over. 'Royalty aren't like us after all.'

Mr Cook snorted with laughter, and everyone joined in except Donald who looked puzzled.

'Has she g-g-got legs?' he asked.

Donald's innocent question prompted another hilarious burst of laughter from everyone.

'Of course she has, dear, they are just hidden under her long dress,' his mother said, picking up a magazine to show him a picture of Elizabeth wearing a knee-length costume, coming down the steps of an aeroplane. It was taken the previous year after she was called back from Australia following the death of her father King George.

Donald looked at the picture, but he frowned. 'B-b-but why did you say she isn't like us?' he said looking intently at his mother.

Rosie smiled. She had known Donald now for nine months. In that time he'd surprised her many times with questions that proved he was as capable of reasoning as she was. The years he'd spent at Carrington Hall with no stimulation had clearly stunted him, but just as soon as he was with someone prepared to explain and discuss things with him, he seemed to take great leaps forward.

Rosie moved across the room to sit in a chair beside him. 'Your mother means that she's led a different life to ordinary people,' she said. In the last week, in preparation for today, she had spent some time explaining to him the purpose of the royal family and what the Coronation meant. He was a bit confused now that the conversation had turned to the Queen having bodily functions just like anyone else. 'She is just a lady, the same as Susan, Alicia, your mother and me. She eats dinners, goes to bed and has baths just like we do. But because she was a princess and they knew that one day she would be Queen, she has ladies-in-waiting and servants to help her dress and do everything for her. She doesn't go out on her own, go on buses or to the shops. That's what your mother meant about her not being like us.'

Donald looked at Rosie for a moment and then gave a huge grin. 'She's the same as me then,' he said. 'I d-d-don't go out on my own, and p-p-people help me with everything.'

'Yes, you're very special too,' Rosie said with a smile. 'And when the Queen comes by this afternoon, you can wave to her from the window.'

Norah Cook held her grandchild in her arms, but she was watching and listening to this exchange between her son and his friend with great interest and affection. On the face of it, Rosemary Smith was just an unusually kind-hearted, pretty young girl, filling in time at Carrington Hall until she was old enough to train as a nurse. Norah had imagined until today that she came from a fairly large, lower middle-class family, where a scarcity of money yet a great deal of love had produced a capable, intelligent and caring person.

It was only this morning that a chance remark revealed she was an orphan. This was something of a surprise and Norah would have liked to find out more, but the speed at which the girl managed to steer the conversation away from herself made her suspect that Rosemary's childhood wasn't a bit as she had supposed.

Since then Norah had been observing Rosemary closely, analysing everything. It was the first time she'd seen the girl since she'd had her hair cut, and without the unflattering maroon uniform and cap to distract her, she felt far more able to accurately assess Rosemary's true character.

The short coppery urchin cut was a little avant-garde in a period where most young girls favoured permed, blonde locks, and it gave her a delightful pixie image. Her apple-green costume with its flared mid-calf skirt and fitted jacket flattered her slim figure, while the bright colour enhanced her pink and white complexion. It was clearly a cheap outfit, perhaps bought in a street market, but on her it looked chic, not tawdry.

Adding all she had observed today to what she already knew about her, Norah felt Rosemary was something of an enigma. Basically a little country girl with her soft Somerset burr, her love of flowers, patience and gentleness, yet there was a steelier side too. Although unfailingly polite, she wasn't servile. She liked challenges, she was also very adaptable. Norah knew by the awed expression on the girl's face this morning that she had never before set foot anywhere as smart as this apartment. She was probably unaccustomed too to meeting people of a different social class, but yet it barely showed as she pitched in with the children, offered to make tea, and quietly fitted in with the family as if she were part of it.

It had been gratitude which had made Norah and Frank ask Rosemary to join them today. Before her arrival at Carrington Hall Donald had often been fearful, sullen and withdrawn when they visited. Now thanks to her interest in him, he was almost the way he had been as a little boy, sunny, engaging and loving. In truth she felt they owed Rosemary far more than a ringside seat for the Coronation.

Matron hadn't liked it one bit when they informed her of their plans for today. Just as she'd always claimed Donald put on his bad moods purely to upset them, she insisted a day out with them would set him back even further. She was even less pleased when asked if Rosemary Smith could join them too, and had suggested she wasn't a girl to be trusted. But Norah didn't believe that for a minute and she could be very insistent, especially when she had a long-term plan in mind.

Today wasn't just a day out for Donald. It was intended as a test to see if he was stable enough to bring home for good. Through Rosemary and their secret telephone conversations, both Norah and Frank were convinced the girl was right in saying Donald was no danger to anyone, providing he had a little supervision. Just looking at him now, seeing his happiness at being surrounded by his family, confirmed they had made a grave mistake in allowing outsiders to influence them into sending him away.

Norah's thoughts about her youngest son were interrupted by her discovering that the baby had wet her dress. 'I think Robin has been affected by the subject of lavatories,' she laughed, getting up with the baby in her arms. 'I'll go and change him and then make some tea and sandwiches, before the crowning,' she said.

'Let me do it,' Rosie said, holding out her arms for the fat, smiling baby.

'Do you know how to?'

'Of course I do,' Rosie grinned. 'I used to change my little –' she stopped, suddenly aware she was about to say 'brother' '– cousin, all the time,' she added quickly.

'Is that okay with you, Alicia?' Norah asked. She didn't like to take liberties with her daughter-in-law; she could be very possessive about her children.

Alicia nodded and smiled warmly at Rosie. She might have only met this girl for the first time a couple of hours ago, but she understood exactly why her in-laws thought so highly of her. She was a natural mother, and both Clara and Nicholas had taken to her immediately. 'If you really want to,' she said. 'All his things are in the bathroom. I'll help Mum with the sandwiches.'

As Rosie disappeared out of the door with the baby in her arms, Michael got out of his seat. 'Suppose I take the kids and Donald for a quick walk around the park?' he suggested to his mother. 'It's going to be at least half an hour before they get to the crowning ceremony and they're getting a bit restless.'

Norah hesitated. She was all for the idea of Clara and Nicholas going out for a while, but she wasn't so sure it was a good idea to take Donald too. He hadn't been out on a street for years and the huge crowds and the noise might make him nervous. She looked to her husband to make the decision but he was talking to Susan and didn't appear to have heard what Michael suggested. To her consternation, Donald had heard though and he jumped up, grinning broadly.

Norah looked from Donald back to her older son. She wished Michael had consulted her out of Donald's hearing. She was afraid he might fly into a tantrum if she refused to let him go. Clara touched her arm. 'Don't worry, Granny,' she said. 'We'll look after Uncle Donald. I'll hold his hand very tightly.'

Norah sighed. Nicholas and Clara were already holding each of Donald's hands, and with Michael insisting too she felt powerless. Michael and Donald were so alike physically and there had always been a very strong bond between them as Michael had looked after Donald a great deal as a boy. She knew too that Michael felt guilty that he didn't see his younger brother very often now that he had a family of his own. He wanted time alone with him.

'Very well,' she agreed reluctantly. 'Just be careful.'

It was some ten minutes later that Frank came out into the kitchen where the women were making sandwiches. 'Where is everyone?' he asked, sitting down at the central table and picking at some sliced ham.

The apartment was large, with two bedrooms, a dining-room and a big family-sized kitchen aside from the huge drawing-room. It had such thick interior walls it was quite possible for the children to be playing in one room without being heard.

'Rosemary's changing Robin, and the others have gone out,' Norah said as she carried on buttering bread.

Frank looked up at her. 'Not Donald too?'

Norah hastily explained.

'I don't believe it!' Frank said in alarm, moving his seat back with such force that it fell over with a clatter. 'Whatever were you thinking of, woman? It's like a circus out there. Donald can't cross a road on his own, let alone cope with all those people.'

Norah looked at her husband with some indignation. Like Michael he was kind-hearted, but he was a big man with a big voice and he tended to forget when he reared up that he made people nervous.

'It was all talked about while you and Susan were in the room,' Norah retorted. 'So why didn't you say something then instead of snarling at me now?'

Frank shot her a withering look as he made for the door. 'I didn't hear you. And I sometimes wonder if anyone in this family has a brain. I'd better go and find them and bring Donald back.'

Along the passage, Rosie was oblivious to what was going on. Robin was lying on a towel on the bathroom floor waving his chubby legs in the air; she was kneeling beside him washing his bottom. She thought that next to Alan he was the nicest baby she'd ever known.

She lingered over the task, tickling him to make him

laugh, playing 'this little piggy' with his toes, and wishing that she had a job looking after babies rather than minding mentally deficient adults.

Miss Pemberton had urged her not to be too hasty in changing her job and she'd dismissed Rosie's ideas that something bad was going on up on the second floor. She pointed out that many people who worked in mental institutions were a little odd, but that didn't mean they were cruel. Her view was that Rosie should give the job a full year, and look around London properly before deciding what to do next.

Yet it wasn't Miss Pemberton's opinion, as much as she valued it, that stopped Rosie from leaving Carrington Hall.

It was Donald.

He had crept into her affections without her really noticing, and each time she thought of moving on she found herself thinking of what it would do to him to suddenly find himself without his special friend. The other girls teased her, saying he sat in the corner and hardly spoke when it was her day off. So how could she leave when he depended on her so much?

On days when Carrington Hall got her down she mentally listed all the things in her life that were good: she had friends, her bust had finally grown enough for her to wear a bra, even if she did have to make it a padded one so she could wear fashionable tight sweaters, without looking like Olive Oyl; she'd even grown an inch to a respectable five-foot-four; at dances with Linda and Mary she found she could chat to boys easily, though she hadn't yet met anyone she liked enough to make a date with; and she knew her way round many parts of London, and once the weather got better she intended to explore further afield.

Then there was Thomas. She'd met him twice for supper in Finchley since Easter and it felt so good to be with someone she didn't need to hide things from.

Alan's adoption was in hand and would almost certainly be finalized this summer, but they didn't speak of that much. They hadn't spoken of Cole or Heather again either. It was almost as if by unspoken agreement they'd moved up a floor, leaving down below all those things which had hurt them both.

Their conversations were all about what was happening in the world now, of films, books and music. Thomas was good for her, he challenged things she said, made her think for herself rather than repeating things she had been told. He said she was good for him too because she reminded him he was still a young man, made him laugh and even made him forget he had only one leg.

Donald was also on that list of good things. Right at the top. He was her undemanding friend, willing pupil, sometimes her child. Because of him she could bear Matron's spite and prying, she could close her ears to the noises from upstairs, Maureen's dirty habits and the claustrophobia of being shut in all day when the sun was shining outside. He might be simple, but he filled a deep need inside her. To see his bright smile when she walked into the dormitory in the mornings lifted her spirits and it was so fulfilling to teach him little things. It was her hope that his parents would take him home as this was the only way she could leave Carrington Hall happily.

'Up you come,' she said to Robin, lifting the clean dry baby up into her arms and kissing him. 'Let's go and see what your brother and sister are up to.'

As Rosie walked back down the passage towards the drawing-room she heard Mrs Cook's voice ring out from the kitchen.

'Oh, where are they, Susan? I shouldn't have let them go, and now Frank's out there too. What if Michael leaves the children to run off after Donald?'

Rosie felt a stab of anxiety. Mrs Cook sounded upset. She stopped short at the kitchen door. Mrs Cook, Susan and Alicia were in there in a huddle; all three looked towards her and their faces were strained. 'What's wrong?' Rosie asked. 'Has something happened to Donald?'

Mrs Cook explained. 'Then Frank went out to look for them,' she added. 'Now Roger has gone too. Do you think Donald might run off?'

'He wouldn't intentionally,' Rosie said, but her heart plummeted. She couldn't believe a sensible adult like Michael would be so irresponsible as to suggest taking him out. It didn't bear thinking about what might happen if someone frightened Donald, or they just got separated in the crowd. He had been locked away for nine years, deprived of any chance to think for himself and she doubted he had any sense of direction. He wouldn't be able to tell anyone where his parents were, and if he was really upset she didn't think he'd even manage his full name. 'I'll go out and look around too.'

'You might get lost as well,' Alicia said and started to cry.

Rosie realized Alicia was frantic that her two children might at this moment be all alone somewhere and she hastened to reassure her. 'Michael would stay with Clara and Nicholas whatever happened,' she said more calmly than she felt. 'He's bound to bring them back here first, even if he's lost Donald.' She passed the gurgling Robin back to his mother and turned away towards the front door, picking up her raincoat as she went.

'Be careful, Rosemary,' Mrs Cook called out, her voice squeaky with fright.

It was raining heavily now and it took Rosie some time to fight her way through the crowd, the sea of umbrellas and the barriers to cross the road. She had just got inside the gate of Green Park when she caught a glimpse of Michael's head through a gap in the crowd. He was some twenty yards from her and there were too many people surrounding him to tell who he was with.

Rosie elbowed her way through the throng. It was difficult because she was going the opposite way to them.

From time to time she had to jump to see over people's shoulders to check she wasn't going right past Michael.

'Michael,' she yelled and wriggled round the last few people separating them. Clara and Nicholas were with him, but not Donald. Both children looked frightened. 'What happened?' she asked as she got nearer.

'Some mounted police came by and Donald just took fright,' he said shrugging his shoulders. 'I tried to follow him, but I couldn't with these two. You can't see anything through the crowds. Heaven only knows where he is now.'

'Take the children back to Alicia,' Rosie said without thinking how presumptuous it was for her to give orders to a grown man. 'I'll carry on looking. Which way did he go?'

'I didn't see, he just disappeared, but it was about halfway towards the Mall when he bolted.'

Rosie didn't stop to say anything more and shot off down through the park. She jumped up on each bench she came to to survey the crowd, looking for that familiar blond head. But she couldn't see it.

Her pulse began to race. She tried to picture what he might do once he found himself alone and that made her even more scared. He might just grab hold of someone he liked the look of and give them one of his frightening bear hugs, and who knew what that might lead to! On the other hand if he was really scared he might just stand and cry. Most adults would approach a crying child to ask what was wrong, but a grown man was a different proposition. People fought shy of the mentally handicapped and today of all days, when they were intent on finding a position to see the procession, they certainly wouldn't want any hindrances.

All she could do was keep on looking, she wished she was taller so she could see over people's heads. Umbrellas and the rain obscured so much. Stupidly, she hadn't even thought to ask if Donald had put on a raincoat, or what colour it was.

As she got to the other side of the park near the Mall, the crowd was even more dense than it had been in Piccadilly. It was impossible to see anything other than the people closest to her. Worse still, she was being swept along by them, trapped on all sides. Realizing this might be happening to Donald too she knew she must find something to climb on to so that she could survey the crowd.

Once out on to the Mall Rosie clawed her way against the flow of people back to where she could see a high wall. Dozens of people had already taken up every available inch on it as it was one of the best vantage points. Taking her courage in both hands she reached up and wiggled one man's shoe. He looked down at her in surprise.

'Can you help me get up there for just a minute,' she shouted. 'I've lost someone and it's about the only place I might be able to spot them from.'

She felt she'd approached a decent sort. He was a tough-looking working man in a cloth cap, not so different from the men around Catcott. Besides he had a warm smile.

'You can sit on me lap if you like,' he laughed down at her. 'Give us yer 'and, I'll 'aul you up. I'm not giving up me space, not even for a pretty little thing like you.'

Rosie held up her two hands and he grabbed them, dragging her up; his friend beside him caught her round the waist and suddenly she was up between them.

'Who you lost?' the first man asked. 'Your boyfriend or your ma?'

'Neither,' Rosie said, struggling to her feet between the two men. His cockney accent reminded her of Heather. 'I've lost a patient from the home where I work. He's about six-foot tall, twenty-four, with blond hair. He's never been in London before and he's a bit simple.'

The view over the Mall was astounding, she had never seen so many people in her entire life. It was like seeing the Christmas Market at Midsomer Norton a hundred times over, and the crowds were so closely packed it was impossible to make out anything about anyone. She realized she was looking for the proverbial needle in the haystack.

The word was passed along the wall that she had lost someone, and suddenly a pair of binoculars was passed to her.

Rosie scanned the crowd again and again. She could see detail now with the binoculars, a small girl on her father's shoulders, hats of all colours, redheads, brunettes and blondes, but no Donald.

She sighed deeply and passed back the binoculars. 'Thanks anyway. I suppose I'll just have to go to the police.'

'If we see anyone who looks like 'im, we'll 'old on to 'im for yer,' the man said. 'What's 'is name?'

'Donald Cook,' she said. 'Tell him to wait for Smith, will you?'

She was just going to ask to be helped down again, when she looked to her right and Buckingham Palace. In a flash of intuition she knew Donald would make for it if he'd come down this far. She'd shown him some pictures of it just a couple of days ago and he would almost certainly recognize it.

The men lowered her down again and she set off towards the palace. The crowds were virtually impenetrable the closer she got. It seemed the whole of England was determined to see the crowned Queen come on to the palace balcony later to wave and everyone was jealously guarding the tiny space they'd managed to find for themselves. But pure terror made her strong enough to push her way through. She had to find Donald soon. A gut feeling told her wherever he was he was badly frightened and although Donald wasn't ever violent, he just might turn that way if he felt threatened.

Miraculously as she got to the end of the Mall where the road swept round on both sides of a big statue, she saw a slight thinning of the crowd. She darted into the space and elbowed her way right down to the barrier holding the crowd back from the road.

'Oi, this is my space,' a woman sitting on a camp stool said indignantly. 'I've bin 'ere all night keeping it. You ain't barging in now and spoiling my view.'

Rosie quickly apologized and explained her predicament.

'Well, that's all right as long as you shove off once you've looked,' the woman said. 'You wouldn't believe what some cheeky buggers 'ave bin doing.'

As Rosie was peering across the road towards the palace railings where the crowds were at their most dense, she had a strange feeling that she was close to Donald, even if she couldn't see him. There was a black police van right outside the palace gates and she could see frantic movement amongst the people gathered there, almost as if a fight had started. A sort of buzz went around amongst the group she was in the middle of, people standing on tiptoe to see and craning their necks.

Two policemen appeared to be dragging someone out of the crowd there. The rain was coming down heavily now, making it even more difficult to see what was going on, but as Rosie saw a brief flash of blond hair, without stopping to make certain it was Donald, she scrabbled up over the barrier and out into the road.

'They'll arrest you,' the woman bawled out behind her, but Rosie ran on regardless.

It was Donald. He was struggling as the police tried to bundle him into the van.

'Let him go!' Rosie shouted as she ran towards him.

From out the corner of her eye she saw other policemen rushing forward to head her off, but she was determined.

'Smith,' Donald yelled out as he saw her and the police must have loosened their grip on his arms momentarily, because he broke away from them and ran to her like a child, arms outstretched, meeting her in the middle of the road.

His face was tear-stained, he had a cut above one eye and his raincoat was torn. He looked wild and distraught.

'Donald,' was all Rosie could exclaim as he trapped her in a fierce bear hug. 'Thank God I've found you.'

One lot of police were trying to shepherd them out of the road, Donald was trying to stutter out to Rosie what had happened to him and the two policemen who'd been trying to get him into a van were shouting above him asking who he was and what was wrong with him. Although Rosie was joyful at finding Donald, she was reluctant to tell the policemen in his hearing that he was simple.

'I must get him back home quickly,' she insisted, once they were back by the police van and the second lot of police had withdrawn. 'His family will be worried sick because he's just come out of a home for the day. He hasn't done anything wrong, has he?'

'Not apart from pushing his way down the front to the palace railings,' the older of the two officers said. He had a stern expression and he was looking hard at Donald as if trying to gauge if he was dangerous in any way. 'But on a day like today that's practically a hanging offence.'

Rosie was aware that was just a turn of phrase, but it still made her shake.

'Who hit him?' she said.

At this point a police car drew up and the policemen left Rosie and Donald momentarily to go and speak to them.

'Someone in the crowd took a swing at him,' a voice said at her elbow. 'And if I were you, love, I'd scarper with him before the police come back.'

Rosie turned to see the voice came from a stocky young man with light brown curly hair and twinkly blue eyes. He was wearing a long brown raincoat and he had a red, white and blue rosette pinned to the lapel. 'I was just by him,' he went on. 'It could've turned much nastier, especially with so many children around. But you look white as a sheet, and you're wet through. Let me help you get him home before they insist on taking you both down the police station.'

Rosie wasn't going to let that happen. Mrs Cook would be beside herself with anxiety as it was and Rosie remembered she didn't even know the telephone number at the flat so she could ring them and tell them that Donald was safe. She had to get back there now, otherwise the whole day would be spoiled for everyone.

'I've only got to get back up through the park again,' she said, clutching Donald's arm and edging away from the police. 'The flat's on Piccadilly. But I'll be all right on my own.'

'You need help,' he insisted and with that he took Donald's other arm and started off back across the road with him towards the park. Rosie had no choice but to fall in with the two men.

Once in the park and away from the police, the young man paused for a second. 'I'm sorry. I must seem very bossy,' he said, grinning at Rosie. 'I'm Gareth Jones. I got separated from my mates too, so I know how your friend must feel.'

Rosie introduced herself, said she appreciated his kindness, but really there was no need for him to go any further with them.

'Look, love,' Gareth said, giving her a sharp look that implied he understood Donald wasn't quite the ticket. 'He's wet and cold, he might even be in shock from that punch. I'm taking you both right home so I know you got there safely.'

Donald held Rosie's hand tightly as they walked through the park and he didn't say a word. She thought Gareth might be right, he could be in shock. Fortunately the crowds were thinner now; presumably they'd all now managed to find places to watch the procession. Rosie explained to Gareth exactly where the flat was.

He was a very resourceful man. When they found they

could no longer cross Piccadilly, he led her down into Green Park subway and up the stairs on the other side. She wouldn't have thought of that herself. Donald was crying when they came up on the other side of the road, the crowds were dense again and Rosie felt he was getting panicky because he could no longer walk by her side. Gareth sensed this. 'Hold on to my belt tightly,' he said. 'And you hold on to Donald's,' he shouted back to Rosie.

The final struggle through the jostling throng to the glass doors of the apartments was desperate, as no one was giving an inch. But Rosie's relief when she saw Mr Cook rushing down the stairs to unlock the door, and the joy on his face as he saw his son beside her, wiped out the last terrible hour.

'You found him! You angel,' Mr Cook exclaimed, his already ruddy face growing even more flushed with delight. 'We rang the police but they said there was as much chance of them finding him today as flying to the moon.'

Before Rosie could explain anything, who the stranger was with them, or how Donald had got his cut eye, the entire family came spilling down the stairs to greet them. Everyone was talking at once. Mrs Cook and Susan had tear-swollen eyes and Mrs Cook enveloped both Donald and Rosie in a fierce, emotional hug.

'We've all missed the crowning,' Susan said, catching hold of Rosie's shoulders and squeezing them affection-ately. 'None of us knew what to do. The men have been in and out like a dog at a fair. The kids were crying because they thought you were lost too.'

It was only then that Rosie managed to get a word in to introduce Gareth, and explain how he'd helped them get back.

'Well, you must come and join the party too,' Mr Cook said with a beaming smile and thumping Gareth's shoul-der. 'It's the very least we can do. Come on in, son. We're very grateful to you.'

Gareth looked shocked. 'I can't join in your family party!' he said.

But Mr Cook insisted, saying that but for his help there would be no party, and led the way back upstairs. Alicia took their wet coats, Susan brought tea for them. Then as Michael took Donald away to the bathroom to bathe his face and find him some dry clothes, the rest of the family wanted to know all about Gareth.

As Rosie sat back and watched the family's warm reaction to a complete stranger, she found herself comparing their code of behaviour to the one she'd been brought up with. Strangers were never welcomed at May Cottage; even men who called on her father in the line of business were rarely invited indoors. She wondered what Cole would have made of the Cooks. They certainly didn't fall into any of his classifications of people.

Throughout her childhood she had been conditioned to believe that people with money and class were all snobs who looked down on common working folk. Cole despised the middle classes even more because he said they aped 'their betters'. As for the ordinary working people, in the main he dismissed those too because they were so servile and lacking in daring. As she watched and listened to the Cooks, she felt they were the kind of people she should aspire to be like. They were neither snobs nor sycophants. They were in a class all of their own.

Gareth appeared to be comfortable with them too, despite being a working man with a London twang to his voice. 'I work on the railways, at Clapham Junction,' he said. 'I came up with a group of the lads, but I got separated from them an hour or so before I saw Donald down by the palace. It was lucky Rosemary got there when she did – another moment or two and the police would have had Donald in the wagon off to heaven knows where.'

Donald came back from the bathroom with a sticking plaster over his eye and a dry pair of trousers on. He was none the worse for his ordeal. Just like a child, the moment he was safe again he gloried in the adventure and didn't even mention the man who had hit him.

'I saw the p-p-palace,' he boasted. 'And the soldiers with the f-f-fur hats.'

Rosie was very much the heroine of the day. As they all waited for the procession to come by, everyone wanted to know exactly how and where she found him and seemed to think she was extraordinarily clever. After being the most junior member of staff at Carrington Hall and either being ignored or blamed for anything which went wrong by her seniors, it felt good to be admired and cosseted. Along with that was this extraordinarily handsome young man sitting beside her, asking questions about where she worked and telling her he knew Woodside Park well.

As his hair dried it fluffed up into tight little corkscrew curls, his eyes were a brilliant blue and he had an engaging dimple in his chin. Rosie wondered how old he was. He looked about twenty-two, but he had the confidence of a much older man.

'My parents live in Mill Hill, which isn't far from there,' he said. 'My dad's a coal merchant, good Welsh stock see,' he added, lapsing jokingly into a Welsh accent. 'I tried hard to get away from coal, but now I'm a train driver and I'm still dependent on the stuff.'

At last the procession finally arrived. First just distant drums and a hush out on the street, then a roaring as people further away got their first glimpse of the golden coach. The entire family rushed to the windows, opening them wide despite the driving rain, and the noise from the crowds below filled the room, drowning all conversation.

It was so magnificent that Rosie cried. To see such a procession on television was thrilling enough, but television could only give glimpses and not the colour or the detail. The red and gold uniforms, the jingle of spurs on shiny boots, the sheen on the horses' flanks, the Yeomen of the Guard, the Household Cavalry, footmen and coachmen, it all exceeded her wildest imagination. The golden coach was pure fairyland, so much more exquisite than illustrations had led her to believe. Rosie leaned right out of the window as the coach approached and she waved frantically, and to her amazement the young Queen in her crown and ceremonial robes looked right up at her, lifting one hand in salutation, almost as if she knew that this particular subject would hold that memory in her heart and mind for her entire life.

A year ago Rosie had had only one decent dress to her name; she'd been a barefoot ragamuffin who'd never been out of Somerset. London and royalty had been as inaccessible and distant as Africa or Australia. But here she was now, leaning out of a window from a grand apartment in Piccadilly, holding a Union Jack and shouting herself hoarse, and the Queen had actually waved at her.

'You will stay and have tea with us?' Mrs Cook asked Gareth after the long procession had passed and the crowds below had begun to disperse, some making tracks for home, but still more flooding into Green Park to try and get to the palace for yet another glimpse of the entire royal family when they assembled later on the balcony.

'That's very kind of you, Mrs Cook,' Gareth said with a shy grin. 'But I ought to try to find my friends now. Thank you so much for letting me see the procession with you. I doubt if I'd have found a better view anywhere, or such good company.'

Rosie found herself staring at Gareth in open admiration. He might be only a coal merchant's son, but his confidence, dignity and manners were as impeccable as both Michael's and Roger's.

'Well, I hope we run into you again one day,' Mrs Cook said. 'And thank you once again for rescuing my son and Rosemary. Perhaps you'd like to show Gareth out, Rosemary?'

After Gareth had said his goodbyes to everyone, Rosie

went out into the passageway with him and found him his raincoat.

'It's still very wet,' she said, feeling the shoulders. 'What if you can't find your friends?'

'I'll find them. They'll be in the pub by Charing Cross, I expect. If not, I'll go on home to my digs in Clapham. But before I go, would you come out with me one night?'

It had been quite a day for shocks and Rosie's mouth fell open in surprise. She'd met a few boys at dances, even had a kiss or two as they walked her home. But Gareth was a man, not a boy. She didn't know what to say.

'I d-don't know,' she stuttered.

'Will you at least think about it?' he said in a pleading voice.

Rosie looked at him through her lashes. He had endeared himself to her just by being kind to Donald; his bright twinkly blue eyes, clear peachy skin and that wide, beguiling grin were so very attractive. She liked him. But a date!

'Okay,' was all she managed to say.

'Is that okay to coming out or just to thinking about it?' he grinned.

All at once Rosie knew she would kick herself later if she let him go without a proper answer.

'Both,' she said and smiled because she suddenly knew that this was what Linda called a 'twist of fate'.

'Next Wednesday evening?' he asked, raising one dark eyebrow. 'I'm working the evening shift right up till then.'

Rosie nodded. It seemed an awfully long way off. 'Shall I write down the address?'

'No need, I know where Carrington Hall is. And I'll come to collect you at half past seven,' he said, and with that he opened the door and was off down the stairs. It was only after he'd disappeared out on to the street that Rosie realized Matron wouldn't approve of a young man calling at the home.

'Have you had a good day, Rosemary, despite Donald

running off?' Mr Cook asked as he drove her and Donald home at eight that evening. The rain was even heavier now, and the streets deserted once they got out of central London. Donald was in the back seat, almost asleep.

'It was the best ever,' Rosie said with a deep sigh. 'I'll never forget it, however old I get.'

After Gareth had left they'd had a huge tea, with ham, chicken, salad and sherry trifle. Then Mrs Cook had brought in a cake which she said she'd bought at Fortnum and Mason. It was iced like a wedding cake, with a tiny gold coach and all the horses sitting in the middle. Mrs Cook had given her the coach to take home as a souvenir. She had it wrapped in a paper napkin, along with a chunk of cake to share with the other girls when she got home.

On top of that she had a date arranged. She could hardly wait to tell the girls that.

Frank Cook looked sideways at Rosemary and smiled to himself. She was such an engaging young woman, so sensible, practical and calm, but there was another side of her which he'd glimpsed as she watched the procession. She was excitable too, full of fire and laughter, yet he had the distinct feeling she'd been forced to subdue this side of her for some reason.

He could see exactly why that young train driver rushed to help her. The little cap of glossy coppery hair, those forget-me-not eyes that seemed to question everything, the dusting of freckles on her nose and that ready warm smile were all so delightful.

'I hope you'll join us again on other days out with Donald,' he said.

'I'd like that,' Rosie replied eagerly. 'But maybe you should pick a place with no crowds next time!'

Frank laughed. He had a perfect place all mapped out in his mind. But he didn't think he ought to tell her where that was just yet.

Chapter Ten

At seven in the morning, the day after the Coronation, Rosie was just unlocking the outer door which led to the day room and dormitories on the first floor, when Matron came huffing and puffing up the stairs. She had her special tight-lipped expression on her face which Rosie had come to know always meant trouble.

Rosie was still puzzling over the unexpected sour note the day before had ended on. She hoped Matron's appearance now wasn't connected.

Mr Cook had got Donald and Rosie back to Carrington Hall at around eight-thirty. She said goodbye to them in the hall, leaving Mr Cook to hand over his son to Matron and to explain how he got the cut on his forehead, and went straight off to find Linda, Mary and Maureen to share out the cake and tell them all her news.

All three girls were in the downstairs staff sitting-room listening to the wireless, the small room thick with cigarette smoke. Rosie was so excited that she didn't notice the other girls' coolness towards her immediately. She sat down in a spare chair and rattled out the tale about Donald getting lost. It was only when none of the girls laughed or asked any questions that she realized something was badly wrong.

'What's the matter?' she asked, looking from one to the other, suddenly chilled. 'Has something happened while I've been out, or are you cross with me?'

The furtive glances they exchanged with one another seemed to confirm it was the latter.

'But what have I done?' Rosie asked in bewilderment. 'Come on, tell me.'

Linda, who was never one to hedge an issue, spoke first. 'If you must know, it's you getting all this special treatment,' she said bluntly. 'I've never 'ad much time for Donald. So I wouldn't 'ave expected 'is folks to ask me, but today was supposed to be my day off. I could'a gone 'ome to me mum's to join in their street party. But I was bleedin' well told I gotta 'ave Friday off instead. That ain't bloody fair.'

'I didn't ask for the day off,' Rosie retorted with some indignation. 'Mrs Cook asked Matron. I didn't even know about it until Matron told me.'

'But why you?' Mary piped up indignantly, her usually gentle blue eyes flashing with spite. 'Maureen and I have been looking after Donald for years. Why don't we get any appreciation?'

Mary was normally so easy-going and generous-natured that it was obvious someone had been working on her. Rosie was tempted to point out in her own defence that neither Mary nor Maureen ever spent more than a couple of minutes a day talking to Donald. They were kindly enough towards him, but they both tended to use him merely as an extra pair of hands on the ward and treat him as an irritation when he dogged their footsteps. But to say that would only make the present situation worse.

Both Mary and Linda mellowed marginally after Rosie said she was sorry, produced the cake and made them a new pot of tea. She was dying to tell them about Gareth, but under the circumstances she thought that might be a mistake, so she asked them about their day instead.

It was only as Linda described how Tabby had clawed at Simmonds when she'd brought up the tea to the day room, and how Archie had seized the opportunity to pick up the teapot and fling it across the room, that Rosie noticed how silent Maureen was. Usually it was she who relished telling such tales, three patients with minor scalds and a domestic with a clawed face was her idea of an exciting day. All at once Rosie knew she was the perpetrator of all this bad feeling.

Rosie fully intended to tackle Maureen about it once they were alone in their room, but she fell asleep waiting for Maureen to come up. So far this morning there had been no opportunity to bring up the subject again either.

'You can lock that door up again,' Matron said in a crisp voice from her position on the stairs. 'I want you up on the second floor in future.'

Rosie wheeled round in alarm. 'Me? Upstairs?' she gasped.

'Well, I wasn't talking to the wall,' Matron retorted sarcastically. 'Give me that set of keys, you won't be needing them any more.'

There was nothing unusual about Matron suddenly ordering one of the more senior girls upstairs. In an emergency they were often called up for a couple of hours. But the spiteful expression on Matron's face and the demand for the keys meant this was permanent and intended as a punishment. Rosie surmised it was Matron's way of exacting revenge for her having had the audacity to get herself invited out by the Cooks.

Rosie turned back to the door, pushing it open a little. 'Can I just go in here first and tell the patients where I am?' she asked. She could imagine Donald being very upset if he didn't see her this morning.

'Don't be ridiculous,' Matron snapped. She stepped forward, pulled the door shut with a bang and pocketed the keys. 'As if they care where you are! You do have such an inflated idea of your own importance.'

Rosie's heart sank. To argue would just result in further trouble, so she had no alternative but to follow Matron meekly up the stairs.

As Matron unlocked the outer door to the closed ward a babble of noise and a stink of excrement wafted out. But once they were through the second locked door it grew far worse, making Rosie gag and recoil in horror.

The stench was appalling, as bad as any pig farm, and the noise was terrible. Hammering noises, yelling, shouting and wailing.

'You'll soon get used to it,' Matron smiled maliciously as she saw Rosie's stricken face, and she grasped her arm firmly. 'The smell will go once they've all been cleaned up. You'll learn to live with the noise.'

Rosie's heart plummeted even further as she was led unwillingly down the corridor for there wasn't even a comforting similarity to the first floor. The corridor there was wide and bright, the several long, narrow windows between the various rooms bathing the area in natural light from both sides. This floor looked just like a prison landing, no windows, only dozens of locked doors, each with a small viewing panel. Even the ceiling was lower, creating a claustrophobic atmosphere, and it was lit by harsh strip lighting.

As Rosie passed along and she saw a grotesque face flattened against one of these panels, tongue lolling out, eyes rolling, all the revulsion she'd felt on her first night in Carrington Hall came back with a vengeance. She had always been so curious about this floor, but all at once she sensed it was going to be far worse than even her wildest imaginings.

As they reached the office, which was at the far end of the corridor, Saunders, the male chargehand, was just putting on a short-sleeved maroon jacket that matched his trousers. Staff Nurse Aylwood was sitting at the desk, checking some notes. They both looked round as Matron came in with Rosie.

After the oppressive atmosphere in the corridor, the office was surprisingly pleasant with a view of the fields beyond the back garden and an early morning breeze coming through an open window.

'Smith will be working with you in future,' Matron said curtly, without even the most cursory of introductions.

'She thinks she's a cut above the rest of the staff, so start her with an initiation into the morning routine immediately. That should cut her down to size.'

As Saunders and Aylwood looked at Rosie with unmistakable hostility, she quaked with fear. They were both very big people, and she felt dwarfed by them. Saunders was some six foot one or two, and perhaps fourteen or fifteen stone. Aylwood's height was not so apparent while she was sitting down, but her shoulders and forearms were hugely masculine, and her eyes as dead and cold as a cod on a fishmonger's slab.

'It's no picnic up here,' Aylwood said in a voice as cold and unwelcoming as her eyes. 'So you'll do exactly as I tell you. This is no place for giggling squeamish schoolgirls.'

Rosie looked at the three adults and saw a similar malevolent look on all their faces. Saunders's pale eyes narrowed and he smirked. Aylwood was now standing, her big arms folded across her chest, and she was sizing up Rosie with clear resentment. Matron's close-set eyes glinted with pleasure. All at once she knew they were all in league in some way.

From down the corridor came a guttural bellowing accompanied by frantic thumping on the door. Rosie's blood turned to water.

Matron turned and left without another word. As her feet tapped off down the corridor, both Aylwood and Saunders took down large green rubber aprons from a hook on the wall and put them on over their uniforms.

'Scared?' Aylwood asked, raising one thick grey eyebrow. She had a very deep voice with a hint of a Newcastle accent.

Rosie nodded. She saw no point in trying to hide it.

Aylwood gave a ghost of a smile, but there was no sympathy in it. Her face had an unhealthy grey tinge, her skin looked as if it was stretched over her bony features. 'Well, that's the first thing you have to overcome then,' she said. 'They're animals up here, and they sense fear

306

and play up to it. Don't give 'em an inch and don't ever turn your back on them.'

For the first time in her life, Rosie was tongue-tied. She wondered why just yesterday she'd been allowed to be so happy, then today it was all snatched away.

Saunders handed her a rubber apron too. 'It's got its compensations up here,' he said with a leer. 'Once they're cleaned and fed, there's nothing else to do.'

Aylwood gave him a peculiar look. Rosie couldn't tell if it was disapproval or warning. 'Come with us now,' she said, nudging Rosie out of the door and into the corridor. 'You'll just observe this morning, but mind you watch us closely because tomorrow's my day off and you'll be taking my place with Saunders. We have to work fast to get them all cleaned up before we feed them.'

Rosie had never considered herself to be squeamish. Right from when she was a small child she'd emptied buckets of slops, seen rabbits skinned and chickens gutted. Since coming to Carrington Hall she'd seen so many unpleasant sights and cleaned up so many disgusting messes that she thought there could be little more to shock her. But when Aylwood unlocked that first door she reeled back in disgust. It was like a stinking medieval dungeon. She had to clamp her hand over her nose and mouth to fight the nausea.

The room was around nine foot long and perhaps six foot wide, almost dark because the only light came from a twelve-inch barred window right up by the ceiling. The patient, she couldn't tell if it was male or female as its hair was cropped short, was crouched on the floor, daubed with faeces. It was making a low moaning sound, rocking back and forth on its heels, face hidden in its arms. The bed and floor were as filthy as the patient and the smell so appalling Rosie couldn't breathe. As Saunders and Aylwood marched in to grab the patient's arms and pull it to its feet, it let out a snarl of anger.

'This is Monica,' Aylwood said, turning her head just

slightly to where Rosie cowered in the doorway. 'She's thirty and she never speaks.'

Rosie could hardly bare to look. The woman wore nothing but a rough linen shift and her legs and arms were no thicker than a small child's. But it was the face rather than the filthy state she was in which really appalled Rosie: contorted, bestial and savage. Her lips were drawn back revealing yellow teeth.

'She's the worst here,' Saunders said as he and Aylwood dragged the woman towards the door past Rosie. 'She isn't human.'

Rosie thought she had never seen anything so vile as the way Saunders and Aylwood dragged that demented, shrieking woman along the corridor to the bathroom, her feet scrabbling uselessly at the floor. Yet she had no choice but to follow.

The bathroom wasn't like the ones downstairs. There were two baths in it, one with a solid contraption over it which suggested patients were immersed, then locked in with only their heads sticking out. The rest of the space was taken up by a large white-tiled shower area, divided into three with metal partitions in-between. Aylwood manhandled Monica into the corner with Saunders holding her tightly from behind the partition, then Aylwood turned on the water and jumped back.

Monica's scream proved the torrential water was icy, and the force of it made her cower back into the corner. But Saunders merely reached up and redirected the shower head right on to her and held her securely beneath it. To Rosie's further horror, Aylwood picked up a long-handled brush and began to scrub Monica with it, her face, head and body. Monica's shift slithered down to the shower floor at almost the first thrust of the brush and her body was so emaciated and covered with bruises that Rosie averted her eyes. She was acutely reminded of disturbing pictures she'd seen of inmates of the concentration camps in Germany.

'There isn't any other way to clean her,' Aylwood shouted over the roar of the water. 'So take that look off your face.'

Rosie was absolutely certain there must be a kinder way. It was like watching a cow or pig being scrubbed down ready to go to market, but no farmer she'd ever met was as rough as these two. Aylwood whacked the woman on her back, forcing her to bend over, then thrust the brush up between her legs to wash her there with almost vengeful pleasure.

Such barbarism was made worse by knowing that tomorrow Rosie would be expected to take Aylwood's place. She just knew she couldn't do it.

Monica continued to yell, but slowly it became less strident and interspersed with gasps and finally they turned off the shower. Saunders held her while Aylwood rubbed her down with a thin grey towel. They forced her arms back into a clean linen shift, then dragged the woman back down the corridor to a different room. Here without a word to Monica they forcibly pushed her in, then Aylwood locked the door.

As they went back down the corridor to fetch another patient, one of the domestics, Coates, was just finishing scrubbing out the room Monica had vacated.

'Coates cleans out the rooms as we do the patients,' Aylwood informed Rosie curtly. 'If she's slow tomorrow when I'm not here, shout at her. It causes problems if there isn't a clean room to put them back in after their showers.'

Rosie didn't think she'd ever have the nerve to even ask Coates to hurry, let alone shout at her. She was an ex-mental patient like all the domestics, a big raw-faced woman with purple hands the size of hams, who constantly muttered to herself. It was common knowledge that even Matron was nervous of upsetting her.

There were only nine patients in all, five women and four men. Rosie was surprised by this; she had always supposed there to be at least fourteen or so, and there were enough rooms up here for that many. Of these nine, only three more were dirty, two men and Mabel, the woman Rosie had heard wailing on her arrival at Carrington Hall. She had imagined someone able to keep up such a constant noise to be robust, a sort of stereotype madwoman like the wife of Mr Rochester in *Jane Eyre*, but she was nothing of the kind.

Mabel was just a frail old lady, so thin she could barely stand on her own, and her back was deformed. Her white hair was sparse, she hadn't a tooth in her head and just one glance told Rosie that she wailed merely because she was in pain. Her heart went out to her. She wanted to pull Aylwood away from her, insist that Mabel was put in a wheelchair to take her to the bathroom. But she didn't dare do or say anything.

Another two men and one woman were just wet, but all of them received the same appalling treatment as Monica, even though they showed no inclination to fight, and one of the men was so infirm and shaky he could barely stand. The last two females, one a young girl called Angela, the other a strapping great woman called Bertha, almost as tall and as heavy as Saunders, were allowed to use a toilet and then wash themselves under a warm shower, but Aylwood and Saunders still stood menacingly over them, allowing them no privacy.

Maureen had related many hideous tales of brutality at Luckmore Grange, including a description of bathing much like this, but Rosie had never imagined for one moment that such things could be condoned in a private home. In truth she had always suspected Maureen of wild exaggeration anyway.

Now in the face of what she'd seen, she did believe Maureen. She was appalled to think that she'd heard those terrible noises for so long, and been so suspicious, yet allowed herself to be convinced by others that it was none of her business. What sort of person was she that she could work, eat and sleep in a place, sensing that something was badly wrong, yet do nothing, say nothing?

Perhaps she was mistaken in thinking Aylwood and Saunders enjoyed humiliating and hurting these unfortunate people. Maybe time and experience would prove that they were merely callous rather than cruel. But all the patients had bruises and scars on their bodies. Every one of them had cowered away from their keepers like frightened dogs as their cell doors were opened. The rooms they were returned to had the mattresses and bedding removed for the day, leaving only the bare wooden base of the bed which was securely fixed to the floor. They had nothing, no clothes, shoes, personal possessions and absolutely no comfort. It was barbaric.

Rosie was acutely embarrassed to be forced to stand beside Saunders watching Angela and Bertha washing themselves. They looked perfectly capable of doing it unsupervised and even if a man was needed there for safety he could at least turn his back on them. She stole a sideways glance at him. He was watching Angela closely as she soaped her breasts and stomach, his tongue flickering across his lips.

Unlike the other patients, Angela was young and quite pretty, perhaps twenty-four or twenty-five, and her thick black naturally curly hair hadn't been shorn off. She had a curvy, well-rounded body with small pert breasts and taut buttocks. There was a savage look in her eyes, and she was muttering and grunting just as much as some of the others had, but there was nothing repulsive about her.

The hairs on the back of Rosie's neck stood on end as she saw Saunders's response. Although she had no real experience of such things, she was sure that he was becoming aroused by looking at Angela. His expression reminded her uncomfortably of the way Seth had looked at women. She looked inquiringly towards Aylwood, perhaps hoping to have this thought squashed, but instead she saw an equally lascivious expression in her eyes too. But as if she sensed Rosie watching her she smirked.

'I bet you're wondering what she's doing up here?' she asked. 'She looks harmless, doesn't she? But believe me, Smith, she's the most dangerous patient in Carrington Hall, far worse than Monica because she's entirely unpredictable. She was down on the first floor when she first came here, until she attempted to strangle another patient. She tried to blind Sister Welbred with a fork once. She's bitten and clawed everyone. She's like a cobra, and you never know when she's going to strike. So don't give her an inch.'

The bathing was completed by half past eight, and by then Rosie had seen enough to want to run out of Carrington Hall and never return. But if she thought the bathing was inhumane, breakfast was to prove even worse.

Saunders went to one end of the corridor with Simmonds in tow. Aylwood and Rosie began at the other end. Rosie had a small tray shoved into her hands at the first door, a bowl of almost cold porridge, another bowl of equally cold scrambled egg, two slices of bread and marge and a mug of tea. Aylwood unlocked the door and walked in, then made Rosie stand with her back to the door to prevent the inmate making a break. This first patient was one of the old men; she wasn't even told his name. He was sitting on the bare wood of the bed as Aylwood handed him the porridge. He lifted the bowl to his lips, sucking it down in one noisy slurp, then held his hand out for the scrambled egg which he ate with his hands. From starting his porridge to the final guzzle of his tea, the whole thing took less than two minutes. As they locked the door behind them on the way out, Rosie glanced back through the window and saw he was picking the spilt food off his shift and eating that too as if he was still hungry.

The next room was Mabel's and she was already wailing again, lying down on her side on the bed rocking herself. Her thin bare legs were covered in hideous, bulging purple veins and she made no move to sit up for her food. Aylwood poured the porridge into a spouted feeding cup, added more milk and stirred it round. She advanced on Mabel, hauled her up by the shoulder, then holding the old lady's neck in a vice-like grip, she literally poured it down her throat. Mabel was gagging as it went down, her arms waving frantically like sails of a windmill, but Aylwood didn't slow down. When the cup was empty, she poured the tea into it, and that was force-fed too.

For some reason she wasn't offered scrambled egg, perhaps because feeding her that required too much effort. Once the last dregs of tea were finished Aylwood indicated to Rosie that the job was completed, then locked the door behind them, leaving Mabel to her wailing again.

This procedure was repeated with everyone. No attempts at conversation or cajoling. If they didn't eat willingly and fast, they were force-fed. Angela ate her porridge willingly enough, but knocked the bowl of scrambled egg out of Aylwood's hand. Aylwood slapped her hard across the face, then holding her neck she forced the woman to get down on the floor and gobble up the spilt food like an animal.

Monica didn't get any breakfast at all. Although she calmed down after her shower, Aylwood none the less gave her an injection which knocked her out. Rosie wondered if that was the reason Monica was so thin. If this happened every day she probably hardly ever got a meal.

Rosie was sitting on a chair in the corridor when Dr Freed arrived to do his rounds soon after ten that morning. She had been told by Aylwood that her duties until dinner time at twelve were merely to patrol up and down the corridor at regular intervals checking through the viewing panels. She didn't even say what Rosie was supposed to be checking for, or what constituted an emergency. It sounded as if she just wanted the new girl out of her hair so she and Saunders could read their newspapers in peace.

All was quiet again. The patients, except for Monica, were sitting on the floor, just staring into space. Monica was out cold on the bed base without even a pillow or blanket. As Dr Freed came in escorted by Matron, Rosie jumped to her feet. She had seen the wiry little doctor innumerable times before downstairs, but she'd never spoken to him as Matron always accompanied him there too. He examined the patients in the treatment room next to the office and even if there were any instructions for the staff, they were rarely told about them.

'Smith! Tell Staff Nurse Aylwood Dr Freed has come to do his rounds,' Matron called out.

Rosie did as she was told, hoping that she'd get an opportunity to speak to him later on, but she didn't. Saunders ordered her to go and make tea for them in the tiny kitchen at the end of the landing and by the time she got back to the office with a tray, Aylwood was there, sitting in an easy chair lighting up a cigarette. Saunders was perched on the desk talking to her.

'I made some for the doctor, too,' Rosie said nervously. 'Is he in with one of the patients?'

Aylwood gave her a withering look. 'He's gone. Leave his tea, I'll drink that too. Get on back to the corridor.'

Rosie slunk out, but there on her seat she could hear Aylwood and Saunders talking. She gleaned that the doctor had recommended electric shock treatment for Mabel and for one of the men. They didn't even mention Monica.

As she sat there in the corridor without even a window to see out of, it suddenly occurred to her that she knew no more about mental illness now than when she had arrived here last September. She knew most of the patients downstairs were born with some brain damage. But what about the ones up here? Were they normal until some tragedy or trauma tipped them into the dark terrifying world they lived in now? And if this was the case, surely something could be done to help them?

It was sad enough downstairs to see adults just shuffling around all day with nothing to do, but at least they had the companionship of the other patients, the staff talked to them, and they could look out of the windows. These poor people up here had absolutely nothing, totally isolated, locked away from any human contact. Even the tiny windows in their cells were too high up for them to see out of. Rosie thought it would be better to die than be forced to live that way.

Rosie had never known time pass so slowly as it did that morning. Downstairs there had been the routine of cleaning and bed making, and chats with the other girls and patients to speed it along. But Coates did all the cleaning herself, and there was no one to talk to. Saunders was lounging in a small rest room further down the corridor, reading a newspaper and chain-smoking. Aylwood appeared to be doing some sort of paperwork in the office. Except for when Nurse Gladys Thorpe came up to help Aylwood take Mabel downstairs for her electric shock treatment there would be no further visitors to the ward until Simmonds arrived with the dinner trolley.

Sitting alone on an upright chair out in the corridor, listening to the sounds of human misery all around her, heads banging against walls, low plaintive crying and every now and then a yell of outrage, Rosie fought back her own tears and tried to think what she must do to get out of here.

It was obvious that pleading to be sent back downstairs was pointless. In fact, if she showed Matron how distressed she was at being here, that would only delight her. If she caused a scene, she might get the sack. Getting the sack looked far more attractive than having to face this ward again tomorrow, but where would she go once she was chucked out? She had less than two pounds in savings, and that wasn't even enough to get a room. Would Thomas put her up until she found a new job?

She was certain he would, in an emergency, but was it

fair to ask him? People would talk about a young girl staying alone with him in his flat and his boss would almost certainly disapprove. Maybe she could telephone Miss Pemberton tonight and ask her advice? But wouldn't she think Rosie was spineless and wonder what sort of nurse she'd make if she wanted to bolt at the first sign of unpleasantness?

Then there was Donald. She knew he was always withdrawn on her day off, but he had a good enough concept of time to understand she'd be back the following day. How was he going to cope when she didn't return? What if he threw one of his tantrums and got punished with electric shock treatment?

Just the thought of that made her eyes prickle with tears and her stomach contract with fear. Matron would almost certainly blame his day out as the reason for his bad behaviour. Without Rosie to act as a go-between Mr and Mrs Cook might well give up any thought of taking him home for good. What would become of him then? He had come on so well, but without the special treatment he'd grown used to from her, he'd soon revert back to the way he'd been before.

Then there was Gareth. Next Wednesday he'd be coming here to call for her, and she didn't know how to contact him to arrange to meet him somewhere else.

Rosie sighed deeply. Gareth wasn't really important, at least not compared with Donald or the patients up here who were being ill-treated. But what was she going to do?

She felt so angry too that the other girls who she thought of as good friends hadn't confided in her about what went on up here. Why hadn't they? Were they so hard-hearted they didn't care, or were they all so afraid of Matron they didn't dare speak out?

This feeling of utter helplessness was very familiar. She had felt this way after seeing what Seth and Norman did to Heather. If she had done something then, told her father, or even admitted to Heather she knew, maybe Heather would be alive now.

Then there were all the times when her father and brothers had laid into Alan. Why hadn't she told her teacher? Maybe she had some sort of excuse then, she was only a kid herself and she was afraid they would take Alan from her. But she was an adult now. If she kept quiet and ignored something she knew to be totally wrong, didn't that make her every bit as bad as Saunders, Aylwood and Matron?

Rosie's reverie was cut short by the sound of Simmonds coming through the outer door with the dinner trolley. She stood up wearily. Breakfast was bad enough, she could hardly bear to think what might be in store for her with dinner.

At the end of the day when Rosie came off duty she was very close to breaking down. Her head ached, she felt sick, and as the long day had worn on, more and more horrifying things had come to her notice. If the patients needed to go to the lavatory, they were supposed to call out or just wait until meal times when staff unlocked their doors and escorted them there. Although one or two of them seemed to manage this, the rest couldn't, and the mess they made was left there on the floor until the next unlocking time, which was the reason all bedding was taken away during the day.

More alarming still was that after tea they would be locked up again until seven the next morning, and from what Rosie could make out, after ten-thirty there was no one continuously on duty, only Sister Welbred coming up from the floor below now and again.

When Rosie had first arrived at Carrington Hall, she'd thought the staff was huge and in fact wondered how they could all be occupied. But over the past months she'd soon discovered that housekeeping duties were the most onerous, not the nursing side at all. By watching people going on and off duty she'd worked out for herself that the second floor had a considerably smaller staff than the first and this had always puzzled her.

Now after a day up there she understood why that was. With patients locked up like caged animals, aside from the early morning cleaning and feeding, there wasn't any call for more staff. As for the story that Matron stayed up here all day, that had turned out to be untrue. Saunders told her she never came up unless there was an emergency.

Rosie went reluctantly down to the staff dining-room. She didn't really want any tea, only an aspirin for her headache and a walk outside to get rid of the disgusting second-floor smell which she felt was clinging to her. She didn't even want to see the other girls because she was convinced now they must have known last night what she was in for today. She still had no idea what to do; she was friendless and helpless, but she felt compelled to hold on to the last vestiges of pride, and if that meant seeing the people she felt had betrayed her, then she wasn't going to dodge it.

Thorpe, Maureen, Mary, Linda and Simmonds were all eating their tea. She heard them talking and laughing even before she reached the dining-room. But as she walked in they all fell silent for a moment, then leaning closer to one another they resumed their conversation and totally ignored her.

Rosie couldn't tell if they were sending her to Coventry because of yesterday, or because Matron had ordered it. She took a place at the end of the table, furthest away from them all. Pat Clack plonked a cup of tea and a ham sandwich down in front of her, without even her usual smile. Rosie drank the tea in silence, and steeled herself against crying.

Maureen and Mary left the dining-room soon after she came in. Thorpe and Simmonds followed soon after. Linda was still sitting there, eating a large slice of fruit cake, but she didn't speak. Rosie gulped down her tea, but left the sandwich on the plate and got up to go, but as she went out into the passage Linda came up behind her.

'Come into the sitting-room,' she whispered. 'I gotta talk to you.' With that she took off like a scalded cat along the passage.

Rosie was puzzled. She looked around, expecting to see Matron somewhere close, but there was no one. Pat Clack was alone in the dining-room, clearing the table. She couldn't even hear distant voices. She hurried into the sitting-room to find Linda lighting up a cigarette, looking very tense and white-faced.

Rosie sat down. Linda checked outside the door, then closed it. 'I 'ad to say sommat,' she said, taking a big drag on her cigarette. 'We've all been told not to, but that don't seem fair to me, so I'm sticking me neck out.'

'But why? What's going on?' Rosie asked. 'And why didn't any of you ever tell me what it's like up there?'

Linda shrugged. 'Forget that for a minute. I ain't got that long,' she said hurriedly. 'I know it ain't too good up there, but then it ain't no different to other loony-bins. What I wanted to warn you about is Aylwood and Saunders, they ain't the sort to mess with, so keep quiet and say nothing, whatever you see.'

To receive such a warning without a proper explanation rang further alarm bells in Rosie's head. 'But I don't understand! Okay, so Matron's got it in for me and she wants you all to send me to Coventry, that's weird and nasty enough. But don't any of you feel any sympathy for those patients?'

Linda shrugged again. Her dark eyes were blank, her thin mouth set in a straight line. She didn't look as if she cared a jot about the patients' predicament. 'They'd get the same wherever they was,' she said. 'So no, I don't feel no sympathy for them. But I do for you.'

'Linda, stop beating about the bush and tell me what's going on,' Rosie said more forcefully. 'Why exactly was I sent up there? Was it just to get even with me because I went to the Coronation, or because Matron hopes it will make me leave?'

A little warmth came back into Linda's dark eyes. 'Yeah, I reckon it's a way to get rid of you,' she said, scratching at her bad skin as if such a disclosure worried her. 'See, the old bat has got a *thing* about you. The day after you arrived she warned all of us that we weren't to discuss the second-floor patients or the staff there with you. And we didn't because we knew Maureen would soon tell 'er if we did. Maureen's a sewer rat, she'd grass up anyone for ten fags. She was loyal to you for a while because you was the only one that was nice to 'er, but she started to get narky when Donald got to like you more than 'er.'

Rosie nodded. Maureen was quick-witted, maybe she'd guessed that she was in regular contact with Mr and Mrs Cook and yesterday's invitation had made her jealous enough to tell Matron. That would explain too why Matron wanted to get rid of her. She couldn't sack her for that without proof, but nudging her out the door was another way.

'What should I do, Linda?' she asked. She had to put her trust in someone, and Linda was at least straight-talking.

'In your shoes I'd be out of 'ere so fast my feet wouldn't touch the ground,' Linda said emphatically. 'There's not many of us got the stomach for the second floor, but neither me, Mary or Maureen 'as been expected to do anything more up there than feed the calmer ones and clean up the odd mess on the floor. Saunders and Aylwood 'ave always done the real grim stuff and they love it. But the shit and the ugliness up there, and whether you can handle it or not, ain't really the point I'm trying to make. Maureen seems to think Matron knows something bad about you. Now that is dangerous, 'cos she'll use it. Is there sommat?'

Rosie's stomach lurched and her head spun for a moment. So that was it. Matron was waiting for her to complain, then she'd threaten to expose her. She took a deep breath and forced herself to look blank. 'Maureen's got too much imagination for her own good,' she said. 'Just tell me why you think Aylwood and Saunders could hurt me in some way?'

Linda looked hesitant. 'Don't you go telling anyone I said this, but from what I've 'eard and seen up there, both of them are real nasty weirdos. Matron took 'em on, knowing all about 'em, same as she did almost everyone 'ere but you, and I reckon they've got some big fiddle going between them.'

'But the owner, Mr Brace-Coombes!' Rosie started to protest.

Linda smirked. ' 'E don't come 'ere any more, do 'e? From what I've 'eard it was a showplace when 'is wife was an inmate. But when she snuffed it, 'e just let Matron take over. I ain't seen 'im 'ere more than twice since I come. Doubt 'e's got the foggiest idea what goes on and cares even less.'

Rosie felt confused. She had a gut feeling that Linda wanted her to clear off immediately for more reasons than she'd stated. Although the girl hadn't said as much, the implication seemed to be that if she stayed, she could expect no help or sympathy from anyone, including herself. Rosie wondered fleetingly if Matron had something on her too. Now she came to think about it, Linda was as evasive about her past as she was.

'I'd better go,' Linda said. She put one hand on Rosie's shoulder and squeezed it. 'Look, I'm really sorry about all this, you're too young and bleedin' idealistic for a place like this. Get out now, love, before you get 'urt. And keep your distance from Saunders.'

Rosie nodded, as if in agreement. 'Thanks for being so frank with me,' she said. 'Will you just do one more thing for me? Would you tell Donald in private where I am and that I miss him. Explain I can't get in to see him just now.'

Linda arched one eyebrow. 'Sure, just as long as you do one thing for me too.'

Rosie nodded.

'Mind you only feed Maureen information you want to get back to Matron. Like you're looking around for a new job!'

Fortunately Maureen wasn't there when Rosie got back to their bedroom, as she might have been tempted to choke her. She quickly changed out of her uniform, put her raincoat over her arm and went back downstairs before anyone could ask where she was going.

It was just before seven as she left Carrington Hall. By quarter to eight she was in Flask Walk, Hampstead, ringing Thomas's bell.

He took some time to answer the door. As she saw him limp across the shop on his crutches, his empty trouser leg flapping, Rosie felt very guilty that she was about to burden him with her problems. He had settled down for the evening and she guessed he wouldn't like her to see him without his artificial leg.

'Rosie,' he exclaimed as he opened the door, but his smile was so welcoming it at least banished the fear of rejection. 'What a nice surprise! What brings you here?'

'I needed someone to talk to,' she said. 'I'm sorry if it's not convenient, but you're the only person I can trust.'

'Any time is convenient if it's you,' he said with a laugh. 'Good job I tidied up a day or two ago.'

Rosie had often wondered what Thomas's flat was like – she had expected a bachelor to be very untidy, but to her surprise there was no clutter and only a minimum of furniture. He showed her his small workshop first as they passed it on the narrow stairs. A bench with a bright lamp, a stool and his tools laid out in rows like a surgeon's beside a dismembered clock. From there they went up another few winding stairs to a small landing, the minuscule kitchen and bathroom at the back of the building, and his bedroom which he didn't show her. His living-room was at the front, looking out on to Flask Walk. This was all painted white, with dark red curtains. The evening sun was coming in the windows and the low ceiling gave the place a cottagey feel. He didn't have many possessions: two rows of books on shelves, two easy chairs and a small round table covered in a red cloth in the window, a wireless and a lamp on a sideboard. But the starkness was relieved by two large bright pictures at either end of the room. One was of a golden cornfield against an azure sky, the other of a white thatched cottage with a faded green door and long waving grass surrounding it.

Rosie was so taken aback by the serene beauty and simplicity of the scenes that her pressing problems were temporarily forgotten. 'Did you paint them, Thomas?' she asked.

He nodded but looked embarrassed and even when she moved nearer to examine them in more detail, he didn't make any comment. Close up Rosie could see by the delicacy of the strokes and the careful shading of the colours that they weren't the daubings of a novice, but an artist of some talent. She wondered why he'd never mentioned before that he could paint, and indeed why he was so unforthcoming now. 'Did you do them when you were in hospital?' she asked over her shoulder.

'What makes you think that?' he asked in a defensive tone.

'I don't know,' she shrugged. 'There's something dreamy about them, as if you painted the scene from a memory.'

'You are very perceptive,' he said, then cleared his throat as if he'd decided he would speak about it after all. 'In fact I was trapped in a ward of men who cried out in pain night and day. I used to get the nurse to wheel me out on to the veranda to paint. It was my only way of escaping. Both these two pictures were images of England I kept in my head all the time out in Burma.'

'Why haven't you ever told me before that you can paint?' she asked quietly.

'It never came up.' He turned away from her. 'Besides, I don't do it any more, so it isn't relevant.'

Rosie had good reason to know that it was often the things which people tried to hide about themselves which were the most important.

'I think it is relevant,' she said, looking back at the picture of the cottage. She knew nothing about art, but she knew that what she was seeing was something special. She could look at this picture every day and never grow tired of it. 'If you have such a talent you should use it.'

Thomas laughed, but there was a hollow ring to it. 'Talent? It's just a daub!'

'That's rubbish, and you know it,' she snorted. 'If you really thought that, you wouldn't have had it framed and hung it on your wall. My guess is your real reason for not doing it any more is because it reminds you of life before you lost your leg.'

Thomas just looked at her. She knew then that she was right.

'Well, Miss Bossy Boots,' he said eventually. 'If you're through with the amateur psychiatrist bit, perhaps you'd like to tell me what brings you here tonight?'

Over a cup of tea Rosie told him what had happened, both seeing the Coronation and today's events. Thomas let her get it all out without interrupting or making any comment. Even though she managed to describe the vile scenes she'd witnessed quite calmly, it was obvious she was stunned and appalled.

Thomas felt rage welling up inside him as he listened. He could scarcely believe that professional nursing staff were not only cruel enough to inflict such misery on helpless patients but also to allow an innocent sixteen-year-old to watch their atrocities.

He looked at Rosie and saw she was as fresh and pretty as always in a white short-sleeved blouse, her short hair-style gleaming in the evening sun, but yet as he looked closer he saw that her blue eyes looked haunted.

His initial reaction was just to protect her, to keep her here tonight, try and make her forget what she'd seen and help her find a new job as fast as possible. But as Rosie went on speaking he realized she was far more incensed by the suffering of the patients than finding herself forced into such a loathsome job.

'The thought of going back into that ward tomorrow makes me sick to the stomach,' she said finally. 'But I can't just run away, can I?'

Her humanity touched him deeply. He had learned the art of looking the other way while atrocities were committed back in the camp. The word for it there was survival. But Thomas felt sure that each and every man who like him had been in that position found it difficult later on to live with their cowardice.

He thought it might be the same for Rosie. If he encouraged her to leave now without attempting to do something to help those patients it might very well become another burden of guilt for her to carry with her.

'There's a bolthole here if you need it,' he said. 'But I think you want to do something more positive than just run away, don't you?'

'I don't know, Thomas.' She ran her hand distractedly through her hair. 'I'd like to do something, anything, to help those poor people, but I'm the most junior chargehand. What experience do I have? I haven't even been inside another asylum to see what they are like. How can I do anything?'

Thomas thought for a moment. 'You could do a great deal,' he said at length. 'Not by tackling anyone head-on yourself, but by gathering information and giving it to someone who is better-placed to deal with it.'

'But who is better-placed?' she asked bitterly. 'After what I've seen today I'll never believe in doctors or nurses again. In fact I don't think I'll ever be able to trust anyone.'

'Well, there's Miss Pemberton for a start,' he said.

Rosie opened her mouth to make an angry retort.

'She couldn't know such terrible things were going on at Carrington Hall,' Thomas said quickly, 'or she wouldn't have sent you there. I guarantee that she'll move heaven and earth to get things changed just as soon as I tell her. Then there's Mr and Mrs Cook too. I can't see them refusing to help when their own son might be at risk.'

'Should I ring them and tell them?' Rosie's voice rose in panic as if she felt unable to alarm them in such a way.

'Let me speak to Miss Pemberton first,' Thomas said gently. 'She'll know the best way to tackle it. I'll ring her later tonight if you like and talk to her about it.'

Rosie fell silent for a moment or two.

'What is it?' Thomas asked.

'What if Linda was right and Matron does know all about me,' she blurted out, her eyes turning almost navy blue with anxiety. 'She's bound to tell everyone, especially if she realizes I'm responsible for making trouble.'

From what Rosie had said, Thomas felt that Matron Barnes was not only an affront to the nursing profession, but an evil, conniving woman who was lining her own nest at the expense of the patients.

'I think you'll have to prepare yourself for that, Rosie,' he said bluntly. 'You know what they say about "you can't make an omelette without breaking a few eggs". But awful though that may seem, you must hold on to the fact that you have done nothing personally to be ashamed of, whereas she has a great deal. Either myself or Miss Pemberton can remind her of that!'

Rosie half smiled at Thomas's hint at blackmail, but she was still a little uncertain. She wanted to do as Thomas suggested, and she knew she was perfectly capable of being as sneaky as Maureen if she put her mind to it. But could she actually go back there, and stand by and watch terrible things happening day after day without breaking down?

Thomas watched her face and, guessing what she was thinking, he felt deeply for her. She was in for a rough ride, that much was certain. But yet it might be the making of her, a chance to do something she could be proud of.

'Do you care enough to speak out for those patients on your ward?'

He watched her face and saw a flame of courage light up in her eyes.

'Yes,' she said. 'I do.'

'And are you tough enough to clean up and feed those patients for a little longer, and brave enough to risk being exposed as a murderer's daughter?'

Rosie gulped. She thought of people sneering at her, whispering behind her back, but then she made herself remember Aylwood with that brush, and Monica's screams, and Saunders leering at Angela. 'Yes, I think I am.'

'Good girl,' he said, leaning forward in his seat and clapping one strong hand over her smaller one. 'Now, as from tomorrow you must keep a day-by-day report. Everything you see which seems wrong or cruel you must jot down; the time, the patient concerned, and who did it. Listen at doors, keep your eyes open.'

'I'll feel like Mata Hari,' she giggled nervously.

'It won't be for very long. I'll get you help somehow and you can come here any evening if it helps. Post me the daily reports for safety if you aren't coming over and ring me at the shop if there's any emergency. You'd better run along back there now and behave normally, but I'll get things moving my end. Have you got the Cooks' telephone number on you? Miss Pemberton might need it.'

Rosie felt very much better as she rode home on the bus. She had a goal now, and although she dreaded tomorrow morning, at least she could think that every moment spent in the ward served a clear purpose. Perhaps too she could find a more humane way of washing the patients to-morrow, or other small things to alleviate their misery.

327

She must stop dreading the job and think of it as a challenge.

It was half past ten when Thomas hobbled back up the stairs from the shop telephone. But for once he didn't feel like a cripple, but a soldier going into battle.

Violet Pemberton sounded almost faint with shock when Thomas told her the story, and like himself her first reaction was to get Rosie out of there. But after a few minutes of discussion she came round to his way of thinking. She said she was certain that Lionel Brace-Coombes was unaware of what was going on, but she would speak to other contacts who knew the home to find their views on this. It was her suggestion that they leave Rosie for about a week to compile her diary, then she would call on Lionel and ask him if he could make an unexpected visit to the home because she suspected something was badly wrong. As she pointed out, it would be very wrong of them not to give the man a chance to prove he hadn't condoned brutality and neglect at the home. And only a guilty man would refuse to do as she suggested. She intended to speak to the Cooks too and enlist their help.

As Thomas limped into his living-room he glanced across and saw his painting of the cottage, and half smiled as he remembered Rosie's questions about it earlier in the evening.

She was a smart girl. Not quite right about why he didn't paint or draw any more, but close. Once he'd never been without a sketch pad, seizing the odd free moment while working at Smithfield market, Sundays down by the docks with Heather beside him. He'd had a dream of becoming an artist, though in those days he couldn't afford decent paper or anything more than water colours.

Later in the camp it had become his lifeline, drawing on anything he could find, bits of old planking and bark once the precious supplies of paper ran out. Some men drew their mates, or the guards, but not him; he drew scenes from home, flowers and birds, anything to keep up his optimism and take his mind off hunger.

These two paintings had been the only ones out of dozens he'd done in hospital which he could bear to keep and look at. He'd been trying to preserve his sanity by painting the images which came into his mind, but all except these two were ugly, dark scenes, of emaciated men carrying bamboo coffins, queuing for a bowl of rice, staggering under heavy baskets of stones, of a man tied spread-eagled to poles, while a grinning Japanese guard whipped him almost to the point of death. He'd destroyed those pictures and put the paints away, vowing he'd never touch them again.

If Rosie could march back to Carrington Hall so bravely, and risk exposing all her old demons, to help a handful of forgotten people who would never even know it was she who saved them, then perhaps it was time he found the courage to face his own demons too.

Rosie discovered the next day that although finding a faeces-daubed room was no less disgusting the second time around, there were indeed ways of making the patients' bathing less horrific. There was no choice but to don the big rubber apron, or to grab Monica firmly by the arms and drag her to the shower, but by smiling and batting her eyelashes at Saunders she managed to persuade him that warm water washed better and quicker than cold. He shouted at her loudly when she refused to use the long-handled brush and instead took a cloth and soap to Monica. His argument was that she'd be soaked, or that Monica would claw at her, but while holding the patient there was little he could do about it, and Monica stopped screaming almost immediately.

Rosie didn't know enough about any of the patients to ascertain whether they'd all been a bit calmer today than they were yesterday, or if her gentler approach was what lessened the struggling and screaming. It could of course have been merely that she was a new face, or even that she was becoming immune to the screaming herself.

Fortunately Saunders wasn't as vigilant as Aylwood. He lost interest when she was drying the patients. He moved back to look out of the window which gave her an opportunity to examine more closely some of the scars on their bodies which he claimed were self-inflicted. Rosie knew they weren't; she'd seen too many lacerations in the past from canes and belts to be fooled, and the sort of bruises she was seeing on buttocks, thighs and shins could only come from a heavy boot. She glanced at Saunders' stout brown brogues and shuddered.

When all the patients were clean again and back in their rooms, Rosie felt almost euphoric. She knew of course that tomorrow Aylwood would be back and that almost certainly Saunders would follow her lead and revert back to the old bathing methods, but she was optimistic that the staff nurse might be lazy enough to relinquish the chore to her. As soon as Simmonds arrived with the breakfast trolley though, Rosie saw that if Saunders was deprived of one sadistic act, he had to find another.

Mabel was the first victim of his spite. Like the previous day she was lying on the bed board, wailing as Saunders unlocked her door. Rosie was just behind him carrying the feeding cup of very runny porridge Simmonds had handed to her. Saunders grabbed hold of the old lady by one arm, yanked her up into a sitting position, and without waiting a moment or two for her to catch her breath, he just tipped her head back and began to pour the contents into her mouth.

Rosie could not credit what she was seeing. He poured the porridge so fast Mabel couldn't possibly swallow it quickly enough and it began to run out of her nose.

'Don't,' Rosie yelled, rushing forward to try and stop him. 'You'll choke her.'

He stopped just long enough to grin maniacally at Rosie.

'I haven't got all day to pander to her,' he said. 'Besides she's used to it this way.'

Rosie shook with anger and nausea as he continued. To be forced to watch that poor deformed little woman, bravely trying to gulp it down, her hands fluttering uselessly in a vain protest, was one of the most distressing sights she'd ever seen. Rosie had an overwhelming desire to pick up the entire porridge pot from the trolley, tip it over his head, then kick him in the genitals.

She could do so little to make amends afterwards. She wiped Mabel's mouth and nose and gently helped her back down on to the bed board, but Saunders was waiting to lock Mabel in and move on to the next patient.

Fortunately Saunders obviously found feeding patients beneath him, and after Mabel he ordered Rosie to see to all the ones who couldn't do it themselves, as he stood by the door with his arms crossed, tutting at how long she took. Monica hadn't eaten more than a couple of mouthfuls yesterday when the spoon was in one of Aylwood's hands, while the other gripped the back of Monica's neck. Rosie didn't copy this cruel method; she held Monica firmly; but gently around the shoulders, at times encouraging her by stroking her, and talking softly as she would have done to a child. To her delight Monica's mouth opened of its own volition, the food wasn't spat back and she didn't fight her.

Later on in the morning, as Coates was cleaning the corridor floor and Saunders sitting reading in the rest room, Rosie went into the office and stole a look at the patients' notes lying in a heap on the desk. She had hoped to discover if there was a good reason why some of the patients like Mabel were given so little to eat. A bowl of runny porridge didn't seem enough; even though she had no teeth she could have managed scrambled egg. But she was disappointed, there was nothing in the notes that she understood aside from a temperature chart. Dr Freed's handwriting was illegible and Aylwood hadn't added anything further. She came to the conclusion that the only ones who got a decent meal were those still able to feed themselves.

There was a filing cabinet tucked into a corner and a quick try of the drawers proved it unlocked. She didn't dare investigate it now, not until she'd discovered what Saunders was doing and his plans for the rest of the morning. So she decided to go and find him and see what she could find out. He was still in the rest room, reading the newspaper. Rosie plonked herself down beside him.

'Have you seen this about Edmund Hillary conquering Everest?' he asked, waving the paper excitedly at her. 'The first man to reach the summit,' he said as if she didn't know, and began to read her some extracts.

Under any other circumstances Rosie would have been anxious to read all this herself and discuss it with almost anyone as she thought it was a wonderful, brave achievement. But she had much more important things on her mind today than mountaineering, and too much disgust for this man to hold an unnecessary conversation with him.

'What's up?' he asked as she began fidgeting.

'Bored,' she said. 'What on earth do you do up here all day to pass the time?'

'This,' he said, rustling the paper. 'I read them all, every word.'

Rosie looked sideways at him. He was such an awful-looking man, and now she knew how sadistic he was she could hardly bear to breathe the same air as him. She wondered what prompted him to work with the mentally handicapped. Was it because he was always a bully, or had the job brought that out in him?

'Are you married?' she asked.

He grinned wolfishly. 'Was once, but I dumped her while I was in the army. I saw no sense in paying for a woman back home while I could get them for free anywhere.'

Rosie winced. It was very odd that she had likened him

to Seth the first time she saw him, as physically there wasn't even the faintest resemblance. But that brutish remark was exactly the kind Seth would have made. Linda's warning that she should keep her distance from him rang in the back of her head, but she needed to stay beside him a little longer to try and build up some kind of trust.

'Could I clean the office?' she asked. 'I'm bored with nothing to do. I'm not used to it.'

'Aylwood doesn't like anyone poking around in there,' he said, giving her a sideways glance. 'I can find something to stop you being bored if you like!' he added with a leer.

Rosie shuddered. She was sure that was a sexual innuendo. 'I'm not that bored,' she said quickly and got up and walked away to go and check on the patients.

It gave her a pang in the heart to see them. Monica was sitting on the floor hunched up in the corner, her shorn head on her knees with her wasted arms protectively round it. She was calm today, and her face had lost that bestial look she'd had yesterday. Rosie wondered if she was still under the effects of the powerful sedative she'd been given then, or whether she fluctuated between rages and silence all the time. She wished she knew the patients' case histories. She thought it would help to understand them, but she guessed that both Saunders and Aylwood would scoff at that.

There was a puddle on the floor, so Rosie went back and asked Saunders if he could let her have the keys to go in and mop it up.

'You're kidding!' he said looking at her scornfully. 'We don't open the door again until dinner time.'

'But she's almost sitting in it,' Rosie protested.

'Serves her right,' he said, and picked up his paper again.

'Why can't they have a chamber pot in there?' Rosie said, trying very hard to keep her anger under control.

Saunders glared at her over his newspaper. 'Are you

an idiot or what?' He sounded exasperated now. 'Would you like a pot of shit thrown at you when you opened the door?'

Rosie turned away. He could be speaking from experience of course, but that still did not excuse his not allowing her to go in and clean the floor. She wondered how he'd feel if he had to sit in his own pee all morning.

At each viewing panel her heart sunk lower. Bertha was pacing up and down muttering, pounding on the door now and then. Angela was sitting on the floor twisting and untwisting a lock of hair in her fingers and cackling to herself. One of the old men was standing facing the corner, making strange faces; another was playing with himself for comfort. Mabel was now lying on the floor wailing, rocking herself to and fro, her shift soaked with urine. Rosie fixed all these scenes in her head so she could write them down later. She wished she could get into the office and search that filing cabinet. She doubted she'd ever get in there once Aylwood was back.

At around three that afternoon Rosie was almost falling asleep in her chair in the corridor when Saunders prodded her. It was very hot and airless and for the first time that day it was quiet everywhere. She thought perhaps the patients were affected by the heat too.

'Go on in the office and get your head down,' he suggested. 'I'll sit out here for a while.'

Suddenly she was wide awake, seeing a golden opportunity which was unlikely to present itself again. Even when Saunders went downstairs for his dinner, Gladys Thorpe had come to relieve him. She'd always thought Gladys to be a caring person, even if she was a bit slow, but when Rosie attempted to draw out her opinions about this ward, the nurse's face tightened and she said, 'It's not for me to discuss it.' Rosie was more shocked by Thorpe's attitude than she was by the chargehands'; she was after all a trained nurse. If Rosie hadn't been afraid it might get back to Matron, she would have torn her off a strip.

'It's so hot up here,' Rosie said, waving her hand like a fan. She had a strong feeling Saunders was offering a favour which he'd expect to be returned. 'Is it always like this?'

He shrugged and his small pale eyes looked vacant. 'I suppose so. You get used to it. I could try and get some windows open. It's turned much warmer outside. I think the summer's come at last.'

Rosie went into the office, took the easy chair in the corner by the filing cabinet and put her head back. She could hear Saunders walking up and down the corridor, his shoes had steel 'Blakeys' and the keys on his belt jingled. Each time he paused she could mentally picture which one of the rooms he was looking into.

She knew when he sat down right at the far end of the corridor by the scraping noise the chair made on the floor, and quickly she opened the filing cabinet. The top drawer appeared to be just a place to put old reading matter, everything from back copies of the *Nursing Times* to a couple of battered paperback thrillers. She silently closed that and opened the lower drawer. To her delight it held the patients' files. Two sections clearly marked, one as ex-patients and the other current.

Taking out the one marked Monica Endlebury, she began to skim through it, one ear cocked for Saunders. Right at the back was a typed case history.

It seemed Monica had been a normal child, though a little highly strung. In 1938 when she was fifteen she was sent to Paris to live with an aunt because her parents thought it would broaden her horizons. A year later when the war started her parents wrote and asked her aunt to send her home. Monica disappeared.

It was in the autumn of 1944 that people in the rural area around Reims began reporting sightings of a savage-like woman dressed in rags, living in the woods. Two men claimed they'd tried to speak to her but she had sprung at them like a wild dog, then disappeared again. In early

January 1945 two young boys out hunting for rabbits heard a moaning sound coming from what looked like a makeshift camp. They investigated and discovered the woman half buried by leaves, on the point of death from cold and starvation.

She was taken to a local hospital, and as she was nursed back to health they realized that she was English from odd words in her demented babblings. They passed on a physical description of her to the British Embassy, who eventually not only got her back to England and into Friern Barnet Mental Asylum, but also contacted her parents.

Rosie was just flitting through a long, detailed report by a psychiatrist who believed that Monica had been kept prisoner for some years and subjected to every kind of sexual perversion, when she heard Saunders's footsteps. Hastily she stuffed the file back into the drawer and closed it, then slumped back in the chair as if she was fast asleep.

She felt Saunders was standing in the doorway for quite some time watching her, but then just as she felt she must open her eyes and speak, he walked away. She listened for some few minutes before going back to the files. She could hear him unlocking cell doors and a louder babble of noise as he went in. She remembered then how he'd said he was going to try and open the windows a little, and assumed this was what he was doing.

Once his footsteps were back up the other end of the corridor, she opened the drawer again. As much as she wanted to know more about Monica and how she came to end up in Carrington Hall, she didn't dare waste any more time reading case histories. What she needed were relatives' addresses.

To her disappointment there were none. She could only assume they were kept downstairs in Mrs Trow's office. She was desperate to read more about all the patients, but feeling certain her luck couldn't hold out much longer, she put the files away and closed the drawer.

It was just gone four o'clock when she looked out along

the corridor. To her surprise Saunders wasn't sitting out there, and she was instantly alarmed.

Her first thought was that he'd come back to the office without her hearing him, seen her reading a file and slipped out to tell Matron. But as she stood in the doorway mentally planning excuses for poking her nose into things which didn't concern her, she noticed that the door of Angela's room was just slightly open.

The doors didn't lock from the inside, a precaution against patients grabbing keys and locking themselves inside. She thought that Saunders must be in there opening the window, but bearing in mind what Aylwood had said about Angela being the most dangerous on the ward, she thought she'd better go and see if everything was all right.

She was halfway down the corridor when she suddenly realized that Saunders couldn't possibly open those small high windows without taking something in with him to stand on. Furthermore, if he was occupied with this, how could he prevent the inmate darting out? She stopped short, thinking back to his unusually solicitous suggestion that she take a nap in the office. Why not the rest room? Unless of course it was because it was almost opposite Angela's room.

The way he'd looked at Angela in the shower came back to her, and with it came a blinding flash of intuition of exactly what he was doing in her room. She crept forward on tiptoe. She felt queasy, knowing in her heart that she was going to see something appalling, but none the less having to look.

When she peeped through the viewing window it was almost like a flashback to the terrible scene impressed on her mind since childhood. Different characters perhaps, and shot from a different angle, but the same equally brutal act.

Saunders's large body almost concealed the small woman trapped beneath his bulk. His mottled bare backside was pumping up and down, and Rosie had to stand on her toes in order to peer down to get the whole picture.

His trousers were round his ankles, and he had Angela forced on to her face on the bed board. She was holding her hands awkwardly above her head and her wrists were tied together with a cord. As she wasn't making a sound, Rosie thought he must have gagged her with something, but she couldn't see Angela's face, only the storm of black curly hair.

Saunders's grunting was so disgusting she retched, and that moment of enforced hesitation as her mouth filled with bile gave her just enough time to think before rushing in to intervene.

It felt like the worst kind of cowardice as she crept back along the passage away from the cell: again another guilty reminder that she hadn't tried to stop her brothers using Heather either, or told the police what they'd done, but common sense told her that she was no match for Saunders inflamed with animal lust.

Standing in the office doorway she shook from head to toe, not knowing what to do. She had no doubt the man had been using the girl on a regular basis for months, probably ever since she came here. Maybe others too for all she knew.

A sudden clinking of keys alerted her that he had finished his horrible business, yet she couldn't move from her position in the doorway. She watched him coming out, turning to lock the door behind him, and suddenly Angela began to scream.

Rosie had never heard a scream like that one. Her blood curdled at the savagery in it, and involuntarily she moved closer.

'Don't look so worried,' Saunders said in a hearty voice as he walked towards her, hands out to ward her off. 'She's always the same if you go in there unexpectedly without food in your hands. I tried to get her window open but she started pummelling me. Had a nice kip? You were well away when I looked in earlier.'

Rosie had to turn away. Her face would have told him she'd seen everything. She couldn't wipe out the look of contempt which she knew was in her eyes, or the angry red flush on her cheeks.

She vomited later in the lavatory. Angela was still screaming and she'd set off some of the others and Rosie knew now what Bedlam must have been like. How could she stay here after seeing that?

'Bad day?' Linda asked over tea. Everyone else had gone, and apart from Pat Clack in the kitchen they were alone.

Rosie could only nod. She couldn't eat anything, it all seemed to stick in her throat. She needed to tell someone, anyone, but yet she knew there was no one she could trust.

'Come out with me tonight, that'll cheer you up,' Linda said with a grin. 'We could get the tube into the West End and wander about eyeing up the blokes.'

Rosie appreciated Linda trying to cheer her and defying the order not to speak to her. It was kinder still to offer her a night out, but she didn't think she ever wanted to look at another man in her entire life. They were all despicable, her father, brothers and now Saunders. For all she knew Thomas might have some secret perversion. She thought she might come to hate all men.

Chapter Eleven

Thomas ushered Miss Pemberton up the stairs and into his living-room before saying anything more than the usual pleasantries. Mr Bryant was about to close the shop, but he was an inquisitive man and Thomas didn't want his employer quizzing him about who she was, or listening to their conversation.

A week had passed since Rosie came to Thomas with her shocking story and although he and Miss Pemberton had spoken twice on the telephone in that time, she hadn't given him any warning that she was coming up to London today. He was even more taken aback by her rather fetching appearance. When they had met at Easter she had looked the embodiment of a social worker, middle-aged, a touch masculine in a tweed suit and stout shoes. But today she looked ten years younger in a very feminine lilac short-sleeved summer dress, dainty shoes and a pretty straw hat.

'If I may be so bold, you look stunning, Miss Pemberton,' Thomas said once he'd closed his living-room door. 'And I'm very grateful to you for coming all this way.'

'If you're bold enough to say I look stunning, you are quite bold enough to call me Violet,' she said with a smile. She liked Thomas Farley. Although she had only met him in person once before and the rest of their acquaintance was through telephone conversations and letters, she found him rather alluring. This quality had come across without seeing him, via the interesting and intelligent statements in his letters and the rich, deep tone of his voice. It grew stronger still when she saw his warm brown eyes, and the way his full lips curved into a half smile while she was talking to him, as if he was secretly amused by her. She very much liked the lines on his face because they told tales of hardship, adventure and experience and also confirmed why he had this wealth of compassion and sensitivity. He was amusing too; somehow he'd managed to hang on to that irreverent, sharp humour that East Enders were renowned for. In truth he was more of a real man with just one leg than most able-bodied ones. And if she'd been fifteen years younger she'd have been tempted to make a play for him.

'I don't know why you should be grateful I called. It is I who am indebted to you, Thomas, for helping Rosie in her hour of need. Besides, I like to think we are friends,' Violet added.

Thomas grinned at her forthright statement. It evoked good memories of other equally plain-speaking Queen Alexandra's nurses he'd known. He owed his life and sanity to such determined women. He was touched she considered him a friend.

'Do sit down,' he said, removing a shirt from one of his two chairs. 'Had I known you were calling I would have tidied myself and this place up a bit. Would you like some tea? Or something stronger?'

'Tea would be lovely,' she said as she sat down and removed her hat.

Thomas felt a little foolish offering her alcohol at five in the afternoon. He had come a long way from his slum-child roots but he still felt he had a great deal more to learn about etiquette. 'Rosie has compiled us quite a dossier,' he said quickly to cover his embarrassment. 'She called last night with yesterday's report. But she won't be coming again this evening as she's got a date.'

He half expected Violet to look disapproving, but instead she smiled with real warmth and her soft grey

341

eyes twinkled. 'Well, that is good news. I've been so worried about her. Who is this young man?'

'Gareth Jones. He's an engine driver. She met him on Coronation day – apparently Donald got lost and Gareth helped her find him. I'm very glad she has someone to take her mind off this awful business, the strain is beginning to tell on her. But let me give you her notes to read while I make the tea.'

As Thomas made the tea in his tiny galley kitchen at the back of the house, his mind was on Rosie yet again. In fact when he came to think about it, she'd hardly been out of his mind for the entire week. He hated the thought of her in Carrington Hall, especially since he'd read her report about Saunders. Again and again he'd been tempted to call a taxi and go over there to get her out. He kept wondering why he felt this way about her; it wasn't rational or normal to feel so attached to a girl who was no relation, especially one so young and with such a background. In dark moments he wondered if he needed to see a shrink.

'Don't be so stupid,' he said aloud, his voice drowned by the sound of the kettle whistle. 'There's nothing wrong with you that couldn't be put right by a few pints in friendly company. You spend too much time alone, that's all.'

Violet was just finishing the last page of Rosie's report as Thomas came back in with the tea tray. 'Rosie would make an excellent reporter,' she said looking up at him. 'She writes so clearly and concisely, one wouldn't expect that really from a girl of her background.'

'She'd make a good detective too,' Thomas grinned. 'The way she managed to find out that Aylwood had been injecting patients with insulin to keep them in a coma, without it being written up by Dr Freed. And then that bit about how she waited in the bathroom watching out for Saunders impressed me. Did you notice she timed his visit exactly: arrived at 9.20; left at 9.52. Fancy him having the nerve to come back during the evenings via the fire escape to carry out more evil deeds!'

Violet blushed. She was mortified to think she'd sent Rosie to Carrington Hall without checking it out first, and felt terribly guilty because she'd dismissed the girl's complaints and suspicions at Easter. She should have taken them more seriously, Rosie wasn't one to be hysterical or exaggerate. Now the poor girl was being robbed of the last of her girlish innocence by Saunders. She felt totally responsible.

'I find it inconceivable that the Matron could leave that floor without someone on duty at night,' she said, shaking her head. 'She should be horse-whipped. One of those patients could have a seizure, a fire could break out, anything.'

Thomas agreed wholeheartedly but pointed out that such a callous disregard for the patients' well-being might make it far easier for them to make all their other allegations stick. 'Mr Cook, Donald's father, called in there without any prior warning on Saturday afternoon,' he went on. 'He rang me later to report on what happened. As usual at that time, Matron was out and he spoke to Mrs Trow, who was very reluctant to let him see his son without Matron's permission. Whilst in her office he managed to get a quick look at a staff rota. According to that, Staff Nurse Wilkinson is on night duty with a chargehand by the name of Giles. Rosie tells me she has never heard of or seen anyone with either of those names.'

'You mean Matron is pocketing the wages of two non-existent employees?' Violet's eyes nearly popped out of her head with shock.

'Well, it looks that way,' Thomas nodded. 'And Rosie is convinced that most of the staff taken on by Matron are probably in her debt in some way. It would be very interesting to check out their records. I can bet we'll find some rattling skeletons.'

'One of the reasons I came up so quickly was because

yesterday I contacted an old colleague of mine, Molly Ramsden,' Violet said. 'Molly was the first Matron at Carrington Hall: I recommended her to Lionel when he was setting up the home. Regretfully she had to leave to care for her sick mother in 1940, and Freda Barnes, who was a staff nurse then, took over as Matron. Molly told me that she went back to visit in 1942, and was surprised to find all the original staff had left. She asked for one or two addresses from Barnes, but she was given the brush-off, and when she asked to see some of the old patients, Barnes virtually showed her the door.'

'Really?' Thomas exclaimed, sitting down to pour the tea.

'Suspicious, I thought,' Violet sniffed. 'I understand that Molly never liked Barnes, and it could be that this incident was merely a case of professional jealousy. But now with what we've learned from Rosie it looks very much as if Barnes was covering up something even then.'

'Does your friend have any contact with any old employees?' Thomas asked, handing her a cup of tea and offering the sugar.

'Only one, Lucy Whitwell, who was employed as cook, again right from the opening of Carrington Hall.' Violet refused the sugar and sipped her tea. 'Whitwell wrote to Molly in 1943, appealing to her to give her a reference as she'd been sacked by Barnes, supposedly for stealing provisions. In the long and bitter letter she claimed that if any provisions had gone missing Barnes was almost certainly responsible, as she held the store room keys. Molly was inclined to take Whitwell's part, as in her time at the home she had found the woman an excellent cook and a very honest woman. So she provided a reference and Whitwell was taken on at a nursing home in Bexhill. She is still there; in fact, they exchange Christmas cards each year. Molly believes she would be very glad to give evidence about her experiences with Barnes should the need arise.'

Thomas thought for a moment as he drank his tea.

'Have you had any further thoughts on why Brace-Coombes allows Barnes to have so much freedom in running his home?' he said at length. 'Or why the doctor there hasn't made any complaints?'

'I've done some checking on him. It seems Dr Freed is well over sixty-five and semi-retired. He has been the Carrington House doctor for some six or seven years and calls a couple of mornings a week. As he has spent his entire working life in mental asylums, he's probably too hardened to notice anything more dramatic than an epidemic or a spate of sudden deaths.' Violet pursed her lips. 'But to be fair to the man, it's quite easy for day staff to have everything shipshape when a doctor always calls at the same time. The patients are hardly capable of making coherent complaints, and if the staff don't bring anything to his notice there wouldn't be any reason for him to be alarmed.'

'And Brace-Coombes?'

Violet shrugged. 'He is only a businessman, not a doctor. I'm sure Rosie has told you he founded the asylum to keep his wife there, and the place was a credit to him. I know that he was devastated when Ayleen died and felt it had to be kept open in her memory. But he found it painful to visit afterwards. I dare say that Barnes found it very easy to bamboozle poor old Lionel into giving her complete authority. It seems she has a talent for manipulating people.'

'That doesn't excuse him.'

Violet's eyes were sad. 'No, it doesn't.'

Along with finding Thomas rather attractive, Violet found him somewhat intriguing. If she hadn't known what his background was, she would have placed him as a grammar-school boy from a lower-middle-class home. Certainly not from an east London slum. But being something of a snoop – she had to be as a social worker – she had made it her business to find out a good bit more about him. A first-class soldier, well liked by his peers and respected by his senior officers. Before the loss of his leg he had been a keen sportsman and was earmarked for promotion. She thought it sad he had ended up as a watch repairer. He deserved better.

'Tell me, Thomas,' she said. 'Before all this cropped up, did you ever doubt a doctor's or a nurse's opinion?'

'Well, no,' Thomas half smiled. 'Because they are trained and I'm not.'

'Quite,' she said crisply. 'In fact, for all you know your leg may never have needed to come off. But you wouldn't have argued with the surgeon's decision would you? We all put our faith in professionals at some time, be it doctors, lawyers, priests or dentists, believing them to be honourable. But in fact I've seen surgeons operate that I wouldn't trust to carve a joint of meat. I know nurses who've been drunk on duty and lawyers who chose to defend their client badly because one of their chums was acting for the prosecution.'

Thomas looked alarmed. 'Well, who can we trust then?'

'A great many people,' she smiled. 'Fortunately the rotten apples are in the minority. I was only making a point about Lionel, because that poor devil is the one who is likely to take the real flak once all this is exposed. We may be able to make certain Barnes never nurses again, with luck she might end up on criminal charges. Dr Freed might get a reprimand, but Lionel is very likely to have his name dragged through the mire.'

'He won't if he instigates the inquiries.'

'And I believe he will, once I've talked to him,' she said. 'I'm staying tonight with an old friend in Highgate. Tomorrow I'm driving out to his home for lunch. I got Rosie into this terrible situation and the sooner I can rescue her from it, the happier I'll feel.'

As Thomas went down the stairs to let Miss Pemberton out of the shop at seven-twenty, Rosie was waiting just beyond the gates of Carrington Hall for Gareth.

Anyone walking down Ridge Lane on a warm summer evening would find it hard to believe that the old house half-hidden by stately trees was the site of so much human misery. The sign on the iron gates gave no indication it was an asylum, it could have been a hostel, or a school. Ivy and clematis scrambling up the walls hid most of the peeling stucco, and two huge peony bushes in full flower distracted the eye from the rest of the somewhat neglected front garden. Earlier on in the day there might be pale, sad faces pressed up against those barred first-floor windows, but at this time in the evening the patients had all been moved on to their dormitories at the back of the house.

The sweet smell of newly cut grass in the gardens of the two bungalows opposite, the sound of children's laughter, mingling with the soft pat of ball on racquet from somewhere unseen and a tinkling of a piano would give any walker a feeling that this was a good place to live, not quite countryside, but not suburbia either. They might spot the pretty girl standing beneath the overhanging sycamore tree and smile, guessing by her nervous stance, her pretty pink and white summer dress and carefully arranged hair, that she was eagerly awaiting her boyfriend. No one would guess that in the past week someone so young could have been subjected to such terrible experiences.

Rosie had been on tenterhooks all day, one moment so nervous she felt she'd have to stand Gareth up, the next counting the minutes till she saw him. All week her mind had been firmly on Carrington Hall, but for the past few hours her mind had been concentrating purely on this date tonight and her own appearance.

Was the pink lipstick she'd bought in Woolworth's too bright? Should she have worn a cardigan? The heels of her shoes were a little worn down, would he notice? Suppose she got a ladder in her new nylons? Would he try to kiss her? And if he did should she let him, or would that make him think she was easy?

The sound of a motorbike coming down the road made Rosie turn. If the rider hadn't waved she wouldn't have realized it was Gareth; she hadn't expected him to arrive on a motorbike.

He wore grey flannel slacks, an open-necked white shirt and a tweed jacket. He stopped a few feet from her, the engine still ticking over. He grinned and ran one hand over his tousled brown curls to smooth them down.

'I half expected to call at the house and be fobbed off with some excuse,' he said. 'I didn't think you'd be waiting for me.'

Rosie was struck dumb for a moment. Not only was the bike a surprise, but he looked even better than the picture she'd held in her mind. The week's sunshine had tanned his face, it made his eyes look like periwinkles and his teeth very white.

'I waited here because Matron doesn't like boys calling at Carrington Hall,' she managed to blurt out. 'I didn't think to tell you that last week.'

He cut the engine but remained seated on the bike, his face crinkled up into an engaging grin. 'I'm not sure how to take that,' he said. 'Do you mean you're waiting here to tell me to get lost? Or have we still got a date?'

Rosie hesitated. In situations like this in films, girls always came back with something saucy which made them seem cute and desirable. But she couldn't think of anything smart to say. 'I meant I'd like to get away from here quickly so Matron doesn't see me.'

'Are you brave enough to hop on the back?' he asked. 'Or shall I park it here and we'll walk somewhere?'

Motorbikes to Rosie brought back only good memories of her brothers and her father; she had ridden pillion with them from when she was a small girl. 'I love motorbikes,' she said and without considering whether it would mess up her hair which she'd spent so long arranging, she leapt on behind him.

'Hold tight!' he said as he kick-started it, and before she

had time to grasp his waist, they were roaring off down the road.

Rosie's knowledge of the geography of north London was limited to the bus route into the city, but Gareth went another way. Within a few minutes they were on a quiet country lane, speeding along with the wind sweeping Rosie's hair into a tangle.

'Are you cold?' he yelled over his shoulder. 'I should have told you I was on a bike, and you could have brought a jacket or a jumper.'

Rosie was a little cold, but it felt wonderful after being trapped inside all day. 'I'm fine,' she yelled back. 'It's so nice to be in the fresh air.'

She was exhilarated by the speed. Pretty cottages, views across fields and woodlands flashed by and the nastier events of the day blew away like dandelion clocks. As she leaned into the bends, her hands on his waist, a cheek against his back, her nervousness of him vanished.

Some twenty minutes later they drove into a small village centred round a green with a duck pond. A few people were sitting on benches outside a pub. Gareth slowed right down. 'Shall we stop here for a drink?' he asked, turning his head to her. 'Riding around is nice, but I can't talk to you.'

Rosie agreed and Gareth parked the bike. 'My hair must look like a haystack,' she laughed as she hopped off, trying to smooth it down with her hands. She hoped she hadn't got mascara running down her cheeks too.

He looked appraisingly at her, and smiled. 'It's windswept but it looks very pretty. Your hair is the first thing I noticed about you, it's such a lovely colour.'

Gareth had a pint of beer and Rosie had lemonade. She expected he would try to persuade her to have something stronger as other boys had, but he didn't. They sat on one of the benches in a patch of warm sunshine, watching the ducks on the pond, and Gareth asked her about Donald.

Rosie had read in advice columns in magazines that a

girl on her first date should ask the boy about his work and hobbies and never talk about herself. But as he had asked about Donald she had no alternative but to explain a little of what had happened since Coronation day. She did her best to make the story if not funny, at least flippant and entertaining, omitting the horror. 'So I haven't seen him,' she finished up. 'I know his father called to see him and I'm sure he explained a bit about where I was, but just the same Donald must be so confused.'

'Your Matron sounds like a right Tartar,' Gareth said sympathetically. 'Why don't you write to your mum and dad and ask them to do something?'

'I haven't got a mum and dad,' she blurted out. 'My mother died when I was six and my dad last year. That's why I came here to work.'

To her surprise Gareth looked deeply troubled, and after the terrible week she'd had, such unexpected concern was very comforting.

'Jesus!' he exclaimed. 'I'm so sorry, Rosemary. That's really tough.'

Rosie shrugged and smiled at him. 'There's lots worse off than me. But don't let's talk about sad stuff. Tell me about you? Did you find your friends after the Coronation? What are your digs like? Were you born in Wales? You haven't got a Welsh accent.'

'Yes, I found my mates. The digs are pretty dingy. I left Wales when I was two and that's why I don't have the accent,' he said, grinning as he answered all her questions in the order she fired them. 'But my parents are still as Welsh as leeks. We come from the Rhondda Valley, my father, grandfather and great-grandfather were all miners, but in 1933 Dad made the break and came to London to look for work. Walked all the way he did, picked berries at the side of the roads, never touched the shilling he had in his pocket for emergencies. It was three years later when he sent for Mum, Owen and me, and by then he had a little coal business.'

Rosie loved to hear stories, especially family ones, and she encouraged Gareth to tell her everything, starting when he got to London.

'I can remember being shocked that London was rows and rows of small dark houses with no green hills beyond,' he laughed. 'The other kids sneered at me and Owen because we talked odd. Owen's two years older than me and he was always getting into fights over it. But the main thing that bewildered me was that Dad kept saying how much better off we were. To me the little two-up, two-down house in Kentish Town wasn't any better than the one we'd left in Wales. What's more, instead of the coal being down the pit, here it was right outside the kitchen door, great shiny piles of it.'

Rosie smiled. His description made her think of May Cottage and the junk outside the door.

'I asked Mum why Dad kept saying we were better off once,' Gareth said reflectively. 'She said the difference was that there was a sign on the front of our house saying "Davy Jones Coal and Coke Merchant", and that meant the coal belonged to us, as did the horse and cart Dad delivered it on, and we had a flushing lavatory too. But that didn't mean much to me then.'

From a very early age Gareth had it drummed into him that it was a man's duty to better himself, and his father was held up as a shining example. Now that he was an adult he could appreciate how courageous his father was to leave the valleys in the middle of the Depression, and try his hand in London. He knew too that there was no luck in what Davy Jones accomplished, only hard work and gritty determination.

'So why didn't you become a coal man too?' Rosie asked.

'Because I love trains,' he said simply. 'I left school just as the war ended. Owen had already been working with Dad for two years, there wasn't really enough work for me too at that time, and besides, I loathed humping coal around. Mum wanted me to be an engineer or an electrician but I stuck out for an apprenticeship with the railways. By the time I was eighteen and got called up for National Service, Dad had made enough money to buy the house in Mill Hill. The house in Kentish Town became the yard office and I was even more hell-bent on being a train driver.'

'Where do you drive trains to?' Rosie asked, imagining him with a soot-blackened face leaning out of the engine wreathed in steam.

'I shunt them up and down in the yard at Clapham Junction,' he said with a rueful smirk. 'Sometimes if I'm lucky I get to be fireman on a local run. But it will be some time I expect before they let me loose as a driver on a passenger train. The old blokes guard their jobs closely, they don't like us keen young ones.'

Gareth's favourite day-dream for almost as long as he could remember had been to drive the *Flying Scotsman*. As a small child he had spent all his spare time at King's Cross and Euston stations looking at the big steam engines with the kind of adoration other kids gave to sports-men and film stars. He collected pictures of them, read every book he could lay his hands on about them. It was an all-consuming passion that until a week ago had never been ousted by anything else other than his motorbike.

'I like trains too,' Rosie said, remembering the advice in the magazines that you had to show enthusiasm for a boy's work and interests. 'Not that I've been on many. In fact, when I came up to London that was the first time. But I'd love to travel more and see the rest of England.'

Gareth grinned. He thought it would be good to show her a few of his favourite engines. 'What on earth made you want to work in a loony-bin?'

'I didn't want to. I wanted to be a nurse,' Rosie replied. 'But I'm not old enough yet, so this seemed a perfect place to fill in the time. I'm thinking about looking for something else now. I don't think I can stand the second floor much longer. The only trouble is I'll have to find somewhere else to live too.'

'I bet my mum would put you up if you were really stuck,' he said impulsively. 'My old room's empty.'

Rosie was touched by his kindness. He was so different from the loutish types she'd met in the past at dance halls. She had a feeling that if she was to tell him the whole truth about herself and Carrington Hall he'd really understand. 'I couldn't expect her to do that,' she said. 'But it's kind of you to offer. I was a bit fed up until tonight, being stuck indoors and stuff. I'm not an indoors person really and coming out on your motorbike has made me feel a lot better. Now tell me about these dingy digs of yours and your friends.'

They sat outside the pub until it grew dark, talking so easily and naturally Rosie felt as if she'd known him for years. He told her more about his family, their home and his mother.

'She's one of a dying breed of women,' he laughed. 'She lives only for the men in her life, cooking, baking, scrubbing. But she irritates me a bit sometimes. Dad's worked his fingers to the bone to buy her a nice house with every luxury you can think of, but she still penny-pinches. Some of the gadgets he's bought her, like an electric kettle, she won't even use. She says it's wasteful to boil a whole kettle when she only wants enough hot water for one cup of tea. She measures it out into a saucepan and heats it up in that. She only uses the vacuum cleaner once a week, the rest of the time she goes round with a dustpan and brush. Was your mother like that too?'

'She was always cleaning too, as I remember,' Rosie replied, glad of an opportunity to be truthful about how she was brought up. 'But our cottage was very primitive, we didn't even have electricity when she was alive, so she was forced to do everything the hard way.' She bypassed any potential minefields by swiftly moving on to tell him about her first job with Mrs Bentley in Bristol and how she had lectured her in 'doing things the correct way'.

'I'm really glad she taught me all those things now,' she giggled after she'd described how the table had to be set just so and how she corrected her speech. 'Or I wouldn't have known how to behave with the Cooks. I didn't know how to lay a table properly, and I suppose I spoke like a farmer. Mr Bentley was nice though, and I loved their garden. I used to tidy it up when they weren't around.'

Gareth looked at her in some amazement. 'I really thought you came from a snooty family like the Cooks,' he said. 'You looked so at home with them in that posh place.'

'I'd never seen anywhere that grand until that day,' she admitted, explaining a little of how she came to be invited. 'I'd just die for a home like that!' She paused, then laughed. 'That's a very silly expression. You couldn't get much pleasure out of it if you were dead, could you? Anyway if I was rich I'd want a garden. I love growing things.'

'Then I'll have to take you home to meet my mum,' he said. 'She doesn't know the first thing about gardening, everything dies on her. Maybe you could give her a few pointers.'

Rosie glowed. It seemed as if Gareth wanted to see her again. After the terrible chilliness at Carrington Hall she so much wanted someone to like her.

As they got back to the motorbike Gareth took off his jacket. 'Put it on,' he said 'You'll be frozen without it.'

'But you'll be cold,' she protested.

'No I won't, not if you hug me tightly,' he grinned. 'And besides, it isn't that far back to your place and I can have it back then.'

It was the best feeling in the world sweeping through those dark country lanes with her arms tightly around his waist. She leaned her cheek against his back again, breathing in deeply that masculine warmth and the smells of the countryside. From time to time he covered her hands with one of his and squeezed them and she felt she wanted to sing and laugh she was so happy.

But all too soon they were back at Carrington Hall. Gareth parked the motorbike some two hundred yards away and Rosie hopped off.

'Thank you for a lovely evening,' she said, at a loss to know what to do or say next.

Gareth got off the bike and put it on its stand, then turning to her he took both her hands. 'When can I see you again?'

'Whenever you like,' she said, hoping that didn't sound too forward. 'I can come out any evening.'

'I wish I could,' he said ruefully. 'But they are always changing our shifts and making us do overtime. Can I telephone you?'

Rosie shook her head. 'Matron doesn't allow us personal calls.'

'Well, let's say Saturday night,' he suggested. 'I'm almost certain they won't make me work then, but I'm worried that if something does crop up I won't know how to contact you.'

'I could give you my Uncle Thomas's phone number in Hampstead,' she said in a moment's inspiration. 'If you couldn't make it you could let him know. If you don't turn up I could phone him.'

Gareth agreed this was a good emergency plan and wrote the number down on the back of his hand.

'But I'll be here at seven o'clock come hell or high water,' he joked. 'We could go to the pictures if it's raining.'

There was a brief awkward silence. 'I'd better go,' Rosie said, taking off his jacket. 'If we aren't in by ten-thirty there's trouble.'

Gareth put the jacket on. 'Have you got time for a kiss?' he asked, and without waiting for her reply he cupped her face in his two big hands and drew her closer.

Rosie had been kissed only twice before, both times

inexpertly by boys she had no desire to kiss back, but the moment Gareth's lips touched hers she felt she wanted to sink into his arms and stay there for ever.

His mouth was so warm and soft, lingering on hers as his fingers ran through her hair. For a brief moment she felt as if they were alone on the top of the highest hill in the world, with the moon and stars twinkling all around them like a sea of diamonds.

'It's almost half past,' he said, stepping back from her, holding on to her hands. 'I don't want you banned from coming out again on Saturday.'

Rosie turned as she went up the path to the staff door and saw him drive on past the gates. The brief flash of his profile looked achingly beautiful. She didn't know how she would get through the three days till she saw him again.

Rosie awoke with a start on Saturday morning and for a moment she was confused. Had the alarm gone off and Maureen switched it off as she'd done before?

She leaned up on one elbow. Maureen was fast asleep, her head almost hidden beneath the covers. Fortunately she hadn't hidden the clock, it was still on the bedside cabinet. Rosie reached out for it and discovered it was only half past five.

Smiling to herself, she lay back down again. Another whole hour to think of how it would be when she saw Gareth tonight. She hoped it would rain so they could go to the pictures; she couldn't imagine anything better than sitting in the dark with his arm around her. Should she wear the green costume she'd been wearing the day of the Coronation or a skirt and blouse? She wished she had a new dress, and some perfume. There wasn't much hope of Mary letting her have a squirt of hers. But she didn't care about the other girls ignoring her now, or what it might be like on the ward today. She had Gareth to think about.

She had just closed her eyes to sink back into some blissful dreams when the sound of raised voices startled her. At first she thought it was Linda and Mary having some sort of squabble, but as she sat up she realized it was coming from further away.

Maureen sat up with a jerk, her eyes wild with panic. 'Have we overslept?' she asked, fumbling on the bedside cabinet for her glasses.

Rosie was tempted to say yes just for the spiteful pleasure in watching the girl scurry about needlessly. But it was nice to hear Maureen actually speak for once. 'No, it's only ten to six,' Rosie assured her. 'Listen, something's going on downstairs!'

They both listened for a moment; the voices were muffled but angry sounding. Both girls got out of bed and went out into the corridor, where they were met by Linda, also in her nightdress. She was just coming back through the door which led to the staircase. 'It's the governor, Mr Brace-Coombes,' she said in hushed, shocked tones. 'I dunno what's going on, but 'e's down there on the second floor with a couple of women. Matron's throwing a bleedin' fit!'

'Let me see,' Maureen said eagerly, pushing her way through to the door, but Linda hauled her back and warned her to keep out of it.

Rosie felt her stomach lurch. She had been over to visit Thomas on Thursday night and he had said Miss Pemberton was in town and that she intended to speak to Brace-Coombes. She guessed that Miss Pemberton had decided to start some action today.

She had been waiting for something to happen, longing for it, but now it had she was scared. How much longer would it be before everyone knew who she was?

'What shall we do then?' Maureen asked Linda. 'Should we get dressed and go down or what?'

'I dunno,' Linda shrugged. 'I don't like the sound of it at all.'

Rosie wondered why Linda looked so nervous. Normally nothing bothered her.

'You could go down,' Maureen said, looking right at Rosie with a malicious look on her face. 'After all, you work there.'

'I don't think any of us ought to do anything until it's the proper time to go down for breakfast,' Rosie said more bravely than she felt. 'Not unless someone calls us.'

It was the longest half-hour Rosie had ever known. She got washed and dressed as Maureen did too. But she could feel the older girl's eyes on her, almost hear her suspicious mind turning over, and she began to tremble with nerves.

'You aren't saying much,' Maureen said at length. 'Why's that? Could it be that rumpus downstairs has got something to do with you?'

Rosie was just going to deny it, but anger at the way this girl had treated her got the better of her. 'Maybe it has,' she snapped. 'If you must know I'm glad Mr Brace-Coombes has decided to pay a visit, it's long overdue. You know better than anyone that there's terrible things going on in this place. I just wonder why you've kept quiet about it?'

'You think you're so special, don't you?' Maureen sneered. 'Of course, it's easy for you, you could go home to Auntie Molly any time you like. Some of us haven't got homes, and we have to put up with things just to keep our jobs.'

At those self-pitying words something just snapped inside Rosie and all the anger she'd kept pent up for so long spilled out. 'You make me sick with your whingeing and whining,' she snarled. 'I've always been nicer to you than anyone else in this place, but you turned against me for nothing. Don't you think it's time you took a good look at yourself to see why people don't like you. You're a snivelling coward, Maureen Jackson, and a sneak. I bet you know every last bad thing that goes on in this place.

Now for once in your life do something worthwhile with it. Go down there now and tell Mr Brace-Coombes all you know.'

She expected Maureen to say something equally wounding back, but instead her face crumpled. 'I can't,' she said and began to blubber. 'I'm scared.'

'Scared of what? Of Matron?' Rosie said contemptuously. 'I doubt she'll even last the day out here now that her boss has got a whiff of the stink on the second floor. What's she got over you anyway?'

There was a moment's silence, and to Rosie's surprise Maureen sank down on the bed and began to sob.

Rosie could never be hard on anyone once they were upset. 'What is it?' she asked. 'Tell me.'

'I did something bad when I first came here,' Maureen blurted out, her hands half covering her face. 'Matron covered it up for me, but she always reminds me. If I say anything today, she'll tell Mr Brace-Coombes and he'll throw me out.'

'What did you do?' Rosie's sympathies were fully aroused now. After all, she had a great deal to fear from Matron too. But if Miss Pemberton was downstairs, Rosie knew that while she wouldn't be out on the streets tonight, Maureen might be. 'Go on, tell me. I might be able to put in a good word for you.'

'I stole Mr Brace-Coombes's wallet,' Maureen whispered.

'You did what?' Rosie gasped. 'When? How?'

'It was years ago, when I first came here. He was talking to some people in the sitting-room. It was in his overcoat pocket out in the hall. I took it. Matron turned the place upside down when he told her it was gone and she found it under my mattress.'

Rosie just stared at the girl. 'And I suppose she said she wouldn't tell him it was you as long as you did exactly as she said after that?'

Maureen sobbed and nodded. 'She told him she found

359

it in the first-floor day room. She said it was one of the patients as they came in from the garden. I've tried to leave here a few times, but she won't give me a reference and she keeps threatening to tell him the truth if I don't tell her other things.'

'Well, a reference from her won't be worth anything after today,' Rosie said bluntly. 'But if you play fair and be honest with those ladies downstairs who are with Mr Brace-Coombes, you might just get one.'

Maureen looked at Rosie through two great pools of tears. She knew by hints Matron had made that this girl was going to come very unstuck soon. She didn't know what it was, but she suspected Rosie must have done something even worse than her. She had been so pleased up until now; she hated Rosie because she was pretty and everyone liked her. Even in the past few days when everyone was ignoring her because they'd been told to, she knew most of them felt bad about it.

'Why are you so brave?' she asked. 'Aren't you scared of anything?'

'Of course I'm scared sometimes,' Rosie admitted. 'I am right now because we don't know what is going to happen. But I'm more angry at what Matron has been doing with this place than anything else. And so should you be. Now stop thinking about yourself and put the patients first. They haven't got the brains or the strength to fight back. You have.'

At six-thirty the bell rang as usual and as Rosie and Maureen walked down the stairs to breakfast, closely followed by Linda and Mary, the second floor sounded ominously quiet.

Linda crept over to the door and peered through the viewing window. 'I can't see anyone in there,' she whispered back to the others. 'Where do you reckon they've gone?'

Downstairs in the staff dining-room everything looked quite normal. Pat Clack had the table laid for breakfast, a

360

smell of frying bacon was coming from the kitchen. The girls said nothing, just helped themselves to cornflakes and tea. Gladys Thorpe came in a few minutes later yawning sleepily; she didn't look as if she'd heard anything. Rosie wondered where Aylwood was – she usually got here first in the mornings and left as they came in.

The cooked breakfast was hardly in front of them before Miss Pemberton swept in wearing a white overall. She gave Rosie a sharp look as if warning her to show no recognition.

'Good morning, girls,' she said in a cool voice, her grey eyes scanning each of the girls' surprised faces. 'My name is Sister Pemberton. Matron has been suspended from her duties and I am here with some assistants to take over for the time being. After you have finished your breakfasts I would like you all to gather in the hall. As we have something of an emergency today, I am relying on you all to co-operate with me.'

She swept out again towards the laundry and seconds later they heard her speaking to the domestics.

'Who on earth's she?' Linda asked in a whisper. 'And what's she done with Matron?'

'Where's Aylwood?' Mary asked, her blue eyes as big as saucers.

Gladys wanted to know what was going on and she seemed to suddenly wake up as the girls told her everything they knew. 'Someone's been telling tales,' she said darkly. 'I wonder who it is.'

Linda looked pointedly at Rosie. Mary gave a little gasp and Maureen dropped her eyes. Gladys looked at their faces, then back to Rosie. 'You?' she said in some surprise. 'Why?'

Rosie hadn't felt any real animosity towards Gladys until the day she'd rounded on Rosie up on the second floor. But once she'd known the nurse was party to all that went on and didn't seem to have even a shred of guilt about it, that, to Rosie's mind, put her in the same camp as Matron, Aylwood and Saunders, even if she wasn't actually cruel herself.

'Yes, it was me,' Rosie pushed her plate aside and stared back at Gladys in defiance. 'And before you say anything more, I'd just like to point out I think all of you are the most pathetic, yellow-bellied cowards to work here all this time and not to speak out about it yourselves.'

She left then, sweeping out into the corridor before they could see her shaking hands or hear her heart thumping.

Miss Pemberton was an excellent actress. As all the girls gathered in the hall in a row, she was looking at a staff rota and barely looked at Rosie.

'Rosemary Smith,' she called out. 'I believe you've been working on the second floor recently?'

'Yes, Sister,' Rosie replied.

'Well, I shall be helping you up there in a moment or two. My assistant Staff Nurse Clegg is already up there, so go on up and join her. Maureen Jackson, you go there too.'

Maureen's eyes behind her glasses looked wide with fright. 'B-b-but Sister,' she stammered.

'Just go, Jackson,' Miss Pemberton said firmly. 'I won't have any arguing.'

As they went up the stairs, Rosie could hear Miss Pemberton asking each of the others to identify themselves and asking them to carry on with their usual duties. Maureen was dragging her feet and when Rosie looked back her face was white with fright.

Staff Nurse Clegg was waiting for Rosie and Maureen in the office on the second floor. She was a big woman with a jolly red face, wearing a dark blue nurse's dress to which she had already added a rubber apron. If she knew anything at all about Rosie she didn't let on. Neither Saunders nor Aylwood was there.

'Which one of you is Smith?' she asked. As usual the smell was appalling, the noise deafening and Maureen had turned from white to green. Rosie introduced herself.

'Right,' Clegg said with a broad smile. 'Now I believe you are familiar with this ward, so we'll start the bathing together. Jackson, you can tag along, an extra pair of hands is always useful. Can either of you tell me if that Coates woman is usually so sullen. I can't get a word out of her.'

Rosie explained that she always cleaned the rooms on her own, and that she was a woman of few words. She took down a rubber apron and gave one to Maureen.

'Come on, perk up,' she said. She didn't know why Maureen was looking so green, it wasn't as if she'd never been on this floor before. 'It won't be so bad without Aylwood or Saunders. And the smell does go once the patients are clean.'

After the terrible sights of the past week, Rosie felt heartened to see a nurse go into action who combined strength with compassion and a sense of humour. She marched into Monica's cell with as much bravado as Aylwood, but she didn't wince at the mess, and as she bent down to help the cowering woman up from the floor, she spoke gently as if Monica was a small child.

'Well you are in a fine mess,' she said. 'Ups-a-daisy, and into a nice warm shower. We'll soon have you all cosy again.'

It was necessary for Clegg to restrain Monica as Rosie washed her, but unlike Saunders she kept up a flow of gentle chat, and as the warm water soothed the patient, she slowly loosened her grip while still watching closely.

'There's some nasty bruises you've got,' she said as she came from behind the partition to towel the woman dry. She stroked her arm in sympathy, tutting over the marks. 'You won't be getting any more of those, my love, don't you worry now.'

If Monica understood what was said to her she showed no sign of it, but for once she willingly allowed herself to be put back into a clean shift and she didn't struggle as they took her back to a clean room.

The same thing was repeated with each patient and

those who weren't dirty were allowed to use the lavatory, with the door half closed to give them some privacy.

Clegg spoke to each patient, explaining that the kinder treatment they were getting today was going to be normal procedure from now on. Like Monica, none of them appeared to be taking in what she was saying, but they were all much more docile than usual. Perhaps it was just because Clegg was a stranger, but Rosie wanted to believe it was because they were soothed by her gentle tone of voice and the lack of aggression.

Miss Pemberton arrived just as they were about to bring Angela out for her shower. Angela's eyes were full of anger, and she was fighting mad, trying to claw at both Clegg and Rosie; her linen shift was soaked in blood and for a moment Rosie thought it was an injury.

'Now, now,' Clegg said soothingly, grabbing the woman's arms firmly behind her back. 'So you've got the curse and you feel nasty, but there's no need for that rough stuff, you've got friends here this morning.'

Usually Angela washed herself, but today she stood under the jet of water glowering and muttering, refusing to co-operate. There was a vivid red bite mark on her breast that hadn't been there the day before. Rosie guessed that Saunders had made another nocturnal visit last night and she wondered if she should say something? She wondered too where he and Aylwood were. Had Mr Brace-Coombes rounded up all the real offenders together somewhere downstairs?

Miss Pemberton took over from Clegg and with Rosie's help washed and dried Angela, put a clean shift on her and a sanitary towel. As they led Angela back to her room, she began to cry and clutched at her stomach.

Miss Pemberton astounded Rosie. She put both her arms around Angela and held her firmly against her shoulder for a few moments, talking soothingly in her ear as if she had no idea of the patient's formidable reputation.

'You are quite safe now, my dear,' she said. 'He'll never

come near you again, I promise you. Doctor will be in to see you soon and he'll give you something for your tummy ache. Now why don't you lie down for a while and rest until breakfast?'

Miss Pemberton ordered that the mattresses were to be left in the rooms with a clean sheet on them. She insisted that the small windows were to be opened as wide as possible and that during the day each patient was to be brought out on a rota basis and given the opportunity to walk up and down the corridor and use the lavatory.

Rosie was cheered by this; Maureen looked even more anxious than before.

'It's doubtful that we'll get any response for several days,' Miss Pemberton warned them. 'I dare say they may become even more aggressive until they get used to it. If you keep people locked up like animals, they begin to behave that way and they resent change. But we must try. Almost all of them have atrophy in their limbs and we must fight this with nourishment and exercise.'

It wasn't until after eleven that morning that Rosie had time to consider what was going to happen next. Miss Pemberton had been rushing in and out, checking on everything from files in the office to patients' charts and the food brought up for them. She'd been in attendance as a new doctor made his rounds and she still hadn't taken Rosie aside for a private word. Apart from a secret smirk here and there she had barely acknowledged her presence.

Clegg was a ball of fire too, unlocking cupboards, checking drawers and files. And in between this she was writing a list of suggestions which included a chair for each of the patients, issuing them with proper day clothes and opening the closed-off room at the end of the corridor as a day room where they could socialize now and then if they were up to it. She was scandalized by the lack of fluids offered to the patients. She could hardly believe Rosie when she said that they had only one cup of tea after each meal, with no offer of water even during the hottest days. She dug out one of several large tins of biscuits from a cupboard and said they were to have them with tea for elevenses, just like the staff, which would be made up here, and ordered Maureen down to the kitchen to bring up mugs.

It was in this lull with Maureen out of the way and with Clegg busy at the far end of the corridor that Rosie approached Miss Pemberton who was in the office looking at some patients' notes.

'I know you are busy,' she said hesitantly from the doorway, 'but have you got a moment to tell me what's going on?'

'My dear,' Miss Pemberton looked up and smiled at her. 'What a little nest of vipers you've uncovered for us, and how remiss of me not to take the time out to thank you.'

'I didn't expect thanks,' Rosie said. 'I just feel awkward. The girls all know it's me who's been telling tales. I dread to think that it will be like at dinner time.'

'You needn't worry about that. I'll have your lunch and Jackson's sent up. In fact I am hoping that by mid-afternoon we'll have some reinforcements arriving, and that we could pop out somewhere in the fresh air for a real talk. Now, can you wait that long?'

Rosie smiled. She wasn't used to being spoken to so civilly. 'Yes, of course I can,' she said. 'It's nice having you here, and Sister Clegg is so very different from Aylwood.'

'I should think she is,' Miss Pemberton chuckled, her grey eyes sparkling. 'We were together in the Q A s. But as she once said to me during the war, "Remember, Pembers, walls have ears, even potatoes have eyes!" So we'll have our little chat later. I've got an interesting proposition to put to you, aside from passing on all the news.'

Maureen came back from the kitchens with snippets of gossip, which she related to Rosie as they made tea together. Rosie found it pitiable that this girl who had been so very spiteful was now trying to creep round her.

But Rosie was only human and she was as anxious to hear the news as anyone, so she put aside her personal views on the girl and listened avidly.

It seemed there were another two new nurses on the first floor, ordering the girls about and making alterations to just about everything. Mr Brace-Coombes and two other gentlemen were in Matron's flat, and Aylwood and Saunders had been in there too for at least some of the time. Pat Clack had passed on this information, and she seemed to think Saunders had been taken away by the police at about ten o'clock. She wasn't sure where Aylwood was, but Simmonds had reported that her room had first been searched and now one of the domestics was packing her belongings.

'I wish they'd tell us all what's going to happen next,' Maureen said. She still looked grey with worry. 'Do you think we'll all get the sack?'

'I shouldn't think so for one minute,' Rosie reassured her. 'Who'd look after the patients? Besides you haven't done anything wrong, have you?'

Maureen didn't reply directly to this, just said she was taking Clegg her tea. Rosie was alone in the kitchen and her mind turned to her arranged date with Gareth.

Under these extreme circumstances she felt very guilty being so concerned about a boy she'd only been out with once, rather than thinking about the patients and the other staff, but yet she couldn't get him out of her mind. Would Miss Pemberton expect her to stay in this evening? Suppose she had plans to take her back with her to Somerset? How would she let Gareth know, and when would she see him again?

Miss Pemberton didn't come back on the ward after lunch until nearly three and Rosie noticed that she seemed to have lost all the energy and fire she'd had earlier in the day. She went into the office with Clegg and shut the door behind her. Rosie wondered if something more had happened downstairs.

It was a beautiful day outside, hot and sunny, but up on the second floor there didn't seem to be a breath of air. The patients were quiet, just a few moans from old Mabel to remind them she was there. Clegg had put an armchair in her room in an attempt to make her more comfortable. It was taken from the downstairs day room, with tubular steel arms, and cushions covered in a waterproof material. Each time Rosie looked through the viewing window Mabel was just sitting hunched up on the bed, looking at the chair. It was a very sad sight. It would take a great deal of kindness and patience before any of the people on this floor began to respond to a new regime.

Rosie was almost on the point of dropping off to sleep in her chair in the corridor when Miss Pemberton came out of the office and beckoned to her.

'We'll go out for our chat now,' she said, but her smile was weak and her eyes looked tired. 'Jackson can take over. Where is she?'

Maureen heard her name mentioned and came scuttling out of the staff room bringing with her the smell of cigarettes and looking very guilty.

Just walking down the stairs felt heavenly after the stuffiness of the second floor; the windows were open wide and a soft breeze brought in the scent of newly mown hay from the field beyond the garden.

Miss Pemberton didn't speak until they'd reached the garden and sat down on a bench under the shade of a tree. 'I'm sorry, Rosie, that I couldn't find time to speak to you earlier,' she said. 'It's been an interminable, very upsetting day.'

Rosie made some sympathetic remarks about the heat, the strangeness of it all, and how early Miss Pemberton must have got up today. Then, unable to wait any longer, she asked point-blank what was happening.

'After the findings in our early morning check today in which we found no staff on duty and neglect to all the patients on the second floor, Mr Brace-Coombes and a business colleague went through the accounts and the drug cupboard,' Miss Pemberton said in a crisp, dry voice, looking straight ahead of her rather than at Rosie. 'It seems your suspicions were correct, Rosie. Along with a failure to maintain a proper standard of care and abusing her privileges, Barnes is also guilty of fraud and misappropriation of funds.'

'And Saunders and Aylwood?' Rosie asked, a little dismayed by the older woman's dull tone and lack of enthusiasm.

'Aylwood was given instant dismissal. It is my recommendation that a full report should be sent to the nursing board and that she should be struck off the register. As for Saunders, that despicable creature,' she winced as if she could barely bring herself to say his name, 'he has been taken to the police station for questioning. It seems he was observed by a police officer entering and leaving late last night, just as you claimed you'd seen him do on previous occasions.'

'But what will happen to him and Matron?' Rosie asked.

When Miss Pemberton didn't answer immediately, Rosie got the idea she was angry about something.

'Freda Barnes – I refuse to honour her any longer with a nursing title – has been sent away,' she finally blurted out. 'Whether criminal charges are laid against her or not is up to Mr Brace-Coombes. He hasn't seen fit to discuss his plans with me as yet. As for Saunders, we have to leave that in the hands of the police. Rape is a difficult enough charge to prove with a woman prepared to testify against him. I'd say it was well-nigh impossible with someone insane.'

Rosie was just about to open her mouth to remind the older woman that she had witnessed him raping Angela, but all at once she realized exactly why Miss Pemberton was angry. She had stormed in here this morning like an avenging angel, found it to be every bit as bad as Rosie had said, and perhaps discovered even more disturbing things. But now instead of seeing the guilty get their just deserts, it seemed as if they were going to get away with it.

'You're angry,' she said in a small voice. 'Does it have something to do with me? Did Matron tell everyone who I am? Is that the reason they're all going to get away with it? Because no one would believe me?'

Miss Pemberton turned in her seat to look at Rosie, ashamed that she hadn't been able to summon up enough energy to feign jubilation at the day's events, or even make up a few white lies.

If Rosie gave evidence against Saunders, he would almost certainly get a long prison sentence, but what would that mean to her? Defence lawyers digging up her family history in cross-examination, a chance of a new happy life vanishing out of the window. Violet wanted that man nailed, and Barnes too, but not at the expense of a kid with a noble spirit who cared enough for the weak and needy to stick her neck out.

Saunders would surface somewhere else. His sort always did. She just hoped the police would keep track of him. As for Barnes, maybe disgrace would be enough punishment, though she personally thought the woman deserved horse-whipping and prison too.

'I'm not angry,' Miss Pemberton lied. 'I'm just tired. I suppose I've just burned myself out today. Barnes did bring the question of your father up, but only to me and I silenced her rather thoroughly. There was no question of anyone not believing you, either; everyone had the utmost admiration for your part in it all. Perhaps Barnes won't go to prison where she belongs, Rosie, but she certainly won't get a position of authority again and she'll never be able to hurt you.'

'But what will happen to Carrington Hall? Will it stay open?'

'For the time being. I've roped in enough temporary

staff to be getting along with for now, though of course its future depends very much on the owner. But for now all the staff still have jobs, including you if you want to stay. But that's what I really want to talk to you about, Rosie.'

Rosie gulped. Surely Miss Pemberton wasn't going to try and make her stay here?

'You've got three or four choices, my dear,' Miss Pemberton went on, smiling at last. 'You could stay here with a rise in salary. You could come home with me to Somerset for a holiday while you think about what to do next. Thomas would put you up at his flat until you found another job in London. Or –' She stopped suddenly.

'Yes?' Rosie prompted, wondering what the fourth choice could be. 'Or what?'

'You could go to Sussex to help look after Donald with his parents.'

Rosie blinked hard and her mouth fell open. She wasn't sure she'd heard that right.

Miss Pemberton laughed at Rosie's astounded expression and all at once her spirits lifted. Let people like Aylwood, Barnes and Saunders wallow in their own dirt. This dear girl was worth so much more, she deserved happiness.

'As you know, it has been their desire to take Donald home for some time,' she went on. 'But they feel they are a little old to be starting out with him again from scratch. They don't want you there as a nursemaid or a domestic, but as a companion to him. Someone to help him adjust to his new freedom, to keep any eye on him and teach him things. They have a fine big house, you would have a nice room and good wages. What do you think?'

'I don't know,' Rosie said. Donald had been on her mind so much since Coronation Day. She had missed him so much, worried about him and been afraid she would never actually see him again. She couldn't imagine anything better than caring for him. In her mind's eye she could see all his family as they had been on Coronation Day. She liked them all and she had no reservations about that side of it. It sounded a job from heaven.

'They know how much you like gardening,' Miss Pemberton smiled as she laid on the temptations. 'They have a large garden, by all accounts, and one of their ideas is that you and Donald could work in it together. You would have regular time off, they have no intention of imprisoning you in their home. They want you to become one of their family.'

At that last sentence Rosie began to cry. Miss Pemberton had been leading her closer and closer to the gateway to heaven in everything she had said, but she'd finally found the right key to unlock it.

'It sounds wonderful,' she sobbed. 'I can't think of anything I'd like better.' She paused for a minute, struggling to find a handkerchief in her uniform pocket.

'But there's a "but" if I'm not much mistaken,' Miss Pemberton said, patting Rosie's knee. 'Now let me guess! It couldn't be the young man you had a date with on Wednesday, could it?'

Rosie blew her nose and wiped her eyes. She felt foolish.

'Yes,' she whispered sheepishly. 'I really like him, and Sussex is a long way from London, isn't it?'

Violet smiled. She could remember one of her old boyfriends cycling fifteen miles in the rain to meet her just for a few hours. A young doctor had once courted her from Leeds when she was in London.

'Love can conquer all obstacles,' she said. 'Besides, he works for the railways, doesn't he? Mayfield has a station, and it can't be more than fifty miles from London.'

Rosie didn't need to consider anything more. No job in London could possibly offer as much as what the Cooks were offering her. Gareth might tire of her, she might get bored with him, and then where would she be?

'I do want to work for them,' she smiled, suddenly

imagining being in the country again, digging in a garden and sharing things with Donald. 'It will be such an adventure. Yes, I do want to go.'

Violet beamed. 'That's the spirit,' she said stoutly. 'Now, when had you arranged to see this young man next?'

'Tonight,' Rosie blushed. She hadn't expected Miss Pemberton to be so understanding. 'Will it be all right for me to meet him?'

'Of course it will. And it will work out just perfectly as Mr and Mrs Cook are driving up tomorrow to collect Donald. They'll be thrilled to find you ready to go with them.'

'Tomorrow?' Rosie gasped. She thought Miss Pemberton meant in a week or two.

'Yes, dear.' She blinked fast in surprise at Rosie's question. 'The Cooks wanted to take Donald away at the first hint of trouble. The only reason they haven't done so is because I was afraid such action would alert Barnes that something was going on. Now what I suggest is that you leave here tomorrow morning first thing in a taxi, telling anyone who asks you are going home to Somerset. Go to Thomas's flat and wait there for the Cooks to pick you up later in the day. That way no one here will have any idea where you are going.'

'Have you told the Cooks about me?' Rosie asked tentatively.

'Only that I came into your life when your father died and arranged for you to work here,' she said. 'That is all that is relevant. As for Thomas, who they've had a few telephone conversations with, they believe him to be a friend of mine, someone I put you in touch with when you first came to London.'

'Do you think I should tell them all about myself?' Rosie asked in a small voice.

'I think that has to be ultimately your decision, my dear. But run along now and have your tea before the rest of the staff come off duty. I'm quite sure you've had enough for one day.'

Rosie had had a bath and washed her hair by the time Maureen came upstairs.

'Simmonds said Matron left this afternoon in her brother-in-law's car,' she said, sitting down on the bed and glancing over at Rosie sitting at the dressing-table. 'She said Mr Brace-Coombes left a few minutes afterwards. But then I suppose Sister Pemberton told you all this when you were having your chat in the garden?'

The sarcasm was laid on with a trowel but Rosie decided not to rise to the bait. 'No, she didn't, actually. She only wanted to know what I wanted to do now. Has she said anything to you?' Rosie was full of excitement and that made her feel a bit sorry for Maureen. She had nothing to look forward to and she seemed so lost and frightened.

'Yes, she said I still had a job if I wanted to stay. But she was a bit frosty. She said I wasn't to communicate with Matron in any way. As if I would want to.'

Rosie had the distinct feeling Miss Pemberton had said a great deal more than that, but she wasn't going to ask. Suddenly the politics in Carrington Hall meant nothing to her.

'It will be much better here now,' Rosie tried to sound encouraging. 'Staff Nurse Clegg's nice, but I don't think Miss Pemberton will leave you on the second floor.'

'As if you care,' Maureen said spitefully. 'I suppose you're going home to Auntie tomorrow?'

'Yes, I am as a matter of fact,' she said. 'And I can't wait.'

'I don't think anyone will stay,' Maureen said and began to cry. 'Donald's going home tomorrow with his mum and dad. Mary's talking about going back to Ireland and Linda said she's only going to give it a week or two because Clegg is contacting all the patients' families to tell them what's happened and she reckons Brace-Coombes will have to close the place down.'

Rosie was torn between sympathy and wanting to get ready for Gareth, but her sympathy won. 'Look, Maureen,' she said, getting up from the dressing-table and going over to sit beside her. She put her arm around Maureen's shoulder. 'You must see this as the beginning of something new, and almost certainly better. Why don't you look around for a new job too, and start all over again where no one knows about anything?'

'It's all right for you, you're pretty and clever,' Maureen sniffled against her shoulder. 'I'm plain and people don't like me.'

'No one around here likes me either,' Rosie shrugged. Neither Linda nor Mary had been up to see her and she didn't think they were intending to either. 'And being clever hasn't got me very far. You've still got a job and I haven't.'

Once she was out of the front door Rosie breathed a sigh of relief. Today had been long and exhausting and Maureen had just about finished her off.

But as she walked down to the gates, reality suddenly hit her. She was free. She would never have to clean another dirty bottom, except perhaps a baby's, she hadn't ever got to go back on either of the wards again. Tomorrow she would pack her clothes, climb into a taxi and enter a whole new world. Donald wouldn't be told she was joining him until after he'd left here tomorrow. She couldn't wait to see his face when his parents called for her in Hampstead. All those things she'd longed to do with him – read books, walk in fields, ride on buses, take him shopping – she could do them all now. It was going to be wonderful.

Filled with wild excitement, her tiredness forgotten, she raced to the gates, opened them and ran out smiling with happiness. And there, just a few yards along the road, Gareth was sitting on his motorbike waiting for her.

They didn't go to the pictures. It was too warm an evening to sit inside in the dark and there was so much to talk about. They drove out into the country and as they walked hand in hand across fields Rosie spilled out all that had happened today, and her part in starting it all. It was such a relief to be able to talk about it. By the time she'd finished she felt as if she'd pulled a plug on a whole bathful of dirty water and watched it drain away.

'I just wish I could have peeped through a window while that old witch was being questioned,' Rosie giggled. 'But Miss Pemberton is very discreet, she probably won't ever tell me the whole story.'

'Fancy you being involved in all this and not saying anything to me.' Gareth looked at her with an expression approaching awe. He hated the idea of her being near a man like Saunders, he guessed exactly what he'd done to the mad woman, even though Rosemary had only referred to it as 'interfering with her'. 'I'd have been out of there on the next bus. I wouldn't have worried about the patients, only myself.'

'I don't believe that,' Rosie smiled. It felt so good being admired, it wasn't something she was used to. 'Anyway, it's a good job I didn't turn tail and run – I wouldn't have got the job with the Cooks.'

Gareth was a little confused because he had a set idea in his head about how girls should be and Rosemary wasn't quite slotting into it. He was glad she was leaving Carrington Hall – he wasn't comfortable with having a girl working in a loony-bin. He thought the Cooks were nice people, but he couldn't see for the life of him why she'd want to bury herself in the country looking after Donald. He would get a lot of stick from his mates if anyone found out what she did. Their girls all worked in offices, shops or hairdressers'.

'Are you really sure that's what you want to do?' he asked. 'I know they are nice people. But it's a long way from London. How will I see you?'

Rosie thought it was better to act cool. She had read in magazines that men were always keener if they had to do all the running.

'Of course it's what I want to do. And you're the one who knows all about trains, so I don't need to tell you how to get there,' she said teasingly. 'But I expect you'll forget me in a few weeks anyway.'

'I won't,' he said, pulling her into his arms. 'I shall be thinking about you night and day, wishing I was with you.'

When he kissed her a little later, it wasn't a gentle light kiss like the one when they'd parted on Wednesday night. This time his arms went right around her and his mouth came down on hers hot and hard.

'I really like you,' he whispered into her neck. 'I want you for my girl, serious like. I didn't intend to say anything like this so soon, but now you're going away I have to. Promise me you'll write to me?'

'Yes, if you want me to,' Rosie agreed, thrilled by his words and by the touch of his lips on her neck. 'I like you too, Gareth. You're the only thing which makes me feel a bit sad about going.'

Gareth saw a glimmer of hope. Perhaps she was only going to Sussex because she had nothing else at the moment. Maybe in a few weeks she'd be tired of it and then he could persuade her to come back to London. He imagined helping her find a room somewhere near him in Clapham, taking her out and introducing her to all his mates. He'd be the envy of them all, none of their girls was so pretty.

He put his arm around her and they walked on until they came to a small copse. 'Let's sit down here,' he suggested.

Soon, sitting down on the grass and kissing led to lying down, and their kisses grew longer and more passionate. Rosie had often wondered what the attraction was for couples who lay in the parks in one another's arms for what seemed like for ever. Now she understood. Each kiss grew deeper, Gareth's tongue probed into her mouth teasingly, and his hands roamed over her back, arms and buttocks, drawing her closer and closer to him.

When his hand stole to her breast the first time Rosie pushed it away immediately, but soon it became a delicious, teasing game, where his hand would come back, and she'd let it linger there for a second or two before stopping him. But each time he touched her there it was harder to push him away. A hot tingly sensation was taking over her body, and although a small voice right at the back of her mind was whispering that she must break away now and cool down, she didn't want to listen to it.

It was Gareth who moved away. 'This is getting out of control,' he said in a curiously shaky voice as he sat up and pulled his cigarettes out of his shirt pocket.

Rosie sat up too, suddenly embarrassed, and pulled her skirt down over her knees. She sat there in uneasy silence for a moment listening to him drawing on the cigarette. Mary had told her that boys wanted only 'one thing' and they'd say anything, do anything to get it. Rosie was confused now: why wasn't Gareth begging her?

He slid his arm around her and drew her back to his shoulder, kissing her gently on the forehead. 'You are so lovely, it's hard to control myself,' he whispered. 'But I'm only human, Rosemary. If we keep kissing like that, I might end up going too far, and I've got too much respect for you to spoil things like that.'

All at once Rosie felt secure. Respect was a word which had never been in her father's or brothers' vocabulary, not where women were concerned. As Gareth used it, surely that meant he believed in true love and marriage, and that sex only happened once there was a wedding ring on your finger?

She turned to kiss him, holding his face between her hands. She could feel the words 'I love you' forming in her mind, but she knew she mustn't say them yet, not before he did.

'You will come to see me in Sussex, won't you?' she asked instead.

'Just try and stop me,' he said with an impish grin. 'It's far too soon to say this, but I think I'm falling in love with you.'

Rosie just looked at him, drinking in those clear blue eyes, the golden tone of his skin and the softness of his lips. She had never felt as deliriously happy as this. All the clouds in her life were at last scudding away.

Chapter Twelve

Thomas stood back and watched Donald rapturously embracing Rosie in Flask Walk. It was two o'clock in the afternoon, he and Rosie had just returned from lunch in a café up by the heath, and now the Cooks had come to collect Rosie.

The reunion was very touching. Both Donald and Rosie were crying and laughing at the same time, and Donald looked as if he would squeeze the life out of her. Frank Cook, his arm around his wife, was grinning broadly, obviously thrilled to be taking his son home. Norah's face was buried in her husband's big chest, so Thomas couldn't see if she was crying too, but he was sure she was.

'Come on in for a cup of tea,' Thomas suggested. Seeing this young man whom Rosie had spoken of so often at last and knowing he was off to a happy new life had brought a lump to his throat.

'That's very kind of you, Farley,' Frank's big voice boomed out, 'but I think Donald has had almost too much excitement for one day already. If we can just take Rosemary's belongings, we'll whisk the pair of them away home.'

Thomas felt a sudden and irrational pang of jealousy. 'But you can't,' he objected. 'Surely you can spare a few minutes?'

Norah Cook let go of her husband, wiping her eyes with the back of her hand. 'Frank's right about him being overexcited.' Always sensitive to others, Norah had picked up on the tension in Thomas's voice. She thought perhaps he was nervous of two comparative strangers taking Rosemary away with them, without checking them out first. She found that touching. 'But this won't be a goodbye, only an *au revoir*,' she said with a smile. 'You must come down and stay for a weekend with us in Mayfield soon, Thomas. Then we can all get to know each other properly.'

'They're right.' Rosie disengaged herself from Donald's arms and went over to Thomas, taking his hands in hers and looking up into his face. 'We should get Donald home quickly. And you will come to Mayfield, won't you?'

Thomas nodded. He didn't quite trust himself to speak. Rosie had arrived at the shop this morning just after nine with her luggage, and it was as if a warm, sweet-scented summer breeze swept into the room with her. She was so happy and bubbly; he'd never seen her that way before and it made him feel happy too. They had gone up on to the heath to sit in the sunshine and she'd excitedly spilled out all the events of the day before, and her hopes for the future.

'Just you remember to write to me,' Thomas finally managed to say. He didn't know what was the matter with him. 'Now, let's get your luggage into the car. Did you bring the gardening book downstairs?'

Rosie stepped inside the shop. She had left her suitcase and a couple of smaller bags there. Thomas had given her a huge, glossy book about gardening this morning as a going-away present. It was the best present she'd ever had and she couldn't wait to start reading it. 'I've already put it in my suitcase,' she said. 'I can't thank you enough for it. I'll read every single word and become a master gardener.'

She stood on tiptoe then, took his face in both her hands and kissed his cheek. 'I expect you to have some drawings to show me next time I see you,' she said in a low voice close to his ear. 'And find yourself a lady friend!'

Thomas stood and waved until the Cooks' Jaguar disappeared out of sight down Haverstock Hill. Then he turned and slowly walked back to the shop. He had a feeling he did know what was wrong with him. Perhaps he did need a shrink after all; thirty-one-year-old men with only one leg didn't fall for pretty sixteen-year-olds. It was ridiculous and utterly hopeless.

'Do sit back on the seat properly, Donald,' Norah Cook said with a note of exasperation in her voice. It was two hours since they'd picked up Rosemary, and her hopes that Donald would settle down with her beside him on the back seat were proving to be vain ones. He had wriggled and squirmed the whole way, turning this way and that, and commenting on everything from shops and cows in fields to different cars, and firing questions to the point where Norah felt she could hardly bear it a moment longer. But now as they grew nearer to Mayfield and he recognized a few landmarks, so his glee had become overpowering. 'And could you try and be quiet for five minutes?'

Yet while Donald had grown steadily noisier as the journey progressed, Rosemary had grown quieter. Norah wondered if she was brooding on all the awful scenes of the past ten days, or maybe feeling she'd been railroaded into this job. But she couldn't ask her now, not in front of Donald.

Rosie *was* deep in thought, but she certainly wasn't dwelling on Carrington Hall. That was one place she never wanted to see or think about again. She had left before nine o'clock this morning with only the briefest of farewells and without even a backward glance. Yet although she felt today was the start of a happy new life, it could well be likened to jumping out of an aeroplane without checking first that she had a parachute strapped to her back.

Last night she'd lain awake for hours just thinking about Gareth. She liked him so much, but did he really like her enough to come all the way to Mayfield to see her?

She was concerned too about Thomas and Miss Pemberton. Would they stay in touch as they'd promised? They had no real need to, not now Alan's future was decided and she was off to a new job, but the events of the last week or so had emphasized the importance of these two people in her life. They were a substitute for family, two people who knew all about her, whose advice, friendship and affection she valued above all else.

But it was Donald who was her main concern. As he sat wriggling beside her, overexcited, assaulted on all sides by views, sounds and sights he'd been shut away from for so long, she wondered if she was really capable of guiding him through all the potential minefields she knew were waiting out there.

Life in Carrington Hall had been very regimented and ordered for both of them. At any given time of the day they both knew exactly what was expected of them. There were no decisions to make, they lived by strict rules.

But now the rules were gone. No more locked doors, no bells ringing to tell her to get up, no permission needed to go outside, no uniform. Rosie wasn't going to be entirely free, she would still be answerable to Mr and Mrs Cook, and because she would be living in their home she would be bound by their code of proper behaviour. But it would be quite different for Donald. He was the prodigal son returning home.

It was this which made her apprehensive. Too much freedom, too soon, could well be disastrous for him. Locked away since he was fifteen, he knew nothing of the outside world. What if he ran out of the house and gave some old lady one of his bear hugs? Or if he took something from a shop not realizing everything had to be paid for, or even wandered into someone else's home? There would be no alarm bell to ring for help in Mayfield. No other staff to commiserate with if things went badly. Of course his parents would be there, but somehow she didn't think Mrs Cook would be very strong in a crisis. She still thought of Donald as a young boy, and so he was in many ways. But his body had grown into a man's while he'd been away from her, he'd picked up habits that might appal her. Rosie wondered if she was aware of all this.

But as they drove into Mayfield and Rosie got her first glimpse of the village that was to become her home, she put aside her anxiety and became as excited as Donald.

There had been so many pretty villages on the way down from London. But there was something about this one that left the others in the shade. The houses and shops in the main street were all joined together in a terrace, yet no two of them were the same. Some had red hung tiles down to the ground-floor windows, some had white painted weatherboard. Some had front gardens and picket fencing, some had front doors opening right on to the pavement. Here a shop with bow windows and a roof so low it looked as if it had been lifted only slightly to slide in an upstairs window. There a three-storey house with majestic pointed eaves. There was absolutely no uniformity, unless you counted the tubs and window boxes of bright flowers. Here a white painted lattice porch, next a few red-tiled steps up to a cottage with roses round the door, and then an open stable-type door with a canary in a cage swinging above it.

Rosie felt that if she couldn't make her new job work here in such a heavenly place, then she wouldn't have a hope anywhere else in the world. Then Donald clutched at her arm. 'Look!' he squeaked with excitement. 'Home.'

Mrs Cook turned to look at her son, her eyes brimming with tears of joy because she had feared he wouldn't remember his home. Rosie couldn't speak either. That first glimpse of The Grange as Mr Cook turned into the drive took her breath away.

Old trees formed an archway over the gateway and the weathered, soft grey stone house beyond looked like a mansion to her. It had the sort of Gothic windows she associated with churches, and they were framed by long tassels of purple wisteria. Jasmine scrambled up around the arch of the front door, and a fat fluffy grey cat sat on the doorstep as if to welcome them. But better than the splendour of the house was the garden. Even in magazines she had never seen one so lovely. A lush smooth lawn, dotted with rhododendron bushes, swept around the house; there were shrubs and trees such as she'd never witnessed before and, without seeing it, she knew the area at the back of the house would be better still.

'It's huge,' she gasped, and Mr Cook laughed.

'Not so big as it looks from the outside,' he said. 'It's probably the best example of wasted space you're ever likely to see, Rosemary. I think the man who built it two hundred years ago just made it up as he went along without a real plan. Just look at that long sloping roof towards the back! If he'd put on a conventional one, there could be two more bedrooms upstairs. But we love it, warts and all.'

Once inside, Donald's memories came tumbling out over themselves as he joined in the tour of the house. 'This was my room,' he shouted out gleefully as they entered one with a low steeply sloping ceiling. 'I m-m-made a house in the c-c-corner.'

'He did too,' Mr Cook said with a smile. 'He dragged up a big laundry basket and used to curl up in it sometimes and go to sleep.'

Rosie thought the sitting-room which even had a television was the most delightful room of all. It was all pinks and greens with great fat armchairs and dozens of photographs of the entire Cook family, and french windows opening up on to the garden.

It was a large house, but still cosy, full of sunshine and character. 'Lived-in' was the expression which sprung to Rosie's mind. Although there were flowers in every room on polished tables, there were books, knitting, and magazines strewn about too. Odd stains on the carpets proved that children still romped here. Some of the furniture was shabby and old, but some was valuable and old like pieces she'd seen in Hampstead antique shops. She loved it.

As for the garden, her eyes filled with tears as she explored it. There was the pond Donald had spoken of, its surface smothered in waterlilies, fat goldfish lurking in its depths. A white painted summer house, a pretty rock garden, a vegetable patch tucked away behind a rose-covered trellis and a herbaceous border that made her fingers itch to weed it. Donald leapt on to the swing hung from a large chestnut tree and shouted for her to push him. Rosie had never seen such blissful happiness in anyone's face, and she knew then that whatever problems might crop up with Donald she was going to make sure he was never sent back to another asylum.

After a meal of chicken casserole in the kitchen, which had apparently been prepared by a lady called Josie who came in a couple of mornings a week, Donald went into the sitting-room with his father and Rosie helped Mrs Cook with the washing-up.

'Donald is very thin,' Mrs Cook said thoughtfully as she rinsed the plates. 'We must build him up again with good food and plenty of exercise. His table manners are a disgrace. I shall have to take that in hand, and of course he must have a decent haircut immediately before we can take him out anywhere.'

Rosie knew Mrs Cook was only being motherly and wanting to make her son look as normal as possible, but the bit about his table manners reminded her sharply of Mrs Bentley.

'He didn't get to use a knife and fork at Carrington Hall, only a spoon,' Rosie said pointedly. 'But he'll soon learn to use them again, just by watching us.'

'I do hope so, dear.' Mrs Cook's blue eyes looked anxious and a trifle disbelieving. 'I noticed he wipes his nose on his sleeve. We'll have to break that habit too. I suppose it can't all be done in a day though.'

'He learns fast,' Rosie said quickly. 'Speaking of that, have you made any plans yet about what you want me to do with Donald each day?'

Mrs Cook looked askance at Rosie. 'He'll just be here with us! There'll be walks, a bit of shopping, that sort of thing. Later on, when he's had a bit of a holiday, maybe we can plan a little further ahead.'

Rosie's heart plummeted. Mrs Cook was very kindly, but she was clearly intending to indulge her son and make up for all the lost years. She wasn't being practical, or doing Donald any favours. He was used to strict discipline, and if it disappeared overnight he was likely to behave like a greedy child let loose in a sweetshop.

She took a deep breath. 'I hope you won't think I'm speaking out of turn,' she said in a shaky voice. 'But I think we must give him some kind of routine right from the start. He's bound to feel very disorientated until he gets used to being here. So I think we ought to try and keep things as much like being at Carrington Hall as possible for a while.'

'Whatever do you mean?' Mrs Cook's voice rose to a surprised squeak. 'I would think you of all people would welcome sweeping away such memories.'

Rosie blushed, but she was determined to get her point across. She explained how Donald had always helped the chargehands and how much he'd enjoyed doing it. Mrs Cook sat down at the table to listen properly and Rosie went on to tell her the worries she'd had on the way down here.

'He needs firm guidelines,' she insisted. 'He was the smartest person on his ward and because of that he got little privileges that the other patients didn't get. If you just let him wander about aimlessly, he'll lose that feeling of his importance. I thought that perhaps after breakfast we could do some little jobs together. Maybe making beds, cleaning shoes, sweeping up the terrace, easy things at first until he gets the hang of it. Then later I could have some quiet time with him, looking at books or doing a jigsaw puzzle.'

Mrs Cook smiled at last. 'Well, that doesn't sound too onerous. And what had you thought of for the afternoons? I'm pretty certain you've got that worked out too.'

That last remark had a touch of sarcasm, but Rosie had to stand her ground. 'Working in the garden, or going for a walk. But I think we should keep him right away from people and the shops in the High Street until he's had time to get used to us and the house.'

Rosie squirmed a little as Mrs Cook looked thoughtfully at her for a moment. Although she was a small woman and her nice clothes and well-manicured nails all suggested she had a fairly idle life, Rosie had already discovered in the couple of hours she'd been here that this wasn't so. Apart from Josie coming in to do some of the heavy work, she was very much a housewife. She cooked, cleaned, made clothes for her grandchildren, and the pantry was stuffed with her home-made preserves, jams and pickles. She had also been a very good mother and Rosie felt that she must seem very impudent telling Mrs Cook how to treat her own son.

'Fair enough,' Mrs Cook said at last, nodding her head. 'I believe he went to bed early at Carrington Hall, so maybe we'd better stick to that too for the time being.'

Rosie breathed a sigh of relief. It was said now, the air was cleared. She just hoped Donald wouldn't sense that his mother wasn't entirely in agreement with her and play them one against the other. He was perfectly capable of that. 'I'm a bit worried about him at night though,' she admitted. 'He's been so used to the other men in the dormitory, he might not like being alone in a room.'

She had seen the rooms both she and Donald were to have. Donald's was the one he'd had as a child, newly decorated in blue and white stripes, and hers was across the landing, at the back, a small but very pretty pink and white room with a similar sloping ceiling to Donald's. She wasn't sure if she'd hear him call out from there.

'Maybe I could sleep outside his door for a few nights?' Rosie suggested. 'Just to make sure he doesn't get up and go wandering.'

Mrs Cook looked aghast at that idea. 'My dear,' she said, raising her dainty eyebrows, 'we didn't bring you here to be some sort of guard-dog.'

Rosie giggled. 'I didn't mean lying on a mat – perhaps a camp-bed tucked up by the banisters. You see, after all the locked doors in Carrington Hall he's going to want to explore everywhere. He'll be like your little grandson Robin for a while, wanting to touch and look at everything. But he won't see the dangers in ordinary things like matches, sharp knives and suchlike. He might be clumsy too, and break things.'

Rosie's point was proved only a few moments later as Donald knocked over a vase of flowers on a low table in the sitting-room. The glass vase smashed, the water spilled all over the table, and when Donald went to pick up the glass he cut his finger. He began to cry when he saw the blood.

Mrs Cook put an Elastoplast on the cut. Rosie mopped up the water and she noticed that Mr Cook was looking fearfully around the room as if wondering what else they ought to move.

Rosie did sleep on a camp-bed. It was just as well because Donald came lumbering out of his room three times during the night. The first couple of times Rosie escorted him to the lavatory, then took him back to his room and tucked him back into bed. The third time it was dawn and she took him down to the kitchen to make him a drink.

'You must stay in your room at night, Donald,' she said firmly as she filled the kettle. 'I need my sleep even if you don't.'

He looked so very young and boyish sitting there at the kitchen table in his striped pyjamas.

'It's t-t-too quiet,' he said.

'Quiet at night-time is good,' she said, putting one hand on his shoulder and squeezing it affectionately. 'It means all the birds and other creatures are tucked up fast asleep just like you. There's nothing to be afraid of; your mother and father are close by, and so am I.'

Rosie was more worried now than she had been when she spoke to Mrs Cook. Between the evening meal and Donald going to bed, some of the problems she'd anticipated had already reared their heads.

Mrs Cook just couldn't imagine the difference between the bleak day room with nothing to look at, and her treasure-filled sitting-room. Even Rosie had a strong desire to pick things up and look at them. But each time Donald touched something, his mother stiffened, afraid he was going to drop it. When she did reprimand him, her ladylike manner and soft voice didn't cut any ice. When his father saw this, he roared at him, and that frightened Donald half to death.

Rosie was afraid he might fly into a tantrum before long, if they kept saying no. With so many easily accessible things to hurl around, she didn't like to dwell on the mayhem he might cause. Another problem was that none of them could possibly guess what he might want to investigate next. They had left him alone in the sitting-room watching the television for a few moments, and when they came back he had raided the coal scuttle and lined up the lumps on the carpet like a row of soldiers. She was scared his parents might lose patience with him. They were middle-class people with a beautiful home, and at their age it would be very difficult to adjust to having their comfortable life disturbed. She was also worried they might come to blame her for suggesting that Donald was capable of living at home in the first place, and then for not being vigilant enough.

Before Rosie took Donald back upstairs she opened the curtains over the doors which led on to the terrace so he could see the garden and the first rays of sun lighting up the sky. As they stood for a moment watching and listening to the birds sing, Rosie stole a look at him. His face was a picture of wonder. A lump came to her throat. She felt that if he was sensitive enough to be moved by the beauty of a sunrise, he was sensitive enough to learn to look at delicate things without touching, to obey his mother even if she didn't shout at him, to learn to eat with a knife and fork again.

Rosie could see a strong parallel between how she had felt on her arrival at Mrs Bentley's in Bristol and how Donald must feel now: both uprooted, thrust into an alien world, then bombarded with new experiences. Her heart filled with sympathy for him.

'It's time for the birds to get up and look for their breakfast,' she said after a minute or two. 'But too soon for us just yet. So it's back to bed, and this time you'll stay there until I call you.'

After taking Donald upstairs, Rosie sat on his bed for a while and gently stroked his forehead. The anxious expression in his eyes made her think of Alan and it also reminded her again that Donald was to all intents and purposes a small boy. Perhaps they had all made a mistake in thinking he understood what coming home for good meant. Maybe he felt he had to snatch everything at once, just in case it was all gone the next day.

'This is where you are going to stay for ever, Donald,' she said slowly and clearly. 'You aren't ever going back to Carrington Hall, not tomorrow, next week, or even next year. This is your home now, and I'm going to stay with you and look after you.' She bent down and kissed his cheek. 'Now go back to sleep. I'll still be here when you wake up.'

On her fourth night at The Grange, Rosie woke with a start on hearing a noise from downstairs. It was still dark, but as she looked across the landing at Donald's room she could just make out his window, which meant his door was wide open and he'd crept out without her hearing him.

Sighing, she got out of bed and reached for her dressing-gown. She hadn't had more than four hours of uninterrupted sleep since she arrived here. But this was the first time he hadn't woken her. He was growing crafty now, as well as disobedient.

'You naughty boy,' she exclaimed as she walked into the kitchen and found him scoffing food in the larder. He had a large slice of meat pie in one hand and a huge lump of cheese in the other. His cheeks were stuffed with food, puffed up like a hamster's. 'How many times have I told you not to come down here?'

He tried to reply but couldn't manage it. Rosie caught hold of the back of his pyjama jacket, pulled him out of the larder, then snatched the food from his hands.

'You get more than enough to eat during the day. You're just being greedy,' she snapped at him and felt like slapping him too. 'You must stop being naughty, Donald. Now wash your hands and back to bed.'

She forced his hands under the kitchen tap and washed them for him.

'I'm s-s-sorry,' Donald finally managed to say as he chewed the food still in his mouth. 'Don't be cross with me.'

'I will be cross with you until you stop this,' she said fiercely. 'And I won't be your friend any more.'

She frog-marched him back up the stairs, tucked him into bed and then went back to her bed.

Rosie was in despair, tired, anxious and so very afraid she'd been mistaken in thinking Donald could cope at home. Mr Cook had threatened to put a lock on his bedroom door yesterday, but Rosie had talked him out of it, saying it defeated the object of bringing him home. Now she wanted a good night's sleep so much she was tempted to ask Mr Cook to do it.

It was tough enough during the day. Donald didn't sit still even for a minute, examining this, poking into that, knocking things over. He'd even wet himself several times because he was too afraid of missing something while he was in the lavatory. Rosie felt he would calm down eventually, but his parents were at the end of their tether.

It seemed like only moments later that Rosie awoke to another noise. It was light again, she guessed about six in the morning, and the sound was Donald retching. Wearily she got up and went into him. He was lying in a heap of vomit – it was in his hair, all over his pyjamas and bedding, cascading down on to the floor – and judging by the sheer quantity of it, he'd eaten half the contents of the larder before she'd caught him.

'That's what comes of being so greedy,' she said, sickened at the thought of clearing it up when she was so tired. 'Get up and come into the bathroom.'

Sympathy overcame her as he knelt by the lavatory bowl vomiting up still more. In Carrington Hall he'd grown used to a bland diet of mushy food. He had forgotten how to chew properly and his stomach couldn't possibly cope with the vast amount of cheese, meat pie and ham he'd stuffed into it. Perhaps he'd learned a valuable lesson at last.

Once there was nothing left in his stomach, she washed him, got some clean pyjamas and tucked him into her camp-bed. He fell asleep almost immediately and Rosie paused for a moment, just looking down at him, before going back into his room to clear up the mess there. She thought how cruel nature was sometimes: in sleep there was nothing to show he was different from any other man. He was handsome enough to attract any girl, but a simple accident at birth had robbed him of a career, marriage and children. She wondered what would become of him when his parents grew too old to look out for him.

*

Two weeks later on a Friday morning, Rosie was kneeling on the grass planting out summer bedding plants when Mrs Cook came out with a tray of soft drinks and biscuits for elevenses. She looked very pretty in a loose-fitting print dress, her white hair fluffy around her small face. No one would guess she was in her sixties; she had the grace and quick movements of a much younger woman.

Donald was mowing the grass, but at the sight of his mother he came gambolling across the lawn. Two weeks of fresh air, sunshine, exercise and good food had done wonders for him. Dressed in only a pair of khaki shorts, his hair streaked by the sun, he had the look of a tanned, but rather thin beachcomber.

'Sit down before I give you your drink,' Mrs Cook said reprovingly as he lunged towards the tray. 'We don't want spills, not even in the garden.'

She put the tray down on the garden table. Donald sat down on the grass and held his hands up expectantly. Rosie came over and joined them, sitting at the table.

Rosie had caught a glimpse of herself in the dining-room window earlier, and smiled when she realized that she had reverted to the way she'd looked back at May Cottage. Her hair had grown quite a bit and it was a mop of curls again, more freckles had sprung up on her nose and her cheeks were bright red. Even the cotton dress she wore to garden in was shabby and dirt-smeared, and her feet were bare.

She had been very surprised to find the Cooks didn't give a jot about appearances. On her first three or four days here she had worn a smart navy blue skirt and white blouse, but they had jokingly reminded her that she wasn't a maid, and old clothes were the order of the day at The Grange, especially when out in the garden with Donald. They seemed to get great pleasure out of seeing her untidy but happy.

'We've achieved so much in two weeks,' Mrs Cook said

to Rosie with a satisfied sigh. 'To think for the first few days I was in despair.'

Looking back, Norah felt a little foolish that she'd expected Donald would behave perfectly from day one, and that she hadn't anticipated the adjustments that she and Frank would have to make. If Rosie hadn't been here, heaven only knows how they would've coped.

Rosie reached down to stroke Donald's head. 'Tell your mother about the story I read you last night, Donald?'

She sat back with a satisfied smirk as Donald related the tale of 'The Cat Who Walked by Himself', from Kipling's *Just So Stories*. His description was a bit muddled, but he hardly stuttered at all. He loved having stories read to him, and now he'd cottoned on to the concept of reading, he wanted so much to learn to read himself. Writing was far harder for him: he had been denied pencils for so long that he seemed unable to control one now, but maybe with practice he'd improve.

Yet it was out here in the garden that Donald had really come into his own. Like Rosie he seemed to have an affinity with nature and growing things. Although he was clumsy indoors, he could handle a small plant with the utmost delicacy, and being outside seemed to work off much of his excess energy. He had remembered all the things she'd taught him about flowers and weeds back at Carrington Hall, and he delighted in using the mower and digging in the vegetable patch.

As the Cooks' old gardener had retired a year ago and Mr Cook had been struggling to keep things tidy, he was only too pleased that Rosie and Donald were so enthusiastic. To encourage them further, he had brought home the trays of plants Rosie was now bedding out. In private he had admitted to Rosie he believed it was work that Donald needed rather than his mother's brand of mollycoddling, and if Rosie wanted to stay with him in the garden all day, that was fine by him.

Rosie did want to stay in the garden; to her it was

heaven, even in the rain. In the evenings she studied the gardening book Thomas had given her, and the many other books she found in the house. Day by day her knowledge of plants, flowers and trees was expanding.

Steadily, Rosie was also growing fonder of the Cooks. Maureen had been wrong in saying they were rich. They were comfortable, the house was lovely and they had a smart car, but they weren't rolling in money. The house and the business had been inherited from Frank's parents. The business was manufacturing tractors and other farm machinery, yet it was only during the war when special government contracts came Frank's way that he had really made it pay.

Norah came from a poor family in a nearby village, and although she moved into the big house when she married Frank, life was a struggle as his parents were old and sick and she had to nurse them. In fact the friend who'd lent them the apartment in Piccadilly was one of only a very few rich friends; almost everyone else they knew was quite ordinary, and some of Norah's old school friends even lived in farm cottages not so different from May Cottage. As for Frank, he was more comfortable having a pint over in the pub with working men than mixing with the many professional men who lived in the village.

They both had a strong social conscience. Norah was always popping out to check on old people in the village, and she took an active interest in a local unmarried mothers' home. Frank was involved in raising money to send farm equipment to poor countries, and until quite recently he'd run a scout troop.

But of all the things Rosie liked about them, it was their openness she admired the most. Nothing was hidden. They didn't whisper between themselves, and if one of them was angry, they said so. Over meals they discussed anything and everything, from the local gossip to business, current affairs, and their family, often stopping to explain a point here and there to Rosie so she understood who or what they were talking about. They never made her feel awkward or excluded, and even more importantly, she felt valued.

Norah had given Rosie Saturday as her day off because Frank was home then to help with Donald. Last Saturday Rosie had caught the train to Tunbridge Wells to look around, but it had rained all day and she'd come home by three, looking, Norah thought, as if she'd felt very lonely on her own. She hoped Rosie might get to know some of the village girls soon, and get out to a few dances or parties. She might be very fond of Donald but it wasn't healthy to spend all her time with him.

'Now what time is Gareth coming tomorrow?' Norah asked.

Rosie's smile spread from ear to ear. 'His train gets in at eleven.'

'What are you going to do with yourselves?' asked Norah. 'Or is that privileged information?'

'I don't really know,' Rosie said. Gareth had written to her five times since she'd got here and it had taken some wangling for him to get the next day off. 'Just explore locally, I expect.'

'Well, bring him home for tea around five,' the older woman suggested. 'I'd like to see him again, and I'm quite sure Donald and Frank would too. Now I'd better go indoors, I've got dozens of letters to write. Donald, put your shirt back on for a bit. I don't want you getting burnt, and the sun's very hot today.'

Once his mother had gone inside, Donald went back to the lawnmower, and Rosie returned to the planting, but her mind was now on Gareth. These last two weeks had flown by in many ways, yet it seemed like an eternity since she had said goodbye to Gareth outside Carrington Hall.

Every single night she'd relived his kisses as she lay in bed, growing hot and tingly all over.

These feelings were so confusing. They felt wonderful, exciting, just like everyone said love was, but yet they made her ashamed too. She tried to tell herself that what she felt for Gareth had nothing in common with what she'd seen Seth and Norman do to Heather, or Saunders to Angela, but a small voice kept warning her it was related, and that all men were animals.

Yet Mr Cook was so loving to his wife. He was attentive, they were kind to each other, interested and warm. Rosie wanted a marriage like that too one day.

'Rosie!'

Rosie was startled to hear Donald calling out her real name. She jumped to her feet blushing. Donald had found it hard to change from calling her 'Smith' to Rosemary and he soon shortened it to Rose. She knew adding the 'ie' was just a natural progression from that, just as she sometimes called him 'Donny', but still it gave her a jolt.

He was walking towards her with the grass box in his hands. 'It's f-f-full up,' he called out. 'Dad said I had to p-p-put it on the commode.'

Despite being so taken aback Rosie had to laugh at him using the wrong, yet rather appropriate word. 'It's compost, not commode,' she said. 'Come with me, I'll show you where it is.'

The compost heap was in a corner by the vegetable patch, fenced off with some corrugated iron. They tipped the grass cuttings on to it, then stopped to look at the runner beans they'd planted last Sunday afternoon after Mr Cook erected the poles. Rosie was delighted to see the small plants were growing plump and starting to wind themselves round the poles. She had always grown beans down in Somerset, and perhaps it was that reminder of the past, along with Donald's suddenly calling her by her real name, that cast a little cloud over her security.

A couple of days earlier Mrs Cook had asked her about her childhood and her parents dying. They weren't deeply probing questions, just friendly interest. Rosie had been able to answer quite easily just as she had with the girls back at Carrington Hall. But there were gaps in her story, like the fact that she had three brothers, that Thomas's sister became her second mother, and of course that her father was a murderer. Just then, as if to remind her of the dangers of omitting great chunks of her background, she noticed that there was some bindweed growing next to one of the bean plants, threatening to take over the pole and choke the bean.

She tore it out, scrabbling at the soil with her fingers to make sure she had roots and all.

'Why did you pull that one out?' Donald asked. Rosie showed him the difference between the weed and the vegetable and explained what would happen if it was left to grow.

She felt faintly sick as they went back into the flower garden to finish off the bedding plants. The beanplant seemed to represent her, growing well because it was in good soil, and given the right conditions it would grow into a strong, healthy plant that could withstand the odd summer storm. The bindweed was like the lies and the half-truths she'd told. Seemingly gone now, it was only a matter of time before it raised its head again, and next time she might not notice it creeping up on her until it had smothered her.

Seth and Norman were out there somewhere. For all she knew, they might one day try to find her. There were people back in Somerset who knew who she was. Miss Barnes knew too, and whatever Miss Pemberton said, she might just pass it on.

As she placed the bedding plants in the soil, she knew she ought to tell Mr and Mrs Cook everything about herself, and Gareth too when he came tomorrow. Yet even as she rehearsed what she would say, she knew in her heart the words would never pass her lips. She couldn't bear the thought that they might reject her.

*

As Rosie was dropping off to sleep that night, her mind on Gareth's kisses, she would have been surprised to find that Thomas was thinking about her mouth and trying to sketch it from memory.

It was very hot and airless in his flat, the windows were wide open, and he was wearing only a pair of old trousers as he sat at his table with a sketch book.

The half-completed picture of Rosie was excellent, aside from her mouth. He had perfected her hair, and the impudent look in her eyes, defiant chin and straight little nose were just right. But try as he might, he couldn't capture her lips.

He had managed to convince himself in the last week that his affection for Rosie was nothing more than paternal. She'd lost her father, he'd lost his sister, one didn't need to know much about psychology to understand why they should be drawn together. After all he wasn't jealous when she told him in a letter how much she liked Gareth. Neither was he brooding about her being so far away and wondering when he was going to see her again.

Why, then, was he drawing her?

Gareth was leaning out of the window as the train came down the track, and Rosie's heart leapt at the sight of his brown curls and waving arms.

It was another glorious sunny day, heat shimmering on the tracks and not a cloud in the sky. The train came chugging in, belching out hot steam and smoke, and Gareth leapt out of the carriage before it even stopped.

He was wearing a dazzling white open-necked shirt with the sleeves rolled up and grey flannel trousers, his jacket in his hand. Rosie thought he must be the most handsome man in England.

'I wanted to get up in the engine and stoke it myself!' he said as he hugged her, regardless of the curious stares from the guard and ticket collector. 'It seemed so slow.'

'It's right on time,' she said, a little embarrassed and

unsure of herself now the moment she'd been dreaming of for days was finally here. 'What would you like to do now?'

'Get off this platform and find somewhere quiet where I can kiss you,' he said, putting his arm around her waist and leading her out of the station as if he, not she, was the one who knew the place. 'Then I'll settle for a cup of tea.'

He kissed her for the first time just outside the station, drawing her into his arms under the shade of a tree, and he held her so tight and for so long that Rosie could hardly breathe.

'I've got you a present,' he said when he eventually came up for air, and delving into the breast pocket in his shirt he brought out a tiny tissue-wrapped parcel.

Rosie smiled up at him; it was enough to just see him again without a present too. Her heart was too full to speak.

'Go on, open it,' he urged her.

It was a tiny silver heart on a chain.

'Oh Gareth,' she whispered in awe as she held it up. 'I've never had a real piece of jewellery and it's so pretty.'

'Not as pretty as you,' he grinned. 'Let me put it on you. That's if my clumsy fingers can do the clasp.'

Rosie's fingers kept stealing up to the heart as they walked into the village hand in hand. It was like confirmation that everything he'd said in his letters was true, that they had a future together. She felt so very happy it was all she could do not to stop everyone they passed, show them the heart and tell them what it signified.

She showed him the shops, pointed out all her favourite cottages and took him past The Grange, telling him they'd been invited back to tea. As she expected he was suitably impressed, and once they were sitting in a tea shop she told him everything that had happened since she got here.

'You really like it, then?' he said, raising one eyebrow at her enraptured description of the house's interior.

'It's wonderful,' she gushed. 'I've never been so happy. Donald was a real pain at first but he's settled down at last, and the Cooks are so kind.' But realizing that she'd gone rather overboard with this litany of praise, she blushed. 'I'm being boring, aren't I?'

'No,' he smiled. 'I'm glad you're happy. Of course I half hoped you wouldn't be, so I could persuade you to come back to London. But you look so pretty, so sparkly, I haven't got the heart to throw any dampers on it.'

The day just flew by. They bought a couple of meat pies and a bottle of lemonade and walked through the fields towards Heathfield, stopping on the top of a hill to look at the view, eat their picnic and talk.

Gareth was excited too because he'd been out all week as a fireman on a passenger train. He spoke of the engine so lovingly he could have been describing another woman, and the enthusiasm with which he described all the stations they'd called at made it sound like a hot date. He said it was just a holiday relief, but the foreman said he'd be putting his name down for a permanent post soon.

Rosie wasn't that interested in engines and stations, but remembering how patient he'd been when she'd gone on and on about The Grange and the Cooks, she made out she was fascinated.

'Can you come up to London in two weeks' time to meet my parents?' he said once he'd told her everything about his job.

Rosie nodded, thrilled that he was taking her so seriously.

'I'll be working on the early shift,' he said. 'But I can get off at twelve and meet you at Victoria and take you straight there. They really want to meet you. I think Mum knows you are someone special. If you could manage to wangle having the Sunday off, you could stay the whole weekend because I've got that Sunday off too.'

They found a little stream and paddled, then lay in each

other's arms kissing, but all too soon it was time to go back to The Grange for tea.

'What a nice boy he is,' Mrs Cook said as she and Rosie washed up after tea. They could see Gareth down in the garden watering the plants with Donald. 'So well mannered and kind. In my opinion they are two of the most important things in a man. When you meet his mother you must look closely at her, though – it's my belief that mothers form their sons' characters. If you see anything you don't like about the mum, as sure as eggs are eggs he'll turn out to have the same traits.'

Rosie giggled at this. Mrs Cook had a great many home-spun theories about people. Although she was a very kind woman in the main, she often dismissed people because their eyes were too close together, their lips too thin, or their eyebrows met in the middle. She said that in men this was a sign that they were born to be hanged. Cole's eyebrows hadn't met in the middle though, so that sat that theory on its heels.

'You might laugh,' Mrs Cook said indignantly. 'Frank's mother was a hoarder. She kept everything, from pieces of string to old envelopes. This house was crammed top to bottom with useless stuff when she was alive. Frank said he loathed it. But what did he start to do once his mother had died and I'd got rid of it all?'

Rosie smiled. 'That's not so bad. There're worse things.'

'That's very true, Rosemary.' Mrs Cook's small face took on a slightly pensive expression. 'You watch out for meanness and bad temper. Those are the things which cripple a marriage. But I'm running ahead of myself. You've only had a couple of dates with the boy. Go on out in the garden with him now. You can tell him you can have that whole weekend with him. The sooner you check on his mother, the sooner you'll know if he's the one for you!'

*

Gareth's train was the eight o'clock, and they left The Grange at quarter past seven to take a slow walk down to the station. Gareth put his arm around her and kept stopping to kiss her all the way there.

'I don't know how I'll survive another two weeks without seeing you,' he said sorrowfully, and his blue eyes mirrored the sad tone of his voice. 'I haven't even got a picture of you to look at. Tell me, Rosie, do you care for me?'

Just as when Donald called her Rosie, it caught her short. Donald had said it again in the garden just now as they were watering the plants; she supposed that's where Gareth had picked it up from.

She took a deep breath. 'Of course I do. I wish you were close so we could see each other all the time –' She broke off, wanting to say so much more, but she couldn't find the right words.

'But I'm going too fast for you?' he asked.

That wasn't what she'd meant at all. What she wanted was the right moment to tell him about herself, the whole truth, before they went any further.

'Sort of,' was all she could manage.

'Well, I'd better slow down then,' he said and grinned sheepishly. 'My mother tells me I'm too impulsive.'

'We'll have more time when I come to London,' Rosie said and reached up to stroke his face with one hand. 'Now we'd better get a move on or you'll miss the train.'

That night Rosie couldn't sleep at all. She was so hot. The window was wide open, but there wasn't even enough breeze to make the curtains flutter. Her bed felt like a huge hot-water bottle and all she had over her was a sheet. Her breasts felt tingly, and each time she drifted into thinking about Gareth's kisses it felt as if a string was tied inside her and someone was tweaking it. She wanted everything, now. To be absolutely certain that this feeling she had about Gareth really was love, to be convinced he really loved her. She wanted to speed things up, to discover just what making love was about.

Yet she knew in her heart that until she could trust Gareth enough to tell him her secrets, she didn't dare allow herself to fall any further.

Chapter Thirteen

Rosie sat straight-backed in an armchair, her hands in her lap as she smiled nervously at Mrs Jones sitting opposite her. She wished Gareth would hurry up and come back into the room. His mother was studying her silently and intently, and Rosie found it extremely unnerving.

'I suppose we ought to be glad of the rain,' Rosie said in an attempt to start a conversation, glancing over her shoulder towards the rain-splattered window behind her. 'The gardens needed it. The lawn down at The Grange was getting quite brown.'

It had been bright sunshine when she left Mayfield this morning and she thought she looked the picture of elegance in her new, pale blue shirt-waister dress, high-heeled sandals and white cotton gloves. But it began to rain as she got nearer to London, and by the time she got off the train it was bucketing down. Fortunately she did have her raincoat folded up in her overnight bag, but she wished she'd thought to bring a cardigan and a change of shoes too.

Gareth met her at Victoria Station but he had his motorbike, so by the time they arrived at his parents' house in Mill Hill, Rosie's raincoat and sandals were sopping wet and her hair dripping, which was hardly the way to impress his mother.

Rosie had imagined Mrs Jones to be a big jolly woman, but in fact she was small and slender with greying hair pulled back tightly from her face. Despite the severe hairstyle she was very attractive, with good bone structure and an unlined face. She shared her son's dark skin tone and his brilliant blue eyes, but she didn't smile, and she was very disapproving, tutting about their wet clothes before she'd even welcomed them.

'Fancy Gareth picking you up on his motorbike in such weather,' she said in a sing-song Welsh accent which had an acid edge to it. 'And you should have more sense than to get on it.'

Rosie was so taken aback by such a chilly reception that she said nothing and accepted the towel to dry her hair and a pair of slippers gratefully. Gareth disappeared upstairs to change and Mrs Jones ushered her into the lounge.

Even if Gareth's mother wasn't as she expected, her semi-detached suburban house was. Everything was just so. The red cushions sat in a neat row on the grey settee, an embroidered firescreen of a lady in a crinoline hid the empty hearth, and a highly polished brass companion set shaped like a knight in armour stood next to it. Mr Jones's armchair had a small table beside it with his pipe, spills and matches tidily arranged in front of the wireless.

Knowing so much about the Joneses' earlier life, Rosie could well see why such a woman would become house-proud. The snowy nets at the windows and the strong smell of lavender polish told of a woman who knew what it was like to struggle to bring up two small boys and keep things clean with a coal-yard just outside their kitchen door. She understood too how heavenly it must have been to move to a brand-new house after the war, and the way Mrs Jones kept it reflected her pride in her husband for taking her and his family up in the world.

As Mrs Jones offered no comment about the rain or her garden, Rosie tried another tack. 'This is a lovely house,' she said. 'So nice and bright. Do you get the sun in here all day?'

They were in a very modern, L-shaped lounge with a small hatch going through from the dining part into the kitchen. Rosie wondered why they'd chosen red and grey for a colour scheme; it seemed a bit dreary to her.

'Yes, the sun comes in all day. But it's a nuisance as it fades the curtains and the carpet,' Mrs Jones retorted sharply.

Rosie liked sunny rooms and she didn't think she'd care about fading. She also wondered how such an attractive woman with so much – this home, two fine sons, and a loving husband – could be so disagreeable.

'I hope the rain doesn't last the whole weekend,' Rosie said. 'Gareth was going to show me a bit more of London on his motorbike.'

At this Mrs Jones pursed her lips. 'I wish he'd buy himself a little car. I worry about him all the time when he's out on that bike. Our Owen's got a nice little Ford Prefect.'

'Go on, say it, Mum!' Gareth said from the door. 'But then our Owen doesn't waste his money on taking girls out.'

'Oh Gareth,' Mrs Jones gasped, putting her hands up to her mouth as if deeply shocked, 'I've never said such a thing!'

Gareth just grinned. Rosie guessed this was something she'd said repeatedly, and he wanted to embarrass her.

'What are we having for dinner then, Mum?' Gareth asked.

'The usual Saturday meal,' she replied, and got up from her seat. From the way Gareth's face fell, Rosie guessed he was disappointed, and she was soon to find out why.

It was boiled eggs and bread and butter.

Rosie wasn't hungry, because Mrs Cook had given her a packet of sandwiches to eat on the train, so boiled eggs were fine by her. But what did hurt was that Mrs Jones was making it plain she didn't consider her son's new girl-friend important enough to make a special effort for.

'What did your father die of ?' she asked almost as soon

as they sat down to eat. Mr Jones and Owen were still out working. Apparently, they never came home on Saturday until around five.

'He had a heart attack,' Rosie said, peeling off the top of her egg.

'And your mother?'

'She got an infection after she lost a baby.' This was something Miss Pemberton had suggested.

'Gareth said you were only six when she died. Who took care of you?'

Rosie was a little heartened that Mrs Jones wanted to know all about her. She hoped her brusque manner was just shyness. 'My dad and my auntie,' she said. 'When Dad died, Auntie got me the job at Carrington Hall.'

'She didn't do you any favours!'

'Mum!' Gareth rebuked his mother. 'Don't be so sharp.'

'Oh, I didn't mean it in a nasty way,' Mrs Jones said. She put her head on one side and Rosie thought she looked like a little bird. 'I just couldn't imagine sending one of mine to work in an asylum. And now you're looking after the boy you met there. There's stern stuff.'

That sounded very much like a reproach, not admiration, and it made Rosie feel extremely uneasy.

'Donald is like a big kid, Mrs Jones. I really like looking after him, and his parents are the nicest people I've ever met.' She paused, searching for something to add which might bring some approval. 'The reason I went to work at Carrington Hall to begin with was because I thought it would be good experience before starting nursing training.'

'Fancy,' Mrs Jones said, pursing her lips. 'And where will you do that?'

'I'm not sure yet, I can't apply till next year. But I'd like it to be a London hospital.'

Silence fell, and Rosie suspected the woman disapproved of nursing for some reason. 'Of course I might change my mind before that,' she said, in an attempt to find out what Mrs Jones was thinking. 'I love gardening too. I could become a gardener.'

'A gardener?' Gareth exclaimed. 'You're joking, aren't you, Rosie? Girls can't do that!'

Although Rosie loved gardening more than anything else, it hadn't actually occurred to her to consider it as a possible career. Apart from one or two posh ladies like Gertrude Jekyll who did become famous for it, she didn't think there were any women gardeners. But when she saw Mrs Jones's mouth fall open in shock, for some perverse reason she couldn't resist persevering.

'Why not? They did it in the war. It's an old-fashioned idea to think that only men can dig and prune bushes. As for planting out and weeding, it's usually women who do that anyway. I should think women would make better garden designers than men too. They've got more imagination, for a start.'

'Well.' Mrs Jones folded her arms across her chest and pursed her lips. 'I never heard such a thing before.'

It stopped raining later and Rosie and Gareth went for a walk down to the shops in Mill Hill.

'I'm sorry Mum was a bit funny with you,' he said sheepishly. 'I don't understand why. But why on earth did you say that about being a gardener? She'll think you're really strange now.'

Rosie stopped in her tracks to look at him. She was deeply hurt by his mother's attitude; even when they were washing the dishes she hadn't warmed up. She also felt indignant that Gareth hadn't warned her in advance about her, and she had no intention of kowtowing to either of them.

'I am a bit strange,' she said in defiance. 'Look! I'm not the delicate little girl you seem to think I am, Gareth. I had a tough childhood, left to fend for myself most of the time. But one thing I've learned from that, and from things that have happened since, is that I have to make full use of the talents I was born with. I'm good at gardening and I love it. So why shouldn't I make a career out of it if I want to?'

Just a few days earlier Mr Cook had said he might offer Rosie and Donald's services as gardeners around the village. Rosie had taken it in the spirit in which it was intended at the time, a bit of a joke, nothing more. But now, in the face of opposition, her opinion hardened that it was exactly what she *did* want.

'No one ever made a career out of gardening,' Gareth scoffed. 'It's just a job they give to people with no brains, the same as dustmen.'

Rosie smarted. 'Now look here, Know-it-all Jones,' she snapped. 'I want to do something with my life. Whether that is nursing, gardening or something entirely different is up to me, however strange you and your mother find it. I don't want to work behind the counter at Woolworth's and end up marrying someone who'll expect me to be at his beck and call for the rest of my life. And I want more than just cleaning windows, plumping up cushions and polishing brass to keep me happy.'

'That's taking a pop at my mother,' Gareth retorted, his mouth tightening.

'Perhaps,' Rosie sighed, a little ashamed of herself. 'But she hasn't been very welcoming, has she?'

'I think she's a bit jealous. She and I have always been so close,' he said. 'Owen's more for Dad. I'm the one who talks to her, makes a bit of a fuss over her. I suppose she's guessed I've fallen in love with you.'

Although Rosie's heart leapt at being told that he loved her, the moment was entirely spoiled by hearing it tacked on to an explanation about his relationship with his mother. Her feelings were already bruised, now she felt cheated.

'I think I'd better go home tonight,' she said. 'Your mum doesn't approve of me and I don't want to be somewhere I'm not welcome.'

'No, Rosie, please don't do that,' he begged her, catching hold of her and trying to hug her there in the street. 'Look, I'll take you out somewhere this evening, and tomorrow if it isn't raining again we'll go out into the country on the bike.'

By the time they got back for their tea, Rosie had forgotten her threat to go home. After their little spat Gareth had made her laugh, and it had been nice looking in the shops, walking hand in hand, and having a milkshake in an ice-cream parlour with tall stools, just like she'd seen in American films. It was exciting to be back in London with all the crowds doing their Saturday shopping. A crowd in Mayfield was never any bigger than six people. But best of all was just being with Gareth again, talking about all they'd done in the two weeks since they'd last met and laughing together as Rosie told him all the daft things Donald had said and done.

But as they went indoors, Mrs Jones was on her hands and knees rubbing at the parquet flooring in the hall. 'Your dripping coat took the polish off my floor,' she said, looking up at Rosie accusingly.

Rosie felt suddenly chilled to the bone. 'I'm *so* sorry,' she said in an icy voice. 'But Gareth didn't warn me that people took their shoes and coats off in the front garden here.'

Gareth looked alarmed at this sarcastic remark.

'Well, you are a little madam,' Mrs Jones said, getting up off her knees, her thin lips set in a straight line. 'The moment I saw you I knew you'd been brought up without any respect for anything or anybody.'

Rosie was so staggered by this unjustified statement that for a moment she could only stare at the woman in amazement. 'I think I'd better go home, Mrs Jones,' she said after a second or two. 'I can see I'm not welcome here and it was a mistake coming. So if you'll just get my bag for me, Gareth, I won't need to step any further on to your mother's clean floor.'

'Hoity-toity,' Mrs Jones shot back, folding her arms and pursing her lips. 'Been used to better than this, have we?'

Rosie looked at Gareth fully expecting him to say something to stop his mother's nastiness, but all he did was stand there gawping stupidly. A surge of anger welled up inside her.

'No, I haven't actually,' she snapped back at the woman. 'The cottage I was brought up in was probably very similar to the place you had in Kentish Town, not much better than a slum. In fact I'd never seen a polished floor till I worked in Carrington Hall. But where I come from it's the warmth of the welcome we give our guests which counts, not how posh our house is.'

Mrs Jones's thin eyebrows shot skywards.

'Get my bag please, Gareth,' Rosie added. 'I'm leaving.'

When Gareth disappeared obediently up the stairs without a word, Rosie knew he must know a whole weekend here was now out of the question. Mrs Jones got down on her knees again and continued to rub at the floor, even though there was no discernible watermark to be seen. Rosie waited, nose in the air.

Gareth came back down the stairs, seconds later, her bag in his hand.

Rosie opened the front door. 'Thank you for the lunch, Mrs Jones. I'm sorry I put you to so much trouble,' she said. She held out her hand to Gareth for her bag.

'I'm coming with you,' he said, and without even turning to look at his mother he followed Rosie out.

'There's no need for you to come,' Rosie snapped at him once he'd shut the door behind him, trying to snatch her bag from his hand. 'I know the way back to Victoria.'

Gareth wouldn't let her have the bag, so she walked out of the garden gate without it, and he followed. 'I'm sorry, Rosie,' he said, catching hold of her hand once they were in the street. 'She can't help the way she is, it's her nerves. She has bad days and this is just one of them.'

Rosie began to cry as they walked in silence towards

the bus stop. She'd looked forward to this weekend for so long, and it had all gone wrong.

'Don't cry,' Gareth said. 'I'll talk to Mum when I get home tonight. I promise you she'll never be like that to you again.'

'She won't get the chance,' Rosie said. 'I wouldn't go there again even if you paid me to. She was hateful, Gareth.'

He pulled her into a shop doorway and held her tightly until she stopped crying. 'I meant what I said earlier,' he whispered. 'I love you, Rosie. If it came to choosing between you and my mum, I'd choose you.'

Rosie felt too miserable to ask why he hadn't stuck up for her. All she could think was that her happy dreams had gone down the pan, and that spending two pounds on a new dress and her train fare had been such a waste of money. But Gareth kept cuddling her, whispering endearments in her ear, until the anger and hurt began to fade.

'Don't go home till the last train,' he begged her as they walked to the bus stop. 'It's not till nine, so we can go up West for a bit and look around.'

The top of the bus was almost empty. They sat in the back seat, and as it trundled slowly through the traffic towards the West End, Gareth tried to explain about his mother. 'She hates London,' he said. 'You see, when Dad brought us up here she had to leave all her family behind – she had five sisters and three brothers all in the same village, and then there were all their children and her parents too. She wasn't too bad when Owen and I were little, she had plenty to do just keeping us clean; you can imagine what it was like living in a coal yard. And during the war people were friendlier too, neighbours popped in and out, they helped each other. But once Dad bought that house and first Owen went off to do his National Service, then me, she was all alone. Dad doesn't help much, he stays out of her way when she's having her funny turns. See, he thinks she should be happy just having a nice house.'

'But if she's lonely, why isn't she pleased to see new people?' Rosie thought that Mrs Jones was a candidate for a loony-bin. She agreed entirely with Gareth's father: she couldn't see how anyone could be unhappy if they had enough to eat and a nice house and garden. She thought the woman should be grateful she had so much.

'If I knew the answer to that, perhaps I could cure her,' Gareth sighed. 'I really thought she'd warm to you. I'm sorry, Rosie.'

It wasn't Rosie's first experience of victimization. As a child most people had avoided speaking to her because of her father and brothers; Mrs Bentley hadn't liked her, neither had Matron. She thought Mrs Jones was every bit as nasty as the other two women, and she wouldn't lose any sleep about never seeing her again. But she didn't want to lose Gareth.

'I'm sorry too that I was rude to her.' Rosie leaned her head against his shoulder wearily. 'She just made me so angry.'

'Let's forget it,' he said. 'She might be my mother, but you're my girl and it's you who is really important to me.'

The West End looked very different from how it had been at New Year when she came with Linda and Mary. There were still huge crowds, but by daylight without the neon lights it wasn't so magical. She recognized the pub they'd been in that evening and to her surprise it was called the White Bear, the same pub Heather said she'd gone to for a drink with Cole the night he asked her to be his housekeeper.

They window-shopped in Regent Street, then went back down to Piccadilly and sat in the window of a café eating egg and chips, watching the people go by. There was a different atmosphere to the area now the shoppers and office staff had gone home. Every few minutes a throng of people would suddenly erupt out of the stairways from the tube below: groups of girls in strappy cocktail dresses, stoles around their shoulders, with carefully made-up faces and every hair in place, making for the Empire in Leicester Square; young men in smart lounge suits, and with Brylcreemed hair, stopped on the corner to have a cigarette and watch the girls. There were couples wandering hand in hand, just as she and Gareth had been doing, and taxis sped around Eros providing only the briefest glimpse of more elegant, older people on their way to theatres.

'I wish it was dark so I could see the lights again,' Rosie said wistfully, then went on to tell him about her evening out with the girls in the West End.

'I'll bring you up here again when the nights draw in,' Gareth said. 'There's all sorts come out, not just the crowd we see now who are off to the dances, but actors and actresses, gangsters, ladies of the night.'

'Really? How do you know?'

'Owen and I used to come up here a lot just after the war. I was only fourteen then, and Owen was sixteen.' He grinned wickedly. 'Owen always wanted to find a girl, but he never had the nerve to go up to one. We used to spy on them and follow them when they picked up a man. Then one night when Owen was just about seventeen, he offered a girl two shillings. Know what she said?'

Rosie shook her head. 'Tell me.'

'She said, "For two bob you can just about afford one of the old crows up Berwick Street. A nice-looking boy like you should be able to get it for free anyway." Owen was so embarrassed he never wanted to come up here again.'

'Would you pay someone for that?' Rosie asked. She really wished she could see one of these girls; the thought of it made her strangely excited.

'Never,' he said, looking astounded that she felt the need to ask. 'When I was in the army some of the other lads did, but not me. Sex isn't anything unless you love someone.'

Rosie smiled. She wanted to ask if he'd loved anyone else enough to try it. But she didn't. She didn't want to know about other girls in his life.

The time went by quickly, and suddenly it was half past eight. They rushed down into the tube station but it was ten minutes before a train came. They had to change at the Embankment, and then to their horror the train stopped in the tunnel between Westminster and St James's Park. Minutes ticked by.

'I'm going to miss the train,' Rosie said in alarm. 'What am I going to do?'

'It'll be all right,' Gareth insisted. 'It only takes a couple of minutes to get up into the mainline station. We can run.'

They did run, like the wind, up the stairs two at a time and across the station to platform three, but the gates were just closing and the guard was waving the flag.

Gareth begged the man to let Rosie on to the platform, but he would have none of it, and as they watched helplessly, the train pulled out. Rosie burst into tears.

'It's okay, we'll go back to Mum's,' Gareth said, cuddling her.

'I'd sooner spend the night here on the station than at your mum's,' she said through her tears and meaning it. She'd trusted Gareth to give her a good weekend and she felt he was responsible for everything that had gone wrong. 'This whole day has been a disaster.'

Gareth just held her for a moment. 'You could come home to my digs,' he suggested eventually. 'It's not very nice, but it's better than trying to sleep on a bench.'

'But your landlady?' she sniffed. Gareth had said in his letters that she was a dragon.

'On Saturday nights she always goes to the pub,' he said. 'I could easily get you in my room and she'll be too drunk when she gets home to worry about me. She never gets up till gone eleven on Sundays either. We could slip out before she wakes up.'

'But where would I sleep?' Rosie said nervously.

'In my bed, of course. I can sleep on the floor.'

'But –'

Gareth put one finger on her lips. He was smiling and his eyes twinkled. 'I'll be a real gentleman, I promise you.'

'Are you sure?' she asked.

'Cross my heart and hope to die,' he said, making a slashing gesture across his throat. 'I told you earlier that I love you, Rosie. I want you for ever, not for just one night.'

Those words rang in her ears as they caught the train to Clapham Junction. Even the sound of the train wheels seemed to be repeating them over and over again. It was dusk now, the sky a brilliant fiery red, and with Gareth's arm around her she felt safe.

Paige Street in Clapham was every bit as grim as Gareth had said. Worse even than a slummy part of Bristol she'd wandered into once by mistake. Even the glorious sunset and the deepening dusk couldn't mask the aura of poverty that slipped out of every open door in the soot-blackened terrace. There were no front gardens here, no trees or flowers. Babies were crying, the smells of drains and frying chips wafted past them, and the few children who played ball in the street looked thin and pale.

'This was what it was like in Kentish Town,' Gareth said, holding on to her hand as if he thought she might turn tail and run. 'I hated it when I first came here, but you can get used to anything. At least the people are friendly – that's more than can be said for the neighbours in Mill Hill.'

Rosie could see he was very embarrassed. He really thought she had never seen poverty or dirt before. But she made no comment; this was not an appropriate moment to try and describe how she had been brought up.

Number 41 was near the end of the street, no worse or

better than the other houses. Gareth opened the front door with a key, paused in the narrow hall to listen, then beckoned her in.

The entire house was silent and it smelled of fried onions. Perhaps it was as well Gareth didn't switch on a light. The banister felt gritty under her hand and the stairs were just covered with oil cloth or lino.

His room was right at the top, at the back of the third floor. Rosie had braced herself for squalor, so she was quite taken aback when he switched on the light. It was a very small room but clean and tidy. A single bed covered with a pale blue counterpane, a chest of drawers and one easy chair. The window was open wide, there was a rug on the floor, and even the blue and white striped curtains were decent and looked as if they'd been starched.

'It's a nice room,' she said with some surprise, looking at his well-ironed shirts hanging from a small rail fixed to the wall. She guessed his mother still washed them for him. 'I imagined something much worse.'

He seemed bowled over that she approved. 'Mum thought it was awful when she came here once. We had a row about it.'

'It's clean and comfortable,' Rosie said, sitting down on the bed experimentally. 'What more could she want?'

'For me to live at home,' Gareth grinned. 'Mrs Kent made the mistake of telling Mum she liked a drink. That's what really did the damage. She thought I was going to be led astray.'

Rosie knelt on the bed and looked out of the window while Gareth went down to the kitchen to make them a cup of tea. Darkness had finally fallen and blotted out the ugliness. This house was taller than the one behind it, so she had a panoramic view of thousands of lights. After Mayfield it was very noisy: music coming from several different directions, people shouting and laughing, and the sounds of train doors slamming and guards calling out from the station where Gareth worked.

She remembered then how back at Carrington Hall it had seemed so important to become a real Londoner. She wasn't sorry she'd moved to Mayfield, she loved it there, yet a small part of her still longed to widen her experience, satisfy her curiosity and explore every part of the city.

Linda had often spoken of the East End. Sometimes she made it sound like one big party where everyone knew everyone else; at other times she spoke darkly of the filth in the slums, the overcrowding and the stink of the docks. As Rosie looked out on all the lights she realized that this area, Linda's East End and the West End were the real London, and if she was ever to find out what really made the city tick, she had to study them and the ordinary people who lived there. Places like Hampstead, St John's Wood and Highgate were not the city's heart.

This afternoon Gareth had given her glimpses into that heart. He'd spoken of the pubs, greyhound racing and football matches. All his workmates lived around here – some in this house – they went out together at night, and it sounded like great fun.

She was just trying to picture herself living in a little room like this, getting dressed up smartly to work in an office, going up to the West End on Saturday nights to a dance with a crowd of other girls, when Gareth came back, interrupting her thoughts. He was carrying two mugs of tea and a plate of sandwiches.

'Good old Mrs Kent,' he said, smiling broadly. 'She might be a boozer and a dragon when you cross her, but she always leaves us lads a snack.'

By eleven they had turned out the light. Rosie was in bed in her nightdress, with Gareth, still fully dressed, lying on top of the covers cuddling her. It had begun to rain again and it was growing a little quieter outside. It felt so good to be along together, holding each other.

'Are you sure Mrs Kent won't come up here?' she asked sleepily. Gareth had shown her where the bathroom was on the floor below, but she hadn't lingered in there for fear of being caught. She just hoped she wouldn't need to use the toilet during the night.

'She can't manage one flight of stairs when she's been drinking, let alone three,' he laughed softly, kissing her neck. 'Besides, she never comes up at night, not unless someone's making a noise. We're quite safe.'

A little later a door slammed. 'That's her now,' Gareth said. They both half sat up to listen and heard her stumbling down the passage towards the kitchen. There was a rattling of china, some running water, then the back door opened and she went outside.

'She uses the outside lav when she's like that,' Gareth chuckled. 'One night she fell asleep out there. It was a good job she left the whistle on the kettle – I heard that and went down and woke her up.'

'What does she look like?' Rosie asked. She liked to picture people.

'Fat, forty and bleached blonde,' he said. 'Mum thinks she's a bit of a floozy, but she isn't. She's just a bit lonely. Her husband was killed in the war.'

Mrs Kent came back indoors and they heard her speak to someone else who'd just come in.

'That's Steve. He's on the first floor,' Gareth reported. 'He works for the railways too.'

It was after one before the house finally sank into silence. Until then there had been doors banging, the toilet flushing and someone coughing. The rain was lashing against the window and it was very snug in the bed as they lay there whispering to one another.

'Can I get right under the covers? I'm cold,' Gareth said.

'Of course you can,' Rosie replied without any hesitation. She had been a bit cramped with the covers pinned down by his body, and besides he'd been as good as his word and hadn't attempted to take any liberties with her. He took his clothes off, all except his pants, and crept in beside her.

Rosie realized the moment she felt his bare chest that it wasn't going to be so easy to prevent any intimacy now that his skin was touching hers. They just seemed to melt into each other as they kissed, and each kiss was longer and more passionate than the one before.

When his hand stole under her nightdress to fondle her breasts, she did attempt to stop him but it was half-hearted, for she was getting as carried away as he was. Next the nightdress came right off and he moved down the bed to kiss and suck at her nipples.

She felt as if she was being drawn into another world, where nothing but his lips on hers, the touch of his hands and the pressure from his body counted. She had lost all will to stop this game, even though she knew it was dangerous. When he pulled off her knickers and touched her there, all she could think of was caressing him too to make him feel as good as she did.

She felt no shame when his fingers probed deep inside her. It was like a thirst which had to be quenched no matter what. She put her hand round his penis and they rocked together, pleasing and teasing each other at the same time. Nothing had ever felt as good as this before and she wanted it to go on for ever.

Until now Rosie had always believed that sex before marriage was instigated and probably forced by the male, and she had no real sympathy for girls weak enough to let it happen. But as she found herself fondling and exploring Gareth's body, her own writhing beneath his in equal passion, she lost all her inhibitions. She wanted him so much that all reason was gone.

It was Gareth, not her, who stopped short at the point of entering her.

'We mustn't,' he panted. 'You might have a baby.'

The word 'baby' was enough to cool her down, bringing with it memories of Heather and her father. Her legs closed involuntarily.

'I want to, so much,' Gareth whispered, his penis as

hard as a rock against her. 'I never wanted anything more. But we have to wait, at least until we're engaged.'

Rosie held him to her tightly, loving him even more because of his strength of character, and more than a little ashamed of herself at letting things go so far.

Exhaustion made them sleep eventually, and Rosie awoke to find the room full of sunshine, with Gareth leaning up on one elbow just looking at her.

'You look so beautiful,' he whispered. 'I get a lump in my throat just looking at you.'

Rosie giggled. She didn't believe she was beautiful. She thought he was. His brown curls were damp with perspiration, his blue eyes like the periwinkles out on the moors; even the dark shadow on his dimpled chin was oddly attractive.

'What time is it?' she asked.

'Nearly eight. We ought to get up before anyone else does.' He pushed the covers down and looked at her breasts. 'I wish we could stay here all day.'

It seemed funny that during the night Gareth had explored every inch of her body, yet now she felt embarrassed by him looking at her. She blushed and reached over the side of the bed for her nightdress and hurriedly put it on.

'One day when you're really mine I'll take all your clothes away and keep you naked all day!' he said with a smile.

Rosie was scared when she was washing in the bathroom. Someone tried the door and she froze, thinking that perhaps they were waiting outside. But whoever it was had gone by the time she got out, and she hurried back to the comparative safety of Gareth's room.

It was just before nine when they crept downstairs. The house wasn't as bad as Rosie had imagined last night in the dark: it was clean and bright, though a little stark. Snores came from behind the closed doors and with every step Rosie was sure Mrs Kent would appear at the foot of the stairs.

Everything sparkled as they walked down to the tube station. The heavy rain in the night had washed the dust off trees and scrubbed the pavements clean. Even dogs out on an early morning cruise of the neighbourhood looked happy.

'I wish I'd taken my bike from Mum's yesterday, we could've gone for a ride today,' Gareth said. 'I'll have to go home tonight and collect it. I'm not looking forward to that.'

Rosie was so happy this morning she felt big enough to even feel a little sorry for his mother.

'Tell her I'm sorry,' she said. 'Maybe I'd better write her a little letter too?'

'Leave well alone,' he said with a shrug. 'She'll come round eventually. Now, how about going to Petticoat Lane Market and afterwards I'll show you the Tower of London?'

It was a wonderful day. The sun shone, the Thames glittered, everyone in the market seemed to have a smile on their face. Rosie tried on fancy hats on one stall, making Gareth laugh as she posed and pulled faces. He tried first a bowler and then a trilby, and she laughed until she had a stitch. They ate huge bacon sandwiches from one stall, then tried jellied eels from another. She told him how down in Somerset the eels came slithering out of every ditch and river at a certain time of the year when they had to mate. Gareth said he would slither on his belly all the way to Mayfield next time he had the urge to mate with her.

Late in the afternoon they caught a bus to St James's Park and lay on the grass to cuddle and kiss, along with countless other couples. A band was playing to a large audience in deckchairs, while children fed the ducks and played hide and seek around the trees. A stop-me-and-buy-one man came round on a bike and Gareth bought Rosie a triple-sized cornet.

It was just about six, an hour before her train was to leave from Victoria, and they were sitting in the tea house in St James's Park. Gareth was relating a story about his first day at school in London, when Rosie was brought up sharply, remembering that she'd intended to tell him the truth about herself today.

His face was crinkled up with laughter, his eyes so tender, and she knew she couldn't spoil the day by telling him now.

On their way to the station they stopped to look at Buckingham Palace. Bright sunshine made the scene so much more beautiful than it had been on Coronation Day. The Guards' red jackets and black busbies stood out in sharp relief against the white of the palace, and every window twinkled. It was peaceful too, only a handful of tourists looking through the railings and so little traffic passing by.

'I knew you were meant for me even then,' he said, looking across at the spot where the police had tried to bundle Donald into the Black Maria. 'My heart sort of lurched when I saw you.'

He turned to her, cupping her face in both his hands, and his eyes weren't laughing now but were filled with tenderness. 'I love you, Rosie,' he said.

Rosie felt winded. She knew without any doubt that what she felt for him was love too. 'You don't know enough about me,' she blurted out. 'You mustn't say such things until I've told you everything.'

'I know everything I want to,' he said, kissing her on the nose. 'You are bright and beautiful, you're kind and giving. All I want to know now is, do you love me?'

Her head was telling her to make a joke, break the spell and then make him listen to the whole truth before he committed himself any further. But she couldn't. She didn't want that tender look to fade from his eyes. She wanted him to kiss her and convince her they really were made for one another.

'Yes,' she whispered. 'I love you too.'

As he kissed her she knew she had passed the point of no return.

Chapter Fourteen

Thomas slumped down on to the grassy path around the edge of the recently cut wheatfield. It was the end of August and he'd come down to Mayfield to stay for the weekend.

'Is your leg hurting?' Rosie was instantly solicitous, although she'd been forcing the fast pace on this walk across the fields. 'I'm sorry. I didn't think. I just so much wanted you to see everything.' She put two fingers in her mouth and gave a very unladylike whistle for Donald, who had gambolled on ahead of them to climb a haystack.

Thomas thought Rosie was priceless. Since his arrival yesterday she had shown him so many different sides to her character. The zealous gardener who went down to the greenhouse to water her seedlings even before breakfast. The little mother fussing over Donald because he had a splinter in his finger, then immediately after the shrew who shouted at him for knocking over the cat's milk. The cook who'd made a superb steak and kidney pie for dinner last night, and the loving, caring companion who guided Donald's hand so carefully when he tried to write his name. She had come in from picking runner beans for lunch today with mud-streaked legs, hands and face, and even before she'd washed it off spoke of cultivating a more sophisticated image because she thought Gareth liked girls like that.

She'd disappeared upstairs later and come down in the pretty pink cotton dress she was wearing now, moaned that her nails were a mess and said in future she would wear gloves for gardening. They were hardly out of the door for his walk before she asked him if he thought it was possible for her to become a gardener, and if she would need to go to college or some kind of training place. Then she'd proceeded with this forced route march, talking non-stop about Gareth.

The loud whistle somehow put the cap on it. Such a dainty, feminine little thing resorting to such loutish tactics!

'What's so funny?' Rosie asked, looking down at Thomas on the grass laughing his head off.

'You,' he spluttered. 'You are the most extraordinary girl I ever met. Part tomboy, part beauty queen. Nurse, gardener, urchin and mother. Just teach me to whistle like that. I always wished I could do it.'

Rosie sat down, waving to Donald to come and join them. 'It's about the only useful thing I learned from Seth,' she said with a grin, and demonstrated how to roll up her tongue, then blow. 'Tell me seriously, Thomas. Could I be a gardener if I wanted?'

'I believe you could be the first woman to set foot on the moon if you really wanted to be,' Thomas replied. 'But it's no good asking me about such things, I'm a townie. Ask Mr Cook. He'll know.'

'But he might think I want to leave, and I don't,' she said earnestly. 'I sort of thought I might be able to learn a bit at night school, and be with Donald during the day. I've been reading all these books about famous gardens and how they designed and laid them out. I'd give *anything* to be able to do that.'

Thomas looked at Rosie. Her cheeks were flushed bright pink, not from the brisk walk in the sun, he realized, but because of how passionately she cared about the subject. Frank and Norah had already pointed out the difference she'd made to their garden. Now Thomas could see for himself she really was seriously committed.

'Well, tell Frank all that,' Thomas said. 'I'm sure he'll

do what he can. Meanwhile you can learn a lot from books.'

Rosie stood up and moved away a few feet, shielding her eyes from the sun to check where Donald was. Thomas looked up and saw that, with the sun behind her, her thin cotton dress was almost transparent. He could clearly see her small breasts, the faint curve of her belly and the outline of her buttocks. His mouth went dry, his stomach turned over. It was one of the most beautiful pictures he'd ever seen, but one he wouldn't even dare contemplate, let alone paint.

'God help me,' he muttered as he turned away and struggled awkwardly to his feet. It wasn't paternal or brotherly love he felt for her, such feelings were calm and pure. What he felt inside him was a dormant volcano, bubbling away, biding its time before it would rise up and spill over. He didn't think there was any way to keep it down.

Six weeks later, Rosie and Mrs Cook were bottling plums in the kitchen. It was October now and a wet and windy evening. Mr Cook and Donald were in the sitting-room watching television.

At the sharp crack of a branch against the window, Rosie paused in packing the fruit into Kilner jars and went over to the terrace doors to look out. The kitchen lights cut a golden swathe through the darkness, right out across the rain-soaked terrace and on to the lawn. Leaves were swirling feverishly around, unable to settle on the ground because of the strong wind.

The scene prompted an immediate and sharp memory of the previous autumn. During her father's trial the weather had been just like it was now, and she had spent a great deal of time staring out of the windows at Carrington Hall, feeling unutterably miserable. Yet as unwanted as the reminder was, it served as a kind of milestone. She could look back and see how far she'd come since then.

Turning away from the window she half smiled at Norah Cook, who was stirring a pan of syrup on the stove. 'I never used to like autumn,' Rosie said. 'I always thought it was a sad time because everything died. But I don't feel sad this year for some reason.'

Norah nodded in agreement. 'I know exactly what you mean, my dear. It's usually my least favourite season too. But this year I feel positively invigorated. I'm so looking forward to Harvest Festival, Guy Fawkes' Night, cosy evenings by the fire, starting the Christmas puddings and cake, everything autumn offers. But then I'm sure you know why. They all seem so much more special now Donald is home with us.'

Norah couldn't explain to anyone just how much her life and marriage had been enriched by having her son back home again. To do so would mean admitting how empty it had been before. For in the nine years Donald had been away from her and Frank it was as though a blight had slowly crept over their once almost perfect marriage. To others, including their two older children, they still appeared to be the ideal couple, but their deference to one another in public was just force of habit. Alone in their home they barely spoke to one another; often they were like strangers, both wrapped in private guilt and resentment which they couldn't air.

Almost as soon as Donald set foot back in the house, his presence seemed to banish that blight. At first it was through sharing the anxiety about his difficult behaviour, wondering if they'd done the right thing by bringing him home, but slowly as their son settled down, their anxiety turned to joy and in their happiness they turned to one another again like young lovers.

Rosie was in much the same position as her employers, unable to adequately describe the state of bliss she found herself in daily. Each morning when she woke up in her pretty room and looked out over the garden and the fields beyond, she gave thanks for finding herself in a beautiful home where she was valued and needed. She had real freedom now, of choice, of expression, without any fear of being belittled. She could plan each day for Donald knowing she would get his parents' full support, and they made her feel as if she was a member of their family.

She had Gareth who loved her too, and a new friend called Judy who worked in the village baker's. They usually went to the cinema together one evening a week, and if Judy's Saturday off coincided with one when Gareth had to work, the pair of them spent the day shopping in Tunbridge Wells. But now, on top of all that, Rosie was about to embark on a small gardening business with Donald.

'Who would have thought six or nine months ago that Donald would be capable of working for his living?' Rosie went on. 'I'd almost like to see Matron again, just so I could show him off.'

Norah winced at the reminder of that awful woman who'd lied to her and Frank so often and so plausibly. She didn't like to dwell on the unnecessary suffering she'd caused the other patients.

'I do hope for your sake Gareth won't be difficult about your business,' Norah said thoughtfully as she stirred her pan. 'You've put so much effort into getting it organized, and I know how much it means to you, but I get the impression he doesn't much like the idea.'

'But why should he mind?' Rosie asked. 'I mean, it won't affect him in any way. I'll still be living here, and Donald will be with me all day. You and Mr Cook are the only ones who might be put out. Not him. Whenever he comes down at the weekends I'll still be here, sitting in the kitchen as always!'

The kitchen had become Rosie's favourite room at The Grange. By day it was a light, sunny place, and by night the Aga kept it snug and warm. It was a cheerful room for long chats after meals, or lounging on the old settee listening to the wireless.

Paintings of Donald's had joined those of the grand-children up on the walls. The pretty china on the dresser shared space with Robin's baby toys and old letters, and a partially completed jigsaw puzzle stayed on a wooden board, ready for anyone who had the time or inclination to add a few more pieces. Rosie often wondered what houseproud Mrs Jones would make of the clutter. She thought she'd probably sniff with disapproval.

'You've got a lot to learn about men,' Norah replied with a touch of cynicism, wiping her hands on her apron. 'Most of them don't like their women to have ideas or aspirations which don't include them. Look at Susan and Roger. She had that secretarial job she loved and when her boss asked if she would accompany him to America on a business trip, Roger sulked until she turned the offer down. So her boss found a more ambitious secretary and now she's been relegated back to the typing pool.'

'But Gareth isn't sulking exactly,' Rosie said defensively. 'He just thinks I'll get overtired and when I see him I'll have dirt under my nails.'

'Too tired for him, he means. Maybe he's afraid you love gardening more than him.'

'I'm not going to be put off by something as daft as that,' Rosie said with some indignation. 'You do think the gardening is a good idea, don't you?'

Norah's mind began to wander. She had liked Rosie right from the first day they met, but over these past months, watching her with her son, liking had grown into love. They would have been perfectly content if she'd just kept Donald happy, but she had gone far beyond that. She'd allowed him to be a real man by teaching him a trade.

He could cut grass, prune trees and bushes, dig and plant. He could follow instructions, but also use his own initiative too if he was alone. Watching him work in a garden, no one would even guess he was mentally retarded. He was as strong as any other young man of his age, having built up his muscles along with his skills. Should anything ever happen to either Frank or Norah, he could not only survive but earn his own living.

But what of Rosie? She was almost seventeen, quite old and confident enough to reach out and grasp what she wanted from life, yet it seemed to Norah that if she had a failing, it was wanting to please too much. She planned every day around others, she didn't ever stop to consider that she had rights too. While this made her the most perfect of employees, and gave Norah peace of mind because she knew her son was of paramount importance to Rosie, she could also see that others might take advantage of such selflessness.

On the face of it Gareth was the ideal boyfriend, a nice, steady, hard-working lad, head over heels in love with Rosie. But Norah had noticed Gareth called all the shots. He fitted Rosie in between his work, football matches and seeing his friends, expecting her to drop everything she was doing at a moment's notice when it was convenient for him.

He was a real town-dweller too. He liked pavements beneath his feet, busy streets, crowded pubs and people around him constantly. He didn't seem to be aware that Rosie was happiest with the wind in her hair and grass beneath her feet and cared far more about nature than trains and motorbikes.

Gareth was no different from most young men of his class and age group. Born during hard times in the thirties, their characters formed by early poverty and growing up through the war years, they hadn't had the stimulation of books, art or music to give them a yearning for something more than their parents had. Even now in the fifties, when films and television gave them glimpses of the dawning of a new age of prosperity, when there were jobs for all, a National Health Service and new houses replacing the old slums in the cities, lads like Gareth still thought like their fathers.

Gareth's ambitions didn't run to more than driving a big steam train, a little house in the suburbs and a dutiful wife at home with the children. Norah wasn't scoffing at his humble aspirations, but she felt Rosie was entitled to, and deserved, the chance to spread her wings a little before committing herself to a way of life that might prove stultifyingly dull. She would like to see Rosie going out dancing with Judy and indulging in a little more girlish giggling and silliness. She also thought she ought to look around at other young men.

Rosie never said much about her childhood. Norah sensed by the lack of nostalgic stories, and by a certain subservience to men, that her father had been a brute. If so, it would be a crying shame if she allowed herself to slip into another man's shadow, or allow his dreams to supplant her own.

'A good idea?' said Norah, returning from her thoughts. 'Frank and I both think it's a brilliant idea. We're behind you one hundred per cent. I'm not trying to pour cold water on it. I want you to succeed and I believe you will. All I'm trying to do is make you aware that there may come a time when you have to choose between gardening and Gareth.'

Rosie said nothing more as she stacked the Kilner jars on to trays ready to put in the oven. She understood what Mrs Cook was trying to say, but didn't believe it would ever come to that. Gareth loved her. She loved him. She also wanted this business and she was determined to have both.

The gardening idea had come about soon after Thomas came down for the weekend. Rosie had spoken to Mr Cook as Thomas suggested, and he pointed out that there were college courses in horticulture, but they were directed more at farming than gardening. He thought gaining experience was the most important part of starting a career and he suggested asking around the

433

neighbourhood to see if anyone wanted help with their gardens.

In the run-up to the Harvest Festival many neighbours came to The Grange to discuss the arrangements with the Cooks for the annual party in the village hall. All of them were amazed to see the improvements to the garden. They admired Rosie's runner beans, the rows of carrots, onions and cabbages. They saw the trays of perennials she'd sown from seeds, took home with them a fresh lettuce or a couple of small plants, and before long word got around that she was a bit of a gardening expert and her assistant Donald was a tireless worker. When Rosie put a card in the post office window offering their gardening services by the hour, Mr Cook was pleased but apprehensive. He knew the prejudice which still existed in the village about his son.

But old Mrs Tyler who had the cottage next to the post office was keen. She'd been widowed a few years before and, because she was crippled with arthritis, her once pretty small back garden had turned into a jungle. She had no problem with Donald – she'd never believed he was the one who hurt that little girl all those years ago, and was delighted he was home again. She was happy to pay them each two shillings an hour.

It took just a few hours' work to get Mrs Tyler's garden back into shape. They pruned her roses and tied them to the trellis, dug out all the weeds and cut back the big shrubs, Mrs Tyler was delighted and almost everyone who came by her cottage was invited to see their work. Soon they had another job offer from a newly married couple who were both out working all day. This garden was far more of a challenge to Rosie because it was just a sloping lawn with a thin border around it. The couple wanted something more imaginative and asked Rosie for ideas. She suggested they had the part of the lawn nearest to the house dug away and a retaining wall built with a couple of steps up to where the lawn levelled out above.

The area by the house could then be paved so they could sit outside when the grass was wet.

They jumped at her idea, hired a couple of men to dig it out and do the bricklaying and paving stones, then invited Rosie and Donald back to carry on with the plan and to plant the garden out. They dug out gently curving flower beds around the lawn and a border next to the retaining wall so that eventually flowers would cascade down over it. It was too late in the season for bedding plants, but Rosie offered to come back in October to plant spring bulbs and perennials around the new shrubs for a good show next year.

Aside from the odd request to do mowing and weeding, there had been no further offers until a few weeks ago, when suddenly it seemed that everyone wanted their gardens tidied for the autumn, spring bulbs put in and a general inspection to see where improvements could be made for the future.

Rosie had no real idea how to organize it all, but Frank Cook did. He sat down with her one evening with a large diary and showed her how to allocate her time to her 'clients', giving them each a couple of hours twice a week. He pointed out that she mustn't overreach herself because it might rain for days on end, and that she'd have to be flexible and do the digging jobs when the weather permitted. He explained too that along with charging for her time, she also had to charge for compost, bulbs and the plants she provided. As he said, it wasn't intended to be a charity, it was real work. He got someone in his office to type up and duplicate a small leaflet which would explain all this to the customers: the money for materials was to be paid for in advance, then the hourly charge settled at the end of each week.

It was Rosie's hope that although there would be no work in the winter months, come the spring she'd be asked back to continue. Meanwhile she could grow summer bedding plants in the greenhouse at The Grange, and next year she would be able to sell those on too. Mr and Mrs Cook insisted Rosie should still be paid her two pounds ten shillings a week from them too, as Rosie would in effect still be looking after Donald. Rosie thought this was wrong as she could see she wasn't going to have time to do the jobs she normally did around the house. So finally they reached a compromise. Rosie was to receive half-pay, unless she earned less than that in the week from gardening, in which case the Cooks would make it up to her normal wage.

Later the same evening Rosie was just wiping down the kitchen surfaces when the telephone rang.

'It's for you, Rosie,' Frank Cook yelled from the hall. 'It's Thomas. I'm just packing Donald off to bed. I'll tell him you'll be up later to say goodnight.'

Rosie smiled, not just at the prospect of a chat with Thomas, but at the way the entire family had all gradually adopted her true name. It had started with Donald, then Gareth, and now they all used it, including little Robin, though he only managed 'Osie'.

It didn't unnerve her any more. She hardly ever thought about the events of the past or her family now. As far as she was concerned it said Rosemary Smith on her insurance card, and that was her real name. She had gone so far down the road now that it would be impossible to tell either the Cooks or Gareth the truth. Even guilt had been banished, her father's sins weren't hers. She didn't care where her brothers were, or what they were doing. She had a new life now and she didn't look over her shoulder.

Thomas had just got her letter telling him about her business and he wanted to congratulate her. 'When do you start properly?' he asked. He knew she'd been gardening for other people part-time for some weeks.

'Monday morning. We're working from nine till twelve at one place which needs a great deal doing. Then from three to six at another. I just hope the weather clears a bit by then. The rest of the week we've slotted in lots more jobs, and eventually we hope to be working from eight in the morning right through till dark.'

'Now don't you go overdoing it,' Thomas reminded her. He asked how Gareth was. The last time Rosie had been to London to meet him, she'd stayed at Thomas's flat overnight and the three of them had gone out together for supper.

'He's fine, he's got his promotion to fireman and he's backwards and forwards all day to Brighton.'

'Has his mother come round yet?'

Rosie sighed. 'Not really. But then I told you in a letter how it was when I went over for Sunday dinner, didn't I?'

It was the same weekend she had stayed at Thomas's. Gareth had come to collect her on his motorbike on the Sunday morning and promised everything would be fine. It wasn't as bad as the first visit, but that was mainly because Mr Jones and Owen were there too. They were very nice, as warm and friendly as Gareth was, but his mother had stayed tight-lipped the entire time. She improved marginally as Rosie was leaving and offered to knit her a cardigan. Rosie hoped that was a sign of acceptance, but still she dreaded another invitation because it was such a strain.

'But you're still in love?' Thomas asked. 'Even if his mother is a witch.'

'Yes,' she admitted, smiling down the telephone. 'He's wonderful. It just gets better and better.'

'What plans have you got for your birthday?' Thomas asked. 'Are you coming up to London?'

Rosie wasn't sure how to answer this. In fact Gareth was intending to take her to a small hotel in Brighton for the weekend, but she couldn't say that. She was currently working on a white lie which involved a fictitious aunt of Gareth's who was going to put them up.

'I'm not quite certain yet,' she said hesitantly. She hated telling lies, especially to Thomas. 'I've got so much on my plate right now and it's a couple of weeks off anyway.'

'You're welcome to stay here,' he said. 'I'll even go out for the evening in the cause of young love!' he added. 'But let me know. If you aren't coming, I'll need to send your present by post.'

When Thomas rang off, Rosie went upstairs to say goodnight to Donald. He was sitting up in bed reading the *Beano*.

'Is Thomas coming here to stay?' he asked.

'Not for a while yet,' Rosie replied, sitting down on his bed. 'He just rang to say how pleased he was about our gardening business.'

'Did you tell him about the new wheelbarrow?'

Rosie smiled. Mr Cook had brought them a brand new aluminium one which was a great deal lighter than their old wooden one. Donald loved it. He treated it like another man would his first car.

'No, I left that for you to tell him next time he comes,' she said. 'Now it's time you went to sleep.'

Donald obediently put down his comic and snuggled down under the covers. Rosie moved closer to tuck him in and kiss him goodnight.

'Rosie,' he said thoughtfully, looking up at her. 'If you marry Gareth, will you go away and leave me?'

Rosie was stunned for a moment. At night she sometimes pondered on this herself, wondering how Donald would react if she were to leave, and also how she would feel about leaving him. But she hadn't realized Donald was smart enough to think this through for himself.

The truth of the matter was that it would be a huge wrench leaving him. He had a place in her heart that no one else could ever fill. He was brother, child and friend all rolled into one. She looked at him now and saw the complete trust in his blue eyes.

'I hope that if we do get married, then we'll be able to

live somewhere near here,' she said truthfully. 'And we'll carry on with our gardening while Gareth drives his trains. But you mustn't worry about that. Even if we do get married, it won't be for a long time yet.'

Two weeks later, on a Saturday afternoon, just a couple of days after Rosie's seventeenth birthday, she and Gareth were up in the bedroom on the second floor of the Regent guest-house in Brighton.

'They must know I'm not really Mrs Jones,' Rosie said, spluttering with laughter. 'I bet they're all talking about us down there.'

Gareth had bought her a wedding ring from Woolworth's and she'd taken great pains to display it. But even in her new green coat and smart brown velour side-tilted hat, she knew she couldn't disguise how young she was or conceal her embarrassed blushes when the landlady asked them if they'd like early morning tea in bed tomorrow.

'We will be married one day,' Gareth said, pulling her into his arms and showering her face with kisses. 'Imagine having a bedroom just like this one.'

Rosie looked around the room gleefully. From when she'd been a small child she had always looked at hotels and guest-houses in Weston-super-Mare and wondered what it must be like to stay in one. She wasn't a bit disappointed by the Regent. It had red and gold carpet right up the stairs, and the sort of striped wallpaper she had always imagined rich people had in their homes. A quick glimpse of the dining-room had revealed more elegance, snowy white tablecloths on each table, and napkins standing up like little pyramids. But this room to her mind was almost as nice as Mr and Mrs Cook's bedroom: a big double bed, a kidney-shaped dressing-table with a chintz frill around it, and better still it overlooked the promenade and the sea.

She wasn't going to worry now about how she would

describe Gareth's Auntie Mary in Brighton when she got back home. They needed to be alone together. If she was old enough to run a little business, then she was old enough to spend the night with the man she loved.

'Shall we go out and explore?' Gareth asked. 'Tea isn't until half past six and I'm starving now.'

'It's "dinner" in posh places,' Rosie giggled. 'But yes, let's go out. I want to look at the sea.'

It was very cold and windy on the promenade, the sky like lead, but Rosie turned up the collar of her new coat, pulled her hat on more securely, tucked her hand into Gareth's pocket, and gazed at the sea in delight. The only proper resort she'd been to before was Weston-super-Mare, and though it had a lovely sandy beach while this one had only pebbles, the sea had been brown, not the clear, greeny blue it was here. The waves were huge, crashing down with such noise and force that it was hard to hear what Gareth was saying. She loved it. She wanted to run down the beach, wave her arms around and shout like Donald did when he was excited.

They went on the pier and put some pennies in the slot machines. Gareth tried to win her a teddy bear by working a mechanical crane, but the money ran out before he managed to grab it. They had a hot-dog each and some candyfloss, then went on the dodgems.

Later in the afternoon they found the Lanes, where all the little antique shops were. Rosie thought it was a bit like Hampstead and insisted that she paid for them to have tea and cakes in a posh tea shop with bow windows.

It was even better inside than it was outside, with a roaring fire, copper pots hanging from the beams, and embroidered tablecloths. Rosie gasped as the waitress brought them a two-tiered glass stand with at least a dozen cakes on it. She waited till the girl was out of earshot and leaned closer to Gareth. 'Surely they don't expect us to eat them all?'

She thought Gareth looked like a real man-about-town.

He was wearing his dark suit and he'd borrowed a grey tweed overcoat from Owen.

'I think they just charge us for what we eat,' he said nervously, looking around to check on what other people were doing. 'I've never been anywhere like this before.'

'We'll soon get used to living like this,' Rosie said airily, as she poured the tea. 'One day when I'm a famous gardener we'll eat out like this every day.'

Gareth didn't laugh and she sensed she had hurt his feelings. 'You'll be driving the *Flying Scotsman* by then,' she said quickly.

He took her hand across the table and for a moment she thought he was going to do something romantic like kiss her hand, but instead he looked at her nails. 'You won't be welcome in smart places with those,' he said sharply.

Rosie snatched her hand away, cut to the quick with embarrassment. All her nails were broken, and although she'd scrubbed them well they did look awful. She also had calluses on her palms from digging, and a few scratches. All at once she noticed that the wedding ring was beginning to tarnish too.

'Your hands aren't so perfect either,' she snapped back. 'And don't be nasty about the gardening, otherwise I'll go home.'

Gareth apologized and they moved on to talk of other things, but Rosie found herself terribly aware of her hands. And when she handed Gareth a ten-shilling note under the table to pay for the tea she knew he hated accepting it.

After all they had eaten during the afternoon, Rosie found it hard to do justice to the braised steak dinner served at the guest-house. Gareth had no such problem: he wolfed it down and finished up Rosie's too. There were only four other guests. A middle-aged couple who kept looking across at Rosie and Gareth and smiling, and two elderly ladies who complained about everything.

'What shall we do now?' Gareth asked when they'd finished. It was only just after seven, and the wind had grown even stronger while they were eating. It rattled the window frames and made them very aware of just how cold it would be outside. 'We could go to the pictures. I noticed that *Genevieve* is on just up the road.'

Rosie felt stuffed with food and so sleepy that she really fancied just going upstairs to cuddle, but she felt sure the landlady would earmark them as a couple away for a dirty weekend if they did that, so she pretended to be enthusiastic.

The walk in the cold wind woke Rosie up again, and the film was as wonderful as all the critics had said. They stopped in a pub on the way back and Rosie had her first port and lemon, which Gareth told her was what ladies drank. She didn't enjoy it much and thought it tasted like cough mixture. But she liked the effect. It made her feel all warm inside, so she had a second one.

Gareth was in bed when Rosie came back along the passage from the bathroom in her nightdress. 'I was beginning to think you'd run out on me,' he said, sitting up. 'What on earth have you been doing all this time?'

'None of your business,' she laughed, cheered by the fact he was wearing a pair of pyjamas. She hopped into bed beside him.

She had in fact spun out washing and cleaning her teeth because she was suddenly and inexplicably stricken by panic. Gareth had always maintained that they would wait until they were married before making love properly, but Rosie thought it might be a different story once they were tucked up in that big bed. During the summer, out in the fields around Mayfield, there had been many times when they had come very close to going the whole way; all that really held them back was the fear of being seen by someone. Suppose they couldn't help themselves tonight? What if she got pregnant? She wanted to marry Gareth more than anything else in the world, but she didn't want to get pregnant; not just yet.

Gareth pulled the cord above the bed to turn off the light, then drew Rosie into his arms. The wind was howling, waves were pounding on the shore, and it felt so good to be in the warm listening to it.

'I'm sorry I said that about your hands this afternoon,' Gareth remarked unexpectedly, cuddling her tightly. 'I don't know why I say things like that. Sometimes I'm just like my mum.'

'I love you anyway,' she said, wriggling still closer and lifting her face to kiss him. Passion flared up the instant her lips touched his. They rolled together, kissing, stroking, fondling and holding. Her nightdress came off, then Gareth's pyjamas, and as their two naked bodies ground against one another, their desire intensified.

Gareth licked and sucked at her breasts until she was crying out for more, wantonly directing his fingers into her. She was swept along by a huge tidal wave of pleasure, growing ever closer to the point of release she'd only found before with her own fingers. She had lost all control, her earlier fears were forgotten. All that mattered now was fulfilment. She writhed under him, aching for the moment when he would lose his self-control and take her. But as she clawed at his back, thrusting her hips closer to him, he suddenly moved away from her, turned and went down under the bedclothes. He pushed her legs apart and began kissing her private parts.

Astonishment made her stiffen. She had never heard of men doing such a thing, and it seemed a very crude act. Even worse, Gareth's chin was stubbly and it rasped against the lips of her vagina.

'It hurts,' she whispered, trying to move his head away from her. But if he heard, he showed no sign of it. With one hand he spread her thighs wider apart, and with the other he thrust his cock into her mouth, giving her no chance for further protest.

Linda had once spoken of this; she had called it 'giving a man a gobble'. Judging by the cheerful way she'd said it, she didn't find it repulsive at all. Mary had taken the opposite view. She'd said it was disgusting and no man would ever stick his thing in her mouth and live to tell the tale. At that time Rosie had never even held an erect penis in her hand, but she had had the idea that if you were really in love with a man you'd probably want to please him.

She tried very hard to think only of that now, but found she just didn't like it. Gareth's cock smelled funny and tasted salty, and she was afraid her teeth would hurt him. When he pushed himself even further into her mouth she gagged, and all the pleasure she'd been feeling such a short while ago vanished.

Aside from her distaste at being forced into taking him in her mouth, she felt like she was being rubbed with sandpaper down below by his chin. When she tried to draw the lower part of her body away from him, he grabbed her even more fiercely and pushed himself further still into her mouth. In a desperate effort to get free, she caught hold of him by the hip bones to try and push him off her. But as she moved her head back and a little street lighting from outside shone in through the curtains, she caught sight of his balls dangling and she retched.

Gareth was oblivious to anything but his own pleasure. 'Suck me!' he ordered, jabbing his fingers inside her hard, perhaps believing she was as aroused as he was. 'Come on, don't stop now, I'm coming!'

Rosie's eyes filled with tears. She had brought him to a climax with her hands many times and felt no disgust about that because he had always been holding her, whispering endearments, and petting her gently too. But this was quite different. There was no tenderness, just bestiality.

444

His chin was digging into her groin, his breathing beneath the bedclothes was laboured and he was muttering something too. Each time he thrust his fingers into her she wanted to scream out with pain. Then, just as she felt she could bear it no longer, he arched his back, let out a gasping breath and pushed her head to one side.

His body was jerking in a spasm. She felt him spurt against her neck, and then he was still.

'That was fantastic!' he murmured, his face resting on her stomach.

Rosie just lay there, stunned, silent tears trickling down her cheeks. She was confused and angry because she felt dirty and used. On the other hand, she felt saddened and guilty, because surely if she loved Gareth as much as she believed she did, his pleasure would be more important than her own feelings.

He turned round in the bed and took her in his arms.

'That was the best,' he said sleepily. 'Fred at work told me him and his missus used to do it like that before they were married. He was right, it's better than a wank.'

He fell asleep moments later. But as Rosie lay there still cradled in his arms she was smarting at his vulgar words. Her vagina was stinging, she felt cheated, but what really shamed her was that he'd discussed something so intimate with a workmate.

Seth slipped into her mind. She could only suppose that was because Gareth's crudity was reminiscent of the way he used to speak. She shivered. All these months she'd never given her brother a passing thought. But now, on a night which should have been blissful, he was back, reminding her of all the things she thought she'd forgotten.

At noon the next day as they walked along the promenade, buffeted by the strong wind, Rosie wished she was back home at The Grange. She could be sitting in front of the sitting-room fire, reading the Sunday newspapers. It was so terribly cold, her feet were like blocks of ice, and everything – the sea, the sky, the houses – looked grey and dingy.

She didn't want to voice her opinion though. Gareth was glum enough already, and any resentment she still harboured about last night had vanished in sympathy when the landlady asked him for an extra pound for their evening meal.

Rosie knew that Gareth had felt sophisticated when he planned his weekend. He hadn't known they would be expected to leave their room immediately after breakfast, or that everything in Brighton would be closed on a Sunday. He certainly hadn't expected it to be so cold. But it was the extra pound which really threw him. He hadn't budgeted for it, and when it was added to all the other slightly embarrassing moments of naivety and awkwardness, it made him feel a complete failure.

'Let's have a cup of tea,' she suggested, trying to pretend she was really delighted about everything. 'We could go to that café on the pier. I expect it's open.'

'I don't want a cup of tea,' Gareth said grumpily. 'I want a pint, but I've only got about five shillings left.'

'I've got some money,' she said quickly.

He gave her an odd sort of look, disapproval at her offering to pay, mixed with relief.

'Look, Gareth, I know the guest-house cost more than you expected,' she said, tucking her hand through his arm and huddling closer to him. 'The least I can do is buy you a drink.'

'I don't take money from girls,' he retorted.

'I'm not just any girl,' she said evenly. 'You didn't mind me paying for tea yesterday, and anyway I'm your girl and we should share expenses. I earn nearly as much as you, after all.'

The moment the words left her mouth, she knew they were the wrong ones. His face flushed with sudden anger.

'That's right, rub it in,' he said bitterly. 'I'm no good for anything, am I?'

'Don't be ridiculous,' she snapped back. 'I didn't mean anything of the sort.'

She managed to talk him round and led him to the nearest pub. Once he had a pint in his hand he apologized for the second time that weekend. By the time he'd got the next one down, which Rosie had pushed a ten-shilling note into his hand to pay for, he was happy again and even joined in with some other men playing darts.

Rosie sat on her own, with a small glass of cider in front of her. The pub was a grubby, smoky place with a smelly paraffin heater. The only other women in there were two shabbily dressed elderly women sitting in a corner.

She watched Gareth playing darts. He was immersed in it, his tongue peeping out between his lips as he eyed up the target, poised to aim. He'd forgotten about her; these three men he'd only just met were now far more important. In a flash Rosie saw that this was how he was in London, down the pub with the lads, or off to a football match. He wouldn't change when they got married, any more than her father had when he and Heather became lovers.

Common sense told her that it was this way for most women in England. Men brought home the money and in return they got hot dinners, their clothes washed and sex on tap. She didn't know why she felt so disappointed to find Gareth was the same. The male Cooks were the only men she'd ever known to behave differently.

When they left the pub at closing time, Gareth was drunk. He'd had six pints in all. 'What'll we do now?' he said, slurring his words and swaying on his feet.

'We collect our bags from the guest-house and go home,' Rosie said, trying very hard not to be cross with him. 'It's too cold to wander around, and anyway there's nothing to do.'

It seemed a very long way to the station because Gareth kept stopping. She didn't like him drunk one bit. His voice was too loud, people kept looking at him disapprovingly because he was weaving all over the pavement, and every now and then he clumsily tried to kiss her. But when he stopped in a doorway and opened his fly to pee, Rosie lost her temper.

'That's disgusting,' she snapped, then walked away and left him there. It was bad enough that Gareth had brought Seth back to mind last night, but to see they had other nasty habits in common was the last straw.

They had to wait an hour for the train, but even the cold didn't sober Gareth up. Fortunately there were few people about, and when the train finally arrived they got a compartment all to themselves. Gareth fell asleep immediately they were on the train, his mouth hanging open and his head lolling against her shoulder. She knew she couldn't take him back to The Grange in that state.

As the train approached Mayfield she woke him. 'I'm getting off at the next stop,' she said. 'You stay on and go straight back to London.'

'Whass the time?' he asked, his words still slurred.

'Nearly five,' she said. 'There's no point in you coming back with me, you'd only have to turn right round and get the next train back.'

'Thass all right then,' he said, flopping right down on to the seat. His eyes were almost closed, he stank of beer and cigarettes, and his mouth was almost as sloppy as Donald's. 'I'll be back in time to meet the lads.'

'You meet them,' she snapped as she lifted her bag down from the luggage rack. 'They're welcome to your company.'

Outside the station Rosie jammed her hat on more firmly, pulled up her collar against the cold wind, then lifting her bag walked swiftly home. It was already dark and Mayfield was as deserted as she felt.

'You might love him,' she muttered to herself. 'But you aren't going to let him walk all over you. And don't you dare cry.'

Chapter Fifteen

Percy Arkwright, station master of Mayfield station, diligently swept the puddles of rain water off his platform. But although he appeared to be entirely engrossed in ensuring the passengers alighting from the seven-fifteen wouldn't get wet feet, in fact he was far more interested in the young couple awaiting the train for London.

It had been raining continuously for the past three days, and it was only now on Sunday evening that the sky had at last brightened and weak sunshine was doing its best to break through. Normally at this time of an evening in August, Percy would be expecting dozens of people to spill off this train after a day trip to the coast, but tonight he doubted there would be any more than five or six dejected looking holiday-makers.

Percy knew just about everyone in Mayfield regardless of whether or not they were regular passengers. He had only landed the job as station master after the war, but he'd been born in the village, and aside from time away as a railway apprentice and his spell in the army, he'd lived here all his life.

Old friends from his childhood used the early morning trains, working men and women in the main, carpenters, mechanics, nurses and shop assistants in neighbouring towns. Around eight in the morning the bowler-hat brigade arrived. Bankers, lawyers and accountants who were relative newcomers to the village and travelled to London first class. Later in the morning he would see the smartly dressed wives of these same men going off for a day's shopping in Tunbridge Wells. He met their children too as they travelled to and from school; some were cheeky little sods who needed a clip round the ear, but others were decent sorts whom he often rewarded with a sweet or two.

But of all the more regular visitors to his station, Percy had a particularly soft spot for this young couple. For over two years now he'd been almost a part of their courtship. He'd witnessed the happy reunions on Saturday afternoons or Sunday mornings, then the sadder partings on a Sunday evening, when they clung to each other until the very last moment before young Gareth boarded the train. He couldn't count the times that he'd got a lump in his throat as Rosie ran with the train, waving and blowing kisses, and seen her mopping her eyes before going home alone.

She always met him and saw him off, regardless of rain or snow, and it made Percy glow to see such devotion. Tonight, however, he sensed something was wrong. They weren't locked in each other's arms as they usually were. They were standing close, looking at each other, not actually arguing but with a certain hostility about them.

In the two years Percy had been observing them, they had both changed. Gareth had been just a lad when he first came, lean and eager-looking, with tousled curly hair and a wide, wide smile. He was a man now, heavier, fatter in the face, broader in the shoulders, his hair cut very short. Sadly, his sparkle and youthful enthusiasm seemed to have disappeared, along with his boyish curls. Nowadays he rarely smiled at Percy, much less stopped to chat about trains as he once had. In fact the only conversation they'd had in recent months was when Gareth pompously informed him he'd been promoted to engine driver on a passenger train.

Rosie had been a pretty girl with an endearing impudent grin, but she'd been too thin then and very pasty. Two years of healthy outdoor living had transformed her into a curvy, radiant beauty, with an aura of natural confidence and a bounce in her step.

Tonight she looked the way she always did when she was with Gareth, fashionable and stylish, in a green dress, high-heeled shoes and lipstick, her hair gleaming like molten copper in the weak sunshine. But Percy personally preferred the tomboyish way she looked when she trundled her wheelbarrow past the station during the week. There was something very appealing about a pretty girl in dungarees with windswept hair and a few dirt smears on her rosy cheeks. She was the kind of girl who made the day a little brighter just by being there, and Percy knew he wasn't the only person around here who felt that way.

Percy leaned on his broom for a moment and watched them. He had an inkling of what was wrong tonight. Young Gareth was a dyed-in-the-wool city man, who only really liked the countryside when he was steaming through it on his train. Perhaps he'd finally realized Rosie and he were on quite different tracks.

Percy was almost spot on. Gareth was sulking, just as he had been since arriving on Saturday afternoon to find it too wet to do anything but stay indoors at The Grange. But now, after a long, dull weekend with no chance to be alone with Rosie, he was blaming her for his boredom.

'I don't know how much longer you expect me to put up with this,' he said. 'If you'd started nursing last year, like you said you were going to, at least you'd be in London. But you think more of your damn gardening and Donald than you do about me.'

Rosie sighed. He'd been spoiling for a fight all weekend, picking on every last thing he thought might upset her. She was tempted to say she did prefer gardening and Donald's company when he was so objectionable, but his train would be here in five minutes and she didn't want to part on a sour note.

'That's not true,' she said.

'Yes, it is. A year ago you were dying to get married, but now you hardly ever mention it.'

'I'd get married tomorrow if you got a transfer down here,' she said heatedly. 'We could easily find a nice little cottage to live in. I don't understand why you are so set on staying in London.'

'You know why,' he said, his voice raised as it always was when she broached this subject. 'I've waited a long time to be a train driver. I won't settle for ticket collecting or working in a signal box, which is what a transfer would mean. Besides, my family are in London, and I don't like the country anyway.'

The distant chugging of the train coming along the track was a timely diversion. Gareth pulled out his pocket-watch to check it, just as he did with every single train. Rosie used to find this endearing. Tonight, however, it irritated her and she had an urge to slap the watch out of his hand.

'Right on time,' he said. 'I expected it to be late because of the heavy rain.'

He kissed her then, long and hard, but it didn't make Rosie feel any better. She knew the time in between before they saw each other again wouldn't change anything. Their problems would only be shelved, to be picked over again next time they met and never resolved.

'Goodbye, sweetheart,' he said, picking up his overnight bag as the train came in. His eyes brightened as if the train itself was more important than her. 'I'll phone you later in the week.'

The train pulled off. He lowered the window and leaned out, and Rosie ran along the platform with it just as she always did, waving and blowing kisses. But tonight she didn't feel the usual unbearable sadness at parting from him. It was almost a relief to see him go.

She didn't go straight home to The Grange, but went for a walk instead. The song 'Love and Marriage' by Frank Sinatra, which had been in the hit parade earlier that year, kept springing irritatingly into her mind. The trees were dripping and her shoes weren't suitable for walking on wet grass, but the air was fresh and sweet after all the rain and she needed time, alone, to think.

The weekend had been tortuous. In fact their relationship had been on a gradual downward spiral for some months, ever since Rosie admitted she had given up the idea of becoming a nurse. Gareth claimed she had been stringing him along all the time.

It hadn't seemed that way to Rosie. Maybe she shouldn't have assumed Gareth shared her vision of a wedding in Mayfield church, a cosy little cottage and the Cooks close by. But if Gareth really had hated this idea, why had be taken so long to come out with it?

Now he was saying that if she really loved him she must give up her gardening and the Cooks and move to London to get what he called a 'proper' job. He spoke of getting a couple of rooms somewhere near Clapham, and putting their name down for a council house. He didn't seem to understand he was asking her to throw away everything she had worked so hard for.

She wasn't entirely against the idea of living in London. At times it looked like a tempting adventure, starting out again, together, building a home, seeing all that London had to offer. Maybe she could even persuade him into letting her do gardening there. Thomas said there were plenty of rich people who were always looking for help with their gardens. Yet how could she just up and leave Donald? Setting aside that she loved him and his family, in their time together they had gone from being nurse and patient to teacher and pupil, until at last they'd become equal partners by pooling their talents.

Gareth always sneered when she tried to explain this. He said Donald could easily carry on alone mowing lawns, pruning trees and planting flowers. That much was true, he could; but Rosie was the one with the organizing ability and the creativity. Just as she relied on Donald's physical strength to get the work done, so he depended on her to plan, find new clients and make sure they got paid.

Their business was thriving, they were making real money, more most weeks than Gareth made as a train driver. They had won the respect and admiration of everyone in the village. They were very proud of what they'd already achieved and Rosie wanted them to do much more. At night she worked on designs, she studied books on rare plants and famous gardens, and she knew if she was ever offered the opportunity to plan a garden herself from scratch, she could manage.

As much as she loved and wanted to marry Gareth, she also wanted to work at her chosen career. Could she do that if she was Mrs Jones, the train driver's wife?

Maybe she was being ridiculously pessimistic. Other girls of her own age thought no further than getting married, having a home of their own, and waiting for their first baby. Wouldn't that be fulfilling enough for her?

Being close to Gareth's mother was another problem. In two years Rosie hadn't grown to like the mean-spirited, sharp-tongued woman any better. Doubtless it was Mrs Jones who had poured cold water on the idea of a country cottage, who insisted her son could never be happy with Rosie unless he got her away from the Cooks to London. Once they were married, Rosie knew the woman would poke her nose into every aspect of their life. But it was Gareth's dislike of the country that worried her even more. It said they were totally incompatible.

She climbed up on to a stile and sat down on it. In front of her was a field of golden wheat, gently swaying in the breeze. Beyond that was a small wood where nightingales sang. As she sat there revelling in the beauty and tranquillity of the scene, she wondered how anyone could prefer London's grimy streets to this. She remembered how Donald had been when she had first brought him out here. He had sat on this very stile just gazing at the view with a broad smile on his face. Like her he never tired of it, whether it was spring when the first bright green shoots sprang out from the soil, autumn when the farmer ploughed the field and hundreds of birds came down for the rich pickings he uncovered for them, or winter when the bare soil was frozen into stiff, frosted furrows. It was at its most beautiful now, yet Gareth had remained unmoved by it.

In fact, Rosie had found few things that did move Gareth. The sight of the *Brighton Belle* or the *Flying Scotsman* with a full head of steam got him excited. His eyes grew misty when he looked at a powerful motorbike, and he became emotional when Wales beat England at rugby. But nature didn't touch him at all.

There were other areas in their relationship which worried her too. He could go out drinking with his pals in London and cheerfully spend half his wages in one night, but with her he insisted on getting the cheapest seats at the pictures, and if they went out for the day somewhere, he would always find a grubby little back street café to eat in.

He was also a very selfish lover. Rosie sighed deeply. Perhaps she was to blame for this. Why didn't she tell him she felt like a whore when he pushed her into masturbating him without trying to please her too? He seemed to think that protecting her from getting pregnant was an act of selfless love, but to her it appeared unnatural, cold and calculating. The trouble was she'd left it too long to start complaining now.

'So what is it you love about him?' she asked herself aloud.

That question was like asking why someone adored the sea, thrilled to a particular piece of music or wept at a film. She couldn't analyse what it was about him that made her pulse quicken as she ran to meet him at the station, her knees shake when he kissed her; it was pure emotion. She wanted to make love with him, walk down leafy lanes holding his hand, cook him meals, have his children. It didn't make sense. But then what made some men want to climb mountains, others to be a butcher? Everyone was different, and they didn't march to the same drumbeat.

Above all else, though, Rosie was stubborn. In the main it was one of her greatest assets: she never gave up on a difficult job, finishing it when everyone else was sure she'd abandon it. She wasn't going to give up on Gareth either, even if common sense told her it might be better to. Next time she saw him she would try and iron out some of the serious differences between them. There had to be a solution.

Back at The Grange, Norah and Frank were taking a stroll round the garden together. It was at its best: the rain had made the lawn a lush green again and the herbaceous border was a riot of colour. Donald was indoors. They could hear him playing 'Rock Around the Clock' on the radiogram. He loved rock 'n' roll music; he bought a new record every week with his gardening money, but this one was still his favourite. Often in the evenings he and Rosie practised jiving together. Donald was surprisingly good at it, as long as he didn't get too excited.

'What's happened to Rosie and Gareth?' Frank asked his wife. 'They used to seem so perfect together, but not any more.'

'I know,' Norah sighed. 'I thought they were for ever too, but Gareth's changed, hasn't he? He's becoming so opinionated and pompous. Did you hear him holding forth to Michael on Saturday about third-class travel being abolished? Poor Michael didn't know what to say, he didn't have any views on it one way or another, and to hear Gareth going on you'd think we were aristocrats with no understanding of working-class people.'

Frank stopped by the pond and sat down on one of the big stones beside it. The water lilies were so thick on the surface he had to part them to see the fish below.

'It's the way he belittles Rosie which worries me more than anything,' he said thoughtfully. 'I can understand his sarcasm towards Donald. He's jealous of Rosie's affection for him. But he never misses an opportunity to ridicule her gardening. You'd think he'd be so proud that she's entirely self-taught. She astounds me the way she's learned all about fertilizers and making compost, laying paths and building walls, along with acquiring an almost encyclopaedic knowledge of plants. I want to shake him and knock some sense into him.'

'I suppose frustration is at the bottom of it,' Norah said quietly, sitting down beside her husband and leaning against his shoulder. 'I used to worry that Rosie would come home one day and tell us she was pregnant. I'm very glad of course that they're so sensible and controlled, but it's not exactly normal in a couple who love each other so much.'

Frank grinned and picked up her hand to kiss her finger tips affectionately. 'No one could ever accuse us of being sensible and controlled,' he said. 'I seem to remember we were like rabbits once we got started.'

Norah blushed. Why she didn't find herself pregnant before they married had always been a mystery to her. 'Somehow I don't think the control is on Rosie's side,' she said. 'I think he makes all the rules. I suspect that fearsome mother of his has warped him to a certain extent. Have you noticed he rarely reveals anything personal about himself?'

'Well, I suppose we could say the same about Rosie,' Frank said evenly.

'No, it's not the same,' Norah disagreed. 'Rosie doesn't like discussing her childhood, but she is open about her feelings and about what she wants out of life. I feel as if I know her inside out.'

Frank smiled. 'So what does she want, aside from Gareth?'

'The same as most women. A decent home of her own, a kind, loving man and a parcel of kids. Sometimes I'm very glad she feels so strongly about Donald. But for him she might have gone off to London a long while ago. At least it's holding her back from making any rash decisions.'

They both looked round as their son stepped out on to the terrace by the kitchen. He was pretending to play the guitar and was entirely oblivious to his parents watching him. Hardly a day went by without them considering how much Rosie had enriched his life. They liked her for herself, but they loved her for what she'd given Donald.

No one in the village was suspicious of him now. They knew he was nicknamed Dopey Donald, but because Rosie pushed him and encouraged him, he had found his niche as a 'character' rather than someone to be feared or avoided. His love and appreciation of gardening had endeared him to a great many people, and the fact that he'd proved himself to be reliable and hard-working made people trust him. Yet however steady and confident Donald was now, both his parents knew that when Rosie did finally leave, he would find it hard without her. She was, after all, his one true friend.

'I suspect Gareth will become overbearing once she's married to him. He's very set in his ways and he doesn't approve of women with minds of their own,' Frank said with a frown. 'Do you think we should talk this over with Thomas? Maybe he could influence Rosie. She sets great store by his opinion.'

Norah didn't answer for a little while. In the two years Rosie had been with them, Thomas had been a regular visitor and he'd become a close friend to the entire family. He was a fascinating man, intelligent, sensitive, warm-hearted and great company. His experience and disability had given him great insight into others, and he had a wonderful sense of humour. Norah often wondered if there was more to the friendship between him and Rosie than just the nasty business at Carrington Hall. She sensed some sort of deep, mysterious and unexplained bond between them. It was almost as if Thomas had known

458

Rosie since she was a small child, though she knew that wasn't possible.

'It might be an idea,' Norah said. 'But Gareth resents Thomas almost as much as he resents Donald. What a jealous man he's turned out to be! Rosie is so smart about most things, but she's blind and deaf where he's concerned. You say you want to knock some sense into Gareth – well, I wish I could do the same to her.'

While Norah and Frank Cook were caught up in their concern for Rosie, Freda Barnes, former matron of Carrington Hall, was thinking about her too. But her thoughts were entirely malevolent.

Two years on from the humiliating ejection from her job and home, she was still in the same basement flat she'd been forced to take in London's Camden Town. The severely straitened circumstances she was compelled to live in, the loss of prestige, family and friends, had turned her into a rapidly ageing and bitter woman.

She had two rooms, a kitchen and a lavatory. The bath was in the kitchen, and with a cover on top it doubled as a table. The bedroom walls ran with damp, so she was forced to eat, live and sleep in just one gloomy room that never saw a ray of sunshine.

The neighbours who saw the short, fat woman with iron-grey straggly hair waddling down the street each evening were unlikely to even pass the time of day with her, much less guess that for most of her life she'd been a respected and highly qualified nurse. They had heard that she snarled at the young couple in the flat above her for taking their rubbish down to the dustbins outside her door before ten in the morning and banged on the ceiling with a broom when their baby cried in the night. In Camden Town almost everyone was poor, so they didn't mind the woman's shabby, grubby appearance. But in a place where life was tough for everyone, they had no time for disagreeable people with sour faces.

Freda didn't want anyone to speak to her. She thought her noisy, common neighbours were well beneath her, and for the first few weeks after she moved in at 13A Harmood Street she thought it was only a matter of time before she found a post as housekeeper or lady's companion and moved to more dignified surroundings. But soon it became clear that no one was going to employ a woman of her age without references. Prospective employers guessed by her manner and speech that she'd once had a position of authority, and their suspicions were aroused when she claimed she had spent the last fourteen years nursing a sick relative. As the weeks turned to months, and she put on a great deal more weight, her slovenly appearance and a certain desperation in her eyes precluded every type of work but office-cleaning.

She fought against this for some time. It was demeaning and poorly paid. But as she began to eat into her savings, she just had to accept it was the only job she was likely to be offered. Worse still, she realized that the dark, damp flat was to become her permanent home.

Apathy set in. At first she intended to paint the flat, buy new curtains and join the local church to meet new people. But as each day passed her will slowly weakened to the point where it became difficult to even take a bath, wash her clothes and maintain a proper diet.

Now, two years on she hadn't noticed that the black mould had crept right up the walls, that she hadn't dusted in weeks, or that the newspapers she bought daily were growing into a small mountain in the corner of the room. She stayed in bed until ten, walked to the shops to buy her newspaper, then came home to read it cover to cover. At five she left the flat to walk to Tottenham Court Road to start work. It was usually around eleven when she came home and she went straight to bed. Sometimes a whole week could go by without her speaking to a soul.

Once she'd grown used to the idea of office-cleaning, she did find that it had its advantages. She worked alone in the narrow four-storey office block and it was easy enough to clean. Built in 1947, it had the advantage of being modern with all its floors covered in lino. Besides the small foyer which she had to scrub and polish, she had only to clean the toilets, sweep, dust the desks and filing cabinets, and empty the waste-paper bins. She could easily do the entire job in three hours, but she spun it out to five by reading any newspapers that had been left behind.

Sundays were the worst day of the week because there was no work to go to and all the shops were closed. The empty, lonely hours stretched out in front of her and as she sat by her window, seeing only the feet of people passing by up on the street level, she was always reminded of Carrington Hall. Sundays had been so pleasant there. The vicar would call for a service in the morning and in the afternoon she was frequently invited out to tea; then she would go to church in the evening and quite often there was supper later to round off the day.

There were so many things she missed, not just from the Hall but from her entire nursing career. Her clothes had been washed and ironed in the laundry, meals were cooked for her, her room cleaned. Junior staff had looked up to her, and there had been discussions with doctors and meetings with patients' relatives who were always so unfailingly grateful.

Lionel Brace-Coombes's last words to her still rang in her ears. He had called her 'an affront to the nursing profession. For your own twisted ends you allowed mentally deficient patients to be abused and neglected. You betrayed the trust I had in you by lining your own pocket with money intended to maintain care and safety in Carrington Hall. I have enough evidence against you to have you sent to prison; the only reason I am not pressing criminal charges now is because I believe by doing so that several innocent young women in my employ might be damaged further by being asked to give evidence against

461

you. You will leave here today, but should it ever come to my ears that you have tried to contact any of my staff again, or make trouble for anyone you knew here, I will come down so hard on you that you will live to regret it.'

Yet her acrimony wasn't directed at Lionel Brace-Coombes. To her mind it was that guttersnipe Rosie Parker who had wrecked her life – a troublemaking sixteen-year-old who knew nothing of nursing! Each long, miserable day the bitterness towards this girl ate away at her like acid. Night after night she lay awake trying to think of some way of exacting her revenge on Rosie Parker. But she had no idea where the girl was, and even less idea of how to go about finding her.

Violet Pemberton was the only person likely to know where she was, but Freda knew she'd get no assistance from that quarter. She thought of hiring a private detective, but with less than six hundred pounds to her name in savings she wasn't in a position to do that. One of the reasons why she read every newspaper she could get hold of was in the hope that the Parker brothers might one day make an appearance in the tabloids. She doubted very much that they'd stayed in Somerset after Seth was acquitted. It was far more likely they'd come to London to live. They might just come up again one day in the news on criminal charges and that would lead her to finding out where their sister was. It was a long shot, but searching the papers daily was better than twiddling her thumbs.

Today, for the first time since moving to Camden Town, she felt optimistic. She had enough energy to put clean sheets on her bed and to tackle the kitchen. She even intended to have a bath and wash her hair later. All because she was ninety-nine per cent certain she'd tracked Seth Parker down. It had been well over a year ago when she read about a scrap-metal merchant in north London being fined in court for selling lead stolen from churches. It had jogged her memory – hadn't Cole Parker and both his sons been scrap-metal dealers?

Time was the one thing she had plenty of, so she got herself a map, marked off areas where scrap yards were likely to be found, and two mornings a weeks she went out looking. She didn't think for one moment that the Parkers would still be using their own names, but she had pictures of them cut from the newspapers at the time of the trial.

It was some time before it dawned on her that the negative responses she was getting to her questions in scrap yards might be due to her appearance and manner. It was only when a burly man threatened to turn his dog loose on her that she realized she was perceived as some kind of professional snoop. After rethinking her strategy, she cleaned up her act and posed as a public health inspector, calling on houses close by yards.

She soon discovered many housewives more than willing to talk. They listed their complaints eagerly, everything from noise, dirt, vermin and fear for their children. Although few of these women knew any employees in the yards by name, they were only too willing to give their views on criminal activity they'd observed. Finally, after some six months, when she had enough useless gossip and hearsay to fill an entire book, one woman in Acton looked at the picture of Seth and said she had seen him at the yard across from her house on several occasions in the past. She said he used to come in a lorry, unload it and then drive away. The reason she remembered him so well was because she hadn't liked the way he leered at her fifteen-year-old daughter. She said she had written down the name on the side of the lorry – Franklin's Haulage – because of this.

Freda had traced that name eventually through another haulage company to London Bridge. She didn't dare go into the office to inquire. The business was situated under a railway arch, a dank filthy place where two rough-looking men were stripping down an engine, and what passed for an office was just a kind of counter and a few shelves.

An inquiry in a nearby café proved helpful but somewhat intimidating. She learned from the woman who ran it that Del Franklin, the owner of Franklin's Haulage, was 'a nasty bastard' who had a finger in many pies, all of them 'bent'. She was advised to go away and leave well alone. Freda apologized profusely but showed the pictures of the Parkers anyway. To her amazement the woman nodded and agreed Seth had been in for meals now and again. She told Freda he'd once boasted to her that he ran a scrap yard for Del in Lewisham.

Lewisham, Freda discovered, was a big place and there were a great many scrap yards to look at. But finally last Friday, after what seemed like a lifetime of dead ends, Freda found the one in Morley Road. There was nothing about it to build up her hopes. Like so many of them she'd seen, it was an old bomb site, this one tucked away at the end of a terrace of dingy Victorian houses. She peered through the fence but couldn't see anyone around, so going back to her old routine she knocked on the front door of the tidiest house in the street.

A young woman with frizzy hair and a toddler on her hip answered. Freda smiled ingratiatingly.

'I'm so very sorry to disturb you. I'm from the public health department and I just wanted to ask you one or two questions about the scrap yard down the street. We have reason to believe it may be a health hazard, particularly to small children. Could you spare me a few moments?'

As she expected, the woman asked her in and even made a pot of tea as she launched into a tirade of complaints.

'It's quiet enough now,' she said, two angry red blotches coming up on her cheeks, 'but by the middle of the afternoon it's hell. They break up cars, they come in with load after load of rubbish. They're there till well after dark, they light stinking fires, and they make so much noise the kids can't sleep. It's driving us all mad.'

Freda looked around her as the woman spoke. She

thought it was a typical working-class home, a bit dark and poky, cheap furniture, but clean and neat. When the child toddled over to Freda she picked it up and let it play with her bunch of keys.

'It must be miserable for you,' she said, smoothing the child's hair in an affectionate display. 'Can you tell me anything about the man who owns it? His name? Where he comes from?'

'There's several men there, we don't really know which of them owns it,' the woman said with a shrug. 'Most of us around here are too scared of them to even attempt speaking to them.'

'Do either of these men work there?' Freda asked, getting her press cutting out of her handbag. 'Strictly between ourselves, we've had a series of complaints about these brothers in other parts of London.'

The woman took the faded newspaper picture. If she wondered why a public health official should produce something so crumpled and unprofessional, she didn't show it. Instead she gasped.

'Yes, this is one of them,' she said pointing to the picture of Seth. 'Mind you, the other one looks almost the same, so I couldn't swear which one it is. He never looks smart like that, he's always dirty and needs a shave. Some of the other women down the street say they've seen him squatting down to do his toilet in that yard. It's disgusting. I hope you can do something about it.'

Freda's heart leapt with delight and gratitude. 'Of course we will do all we can to get the yard closed,' she assured the woman. 'But I must ask you to keep my visit here today under your hat. To get a successful prosecution, other officials from the public health department will be making undercover visits to the yard in the next few weeks. A leak at this stage could put the whole case in jeopardy. Not only does it give the offenders time to start cleaning up, but we've often found they can be very unpleasant towards the people they believe have talked

465

about them. You and your husband have had more than enough to put up with already, without further trouble.'

The young woman's anxious expression confirmed she would say nothing.

'One thing more,' Freda asked as they walked together to the front door. 'I don't suppose you've ever seen a young girl over there, have you? She's about five foot four or so, slim, with coppery-coloured curly hair, around nineteen?'

The woman shook her frizzy blonde head. 'No. There's an older woman, in her thirties, calls sometimes, but that's all. I don't think any young girl in her right mind would go in there with those men, they all look so dangerous to me.'

Freda paused for a moment once back on the pavement outside the house. She hadn't actually thought beyond the point of finding one of the Parkers, and she knew she should make a proper foolproof plan before approaching them. But her curiosity about Seth Parker was so great that she really wanted to see him for herself, just to make certain that all the long months of searching were finally over.

As she glanced back down the cul-de-sac, to her surprise she saw a tall young man jump up on to the top of a heap of old cars. He was wearing nothing but a pair of shorts, and his bare chest and limbs were tanned a golden brown. Her heart leapt with excitement: even at a distance of some forty feet, she was sure it was Seth Parker just by the insolent way he stared around him. This same insolence was something that had been mentioned several times during the trial and caught so clearly in the artist's sketches. She didn't need to go any closer.

That evening for the first time since she began her office-cleaning job, Freda hurried to finish. In her mind she was preparing a letter to Seth Parker, and she couldn't wait to get home to write it.

She had mulled over every plausible reason she could

give for needing to find Rosie, and thought long and hard about what would prompt Seth to give her the address. She decided that money was the only likely inducement.

Seth was whistling 'Mountain Greenery', but stopped short in surprise when a postman walked into the scrap yard on Monday morning.

'Got the wrong place, ain't you?' he called out from the shed doorway. 'Since when did we get letters?'

'You don't know a "Mr S. Parker" then?' the postman said with a glance at the letter in his hand. 'It's addressed to the scrap yard in Morley Road.'

Seth was so shocked he almost dropped the cup of Camp coffee and condensed milk he'd just made. No one knew his real name, not Del or anyone else. They all knew him as Stan Willmot, though some of the lads called him Tom Pearce because of his West Country accent.

'Let's have a look at it then.' Seth almost leapt across the path towards the postman, practically snatching the envelope out of the man's hand. 'Maybe it's for Stan. I dunno his other name.'

Seth saw it was a woman's writing and the postmark was Camden Town. He wondered if he'd given his real name to some bint when he was pissed.

'Oh yeah, that's for Stan,' he said, hoping postmen weren't in the habit of checking up who was who. 'I'll give it to him when he gets in.'

Once the postman was out of sight, Seth sat down on a couple of tyres, lit a cigarette and opened the letter. The spidery handwriting was hard to read, and reading wasn't his strong point anyway.

'Dear Mr Parker,' he read. 'I believe you to be the brother of Rosie Parker who was employed at a nursing home in north London where I am a staff nurse. Rosie left us some two years ago without leaving a forwarding address and I am very anxious to trace her as one of our patients died recently leaving her a small bequest. I shall be coming to

467

Lewisham on Friday morning of this week and I hope it will be convenient to pop in to speak to you about this matter. Yours sincerely, J. Marks.'

It took several readings before Seth worked out what all the words were, and he wasn't sure what 'bequest' meant. He hoped it was money. His first thought was that the woman was coming here to hand it over, which was fine by him. He had absolutely no idea where Rosie was, and if he did he'd be sticking a fist in her face, not passing on cash.

Seth's brain was often slow. It was only hours later that he began to wonder how the woman had found out where he worked. He thought he'd covered his tracks so well that no one would ever find him.

Being discovered, and in connection with his sister, brought back the full force of his anger towards her. As Seth saw it, because of Rosie his father was dead and Norman had legged it off up north somewhere. Cole getting hanged was bad enough, but losing his brother hurt far more. Seth had fully expected that after the trial he and Norman would find themselves a little place together, and their life would go on much the way it had been before, but Norman had walked out on him. Even now, getting on for three years later, Norman's angry words still stung: 'I hate you, you lying bastard. I never want to see you again. I want to forget I ever had a brother. Don't try and follow me. You and me are finished.'

May Cottage, and all that fine furniture in the parlour which he could have sold for a bob or two, had gone, and suddenly everything he'd taken for granted in life was gone too. He'd been *someone* back in Somerset. He could walk into any pub and he'd be bought a drink; people respected him, they did what he asked. Seth didn't like big cities, there were too many men tougher and brighter than he was, and he'd found without Norman to back him up he wasn't quite as fearless as he'd always believed.

This was why he'd fallen in with Del and his cronies.

He didn't much like being treated like a dumb country boy and called 'Swede', their name for anyone who came from out of London. But he got paid a good screw each week because he knew the scrap business inside out, could be relied on to keep his trap shut and was handy with his fists. Most of the time he counted himself lucky.

Yet just now and then he had attacks of pure fright, usually in the middle of the night, when he woke up to find he'd pissed the bed again. He'd been thrown out of more lodgings than he could count because of it. He blamed it on missing his father and brother, and the moors he'd grown up in and could never go back to. That brought him right back to Rosie, and his hatred for her grew stronger each night it happened.

He knew he was living on a razor's edge. These London blokes he worked for were real villains. They might look like a bunch of diddicoys, but they were sharp and dangerous, involved in everything from bank robbery to vice. They had no loyalty except to their own, and Seth was well aware that they wouldn't think twice about running out and leaving him to carry the can if things got a bit hot. They were jealous too because women fell over themselves for him. The truth of the matter was that Seth had no real interest in women. He liked a quick screw, then he was off. But the lads didn't know that; they thought he had it made.

On Friday morning at eleven, Freda walked into the scrap yard and went straight to the shed. It was raining hard and she had great difficulty bypassing the many puddles. She had some sympathy for the people in Morley Road. The yard really was a terrible place: dozens of cars in the process of being stripped of useful parts, old cookers, baths, sinks and water tanks piled up high. It stank, too, of burning rubber, petrol and something even more unpleasant which she recognized as excrement.

'Mr Parker!' she called out as she tentatively tapped on

the half-open door of the shed. 'It's Miss Marks. May I come in?'

She hoped she looked the part. She had put on her old navy blue raincoat and a felt hat, she had her SRN badge pinned to her lapel. She could easily pass for a district nurse.

She smelled Seth before he came to the door. It was the same smell – sweat and urine – that lingered around patients in Carrington Hall. She immediately knew that he was a bed-wetter and that he was most likely living in the hut. Fighting back her revulsion, she prepared a smile for him.

He was undeniably an extremely handsome man; the court sketches, press photographs and her view of him last week hadn't done him full justice. He was wearing a filthy shirt and grease-encrusted trousers, yet the face above them was all she really saw: hair as black and glossy as new tar, dark sparkling eyes, golden skin and white flashing teeth. He was in desperate need of a shave, along with a bath, but considering his background that was hardly surprising.

'It's a bit rough in here,' he said, but after looking at the rain he beckoned her in. 'Sorry about the stink too. I think someone got in here last night.'

The shed was perhaps twelve feet square. An old table stood near the door, and sacks and boxes spilling over with rags took up much of the rest of the floor space. In a corner were a couple of old car seats with a heap of sacks and blankets on them; a suit and a clean shirt hung on a nail on the wall. As Freda had surmised, he was living here. Remembering what she'd learned from the newspapers about the way he and his family lived, she wondered where Rosie had got her airs and graces.

'You got my letter then?' she began. 'I'm so anxious to find Rosie to get this bequest settled.'

Seth had asked someone what that word meant. He'd been told it could mean money or a gift. He'd also been told it was extremely unlikely to be left with him to pass on.

'I don't rightly know where she is,' he said, scratching his head. 'I ain't seen her for a couple of years. I could take what you've got and pass it on when she turns up. But I can't say when that'll be.'

Seth had discovered soon after arriving in London that sometimes it paid to act like a dumb country boy. He'd purposely hung on to his Somerset accent because he'd found it made people trust him.

'I can't do that, Mr Parker, much as I'd like to,' Freda said. 'It isn't allowed. I have to give it to her directly, or else it has to go right back to the solicitor's office and stay there until they can find her.' She paused long enough for that to sink in.

'But owing to your family circumstances, that might prove embarrassing for Rosie,' she went on. 'You see, your sister called herself Smith at our nursing home. I was the only person to whom she confided her true identity.'

Seth's mouth fell open. It hadn't occurred to him that this woman would know about Cole. It was even more surprising to find she was prepared to do something for his daughter when she did. The sort of people he mixed with wouldn't turn a hair if he told them his father shot a policeman or bludgeoned another villain to death; they would even look up to him. But murderers of women were a different matter. Seth had never confided in anyone about himself. He was amazed that Rosie had.

'How much are we talking about?' he asked. He felt very uncomfortable knowing she knew so much about him and his family. He wished he'd tidied himself up, met the woman at the gate and taken her to a café for this talk. At least there he could have walked away from her if necessary; here he felt trapped.

'Something in the region of a thousand pounds,' she said glibly. 'If you don't know where she is, perhaps you know someone else who might?'

Seth shook his head. The thought of Rosie coming into all that money for doing nothing more than being nice to some old codger made him feel green with envy. But at the same time his natural greed was telling him he could overcome his anger at Rosie if he could get a share of it.

Freda could almost track his thought processes. 'Do you know a Miss Violet Pemberton?'

Again Seth shook his head.

'She was the social worker who took your brother and sister away,' she said gently. 'I am absolutely certain she knows where Rosie is, but she's unlikely to pass on the information to me as it was she who shielded Rosie from the press to the time of the trial and gave her a new identity. She is very protective. But as you are Rosie's brother, she may be prepared to tell you.'

The name finally rang a bell. He did remember his barrister speaking about her. It was that old biddy who'd talked the police into dropping the lesser charges against him. 'Do you know where she lives?' Seth asked.

'I have her address in Somerset. If I could count on you to see her and get Rosie's new address, I would pay you your expenses out of the bequest.'

Although Seth was slow, it suddenly dawned on him that this woman couldn't possibly have kindly reasons for wanting to find his sister. If she meant well, she'd merely have written to this Miss Pemberton, or else instructed a solicitor to do it.

He perched on the edge of the table and just looked at the woman. The nurse-type coat and hat had detracted from her face at first. Now he saw she had a mean mouth and her eyes were very close-set. He wondered if she really was a nurse, and what Rosie might have done to make her search her out.

'How much "expenses" are we talking about?' he asked, narrowing his eyes. 'I'd need to have time off work, petrol money, and maybe a night in a hotel. I don't much care if I never see my sister again, so I'd have to have something for my trouble.'

Freda thought for a moment. This man wasn't as dense as she'd expected. She suspected he was on to her. But she needed his help and she had a strong feeling he'd get Rosie's address somehow if she made it worth his while.

'Ten pounds straight away. Another ten if you get the address.'

Seth just laughed at her. 'Are you loopy? I make ten quid just sitting here all day. Make it twenty-five now and the same again when I get the result, and I might think about it.'

Fifty pounds was a great deal of money to Freda, but she'd come so far she didn't see how she could back off now.

'Okay, fifty pounds altogether. But fifteen now and the balance when you get me the address.'

Seth agreed so willingly that Freda realized she could probably have settled for thirty, but the deal was done and she had to hand over the money and Miss Pemberton's address.

'Will you see to it quickly?' she asked. The stench in the shed was making her feel queasy, and even if the man was handsome there was also something repellent and dangerous about him. 'I must get it all tidied up and I'm sure you want Rosie to get what's coming to her without any further delay.'

'Aye, I do that,' he said with a touch of irony in his voice. 'Now, where do I contact you?'

'Just drop me a line when you've got the address. I'll come here the next day,' she said. 'You've still got my letter with my address?'

He nodded and Freda backed away towards the door. 'Thank you. I'm very grateful.'

It was only as she walked down the road back towards Lewisham High Street that Freda suddenly sensed that Rosie was going to get extra trouble now that Seth was involved. She had a feeling that as soon as he had her address he'd be after her. Maybe she wouldn't even need to exact any revenge personally. He looked capable of being anyone's worst nightmare.

Chapter Sixteen

'Be careful, Rosie!' Donald called out as she began to climb up the ladder set against an overgrown fir hedge with shears in one hand. 'Let me do that.'

'You aren't as quick as me,' she called back, laughing down at his upturned anxious face. The truth was she didn't entirely trust Donald with shears. He usually got a bit carried away, until the hedge resembled a skeleton. This one only needed a couple of feet of straggly growth cut off the top to make it square again.

Rosie loved trimming hedges, especially on warm sunny days. The Bakers' garden was one of the nicest she'd worked in: it was a series of terraces up to the lawn at the top, where she was now. The Bakers had grown the hedge as a shield against northerly winter winds which swept across the high part of the garden, killing all but the hardiest plants. Now she was at the top of the ladder the breeze was delightfully cooling, and she could see right across the fields as she worked.

She was especially happy today. Gareth had telephoned the night before and seemed to have had a change of heart since last weekend because he thought he might be able to get a transfer working out of Tonbridge. A week on Saturday he was going to take both her and Donald down to Eastbourne for the day. This was why Rosie was wearing just a pair of shorts and a thin sleeveless blouse today instead of her usual dungarees – she wanted to get her legs brown before exposing them on the beach.

Thomas was coming down this evening too, and staying

for a few days. She hoped the good weather would last as he always enjoyed coming along with her and Donald to watch them work, but it wasn't very nice for him if it was wet or chilly.

She wondered if Gareth's change of heart and suddenly being pleasanter about Donald was because of the letter she'd sent him. She had been so cross after last weekend that she'd written to say she was beginning to have regrets about him, and that maybe they didn't have enough in common to get married. He didn't mention the letter, but then that was typical of Gareth. He would never talk anything through properly.

'Don't stretch so far,' Donald called out from below. 'Come down and we'll move the ladder.'

'Mind your own business,' she called back. Donald had become very bossy in the last year. It was good to find he'd learned so much that he wanted to take control, but irritating too when he thought he knew best. 'You can't see what I'm doing from down there.'

It was fun clipping a hedge. She always imagined she was cutting a giant's hair, a bit off here, a bit more there, then down the ladder to check on her progress. She fancied learning how to do topiary. It would be such a thrill to make a peacock like the one she'd seen in a garden over in Heathfield.

She paused for a moment to check her work. Then, noticing a bit she'd missed to her right, she stretched out to snip it off and all at once the ladder shifted under her feet.

'Donald!' she shrieked, clutching on to the hedge and letting the shears fall. 'The ladder!'

The clump of hedge just slipped through her hands as the ladder slid to one side, and suddenly she was falling sideways towards the terraces.

She landed face down, smacking her knees on to the wall of the terrace. Her upper body lay across the plants and the pain was so acute she couldn't even scream. She heard Donald yell out and his feet come thundering up the garden, then all at once he was lifting her up in his arms.

'Put me down on the grass,' she managed to get out. 'Then go and get some help.'

He was very gentle, but even so her legs hurt so much she screamed out as he laid her down.

'I'm sorry,' he said. 'I sh-sh-should have stayed holding the ladder. It's my f-f-f-fault.'

Rosie opened her eyes and saw he was crying. 'It's not your fault,' she managed to croak out. 'Just go and get help. I think my legs are broken.'

It was odd the things she thought of as she lay there with the sun beating down on her, pain in her legs growing stronger by the minute: that the Bakers would be cross she hadn't finished the hedge by the time they got home this evening; that she must have squashed all the flowers in that bed; and that the hedge trimmings must be gathered up. Then she thought of Gareth. He would be cross too if they couldn't go to Eastbourne and he'd want to know what she was doing up a ladder. She wouldn't be able to see Thomas either if she was in hospital. She lifted her head once, enough to see her knees, and the sight made her feel faint. They were just a bloody mass.

Donald seemed to be gone for a very long time, but at last he came rushing back through the side gate of the cottage carrying a bottle of water. 'I g-g-got Mrs Jackson in the sh-sh-shop to phone for an ambulance,' he said breathlessly. 'Then I ran home to tell M-m-mum. She's coming, but I ran on w-w-without her. I've brought you some w-w-water too.'

He sat beside her, gave her a drink, then wetting a handkerchief he wiped her face with it. His face was contorted with anxiety, his stutter had returned, and Rosie knew he was blaming himself. But rather than this disturbing her, she suddenly realized just what that meant. She had grown so used to being with him day after day that she barely noticed his progress any more. Two years ago she doubted he would have had any conception of another person's pain, or felt any responsibility for it. His reactions today had been like any normal man's, from the time when he urged her to be careful, through lifting her off the wall and going for help. She reminded herself to ask Mrs Cook if he thought of the water all on his own, or if she gave it to him.

'It's okay,' Rosie said weakly and lifted her hand to touch his troubled face. 'It was an accident, and my fault because I wasn't thinking what I was doing. You've done everything right.'

'Well, young lady, it's your lucky day,' the doctor said as he came into the cubicle with the X-ray in his hands, some three hours later. He was quite old, perhaps even sixty, with white hair and a beard like Father Christmas, but he'd been very sympathetic to Rosie and he'd even managed to make her laugh a couple of times. 'I think you must have cast-iron knees because there are no broken bones. They are going to be very sore for a while, and I don't think you'll be walking, much less climbing ladders, for some time.'

Rosie was so relieved that she began to cry and laugh, both at the same time.

Mrs Cook and the ambulance had arrived at the cottage simultaneously. Donald had insisted on coming with Rosie to Tunbridge Wells hospital, and somewhat reluctantly his mother agreed, promising to come on later when her husband got home from work. From the moment Rosie was brought into this cubicle in the accident department she'd been convinced it was only a matter of time before they whisked her away to a real ward where she would stay for several weeks.

'Does that mean I can go home?' she asked.

'It certainly does, after we've put a clean dressing on those wounds,' he said. 'Your friend's parents are here now, I believe, so I'll just speak to them for a moment and warn them not to let you out dancing for a week or two. Then you can go.'

It was Donald who carried Rosie up the stairs to her room. It hurt terribly to even attempt bending her knees. Coming home in the car she'd had to sit sideways on the back seat with her legs out straight over Mrs Cook's lap.

'I'm going to look after you till you're better,' Donald said as he put her down gently on the bed. 'And I'll do all the work on my own too.'

Rosie let him plump up the pillows behind her back and just smiled at him. Perhaps it was because of the role reversal that she found herself trying to picture exactly how he was three years ago when he grabbed her on her first evening in Carrington Hall.

He'd been so pale and thin then. An awful haircut and clothes which were too big for him had added to his neglected appearance. But when she came to think about it, the thing which had really repelled her was his wet, sloppy mouth. Now as she looked at him, she saw his mouth wasn't that way any more. It was still wide of course, fleshy lips that easily curled into a smile. But it wasn't sloppy. Somewhere along the line, without her ever noticing, that had gone, along with the stutter, and the bouts of rolling on the floor when he got excited.

'What are you smiling for?' he asked, his blue eyes looking wonderingly at her.

'Because I love you,' she said. 'And because you've been so smart today.'

He gave her one of his special radiant 'I love you too' smiles. It dulled the pain in her leg and soothed her anxiety about what Gareth would say when he heard about the accident. In some strange way it was the justification she needed for putting Donald's well-being and happiness before Gareth.

Thomas arrived at nine that evening. Rosie heard

Donald greeting him at the front door, then launch immediately into the story of the accident. Still talking at a hundred miles an hour, he brought Thomas straight up to see her.

'Poor old wounded soldier,' Thomas said in sympathy as he came in the bedroom. 'I bet it hurts like hell!'

'It serves me right,' Rosie shrugged. Now that she was sitting up, her legs straight out in front of her, the sensation had become more of a throb and ache rather than the earlier acute pain. 'At least they aren't broken.'

'I'll have to check daily for gangrene,' Thomas joked. 'Donald and I can saw them off if necessary, and I'll teach you to walk with a peg leg.'

Donald instantly looked alarmed. He didn't understand adult jokes. 'You can't cut her leg off!' he gasped.

'Thomas is just teasing me,' Rosie said gently. 'Now why don't you go and get him a drink, then I can tell him how clever you've been today.'

After Donald had gone, Thomas pulled up a chair by her bed and sat down, easing his leg out in front of him. 'Well, this puts us on the same level,' he said with a smile. 'At least I can have your undivided attention for a couple of days without you springing off here, there and everywhere. Is there any news aside from this tragedy?'

Rosie gave him a quick update on the continuing success of their gardening business and her observations about Donald today, and she mentioned that Gareth had spoken of getting a transfer to Tonbridge.

Donald came back with a large whisky and soda for Thomas and said his mother was making him some supper too.

'I'd better go on down in a minute and leave you to sleep,' Thomas said. 'We'll have all day tomorrow to chat. Now don't go worrying about that half-finished job. I'll pop round there with Donald in the morning and check out what needs doing. I can't promise to finish the hedge, but I can supervise Donald and hold the ladder for him.'

As Thomas went downstairs he felt ridiculously shaky. He was always worrying about Rosie having an accident while she was working, imagining her lying helpless in agony in an isolated garden, with Donald too distraught to leave her side to get help. He had never admitted these fears to anyone, least of all to Rosie. She would only have laughed at him and called him a worryguts.

He found it odd how losing a leg had altered his perception of danger. When he'd joined the army he'd never once imagined he could be wounded, let alone killed. All the time in the camp when he saw others dying of tropical diseases, he refused to believe he might catch one too. Even when that ulcer spread so rapidly on his leg he was convinced it could be stopped. But perhaps the discovery that he was not special enough to be spared was the reason why he now saw terrible dangers lurking out there for Rosie. She was as fearless and light-hearted as he once was, leaping up ladders, climbing trees, often with implements in her hands that could maim her so easily. But what could he do? He couldn't tell her that to see her in pain was more than he could bear.

A stronger man would go right away, turn his back on that sweet affection she gave him, knowing it served only to torment him more. A braver man would perhaps admit how he felt and risk complete rejection. But he was no longer strong or brave. He was clinging on to what he had like a life-belt: her friendship, trust and affection. Most days it was enough.

Rosie didn't go to sleep for quite some time. She could hear Thomas and the Cooks' voices wafting up from below in the kitchen and it felt good to know they were all close by. A soft, warm breeze wafted in through the open window, she heard an owl hoot in the distance and it reminded her of summer nights down in Somerset. She thought about Alan. He was nine now, and in the last report from Miss Pemberton she said he was clever enough to pass his eleven-plus and go to the grammar school in Taunton. Rosie didn't feel any sadness about him now. He was so very happy with Mr and Mrs Hughes, Thomas had made the right decision to let him be adopted. She just hoped that one day she might get to see him again.

Her last thoughts as she drifted off to sleep were of the orchard at May Cottage. She saw herself and Alan chasing the hens into their coop at sunset. She could feel the long grass beneath her bare feet, see the sun gradually sinking down into the moors. When she was very little she had believed that the vast expanse of flat land she could see from a perch on the orchard fence was the entire world. She knew better now of course, but tonight she felt as if all that really mattered to her was here in this house.

As Rosie was dropping off to sleep, Seth was eating fish and chips in a small, dark blue Morris van parked in a remote part of the same moors she'd been picturing. He'd left London at ten that morning and gone straight to Chilton Trinity to check out where Miss Violet Pemberton lived. Then he'd driven into Taunton to while away the time until he could put his plan into action.

Seth was slow-witted, but he wasn't a complete fool. A social worker who had been responsible for taking his brother and sister into care and knew everything about the Parkers wasn't likely to welcome him turning up on her doorstep, and she certainly wasn't going to give him Rosie's address. So he planned to break into her cottage once she was asleep, find the details he needed, then scarper back to London.

Burglary was something Seth knew all about. Right from the age of fourteen he'd been an opportunistic thief, nipping through an open door and grabbing what he could stuff in his pockets. Later on, after the war, he'd progressed to breaking and entering houses in Wells and Glastonbury. He'd never bothered with doing big houses

– wealthy people paid too much attention to security and they rarely had cash lying about, which interested him far more than stuff that he'd have to fence. Over the years he'd done dozens of jobs when he was short of readies, and cottages like Miss Pemberton's were the easiest of all. Hers stood on its own, backing on to fields, and he'd observed this afternoon that there was only an old lady living next door. When this old girl went toddling off to the village shop, he'd nipped in round the back of Miss Pemberton's and taken a good look round.

Aside from a tiny kitchen there was just one large room, with stairs leading up. Her desk was right under the back window, an address book lying on it beside the telephone. If he hadn't been afraid the old lady next door might return suddenly, he might have smashed the window and grabbed it then and there. But he'd spotted one or two other things which were worth having anyway, and she might have a bit of money tucked away too. It would have to wait until later.

Seth finished his fish and chips, put on a dark jumper and leather gloves, then tucking his jemmy, a sharp knife and a torch into his belt, and his cigarettes into his pocket, he got out of the van and climbed over a five-barred gate. It took quite a while to walk across the fields and reach the hedge enclosing Miss Pemberton's garden. It was a lovely warm night, masses of stars in the sky, and enough light from the moon to see where he was going without needing the torch.

He felt powerful again because he was back on home territory. In London he never felt entirely in control of his life; he was a mere runaround for Del Franklin and his boys, and more often than not he suspected he was their patsy. Perhaps after tonight he could make the break from them and move on to something better.

Two minutes later Seth was watching Miss Pemberton from the safety of her garden shed. She'd drawn the curtains at the front of the cottage, but left the back ones open and with the light from a couple of table lamps he could see her clearly. She was sitting on a settee with her feet up on a stool, her glasses on, reading a book. To his delight she was older and smaller than he'd expected, just an ordinary, plump, middle-aged woman. Seth struck a match, lit a cigarette and checked his watch before blowing it out. It was almost eleven. He guessed a woman of her age would go to bed soon; the old woman's house next door was already in darkness. He planned to wait another couple of hours before going in to make sure she was sound asleep.

A few minutes later she got up from the settee and went into the kitchen. The glass in the door there was reeded, but he could see her silhouette and he guessed she was making herself a hot drink. She opened the back door to let her cat out, but although she locked it afterwards, she didn't close the little window beside it. The kitchen light went out, then she went back into the living-room and turned the lights out there too. A few seconds later the light came on upstairs and he could see her drawing the curtains.

He heard the toilet flush and water running, but still the bedroom light stayed on. The wooden box he was sitting on was uncomfortable. He wanted to unfold one of the deckchairs stacked against a wall, but he was too scared of knocking something over. Finally, about half an hour later, the light went out.

Seth moved to the floor, leaned back against the box and lit another cigarette. He hadn't known such utter silence since his days back at May Cottage, and it pleased him. In London there was always noise at night, banging car doors, tyres screeching, drunks shouting. He thought back to nights like this when he went out catching eels with Norman. If they stayed quiet they could actually hear the eels slithering, and when they caught them and put them in a bucket the sound of their skin rubbing together was almost like listening to hot sex. He missed those kinds of things – and Norman. He still didn't fully understand why his brother ran out on him; they could have had such a good life together.

His eyes were used to the gloom by now and he studied the contents of his hidey-hole. The orderliness of it said a great deal about the woman's character. Garden tools hanging from hooks, a neat stack of flowerpots, pots of paint on a shelf and brushes in a jam jar. It even smelled clean in here. From what he'd seen of her cottage, that was equally orderly. It was going to be a doddle. He could be in and out within ten minutes.

At half past one Seth crept silently up the garden, slid his hands through the small window, reached the lock on the door, turned it and went in. He had always prided himself on his stealth. A teacher at school had once said he moved like a cat. He went straight to the desk, but to his disappointment the address book he'd seen earlier was no longer there. Taking his torch from his belt, he flashed it around the room. The beam caught two nice silver candlesticks, a couple of photograph frames and a carriage clock which looked as if it might be valuable. But he had to find Rosie's address first.

Holding his breath, he gingerly opened the top drawer in the desk. It was full of stationery. The next drawer down held some cardboard files. He opened one, then another, but all the correspondence was typewritten and unlikely to be from Rosie. The last drawer had ordinary letters, a whole clump of them held together with a paper-clip. He put them on the desk and, holding the torch so he could see them properly, he turned them over one by one.

'Get out of my house!'

Seth nearly jumped out of his skin at the sound of the woman's commanding voice. He hadn't heard so much as a creak from upstairs. He turned in astonishment and dropped his torch. It spun on the floor for a second or two and Seth was rooted to the spot in fear as the beam of light flashed round the room, showing her ghostly figure at the top of the stairs.

'There is nothing in this house to steal, you scoundrel!' the woman said in a crisp, cold voice. 'Get out immediately!'

Suddenly the overhead light was switched on and Seth was astounded to see that the woman was brandishing a heavy stick of dark shiny wood. She came down the stairs towards him and his legs turned to jelly.

'I've killed snakes out in Africa with this stick,' she said quite calmly. 'And I won't hesitate to hit you with –' She stopped abruptly, her eyes opening wider. 'Good heavens, you're Seth Parker!'

It was bad enough to be caught red-handed, but even worse to find himself recognized by a woman he'd never met before.

'I want my sister's address,' he managed to stammer out. 'Give it to me now or you'll be sorry.'

'I think not,' she said, and came further down until she was almost at the bottom of the stairs. 'I'm going to pick up the telephone and call the police.'

It was her calm and her self-assurance which unnerved Seth. He'd been disturbed before on burglaries and his victims had always been so terrified of him they backed away. She was such a small woman too. Even standing on the stairs, her eyes were below the level of his, grey, steady and utterly fearless.

Seth took a menacing step towards her, expecting her to back off, but instead she raised the stick and brought it down hard. Had he not jumped to one side, she would have caught him on the shoulder. But Seth was a street fighter, and as the stick came down below its intended target, he grabbed the end of it with one hand and with the other he caught her by the shoulder.

'Drop it!' he roared, pulling her off the stairs. She was much stronger than she looked and she struggled desperately to get away from him. But she was no match for Seth and he soon wrenched the stick out of her hand.

He lifted the stick above his head, ready to bring it down on her.

'Don't,' she called out. Yet to Seth's ears it sounded more of a threat than a plea for mercy and for one brief second Seth wanted to let her go. There was defiance in her cold eyes; she wasn't even cowering from him. She had real courage.

Seth respected bravery, and deep down in his heart he knew he had little of it and it shamed him. But just as he'd often watched a hawk hovering in the air and admired its sheer beauty, yet still felt compelled to lift his gun and shoot it, so he lifted the stick and brought it down hard on her head.

She just collapsed like a meringue struck with a spoon. Seth watched her slither down to the floor in some surprise. Somehow he'd expected her to be more resilient than that. She landed on her knees, holding her head in her hands, her eyes at last wide with terror. 'Please don't do this, Seth,' she whimpered.

He looked scornfully at her. Her courage was gone now, she was just another pathetic woman pleading with him as they always did. He had no desire to kill her, but he knew he must. She knew who he was.

Taking the stick in both hands, he brought it down again on her skull. She keeled over and he continued to beat her jerking, bucking body as if she were a sack of hay he wanted to flatten. It was only when her dressing-gown turned red with blood that he paused. She was still at last, and he knew she was dead.

He dropped the stick beside her. It took a couple of minutes before he realized the enormity of what he'd done. She looked like a broken doll covered in strawberry jam. In panic he rushed for the back door, but as his lungs filled with fresh air and the moment of nausea left him, it occurred to him that he must make it look like a real burglary. Going back into the room, he averted his eyes from her body and drew the curtains at the back window.

He was systematic now. He finished checking through the letters, but there were none from Rosie. He opened the desk drawers and scattered the contents on the floor, then went through every other cupboard and drawer in the room. He came across a nice silver bangle which he put to one side, along with the photo frames, candlesticks and carriage clock. But still he couldn't find the address book, so he went upstairs.

For some reason the woman's bedroom unnerved him. It was so bare, just a narrow bed, a chest of drawers and a wardrobe, no feminine frippery, perfume or cosmetics, not even an ornament or two. On the wall was a photograph of her taken when she was much younger. She was in a nurse's uniform, flanked by several smiling army officers. Seth wondered momentarily why she had never married.

The address book was by her bed, alongside a half-written letter. He snatched it up, but before pocketing it checked to see if Rosie was in it. There was a Rosemary Smith amongst the 'S's, at an address in Sussex. He thought about it for a moment, and felt it must be her. But if it wasn't her, well, that was Miss Marks's bad luck.

A rummage through a handbag produced seven pounds and a bit of loose change. He stuffed that in his pockets, then turned off the light and went down to collect the things he wanted to take. Two minutes later he was leaving the way he had come in, taking care to lock the door behind him.

Seth was halfway to London before it dawned on him that once the news of this murder got out, Miss Marks would guess he was responsible. His stomach heaved, and he just had time to pull over on to the side of the road and lean out of the window before he was violently sick. He sat there at the roadside in the dark for some fifteen minutes, trembling with fear. What was he going to do? One side of his brain told him that Miss Marks was crooked enough to be persuaded to keep quiet, but the other said he couldn't count on it. If he didn't take her Rosie's address, she'd be mad and come looking for him again; if he took it to her and got the rest of the money, she'd know for sure that he'd been there.

He had no choice but to kill her too.

It was then that he realized his clothes were splattered with blood. Fortunately he had a pair of overalls in the back of the van, so he got out and put them on, wiping his shoes with a clump of grass before continuing his journey.

He was very tired by the time he reached the outskirts of London and the sky was growing light. He didn't dare delay getting to Camden Town but he was so very scared. He had no way of knowing if Miss Marks lived alone. There was no time to check her out, as he had Miss Pemberton.

Driving slowly down Harmood Street he saw that 13A was a basement flat and he felt a certain relief. It would have been much more difficult if she'd lived in a couple of rooms upstairs. He parked around the corner, and after copying Rosie's address from Miss Pemberton's address book on to a scrap of paper, he took a heavy claw hammer from a tool-bag in the back of the van, tucked it into his belt, then buttoned his overalls up over it.

Seth rang the bell on the basement door. It was nearly six now and people were coming down the street on their way to work. He stood back in case anyone should glance down into the basement area and see him. It stank of dustbins and cats' pee. It wasn't the kind of place he would have expected a nurse to live in.

'Who is it?' she called out through the locked door.

Seth looked up towards the street nervously. He hoped there was no one within earshot. 'It's Seth,' he called back. 'Sorry to call so early, but I've got what you wanted.'

The door opened but she had the chain on, and Seth could only see half of her face.

'I told you to write,' she said in an irritable voice.

Seth took a deep breath. 'I know, but I've got to go up north to work today and I'll be gone for weeks. I thought you were in a hurry for it.'

She hesitated. Seth wished he could see her clearly. 'You can wait till I get back if you like,' he said, shrugging his shoulders and turning as if about to walk away. 'But I had to come this way and I thought you'd want it.'

'You'd better come in, then,' she said, and closing the door she took off the chain.

Seth smiled with all the charm he could muster as she reopened the door. 'What a task you set me,' he said, stepping over the threshold before she could change her mind. 'That Miss Pemberton was like my old school-teacher, a real dragon.'

Freda was only half awake, but even so she was alert enough to realize she must be careful with this young man. He would want the rest of his money, and she wondered how she was going to get it out of its hiding place without him seeing how much she had.

'Any chance of a cup of tea?' Seth asked cheekily once he was right inside her room. 'I've had a long drive.' He was somewhat stunned by the squalor. He'd frequently lived in worse, but the way Miss Marks spoke and her haughty manner had given him the idea she would live graciously. There were piles of old newspapers, dust and grime everywhere, and even her recently vacated bed looked as grubby as many he'd slept in. He didn't want tea or to stay here for a moment longer than necessary, but at the same time he didn't want to appear too hasty in case she became alarmed.

'Let me see the address first, then I'll put the kettle on,' Freda said. She was not only thrown by this unexpected visit, embarrassed by him seeing where she lived, but also very wary of being tricked by him. She wouldn't put it past him to give her a false address.

'She's in Sussex. In a place called The Grange,' Seth

said, pulling the scrap of paper out of his pocket. 'Sounds a bit posh. Maybe it's another nursing home.'

Freda gasped. The Grange was the home of Mr and Mrs Cook. She felt a surge of white-hot anger at herself for not considering earlier that Rosie might have gone to them.

Seth saw her reaction and was puzzled by it. 'You know that address, don't you?' he said.

'Well, yes,' she admitted. 'I'm just surprised to find Rosie didn't tell me or anyone else that she was going there to work.'

'Well, the deal's still the same whether you knew the address or not,' Seth said quickly. 'And it took a bit of persuasion to get it out of Miss Pemberton too.'

'Let me make the tea,' Freda said quickly. As she turned to go out into the kitchen, she picked up her handbag and took it with her. She knew she had less than three pounds in there, but she didn't trust Seth not to riffle through it the moment her back was turned. 'Sit down. I won't be long.'

She filled the kettle and put it on the gas, then glancing back into the other room to make sure Seth was still sitting down by the window, she bent down and groped under the cooker for the tin box where she kept all her personal papers and cash. It took only a couple of seconds to pull out the notes from a bundle. She put them in her handbag and, putting the address in the box, replaced it under the cooker.

'Do you take sugar?' she called out a couple of minutes later, relieved she'd managed this sleight of hand without him seeing anything.

'Yes, two please,' Seth replied, and slid his hands into his leather gloves. He was shaking with fear now. It was broad daylight outside, more and more people were out on the streets going to work, and he'd heard someone moving about in the flat above. He had to do what he'd come for and get out quickly.

He heard her turn the tap on again. He stood up,

unbuttoned his overalls, took the hammer from his belt, and walked stealthily across the room towards the kitchen. She was bending over the sink swilling round the teapot as he looked in. Lifting the hammer above his head, Seth clenched his teeth and lunged at her, hitting her with full force on the back of the neck.

Freda Barnes didn't call out. She just slumped forward over the sink, the teapot falling to the floor and shattering.

Seth hit her again, even harder, then, heaving her back on to the floor, he checked her. Her eyes had rolled right back into her head, her mouth was hanging open. She was dead.

He looked down at her in disgust. Her dressing-gown had come loose and he could see down the front of her nightdress. Her tits were huge and flabby and her stomach bulged out beneath them. He kicked her hard in the side for good measure, then reached for her handbag.

As soon as he saw the notes folded just inside it, he knew she must have got them from somewhere out here in the kitchen. It took him only a few minutes to find her box hidden under the cooker and the wad of notes concealed in it, along with the address he'd just given her. He smiled with pure delight; judging by the thickness there was over five hundred pounds. He was glad he'd come.

Seth paused before letting himself out, looking around him one last time. He'd found a few nice pieces of jewellery in a drawer, which, together with the cash she had, puzzled him. Why was she living in such a grim place? More important, however, was why was she so anxious to find Rosie. The two things seemed to be connected, but he couldn't see how or why.

Chapter Seventeen

Mrs Underwood looked speculatively at the two bottles of milk in the porch as she waited for Miss Pemberton to answer the door. She thought one of the bottles must be from the day before as it was separating, yet her neighbour's downstairs curtains were still drawn and it was after ten in the morning.

Una Underwood was the seventy-year-old, stick-thin, wizened widow who lived next door to Violet Pemberton. They had a friendly but not close relationship. The social worker often went out early in the morning and returned late at night, so sometimes they didn't see each other for days on end. But Violet always asked Una to feed her cat if she was going to be away overnight.

Una was puzzled. She had called round as the big tabby had been mewing hungrily around her door earlier. Then she'd noticed Violet's car was still in its usual parking place just up the road. Walking round the back of the cottage, Una tried the back door. It was locked. The living-room curtains at the back were drawn, so she couldn't see in. She thought that was very odd too. Violet never drew them in the summer, she always said she liked to watch the sun go down. Even if she had gone off early in the morning by train and forgotten the cat and the milk, somehow she couldn't imagine her tidy-minded neighbour not pulling back the curtains before she left. Una decided she must get another neighbour with a telephone to ring the welfare office in Bridgwater to find out if Violet was away on business.

An hour later PC Hargreaves, the local policeman, rode up the lane on his bike as Una was polishing her brass door knocker.

'Morning, Mrs Underwood,' he called out cheerfully. Resting his bike against her hedge, he took off his helmet and wiped his brow. 'Whew! It's hot today. I hear you're a bit worried about your neighbour.'

'I'm probably being a terrible fusspot,' Una said anxiously. She didn't like people to think she spent all her time watching her neighbour's comings and goings. She explained about the car, the milk, the drawn curtains and the cat. 'I got another neighbour to telephone her work, but they haven't seen or heard from her either for two days. She does get called away on cases sometimes, but it's not like her to forget to ask me to feed her cat, or to phone in to her office. I'm afraid she might be in there, too ill to answer the door.'

'Well, let's put your mind at rest,' he said soothingly, patting the old lady's thin shoulder. 'Would you like to come round there with me? I might have to break a window to get in.'

Una looked even more worried then. 'I hope she won't be cross with me,' she said. 'I wouldn't want anyone breaking my windows.'

'I'm sure she'll be pleased that you cared enough to watch out for her,' he said. 'And if she is ill, she'll be very grateful.'

They walked round to the back of Violet's together.

'Well, that's a bit of luck,' the policeman said with a smile as he saw there was a small window open by the back door. 'I'm always telling people to shut their windows when they go out, but all the same it's handy to find an open one in an emergency.'

He put his arm in and turned the key in the back door. Una went to follow him in. 'No, you stay there, Mrs Underwood,' he said. 'I'll just take a look round on my own first.'

Una knew by his gasp a couple of seconds later that he'd found something wrong, and despite what he'd said she darted in.

She wished she hadn't.

It didn't look like Violet at all. It was more like seeing a sack of bloody offal lying on the floor. There were flies all over her and a horrible, sickly sweet smell. The room was strewn with papers. It was the most terrible thing she'd ever seen and her legs just gave way under her.

It was the early evening of the same day, and Rosie, Donald, Thomas and Frank Cook were all sitting out on the terrace just outside the kitchen, drinking tea. Norah was inside, joining in the conversation through the open windows and doors as she prepared the evening meal. They were all laughing as Donald told them about getting Thomas home today. Thomas, it seemed, had got carried away in his enthusiasm to help out with the gardening, and by the end of the afternoon his leg was hurting badly. Donald had forced him into the wheelbarrow and trundled him home in it. Apparently they had been seen by quite a few neighbours and Thomas had made it even funnier by giving regal waves as he passed them.

When they heard the six o'clock pips on the wireless, Frank called out to Norah to turn it up so they could listen to the news. Donald immediately got up and went off down the garden. Rosie stood up tentatively. Her knees were stiff and sore, but she thought a little walk might help them.

'A middle-aged woman was found brutally murdered today in her cottage in the village of Chilton Trinity in Somerset.'

Rosie stopped short at hearing the name of a village she knew.

'The victim has been identified as Miss Violet Pemberton, a social worker. It is believed she was killed when she interrupted a burglary in her home. The Somerset police are conducting a house-to-house search as the killer is thought to be a local man.'

'Violet!' Thomas gasped, rising out of his seat. 'Did I hear right? They did say Violet Pemberton?'

Frank nodded and Rosie sat down again with a bump, too astonished and horrified to speak.

Norah stuck her head through the window. 'Did you hear that?' she asked. 'Poor woman!' On seeing Thomas and Rosie's stricken faces, she quickly withdrew from the window and came out on to the terrace, drying her hands on a tea towel. 'You don't know her, do you?'

Thomas nodded. He didn't trust himself to speak. He wanted to reach out for Rosie to comfort her, but he was unable to move a muscle.

Norah just stood looking at them both for a moment, and suddenly she remembered who they both knew who lived in Somerset. 'It's not your friend, is it? The lady we met at Carrington Hall?'

Thomas managed to pull himself together enough to confirm it was.

Frank was slower to catch on about who and what they were referring to. 'What a ghastly thing! And to hear it just like that on the wireless!' he said in a voice which seemed to boom right round the garden. 'I thought they didn't announce a victim's name until all relatives had been informed?' he added in some indignation.

'She didn't have any relatives,' Thomas said in a small croaky voice.

Frank and Norah were both speaking at once, but Rosie felt as if all her blood was draining away. She couldn't move, speak or even hear what was being said. All she could feel was an intense anger welling up inside her that someone, some louse of a thief, had taken the life of a woman who was so precious to her. She gripped the arms of her chair and the anger she felt rose up and spewed out in a bellow of outrage.

'Rosie!' Norah gasped, shocked still more by this

primitive outburst than she was by the news. 'Rosie, what is it?'

Thomas was out of his chair and over to Rosie in a flash. He caught hold of her firmly and shook her gently to stop the screaming. 'She's in shock. Violet meant a great deal to her,' he said, enfolding the girl in his arms. 'Could you get her some brandy?'

Later that evening when Rosie had calmed down enough to reason again, she wondered how she would have coped without Thomas. He had taken her into the sitting-room, away from the others, and held her in his arms. He let her cry and shared her grief because he fully understood the significance Violet had held in her life. The woman not only knew the full horror of all that had happened at May Cottage, but had helped Rosie put aside her shame and rebuild her life. Thomas knew Violet had never seen Rosie as just one of her 'cases', but had been aunt, friend and adviser. Had she lived, Thomas had no doubt this often brusque but caring woman would have been at Rosie's wedding, godmother to her children. It was a terrible, wicked loss.

Thomas cried along with Rosie. He too had a great deal of affection for Violet. Along with organizing his nephew's happy new life, supporting and advising him throughout the subsequent adoption, she had also become a friend.

Rosie knew the Cooks couldn't be expected to comprehend her enormous sense of loss. All they really knew about Miss Pemberton was her active role in getting Matron thrown out of Carrington Hall. Even though they were aware Rosie had continued to correspond with her over the last two years, the Cooks had never had any reason to suppose that these were anything more than duty letters, occasional progress reports because the woman was interested in her.

She wished she could tell them the whole story now, if only so they could understand.

'Should I tell them everything?' she asked Thomas.

'I don't know,' he said truthfully, his brown eyes soft with concern for her. 'I did think when you first came here that it would be better for you to make a clean breast of it all and be done with it, but so much time has elapsed now and they care so deeply for you. But to be suddenly faced with such news might put a strain on your relationship with them. And what good would it do telling them now, Rosie? It might help them to understand your grief about Violet, but that's all.'

She shamefacedly admitted then that she'd never told Gareth either.

Thomas sighed deeply and hugged her tightly. 'Oh Rosie! How could you possibly plan to marry a man without telling him something so important? I always assumed you'd told him right at the start.'

'There never was a right moment,' she said in a small voice, her eyes downcast.

When Rosie went into Donald's room later to say goodnight to him, he was sitting up in bed as always reading a comic, but instead of giving her his usual welcoming smile he looked at her reproachfully.

'Why have you been crying and talking to Thomas all evening?'

Rosie wasn't sure how to answer. He was adult in many respects, but there were large areas in which he was still a child and as such they all avoided discussing distressing things in his hearing. 'Because the lady who we heard about on the news was an old friend of mine, and of Thomas's. I couldn't talk to you in the same way about her because you didn't know her,' she said eventually.

'But you shut me out,' he said, and his lip quivered.

'I didn't want you to see me upset,' she said, sitting down beside him and taking his hand in hers. 'That's the only reason.'

'But I looked after you when you hurt your knees,' he

said. 'I can look after you whatever happens to you.'

Rosie's eyes prickled at his staunch retort. He might see the world and problems from a child's simplified viewpoint, but his loyalty and affection were truly adult.

She doubted somehow that Gareth would take such a liberal stance.

Three days later on Monday morning Donald and Rosie were in the greenhouse thinning out some wallflower seedlings. Thomas had gone back to London on the train the night before, and as Rosie's knees were healing well she felt it was time to get back to a little work.

The newspapers had been full of Miss Pemberton's murder over the weekend. The police hadn't arrested anyone yet, but it was thought that the murderer was someone she knew. As her social work brought her into contact with so many people from all walks of life, sifting through them would take some time.

Rosie had been very sad to see Thomas leave. He'd comforted her, helped her through the shock, and pitched in to help Donald with the gardening while she was unable to get around. But she was feeling a little less fraught today. She hoped that by the time she saw Gareth at the weekend she would be more like her old self.

He had been very sympathetic about Miss Pemberton when she spoke to him on the phone, but quite callous about her bad fall. He'd said climbing ladders was men's work and it served her right.

Rosie was sitting on a tall stool, and as her mind turned to the now-cancelled trip to Eastbourne on Saturday, she glanced down at her bandaged knees and sighed. They didn't hurt that much now, it was a dull ache mostly, but she couldn't walk far and they looked hideous under the bandages. Gareth would undoubtedly use them as more ammunition as to why she should give up gardening.

'That sounds like Dad's car,' Donald said, interrupting her thoughts.

Rosie listened. It did sound like the Jaguar coming into the drive, but the greenhouse was in the far corner of the back garden and their view of the drive at the side of the house was obscured by bushes.

'He wasn't supposed to be coming home for lunch today,' Rosie remarked. 'Besides, it's only twelve o'clock.'

Donald downed tools and rushed out to see. Rosie smiled as she watched him run across the garden. In the past she had likened him to an excitable puppy; now he was growing into a nosy dog who always had to know exactly where everyone was and what they were doing.

He disappeared round the side of the house. Rosie heard him call out to his father, but she continued with the pricking out. It was some minutes later that Donald appeared again, through the kitchen door. He was eating a freshly baked cake and had a shopping bag over his arm.

'Mum wants me to go to the baker's,' he bawled out from the lawn. 'She wants you to come in for a moment.'

'Okay,' Rosie called back. She wiped her hands on a piece of rag and hobbled up the garden to the house. Although the kitchen smelled deliciously of cake, and the metal cooling tray was piled high with rock buns, the moment Rosie stepped into the room she knew something serious had happened. Norah was sitting at the table, her husband standing beside her with his hand on her shoulder, and they both looked anxious. Rosie surmised they must have something to say to her that they didn't want Donald to hear and that's why they'd sent him on an errand.

'What's happened?' Rosie asked, before she even went to the sink to wash her hands. 'Is it something to do with Donald?'

Frank's face was usually ruddy, but now it was quite pale. He sat down heavily next to his wife and they looked at one another as if trying to decide which of them should tell her.

'It's nothing to do with Donald. There's been another murder,' Frank blurted out.

Rosie forgot her dirty hands. 'What? In the same village?'

Frank made an odd sort of growl in his throat. 'No, in London.' He stopped and wiped his hand across his forehead. She'd never seen him look so fraught before. 'You'd better sit down,' he added. 'This is going to knock you for six too.'

'It's Freda Barnes, Rosie,' Norah said in a weak voice. 'Frank read it in the paper at work. That's why he came home.'

'Matron!' Rosie's mouth dropped open in shock. 'Are you sure?'

'Explain, Frank,' Norah pleaded, and began to cry. 'I can't tell her.'

Rosie listened as Frank hurriedly recounted how he'd opened the daily paper and read a report that a second middle-aged woman had been found murdered, this time in a basement flat in Camden Town. Her body had been lying there for several days before it was discovered. When he read her name and realized it was the ex-matron of Carrington Hall, he was so alarmed he had to come home.

He took the folded newspaper from his pocket and put it on the table. 'You can read it for yourself, Rosie. They have pointed out similarities in the two brutal murders, both middle-aged spinsters living alone, killed within eight or nine hours of one another, both ex-nurses, and in both cases there was no sign of forcible entry to their homes. What really worries me about these reports, though, is that the police appear unaware that the women were known to one another too. Unless we tell them about the real connection between them, they might go off on the wrong track.'

'Connection?' Rosie repeated.

'Carrington Hall,' he said. 'It could well be that dreadful chap Saunders.'

'Surely not!' Rosie gasped.

'It could be,' Frank said with a knowing nod. 'We already know he's a brute, and he may well have held a grudge against both Barnes and Miss Pemberton after he lost his job.'

Rosie felt queasy as she quickly read the newspaper report. Barnes's landlord called several times between Friday and Sunday for his rent, but she wasn't there, which was very unusual. Finally, thinking she may have left without telling him, he used a spare key and went in. He found her body in the kitchen. She had been struck on the back of the neck with a heavy object.

Although Rosie had no reason to mourn Barnes, it was still shocking to hear she had died in such a way, and it brought back a renewed sense of grief at Miss Pemberton's death. She began to cry.

Frank came round the table and put his hand on her shoulder. 'Brace-Coombes will almost certainly speak to the police the moment he hears the news. But you knew both women very well, Rosie, and quite a lot about Saunders, so you might be able to help them far more than he could. I think we should ring the police station now and ask someone to come over.'

Rosie's heart began to flutter and her stomach turned over.

Police weren't like ordinary people. You couldn't tell them you knew two murder victims and leave it at that. They would want to know how and why she came to know Miss Pemberton. Before long she would be forced to reveal her real identity.

'Well, what do you think, Rosie?' Frank asked. He thought she looked a bit vacant. That wasn't like her at all.

Rosie was thinking hard.

Mr Cook might be right about Saunders bearing a grudge against both women, especially if he'd ended up in prison for what he'd done at Carrington Hall. Yet Freda

502

Barnes didn't get him into trouble, and neither did Miss Pemberton. It was *her* who'd spilled the beans about him. Mr Cook's word 'connection' came back into her mind. Suppose *she* was the connection between the two women?

The room seemed to swirl around her. What if Saunders went to both women's houses trying to find her? Then for some reason he'd killed them.

'Rosie, are you all right?' Norah asked. 'You've gone as white as a sheet! You poor thing, let me make you a cup of tea.'

'I'm all right, thank you.' Rosie heard her automatic polite response, yet she felt remote, as if she wasn't even in the same room as the Cooks. Another idea was pushing its way into her head, a wild, sickening one she didn't even want to consider. There was someone else out there who might want to find her.

Seth.

A vivid picture came into her mind. It was of the last time she'd seen her brother, that afternoon when he'd attacked her in May Cottage. He'd been crazy with hate for her that day, and for all she knew that hatred might have been raging inside him ever since.

All at once Rosie knew she must tell the Cooks everything. She could be wrong about Seth. She fervently hoped she was. But she couldn't keep such a dark, terrible suspicion to herself just in case she was right.

She looked at Norah, then back at Frank. They both had such deeply concerned expressions on their faces. Their affection for her was so strong she could almost touch it, and she felt an acute pang of shame that she had selfishly allowed them to draw her into their family, taken all they had given her, yet cheated them by withholding the truth about herself.

'There's something I've got to tell you, before you call the police,' she said haltingly, her mouth drying up with fear. 'Because it will all come out when they speak to me. I should have told you a long time ago, but I was afraid.

503

My real name is Parker, not Smith. My father was Cole Parker. He was hanged in 1952 for murdering two women.'

Norah gasped and stiffened.

'Go on,' Frank said in a stern voice, and moved closer to his wife.

Rosie couldn't meet their shocked eyes as she told the full story. It was like stripping a scab off a painful old wound and reliving the agony of injury all over again. She was swamped with a feeling of total worthlessness.

'I shouldn't have allowed you to bring me into your house,' she finally said in a voice that was only just above a whisper. 'I'm so ashamed and so sorry.'

There was utter silence in the kitchen. Rosie waited, her eyes downcast in readiness for a storm to break over her head.

'Rosie, look at me!' Frank said at length.

She slowly lifted her head to see that Frank had his arm comfortingly around Norah. She was crying against his shoulder.

'What do you expect us to do now?' he asked. He had a tear trickling down his cheek, and she had never seen such a bleak look in anyone's eyes before.

'Tell me to leave,' she whispered. 'I'll speak to the police, then pack my bags and go. I know you won't want me near Donald.'

'Won't want you near Donald?' he snorted, letting go of his wife and standing up.

Rosie cringed. She thought he was going to strike her. She put her arms up around her head to ward off the expected blow.

'Don't cringe from me, girl,' he roared at her. 'I've never hit a woman in my life, and I certainly wouldn't hit you.'

Rosie lowered her arms. Frank caught hold of them, shook her a little and brought his face close to hers. 'Have you so little faith in us that you think we'd turn you out because of your father?'

She couldn't speak. Tears ran down her face.

'Don't you know what you've done for us?' Frank asked with a break in his voice. 'You've given our son a life. Everything Donald can do now is because of you. It's true we might have been able to accomplish some of it ourselves given enough time and patience. But somehow I think our patience would have run out pretty quickly. Now do you really think we would turn our backs on you after that?'

Rosie didn't know what to say.

Norah came over and nudged her husband away from Rosie. Without saying a word she pulled her into her arms and hugged her tightly, rocking her against her shoulder as if Rosie was a small child.

Norah could remember reading about Cole Parker's trial. If she was entirely honest, had she known his daughter was working at Carrington Hall she would have been outraged. But as Frank had pointed out so very clearly, Rosie had earned their affection and respect. She deserved their protection now.

Frank cleared his throat. He wasn't by nature an emotional man, nor one who found it easy to speak about his feelings. But as he looked across at his wife embracing this young slip of a girl who had never had the kind of happy childhood his children had known, his heart went out to her.

'We both love you, Rosie. Love you, just as you are, with whatever baggage has come with you,' he said gruffly. 'You aren't responsible for your father's deeds. You are your own person, a warm, loving human being. If we have anything at all to say about this, it's only to ask why you couldn't have taken us into your confidence before.'

'I was afraid to,' she whimpered against Norah's shoulder.

'Well, you'll never need to be afraid again,' Norah said, and letting go of Rosie she mopped the girl's cheeks with

505

a handkerchief. 'I kind of guessed your father was a brute. I'm just sorry I didn't press you harder about him.'

As she moved away to put the kettle on, Rosie knew she must voice her suspicions about her brother. 'I really hope I'm wrong,' she said bleakly as she came to the end, 'but suppose Seth did go to them to try and find me? He always had a terrible temper, with no respect for women.'

Frank looked at Norah's horrified face, then back to Rosie's stricken one. He barely remembered the Parkers' trial. Every day the newspapers had been full of sensational stories and neither he nor his wife was the kind to revel in ghoulish news. All he really recalled of the case was that the father was hanged and the son acquitted, and he had great faith in the British legal system. 'I can't see any logical reason why your brother should go to such lengths. Saunders is a far more likely candidate,' he said evenly. 'What could Seth want from you that's important enough to kill for?'

'I don't know,' Rosie said. 'But logic wasn't a word he ever understood, and I've just got this nasty feeling about it.'

Talking to the police wasn't anywhere near as terrible as Rosie had expected. Frank knew both the officers who called and he stayed with her for support throughout the interview, speaking for her when she broke down. The two policemen were clearly astounded to hear she was Cole Parker's daughter and even more surprised when she put forward her brother's name as a suspect. But though they said they would check him out, they appeared far more interested in hearing about Saunders. Like Frank Cook, they were of the opinion he had nursed a grudge against the two women since he was thrown out of Carrington Hall.

After the police had gone Frank took Donald out in his car. Donald had been very curious about them calling and his father wanted to distract him, at the same time giving his wife and Rosie time to talk alone.

'Rosie, I really think you must tell Gareth all you told us if he phones you this evening,' Norah said as they prepared the vegetables for the evening meal. She looked agitated, chopping up carrots as if taking out her anxiety on them. 'Your name just might be leaked to the papers now that the police will be looking for your brother. It would be so very cruel for him to find it out that way.'

'I can't tell him something like that on the phone!' Rosie exclaimed. Gareth always used a telephone box and she could just imagine people tapping on the glass asking him to hurry up as she was telling him her life story.

'I didn't actually mean over the phone, rather that you insist he comes down here immediately, or say you are going up there. I'm sure Thomas would put you up for the night if necessary. By the way, does he know anything about this?'

'Yes, all of it,' Rosie said, and explained that he was Heather's brother, and how he'd befriended her after Cole was arrested.

Norah abandoned the vegetables, listening with wide, incredulous eyes, but as Rosie finally told her about Alan's adoption, she began to cry. 'What a good, generous-hearted man he is,' she wept. 'I had always felt there was something more between you two, and that evening when we heard the news about Miss Pemberton I had a feeling you were sharing a secret. But I'd never have guessed at anything like this.'

Thomas rang after hearing of Barnes's murder on the six o'clock news. He too was shaken, and like Frank he immediately suspected Saunders. Rosie poured out everything to him: how she'd had to tell the Cooks, the talk with the police and her suspicions about Seth.

'I'm so glad you've made a clean breast of everything,' he said, and admitted that after he'd returned to London he'd felt he ought to have encouraged her to tell the Cooks while he was still there. He didn't pooh-pooh her thoughts about Seth entirely. 'It strikes me as unlikely,' he said. 'But I did form the opinion watching him in court that he was a dangerous man without any scruples. You did right to put his name forward.'

Thomas agreed she must tell Gareth quickly before he heard it from another source. 'Scotland Yard don't pussy-foot about where murder's concerned,' he said sharply. 'By now they will have issued an all-points alert to bring both Saunders and Seth in for questioning. You can bet your life that by tomorrow both their pictures will be on every front page, and that's bound to mean your father's case will get hashed over again. I wish I could promise you that the police will shield you, Rosie, but I'm afraid I can't.'

Rosie began to cry. She could go to London now, but Gareth would almost certainly have gone out with his mates long before she got there. Tomorrow might be too late.

'Suppose I went over to his digs and told him?' Thomas suggested because she was so worried. 'If I left now, I could catch him when he comes in from work. As a third party who knows all sides to this I could probably present a better case for why you've kept this from him than you could yourself.'

Rosie saw this as a sound idea, if a little cowardly on her part. But even if she did leave this minute and managed to catch Gareth in, he wasn't the most sensitive or under-standing of men, and was quite likely to bawl her out without listening properly. Thomas was good with people and Gareth would be forced to hear him out.

'Do you think you can bear to?' she asked. She knew it was still a painful subject for him too.

'Rosie, I can bear anything for you,' he said with a smile in his voice. 'Just give me his address.'

At half past seven that same evening Gareth answered the knock on his door and grinned broadly to find Thomas standing there. 'What a surprise, mate!' he said. 'What brings you round here?'

Thomas noted immediately that Gareth was ready to go out. He was wearing smart navy blue slacks and a crisp white shirt and he smelled of soap.

'Sorry to come uninvited, but there's something we must talk about,' Thomas said. 'It's about Rosie and it's very important.'

Gareth looked at his watch. 'I'm meeting the lads in half an hour,' he said. 'Is it going to take long?'

Thomas's hackles rose. He'd already said it was important. 'It might,' he said, and edged himself into the small room before Gareth found another excuse.

Jealousy was an emotion that Thomas both despised and refused to succumb to, and in all the time he had known Gareth he had tried to be scrupulously honest with himself about whether it was jealousy which prevented him from taking to the lad. Yet right from the start Thomas had found Gareth to be shallow and limited in his conversation.

In the last eighteen months, however, he had become very pompous and opinionated. Thomas could see it now in his face: he'd put on weight, he had a permanent sneer, and his eyes were cold and suspicious. He just couldn't like him, not even for Rosie's sake.

'Have you seen the news about Freda Barnes being murdered?' he asked.

'Who?' Gareth asked, looking baffled.

'The woman they've just found dead in Camden Town.'

'Oh yeah,' Gareth nodded and grinned. 'What's that to you?'

'She was the matron at Carrington Hall,' Thomas explained.

'Bloody hell!' Gareth's eyes opened wider with interest. 'That's a bit of a coincidence, two people getting killed that Rosie knows.'

'I think it's more than coincidence.' Thomas sat down

on the bed. He didn't think Gareth was ever going to offer him a seat. 'There's a possibility that the killer could be after Rosie.'

Thomas knew it was callous of him to launch into the story with such a dramatic and possibly untrue statement, but he felt he had to grab the lad's attention.

It worked. Gareth sat down on the chair with a thump. 'But why?'

Thomas warned Gareth that what he was going to tell him was likely to upset him and asked only that he should hear him out until he'd finished.

Gareth didn't interrupt, but as the story progressed his eyes narrowed and his colour heightened; even his neck turned red. 'Why didn't she tell me herself?' he burst out angrily as Thomas finished. 'If this hadn't cropped up, would she have married me without telling me?'

Thomas thought Gareth's priorities were misplaced. He would have expected his first reaction to be for Rosie's safety. 'I don't think so. She was waiting for the right moment,' he said gently.

'The right time was when she first met me.'

'Come on!' Thomas exclaimed. 'Could any girl say, "Yes, I'd love to go out with you, but I must just tell you first my father's a murderer." Be reasonable, Gareth. And it got progressively harder for her to tell you as time went on.'

Gareth was clearly incapable of reason as he launched into a volley of accusatory remarks about how his family would feel, his workmates and even his employers.

Thomas cut him short. 'I thought you loved Rosie?'

'I do,' Gareth glowered.

'Well, how about showing some concern for what she's been through?' Thomas said. 'She never had a real childhood. From the age of twelve she kept house for her father and brothers, and she was mother to my little nephew. She had no life of her own, no friends or fun. Then suddenly, without any warning, she finds her father is a murderer.

From then on, through no fault of her own, she is an outcast. No home, no rights, no one at all aside from Violet Pemberton cares a jot about her. I know how it was for her back then, until she went to work for the Cooks, and I can tell you, Gareth, the life she had would give you and me nightmares.

'But she didn't sit about feeling sorry for herself, she used the talents she had to make something of herself. And look what she's done with them! The Cooks would have been content if she'd just kept Donald out of mischief, but she's taught him to read, to do sums, given him some self-respect, and freed his parents from anxiety about him. She's started the gardening business and made a huge success of that. Is it any wonder that she's won the respect and admiration of the entire village? Aside from all that, she's one of the kindest, pluckiest girls I've ever met. You are a lucky man, Gareth, to have such a girl.'

'It's easy for you to stick up for her, you knew the truth about her all along,' Gareth said stubbornly.

'So it's easier for me to see good in a girl whose father murdered my sister in cold blood, than for you who fell in love with her, is it?' Thomas spat at him. 'I'll tell you why I stick up for her: it's because she's a very special person. Whoever named her Rosie named her well. She's risen out of that pile of manure she was born into and become something beautiful. If you can't see that, then there's something badly wrong with you.'

Now that Thomas had worked himself up he couldn't stop. He told Gareth how Rosie had got Alan away from May Cottage, and then went into graphic details of the beating Seth gave her. He described the full horror of what Rosie had witnessed at Carrington Hall and got a certain pleasure from seeing the younger man's face blanch.

'She didn't tell you these things either,' he went on. 'Maybe she'd have aroused your sympathy if she had. But trying to wring sympathy out of people isn't Rosie's way. You think you're such a big tough man, Gareth, but you're just a worm really. You're afraid of the most harmless thing in life – other people's opinions. If you want to know what true courage is, ask Rosie. She's an expert on it.'

Thomas got up then. He knew he'd gone too far and if he stayed any longer he might just throw a punch or two.

'I'm going now. All I ask is that you carefully think over what I've told you and weigh up for yourself whether or not you can accept Rosie's background. If you find you can't, be a man and tell her so.'

As Thomas walked back down the dingy street to the station, tears rolled down his cheeks. He was ashamed of himself for being so hard on Gareth. He should have been more kindly, more persuasive. Had he been cruel just because he was in love with Rosie himself?

Thomas had often tried to chart the moment when his affection and admiration for Rosie had turned to real adult love. There was no doubt in his mind that the seeds were sown when he saw her courage at Carrington Hall, but it wasn't until he felt compelled to begin sketching again that he sensed her real importance in his life.

Those first few sketches were all of Rosie. Yet as he drew her, so he drew on her strength too, and soon he was looking around him, suddenly hungry for new inspiration and challenges. He'd bought an easel, oils and canvases, and painted furiously until the early hours of the morning. Scenes from his childhood, Singapore and Burma, and for each completed one he knew he had Rosie to thank for showing him the key to unlock all those memories, good and bad, and giving him much longed-for inner peace.

Perhaps it was inevitable that he should fall in love with the person who had brought back his old spirit. He'd learned to laugh again, to enjoy company, to look forward instead of backwards with bitterness. He wondered sometimes where such love would lead him. He was fifteen years older than her, he had a peg leg and thinning hair.

He had as much chance of making her love him as having his old leg grafted back on. But as long as he could be just a small part of her life, it was enough.

The following evening at nine, the telephone rang at The Grange and Rosie rushed from the sitting-room, where she was watching television with the family, into the hall to answer it. To her disappointment it was for Frank, and she went back to tell him.

After he had gone out of the room Norah patted the seat beside her for Rosie to sit down. 'I'm sure Gareth will phone,' she said. 'He's probably just sorting out his thoughts before he speaks to you.'

'I think he's already done that,' Rosie said, and a tear trickled down her cheek. 'If he cared for me at all he would have rung me the minute Thomas left him. I bet he went over to see his precious mother and asked her opinion.'

Mrs Cook thought this was probably very true. But she couldn't bring herself to say so. 'If he is influenced more by others than by his heart, then maybe he isn't the one for you, Rosie. But give him time, he may just be in shock.'

Donald had been quietly sitting in a chair throughout this, but when he saw Rosie's tears he got up and came to kneel in front of her. 'I'll look after you,' he said. 'You don't need Gareth.'

Rosie began to cry harder. Donald didn't really understand what was happening. His mother had tried to explain, as you would to a child, that Rosie's father had done something very bad a long time ago and Gareth was cross with her because she hadn't told him. But that wasn't really enough to satisfy him. They had all avoided speaking of the two murders in his presence, but he had heard a few snippets here and there and was intensely curious.

'You mustn't cry,' he said, putting one hand on her cheek and wiping away the tears. 'It doesn't matter if Gareth isn't here with you. If that bad man comes here, I won't let him hurt you.'

Until now all Rosie's anxieties had been centred on Gareth and everyone else she knew, wondering how they would react on discovering who her father was. Yet deep down, almost in her subconscious, she had sensed she was in danger, and that was why she needed Gareth so desperately. She hadn't voiced that to anyone, she had squashed it each time it tried to rear its ugly head.

It was odd that Donald, who couldn't possibly comprehend the complexities of past and recent events, had put his finger right on the crux of the matter.

The next morning Rosie picked up the newspaper from the doormat and saw pictures of Seth and Saunders on the front page. The headline was HAVE YOU SEEN EITHER OF THESE MEN? She took it straight into the kitchen and handed it to Frank, who was eating his breakfast. 'I can't bring myself to read it,' she said in a small voice. 'Will you tell me the gist of it?'

He half smiled and patted her arm. 'Sit down and have a cup of tea,' he said.

Norah was in her dressing-gown, frying bacon at the stove. She had dark circles around her eyes as if she'd had a sleepless night. Donald was still upstairs. 'Tell her quickly before Donald comes down,' she said, looking anxiously at her husband.

Rosie poured herself a cup of tea and topped up Frank's too. She waited while he read the front page.

'There's nothing much new,' he said, folding it back so the front page wouldn't show. 'Just a rehash really of everything they've already said and that the police want to question the two men. A paragraph about Saunders; it seems he has a record of violence. There's a bit about your father too. But there isn't any mention of you.'

Frank was glad Rosie hadn't read it herself. It was a hysterical piece of journalism guaranteed to make half the population run to bolt their doors against the killer on the loose. Yet it made him wonder whether his own house was secure enough, and if indeed he dared go off to his office until one or both of these men were found. But that was foolish. For one thing, there was no positive proof either of the men had murdered the two women. And if one of them had, would they be stupid enough to come here, knowing the police were looking for them?

The post arrived just as Donald came downstairs and he brought it into the kitchen with him and handed it to his mother. She sifted through the letters.

'There's one for you,' she said looking across at Rosie. 'I think it's from Gareth.'

Rosie opened it eagerly, but her smile faded at the first line.

Dear Rosie,

I'm sorry but I'll have to pack you in. It isn't just because of your dad. I know you can't help that, but you haven't been exactly straight with me about a lot of things, like the nursing and coming up to London. You seem to care more about Donald and your gardening than you do about me too. I think we'll both be happier apart.

Best wishes,
Gareth

Rosie read the short, cold letter twice. She couldn't believe that after telling her he loved her for over two years he could just abandon her now when she needed him most. He wasn't even man enough to admit he was shaken by discovering who her father was; he had to blame his change of heart on her caring more for Donald and gardening.

Norah came over to where Rosie sat and put a hand on her shoulder. She had watched the girl reading the letter and guessed its contents by the shocked look on her face. Rosie turned towards her employer, burying her face in her chest for a moment, but steeled herself not to cry.

515

'I'm so sorry, Rosie,' Norah said. She took no satisfaction from finding that her intuition about Gareth had been correct. She had a feeling Rosie was going to find it harder to deal with this than with any of the other tragedies in her life.

'I feel so responsible,' Thomas said to Norah on the telephone one evening a few days later. 'I was too blunt with the lad. I shouldn't have walked out when I did, but stayed until I'd talked him round.'

Norah had telephoned Thomas because she was very worried about Rosie. Since the letter had arrived from Gareth she'd been like a robot, doing everything she normally did, but slowly, silent and expressionless. She hadn't cried or talked about it. She'd gone out with Donald to work, come back at the usual times, eaten meals with them and each night watered the garden, then joined them in the sitting-room to watch television as usual. Yet Norah knew the girl was desperately unhappy and hiding it away wasn't going to help her at all.

Saunders, rather surprisingly, had walked into a police station in Manchester on the day his picture was in the paper. It seemed he was working as a night porter in a hotel and he had a cast-iron alibi for the times both women were killed, as he was on duty from nine o'clock in the evening until nine the following morning. Rosie had only shrugged her shoulders when she was told this. Even the news that he appeared to have escaped any criminal charges for what he'd done at Carrington Hall didn't seem to affect her.

Frank had tried to get a reaction from her about half an hour earlier by telling her that the police had found Seth's van somewhere on the moors in Somerset. Rosie had just looked at him blankly as if she didn't know what he was talking about. Frank hadn't been able to bring himself to tell her that in the van were items which had come from both Miss Pemberton's cottage and Freda Barnes's flat.

He didn't think it wise to confirm to her that her brother really was the murderer.

'If Gareth truly loved her, he wouldn't have needed talking round,' Norah said firmly. 'He'd have come straight down here on the next train to support her. She's well rid of him in my opinion, but that doesn't make it any easier to see her breaking up inside.'

'Shall I come down for a few days?' Thomas suggested. 'Maybe I can get her to talk. I've only got a few watch-mending jobs to do, and I could just as easily do those down there. Mr Bryant owes me several days off and it's our quietest time at the moment.'

Norah had been hoping this was what he'd say. 'That would be wonderful if you could manage it,' she said eagerly. 'Donald's been like a faithful dog, never leaving her side for a moment, but that might be making her worse.'

'I'll be down tomorrow afternoon,' Thomas said without any hesitation.

As Thomas was putting a few tools and a change of clothing into a small bag ready for the next day, Seth was lurking round the back of a Somerset pub, considering which of the five cars parked beside it would be easiest to steal. He was in Brean, where he and Norman used to come to as kids to swim in the sea and play in the sand. It couldn't be called a resort exactly, not like Weston-super-Mare a few miles away. It was just a few houses straggling along the flat coastal road. But there was a holiday camp and several caravan parks. In July and August it was a popular haunt for working-class families, who didn't seem to mind the lack of amenities and appreciated the long sandy beach.

It was a beautiful night, warm and still, the sky like black velvet sprinkled with sequins, but it gave Seth no pleasure to think he could comfortably spend the night on the sand dunes if necessary and sleep to the soothing

517

sound of waves on the beach. He wished he could go to the pub.

Shafts of golden light spilled out through the open windows along with the sounds of chatter, laughter and the clink of glasses. Pat Boone's 'I'll be Home Soon' was playing on the juke-box, and he could hear a couple of young girls giggling round by the front door as they chatted to some lads on bicycles. Seth yearned for company, wished more than anything that he could go and join all those holiday-makers with their sun-reddened faces, drink a couple of pints of cider, play darts and watch the girls. But he didn't dare. Someone was bound to recognize him.

It had been a mistake to come back to Somerset. He should have gone up north somewhere, straight after knocking off Miss Marks. But what with all that money he'd found, he couldn't drag himself away from London. He'd bought himself a flashy suit, stayed in a posh hotel, pulled a couple of girls and drunk himself stupid. Then all at once, before he'd even had time to get his head straight, they'd found the woman's body and to his shock and surprise his face was slapped across all the daily papers, along with some other geezer's.

Rosie had put him in the frame. He knew that with utter certainty, even if the papers made no mention of her. All the hatred he felt for her came back more strongly than ever. He would get even with her if it was the last thing he did.

But some sort of homing instinct made him come back here instead of going down to Sussex or fleeing up north. He'd had the idea he could hole up on the moors for weeks without being spotted while he made some plans. But it wasn't like the old days any more, there were holiday-makers everywhere, camping, walking, caravanning and bicycling. He'd left his van parked in a lane where he thought no one would ever notice it, gone off for a bit of a walk with his shotgun to look for some rabbits, and as he came back the police were crawling all over it. Luckily they didn't see him; he'd managed to duck down behind a hedge. But they left a copper guarding the van and so he'd had to leg it, leaving everything he owned inside. All he had now were the clothes he stood up in, his shotgun and the last hundred quid he'd got from Miss Marks. He smelled bad, he had thick stubble on his chin and he was desperate because he knew there was enough evidence in the van, including that claw hammer, to tie him to both murders.

He had to get away. There were police everywhere. He was sick of hiding in ditches and under hedges, and he was starving because he didn't even dare go into a shop for something to eat, or for some fags or a newspaper. If he could just get down to Sussex and find Rosie, he could force her to help him before silencing her for good. All he needed was a car.

The Standard Vanguard looked the best bet. It was new and he'd driven one of them before for Del. It was also furthest away from the pub, so perhaps no one would hear him start it up and he'd be long gone before they knew it had been stolen.

His luck was in. The car wasn't locked. He slid into the seat and the leather upholstery smelled good. It took only a couple of seconds to wire it up and he was away down the sea road towards Burnham. From there he would go cross-country to Sussex.

As Seth drove across Salisbury Plain much later that night, he was reminded of his National Service days. He'd been stationed at Warminster for some time and they'd often come out here on manoeuvres. Looking back, all his happiest times were in the army. Maybe he should have signed on as a regular.

The soft breeze coming through the window was soothing. All he could see was the road ahead in the beam of the headlights, and the odd rabbit and fox scuttling for safety as he approached. He wished it was dawn so he could watch the sun come up. Next to the Levels this was his favourite place, wide-open space, undulating hills, hardly a house in sight – a wildness that suited his character perfectly. If he could have his way, he'd like to live in a remote cottage somewhere out there in the darkness.

From force of habit he reached over the bench seat for his cigarettes. But as his hand touched the smooth leather, he was reminded he had none.

'Fuck you, Rosie!' he exclaimed. It was also force of habit to blame her for everything. Over the last few days he'd been spending a great deal of time thinking about her and considering the best way to punish her for screwing up his life.

It all started with her birth, now he came to think about it. Up until then it had been just Cole, Norman and him. Of course Ruby was there too, but she didn't interfere much with their life. She just cleaned and cooked and, in his own way, Seth quite liked her. She was soft and gentle like women were supposed to be.

'October it was, and pissing down,' Seth mused aloud. He was nine, Norman eight, and he remembered they came in from school to find that the stove had gone out and there was no tea on the table. Ruby called out from upstairs.

'Get me some help, boys,' she yelled. 'The baby's coming.'

They went upstairs to see her. She was lying in their dad's big bed holding on to the wooden rail on the bedhead. Her face was all blotchy and kind of puffy. Her nightdress had come open in the front and Seth remembered her swollen belly was very white and crisscrossed with little blue veins. One big breast showed and it made him feel sick.

'Seth, run up to the village and get me some help,' she said in a wheezy voice. With that she screwed up her face and started making a terrible noise down deep in her throat. Seth turned tail and ran.

Maybe if he hadn't noticed Tommy on the way to the village he would have gone for help, but Tommy had seen some big eels in one of the ditches about a mile away, and when he asked Seth to go with him to catch some he forgot all about Ruby.

It was pitch dark and nearly eight o'clock when Seth got home. He and Tommy had caught five eels and taken them round to Tommy's granfer's. His gran had given both boys some soup and dried off their wet clothes.

As he walked back into the kitchen, Cole lunged at him and caught hold of his ear. 'You little bastard,' he yelled, pulling him roughly around the room. 'Why didn't you get help for Ruby? She could have died if I hadn't come in when I did.'

Cole shoved him over a chair, pulled down his trousers and took a stick to his behind. But what really stuck in Seth's memory, more than the pain, was the sound of a baby crying upstairs. In the days that followed when he couldn't sit down because his backside was so sore, it was the baby he blamed. In the months afterwards he found even more reason to hate his new baby sister.

Cole doted on her. He boasted down the Crown that he instantly felt something for her because he delivered her himself, and he called her Rosie then and there because she had a mouth like a rosebud. It wouldn't have been so bad for Seth if his father had kept his crowing for other people, but he was always picking the baby up and making Seth and Norman admire her too.

According to Cole she was the prettiest, cleverest, sweetest-natured baby on earth. He would walk in the door from work and scoop her up out of her crib before he even spoke to the boys. On summer evenings he would stroll around the orchard with her in his arms. Once she could walk he took her off down the lane. Seth could still vividly recall seeing the big man almost bent double as he held her hand.

Nothing was the same after Rosie's arrival. She had

Ruby's entire attention, and Cole demanded that the boys help around the house on Saturdays instead of going out to play. In the past Cole had often played football with them in the evenings, but now he sat in the kitchen dangling Rosie on his knee. She got titbits from his plate and, as she got bigger, he bought her hair ribbons and picture books. Seth heard him telling her that he loved her.

Seth was convinced that the only reason Cole bribed someone on the draft board to find him unfit for active service was Rosie, too. One by one all the able-bodied men around Catcott went off to war, but Seth and Norman had to endure the jeers of the other boys who said their father was a coward. Later on during the war, public opinion changed towards Cole because he almost single-handedly supplied the village with rabbits, ducks and other food, but the shame of those first two war years was stamped permanently on Seth's mind.

There were many times when he was tempted to hurt Rosie badly, but he didn't dare. Cole was dangerous when he was angry, and he'd be more than angry if he found his precious little girl had been touched. The only way Seth could find to get at the kid was through her mother, and even though he had little bitterness towards Ruby, aside from bringing the kid into his home, he found dozens of ways to distress her. Cole might have idolized his daughter, but he wasn't as soft with Ruby. If his dinner wasn't put on the table as he walked through the door, if his best shirt wasn't ironed and aired when he needed it, or he thought she'd been squandering his money, then he was likely to slap her.

It was easy enough to distract Ruby while cooking the dinner; she wasn't the smartest woman alive. One favourite trick was to move the clock hands back, then quickly change them when he heard his father's truck. The best shirt could easily fall off the line into mud out in the orchard. He could take some money out of her housekeeping tin and go to the village shop and buy something frivolous and feminine, then leave it somewhere where his father would see it.

Each time Cole slapped Ruby, Seth hoped that she'd run off like his own mother had done. He didn't think she would leave Rosie behind. She cared too much for her.

But Ruby didn't leave. Seth caught her crying often enough. He heard her telling Cole one night that she thought Seth was playing tricks to get her into trouble, which started another row. Soon Cole was sullen towards her and she towards him, but still she stayed.

It was the summer of 1942, when Seth was fifteen, that Cole and Norman went away on an overnight job in Birmingham, leaving him to look after Ruby and Rosie, tidy up the yard and take over his father's fire-watching duties. Seth bitterly resented being left behind. The chances of Catcott being bombed were extremely remote; the most they ever saw of war were planes overhead and a few distant booms from Weston-super-Mare. He had wanted to see the bomb damage in Birmingham. He'd even hoped to be caught up in an air raid so he'd have something to boast about to his mates. As he toiled in the hot sun, humping timber and shifting piles of tyres, his resentment towards Ruby and Rosie grew even stronger.

After tea, Seth went up to his room to have a snooze before going out for the fire-watching. He knew Ruby was intending to have a bath as she'd lit the boiler in the outhouse earlier in the evening. He heard her fill it, then the squeals of laughter from Rosie as she went in first. Then Ruby brought Rosie upstairs and put her to bed.

As he lay there on his bed, thinking dirty thoughts and idly playing with himself, he heard Ruby go back downstairs and add more water to the bath. He waited for the creak and scrape on the stone flags which meant she had climbed in, then crept downstairs to watch her through a crack in the kitchen door.

He had never thought she was beautiful before. But she was that night. By day she always wore her hair up, and the shape of her body was always concealed under a loose dress and apron. He knew her to be twenty-seven and that seemed very old to him. But as he peeped through the crack in the door she was standing up in the bath soaping herself all over, her chestnut hair cascading down over her breasts.

She was all pink, white and curvy, with a small waist and plump little buttocks. As she soaped over her tits and down into that triangle of reddish hair, Seth's cock leapt up like a barber's pole.

She screamed as he came bursting through the door naked, and tried to grab a towel to cover herself. But Seth just leapt on her, tossing her down on to the stone floor of the kitchen, and thrust his hardness inside her.

That all-too-brief, wonderful moment was one he still liked to savour now. She was all wet and slippery. She smelled of soap and her fanny was so hot and tight, so much better than his own hand.

It was like living on a knife's edge when his father came home. Seth was terrified Ruby would blurt out what he had done, yet at the same time he was determined to have her again at all costs. He bought her silence with little threats towards Rosie. She was five now and followed him about like a little sheep. He had only to turn back towards Ruby as he took the kid out for a walk and mime cutting her throat in order to remind Ruby to keep her trap shut.

He didn't get to have her very often. Ruby was clever at making sure she was never alone with him in the house, but sometimes he found a way of coming home in the afternoons without Norman and his father, and then he would pounce. Ruby cried and pleaded with him at these times, again and again she insisted she was going to tell Cole. But Seth knew that each time he screwed her she was less likely to. She should have told Cole the first time.

But then one day in the autumn of 1943, just after Seth's sixteenth birthday, Cole announced he was going up to

Birmingham the next day to price a demolition job and he would take Norman with him. He said he would drop Seth off at the farm near Bridgwater to finish off mending a barn roof they'd been working on together, and if they put his bike on the back of the truck, he could ride it home later in the day.

Seth stayed on the job just long enough so the farmer knew he was there, then got on his bike and rode home. It was raining hard and Rosie was at school. He was convinced Ruby would be more amenable knowing Cole was far away, but he was wrong. As soon as he walked in the kitchen, she picked up the carving knife and threatened him.

'Don't even think of it,' she snarled at him, her blue eyes flashing as dangerously as the knife blade. 'I've had enough, Seth. You can threaten me all you like but you won't be able to hurt Rosie. I guessed you'd come back today and I've got someone to pick her up from school and keep her until Cole gets back. I'm going to tell him.'

'He won't believe you,' Seth retorted. He had an erection already just looking at her heaving chest and imagining those pink tits laid bare.

'He will. He already knows there's something wrong. He's been trying to get it out of me for weeks.'

Seth knew this much was true. Cole had asked both boys if they knew why she was so withdrawn.

'Put that knife down,' Seth ordered her. His stomach was churning; he wasn't sure if it was fear or desire. 'What's the harm, anyway? You aren't married to him.'

She gave a tight little laugh and instead of putting the knife down she took a menacing step towards him. 'I might not have married your father, but I love him,' she said. 'If it wasn't for you, Seth, we'd be the happiest couple in the world. It's you that causes all the problems. You were a strange kid right from the start, and as the years have gone by you've got stranger, crueller and nastier. I was sympathetic at first. I know when your mum ran off it was a terrible shock to you, and I tried to care for you and treat you like you were my son. But you're out of control now. You steal, cheat and lie, you're perverted and vicious. I want you out of this house for ever, before you taint Rosie.'

All at once Seth knew she really meant what she was saying. There was strength and determination in her face, her voice was calm and confident. He had badly misjudged her.

Seth had learned at an early age that sometimes when he was in trouble with teachers at school, or his father, it was necessary to back down, to feign remorse while he considered his next move. He did this now, slumping down on to a chair and covering his face with his hands.

'Please don't tell Dad,' he begged her. 'I'll go away, get a job somewhere and never come back and bother you. Just don't tell him.'

She didn't relent immediately. Still holding the knife threateningly, she launched into a long, bitter attack on him, listing all the unpleasant things he'd done in the past, all the acts of cruelty to Rosie, Norman and other kids in the village she'd found out about. She said she was going to write them all down, along with the times he'd stolen money from her housekeeping purse and his father's pockets, and complaints from neighbours. Finally she gave him his orders. He was to go up to his room, collect his clothes and be gone. She would make her list and if he ever came back she would give it to Cole immediately.

It didn't take more than a few minutes to pack his few belongings. He had nothing more than a change of clothes and one pair of Sunday shoes. When he came back down to the kitchen she had put away the knife and was standing by the sink, her arms folded across her chest.

'Try and make something of your life,' she said in a much gentler voice. 'For your father's sake. He might never tell you he loves you, but he does.'

During her earlier lecture, Seth's desire for her had

flown and been replaced by anger and a need for revenge. But as she spoke of his father loving him, rage swept through him. If it wasn't for Ruby coming here and changing everything, he and Norman would have their father all to themselves. He hated her.

Ruby turned away from him to reach up to the mantelpiece above the stove for her housekeeping tin. In that second Seth saw the small axe they used for chopping up kindling by the back door. He grabbed it.

'I can spare two pounds,' she said without turning back to him. 'I was trying to save it for Christmas, but you'll need –'

She didn't finish the sentence because Seth swung the blunt side of the axe hard across the back of her neck. She toppled sideways, her eyes wide with surprise, and an odd sort of growling noise came from deep inside her.

She may have been killed with that one blow, but Seth couldn't be sure of that, so he hit her again and again.

Digging a hole for her body was the hardest thing of all. He knew it had to be deep, otherwise foxes would get her out. He moved a pile of timber first; then, hidden behind it from the lane, he dug and dug. The first two feet of soil came out easily, but the deeper he went the more compacted it was. Only terror of his father coming back and catching him kept him going. Finally, at three in the afternoon, soaking wet with the rain, he finally carried Ruby out and laid her in the hole. Then he quickly shovelled the soil back on top of her, jumping up and down on it till it was flat enough to move the timber back to conceal the grave.

He was sweating when he returned to the cottage. He took his muddy clothes off in the porch, washed his hands, then ran upstairs with the clothes he'd packed earlier to put them back in his room and filled the same small bag with Ruby's things. When he came back down he wiped up her blood and the mud he'd brought into the kitchen when he'd collected her body. He dressed himself again in his wet, muddy clothes, shut the back door, hitched the bag with her belongings on to his back and made off on his bike to Bridgwater to finish the job there, stopping only to add a few stones to the bag and dropping it into the River Parrett.

Luck and the rain were on his side. He passed no one on the road, and back at the farm his absence hadn't been noticed. In fact at seven that evening when the farmer found Seth hard at work, he complimented him on continuing to work in such weather and asked if it wasn't time he made for home.

Seth pulled over to the side of the road. Remembering that first killing had given him the shakes. He'd never regretted it, Ruby had had it coming to her. In fact he was proud of being smart enough to commit the perfect murder.

Everything had gone his way. Ruby had told the neighbour she left Rosie with that day that she had to go and see a sick relative. When she didn't return everyone commiserated with Cole. They went along with his story that she must have been killed in an air raid. Secretly they thought she'd just run out on him, the same as Ethel Parker had done. So no one ever searched for her.

By day Cole had put on a brave face, and often he acted as if he didn't care that Ruby had left him. But Seth knew better. Sometimes when he heard his father crying at night he felt bad about what he had done. He even tried to make it up to him by working harder.

'If you'd only found a way of getting rid of Rosie, you wouldn't be up to your ears in shit now,' Seth said aloud.

Rosie was like a thorn in his side. Everything came back to her. Norman, Cole and him could have been fine in those days after Ruby was gone, if not for the brat. Cole worried about her being alone in the house after school, about her growing up wild with no one to teach her any manners. He didn't seem to remember that his two boys had been alone after their mother cleared off, and that he often stayed down the pub until closing time, leaving them alone in the house with nothing to eat. Rosie was his pet, his little princess, no other kid in the world was as special as her.

So he found Heather.

The night he and Norman came home and found her there, Seth was livid. It made no difference that she'd cleaned up the kitchen and that they had their first good meal in years. Heather was only a few months older than him. It was insulting that his father should bring a girl like her into their home and let her take over without consulting them. Ruby had been quiet and docile, but not Heather. She bawled out her instructions to them all, from Cole right down to Rosie, and before Seth could say 'sheep dip' they were all taking off their boots in the porch and washing their hands before meals, while Cole was totally taken by her.

Seth was glad to go off to do his National Service. He knew it was only a matter of time before the girl ended up in his father's bed. But what really irked him was that she won Norman round while he was away. When Seth came home on leave, he was made to feel the outsider, a trouble-making nuisance who spoiled the happy family. Norman painted the kitchen for her, Cole papered the bedrooms; as for Rosie, she stuck to Heather like glue, aping everything she said or did.

Seth saw the first chinks appearing before Alan was born. Heather was tired and cross all the time and they'd been fighting. Over Christmas Cole got drunk and he admitted he felt too old to be responsible for another child. Seth saw his chance and hinted that the child she was carrying might not be Cole's. His father reared up in indignation, just as Seth knew he would, but he also knew what a jealous man Cole was and that once seeds of suspicion had been sown, trouble and rows would soon follow.

Seth came out of his reverie with a start, surprised to

see the first light of dawn coming up over the plain. He must have been sitting here for a couple of hours without realizing. He started the car up and went on, but the shaky feeling was still with him. He knew he needed food and a hot drink to put him right again, and a place to sleep where he wouldn't be spotted.

Thomas arrived at The Grange at midday to find Rosie just as Norah had described on the telephone, almost vacant, as if part of her mind had shut down. The way she showed no real reaction to Thomas visiting again so soon after the last time proved she wasn't herself.

'I want you to forget gardening this afternoon,' he said firmly. 'We'll go for a walk instead.'

Thomas hadn't intended that Donald should come too, but when he tagged along he hadn't the heart to tell him to go home. Once they were out in the fields walking towards Heathfield, however, Donald bounded on ahead and Thomas began speaking more seriously to Rosie.

'I'm not going to make light of Gareth rejecting you,' he said, coming straight to the point. 'I know it hurts and it's made you feel worthless. But you must see, Rosie, that he is the worthless one, not you.'

She didn't reply. In fact it was almost as if she hadn't heard him. Thomas caught hold of her arm and pulled her round to face him, tipping her face up to his.

'Do you know what I see in your face?' he asked, looking right into her eyes.

She shook her head.

'I see strength,' he said simply. 'The very first time I saw you back at May Cottage when you came out of those bushes where you were hiding, I noticed it. Your expression then reminded me of East End kids – defiant and quick-witted. You looked like a little ragamuffin in your big shabby dress and your hair all tangled, but I knew right away that you'd be a force to reckon with.'

Rosie grimaced. 'What's that got to do with anything?'

'Because it makes me sad that you have all that strength, yet sometimes you just accept things when you shouldn't. I'm not going to repeat all the old lectures I've given you so many times before about your father's sins not being yours. You know that already. But what I do want to make you see today is that Gareth has actually done you a great favour.'

To Thomas's delight that defiant look flashed back into her eyes. 'He's *what*?' she retorted indignantly.

'A favour,' Thomas repeated. 'Because of him you accepted sliding into a comfortable rut. Ever since you met him, just seeing him when he had time off, you haven't had so much as a glimpse of the outside world. You haven't been to a dance, you haven't flirted with any other boys or sat about giggling with other girls. In fact you haven't got a clue about what other girls of your age get up to. You accepted seeing only what Gareth wanted you to see.'

'That's not true,' she said, brushing away his hand from her chin.

'It is,' he insisted. 'And I can tell you too how it would be if you married him. First, you would spend a year or two in a couple of rooms, you'd make it cosy and you'd visit his parents every Sunday. Then you'd get pregnant and Gareth would pull out all the stops to get you a better home. Maybe he'd get enough money together to buy a little house somewhere near his parents, but more likely you'd get a council house. There's nothing wrong with any of that, so far. But let's just flick forward a few years. You've got your home and a little garden all of your own, two or three small children. But Gareth works long hours to keep all this going; he's grumpy when he gets home, so he takes off to the pub every evening. He wants his home to be just like his mother's, everything spick and span, dinner on the table as he gets in, but he doesn't want to talk to you.'

'It wouldn't have been like that,' she said angrily. 'It wouldn't.'

'Oh yes, it would,' Thomas went on. 'But because you've got a good mind, Rosie, you'd have woken up one day and seen it for yourself. You'd have realized that you'd accepted second best, and you'd have felt cheated. You'd have wanted your children to be out playing in fields. You'd have wanted passion and new experiences – to see the world.'

'All women have to compromise when they get married,' she said stubbornly. 'That's what marriage is all about.'

Thomas shook his head. 'No, it's not, Rosie. It's about sharing a life with someone because you can't live without them. It's about joy and working together to achieve the same dreams. True, there are ups and downs; few people go through married life without hiccups. But you both have to set out on the same path with the same goal in view. You two were never really on the same path, or if you were you came to a fork in it some time ago and went off in different directions.'

'Is that supposed to make me feel better?' she said sarcastically. 'Because if it is, it hasn't worked.'

'No, it's supposed to make you look at it all more objectively. You've discovered that Gareth doesn't have much compassion. He's wooden-headed and blinkered. He wants a wife who will do exactly as he tells her. He only cares about himself.'

Rosie sighed. She knew in her heart that everything Thomas had said was true, but she couldn't bear Gareth to be so maligned. 'It's his mother who's made him like that,' she said. 'She tells him how he should live his life.'

Thomas thought for a moment, remembering all the things Rosie had told him about Mrs Jones. 'Have you ever considered why she is like she is?' he said quietly. 'She didn't want to leave Wales and all her family. She found herself uprooted in a place she never fitted into. It didn't do her any good ending up in a smart home with every imaginable gadget. She just grew bitter. She is a very good example of what might have happened to you.'

'But she didn't have anything back in Wales. They were terribly poor.'

'Money can't buy happiness, Rosie,' he said. 'That has to come from within.'

They walked on then to catch up with Donald, and to change the subject Thomas began to talk about the impending Suez crisis. Rosie didn't appear to have been following world news the way she once did, but he supposed under the circumstances that was understandable.

The three of them sat down on the grass later and Donald pulled a bottle of Tizer and some apples out of his knapsack. It was very warm, the sky was cloudless, and in a moment of silence they heard a lark singing somewhere high above them.

Maybe it was the utter peace that prompted it, or Thomas telling her a story about swimming in the East India docks when he was a kid, but Rosie began to talk about how it was in summer on the Somerset Levels: fishing for eels in the rhynes with only a stick, a piece of wool hanging off it, and a worm tied on to the end; cutting peat into blocks for the fire; and picking great bunches of marsh marigolds to take home to the cottage.

Thomas encouraged her. He felt she'd kept all these good memories locked away for fear they might remind her of the bad ones. She needed to re-examine them; it would help her to think objectively about her memories of Gareth too.

Donald lay on his stomach listening to Rosie and Thomas. Rosie had told him many stories but never ones about when she was a little girl before. He found it puzzling that she laughed about her brother called Seth, because that was the same name as the bad man the police were looking for. It was also funny that she talked about someone called Heather, and then Thomas said that was his sister. But Thomas seemed to like Rosie's stories about Heather and how she found country ways so strange, because he kept laughing. It made Donald laugh too, although he didn't quite understand all of it.

'She nearly had a fit when she found the privy didn't have a flush and that from time to time a new hole had to be dug,' Rosie said, stopping for a moment to explain to Donald what a 'privy' was. 'She used to be scared to go down there at night because Seth told her there were creatures in there that might bite you.'

Thomas then told them about the latrines in the prison camp. 'It was just a long, deep, stinking trench. We had a bamboo rail to hold on to, another one to crouch down on, and that was it – one slip and you'd had it. When I got dysentery it seemed like I was out there all night. You'd hear squeaking and rustling, but you didn't dare look down because if you saw the rats you got so scared you'd fall.'

Donald wondered why Thomas and Rosie were talking about things that had happened a long time ago. Listening to them was a bit like when he tried to read a real book, rather than a comic. He understood some of it but had to keep skipping the big words, and sometimes at the end of the page it didn't quite make sense. He wanted to interrupt them again and again to make things clearer for him, but something told him to keep quiet. It seemed important to just let these two people he loved talk to each other. It was making Rosie happy again.

It was after five when they went home, and as they walked across the last field towards Mayfield village Thomas glanced sideways at Rosie. Her cheeks were pink again, the slight stoop she'd had when they came out had gone, and she was bouncing along, laughing at something Donald was saying.

He remembered then how he had predicted to himself that she would grow into a pretty woman but would never be sophisticated. He had been right on the second count

– he couldn't imagine any hairdresser completely taming that wild mop of curls, or any elegant dress transforming her country-girl style into city chic. But she hadn't grown into a merely pretty woman, she was beautiful: long, coppery lashes framing those sky-blue eyes, that determined pointed chin and upturned nose with freckles like gold-dust across the bridge, and such a soft, kissable mouth. He felt a pang of exquisite tenderness for her. He had been so blunt about Gareth today that he wished he dared be equally honest about his own feelings towards her.

Donald leapt over the last stile and ran on ahead. Thomas went next, slowly because climbing was hard for him. He turned at the other side and instinctively held out his hand for Rosie's. For a moment she just sat astride the stile looking at him, her hand in his. The sun was behind her, turning her hair into a fuzzy golden halo, and the tops of her arms in her sleeveless cotton dress were golden too. He tried to photograph it in his memory, so he could paint it just as soon as he got back to London. He also wanted to be brave enough to put his two hands on her waist and lift her down into his arms, then kiss her.

'Thank you, Thomas,' she said in a soft little voice. 'You always seem to be here for me just when I need you.'

'I hope I always will,' he said, and lifting her hand to his lips he kissed it.

As Rosie lay in bed that night, she found it odd that her thoughts were not of Gareth, as they had been night and day for the past week, but of Thomas. He had been such an important person in her life for so long, and she thought she knew everything about him, but today he'd been different, sort of cruel, yet she liked him even more for that.

He'd pulled a kind of veil from her eyes. Most of what he'd said about Gareth she'd always known deep down,

535

but he'd brought everything to the surface and now she could see it with utter clarity. She wasn't exactly sure she liked such clarity, though. She didn't want to remember Gareth urging her to masturbate him almost the second they were alone together, nor the fact that in the last year he had rarely attempted to please her. She didn't want to think about the nasty jibes he made at Donald or Thomas, and especially not the ones he made about her, that her hair was always a mess, that her breasts were too small and her hands were getting rough like a man's. Neither did she want to admit openly that Gareth was boring a lot of the time, especially when he talked about trains or motorbikes.

That misty image of their married life in a little rose-covered cottage had always been so pretty and comforting, but she knew now that Gareth wasn't really the man she imagined sitting across a candlelit table from, or tucked up in a vast comfortable bed with. She still had to find that man. Yet she did feel sort of refreshed by having had that veil pulled down. She could see further and she had an urge to get out into the world and try new things.

What would it be like to go to dances again? To let some new man kiss her? And these girls he'd said she should be out there giggling with, who were they? Where would she meet them?

Sleep overtook her before she could answer the many questions spinning around in her head.

Chapter Eighteen

Three days after Thomas returned to Mayfield, Seth arrived too. He had crept into the garden at five-thirty in the morning, peered through every downstairs window, and now at seven o'clock he was sitting high up on the garden wall, hidden by the dense foliage of a copper beech, staring right into the kitchen. He was waiting for the occupants of the house to get up so he could take a look at them.

His appearance was now as desperate as his state of mind: unwashed, filthy clothes, and a thick growth of black stubble on his chin. He had abandoned the Standard Vanguard back near Southampton, then walked many miles cross-country before helping himself to a green Rover 90 in a small village. The owner had left a tweed jacket and a flat cap in the back, which offered a little warmth at night and some semblance of a disguise. He'd also managed to buy some food and cigarettes in a village shop run by an old lady. She didn't appear to recognize his face as the one on the front page of every newspaper, but he sensed his luck at evading the police was fast running out.

His heart had sunk when he eventually reached Mayfield and saw where Rosie lived. He had imagined The Grange to be some sort of institution, a school or a nursing home, tucked away in isolation. Instead he'd found it to be a big, posh, private house, with a sleek Jaguar parked in the drive, slap-bang in the middle of a village high street.

Seth knew that village people tended to be more observant than their city counterparts, and judging by the houses and cottages he'd seen so far, this one had a large proportion of wealthy residents. They were likely to call the police if they so much as caught a glimpse of an unkempt stranger, and that made him very jumpy.

On the plus side, however, there were no police at the gate, no dog either, and the number of bushes in the garden made it easy to creep around unseen. He'd also reconnoitred a way in via the field at the bottom of the garden. He intended to hide his shotgun there later, then drive the Rover away to some woods and dump it.

A noise drew his attention back to the house. A small, grey-haired, middle-aged woman wearing a pink dressing-gown was opening the kitchen window as she filled the kettle. Seth frowned. He had assumed that Rosie must be working here as a maid. But if she was, why wasn't she up first? Remembering how astonished Miss Marks had been when he showed her this address, he wished now that he'd asked her why. But then, with hindsight, there was a great deal more he should have found out before he allowed himself to become involved with that old bag.

He had managed to fit part of the story together from newspaper reports. Miss Marks was really Freda Barnes, one-time matron of a private loony-bin, and Miss Pemberton had been instrumental in getting her the sack. The man called Saunders whose face was in the papers too had also worked there. Clearly Rosie had created some mischief while she'd been there, including grassing up the matron and Saunders.

As Rosie wasn't mentioned in any paper he'd read, he'd come to the conclusion she must have informed on him anonymously, the sneaking sniveller. He wondered if that woman in the kitchen knew her real identity? He bet she didn't.

A man came into the kitchen some ten minutes later.

As he was well back in the room, Seth couldn't see him clearly. He was a tall, well-built man, about sixty, Seth thought; probably the woman's husband.

When Rosie suddenly appeared at the kitchen doors, opened them wide and stepped out on to the terrace, Seth almost fell off the wall in surprise. There was no doubt it *was* Rosie, as her unique copper-coloured curls gave her away, but he hadn't expected to find that the skinny kid he remembered had grown into a beauty.

The old tangled mane of hair was gone, the new shorter style was much shinier, and she was taller too, with the figure of a pin-up girl. The confident manner in which she opened those doors, and her casual outfit of dark green shorts and a sleeveless white blouse, suggested she was a great deal more than a maid in this house.

'It's so lovely and warm,' she called back into the kitchen. 'Shall we have breakfast out here today?'

Her voice was another surprise: she appeared to have lost her Somerset accent. Seth's was toned down too from his time in London, but people still recognized his West Country origins. For some reason this rankled more than her appearance as it suggested she hadn't suffered in any way, just slipped miraculously into an easy life.

'Well, you won't have it much longer,' he muttered to himself as he watched her arranging garden chairs around the table.

He soon began to feel very vulnerable, being so close. He was less than eight feet from her. If he as much as sneezed, he would give himself away. But he couldn't move now, he was trapped.

In the next half-hour Seth grew more and more agitated, not just because of his proximity to her but out of jealousy too. She was laying the table for four: a jug of orange juice, marmalade in a pretty pot, and butter in a glass dish, cutlery placed just so. The older woman was frying bacon, and the smell, along with the comfort of the house he'd noticed earlier, tormented him.

He had never had any comfort or glamour in his life – out in all winds and weathers, doing back-breaking work, his meals virtually thrown on the table. Since Cole was hanged, he hadn't even had a place he could call home. He was twenty-eight, but he'd never once sat in a beautiful garden like this, or had a holiday, or been anywhere luxurious. Why should she live in a place with a piano, a television set, thick carpets and all the other trappings of wealth, when he had nothing?

It seemed that the man wasn't joining the breakfast party outside. Seth thought he must be going off to work shortly. He wondered who the other two places were for? Perhaps there were children in the house?

Just after eight a big blond-haired man came into the kitchen. Seth sneered as he saw him go up to the older woman and hug her.

'Mummy's boy,' he muttered. He smirked a few minutes later as the same chap came out into the garden with the *Beano* in his hands and sat down at the table to read it. Seth's reading didn't go much beyond the *Beano* either, but he would have expected someone who lived in a place like this to be reading the *Financial Times*, not a comic.

After a few moments of studying him, Seth came to the conclusion he was simple. He looked normal enough, he was muscular and suntanned, and his light-coloured slacks and short-sleeved shirt had an expensive, well-fitting look, but he was laughing aloud at the comic and his mouth had a slightly droopy look like some of the 'divvies' that worked as labourers on building sites.

Then all at once Seth's attention was diverted by another man coming out on to the terrace. His lean face, fair hair and pronounced limp seemed very familiar. It was a minute or two before he placed him. But when the penny dropped he gasped in astonishment, grabbing the wall for support.

'It's fucking Farley!' he thought. 'What the hell is that bastard doing here?'

Thomas Farley was a man he was never likely to forget. Not only was he responsible for initiating Seth's and his father's arrest, but it was his character, background and testimony in court which had swayed the jury into finding Cole guilty. From the moment the jurors saw the haggard man who'd fought for his country and spent years in a Burmese prisoner-of-war camp only to lose his leg from an infected wound, they were for him. He was a hero, while Cole Parker with his robust health had spent the war years in cowardly comfort and safety. Cole didn't stand a chance.

In the next ten minutes or so, before the older man drove off in the Jaguar and Rosie and the older woman brought out plates of bacon and eggs, Seth scrutinized Farley and listened to his conversation with the man he called Donald.

Farley looked younger than he had at the trial. He'd gained some weight, and even the lined face Seth remembered so clearly seemed to have smoothed out remarkably. In court Farley's expression had remained grim, and he had looked at Cole and Seth with hatred as if he was capable of tearing them apart with his bare hands. Seth remembered how he had made his blood run cold, even though he was a cripple. In fact for some time after his acquittal, Seth had half expected the bloke to come gunning for him.

Life had clearly been good to Farley since then. He looked relaxed and happy as he smiled and chatted. He reminded Seth a bit of his sergeant when he was doing his stint in the army. He had the same kind of cool confidence, the sort other men looked up to – tough and dependable. Seth wondered what he was to Rosie. Surely the man couldn't care for the daughter of his enemy? But if he did care for her, so much the better. Seth could exact a double helping of revenge at one stroke.

Once Rosie and the older woman joined the two men for breakfast, Seth soon gleaned a great deal more information about all of them from the conversation. Farley was a guest, a regular one at that. Rosie was almost a daughter to the woman, though she called her Mrs Cook. Donald, as Seth had suspected, was simple, and he worked as a gardener.

But he still couldn't make out his sister's role here. She seemed very affectionate towards the simple bloke, so maybe she was his girlfriend. But then she was equally affectionate towards Farley. It was really peculiar. Surely Rosie could do better than a cripple or a simpleton? Yet there was also a reference to someone called Gareth, so maybe these people had another son. He wondered where he was.

Most of their conversation, however, seemed to be centred on the day ahead. Farley said he had some work to do, but he'd like to do it out here. Mrs Cook was going to a whist drive at eleven. Rosie and Donald appeared to be going somewhere together, and Rosie spoke of being gone for two hours. There was a great deal more conversation about someone called Robin. Seth suspected from their laughter that he was a small child, perhaps a grandchild.

Seth was frustrated when they finished breakfast. Rosie and Donald disappeared into the house out of sight, but the old woman and Farley stayed in the kitchen washing up. He wanted to move from his hiding place because he was afraid Rosie would leave by the front door and he wanted to follow her. But he didn't dare move until the kitchen was empty.

Minutes ticked by, and to Seth's horror Farley came out on to the terrace again and set up some tools on the table. He had visions of being trapped on the wall all morning. As he was so close to the terrace, just the slightest movement could alert Farley that someone was there.

At last Farley went back indoors and vanished from sight. Seth couldn't see the old girl either, so he took his chance, leapt down into the garden, skirted around behind some thick bushes which surrounded the lawn, and reached the drive.

The front door was actually located on the side of the house, and Seth was startled to hear it opening just as he was about to run past. He dived behind a bush, trembling with fright, assuming that someone had spotted him. He regretted coming here now. It was nearly half past eight. The shops in the high street would be opening any minute. He knew only too well that in country villages people came out early to do their shopping, older people gathered to chat and a lot of holiday-makers might well be there too.

'We'll be home by twelve,' Rosie called out to someone behind her. 'If Mrs Parsons phones, tell her I'll call round this afternoon to give her a quote.'

Seth breathed a sigh of relief. They hadn't seen him.

The bush behind which he'd concealed himself was holly and very prickly, but even when Rosie and Donald walked past him up the garden, he didn't dare come out. A few minutes later they came back, Donald pushing a wheelbarrow loaded with garden tools and Rosie carrying a tray full of small plants. Surely she hadn't become a gardener?

At eleven that same evening Seth was in the field at the back of The Grange, tucked up against the garden wall, concealed by two dense bushes. It was dark now, but sticky hot, as if there was a storm brewing.

It had been very difficult to follow Rosie this morning. The high street was busy, and there was nowhere to conceal himself. Rosie seemed to know everyone; again and again she stopped to chat. Seth had attracted quite a few curious glances, and even though he pulled the cap further down over his eyes and shuffled on as if he was just a farm worker passing through, he felt his presence had been noted and it would be only a matter of time before someone alerted the police that there was a suspicious-looking character in their midst.

Apparently Rosie and Donald ran a gardening business together. He'd spied on her over the hedge of the place where they were working and was amazed to see her digging like a seasoned professional. Unable to get near her because of Donald, Seth had a sleep in a field near by. He woke later to find they had both gone home, so he went back to the car, drove it into some woods, then came back to The Grange and just waited. At four he heard Rosie and Donald come down the garden together. He pricked up his ears, but they went into the greenhouse and their voices became muted. An hour or so later Farley came into the garden and called Rosie out to speak to her. This time Seth heard everything distinctly. He felt they must be sitting on the bench just the other side of the wall, only feet away from him.

Farley had come to tell Rosie about the latest news bulletin. To Seth's consternation, it soon became clear that the entire household knew exactly who Rosie was and also the details of his own movements, which could only have been passed on to them by the police. Farley told her a Standard Vanguard with Seth's fingerprints all over it had been found, and went on to say the police believed he was heading in their direction in a green Rover.

'They're warning the public not to approach him,' Farley said, his voice gruff and authoritative. 'They've posted an officer at the gate here, but you mustn't go out at all until he's been caught.'

'Surely he won't dare come here?' Rosie said, and Seth had a twinge of pleasure at the alarm in her voice.

'It doesn't seem very logical,' Farley replied. 'If I was him, I'd be looking for ways to get out of the country. But who can guess at a man's state of mind when he's already killed twice?'

Their voices slowly faded as they walked back to the house together. Although Seth was shaken to find the police were so close on his tail, he still smirked. They hadn't got the savvy to watch the back of the house too, and if Farley knew how close Seth had been to Rosie today he'd be shitting himself.

Seth lit up another cigarette. He was waiting for everyone in the house to go to bed. He hoped there would be a storm, because it would make his new plan easier.

His original idea had been to catch Rosie alone, well away from the house. As the day's events had made that impossible, he'd had to rethink. But in fact his new plan excited him far more.

He had resigned himself to being captured eventually. But he could go to the gallows a great deal happier knowing he'd pulled a fast one on Farley and the police, as well as getting the ultimate revenge on Rosie. It was going to be the most satisfying act of his whole life, and he wished his mind would dwell on it, but for some reason it kept slipping back to Heather.

He'd had her for the first time when Alan was only eight weeks old. He'd arrived home on a forty-eight-hour pass from the army the night before, right in the middle of a vicious row between her and Cole.

When he got up the next morning, Cole had already gone to work with Norman, Heather had a huge shiner and badly skinned knuckles, and the baby was screaming fit to bust. She was at her wits' end because she had a mountain of washing to do. She looked exhausted and old. It was the first time Seth had ever felt sympathy for her. He had admired the way she tried to fight back the night before – he wouldn't have dared take a saucepan to Cole's head the way she had.

It certainly wasn't desire which motivated him to take her in his arms. She looked terrible, her clothes were stained and her hair hadn't seen a brush for days. But once he was holding her, something overcame him.

Heather was very sexy in her own way. He'd always thought so. Her big backside undulated as she walked, her tits quivered and her eyes sparkled when she laughed. Normally her long, fair hair was clean and shiny, and she had a way of talking to men that made them feel a bit special. That day she smelled all milky, her breasts against his chest were swollen and hot, and as she cried against his shoulder and thanked him for being kind he knew he had to have her.

Seth couldn't remember now how he managed to persuade her to come upstairs with him. Maybe he said he would help her make the beds. But he got her in his father's bedroom, then pushed her down and fucked her.

Funnily enough, he couldn't remember now how it felt, not the way he did with Ruby. She struggled and screamed of course, she cursed him to hell and back, but he couldn't recall the excitement really. The only vivid memory was looking down at her afterwards. Her dress was all rucked up and he'd torn the bodice, milk was trickling out of one of her big swollen breasts, and he remembered he'd pinched her nipple like he was milking a cow, and laughed as milk squirted across the bed.

He knew somehow she wouldn't tell Cole, though she was hysterical afterwards. She flew at him and tried to scratch his face, but she kept saying over and over again that she ought to have known better than to trust him. He guessed that meant she thought she'd led him on, and perhaps she was just too weak after the baby to stand any more rows with Cole.

Seth went back to camp and Heather probably thought it would never happen again. But she was wrong of course. As soon as he was demobbed and back home, he soon found opportunities and, like he had with Ruby, he kept her silent by threatening to hurt her child.

Seth took great pleasure in finding Cole still had no interest in the kid. It meant he could have got away with doing almost anything to him. He was always crying anyway, so a few minor injuries would have gone unnoticed.

Seth couldn't remember how many times he had

Heather before he drew Norman into it – four, five times maybe. It was Norman's first leave after his call-up, and the night before he'd admitted to his older brother that he hadn't lost his cherry yet and all the other men kept teasing him about it. Seth promised to lay on a girl and said he'd show him how to do it.

That day they'd been drinking cider down at the Crown from twelve until halfway through the afternoon. They staggered home to find Alan in his pram in the kitchen fast asleep and Heather upstairs having a nap. She was laying face down on the bed, Seth remembered, her dress caught up slightly so it showed her stocking tops and plump white thighs. He was instantly aroused, so he unzipped his trousers, leapt on the bed and, dragging her on to all fours, pumped it into her.

The most thrilling thing about that time wasn't just her screams or struggling, though that always turned him on still more: it was having a spectator. He glanced over his shoulder and saw Norman with his cock in his hand and that really made it magic. It was like when they were kids again, creeping in the back of the village shop to nick a packet of biscuits or a bar of chocolate from the store room. Mostly they didn't even want what they nicked. It was the shared badness which made it a great adventure.

Alan started screaming downstairs, but that made no difference. It was glorious, better than racing down the lanes on a motorbike together, or swimming naked in the river. After he'd come he made Norman take over, and the excitement on his brother's face was better than watching him open a Christmas stocking.

Norman chickened out after that one time. Once he was sober he would barely talk to Seth, and he didn't come home on leave again for a long time. Heather kept warning Seth that she was going to tell Cole, but she never did.

Seth had it made. He'd managed to create enough conflict between his father and his woman so that all trust was gone. Cole believed in his heart that she'd saddled him with a child who wasn't his own. Heather, not knowing this, rejected all his advances because Cole didn't care about her son. She had to give in to Seth for fear of him hurting her child, and slowly but surely the friction in May Cottage mounted.

Almost every night they had a row. Mostly it was over something petty, Cole going to the pub or her forgetting to shut up the hens. But each row seemed to get more bitter. She would say Cole didn't love her or Alan. He would ask how she could claim to love him when she didn't want him near her. Often it was Heather who started the physical stuff; she would throw something at him, and he would retaliate by punching her.

Seth sat back and gleefully watched it happening. Sometimes he returned from the pub just in time to see the fighting through the kitchen window. At other times it began after he'd gone to bed. It amused him that they thought neither he nor Rosie knew anything of these scenes. He'd finally got his revenge on his father for hurting his mother so much that she left. It absolved him of his guilt at killing Ruby, and it punished Rosie for being born. He believed that any day now Heather would take Alan and leave. He hoped she might take Rosie too.

In the spring of 1949, Cole and Seth were working on a job in Bristol, clearing rubble from a bomb site. Seth was twenty-one, Rosie twelve and Alan just two. Norman was still away in the army but with only a few more weeks' service to complete. They had been staying in Bristol for some time, going home only on Sundays, but one night Cole cleared off on his own, returning two days later with a wide grin on his face and refusing to say where he'd been. Seth assumed he'd found a new woman, and a little later that morning when he was packed off to dump a truck-load of rubble he decided to make a detour to see Heather. He was cautious enough to leave the truck half a mile away and get to the cottage across the moor. If Cole heard he'd been back during the day he'd want to know why.

As soon as Seth saw Heather hanging up washing in the orchard, happily singing as she worked, as if she'd just had a good fucking, he suddenly realized where Cole had been the last two days. It hadn't been another woman, but this one. Worse still, he sensed they'd made up their differences without him there to throw in a few spanners in the works. Heather's smile vanished as she caught sight of him. But instead of running as she usually did, she just stood her ground, hands on hips, and glowered at him.

'Don't even think about it,' she warned him. 'If you want tea or a sandwich, that's fine and dandy. But if you've got anything else on your mind, forget it.'

Her confidence shook him. She looked just the way she had when she had first arrived, young, fresh and strong. Her brown eyes looked unwaveringly into his; that courage he'd once admired in her was back.

'Aw, come on,' he said, uncertain if he was trying to persuade her or pretending the thought of sex hadn't crossed his mind. 'Dad might have been good to you for the last couple of days, but that's just because he's been screwing every bit of skirt in Bristol.'

She half smiled and shook her head despairingly. 'Don't give me that old toffee,' she said. 'You are a maggot, Seth, a lying, stinking, rotten maggot. If I hadn't been so busy making yer dad happy for the last couple of days, I would have told him every last thing you've done, but I didn't want to waste our precious time together talking about you. I'll tell you now how it is. You are going to leave here for good, and if you don't leave by Friday of your own accord, I'm going to tell Cole everything and get him to throw you out.'

Just as he knew Ruby had meant it, so he knew Heather did too. There was absolute determination in her eyes.

He had no intention of killing her, not then. He spoke

to her nicely. He even apologized and agreed to find digs in Bristol. It was only as she turned away and flounced back towards the cottage in front of him with the laundry basket on her hip that he suddenly realized she intended to tell Cole anyway. He followed her. The same axe he'd killed Ruby with six years earlier was lying on top of the wood pile by the outhouse. He picked it up and concealed it behind his back.

Heather stopped by the mangle. Beside it was the old tin bath full of rinsing sheets. She bent down to pick one up, folded it over a couple of times and began threading it into the mangle. 'Go and put the kettle on,' she said dismissively. 'I'll make you a sandwich when I've finished this.'

Seth lifted the axe and struck her hard on the neck from behind. She slumped forward on to the mangle and he hit her again.

Just two strong blows and that was it. Easier than wringing a chicken's neck.

The whole thing was far easier than it had been with Ruby. He was a fully grown man now and much stronger. The earth was softer too, because in recent months he and Cole had dug up a patch of ground when they were trying out a mechanical digger. He had a hole dug within two hours, and the whole thing was over and done with, timber replaced and all, within three. It was only as he finished that he heard Alan crying.

Sick was the only word he could use to describe how he felt. In the heat of the moment he just hadn't thought of the kid. He was down the orchard in his pram, and if Seth hadn't forgotten the little bleeder's existence he would have killed him too and tossed him into the grave along with his mother.

But it was too late to do anything now. Rosie would be back from school soon. If he didn't get back to Bristol within an hour, Cole would be suspicious. Later as he drove away to dump a bag of Heather's clothes, he told himself Cole would eventually hand Alan over to the welfare people.

Leaving that kid alive was the only thing he regretted about that day. He didn't mind Cole crying like a child, and he enjoyed seeing Rosie bewildered and exhausted as she tried to juggle going to school and looking after the brat. But for that scrawny, miserable kid, everyone would have believed Heather had run off because she couldn't stand Cole any longer. Farley would never have started the investigation. Cole, Norman and him would still have been at May Cottage. Rosie would have been married off a year or so ago.

Cole wouldn't have been hanged.

As the first spots of rain began to fall, Seth slung his shotgun over his shoulder, climbed up on to the garden wall and dropped down soundlessly beside the greenhouse.

He felt absolutely no guilt at killing the women. They had got in his way. He hadn't even felt bad about Cole being tried for something he hadn't done. But what did still plague him was that look his father gave him in court as he was given the death sentence.

All through the trial Seth had been convinced that Cole believed someone else had come to the cottage and murdered the women. He couldn't have suspected Seth or he would have spoken out. But when he fixed Seth with those cold, penetrating black eyes, he realized Cole had known that it was him ever since the bodies were found. To this day Seth didn't understand why his father kept quiet. It gnawed at him like a toothache.

He crept stealthily across to the summerhouse and let himself in. The kitchen was in darkness, and he guessed the entire family were watching television at the front of the house. He made himself comfortable on a wicker garden chair and settled down to wait.

The rain was still so light he could barely hear it, but there was a distant rumble of thunder. A little later a light came on in the room above the kitchen, shining a clear path across the terrace and on to the lawn. He sat up and almost cried out with glee when he saw Rosie come over to the window and look out, and he remembered as a kid how she had always spent a great deal of time looking out of her bedroom window. She didn't draw the curtains, and only partially closed the windows. As he watched she began to undress.

Seth could only see her from the waist up, but as she unbuttoned her blouse he had an immediate erection. She was wearing a white bra, and she turned away to remove her skirt or shorts. To his acute disappointment, she moved before taking off the bra, and when she came back into his line of vision she had on some sort of frilly top that looked like one of those cute baby-doll pyjama sets. She stayed for some time by the window brushing her hair, then a dimmer light came on, the overhead one went off, and he assumed she'd got into bed.

Seth had had plenty of time that morning to study the back of the house. The room Rosie was in was directly over the kitchen. There was a plant climbing up a trellis which almost reached her window, and by coincidence it was the very route he'd planned to take into the house if he couldn't grab her during the day. But he hadn't expected to be lucky enough to find her in that very room. He just wished he knew where everyone else was sleeping. He guessed the parents would have a big room at the front, but where were Farley and Donald?

One of them was accounted for a little later when a light came on two sets of windows away from Rosie. The curtains had been drawn, so he couldn't tell which of the men it was, but a sixth sense told him it was Farley.

At half past one Seth was ready. Several lengths of strong rope were strung around his chest; he had rags in his pocket and his knife in his belt; his jacket and shotgun were stashed by the garden wall.

He'd crept round to the front of the house a little earlier.

There was only one policeman on guard. Seth could see the red glow of his cigarette as he sheltered from the rain under a tree just outside the front gate. It took him only a moment to cut the telephone wire outside the house. The policeman never even moved.

It was raining stair-rods now. The rattling sound on the greenhouse and the gravel drive was enough to mask any sound he might make. But best of all was the thunder, booming out like distant guns. Fear was replaced by intense excitement.

Rosie awoke with a start to find something wet and cold pressing on her windpipe. But as she opened her mouth to scream, something was stuffed into it, making her choke. It was too dark for her to see her attacker, but she instantly knew who it was by the smell. Only one person's sweat smelled like that – Seth's. Bucking against his restraining arms she tried to free herself, but he had her pinned down tightly by her bedclothes.

'Well, little sister, I bet you never thought you'd see me again,' he whispered. 'Now, be a good girl and keep very quiet and I won't hurt you or anyone else in this house.'

She tried to scream, but Seth pushed the cloth further into her mouth and she choked again and again.

'Smell,' he ordered in a menacing whisper, his face looming over her as he held her captive. Rosie tried to turn away from his breath. That smelled bad too, but as she did so another, stronger smell reached her.

Paraffin.

She jerked her head back in even greater alarm and she saw by the glint of his teeth that he was smiling.

'Yes, it's paraffin. You left it for me in the greenhouse and I've been pouring it all over the house. Keep your trap shut, don't try to struggle, and I might not strike a match. You know what will happen if I do, don't you?'

Rosie froze. She had no doubt Seth was ruthless enough

to torch the house. He had nothing more to lose. She had to do what he said.

'I haven't come to hurt you. But you got me into this mess and you've got to get me out of it,' he said very softly into her ear. 'So I'm going to tie you up, then lower you out the window. But just remember when you're out there in the garden and I'm up here, one sound – just one squeak from you – and I'll start the fire.'

Rosie knew he meant to hurt her whatever he said, but there was no alternative but to obey him. She couldn't risk him striking a match. Maybe once they were outside she'd be able to get away.

He rolled her over face down, secured her hands behind her back with a piece of rope, tied her ankles with another, then a third thicker one went around her waist like a noose. For good measure he tied another rag round her mouth to make sure she couldn't spit out the gag.

As he lifted her up in his arms to bundle her head first out of the window, all Rosie could do was pray that Thomas would hear something and raise the alarm, but she knew that above the noise of the storm it was un-likely.

Rosie only weighed about eight stone, but it was still a heavy load for Seth to hold on to. As he humped her body further and further over the window sill, she had visions of the rope slipping from his hands and her skull crashing on to the terrace below. She had been in this position with him before when she was four or five, dangled head first over the wall of a pig-sty. But then he hadn't really dared to hurt her.

She was wearing only the skimpiest of nylon pyjamas, and the rope around her middle was cutting painfully into her skin. Miraculously she landed quite gently, but even if she hadn't been tied hand and foot there was no escape. Seth was still holding the other end of the rope, and as she looked up he was climbing out of her room to join her. She held her breath, afraid he would throw a match before leaving. But he didn't. He just came silently down the trellis like a monkey.

Thomas woke up suddenly from an unpleasant dream. It was an old one that hadn't troubled him for some time: all the men were lined up in the boiling sun for 'Tenko', waiting for the Japanese guards to discover there was one man missing. The dream was always vivid, and he'd kind of learned to wake himself out of it. But it always left him with the same gut-wrenching terror and cold sweats, even without reaching the part where one of the guards made them kneel on the ground, heads bent, and then proceeded to walk along the line with his sword raised to select someone to behead.

Thomas never understood why this dream persisted. He'd seen men beaten, whipped and shot by guards, but not beheaded. A psychiatrist at the hospital had said he thought the sword was merely symbolic of everything Thomas feared. Perhaps it had come back tonight after months of respite because of his anxiety about Rosie.

When he heard a clap of thunder, Thomas smiled to himself. It was just a storm that had prompted his dream and he got out of bed and hopped across the room to watch it from the window, taking deep breaths of air to banish his nightmare for good.

Lightning flashed and for a second the whole garden was illuminated. He blinked. He thought he'd seen someone running across the lawn with a bundle over their shoulder, but suddenly the garden was in darkness again. For just a second he stood there, swaying a little as he balanced on his one leg, peering out, sure it was a figment of his imagination. But the image didn't fade from his mind.

He had no crutches or walking stick. So with his empty pyjama-leg flapping, he hopped his way to Rosie's room and as he opened the door he saw her empty bed and the wide-open window with the curtains blowing in the wind. He also smelled paraffin.

There had been many times since his capture by the Japs that he'd felt utterly impotent, but never quite as badly as this. His mind told him to jump out of the window in pursuit, but he knew it was impossible. Instead, all he could do was scream like a banshee to Frank and Norah as he hopped across the landing.

Donald appeared from his room before Thomas reached his parents' door.

'Go and telephone the police,' Thomas yelled at him. 'Seth Parker's got Rosie. He's making his way over the field at the back.'

He expected Donald to stare at him vacantly, perhaps wasting precious minutes asking questions, but Donald shot along the landing, past Thomas and straight down the stairs, taking them three at a time.

Frank emerged from his room rubbing his eyes, hastily followed by Norah. Thomas told them what he had seen.

'Check that Donald's telephoned. I'll go and put my leg on,' he said.

He hadn't even got to his room when Donald called up the stairs.

'The phone won't work. It doesn't even make a funny sound,' he said with alarm in his voice.

'I'll get the policeman outside,' Frank said, running back to his room to grab his dressing-gown.

Thomas was just finishing strapping on his leg when he heard Norah yell out from the kitchen. He pulled on his trousers over his pyjamas, grabbed his jacket and shoes, and rushed downstairs.

Norah was standing in the kitchen, wringing her hands, her expression one of utter terror. The doors on to the terrace were wide open. Rain was lashing into the room.

'Donald's gone after them,' she cried. 'Oh Thomas, he's no match for that man.'

Thomas comforted her as best he could, but there was

little he could say to make her feel better. Donald was strong and fit, and he knew his way about the fields. But the chances were that he would blunder after them like an enraged bull and make the situation even more dangerous.

Frank came back in as Thomas was making Norah some tea. He was soaked through, rain running down his face, purple with anger.

'Some bloody guard! He wasn't there. I had to bang them up next door to use their telephone,' he exploded.

'Are the police coming?' Thomas asked.

Frank nodded, adding that he hoped they'd send men a little more competent than the one they'd left outside. 'Let's hope they switch their sirens on. It might make that animal dump Rosie and run for it.'

As Thomas told Frank about Donald, the older man blanched. 'Damn him,' he exploded, thumping a fist on the kitchen table. 'He'll just complicate things further.'

'He went for all the right reasons,' Thomas reminded him. 'If I had two good legs, I'd be out there now too.'

When the first lot of police arrived some ten minutes later, along with the one who should have been outside, both Frank and Norah had dressed. While two of the men went out into the garden with flashlights, Thomas took the third man, an older officer, upstairs and showed him Rosie's room. The smell of paraffin was still strong, but there was no sign of any having been spilled. They thought perhaps Seth had got it on his clothes while he was holed up somewhere.

Thomas demanded to know why the man supposed to be guarding the house had disappeared, and why indeed they hadn't watched the back of the house too. The officer said he would look into it, and hurriedly left to join his colleagues, who were now over the wall and into the field.

It had been twenty-five past two when Thomas came down to the kitchen to hear that Donald had gone. He reckoned it must have been about fifteen minutes earlier that Rosie was snatched. Now as they waited in the kitchen, desperate for news or something constructive to do, the minutes seemed like hours.

For some time after the police had left, they all reassured one another by speaking of the reinforcements the police had said were coming, the road-blocks being set up, and the promises they'd been given that Donald would be found and brought home immediately. But as time went on they all sank deep into their own thoughts.

Norah silently busied herself by making a pile of sandwiches and a large thermos of coffee. She covered the sandwiches in a damp tea towel, took a pile of small plates from the cupboard and placed them in readiness along with some cups, almost as if she was anticipating a party. But her fear was evident in her jerky movements and her compulsion to constantly wipe down surfaces. Her usually calm, grey-blue eyes were dark with anxiety; her lips trembled as if she was on the verge of breaking down.

Frank appeared to be in a stupor, his chin embedded in his chest. His customary ruddiness, which had always advertised his good health, now seemed dangerously livid. The veins in his forehead were swollen and throbbed visibly.

Earlier they had spoken of Michael and Susan and discussed briefly how, even if their phone line hadn't been cut, it would be unfair to wake them with bad news. Yet Thomas knew they both wished their two older children would suddenly appear at the door.

Thomas felt deeply for this couple he had come to know so well. Some time ago they had told him about that day years ago when the little girl from their village went missing. He knew they were reliving it now, experiencing the same terror her parents had felt all through that long night as search parties combed the woods and fields.

Donald might be a man in most people's eyes, but to them he was still a small boy, who was out there, barefooted in a storm, following a murderer who might very well kill or maim him too. He could almost hear their agonized thoughts. Why hadn't they sent both Rosie and Donald to their son's in Tunbridge Wells for safety once they knew Seth Parker was the killer of the two women? And why had they been foolish enough to trust the police to be vigilant?

But while Thomas acknowledged Frank and Norah's plight, he felt his own pain was far greater. The war had robbed him of his mother, his youth and his leg. As if that wasn't enough, his sister had been taken from him too. Then, like a miracle, his friendship with Rosie had wiped out the bitterness inside him. Right from the time that she'd written those first letters when she was with the Bentleys, she'd enriched his life with her courage and endurance.

Now he might never see her again, and there was so much he wanted to share with her – that he'd finally been brave enough to show his paintings to Paul Brett, an art-gallery owner in Hampstead, just the day before coming down here; that he felt he was on the brink of something wonderful.

Rosie had inspired him, and yet now she might never see that painting which had impressed Paul Brett so much. He'd painted it from memory: a little curly-haired ragamuffin with defiant eyes peeping from behind a wild rose bush.

He couldn't even go outside and join the search for her. One step on uneven and slippery ground and he'd fall over. He was about as much use to the woman he loved as a chocolate fireguard.

Donald, meanwhile, wasn't quite as incapable of thinking clearly as his parents believed. Though he was angry and upset, he still had the presence of mind to grab a dark mackintosh that had once belonged to Michael from a peg in the hall, slip his feet into his gardening shoes, and take the big torch his father used for looking at his car engine in the dark.

He also knew from comics that if you wanted to catch someone by surprise, you had to be quiet and stay invisible. The moment he got out in the field he rubbed mud all over his face and hair. He'd seen someone do that in a film.

Being quick seemed to be the most important thing at first, so he ran like the wind across the field until he reached the stile at the far end, but from there on he flashed the light every now and then to check for tracks. There were clear boot marks in the mud, and imprints of bare toes, which had to be Rosie's. The bad man was taking her to the woods.

It was only as Donald approached the woods that he became scared. He'd never been in them before at night and every tree trunk had a nasty, leering face on it. He stopped for a minute, too frightened to go any further, but as he stood there he heard noises above the drumming of the rain on the trees – cracking, rustling noises and not that far ahead of him. Knowing that Rosie was there, even more scared than he was, gave him new courage. His eyes had grown more used to the dark now, and he did know the woods very well. He didn't dare switch on the torch again, so he tucked it into his pocket and picked up a big stout stick.

He kept to the well-worn path. The man and Rosie were over to his left and pushing through the undergrowth, but his path gradually wound round towards their direction. If he was quick and quiet he could get in front of them, just like the Wicked Wolf did in Little Red Riding Hood.

His plan worked. After walking quickly for about twenty minutes he stopped to listen and he heard them coming towards him.

'Move it,' the man said in a gruff voice, and Donald heard a sound like a cane swishing through the air. It was as if the man had beaten her, but Rosie didn't cry out; there was just a noise like one of them stumbling over something.

Donald hid behind the biggest tree trunk. He wished he'd brought his balaclava he wore in winter. He was afraid his blond hair would show up.

But all at once they stopped moving. Donald strained his ears to listen. He could hear strange sounds but couldn't identify them. He waited, not knowing what to do now, and then the man spoke again.

'This is as far as you're going,' he said.

Donald was relieved at that. He thought the man was going to leave Rosie there and go on alone. He must know the police would be coming to get him. That made it much easier for Donald: he would just wait till the man had gone, and then take Rosie home.

But as the minutes ticked by and the man didn't move in his direction but just stayed there making funny rustling noises, Donald got anxious. He began to creep closer towards them.

'Keep still, you bitch. I can't get it in,' the man suddenly exclaimed, and instinctively Donald knew he was trying to do something very bad to her.

Rosie was beside herself with terror. From the moment Seth had hiked her roughly over the garden wall, then untied her feet so she could walk, she knew he was planning to either kill her or leave her so badly hurt she'd wish she was dead. She couldn't get away from him. He still had the rope tied tightly around her waist, and if she stopped walking he just dragged her or kicked her along. The cloth in her mouth was making her feel sick, and the one he'd used to keep it in place stank of paraffin. All at once she realized that he'd fooled her back in the house. He hadn't spilt paraffin, it was just this cloth she'd smelled.

All the way across the field he kept up a barrage of accusations. She was the reason he'd gone wrong. Right from when she was born she'd caused him trouble. Cole had always cared more for her than for him. She was the reason he had to kill Ruby.

She had stopped short at that, staring at him in horror. He snarled at her, kicked her to start her walking again, and proceeded to tell her in gory, sickening detail just how he did it and why. Then he moved on to Heather.

By the time they reached the woods Rosie was in pain. She had stubbed her bare feet on stones several times, she was icy cold, and the rope around her middle was cutting deeper and deeper into her skin. The rain made her pyjamas cling to her and she was certain Seth intended to rape her. Somehow rape was the worst thing she could imagine. She'd rather be beaten half to death.

Yet above all that was the terrible knowledge her father had been innocent. Hanged for crimes committed by his eldest son, this savage madman. She had always felt guilty that she hadn't told the police everything she knew about Seth. Now she felt utter desolation because by keeping her counsel she had actually helped put the rope round her father's neck.

Praying for rescue was pointless. No one would even know she was missing until the morning, and by then it would be much too late. Tears poured down her face, but she couldn't even speak to plead with Seth.

Going through the woods was far worse than the fields. She stumbled on every stick, she was stung by nettles and pricked by thorns. Then he stopped and tied her to the tree with her feet splayed wide apart, and she knew this meant that rape was going to be the start of it. But he teased her first, taking out a long, shining knife from his belt and running it under her nostrils and down her cheeks, digging the point in just a little way to show what he intended to do.

'That will be last,' he whispered. 'I'm going to cut your face to ribbons, then poke out your eyes. No man will ever want you again, you won't even be able to see how ugly you are or look at your precious flowers. But first you're going to get my big, hard cock.'

Even above the overpowering smell of paraffin, she

could still smell his foul breath and the stink of sweat, and she gagged again. Then he unzipped his trousers and displayed his penis to her, jerking her head this way and that each time she tried to look away.

Ripping the pants of her pyjamas away with one hand, he masturbated with the other. Then when it was hard, he tried to force his penis into her. She tightened every muscle. Whatever he did to her, she wasn't going to let him have this. She had wanted to save herself for Gareth on their wedding night. He didn't want her now, but she'd be damned if her brother was going to take her virginity.

He punched her in the face when he couldn't get it in, but she was beyond caring. He was an animal, a cruel sadistic monster, who had allowed their father to be hanged for killing two women he loved. Her virginity was all she had left and she would fight to keep it.

Suddenly there was a roaring, bellowing sound. For a moment she thought it was Seth, but as she jerked her head round she saw a figure hurtling towards them like a wild bull.

Seth backed away, taken by surprise. He scrabbled for the shotgun that was still slung across his back. But he wasn't fast enough. The figure leapt at him, sending him flying backwards on to the ground, threw himself on top of him and began beating at his head and face with a heavy stick.

It wasn't until her rescuer sobbed that Rosie realized it was Donald.

Chapter Nineteen

Pandemonium broke out in the woods. Shouting male voices, feet thundering through the undergrowth and dancing lights came from every direction to vie with the thunder, lightning and drumming rain. Rosie tried to scream to direct them to her, but the sound was only in her head and she choked again and again as the rag in her mouth was sucked deeper into her throat.

But Donald was yelling for her. In a flash of lightning Rosie saw him clearly. He was sitting astride Seth, head thrown back, roaring like a wounded lion.

All at once uniformed men appeared. She saw the glint of silver buttons, faces ghostly-white in the light of their torches, and the trees seemed to spin before her eyes.

'You're safe now,' a gruff voice said, and his hands felt warm against her cold, wet cheeks as he untied the rag around her head and mouth. As he pulled the second rag from her mouth, the screams she'd stored up burst out.

'Steady now,' the policeman said. 'I'm going to untie you.'

'Donald,' she yelled. Her line of vision was obscured by the policeman's big shoulders, and now she was safe she had to make sure Donald was too.

'He's fine,' the policeman said, glancing over his shoulder to where his colleagues surrounded Donald and Seth. 'Don't you worry about a thing. It's all over now.'

Those words 'It's all over now' kept repeating in her head as she was wrapped in someone's coat and lifted up by strong arms. Her father had often said them when he woke her from a nightmare as a small child. Sergeant Headly had said them as he carried her into Bridgwater Infirmary. Miss Pemberton and Thomas had both uttered them after her ordeal at Carrington Hall. But was it really over this time? Or was there more to come?

'You're the bravest man I ever met,' Thomas said as he washed Donald's hair for him in the bath. It was dawn now: the storm was over and a fresh wind was driving away the last of the cloud. Thomas wished he could wipe out the terrible images which the police, Donald and Rosie herself had imprinted on his mind in the last hour or two, as easily as he could rinse away the mud from this boy's hair.

Donald's eyes shone and his grin stretched from ear to ear. 'I had to stop that bad man,' he said. 'He was hurting Rosie.'

Thomas gulped and turned away so Donald wouldn't see his tears.

When the police had come back to the house, one of them carrying Rosie in his arms, for one split second he had thought she was dead. Reason immediately prevailed, however: policemen didn't carry dead bodies into anyone's house. But she looked like a rag doll wrapped in a coat, her hideously scratched, mud-daubed legs dangling lifelessly over the man's arms.

'She refused to go to hospital,' the policeman said helplessly. Then as Norah came flapping down the hall, directing him to carry her into the sitting-room, Rosie began moving in his arms.

'I'm all right,' she said, in a surprisingly clear voice. 'Take me into the kitchen. I'm all wet and muddy.'

Later on, after the doctor had pronounced her injuries to be only superficial scratches and bruises, they even managed to smile about her concern for carpets and furniture. But at that moment they were all so profoundly stunned at actually having her back, alive and able to speak clearly, that they did as she asked and sat her on a wooden chair.

Donald's arrival a few moments later almost eclipsed Rosie's ordeal. Their first view of him – mud-caked face and hair, blood-stained hands and raincoat – gave them all a turn. But while Rosie sat in silence, wrapped in a blanket, Donald excitedly related a garbled tale about how he'd stopped 'the bad man'.

Once it was established that Donald too was unhurt, Norah took Rosie upstairs to bathe her and put her to bed, and the police took Frank aside to speak to him in private. They left soon after, saying they would call back later in the day in the hope that Rosie would then be able to give a full account of the night's events.

Norah came back downstairs sometime later, grey-faced and shaking. She managed to order Donald upstairs to take the bath she'd run for him, but once he'd left the room she burst into tears as she related to Frank and Thomas what Rosie had told her.

'It was Seth who murdered Ruby and Heather, not his father,' she wept, clinging to her husband. 'Can you imagine! He boasted about it to Rosie and told her all the horrifying details. He said he was going to blind and disfigure her, and he was trying to rape her when Donald charged through the woods and stopped him. She might have no serious external injuries, but heaven only knows what terrible damage he's done to her mind.'

Frank spoke then of what the police had told him in private, how Donald had leapt on Seth and almost clubbed him to death with a stick. They thought Seth's skull was broken and doubted whether he would live to stand trial. He was on his way to a hospital.

There was only one role left for Thomas to fill. He made tea, poured brandies, listened and offered consolation, but the role he was burning for was avenger. He wished more than anything that it was possible for him to have five minutes alone with Seth Parker, for he would make the man beg and plead for death.

In the absence of any opportunity to exact revenge, Thomas chose to pray silently as he gave his help to each member of the family: that Rosie would come through this unscathed; that Donald would never again need or want to use his physical strength to get the better of another man. But most of all he prayed that Seth would survive, so that he could endure the kind of terror he'd inflicted on Rosie, waiting to be hanged.

Thomas poured a jug of water over Donald's head to rinse off the last of the shampoo. Then he handed him a towel.

'I was just like a Red Indian,' Donald said proudly as he dried himself. 'I would have scalped him too if I'd had a knife.'

That boast of Donald's brought a chink of light to Thomas's black thoughts and even made him smile. The lad sounded like an excited six-year-old just back from a feast of Cowboys and Indians at Saturday morning pictures. Fortunately he had no real conception of exactly what Seth was intending to do to Rosie, or in fact how close he'd come to murder himself. He had been guided only by a primitive protective instinct, and within days he'd probably have forgotten all but the glory of it.

For the first time ever Thomas found himself envying Donald's simpleness. He didn't look back over his shoulder at the past, or try to see into the future. He accepted everything as it was. Good food, clean clothes, the love of his family, warm smiles from neighbours and occasional words of praise were all he needed for complete happiness. Thomas remembered how he'd felt in the camp in Burma, when just one tiny piece of meat or fish in his daily bowl of rice was enough to make him delirious with happiness. He wished he could regain that ability to need and want so little.

*

Two days after Seth snatched Rosie from her bedroom, the press were in the garden of The Grange photographing Donald. Overnight he had become a national hero, and because Norah and Frank were afraid that unscrupulous reporters might resort to underhand methods to talk to their son, they had allowed them this one photo-call, strictly under Frank's control.

'Look at them!' Norah whispered scathingly to her husband as they posed for one picture with Donald. She inclined her head towards the end of the garden where people from the village were packed shoulder to shoulder, rubber-necking through bushes, even climbing on to the wall and gate. From time to time someone would shout out extravagant praise, or lead a chorus of 'For He's a Jolly Good Fellow'. The reporters thought it was very moving and were puzzled by Norah's refusal to be photographed with the villagers.

There was an excellent reason for her refusal. Twelve years ago some of these very same people had stood in the same place, screaming hysterically that Donald was a maniac and ought to be behind bars. Norah had forgiven them for that – they were ignorant people who allowed themselves to be caught up in group hysteria. But proud as she was of her son's courage, she didn't intend to share a moment of it with them.

'You don't have to do it,' Thomas reminded Rosie as they came downstairs. They had been watching the noisy scene from a bedroom upstairs and Rosie had suggested that she went out there too and got it over and done with.

'They won't stop telephoning and calling round until I do,' she said in a firm, crisp voice. 'Besides I'm fine now, and they'll like it better if they can see me while I still look beaten up.'

Thomas looked at her appraisingly. She was still very pale and was having difficulty in holding a cup of tea because of her shaking hands. But apart from one badly bruised eye where Seth had punched her and vivid scratches on her arms and legs, she didn't look so bad. He thought she must have a nervous system made of steel, because apart from breaking down when she first told Norah everything Seth had said and done, she had somehow managed to maintain an air of near-indifference to the events of that night.

'Well, just do a quick interview then,' Thomas said, his hand on the half-glass door which opened into the porch. He wasn't convinced that she was as inwardly composed as her exterior suggested. 'If they ask any awkward questions or I think you look distressed, I'll drag you in by the scruff of your neck.'

'Okay, bossy-boots,' she said with a grin. 'Lead on.'

The moment Rosie stepped outside the front door, a buzz went round amongst the journalists and photographers gathered round Donald and his parents further down the drive.

'It's her,' 'The girl's here' and 'It's Parker's daughter' were some of the remarks Thomas heard. As one they turned away from Donald and flocked up the garden towards Rosie.

'How are you feeling, Rosie?' one young reporter shouted out, determined to get something meaty out of her if it was the last thing he did. Donald Cook was a dead loss as far as he was concerned, keen enough to pose for pictures, but he couldn't give a very lucid account of how he'd managed to overcome Seth Parker. What's more, his father had already marked their card and said no one was to print that his son was simple-minded, and without that juicy bit there wasn't much of a story.

'I'm better now, thank you,' Rosie said. She felt intimidated to find herself surrounded by men clamouring to speak to her.

'How do you feel about your brother now?' the same reporter threw in, hoping for an unguarded answer while she was still unprepared.

Thomas bristled at the question and tightened his grip on Rosie's arm. She glanced at him to reassure him. 'He's only my half-brother,' she said. 'I'm just glad he's somewhere he can't hurt anyone else.'

'Is it true that it was him and not your father who murdered Ruby Blackwell and Heather Farley?' another reporter called out.

Rosie lifted her head and looked out defiantly. 'Yes, that's right,' she said. 'Seth told me himself that it was him. My father was an innocent man.'

'But your father must have guessed it was his son who killed them. Why didn't he speak up at his trial?'

'I don't know,' she said truthfully. That was a question she had asked herself again and again in the last two days, and she still hadn't come up with any answer. 'Maybe he hoped Seth would confess, but it's too late to ask him now.'

'Do you hope Seth will recover to stand trial?' someone from the back of the bank of reporters called out.

Rosie knew someone would find fault, however she answered that question. 'I hope he recovers enough to make a confession which will clear my father's name,' she said evenly. 'I haven't thought beyond that.'

'That's enough now,' Thomas said suddenly as the reporters' questions became too probing. He could see they didn't care tuppence about Rosie. All they wanted was more horror to thrill their readers. One had actually seemed disappointed to see she wasn't more badly scarred. He knew they would rush back to their offices and embroider what they'd been told with sensationalism, twisting the truth to make both Donald and her into a pair of freaks from a sideshow. 'I'm taking Rosie in now. You have everything you need.'

'Not quite, Mr Farley. It is Thomas Farley, isn't it, the brother of Heather Farley?' A foxy-faced man in his twenties pushed his way to the front of the crowd, his eyes narrowing with malicious intent. Thomas was pretty certain he was one of the journalists who had practically camped outside the shop in Flask Walk during the trial. 'As the brother of one of the women murdered by Parker, and chief prosecution witness at his trial, I'm somewhat surprised to find you involved here. I'm sure we'd all love to hear how and when you and Rosie came to be such good friends. Was it before or after the trial?'

Thomas couldn't think of any reply, clever or otherwise, so he merely glared at the man for a second, then took Rosie's arm more firmly, wheeled round and escorted her indoors.

Rosie went over to the stairs and sat down, looking questioningly back at Thomas. He was still standing by the porch door, quivering with anger.

'Thomas,' she said quietly, 'what is it?'

'I loathe and detest journalists,' he said vehemently. 'They are the human version of vultures.'

Rosie could understand him being angry at being picked on by that journalist. There was a definite implication that there was something odd, shady even, about them being friends. Yet she thought his reaction was a bit extreme. 'We always knew that someday, someone would ask us that question,' she said. 'Maybe you should just have told him how it came about?'

The front door was still open wide, but they had closed the inner door. It had red stained-glass panels and the sun coming in was turning his fair hair pink. Outside the press were still firing questions at Donald and his parents, but here in the hall they seemed a long way away.

'You know why. I can't stand talking about Cole or Heather. I never see our friendship as having anything to do with them, or what happened. We are separate.'

Rosie was just about to say how good that sounded, when Thomas turned his head to one side. His face had been in shadow until then, but as he moved she saw tears glistening on his lashes. It reminded her that she'd thought

571

he'd changed in some way since Seth abducted her – how exactly she couldn't pinpoint, just less sure of himself, brooding perhaps.

In the last two days she'd had every opportunity to talk about what had happened to her. The police, the doctor, Mrs Cook, everyone was only too keen to listen and give comfort. Yet although she'd told all those people most of what had happened, she still hadn't revealed how she actually felt about it.

That policeman's words, 'It's all over now', came back to her. He was wrong, just as she'd suspected. An incident as traumatic as this one had been, with deep roots in the past, couldn't be forgotten with just a couple of brandies and a hot bath.

In a flash of intuition she knew that it was the same for Thomas as it was for her. Both of them needed to examine their feelings, about the recent events and the old injuries too. Thomas had joked soon after she was brought home about being as useful in her rescue as a chocolate fireguard. Now she realized it wasn't a joke, but a statement of exactly how he felt.

She got up from the stairs and walked across the hall to him. Impulsively she slid her arms around his waist and held him tight. 'It's time we really talked,' she said softly against his shoulder, surprised by how good it felt to hold him. 'After all those people have gone, shall we slip out on our own somewhere?'

His lips brushed against her cheek. 'I was thinking I ought to go back to London. Mr Bryant sounded as if he was losing patience when I phoned him yesterday.'

Rosie sensed this was an excuse. He wanted to crawl back into a hole where no one could question him. But she wasn't going to let him do that. 'You could go back on the evening train,' she suggested. 'That still leaves this afternoon.'

She heard a sigh form deep inside him, almost as if he knew he couldn't fight her will. He took a step back from her and forced a smile. 'Okay, but I don't know where we can go without bumping into someone.'

'I do,' Rosie smiled up at him. 'Trust me.'

'Are you sure about this?' Thomas asked as Rosie unlocked the side gate of Swallows, a small cottage just five minutes away from The Grange.

'Mr Tweedy asked me a while ago to come and make a plan for improving his garden,' Rosie replied with a mischievous grin. 'He and his wife are away on holiday until next Saturday, that's why they gave me this key. So maybe I'm not actually going to plan the garden today, but I need to sit in it for a bit to get the feel of it.'

It was a garden that had been allowed to run wild for several years. The many flowering shrubs overshadowed the small lawn, and a pergola was almost collapsing under the weight of wisteria and climbing roses. Seen now at the height of summer after the recent heavy rain, it was a glorious, colourful jungle and an ideal secluded place to talk freely.

'So what else do we have to talk about that requires so much privacy?' Thomas asked eventually. They were sitting on a bench in the sunshine and had already been through a discussion about Donald and what effect being pushed into the limelight might have on him.

'Something I should have admitted a long time ago,' she said simply. 'You may hate me after I've told you.'

Thomas turned on the seat to look Rosie in the face, disturbed by her words. She had regained her colour since the press had left the house. In fact she'd seemed quite bouncy and normal again over lunch. He hadn't imagined she intended to reveal any deep, dark secrets this afternoon. He thought she just needed to get away somewhere quiet.

'I don't think I could hate you for anything, however bad it was,' he said, putting one hand on her cheek. 'But what makes you want to tell me now?'

573

'Something you said this morning made me see that neither of us can move on in our lives until we fully come to terms with the past,' she said in a rush, brushing his hand away from her cheek. 'I've got this locked away. I think you've got something too. So I'm going to tell you mine, in the hope you'll tell me what's bothering you.'

Thomas felt an unpleasant prickle in his spine. He frowned. 'Something to do with Heather? Did Seth tell you what he did to her?'

'Yes, in crude, graphic detail,' Rosie admitted, hanging her head. 'But that's not it. It's something that happened a year before she disappeared. If I'd told my father then, Heather would still be alive now.'

Rosie had buried the memory of her brothers raping Heather. It hadn't been entirely erased from her mind, any more than she could wipe out the horror of her father's trial and hanging, but she had buried it deeply enough for her to go months and months without thinking of it. When Seth forced her to listen to his boasts about all the other times he'd abused Heather, and that last day with her before he killed her, the true significance of what she'd seen and kept quiet about was laid bare.

Every word stung as she described to Thomas what she'd seen as an innocent eleven-year-old. She could recall all the noises, from the rain outside to the creaking bed, the men's grunts and Heather's cries, just as if it happened yesterday.

Thomas sat very still as she was speaking, but he was clenching and unclenching his fists in a frightening manner.

'I'm to blame,' she whispered when she'd finished. 'If I'd told Dad that night, he would have thrown Seth and Norman out. Dad and Heather would have been happy again. But instead it just went on and on.'

'Why didn't you tell him?' Thomas said in a strangled voice.

'I was scared.' It sounded so weak and pathetic, but yet

she could vividly recall the terrible nightmares which followed that day, and the fear that Seth would do it to her too.

Thomas took a deep breath. He wanted to go and punch that tottering pergola in front of him so it came crashing to the ground, but he controlled the urge.

'You were only a child,' he said at length. 'You didn't fully comprehend what you'd seen, any more than Donald really understood what Seth was trying to do to you the other night.'

'I did,' she admitted. 'I even expected that Heather would run away after that. I just hoped she'd take me when she went.'

Thomas just sat there unable to speak for a moment. He wondered how Rosie could have become such a beautiful person, inside and out, after being exposed to such things.

'So that's why he killed her?' he said eventually. 'She got brave one day and she threatened to blow the whistle on him?'

Rosie nodded.

Thomas slumped forward, his head nearly on his knees. 'Oh Rosie,' he said. 'I don't know which is worse – you carrying that memory in your head, or putting such a terrible picture into mine.'

Rosie began to cry. It had all seemed so simple earlier. She would tell him this shameful dreadful secret and he would get angry enough to bring out whatever it was that was troubling him. Yet all she'd succeeded in doing was giving him more anguish.

'For God's sake, get angry!' she suddenly roared out. 'You are allowed to be angry. It's quite normal! Or did you lose the ability to show your feelings when you lost your leg?'

He straightened up with a jerk, his lean face flushed and his lips curled back.

'Angry! I'm more than angry, I'm furious!' he said in a rasping voice. 'But there's no one left to take it out on, is there? Your father's been hanged, Donald's virtually destroyed Seth, and your other brother is in hiding somewhere. What do you want me to do, Rosie? Beat the stuffing out of you to show what a big man I am? That's what the men in your family do, isn't it? But I couldn't even hurt you – one punch and I'd probably fall over. I'm no use to anyone.'

'I said get angry, not feel sorry for yourself,' she snapped back. 'So you've lost a leg – you've still got plenty of other things going for you. You've got two eyes, two hands and a fine brain. What's a missing leg?'

'I'll tell you what a missing leg means,' Thomas snarled, standing up and glowering down at her. 'It means you can't run to protect a woman you love, you can't fight for her, and she'll never want you anyway.'

Rosie could only stare back into his angry brown eyes in amazement. But as the full realization of what he'd admitted came to her, she felt deep shame at having goaded him into revealing it.

'Oh Thomas,' she whispered.

'I'd better go,' he said, turning away. 'I shouldn't have said that. Forget it.'

Rosie got up and grabbed his arm. 'You were right to say it if it's the truth,' she said in a low voice. 'But I don't agree a woman wouldn't want you just because you couldn't fight to protect her.'

Thomas gave a tight little laugh and looked scornfully at her. 'Wake up, Rosie! So a woman might be able to love a man with a heart condition, a blind man or even one with an incurable disease. There's a touch of romanticism to that. But not one with an ugly stump. I know because other women have seen it, and it killed anything that might have happened stone dead.'

Rosie felt the deep-seated inner pain that had prompted such a speech and it made her wince. She had believed she knew him, but just as she had locked away that image of Heather and her brothers, unable to speak of it, so he had locked this fear of rejection away too. She had always loved him as a friend, confidant, sometimes brother and father figure too. But she wasn't seeing him in any one of those roles now. He was just a man who meant the world to her.

'A woman who truly loved you for yourself wouldn't be put off,' she said tartly. 'And a man can fight for a woman without using his fists. Ever heard of wooing? It's insulting to women to suggest that every single female who might be attracted to you is bound to drop you after one glimpse of your stump. You weren't the only man during the war to lose a limb, and I'm damn sure many of those others have fallen in love, married and had children.'

Thomas squinted at Rosie, the sun in his eyes. 'So how does a man start wooing a woman he's known since she was a little ragamuffin?' he said softly.

Rosie smiled. She didn't have the least idea of how to try to shift a long-standing friendship into a different gear.

'You're the one with all the experience,' she said. 'But I always thought kissing was the way most people get started.'

'I'm too old for you,' he groaned.

'That's a pathetic excuse,' she said, and knowing he wasn't going to make the first move, she did. She stepped forward, took his face in both hands and kissed him lingeringly on the lips.

His arms came round her and suddenly it was him who was kissing her with sensual, soft lips which made her every nerve-ending tingle. Rosie knew then that she hadn't made a fatal mistake; she felt the same hunger she could sense in him.

'You're some sort of demon kisser,' she said, when he eventually let her go.

'Well, everything else is intact, apart from my leg,' he laughed softly, smoothing her bruised eye with his hand, his eyes glowing as he looked into hers. 'My heart, soul and feelings. I've wanted to kiss you for such a long, long time.'

They stayed in the garden until the sun moved away from the lawn and they were reminded it was after five. Kissing, holding and talking, but this time not merely about the past or recent events, but of the future too. Thomas finally told her about his painting and his hopes for an exhibition in Hampstead.

Rosie felt a huge surge of excitement. She had seen him sketching occasionally when he came down here. On her last visit to his flat she'd thought she smelled paint, but as she'd seen no actual evidence that he'd really taken up his old hobby she'd forgotten about it.

'When will this exhibition be?' she gasped.

'Probably in November,' he said, thrilled by her reaction. 'If people like my work, maybe I won't need to stay in London, mending clocks and watches,' he said. 'I could move to the country and work there.'

'While I garden?' she asked laughingly. 'Is that what you mean?'

He held her face tenderly in both hands, looking into her eyes. 'It's too soon to speak of such things, Rosie. I didn't mean to admit my feelings for you today, it wasn't fair of me after the terrible ordeal you've just been through. But now I have, it puts you in an impossible position.'

'It doesn't!' she said indignantly.

'It does,' he insisted. 'You might at this moment think you share my feelings and even believe we can build a future together. But it could just be sympathy and in a few months you might very well see things differently.'

Rosie shrugged. 'I won't.'

Her stubborn expression made him laugh. 'We'll see. Let's take things in easy stages. I'd like you to come up to London for the exhibition. I'd also like to show you around and introduce you to a few people who aren't country yokels. But don't let's think beyond that for now.'

As they walked back to The Grange, Rosie felt as if she was walking on air. Just a few hours ago she could see no further than a day ahead. Everything was flat and grey. Now she felt as if someone had just switched a black-and-white film to glorious Technicolor.

'Something's changed, hasn't it?' Norah said as Rosie came bouncing in after seeing Thomas off at the station that evening.

'Yes,' Rosie agreed, and just stood there in the kitchen grinning foolishly. 'I suppose so. He's kind of moved on from just being a friend.'

Norah smiled. She had suspected at the time of Miss Pemberton's death that Thomas's feelings were more than just friendship. 'I'm very glad for you both,' she said honestly. 'I hope it works out.'

'Do you?' Rosie's eyes were as big as millstones. She had half expected her employer to throw cold water on the idea.

Norah was just about to caution Rosie that she'd been through a terrible ordeal only days before and might be on the rebound from Gareth. But one glance again at the happy face in front of her stopped her.

'I do indeed. You have a great deal in common.'

'You don't think he's too old for me, then?' she asked.

'No. Maybe I would if you were any other girl,' she said with a warm smile. 'But you've always been so mature. In fact I couldn't imagine you having anything in common with a boy of your own age. The only worry I have now is that this might be a reaction to what happened the other night. So take it slowly, Rosie.'

Two months after the afternoon in the garden at Swallows, Rosie was out in the greenhouse potting some cuttings. It was an October Saturday morning and she and Donald were busier than ever tidying up gardens and planting spring bulbs. But it was raining hard, so she'd opted to stay where she was while Donald went to a job on his own. He liked rain, it never kept him indoors.

Everything was calm again in the village. Seth Parker was all but forgotten, since it was pronounced he was unfit to stand trial. Everyone assumed this was as a result of his injuries. It was only Rosie and those closest to her who knew the truth. Seth was considered by the psychiatrists to be insane. He would spend the rest of his life in a secure mental hospital.

For Rosie who had a real idea of just how grim that would be, it was more appropriate for Seth than hanging. She had been sent a report by the psychiatrist handling Seth's case and it seemed all her brother's problems were connected to his mother deserting him. He idolized his father, yet hated him too because he held him responsible for Ethel leaving. In the same way he wanted to punish every woman he met to get back at his mother.

Rosie still didn't know if her father would ever be granted a posthumous pardon. The word of a man mentally unfit to stand trial could hardly be believed. But she had moved on from agonizing over such things. She felt happy and secure again. She had Donald for company, who was none the worse for that night in the woods – if anything it had made him sharper and more confident. Often in the evenings they'd slip across to the pub for a drink and she had got to know many other people in her own age group. Most Sundays Thomas came down, and she'd been up to London to spend the day with him a couple of times. She'd made long-term plans too: she was going to look for clients who wanted their gardens designed rather than just tidied up. Thomas had offered to take her rough layouts and produce professional-looking scale plans for her.

Everything was just about perfect. Except Thomas's reluctance to take things a step further.

He kissed her all the time, so passionately she was sure it would soon lead to something more. But he was always the one who put the brakes on. Rosie wanted him so badly she could think of nothing else, but when she told him this he laughed and made excuses: she was on the rebound from Gareth; she might get pregnant; they had to be absolutely certain first; he wanted the first time to be somewhere special. Anything but the truth, which was that he was afraid of her seeing his stump.

Maybe if he'd invited her to his flat she could have pushed him into a corner. But Thomas made excuses as to why he couldn't do that either. His living-room was now a studio and was a mess; he didn't want her to see it.

It was the sound of the kitchen door opening that drew Rosie out of her thoughts and made her look up from her work. Norah Cook was rushing down the garden, protecting her newly set hair from the rain with an apron over her head.

'Oh Rosie, Gareth's here!' she called out breathlessly before she even reached the greenhouse. 'I told him I didn't think you'd want to see him, but he said you've got to. I think he wants to apologize. I couldn't do anything but invite him in.'

Rosie was so surprised she couldn't think of anything to say for a moment.

'Gareth apologize?' she managed eventually. 'Well, there's a turn-up. He'd better come out here – I've got a lot to do and my shoes are muddy.'

Norah half smiled. It wasn't that long since Rosie would have flown into the house, combed her hair and put on some lipstick before seeing him. Clearly she really had got over him.

'Okay, I'll send him out,' she said, and ran back up the garden.

But as Gareth appeared on the terrace, looking very handsome in a new navy blue suit, Rosie's heart did an unexpected somersault. He'd lost a little weight and let his hair grow a little longer. The endearing curls were back, and she was afraid her old feelings for him were too.

She stubbornly continued potting her cuttings, not even looking at him as he sprinted down the garden. She wished she wasn't wearing such baggy, dirty trousers and that she'd washed her hair last night. She would have felt more confident if she was looking good.

'Hullo, Rosie,' he said from outside the door of the greenhouse. 'Have we really got to talk out here? Can't you come indoors with me?'

'I'm too busy for that,' she said, trying very hard to look disinterested. 'You'll have to come in here. But mind how you go, it's a bit mucky.'

He came right in and perched gingerly on an upturned orange-box. 'You don't seem very surprised to see me,' he said, wrinkling his nose in disapproval at the stink of the compost.

Rosie merely shrugged. She filled another flowerpot with soil. 'Should I be?'

'Well, I thought you would be,' he said. 'You see, I came down to tell you I'm sorry.'

'Sorry about what?' She glanced round at him. He might look the way he did when she first fell for him as he'd lost some weight and let his hair grow, but he still seemed as full of himself as ever, and she could smell beer. Obviously he'd popped into the pub for Dutch courage before coming. 'Sorry that it wasn't my dad who was the murderer but my brother instead? Or sorry I nearly got killed too?' She gave him a long, cold stare.

'I was a mug,' he said, hanging his head. 'I've missed you so much. I want to start all over again.'

Night after night after he'd sent that terse, cold note, Rosie had dreamed of this scenario. If he'd turned up then, she knew she would have forgiven and forgotten because she needed him so badly. Even if he'd written or called to show his sympathy after Seth abducted her, she might have thought more kindly of him. But everything was different now. She had found not only that she could survive without him, but in fact she was a great deal happier. He would have to crawl at her feet before she could forgive him.

Silently she listened to his long litany of woes. He couldn't concentrate at work, he was off his food, no other girl would ever replace her, even his mother had called him a fool to ditch her. He missed coming down here at weekends, he was prepared to move to Tonbridge now, he wouldn't even mind living in the country.

She waited, thinking that any minute he would come to the crucial part and admit what a louse he'd been and show concern for what she'd suffered. She expected him to want to know the details of what Seth had done to her, to be angry that the police hadn't given her better protection. Or even to ask how Donald had been since that night, and if the rest of the Cook family had been affected. But there was nothing like that. All he could talk about was himself.

She let him go on, nodding as if in approval as he spoke of some new houses being built near Tonbridge and how he thought they could put a deposit down on one. But when he got round to saying his mother was prepared to give them her old three-piece suite as she was tired of it, Rosie gripped the edge of her workbench in anger. All at once she wondered how on earth she'd ever imagined herself to be in love with this pompous, self-centred ass.

'How nice of your mother,' she finally blurted out. 'How thoughtful of her to offer me her furniture,' she added, pausing for just one moment to allow the sarcasm to filter through. 'But you can tell her from me I don't want anything of hers in my home, especially not her son.'

Gareth looked astonished. 'But I thought –'

'You thought you were such a catch that you only had to turn up here and say you're sorry and I'd leap into your arms,' she retorted sneeringly. 'Let me spell it out for you. I'm glad you ditched me when you did, Gareth.

I found out then how worthless you were. If you had turned up here today in a gold-plated Cadillac and offered me a place to live in, I'd still tell you to shove off.'

'But, Rosie –'

'Don't "But, Rosie" me,' she snarled at him. 'I expect a man who said he wanted to marry me to be prepared to die for me. He'd certainly catch the next train here if he thought I was in danger or needed his support. I don't want a man who can't share everything, good and bad. Or one who does what his mother tells him to, who cares more about himself, trains and motorbikes than my feelings.'

He managed to look just a little chastened. 'But it was your fault. You didn't tell me about yourself.'

'No, I didn't. But then you never really asked me anything, did you? I'll tell you now why that was, because you were never that interested in me, not as a person. The kind of man I want and need would want to know every last thing about me. From the moment of my birth onwards. He'd care about my interests, want to discuss everything I do, dream and think about.'

'Men aren't like that,' Gareth snorted scornfully. 'Except in books and films. You're living in a fantasy world.'

'I know several men who are,' she retorted, beginning to enjoy herself. 'And one in particular. I just wish I hadn't wasted two years of my life with you, when I could have been with him.'

Gareth's mouth fell open and a crimson flush crept up his neck. 'Who's that?'

'Thomas, of course,' she said airily.

'You fancy a cripple?' he sneered.

She saw red and leapt forward to slap his face. 'He is not a cripple,' she roared. 'He may have lost a leg, but he's twice the man you are. He was just your age when he had it cut off, without anaesthetic, miles from anywhere in a jungle. You couldn't even cope with a bad finger unless your mother was there to dress it for you. You are the real cripple, Gareth, not my Thomas. Now get out of here before I do you an injury.'

Gareth backed away to the door, but he hesitated before moving out into the rain. 'All right, I'll go, if that's the way you want to be. But there isn't a train until four-thirty and I'll get soaked if I go down to the station in this. Can't we go indoors and have a cup of tea?'

All at once Rosie saw the funny side of it all. She giggled. Gareth looked baffled. 'I can't see what's so funny. My new suit will be ruined.'

The giggle turned into a shriek of laughter. 'You may have two legs, but you've only got half a brain,' she said, giving him a push out into the rain. 'Did you really think a new suit and your mother's old armchairs would do anything for me? Didn't you learn anything about me in our time together?'

'You're mad,' he said in alarm, backing away from her. 'As mad as your brother.'

'I am mad,' she yelled after him as he ran up the garden. 'Mad for Thomas like I never was for you.'

After he'd gone Rosie sat on the box Gareth had just vacated and continued to laugh. She thought of his tight-lipped mother in her spotless house and that set her off again. Remembering how Gareth knew train timetables by heart, she rocked with merriment. Tears ran down her cheeks with the laughter, and as she imagined him dodging into doorways all the way to the station she had to hold her sides.

'What's so funny?' Donald's voice from the doorway caught her short.

He was dressed in a yellow waterproof coat, wellingtons and a sou'wester. He looked like the man on the Shiphams fishpaste advertisements.

'It's Gareth,' she said, still spluttering with laughter as she made room for him to come in out of the rain. 'Oh Donald, I wish you'd been here, he was so pathetic. I can't imagine what I ever saw in him.'

Donald tilted back his sou'wester. His face was still a golden brown from working outside and his eyes were the clearest blue. 'Good,' he said, a big smile spreading across his face. 'That means you can marry Thomas, doesn't it?'

'Now what makes you think Thomas would want to marry me?' she asked, reaching out and ruffling his damp hair affectionately.

Donald looked surprised at her question. 'Of course he does. Last time he was here he said he hated going back to London. I said he didn't need to go, he could marry you and stay with us for ever.'

'And what did he say to that?' Rosie laughed. She was always very aware of Donald's limitations. He certainly didn't understand the complexities of adult emotions.

'He said he'd like to, but you loved Gareth, not him.'

Rosie frowned. Donald got people's meanings all wrong all the time. He took everything said to him as gospel, whether it was intended as a light-hearted joke, sarcasm or serious comment. But one thing Rosie had learned was that he was very good at relaying exactly what people had said. He hadn't learned to embellish things, and unless Donald had suddenly acquired that talent, she could entirely believe him. That put a different complexion on Thomas's reluctance to take things a step further. While she had believed his leg to be the only problem, Thomas had seen Gareth as an immovable obstacle.

Rosie wanted to laugh at the absurdity of it, yet she could see there was some truth in that, or at least there had been until Gareth walked into the greenhouse. She had needed that showdown with him – to see him once and for all – to rid her of any romantic illusions she'd once held. She knew now that she never, ever wanted to clap eyes on Gareth again. The relationship was truly dead and buried.

She thought for just a moment. 'Would you finish

potting these for me?' she asked Donald, waving her hand at the cuttings.

'Why? Where are you going?' he asked.

'To London,' she said with a grin. 'To see Thomas.'

Norah was making a cake when Rosie burst into the kitchen to ask if she'd mind if she went to London for the rest of the weekend.

'What, now?' she asked, raising her eyebrows. 'On the same train as Gareth?'

Rosie hadn't considered that, but the irony of it appealed to her. 'I doubt if he'll even recognize me in my new outfit,' she giggled. 'But I'll wait till the last minute before jumping on the train and get in the Ladies Only carriage.'

Rosie arrived at the station with only a minute to spare to buy her ticket. She could hear the train coming in. She waited in the ticket hall for a moment or two until a few passengers had come out, then nipped out to the platform and straight on to the train. She caught a glimpse of Gareth further down as he got into the front coach.

She was so excited and never more sure of herself. Her appearance reflected everything she felt. A couple of weeks earlier she'd taken some money out of her savings to buy a midnight-blue coat with a velvet collar from a very expensive shop in Tunbridge Wells. She had intended to wear it for the first time to Thomas's art exhibition, but today was more important. It was quite beautiful, a soft lightweight wool in the new Princess style which clung to her slim figure. She had a small, matching, velvet skull-cap too, and her curls wound up around it in a fetching manner. Underneath she wore a plain navy sheath dress. It wasn't new but it was smart, too smart to wear in Mayfield.

It had been such a rush to have a bath, wash her hair and do her nails, all in time to catch the train. She wondered what Thomas would say when he saw her.

*

The church clock was striking seven as she rang the bell on the shop door in Flask Walk. She clutched her small suitcase and took a deep breath to steady her nerves. As she heard Thomas clonking down the stairs, she resolved that once they were together for ever, they'd find a bungalow so he didn't have the strain of stairs.

His face broke into a broad smile as he saw her face pressed up against the glass. He flicked on the light and moved faster across the small shop to open the door.

'Rosie!' he exclaimed. 'What on earth are you doing here?'

'I'm here to see you,' she said, and with that threw herself into his arms.

'But why now?' he said, after kissing her. 'And why the case?'

'Because I'm going to stay the night with you,' she said. 'But you'll have to get yourself smartened up because we're going out to dinner first.'

She was surprised he didn't argue. All he asked was if the Cooks knew she was coming here, and said it was lucky he'd collected his best shirt from the laundry. He also said the living-room was a pig-sty and she'd probably want to catch the next train home.

While Thomas was shaving, Rosie went into his living-room. It was messy just as he'd said, pots and tubes of oil paints strewn everywhere, pencil sketches littering the floor, and a recently started painting on his easel. But a finished painting propped against a chair caught her attention. It was of two small girls bent over a battered doll's pram. It was absolutely delightful, but her first reaction was to wonder what prompted such a subject.

Thomas hadn't said what subjects he painted. She had assumed they were all scenic like the two she'd seen on his walls. She had never imagined him painting people.

The picture had a curious timeless quality. The little girls had very worn-looking dresses, in dull colours; the background had a murky tenement or back-alley feel to it. But for the short clothes showing plump legs, they could be two little girls from any period.

Thomas came back into the room adjusting his tie. He paused to watch her looking at the painting.

'Your verdict, milady?' he said.

'It's truly magical,' she said, smiling at him. 'What made you paint them?'

'Because they were there,' he laughed. 'I saw them out of this window one Sunday afternoon and I quickly sketched them. I suppose it brought back images of Heather. We never had enough money for her to have a doll's pram, but I remember her borrowing one once.'

'She used to love taking Alan out in his pram,' Rosie said, suddenly seeing Heather in her mind's eye, pushing the pram fast and letting it go, then running after it to make Alan laugh. She was on the point of reminiscing how much she missed Heather in those first few months after she disappeared, of how she had to push Alan in his pram up to the village to be minded by a neighbour while she went to school, but she caught herself in time. Tonight wasn't the occasion for speaking of sad things.

'So where are we going to eat?' Thomas asked, picking up a clothes-brush to clean his jacket.

'In that posh Italian place up the road,' Rosie said. 'And it's my treat, before you start arguing. I thought of it.'

He raised an eyebrow as if wanting to disagree, but Rosie wagged a finger at him. 'Don't you dare! Otherwise I'll behave like a guttersnipe in there and embarrass you.'

'You couldn't possibly behave like a guttersnipe in that outfit,' he said with a smile. 'Did I tell you that you look like a film star?'

'I thought you hadn't noticed,' she laughed, twirling round for his benefit. 'I bought this for the opening of your exhibition. But I thought tonight was just as important, perhaps more in a way.'

'And why?' he asked, coming closer to hug her.

'Because it's the special night we've both been waiting

for,' she said. 'And because I've got something very funny to tell you.'

The waiter took them to a table in an alcove at the back of the restaurant and lit the candle on the table. Rosie had grown used to eating out as the Cooks often took her and Donald with them to their favourite restaurant in Tunbridge Wells. But that was a brightly lit place, with big silver covers on the joints of meat and sparkling white tablecloths. This place was small, intimate and dark, with checked tablecloths and flowers on the table. She liked it very much more.

They had minestrone soup first. Then, as the waiter brought the main course of chicken and vegetables, Rosie told Thomas about Gareth's visit.

She was good at telling funny stories. She described his new suit and his obvious annoyance that she didn't take him back into the house, then she launched into his litany of misery, adding a few extra things for good measure. All she omitted was Gareth's description of Thomas as a cripple. She changed that to 'being so old'.

Thomas was laughing with her as she got to the part about Mrs Jones's three-piece suite, and although he knew what Gareth must really have said about him, he took some pleasure in imagining the man being so taken aback by the volley of abuse Rosie flung at him. But what pleased him most was to see the joy in her face as she related the tale. He knew she meant every word, and for her to rush off on the train, taking the risk that Gareth would see her and think she'd come after him, was so very flattering.

'So it is finally dead and buried,' she concluded. 'You were daft to think I still held a torch for him. I suppose that's why you've been holding me at arm's length?'

Thomas was somewhat surprised by her direct approach. But then she'd always been so direct about everything. Yet women were funny things, one moment outspoken, the next afraid to say what was on their minds.

In five years of being in Hampstead he'd had many women friends. Before he'd found his heart was in Rosie's keeping, several of them had claimed to love him, some had been to bed with him, yet not one of them had been honest enough to admit that his disability put them off. One in particular had wounded him almost mortally when after a night of passion she'd turned her head away as he got out of bed and loudly insisted he put on his trousers immediately.

'I've been holding you at arm's length for lots of reasons,' he said, taking her hand in his. 'Gareth was the major one. I was afraid you still cared for him, and we all do silly things on the rebound. But that isn't the only reason. There is my leg, and the fact that I'm so much older than you. You see, I value you as a friend above all else, Rosie. I couldn't bear to lose you, so I had to be sure of you first.'

They were both a little tipsy as they walked home. Hampstead Village looked enchanting to Rosie with its bow-fronted shop windows all lit up and with beautiful displays unlike anything she ever saw in Sussex. She was excited by everything – the clear, starry sky, the leaves blowing down on to pavements, the music wafting out of public houses and Thomas's hand in hers.

In a week's time she would be nineteen. If she'd been born to any other family down on the Somerset Levels, she would probably be married with children of her own by now. Yet she was still a virgin. But not for much longer.

Thomas lit the fire in his living-room and produced a bottle of champagne he'd bought for the opening of his exhibition. It was warm because he didn't have a refrigerator, and placing it outside the kitchen window while they were out hadn't really had the desired effect. He wished he'd had some warning that Rosie was coming tonight. He would have changed the sheets on his bed, spring-cleaned the flat and bought candles to make it all more romantic. Yet despite his anxiety, just Rosie's presence was enough to make his heart beat faster. In the soft glow of the fire her coppery curls, pink cheeks and sparkling eyes gave the untidy little room beauty.

Rosie giggled as she sipped the first glass. 'I always wondered what champagne tasted like,' she said. 'I got a book from the library once where the heroine drank it sitting in her bath. One night when I was having a bath in the kitchen, I poured myself a glass of lemonade to pretend I was her.'

Thomas smiled at the mental picture of a skinny teenager sitting in a tin bath imagining such things. 'Maybe one day I can take you somewhere glamorous enough to try it out,' he said. 'But for tonight we can pretend this is a suite in the Dorchester.'

'Have you ever stayed anywhere really grand?' she asked. She liked the champagne and the effect it was having. She moved her chair a little closer to Thomas and took his hand in hers.

'No, I haven't.' He shook his head ruefully. 'I went into Raffles, a posh hotel in Singapore, a few times, but only for drinks. That was splendid, with polished wood floors, big fans keeping it cool and soft armchairs. I used to dream of it a great deal when I was in the camp. But maybe if I sell lots of pictures at the exhibition I'll be able to take you somewhere like that.'

Rosie slipped off her chair and knelt down in front of him, leaning her arms on his lap. 'It's good that both of us haven't ever had much, isn't it? I mean, we can dream about it all together, and plan how we're going to get there.'

Thomas's heart contracted painfully at her words. They made the gulf between their ages and experience so much narrower. Joy and excitement bubbled up inside him like the champagne. At last he felt he was stepping out of a long, dark tunnel into bright sunshine, and before him lay a road lined with all the things that had once seemed unattainable.

Her eyes, looking like sapphires in the firelight, were glowing for him, and her soft lips were waiting to be feasted upon. He was just twenty again, and all the niggling doubts in his mind vanished as he bent to kiss her.

'Let's get into bed,' Rosie whispered some minutes later. She stood up and took both his hands, urging him out of his seat. Her lips were swollen with kissing, her hair as tousled as it had been the first time he saw her.

Thomas wished he could pick her up in his arms and carry her to the bedroom, but Rosie slipped her arms around his waist and led him there herself. He sat down on the bed. This was the moment he'd been dreading, but Rosie sat beside him and kissed him again, gently pushing him on to his back.

'I love you,' she said simply. 'I know you are embarrassed, but so am I and tonight's just the beginning of something wonderful for both of us. So we aren't going to let it stand in our way.'

It wasn't until Rosie knelt up on the bed beside him and slowly began to undress him that he was reminded she had always been a carer, and that she had bathed and dressed adults with worse disabilities than his. She took off his shirt first, running her fingertips across the smooth skin of his chest, kissing his shoulders, arms and abdomen with such tenderness that he felt the embarrassment fading.

Half nurse, half lover, she slowly stripped him of his shoes and trousers, down to his underpants. He held his breath, searching her face for signs of panic or disgust when she saw the stone-coloured artificial leg lying next to his normal, muscular one, but her loving expression remained unchanged. 'You have a beautiful body,' she murmured as her hands moved to the straps. 'This is the last hurdle.'

The leg clanked as she dropped it to the floor and Thomas closed his eyes, gritted his teeth and waited for the expected gasp. But instead he felt a soft hand stroke the scarred stump tenderly. 'There,' she whispered. 'You can open your eyes now. There are no more secrets between us.'

Thomas opened his eyes to see her through his tears. Her face was serene, her eyes soft with love, and she was caressing and looking at his body with adoration.

He pulled her down to him, overcome by emotion. The mouth that met his was as hungry as his own and he knew that they really had leapt over that last hurdle.

'You are an angel,' he whispered. 'I love you so much.'

She climbed off his bed and began to undress herself. Thomas moved himself round into the bed and watched her with awe. Her dress slid down to the floor, leaving her in a cream satin petticoat. Like a practised temptress she lifted one leg on to the bed and unfastened her stocking, peeling it off slowly, then the other. She smiled at him as she lowered one strap of the petticoat over her shoulder, then the other, and slowly the satin slithered down her slender body, leaving her in satin knickers and a matching brassière.

She climbed back on to the bed and it was only then that Thomas realized she was just as embarrassed about revealing her body as he was.

'I've never seen anything so perfect,' he whispered as he slid his hands around her body and unfastened the hook of her bra. Her breasts were small and uptilted, nipples erect in the cold room, her skin creamy with just a hint of pink that reminded him of the inside of seashells. 'Come into bed. You're cold.'

For Rosie it was the best, most thrilling moment in her life as she cuddled into Thomas's warm body. She hadn't expected to be repelled by his leg. Any thoughts she'd had previously were just curiosity. It wasn't ugly as he'd led her to believe, just a thigh ending above the knee and neatly and smoothly gathered together. She didn't understand why anyone would find it daunting. As for the rest of his body, that was just perfect, a smooth and muscular chest, powerful arms and shoulders. She loved every inch of him.

That feeling of love and adoration became even stronger as he caressed her. His fingertips were so sensitive compared with the rough manner in which Gareth had often handled her, and his kisses sent her off on to another, higher plane. He moved down the bed to kiss and suck at her breasts, and her body seemed to melt into his as if they were one. But it was the things he whispered as he was loving her that made it extra-wonderful – how perfect her breasts were, the silkiness of her skin and how much he wanted her.

Her knickers and his underpants seemed to vanish as if by magic. He gently stroked her vagina and gasped with pleasure as she caressed his penis. There was no rush for fulfilment or any sense that this bliss might suddenly end. It was just perfect eroticism which gradually built into an ever-spiralling ecstasy.

With Gareth, the lack of comfort and the fear of being caught when he petted her had all too often prevented her from getting fully aroused, much less given her any real satisfaction. In the last year or so Gareth had only ever been interested in his own needs, and once they were met he became bored. It wasn't so with Thomas. He ejaculated once and whispered apologies, but he carried on petting her and to her surprise and delight almost immediately grew hard again.

It was a feast of pleasure. Every inch of her body responded to his touch, each kiss deeper and more sensual. Rosie kissed all of him too, his back, his stomach, his penis and his inner thighs, right down to his injury, glorying in the sensation that never again would he feel shame about it.

But it was when he parted the lips of her vagina and

used his tongue on her there that Rosie finally abandoned the last of her inhibitions. She screamed out her pleasure, writhed and bucked under his touch, desperate to reach the point she knew she was heading for. Then at last she felt a burning, melting sensation that seemed to come from deep within, and pulling Thomas towards her she demanded he enter her.

Later as she lay in the rosy afterglow, she was surprised that it hadn't hurt. But at the moment of entry nothing crossed her mind except the great need to have him inside her at all costs. It was wonderful, so thrilling, satisfying and tender. Nothing in her life had ever moved her so much. Tears of joy ran down her cheeks. She called out his name and clung to him like a limpet. She felt like a real woman at last.

Rosie awoke the next morning to hear church bells ringing and, as she groggily opened her eyes, she found Thomas leaning on one elbow looking down at her.

'So the sleeping princess has finally woken,' he said. 'I nipped out and asked them to ring the bells because I couldn't manage to wake you.'

'It must have been that champagne,' she said. They had finished the bottle after the first bout of love-making, then started all over again.

'And to think I assumed it was my love-making which exhausted you,' he smiled. 'I hope you aren't going to tell me you don't remember anything about last night?'

Rosie laughed and snuggled closer to him. 'I remember every last detail,' she said. 'I think even when I'm a little old lady I'll remember it.'

As the train chugged away from Victoria Station that evening, Rosie leaned out of the window and blew frantic farewell kisses to Thomas. But all too soon he was out of sight. She closed the window and sunk down on to the seat. She was glad she didn't have to share the compartment in case someone tried to hold a conversation with her. She wanted to be alone with her thoughts and savour the last twenty-four hours.

It had been the best day in her life. They'd eaten breakfast by the fire in Thomas's living-room, then gone for a walk on Hampstead Heath. Everywhere looked so special, the trees in their autumn colouring, the children sailing boats on Whitestone Pond, nannies in uniform out wheeling their charges in big prams, other couples like them wandering hand in hand. Later they had gone into Jack Straw's Castle and had a couple of drinks before going back to Flask Walk for more love-making.

Thomas was very concerned that they hadn't taken any precautions against her getting pregnant. Rosie didn't care one bit if a baby had already got started last night, but she was touched that Thomas cared enough to insist they were more careful in future.

They'd eaten sandwiches in bed, and between love-making they had talked and talked. For the first time he spoke dreamily about his hopes that the exhibition would be a success, and that one day he might only do clock-mending for pleasure.

'I want the same as you,' he whispered as they lay face to face on the pillows. 'A little cottage with roses round the door. A garden with a stream running through it. I want babies of our own, but room for Donald to come and stay. Maybe one day Alan will come and look us up too.'

'It sounds like heaven,' she said, smiling at his serious face and tracing the fine lines around his eyes.

'That dream kept me going when I was in the camp,' he said. 'I used to visualize every piece of furniture, every inch of the garden. But the girl in my dream never had a face. I tried to give her one, I thought of every film star, of girls I knew back home and ones I'd met in Singapore. But the faces never stayed, no matter how hard I concentrated.'

'Does my face stay?'

'That's when I knew I'd fallen in love,' he said with a sweet smile. 'I found myself lapsing into the dream again around the time you first went to work for Norah and Frank. Suddenly it was you there with me in that cottage. Each time I came down to Mayfield and you spoke about Gareth, your gardening and that little cottage you wanted, I felt so sad. You seemed to share my dream, but you had the wrong man beside you.'

'Did you always know he was wrong for me?'

'No, not really. I wasn't struck on him, but at first I thought he was good for you. You gained confidence and extra sparkle. I was happy for you, I really hoped it would work. But as time went on I could see the flaws. You see, he wanted a very ordinary girl, someone he could mould into what he wanted.'

'And I'm not ordinary?' Rosie's eyes widened.

'No, you aren't. You're just like those moors you come from, wild, fascinating, full of mystery and unexplored places. So beautiful and serene mostly, yet with a darker side too, and that's why I find you so intriguing.'

Rosie closed her eyes and listened to the sound of the train. She thought of the Somerset Levels in high summer: waving grasses up to her waist, swans gliding along the rivers, and a grey heron standing on a bank waiting to catch its dinner. She could feel the hot sun on her arms, the cool mud under her bare feet as she paddled, and the scent of meadowsweet all around her.

She remembered her father teaching her to swim on such a day. Seth and Norman were already in the river splashing each other, both as brown as berries, water glistening on their dark skins and slicked-back hair. Her mother was sitting on the grass bank, laughing as Cole held her under the tummy and instructed her how to make her legs move like a frog. He took his hand away later, and it was some time before she realized it had gone and she was swimming alone.

All at once Rosie saw the significance of that memory.

Cole had insisted that she learned to swim so young because he feared for her safety with so much water around their cottage. For years she'd thought of him as a bad father, latterly because of the crimes she believed he'd committed, and before that because he wasn't quite like her school-friends' fathers. But now, looking back, she saw that in many ways he was one of the best. He'd taught her how to be brave, self-reliant and appreciative of the beauty of nature.

Why did he allow Seth to go unpunished? She thought she even had the answer to that now. He loved his first-born, he saw himself mirrored in him, and perhaps at the bitter end, when he'd discovered what Seth had done, he took the blame for his warped character entirely on to his own shoulders. Maybe he hoped his son would be man enough to confess at the last minute, or that the shock of knowing his father had been hanged for his own crimes would bring him to heel.

'Rest in peace, Dad,' she murmured to herself. 'You taught me to swim and a great deal more. I can get by all on my own now, thanks to you.'

Chapter Twenty

Rosie looked reflectively around her as she made her way up the wide, thickly carpeted staircase. It was the same Piccadilly apartment building from where she'd watched the Coronation procession two and a half years earlier. Back then the opulent flocked wallpaper, red carpet, crystal lights and mahogany banisters had been her idea of an entrance to a palace. She could clearly remember a sudden attack of panic when she first saw it, instantly aware that her apple-green suit looked as cheap as it was, and that before the day was out the Cooks would regret inviting someone so common.

She could laugh about those feelings of inadequacy now, for she had no anxiety today about her appearance, nor her ability to hold her own in company, but she had a remarkably similar sensation of butterflies in her stomach, as if something momentous was about to happen. Perhaps that was just because the last visit here had been an important milestone in her life.

'It feels really peculiar being back here again,' she said, turning her head to Norah who was right behind her. Frank and Donald had gone ahead with their luggage.

'It does to me too,' Norah said with a nervous laugh, remembering the heart-stopping terror of that day. 'I just hope Donald doesn't run off again. But then he's not likely to, is he?'

'Of course he isn't,' Rosie said with a smile. She found it touching that Norah still relied on her for reassurance about her son. 'And even if he did get separated from us by accident, he's perfectly capable of asking for directions back here. You don't need to worry about him.'

They were in London for Thomas's exhibition, which was due to open the next day at a Hampstead gallery. Rosie had only expected to be at the Saturday opening-night party, but two weeks ago on her birthday Mrs Cook said she and her husband had another surprise for her. This was it: a whole week's holiday in London. The Cooks were only staying for the weekend, intending to drive home on Sunday afternoon with Donald. After that she and Thomas would have the apartment entirely to themselves.

As they walked through the front door and into the large sitting-room which for so long had been the yardstick by which Rosie measured grandeur, her initial reaction was that it wasn't quite as huge or grand as she remembered. Donald was already sprawled on one of the big settees, Mr Cook looking out of the window at the busy street below. It was of course just the same – the thick carpets as sumptuous, the ornaments and paintings as exquisite. She could still see her face mirrored in the rosewood table, and the curtains she'd once considered big enough to cover every single window in May Cottage with enough left to make a ball gown were every bit as fabulous as she'd thought then. The difference was only within her. She'd become accustomed to luxury.

By five o'clock it was dark outside. The traffic along Piccadilly was growing heavier and noisier, while office workers and shoppers were flocking into Green Park tube station to go home. Rosie lingered at the sitting-room windows before she drew the curtains. Frank had taken Donald along the road to Fortnum and Mason to buy some extra treats for the weekend. Norah was out in the kitchen unpacking a box of groceries she'd brought from home, and Rosie was glad of a few moments alone.

She thought London was so glamorous and exciting by night. Car headlights and neon signs flashing, brilliantly lit shop windows, so much noise and bustle. The Ritz across the street to her left gave her a glimpse of the rarefied world of the rich. She could almost hear the chink of champagne glasses as liveried flunkies hailed taxis for guests and held open doors for elegant women in fur coats. She looked up at the windows above, wondering what the bedrooms were like and which famous people might be staying there tonight. Golden light from the restaurant on the side of the hotel streamed out into the darkness of the park, and through the windows she could see a waiter shaking out a starched tablecloth, another holding up glasses to the light to check for smears. Rosie wondered how much it cost to have dinner there, and silently vowed to herself that whatever it cost, one day she and Thomas would eat there.

She smiled at her audacity as she drew the curtains. Three years ago she would have been awed by just an ordinary self-service cafeteria – she'd thought places like the Ritz were only for the upper classes. But now she knew the entrance requirement for such places was really only confidence: with the right clothes, and enough money, you could do anything, go anywhere.

'What can I do to help?' Rosie asked Norah as she went into the kitchen at the back of the apartment. It was much quieter here, the traffic a mere drone in the distance.

'You could peel the potatoes,' Norah suggested. She was holding a beef casserole she'd brought from home. 'I'll put this in the oven, then I'll make some custard.'

Rosie found the potato peeler in the table drawer and went over to the sink. She liked this kitchen. Aside from a modern gas cooker and a refrigerator, it had remained virtually unchanged since the apartments were built a century before. Large glass-fronted cabinets full of beautiful china lined the walls, there was a big, scrubbed table in the centre, and standing at the sink she could see right down into brightly lit offices and other apartments.

It was almost like seeing into half a dozen theatres, with a different show in each. She could see girls sitting at desks typing in one, in another a businessman was leaning back in his chair, with his feet up and his hands behind his head. She thought he was dictating a letter to his secretary, though she couldn't see anyone else. In an apartment to her right, a slim and elegant woman in a red dress was placing a huge vase of flowers on a baby grand piano; she stopped to tweak them into place, then stood back to admire then. Rosie had a suspicion it was probably the nearest thing to work she'd done all day.

'I wonder what it would be like to go back and live somewhere like May Cottage,' she said thoughtfully, glancing round at Norah, who was bent over by the cooker arranging the oven shelves. 'I never thought it was awful when I lived there, but after living in your house and seeing places like this, how on earth would I cope without all the comfort and modern appliances?'

Norah stood up and smiled. She wondered what had prompted Rosie to think of such a thing.

'I suppose that would depend on the circumstances,' she replied. 'I doubt you'd mind roughing it a bit with Thomas. Or indeed with us, if it was just a short holiday.'

'I didn't mean like that,' Rosie said. 'I was imagining being uprooted, shoved back there permanently, alone, without any money to make it nice.'

'Well, that is a grim scenario, and an unlikely one,' the older woman laughed. 'But I have to admit that after I married Frank and moved to The Grange I hated having to spend more than an hour or two with my parents in their cottage. It was so tiny, so uncomfortable; the beds were hard and lumpy and so very cold. I tried to explain how I felt to my mother once, but she accused me of becoming a snob.'

'Am I becoming a snob too?' Rosie asked anxiously.

'Of course you aren't,' Norah scoffed. 'Being a snob is

looking down on people who aren't as fortunate as your-self. There's absolutely nothing wrong with raising your standards. My mother could have improved her home, she had enough money, but she was too mean. She'd put a coat on rather than add some more coal to the fire, and moaned about the broken springs in her bed but wouldn't buy a new one.

'She always harped on about me "getting things too easily". She didn't see how hard Frank worked for what we had, or that I was looking after his ageing parents at the same time as bringing up Michael and Susan. She made me feel very guilty about everything when she visited me, so much so that I reached the point when I didn't want her to come at all. I hope to goodness I'm never that crabby with my children.'

Rosie giggled. There was absolutely nothing crabby about Norah Cook. She rejoiced at her children doing so well for themselves and doted on her grandchildren.

'Perhaps when I've got children I'd better not tell them about May Cottage,' she said. 'I wouldn't want them feeling guilty about what they've got.'

Norah thought she was edging closer to what was really on Rosie's mind. 'I think you should tell them, but just keep it humorous. I know my children love to hear about their grandparents' oddities. Or is that what you're really worried about? That by telling them about May Cottage you might have to reveal the family history too?'

Rosie thought for a bit before replying. 'I suppose so,' she frowned. 'The one does tend to lead to the other. I mean, if I began to talk about Seth and Norman skinning eels, or the scrap yard round the cottage, they'd be bound to ask what happened to them, wouldn't they?'

Norah sighed. 'For someone so young you can be remarkably astute, Rosie! In your shoes I'd probably invent a few white lies, at least until they were grown-up and able to understand. But let's put things into perspect-ive. You aren't married yet, there are no children either, and by the time some are born and old enough for such revelations, you and Thomas might have had so many adventures together that your children will never hark back further than that.'

'That's a better thing to think about.' Rosie's face brightened. She didn't really know why she'd got involved in talking about such things. 'Besides, after tomorrow Thomas might be the toast of the art world.'

'Indeed he might,' Norah smiled. 'Now, are you going to tell me the state of play with him? I don't want to put my foot in it when we see him tomorrow.'

Rosie smirked, a little embarrassed. She was always surprised by how direct Norah could be. On the Sunday night after Rosie had returned from spending the weekend with Thomas, she had fully expected some sort of lecture. To her surprise Norah asked her bluntly if they had made love, and had they 'been careful', as she put it. She wasn't disapproving. It was quite clear from what she said that she knew all about the joys of passion-filled nights. She was happy for them both, but she just didn't want to see them saddled with a baby before they'd had time to enjoy being alone together.

Since then Thomas had been using all his spare time painting and he'd only been to Mayfield once. Norah had been very sympathetic about the lack of opportunity for them to spend any time together, and she had turned a blind eye to Rosie creeping into his bed late at night. The fact that she and her husband had arranged for them to have this apartment showed they wanted to smooth the lovers' path. As such, Rosie felt compelled to confide in the older woman.

'We desperately want to be together all the time,' she said. 'But I don't see how we can. Thomas can't move away from Hampstead for some time.'

'Well, go and live there with him.'

Rosie's eyes widened and her mouth fell open in surprise. 'Live in sin!'

Norah laughed at Rosie's shocked expression. 'I know, it's not the done thing, at least not now in the prudish fifties. To listen to some people, you'd think they'd forgotten how uninhibited we all were during the war. But Thomas is an artist after all, and he lives in Hampstead which is a hotbed of Bohemian people. As I remember, being separated when you are in love is painful. I dare say Thomas will want to marry you anyway, but I can't see any good reason for hanging around waiting for a ring on your finger, when it's as plain as the nose on my face that you two ought to be together now.'

'But what about Donald?' Rosie asked. 'I can't just up and leave him in the lurch.'

'He'll be fine. It's not as if you'd be going out of his life for good.' Norah came closer to Rosie and put her arm around her waist. 'Heaven knows Frank and I owe you so much, Rosie. You've taught our Donald enough to be able to work and make friends. He'll miss you of course, as Frank and I will, but all of us would rather see you two happy and fulfilled than try to keep you with us for our selfish needs.'

Rosie turned and buried her face in the older woman's warm, perfumed neck. 'I don't know what to say,' she whispered as tears of gratitude came into her eyes. 'Just thank you for being so understanding doesn't sound enough.'

Ever since that night in Hampstead with Thomas, Rosie had thought of little else but wanting to be with him permanently. It seemed ironic that when Gareth had wanted her to move to London she'd raised so many objections. Yet now she didn't care whether she lived in Mayfield, London, Manchester or even Australia, just as long as she could be by Thomas's side.

She remembered so clearly how he had once mapped out her life with Gareth for her, and claimed that one day she would become dissatisfied with the kind of future he offered. At that time she hadn't fully understood what

Thomas was getting at, but she could see it for herself now.

She needed adventure before she settled down with a home and children. There was a huge world out there, and she'd seen only the tiniest corner of it. Thomas had made her hungry to see more. He wanted to go to Venice and Paris to paint, she wanted to see the gardens of Versailles, the Grand Canyon, jungles and deserts. Maybe they could do it all together.

Norah lifted Rosie's face from her shoulder, and holding it in both her hands she looked right into her eyes as if she was delving into her soul.

'Will you take another bit of advice?' she asked. 'Go with Thomas, be happy with him. But make sure you keep your own identity and talent intact, Rosie. You are as much of an artist as he is. The only difference is that the pictures you paint are with living, growing things. Don't allow yourself to be sidetracked from your personal ambitions to be a garden designer by just slipping into becoming the perfect little wife and housekeeper. One of the main reasons you two are so right for one another is that you are both free spirits. So keep it that way.'

Rosie was surprised by such a statement, especially coming from someone who was such a superb role-model for womanly skills.

'You're amazed by me saying that, aren't you?' Norah's eyes twinkled. 'I've been totally content as a wife and mother, and I wholeheartedly believe that for most women it is a fully satisfying and important role. But times are changing, Rosie. There are opportunities for women now that were unthinkable before the war. Look around you while you are here in London, see how things have moved on since you were a child, and imagine how they will change even more drastically in the next ten years. You are young, strong and bold. You know more about gardening than most people three times your age. You can plan, build and design. Don't waste that talent, Rosie. It's precious.'

*

607

'My goodness, you look sensational!' Frank exclaimed as Rosie came into the sitting-room at half past six on Saturday evening. 'Everyone's going to be looking at you instead of Thomas's paintings.'

Rosie blushed. Norah had insisted she bought the new dress this afternoon and the matching suede high-heeled shoes. She'd never imagined herself wearing anything so sophisticated as this black velvet, figure-hugging dress. It had three-quarter-length sleeves with a low-cut back and a spray of gold-beaded embroidery from one shoulder down to just above her right breast. Norah had lent her a pair of gold, dangly earrings and arranged her hair so it was swept up above her ears and held in place with two glittery combs.

'You look like the Queen,' Donald said. 'And you've grown too.'

'It's only the high heels,' Rosie laughed. 'And you look like a prince tonight too.'

Donald's height, wide shoulders and straight back were emphasized by his dinner jacket and bow tie. With his blond hair neatly cut, his bronzed face and bright blue eyes, he would undoubtedly attract attention tonight. Both Rosie and Norah were a little anxious as to how he would cope with that. He wasn't used to strangers and there was nothing about his appearance to warn people he was retarded. But he needed the challenge to prove himself, and they couldn't keep him wrapped in cotton wool for ever.

'And another stunning woman!' Frank exclaimed as his wife came into the room. She was always elegantly dressed, but the turquoise-blue cocktail dress she'd bought this afternoon was far more fashionable than any of her others. The colour suited her, enhancing her blue eyes and grey hair. She looked closer to forty than her real age of over sixty.

'We'd better get going,' she said, and nervously brushed Donald's jacket. 'Have you got a clean handkerchief? And don't you dare sneak drinks when I'm not looking, or we won't take you with us again.'

'No, Mother,' Donald said, like a small boy. 'I'll be really good. I promise.'

Rosie smiled affectionately. Donald and she were in the same boat tonight. Neither of them was used to smart places or mixing with society people. They were both excited and scared at taking a step into the unknown. But she expected that Thomas was even more scared. He had sounded confident enough when she spoke to him earlier on the telephone, he'd even laughed and said he'd be happy if he just sold one or two paintings. But she knew that was just bravado. He was pinning all his hopes on this exhibition changing his entire life.

'Look!' Rosie squeaked with excitement as Frank drove past the gallery in Heath Street, looking for somewhere to park his car. The gallery was in one of the old bow-fronted shops, and the windows were as brightly lit as a Christmas tree. What had excited Rosie was the banner across the window: THOMAS FARLEY EXHIBITION. Somehow seeing his name up in such big letters meant it was really going to happen for him.

It took some time to find somewhere to park. Hampstead was always bustling, but on a Saturday night people came from all over London to eat in its many restaurants or drink in the quaint pubs. The streets were narrow and soon became congested. Rosie had never seen so many smart cars all in one place. But they eventually found a parking spot and walked back down Heath Street to the gallery. To their delight, by the time they got there at least twenty other people had arrived.

'Your invitations, please, sir,' said a small dark man in a dinner jacket as they walked in. 'There is a cloakroom at the far end of the gallery for the ladies' coats,' he went on as he checked the invitations. 'I hope you will have an enjoyable evening.'

Rosie's first thoughts at that moment were that Thomas

had held out on her. He had played down how swish this gallery was. It looked quite small from outside, but in fact the narrow part was merely an entrance hall, and a few feet further down it opened up into a much wider space. It was so very modern, like Scandinavian designs she'd seen in magazines, all white and chrome, with dozens of spotlights and a polished pine floor.

Her eyes darted this way and that. The walls on either side of her each had four small paintings. She wanted to examine them, but the entire crowd were standing shoulder to shoulder apparently gazing at just one picture in the middle of the gallery. Rosie could just make out the top of Thomas's head behind their backs. She turned to Frank, who was just helping his wife out of her coat.

'Do we wander about, or is that some kind of conducted tour?' Rosie whispered, indicating all the people in the huddle. 'Is Thomas talking to them?'

Frank looked and half smiled. 'I think they are asking him questions. Give me your coat and I'll try to catch his eye as I go past. They don't normally have tours as such. I expect that particular painting is something out of the ordinary.'

As he went off with the coats, Donald, Rosie and Norah went over to look at the first group of paintings. 'Look, that's Sparrow's Nest,' Norah exclaimed. This was a pretty, white boarded cottage in the village. 'And that one is old Jack Higgins's tumbledown place.'

Rosie stared at them in awe. She'd been with Thomas when he'd sketched them both, but she'd never imagined they would end up like this. Sparrow's Nest had a misty, early morning look about it, and he'd painted the minute garden in front of it just as it really was, a wild profusion of tumbling flowers. Jack Higgins's place, however, was painted as at dusk, the long shadows giving it a sinister feel. Of the two she preferred the latter: she'd often got goosebumps as she walked by Jack's place, and the painting achieved the same end.

'Rosie!'

She turned sharply at Thomas's voice. He was coming across the gallery towards her, with a wide smile on his face. He wasn't wearing a dinner jacket like all the other men. She knew he didn't own one, and he probably thought such things didn't go with an artist's image either. But he looked smarter than she'd ever seen him before in a light grey jacket, trousers of a slightly darker shade and a bright blue tie she'd given him last year on his birthday.

'You look so gorgeous,' he exclaimed, his eyes reflecting his joy at seeing her. 'My wild rose has turned into a beautiful, sophisticated woman.' He kissed her cheek and hugged her with one arm as he warmly greeted Norah and Donald.

'I hope you won't mind if I can't spend much time with you this evening, but Paul Brett, the gallery owner, has warned me I have to mingle with all the guests.' He glanced round behind him. 'That's Paul,' he said, pointing out a thin, dark-haired, dapper man with a thin moustache who was talking to a small group of people. 'I'll introduce you to him once he's free, but do you mind if I whisk Rosie away for a minute or two? I've got something to show her.'

'Of course not.' Norah put her arm through her son's and smiled at him. 'Donald and I will mingle ourselves, won't we?'

Donald grinned. He looked entirely at ease. 'I'll look after Mother,' he said. 'I like parties.'

People were still standing in front of the same picture, but as Thomas came up behind them they parted, and Rosie gasped as she saw what they were all looking at.

The picture was of her. It was entitled 'Wild Rose' – a girl with a dirty face, tangled hair and a shabby over-large dress, looking out through a wild rose bush.

'Oh Thomas,' she breathed, suddenly overcome by a rush of half-forgotten memories. 'It's so, well . . . beautiful.'

She couldn't say more, for she was carried right back

to that day over three years ago. She could feel the sun on her bare arms as she hung out washing in the orchard, hear the clucking of the hens, smell the scent of meadow-sweet as she watched the man with a limp and a walking-stick coming up the lane. She remembered everything so distinctly, his open-necked shirt, his tilted hat, a knapsack on his back and jacket slung over one shoulder. Heat shimmered on the road, and she felt his weariness. Even before she heard him knocking on the front door or calling out, somehow she sensed he wasn't going to pass by.

Over the years she had often recalled every detail of that day, sometimes with regret that she'd unwittingly been the cause of such an avalanche, but more often with wonder that, after all the horror and shame, he'd become her dearest and closest friend.

Now, as she gazed at this painting, she was staggered that Thomas had kept that first glimpse of her tucked away in his head, that he loved her enough to be able to paint her there, just feet from where his sister lay buried. It wasn't a twee, sugary painting destined for a chocolate box; he had managed to convey the feeling that something dark was going on behind the scenes. It was simply a masterpiece.

Turning to Thomas with brimming eyes, heedless of all the curious glances around them, she stretched her arms out for him. He held her silently for several minutes. She could hear his heart beating and sensed he was trying to find the words to explain why he'd never told her about this picture, and what it meant to him.

Lifting up her chin, he looked into her eyes for a moment, then smiled. 'It represents a new beginning,' he said softly. 'That moment when you came through the weeds was the start of a new era for me. There was terrible pain to come, great anger and hatred, yet through all that I found myself again. Through you, seeing your courage and determination, I was able to really live. It's what started me painting again, and stopped me seeing myself as a cripple. So no more tears. Tonight's another new start. A bright, sparkly new future for both of us.'

Rosie found it hard to contain her tears many more times that evening, seeing paintings which she knew were glimpses into Thomas's very soul. A tenement building with washing hung across the yard was his early life. A woman dozing in a chair was his mother. A jungle scene was part of his memory of Burma, perhaps a view from beyond the barbed wire. Whitestone Pond was there too, and with small children sailing their boats it somehow reflected the optimism he'd felt once he'd arrived in Hampstead. Yet the crippled ex-soldier selling news-papers was how he'd feared he would end his days.

Her heart swelled with pride as she saw that people were spellbound by his paintings. She listened as Thomas spoke shyly to reporters and wished she dared interrupt and inform them what a brilliantly funny man he could be too. When she overheard a couple of art critics pompously speaking of his 'raw talent' and 'primitive technique', she felt like steaming in to give them a mouthful of the kind of primitive abuse she'd learned as a child from her father.

But as the evening wore on, she realized that such criticism was actually praise, for they mentioned Thomas in the same breath as Van Gogh and Monet. Her excitement grew each time she saw Paul Brett cross the room to place a Sold ticket on one of the frames. She heard plummy voices lavishing unstinted praise, and she knew they weren't phoneys only here for the free wine and canapés, but people who truly appreciated art. A little old lady whom she later discovered was Lady Elizabeth Hunting-don said she could hardly wait for the exhibition to close so she could take her painting of Sparrow's Nest home and hang it.

But the picture Thomas had named 'Wild Rose' was still unticketed. Paul Brett was jotting down offers for it; the highest bidder would get it at the end of the week.

Rosie didn't dare to even think of asking Thomas how high the bids might go. She had overheard the sum of forty guineas mentioned at one time, and that stunned her.

Paul was the only person to realize 'Wild Rose' was Rosie. He took a step back when Thomas introduced them and smiled at her as if he'd just solved a mystery.

'Now I understand,' he said, his cool blue eyes twinkling. 'When Thomas showed me that picture, the hairs on the back of my neck stood up. I don't often react to art in that way. When I do it's because I know I've found something really special. I believe you were the catalyst which unlocked Thomas's latent talent. I must take you and Thomas out to dinner one night next week. Perhaps then I can persuade him to paint you as you are now, for me.'

As the evening progressed Rosie found herself losing her nervousness, to the point where she introduced herself to people not just as Thomas's girlfriend, but as a gardener. She soon found that art lovers were invariably garden people too, and when she said she was thinking of moving to Hampstead shortly, several people gave her their cards and asked that she contact them.

To her further delight, Rosie's fears that Donald might show himself and his parents up were unfounded. He took only one glass of wine and moved around with his parents, chatting to people quite comfortably. At one point Rosie heard him telling a middle-aged couple about how Jack Higgins, the man who owned the tumbledown cottage Thomas had painted, had once chased him right through the village when he was a small boy because he thought he'd been scrumping in his orchard. He told them he was too scared of the place to even set foot in the garden. The couple laughed with him and must have been touched by the story, because later Rosie heard they'd bought the painting for twenty guineas.

By ten o'clock, as the last of the guests left, only four

paintings remained unsold. Frank and Norah were slumped wearily on a settee, and Donald was still wandering around staring at the paintings. The two waitresses were collecting empty glasses.

Paul Brett was standing in the middle of the gallery, beaming at all the sold tickets. 'Well, Thomas,' he said. 'What am I going to sell for the rest of the week? Couldn't you rustle up another couple for me tomorrow?'

'And on the seventh day he rested,' Thomas chuckled. 'Not to mention spending the day with Rosie. And you've still got "Wild Rose" to auction off, so don't be greedy.'

Paul turned to Rosie, took her hand in his and lifted it to his lips. 'I wish you both every happiness. Thomas is a great artist, Rosie, and I'm quite certain that you've been his inspiration. I can't thank you enough for that.'

Frank insisted Thomas came home with them. 'There's a spare bed in Donald's room,' he said, winking at the younger man to remind him that for tonight there had to be some propriety, at least until he and Norah had gone home. 'I've got some champagne chilling. We've some serious celebrating to do.'

'Do you know what was the nicest thing tonight?' Norah said much later that evening, back in Piccadilly. Donald had gone to bed – one glass of champagne and he was almost asleep in the chair.

'What was that, my dear? That our bid for fifty guineas for "Wild Rose" has almost certainly been beaten by someone?' Frank said, slurring his words slightly.

Rosie gasped. She knew they had put in a bid for it, but she hadn't known for how much.

'No, dear, not that. And I did tell you to buy the little girls with the pram, just in case, but you didn't listen,' Norah said reprovingly.

'I wouldn't have let you buy one of my paintings,' Thomas said with a slight hiccup. They were all a little tipsy but he was the worst, as people had been plying him with glasses of wine all evening. 'I'll paint one specially for you.'

'You can't give your work away,' she said indignantly. 'That's like asking Frank to give you a tractor for nothing!'

'What would I need a tractor for?' Thomas laughed. 'Besides, I know you'll show it to everyone and I might get a few commissions. But to get back to what you were saying, what was so nice about tonight?'

Norah looked a little embarrassed now. 'Perhaps I shouldn't bring up the subject, but it was just that absolutely no one mentioned the murders.'

Rosie had also noticed this and been surprised by it. She and Donald had had their faces appear in enough newspapers, and Thomas's connection hadn't gone unnoticed by the press either. She had braced herself for someone to bring it up. But there hadn't been even the vaguest allusion to it.

'Arty Hampstead people are too polite,' Thomas said. 'Or maybe they just don't read newspapers.'

'I don't think it was that at all,' Norah retorted. 'It's because it's all forgotten. No one talks about it any more in Mayfield either. It's finally over.'

Rosie didn't comment for a moment. She wanted to believe Norah was right. 'Don't you think it's more likely they forgot because Thomas was the star of the evening, and he's such a fascinating man in his own right?' she suggested. She had seen the wealth of human interest in every single one of his paintings. Each one had a story behind it, enough to keep anyone's interest well away from her and her family. 'We'll have to wait and see before we get too complacent; we don't know what the press will drag up yet.'

'None of them asked me anything about it,' Thomas said. 'I was prepared to snap their heads off if they did, but there was nothing. In fact they didn't even drag up the old stuff about me being a prisoner of war.'

Frank stirred in his chair. He looked sleepily content,

his fat belly bulging over his cummerbund. 'I think you two should stop fretting about the past and look to your futures,' he said. 'My Norah's always right, or so she's very fond of telling me. The whole business is forgotten. The Suez crisis and the sale of premium bonds are the only hot news now. If you want my advice, you two should get yourselves married and concentrate on living happily ever after.'

'Frank!' Norah said sharply. 'It's not for you to put forward such a suggestion.'

'Best one I've heard all year,' Thomas grinned. 'Will you marry me, Rosie?'

Rosie's heart leapt. She had already made up her mind to tell Thomas she intended to come and live with him. But even though she felt she was brave enough to fly in the face of convention, she would be doubly happy with a ring on her finger and calling herself Mrs Farley. She looked at Thomas and smiled, then glanced across to Norah and winked at her.

'As soon as you like,' Rosie replied.

Frank got out of his chair. 'The champagne's finished, but there's some brandy for a toast,' he said, a beaming smile spreading across his face. 'We haven't had a wedding at The Grange since Susan's, and that was so long ago I've almost forgotten it.'

On the following Friday morning, Thomas took Rosie with him to the gallery to collect a cheque from Paul Brett.

It had been a frantic week. Thomas had stayed each night with Rosie, then early in the morning he'd had to go back to the shop in Flask Walk to fit in a few hours of clock-mending before Rosie joined him at one for a hasty lunch. In the afternoon he had to spend a couple of hours at the gallery to meet people who were interested in his work. All but one of the paintings on display were now sold, but Paul hoped he might get some further commissions. On three evenings they had been invited out to dinner, and on the remaining ones Thomas had taken her out to show her a little of London's night life. But now it was at an end. The exhibition was closed. One by one his paintings were being taken down and carefully wrapped for Paul to deliver to their new owners. Tomorrow another artist's work would be hanging there.

'I shall miss your pictures,' Paul said and the mournful look in his eyes showed his sincerity. 'It's been one of the most successful exhibitions I've ever staged, both in sales and in the public's response, but I shall miss coming in and seeing them all here. Each one had become special to me.'

He opened a drawer in his desk and pulled out an envelope. 'This isn't the final amount. Some people won't pay me until I deliver the pictures to them. But I've got a feeling you have something pressing to buy your young lady.'

They were out of the gallery and off up Heath Street before Thomas opened the envelope. He took out the cheque and the attached statement and let out a low whistle. 'Bloody hell!' he exclaimed. 'It's for four hundred and fifty-eight pounds! And there's another eight hundred odd to come.'

He caught hold of Rosie by the waist and twirled her round, breaking into wild laughter, regardless of a group of women shoppers who were watching.

'Put me down,' she yelled, afraid he might fall over.

He lowered her to the ground, but still held on to her. 'Do you know what this means?' he said, his voice bubbling with excitement.

'That you can buy me a ring?' she said. 'That we can go to Venice or Paris?'

'All that,' he gasped, showering kisses all over her face. 'But better still, we can find somewhere of our own to live. I can give up mending clocks and you'll have enough to start a proper gardening business and employ someone to help with the heavy work.'

Rosie kissed him deeply and lingeringly. She didn't care that the group of women were staring.

'I love you so much, Thomas Farley,' she said, cupping his face between her hands. 'I'd love you even if we had to live in a cottage with no electricity and I had to take in washing. But do you know what means most of all to me?'

'What? The fact that I'm on my way to being as famous as Monet?'

'No,' she laughed. 'Because you said that about the gardening. I thought you might suggest I give it up.'

His face was suddenly serious. 'I would never suggest that,' he said. 'You and your plants are like me and the paints – inseparable. One day you'll be as well known as Gertrude Jekyll and I'll paint your gardens.'

Epilogue

1963

The chambers of Wentworth, Dupree and Brownlow in Chancery Lane were somewhat cold, dark and Dickensian, with book-lined walls and heavy wooden furniture from the last century. But Charles Dupree, the senior partner, had a roaring fire in his office, and the heavy snow falling outside his long, narrow windows merely enhanced the cosiness of the room.

'Let me top up your sherry,' Charles said, taking Rosie's glass before she had a chance to refuse. 'We have every reason to celebrate, don't we?'

Rosie smiled. There was a time in her life when she would have been intimidated by anyone in the legal profession, but Charles was not only her solicitor, he had become a true friend. He was short and fat, with thinning hair and a purple nose, and well over fifty, but his jolly personality and deep, resonant voice were what she saw and heard.

Rosie had met Charles at a party in Paul Brett's Hampstead home just six weeks after she'd married Thomas in December 1955. At that time they were still living above the shop in Flask Walk, and because the flat went with the job, Thomas was still trying to juggle mending clocks with painting in his spare time.

Although Rosie had made contact with several people she'd met at Thomas's exhibition almost as soon as they returned from their honeymoon in Paris, and she'd made tentative plans to start work on their gardens in the spring, she was a little frustrated by living in such a confined space with no work of her own to do just yet.

Over a few glasses of wine, she'd found herself confiding this to Charles. At that time she'd had no idea he was a solicitor, or that he had just bought one of the rambling, neglected houses she'd admired in Fitzjohn's Avenue on her very first visit to Hampstead at the time when she worked at Carrington Hall.

She wasn't in the habit of talking about herself, but Charles was intensely interested in both her and Thomas. He had met Thomas at his exhibition, and in fact had bought a painting of the jungle in Burma. Since it had been hanging on his wall he'd found himself wishing to know more about the artist, and having discovered that this pretty young woman had recently married him, Charles went out of his way to engage Rosie in conversation.

Charles was captivated by her. She spoke of gardening in the same passionate way women of his class spoke of ballet or the theatre. He found himself fully understanding her frustration at being shut in a cramped flat when she had been used to wide open spaces. He thought it a shame, too, that an artist of Thomas's calibre should still be spending most of his time mending clocks. In the days that followed, this intriguing couple occupied Charles's mind a great deal. He wanted to get to know them better and he felt they were worth helping.

A couple of weeks later, Charles called round at the shop one evening and put a proposition to them both. They could have the semi-basement flat in Fitzjohn's Avenue rent-free, in return for supervising the workmen he was getting in to convert the rest of the house into flats.

As soon as Rosie and Thomas saw the flat they agreed. It was spacious, and the room overlooking the back garden would make a perfect studio for Thomas. Rosie eyed up the huge, overgrown back garden, and her fingers itched to transform it into something beautiful.

They were ecstatically happy in that flat, especially the first summer. It was like one long honeymoon, with Thomas painting and Rosie working on the garden. They eked out the money Thomas had put aside from his exhibition with Rosie doing a few gardening jobs for other people, and the odd sale of one of Thomas's paintings.

Eighteen months later, when all the upstairs flats were finished and sold, Charles made a second proposition to them. The beautiful garden Rosie had created had increased the value of the basement flat dramatically, and Charles, ever a businessman, couldn't afford sentimentality to stand in his way of profit. Yet at the same time he liked Thomas and Rosie too much to just give them their marching orders. As Charles had a client who wanted to sell a small cottage right in Hampstead Village, he suggested that he gave them a lump sum as a deposit on the mews cottage, and he would arrange a mortgage for it.

Rosie and Thomas were delighted. The big flat, however lovely, was hard to keep warm, and the huge garden took up so much of Rosie's time that she had little left to spend on jobs elsewhere which would bring in more money. They knew too that without Charles's assistance they would not be able to buy a house of their own because their earnings were so erratic.

It was love at first sight when they saw the cottage in Holly Walk: one large main room downstairs with an open staircase, and a smaller room to the side where Thomas could paint. Upstairs were two bedrooms and the prettiest bathroom Rosie had ever seen. The garden was small, but just as if it was intended for them, with a shed-cum-greenhouse at the bottom. Everything about it appealed to them – the stable door, the oddly Gothic windows. It was bathed in sunshine and a fat ginger cat was sitting on the window sill as though ready to take up residence with them. The previous owner had clearly been fastidious and a comfort-lover. Radiators ran from the kitchen boiler, the carpets he intended to leave behind were thick and new, every room was painted pristine white.

Their friendship with Charles took a leap forward once they'd moved into the cottage. He and his wife Julia often came for supper, and Charles found a steady stream of clients for Rosie because he was always showing photographs of the garden in Fitzjohn's Avenue, and praising her talent endlessly.

That year, from mid-1958, was the real start of the change in Rosie and Thomas's fortunes. There was another hugely successful exhibition at Paul Brett's gallery, and as more and more people beat a path to Rosie's door, she soon found herself in a position where she could pick the jobs she really wanted. She concentrated on those where the client wanted a complete make-over for their garden, giving her a free hand to plan it from scratch. She took on casual labour for the heavy work, and used local builders for laying paths and building walls. But the design, the choice of plants and planting out she did herself. It wasn't long before she was regarded as something of an expert. She often heard herself referred to as 'the plant lady'.

But over and above the success and the security of knowing that once again they had money in the bank was the fact that she and Thomas were so blissfully at one with one another. They could be apart from each other for days on end, but they had the freedom to drop everything when it suited them, and take off for a picnic on the Heath, catch a train anywhere on an impulse, or just stay in bed on cold winter days.

Donald often came up to stay, helping Rosie with her projects. Back in Mayfield he had continued looking after most of the gardens they'd started on together. His passion for rock 'n' roll continued – he'd even bought a guitar and learned to play it well enough to delight Rosie and his family with impersonations of Elvis Presley. He played darts in the pub, cricket in the summer, and he was supremely happy.

Norah and Frank came up to stay for a weekend every couple of months. Michael, Alicia and the children visited for a day out every now and then. Clara, Nicholas and Robin had a week's holiday on their own with Rosie and Thomas every Easter. Susan and Roger had two small girls now, but Rosie mainly saw them when she and Thomas went down to Mayfield.

There were the theatre, films and concerts, meals in good restaurants, parties and fun. Hampstead was everything Rosie had ever hoped for, lively, full of interesting, off-beat characters, and yet it felt like the country. She had the man she loved, a wonderful home, and a job she never tired of.

Now she had been offered a once-in-a-lifetime chance: an American financier called Arthur Franklin was having a mansion built in The Bishops Avenue, a road between Hampstead and Highgate often dubbed 'Millionaires' Row'. He wanted a splendid and ostentatious garden created, with grand terraces, pools and fountains. Money was no object; he simply wanted a garden that would amaze and delight everyone.

She was here today to sign the contract.

'I can hardly believe Arthur's chosen me,' Rosie said as she gulped down her sherry. She had spent the last six months, almost night and day, working on the plans. Thomas had transferred her scheme to paper, using all his artistry to convey the richness of her design and the magnificence of her dream.

Charles looked at Rosie and smiled. He could take the credit for introducing Rosie to Arthur, for persuading him that such a small, young woman could indeed handle such a big job. He'd taken Arthur to view other gardens she had planned and created, and pointed out that though they were small projects compared with what he had in mind, her talent and imagination were obvious. But in the end it was Rosie's personality alone which had swung it for her.

She was dressed for the city today, in a dark green suit with a fur collar and a pert side-tilted hat. She had arrived in a taxi and her nails were blood-red talons. Anyone would take her for the owner of a chic dress shop or the wife of a rich businessman.

But Arthur had met her for the first time when she was working in a muddy garden in Hampstead Village, a twenty-five-year-old girl in torn dungarees and wellingtons, with broken nails and her hands so dirty she couldn't even shake his hand, her hair a tousled mop. Yet Arthur had been enchanted by her love of gardens, the joyful way she spoke of magnolias and Japanese maples, and he'd taken the next step to ask her to look at his vast plot of land.

She had ridden there on a bicycle, wearing a shabby pair of men's trousers and plimsolls on her feet. She sat down on a felled tree and asked Arthur what image he wanted to create. She hadn't smirked at his grandiose ideas, or the fact that he didn't know a rose from a tulip. She wanted to know about him, his dreams and aspirations. Arthur had already seen so many snooty landscape gardeners, he sensed that every one of them was laughing up their sleeve at his ideas of Corinthian pillars and grand terraces with statues in the undergrowth. He knew they thought him vulgar and pretentious, and their only reason for trying to get the contract was because of the money.

Rosie did laugh about some of his ideas too, but with him, not at him, and she was hungry for the job, which he liked.

'He chose you because he believes in you,' Charles said. 'He knows it will be years before the garden comes to full fruition. He'll give you every support in getting you the more exotic materials needed and the craftsmen for the building work. But the designing and the planting will be all yours, Rosie. And you deserve such a wonderful opportunity.'

Charles passed her the contract. As she bent forward to read it, he studied her with affection.

Charles had been born with the proverbial silver spoon – educated at the best schools and Oxford, he then slipped happily into his father's law firm. He had never known a moment's hardship in his entire life. Until he encountered Rosie and Thomas at Paul Brett's party, he had never met anyone socially outside his own privileged set. Rosie had enchanted him that first night, because she was so vivacious, warm and funny. Thomas took a little longer to get to know: he was more reserved, an observer rather than a talker. But once Charles had broken through that reserve, he found in Thomas the friend he'd always hoped for.

He heard some gossip about Rosie's family some months after they moved into the flat in Fitzjohn's Avenue. It hadn't made a scrap of difference to his affection for them, but he was intrigued, and delved around until he discovered everything about both her and Thomas's backgrounds. That was a turning point in his understanding of the less privileged. He was faced with two such very admirable and talented people, who through some twist of fate or accident of birth had endured more pain and sorrow than he could possibly imagine.

Charles spent many a sleepless night considering how he would be now if he had returned home at the end of the war with a missing leg, to find his only relatives dead. Or what it must be like to have your father hanged, only to discover later that your brother was the guilty party. He was sure he would never have the strength of character to rebuild his life after such things.

Eventually Rosie told him the story herself. She said that secrets created a wedge between friends, and he admired her for that courage more than anything. She said she still had no idea what had happened to her other brother Norman. She had no wish to trace him either, but she hoped he'd kept out of trouble. She confided in Charles too that she hoped one day Alan would come to see her and Thomas. Charles had promised then that when the boy was sixteen, to his mind an age of reason, he would try and act as a go-between and arrange a reunion for them. Alan would be sixteen in February and Charles had every intention of carrying out his promise.

'Sign where I've put the cross,' Charles said as she came to the end of the document. 'That is, of course, unless you've changed your mind.'

She just laughed and signed her name with a flourish. 'That's it, then,' she said. 'My fate is sealed.'

'There's the money to come yet, and all the back-breaking work,' he said.

Rosie looked at him thoughtfully for a moment. 'Money is a funny thing,' she said. 'It ceases to be of importance once you have enough. It's the creating bit I care about.'

Charles shook his head in wonder. Money was very important to him, but he knew Rosie and Thomas didn't think along the same lines. They would spend it as it came, travelling, having fun together, but it would never become their master. When they were gone, their children – for he was sure they would have some before long – would get a rich inheritance, not money or property, but their father's art, the beauty of their mother's gardens and a sense of pride. He wished he had something so priceless and permanent to leave his own children.

'You won't be able to start work until the weather gets better,' Charles said. It had been the worst winter since 1947; the roads had been blocked with snow, many villages had been cut off for weeks, the mail and milk were brought in by helicopter. 'What are you going to do until then?'

'Lie around reading plant books,' she laughed. 'Pose for Thomas, cook him meals and do all the jobs I normally neglect. Once I get bored with that, I'll hunt around to find some good statues for Arthur. But before I begin to vegetate for the rest of the winter, I want you and Julia to come out somewhere special with us.'

'Now where would that be?' Charles half expected her to say something like sledging, for at times she was still very much a child.

'The Ritz,' she said with a wide, impish grin. 'For dinner. I've always wanted to go there, and you and Julia know your way around posh places.'

Charles raised an eyebrow in surprise. He and Julia often went there, but he had never imagined Rosie had such a hankering. She was in many ways a true Bohemian, far more at home with checked tablecloths and a candle stuck in a bottle.

'Tell me why first?' he asked.

She gave a little sigh and blushed. 'It's like the ultimate challenge,' she said softly. 'The daughter of wild Cole Parker finally making it. Can you understand that?'

Charles could. She had once told him how she used to believe she was marked for life. So she had been. Yet in many ways that curse, or affliction, whatever one called it, had also been the making of her.

'You're on, Rosie,' he smiled. 'But only on the condition that it's my celebratory treat. Anyone can pay to eat in the Ritz. To be taken as a guest has far more kudos.'

'What does "kudos" mean?' she asked. Charles had a habit of using unusual words and she always questioned them.

'It means what Arthur will have with you designing his garden. What people have when they own a Thomas Farley.'

'Really!' Her face lit up and she giggled. 'Don't be silly!'

'Just you wait,' he said sagely. 'Maybe you aren't quite there yet. But you soon will be.'

'I know there are real heroines out there who would put my fictional ones to shame, and I really want to hear about them' LESLEY PEARSE

Is there an amazing woman out there who deserves recognition?

Whether it is someone who has had to cope with problems and come out the other side; someone who has spent her whole life looking out for other people; or someone who has shown strength and determination in doing something great for herself, show her how much she is appreciated by nominating her for an award.

The Lesley Pearse Women of Courage Award gives recognition to all those ordinary women who show extraordinary strength and dedication in their everyday lives. It is an annual event that was launched by Lesley and Penguin in 2006.

The winner and her family are invited to London for a sumptuous awards lunch with Lesley, where she will be presented with a cheque for £1000, as well as a host of other prizes.

Let us know about an amazing lady you know and make a difference to her life by nominating her for this prestigious award.

To nominate someone you know:

Complete the form opposite, or send us the details required on a separate piece of paper, and post it to:

The Lesley Pearse Women of Courage Award, Penguin General, 80 Strand, London, WC2R 0RL

or visit:

www.womenofcourageaward.co.uk

where you can print out a nomination form, enter your nomination details onto our online form and read all about the award and its previous nominees and winners.

The Lesley Pearse
Women of Courage Award

www.womenofcourageaward.co.uk

OFFICIAL ENTRY FORM

NAME OF YOUR WOMAN OF COURAGE:

HER ADDRESS:

POSTCODE:

HER CONTACT NUMBER:

YOUR RELATIONSHIP TO HER:

YOUR NAME:

YOUR ADDRESS:

POSTCODE:

YOUR DAYTIME TELEPHONE NUMBER:

YOUR EMAIL :

ON A SEPARATE SHEET, TELL US IN NO MORE THAN
250 WORDS WHY YOU THINK YOUR NOMINEE DESERVES TO WIN
THE LESLEY PEARSE WOMEN OF COURAGE AWARD

For Terms and Conditions please visit
www.womenofcourageaward.co.uk

LESLEY PEARSE

'AMONGST FRIENDS'

THE LESLEY PEARSE NEWSLETTER

A fantastic new way to keep up to date with your favourite author.

Amongst Friends is a quarterly email with all the latest news and views from Lesley, plus information on her forthcoming titles and a chance to win exclusive prizes.

Just go to **www.penguin.co.uk** and type your email address in the 'Join our newsletter' panel and tick the box marked 'Lesley Pearse'. Then fill in your details and you will be added to Lesley's list.

LESLEY PEARSE

If you enjoyed this book, there are several ways you can read more by the same author and make sure you get the inside track on all Penguin books.

Order any of the following titles direct:

Visit www.penguin.com and find out first about forthcoming titles, read exclusive material and author interviews, and enter exciting competitions. You can also browse through thousands of Penguin books and buy online.

IT'S NEVER BEEN EASIER TO READ MORE WITH PENGUIN